AWAKENING HORDE

SHIELDWALL ACADEMY BOOK 1

M. ZAUGG

CONTENTS

DEDICATION

To my kids who give me the best ideas.

PROLOGUE PART 1: ON SALMAN'S WALL

The clang of the alarm bell stabbed through Turgan's dream, waking him from a sound sleep so suddenly that he sat up and smacked his forehead on the wooden slats of the bunk above him. Despite the pain, his body moved on autopilot, disentangling his limbs from his twisted bedding and shoving his feet into the boots he'd placed beside his bed before falling asleep.

Turgan's heart pounded with adrenaline as his fingers laced the boots with frantic speed. He wondered if his upcoming fourth year at the Mage Academy was going to be like this all the time. Around him, the room exploded into a frenzy of activity. Experienced mage and warrior students scrambled into action as the alarm clanged, calling for reinforcements on Salman's wall.

Thoughts still muggy with sleep, Turgan was just glad he'd slept in his leathers, as Elora had warned him to. In all his father's stories about the Mage Academy, he had been called up only once during a night of watch-call in his entire fourth year. But times were different now. The whole empire was on the defensive. Turgan tried not to dwell on things he couldn't change.

"Section 22, now!" the clerk holding the door yelled. He waved his clipboard as the students rushed past him in a hectic run. "Up top, to the battlements!"

The battlements? Turgan's mind ran over the instructions as he jogged and tightened the straps of his leather vambraces. The glint of his mage tattoos under the arm protectors steadied him, the swirls of indigo light twisting in three hard-earned waves that wrapped around each wrist and represented his repertoire of spells and abilities. At the thought, Turgan felt his water magic swell inside him, making his tattoos pulse with eagerness. Whatever monsters awaited them on the wall, he wouldn't be helpless.

Confidence tightened his focus, and Turgan worked to keep his breathing steady. He ran on the heels of the armored warrior student in front of him. Her broad shoulders and shorter height could be any dwarf mix like him, but the dark hair that stuck out in all directions under the dull metal helm told him it had to be Janil, a younger warrior who, in his opinion, shouldn't even be on the real walls yet, much less the dangerous upper battlements. No, Janil should be in the relative safety of the arrow slits in the lower hallways weaving through the thick walls. Not that he'd ever say that to her. But he resolved to keep an eye out for her, if possible, once they joined the fighting.

Boots slammed on well-worn stone floors. Harsh breathing filled the narrow halls as they ran through the inner hallways that were just cooling from the late summer's daytime heat. Low-level flame core lights did their best to banish the darkness, casting long shadows along the jagged walls.

Their group shifted to the inner wall as they passed a row of arrow slits manned by archers who launched arrows as fast as the apprentices racing back and forth could supply them. The distant roar of beasts bounced in through the open slits in a distorted echo of battle. Turgan sneaked a glimpse through one of the narrow cross-shaped slits in the thick stone as he ran by.

An involuntary shudder ran through him at the dark maelstrom of creatures far below, and he redoubled his efforts, charging forward with the mass of students. They ran up stairwells, one after another, fighting to get to their assigned position in time to help.

Turgan knew he couldn't be the only one wondering how bad it had to be tonight if they were calling on the students for reinforcements. Salman was the capital of the Astan Empire, after all. Positions for mages and warriors on the walls here were plum assignments for top performers. And any beasts had to not only get past the massive tower ring far out on the wild edges of the empire, but also past all the outlying cities before reaching the capital.

Rumor had it that the on-call students were getting pulled onto the wall more and more frequently. Turgan had hoped they'd be assigned to man an arrow slit on his rotation, a nice safe spot to lob spells out at the nightly hordes. But the battlements? The top of the towering walls, higher than five or six homes stacked atop each other, looked impossible for monsters to reach. Lately, though, the hordes had grown so vast that the beasts flew, climbed and even launched other beasts that high. The battlements had become the most dangerous assignment.

Turgan had only been up there once himself, during an academy orientation tour. The view had been impressive while making his stomach churn a bit at the sheer height when he looked over the side.

Ahead of him, Janil stumbled on the top step of the most recent stairwell. Turgan stutter-stepped in order to slip a hand out to grab her upper arm and steady her.

"Thanks," she said, before giving him a sheepish shrug. "Never enough Endurance."

He grinned and nodded, his own lungs burning with effort as he kept pace beside her, trying to peer over the heads of those running ahead of them. Turgan needed to make time for his own physical improvements. It was easy to forget the basics while cramming for the start of his fourth-year skill and spell training.

They rounded a corner. The distant clang of weapons and yells of fighting echoed even louder from the stairwell ahead.

Flashes of light from spells lit up the dim hallway and made Turgan's heart race even faster. He swallowed against a suddenly dry throat and pulled on his water mana. The raging eagerness of the power he'd nurtured and cultivated for exactly this kind of situation helped calm his nerves. If the beasts were threatening his city, he'd do everything in his power to stop them.

"For Astus!" someone ahead yelled out.

Eager yells responded in kind. Turgan's lips pulled back in a fierce grin as the battle fever rushed through him.

Beside him, Janil let out a roar, slamming her gauntlets against her chest as she ran for the stairs.

Whatever monsters had made it this high wouldn't stand a chance against them.

Together, they raced up the last steps and emerged onto the wall . . . and into complete chaos.

If their charging group hadn't hemmed him from ahead and behind, Turgan might have frozen at the sight.

All along the wall, defenders with shields, mana-based or enchanted, did their best to protect the ranged fighters who were pouring damage over the wall and directly down into the murder holes at their feet. Flame, water, earth and air spells lit up the night with so much energy, Turgan felt the wave of the mana slam into him and the other students. More than one jaw dropped in surprise.

Warriors fired arrow after arrow, from bows, crossbows and even the huge mounted ballista. It fired bolts big enough to tear a gaping hole through a monster horde. Some arrows and bolts pulsed with damage and speed enchantments, *whoomphs* of impact mixing in with the roar of the beasts from below.

Warriors drew bows with many times the strength Turgan would ever have. Others fired so fast, he saw more than one apprentice unable to keep up with enough ammunition. Other apprentices refilled and dumped oils and noxious potions over the side, some being lit by attentive flame mages.

It was such an overwhelming display of force that Turgan couldn't believe any horde of monsters could stand against it.

But they did.

Dark shapes flew up from below, limbs splayed and teeth bared as they landed amongst the defenders, each one causing chaos as the ordered defense reverted to a chaotic melee full of clanging weapons, exploding spells and screams of pain from both defenders and beasts.

"To the flame mage, second section down," said a sharp voice from their side. "The five of you. Move it!"

Turgan glimpsed a harried man in a guard uniform pointing ahead before he shoved Turgan in the right direction. The guard's attention moved to the students coming out behind them before Turgan could ask questions.

"Thank Vitur," said the flame mage as Turgan, Janil and three other students skidded to a stop near her, careful to avoid the flaming shield she held flush with the closest edge of the battlements. "You're just in time."

"Mage Bayle!" Janil said in surprise, making the other newcomers turn and stare, as they recognized the academy's lead flame mage.

A stout elf, she usually dressed impeccably and looked composed. But now, Turgan hardly recognized her. With her expression severe and hair pulled back tightly under a leather helm, Turgan could tell the battle wasn't going well. A jagged flap of her leather armor hung, ripped on her left side. She strained to hold a massive flame shield over the two archers focusing below. The sweating men rained down arrows through the murder holes. Behind them, a small crew manned a boiling oil pot, stoking the fire and working continuously to refill it.

Bayle's shield suddenly sputtered as something the size of a small dog slammed into it, letting out an ear-shattering shriek as it hit the raging flames. Turgan and the other students flinched. Teeth flashed and claws scrambled against the shield without finding purchase. A half beat later, the creature fell back into the roiling darkness on the other side of the wall. The wail faded, leaving behind a stench of burning fur that just added to the reek of battle.

"If you've got a shield, magical or material, join me," said Mage Bayle, her eyes tired but arms steady. "Everyone else, we have to hit the Void Matriarch with everything you have through the murder holes! And switch to melee against any of her spawn that make it to the wall."

Turgan's mind scrambled through his studies, trying desperately to find any information on a Void Matriarch as he and Janil sprang into action. The others must have hesitated.

"Now!" the flame mage yelled. "She's water-based. Level 25 and weak to earth or anything powerful you can throw at her."

Level 25! Turgan almost tripped in surprise. The high-powered mages and warriors at the tower ring were supposed to stop monsters that strong from making it inside the empire boundaries. No wonder he was drawing a blank on a Void Matriarch monster. He would have skimmed over anything that powerful, knowing he wouldn't encounter one for years, if ever.

"We've got her down to a tenth health," Bayle rattled off, ignoring their surprise. "But her last-ditch ability is generating more spawns than we can handle. And she's launching them up here easily. We can't let her recover. Hurry!"

Janil had her tower shield out, already positioning herself beside Mage Bayle, looking determined to protect their flame instructor with her life. Turgan skidded to a stop at the closest unmanned murder hole. A student air mage slid into the one just beside him. A gust of wind blew the reek of heated rancid oil over them as Turgan peered through the small gap in the stone for his first glimpse of the Void Matriarch.

She was a huge, glistening mass of black tentacles roiling in frenzied motion as attacks rained down on her in a veritable flood. Along her back, a seething army of dark figures bulged out. To Turgan's astonishment, her tentacles latched onto the balls, and hurled them in a rapid-fire counterattack up the wall that was almost as numerous as the city's defensive strikes.

Identify.

∾

Identify attempt failed. Level difference is too significant.
*Skill Boost: +14 to **Identify** Level 3 - 82/300*

Turgan's eyes widened, and he quickly spammed Identify to max out the points from the high-leveled beast. His breathing quickened as he pulled on his water mana, excitement flaring despite the danger. He also toggled off his notifications, knowing a distraction could be deadly. Identify wouldn't be the only thing he'd be able to advance tonight.

Danger accelerates growth. It was a saying for a reason.

His basic water spells were unlikely to do anything against the water-based behemoth so far below. His Drain might have been an option to suck a critical part of the creature dry, but it required direct contact from him or his staff. Not happening.

Plus, Drain instigated a battle of wills and strength when used against creatures or sapient beings. Turgan didn't fool himself that his spell had any kind of chance against the powerful beast below.

That left his most advanced mage ability, just learned a couple of months ago and barely a few unstable steps into level one: Spherical Spell. It allowed him to turn any of his offensive spells into something he could launch at an enemy, at the cost of a ton of mana.

He blew out a breath and drew on his focus, pushing the energy of his Drain spell out to manifest between his hands. A sudden scream from his left, followed by multiple shouts, shattered his concentration. The water mana, suddenly uncontrolled, exploded in his hands. Turgan quickly directed it outward over the wall, gritting his teeth against the pain as he berated himself. He couldn't afford to waste mana.

A quick glance in the scream's direction showed a cluster of defenders in a desperate fight with a waist-high creature with multiple midnight-black appendages. The beast had overwhelmed a warrior, stabbing down into the screaming man whose flailing knives seemed to glance off the powerful limbs.

All along the wall, Turgan could see more shadowy shapes flying up from below, dark limbs grasping for targets. Forcing himself not to gawk, Turgan focused on his only chance of contributing to the battle.

Eyes scrunched, he cast his Drain spell again, the power straining against his control as he insisted it condense itself and wait for his command to release.

Spherical Spell, he chanted, in his mind, as a viscous dark-blue ball formed between his hands, giving off a parched feel to his mana senses, despite being water-based. He pushed more mana into the ball, watching it grow to the size of a small fist. The memory of the enormous monster below and the injured fighter just down the wall from them forced Turgan to push a bit more into the spell than he usually did. Too much, and he risked the whole mess exploding in his face, but too little, and he might as well have stayed in bed.

Turgan's hands vibrated as he felt bursts of air from the air mage beside him launching dart after dart down below.

Enough. Turgan cut the mana and, with a final push of will, sealed the ball of Drain. Before he could second-guess himself, Turgan peered down through the jagged murder hole, aimed at the center of the vast monster below, and let the Spherical Spell drop. His hopeful eyes followed the ball as it plummeted, the flares of burning oil and flame spells haphazardly lighting the scene below.

PROLOGUE PART 2: A HOLLOW VICTORY

By the time it struck far below, his ball of magic had shrunk, like a snowflake melting on a vast field. At least it impacted the back of the monster, where spawning creatures were still budding to the surface. Turgan thought he could see one of them shriveling where his spell impacted, but he couldn't be sure.

Disheartened but pragmatic, he forced himself to repeat the process, ignoring the small blinking notifications in the bottom of his vision. There'd be time enough to see his gains after the battle.

The next few minutes felt like hours as Turgan poured his mana into Spherical Spells that grew in size by a small amount each time as his confidence grew. He'd even hit and disable one of the spawn creatures mid-air as its creator hurled it toward the top of the wall. The shot was so unlikely, Turgan hoped he hadn't used up all his luck for the night.

He'd forced the battle din to recede into a dull but constant roar as sweat dripped down his face. Both hands busy, he couldn't wipe his face as he formed yet another ball. He'd definitely be thanking Elora for lending him her mana boost ring tonight, and he'd be applying himself even harder at studying and mental exercises to level up his Insight and Intelligence. Watching his mana plummet while using his more advanced spell drove home how much work he still had ahead of him before he'd be an effective wall mage. At least he had the set of mana potions they issued to every mage taking a wall shift.

A vicious shriek pierced the night just behind Turgan, making him spin and lose control of his spell for a second time. Pain stabbed into his forehead. He squinted, watching in horror as another dark form flew over the battlement. One tentacle wrapped around a stone merlon, and the creature used the pivot point to crash over onto the walkway just a few yards from their group. It moved with a speed that was hard to follow in the shadows cast by the mage lights.

A stab of adrenaline-fueled panic pushed Turgan's fear away and cleared his mind to fight. He tried another Identify, but even the spawn was more than five levels above him.

"Behind me," Janil yelled, pushing forward and planting her shield as the creature's large, globular eyes focused on their group.

It retracted its tentacle from the merlon before spinning on multiple claw-tipped legs, a black thing of nightmare, faster than it had any right to be.

"Take it out fast and then focus back on the matriarch," urged Mage Bayle, as she kept her shield aloft with one hand, the other lighting the globes of hot oil raining down below. "She just keeps making more."

Turgan barely heard her. His training took over, pulling his focus where it was needed. Regardless of what else was happening around him, he needed to help stop the spawn, or none of them would survive to fight the beast below.

Janil had her spear out and braced to the side of her shield, but Turgan didn't think the mobile spawn would cooperate by charging them head on. This wasn't a classroom exercise where they had all the time in the world to match the perfect spell or skill to the situation.

A *twang* snapped out behind him. Turgan caught the flash of an arrow shooting through the space toward the spawn. One of the warrior students had shifted their fire to the beast. Arrow after arrow flew toward the monster, at an angle that wouldn't put the other fighters on the wall in danger. But the creature just flipped up on one set of legs, its body tipping up and down to either side extremely fast as it advanced. Most of the arrows passed harmlessly beneath its body.

Turgan's heart fell, and he knew his basic water attacks were unlikely to do much better, but they could be effective stopgaps, hopefully keeping the spawn at bay long enough for the rest of his team to kill it.

Create. Turgan commanded, using just a small amount of mana to pull water from the surroundings and fill the area at its feet. As soon as there were a few inches of water, Turgan switched to his next spell, hoping his remaining mana could maintain the disruption long enough for the others to finish the spawn off.

Churn. The calm pool exploded into a roiling mess as Turgan's mana slammed the water back and forth around the creature's tentacles with a force increased by how close the monster was.

Turgan liked to imagine there was some surprise as the spawn lost its footing to the unexpected attack. It fell into the shallow pool with a sudden splash.

"Get the water away from us! Surround the spawn with it!"

The command came from Mage Bayle, and Turgan obeyed it on instinct, the years of drills making him act before thinking. The last of his mana pulled the small pond of water toward the creature, leaving the stone walkway near their group dry as a bone.

With a strength that made his hair stand on end, a ball of flame rushed past Turgan to slam into the water around the beast. He stared wide-eyed at the sudden explosion of steam that hid the spawn from view. Howls of pain filled the air, and Turgan caught glimpses of limbs thrashing in pain.

"It won't last long," she yelled out. "Kill it while it's down and blind."

Turgan spun back. Dark, flailing limbs were already more visible as the steam dissipated. They didn't need more encouragement. All five students rushed forward together. Janil's spear hit the creature's center, eliciting an angry shriek.

The air mage's darts tore into limbs, doing much better against a closer enemy than the huge matriarch below. His darts sliced deep and sent green ichor spraying everywhere. The archer switched to daggers, flitting around the disoriented creature and stabbing at opportune targets. Turgan saw the wounds hanging open, bubbling unnaturally. An enchanted blade, maybe?

And then it broke out of the steam cloud, or at least a few of the dangerous limbs did. One stabbed out at Janil as she kept the creature pinned, working the spear back and forth inside its torso to do the most damage.

Turgan caught sight of sucker pads on the underside of the limb right before it stabbed the sharp claw at its end into Janil's side. Her leather armor barely slowed the thrust. She cried out in pain but didn't let go of the spear, grinding it harder into the monster.

Turgan threw himself toward the tentacle buried in his friend and used the last of his mana.

Drain! he commanded, pitting his will against the angry monster to give up the moisture that kept it alive.

For a moment, Turgan was sure he'd sealed his fate. A pragmatic voice inside his mind listed things in life he regretted not doing as the cold slimy limb spasmed under his hands, fighting his spell with a wild strength.

Drain! Turgan insisted again, determined that he would at least save one person by his death. He couldn't imagine a worse fate than dying for no reason at all. Digging deep, he pulled with all his strength, physically, mentally and magically.

The smallest flush of water made his palms wet, and a surge of excitement and victory strengthened him further.

Drain. Drain. Drain.

With each pull of the spell, Turgan felt the liquid inside the spawn surge out onto his hands, soaking his bracers and splashing across the front of his leather armor. Teeth bared in a harsh grimace he kept pulling, determined not to stop even as he felt his mana plummet.

From somewhere in the distance, voices yelled in effort and a horrendous bellow rose from below that might normally have triggered an instinct in Turgan to freeze or flee to safety. But his whole world had become the creature before him, not just the limb, but the entire beast. He sucked it dry with drip after drip of mana until a headache threatened, and he knew he was moments from a mana coma.

"Let go. It's dead. You did it!"

The words didn't penetrate, but the hard shove did, breaking his grip on the spawn's tentacle and sending Turgan staggering back a few steps. He shook his head to clear it and blinked at the shrunken creature lying unmoving on the stone floor, arrows protruding in all directions. It looked so pathetic now, a dried husk no more imposing than an empty suit of clothing.

Janil stood with a pained look on her face, one hand pressed to her side and breathing heavily.

The roar of triumph all along the wall startled Turgan. Surprised, he looked around, unsure why everyone would be cheering their victory over a single spawned creature.

Even Mage Bayle stepped back from the wall, her shield dissipating as she let her arms drop wearily to her sides.

The student archer was the first to figure it out. She ran to one of the murder holes and peered down before popping right back up with a huge grin on her face. "We did it. We killed the Void Matriarch!"

Turgan sagged slowly to the hard stone floor, hardly noticing how uncomfortable his wet leathers were.

"Hold still. I've got you," Mage Bayle said as she crouched down next to Janil and placed a hand on her wound. A bare moment later, she waved Turgan over. "Drink another potion and help me."

His mana and health had recovered the barest amount, and Turgan felt stupid that he'd let the headache distract him from using a potion. It only took a moment to knock one back. His headache already easing, he hurried over to Bayle and Janil.

"There's a touch of venom here," Bayle said. "Can you pull it out with your Cleanse? Then I can cauterize and heal the rest."

Nodding, Turgan crouched down next to Janil, doing his best not to look worn out.

Janil gave him a grateful smile before he closed his eyes and placed a hand on her side. He'd recovered just enough mana to reach for the tainted fluid and pull it from the wound in a noxious gush.

Mage Bayle took his place, and a few moments later, Janil let out a sigh of relief and sagged back.

When Mage Bayle stood back up, she gave the watching students a weary but grateful look. "Thank you for your help. You might not be very powerful yet, but every point of damage today was crucial." She cast a glance over at the shrunken corpse. "And keeping the spawn off of us so we could focus down below made all the difference."

Now that his health and mana were recovering, Turgan had the energy to smile. The inevitable excitement after a victory made him eye the corpse with speculation.

Mage Bayle chuckled, and he flushed.

"Don't be embarrassed," she chided. "You earned your share of that creature's level 11 water core, and while there won't be any blood left to harvest, I'm sure the hide, claws and teeth will be worth a pretty penny, too. Or if you can afford to keep the hide and have it made into armor, it would be a step up from what you've got now."

Turgan tried not to flush in embarrassment at the honest assessment as he ran through the crafting students he knew who might do a trade with him for labor.

"And anyone whose name comes up on the damage tally for the matriarch will get a share there, too," Bayle continued. "After the auditors come to an agreement tomorrow, your academy auditors should send you your totals."

All the students perked up at her words as they eyed the creature that had almost killed one of their own, but would instead make them stronger. As Turgan ran over the fight in his mind, he realized how much teamwork had made a difference.

His friends had already moved toward the door leading down and Mage Bayle stood by herself. It gave him the perfect opportunity.

Moving in close, he pitched his voice low and said, "I'd like to learn more from you, Mage Bayle."

She gave him a curious look. "But you're a water mage?"

"It's just, well—" his mouth was dry again, and he stuttered under her gaze, knowing what he was about to suggest could be considered close to heresy. Turgan swallowed hard and tried again. "I just saw how effective we were when both of our magics hit the beast, and it made me think I'd like to explore that idea going forward during fourth year. I know I'll have a water mage adviser, but perhaps I could come to you occasionally with ideas or questions? The beasts are getting stronger, so maybe we need to too?"

Bayle's expression had turned from congratulatory to concern as he continued speaking. She moved suddenly to put herself between him and the other students. Janil had stopped and looked back toward them.

With a strong grip, she pulled him off to one side and stepped in close. "You need to be very careful, young mage," she said in a low tone. "You know magical experimentation is expressly forbidden."

"But I wasn't—" Turgan protested. "Every mage knows experimenting with magic caused the cataclysm and released the monster hordes. I just meant we could plan more effects like the steam—"

"That was a happy accident," she instructed severely. "We may work together as mages and our spells, once cast, may overlap. We can't control that. But it's a basic tenet of our society that the four elemental magics have to be kept distinctly separate. Understand?"

He bobbed his head up and down, but he couldn't help that his mind spun off on a tangent wondering what combining magics might actually do. He shot a quick glance toward the outside edge of the wall and the dead behemoth he knew lay at the base. He spoke again, because he had to know. "And if the monsters keep coming and getting stronger?" He hesitated, knowing he might be skirting sacrilege with his next question. "Won't we need something new to fight them with? To save our people?"

Bayle followed his gaze and started to speak before she let out a sigh, shoulders slumping. She leaned in before whispering, "There may come a time when our traditional ways no longer work. But we're not there yet, and it's heresy to discuss the topic. Understand?"

Turgan met her eyes and saw both weariness and troubled

thoughts there. He nodded his understanding. She gave his shoulder a squeeze before giving him a nudge toward the stairwell.

The others had already left, so Turgan trudged back down the stairs, lost in thought. He knew he had to put such dangerous topics out of his mind. Fourth year started soon and earning the gold to make it this far without washing out meant he might have a shot at making a tower ring team in the future.

A tired grin returned to his face as he ducked into a side alcove and closed his eyes to access his menu and notifications. His grin widened as he saw the gains he'd made to his newly learned Spherical Spell ability, not to mention his Drain and Create.

Those gains and today's loot would give him the perfect boost to start the new school year.

BEST LAID PLANS

RELEASING A SLOW BREATH, Pax pressed one eye against the rough wood of the old barrels in front of him. His fellow Viper, Tomis crouched next to him, having squeezed himself into the small space. He pressed his face to a break between neighboring barrels. Together, they watched the festive atmosphere play out in the huge open space of the city's central square. Thanhil's inner keep reached to the sky on their left.

Pax clenched his jaw, fighting back his fury at watching the cream of the city's family celebrating while his best friend rotted in prison, a captured *shirker* to be forcibly awakened tomorrow. Malnourished and often sick, street rats didn't always survive the Awakening. With no coin or advocates, even if Amil survived the process, he'd still be sold off to the highest bidder as an indentured apprentice, regardless of what class he got.

Pax knew he and Tomis risked the same fate, if they were caught. It made more worry stab through him. By risking capture, he put the future of all his Vipers in danger. But he had to at least try to save Amil.

So Pax stewed, watching the wealthy out in force, proudly displaying their children, oblivious to the plights of those beneath them. Dressed in expensive candidate robes, many of the pampered children looked giddy about tomorrow's prospects.

Pax caught an occasional teen wearing a sullen expression, despite a well-fed face and wearing clothing that would feed Pax's entire crew for months. The adults were deep in conversations finalizing agreements that would give their children the best start to their new lives. So different from the fate of captured street rats.

Titus. Pax forced the old pain back down. His older brother had been caught in the final hunt just before an Awakening years ago, and no one had seen him again. Pax had been hopeful for months, examining every laborer or grunt among the crafters, warriors and merchants. But Titus was gone. Disappeared. Like his parents.

Pax forced his attention back to the square. He had to worry about his crew, his Vipers, right now. The wealthy continued their party, oblivious. Even the backdrop to the party screamed luxury. All the statues in the central fountain had been powered in an extravagant display of water magic. The street lamps glowed with costly flame cores instead of the more mundane oil and wicks used in the poorer sections of town.

Everywhere he looked, men, women and children were dressed in bright colors, full of smiles and a celebratory abandon that he couldn't remember ever feeling, even when his hardworking parents had been alive.

Food vendors called out, holding savory treats high and doing a brisk business. The smell of spicy kabobs and freshly baked buns made Pax's mouth water. He hoped the guard patrols would lighten up enough for him to scrounge through the alleys for leftovers later.

He forced himself to look past the happy throngs to the large stage that they assembled for the Awakening. The huge and sturdy structure had been erected in an open area just past the stone steps leading up to the courthouse and city offices.

Busy laborers swarmed on and around the brightly-lit stage with vague tool-shaped shadows in their hands. A handful of figures called out directions, hands pointing and gesticulating, likely crafters assigned to oversee and speed up the work with their skills. The stage itself was large enough to fit a few houses on the polished wooden expanse. A vast canopy covered the whole thing, protecting everything that had been set up for the ceremony tomorrow.

"Look to the far left," Tomis whispered. "I told you. That's where the governor will speak tomorrow."

Pax scanned the stage, quickly finding the podium of gleaming ironwood standing at one edge. According to Tomis, the governor would use a far-speaking device to announce the results for each youth as the mages awakened them.

Pax gave his friend an acknowledging look. Tomis was a large boy, the mix of dwarf in his heritage obvious in the stout features of his developing man's growth. His chest had filled out while his feet and legs became clumsy and difficult to manage. A rumpled mop of sandy hair flopped over eyes that were often patient and kind when he'd be better served by being harder.

A lifetime of his father's censure had left Tomis frequently looking down, shoulders hunched and expecting a blow. At least his brute of a father had taken him to observe a handful of Awakenings, unlike the rats, who always hid from the bounty hunters. And with tonight's emergency bringing them out of hiding, Tomis' knowledge was critical.

A swell in sound drew Pax's attention back to the square. At the center of the large stage the crafters had built a circular pedestal with ornately carved patterns and gilded accents with just enough room for a single person to stand on. Lit brightly, it stood empty but made Pax shiver as he imagined Amil in chains standing there tomorrow.

The workers had placed four elegant chairs equidistant from the pedestal, at each of the four corners of the compass. They looked like thrones. Crafters had carved and painted intricate depictions of the four elements in such detail that some almost looked alive, even from a distance.

Seats of honor for the visiting mages from the capital.

The mages who forged children into adults, and began one's service to the community. At least if you weren't a shirking street rat. Most of the rats Pax knew would rather starve, alive and free.

Though, for a brief flash, Pax couldn't help wondering what it would be like. A full menu. Completely unlocked instead of the bare juvenile version he had. The possibility of crafting, merchant and martial skills or even the rare ability to use magic had appeal. The street posters promised good masters and a better life for shirkers who awakened to those classes. No one mentioned the all-too-common laborer class.

Pax swiped in irritation as his thoughts triggered his crippled menu.

~

Name: Pax Truesworn
  Race: Mixed Human (monster-touched)
  Age: 16
  Bound Location: Locked
  Class: Locked
  Level: Locked
  Health: Locked
  Mana: Locked
  Attributes: Locked
  Skills/Abilities/Spells: Locked
  Inventory: 1/10 available. Restricted to 10 time-delayed slots
  Assignments: Locked
  Misc.: Locked

~

HE FROWNED. Even his internal inventory was pretty useless. Unawakened children had a thirty-second time delay on placing and removing items from their inventory. This made it impractical to summon or switch weapons during a fight or to stash stolen items fast enough while pickpocketing. Other than a ring his mother had given him and a medallion from his brother, he had nothing much of value. His coin count was barely above zero either, just a handful of copper, barely more than half a silver.

~

Coin Count: 0 Gold, 0 Silver, 52 copper

~

Annoyed, Pax mentally swiped the display away and looked across the square again.

A flash of movement toward the back of the stage caught his eye, and he pushed aside any flights of fancy about the Awakening. Reality was entirely different from daydreams, as anyone living on the streets knew well.

Tomis gave Pax's shoulder a soft nudge. "It's them," he whispered under his breath.

Pax squinted, looking.

A ripple of excitement traveled through the crowd as hands pointed and heads leaned in to whisper to neighbors.

And then he saw them. A group of four people ascended the steps to the stage. The workers parted for them, altering their busy paths like a river did around imposing rocks.

Pax's face split into a fierce grin as he turned to the large mixed-dwarven boy with approval. He leaned close to Tomis' ear. "You were right." Pax barely moved his lips. "They did come tonight. To prepare."

Tomis grinned at the praise and leaned in close, too. "Don't worry, First. It'll be a cinch to follow them back to their inn. We won't lose them."

Pax nodded before turning back. Their plan wasn't complicated. They couldn't free Amil from the guarded prison, and the ceremony tomorrow was too dangerous to approach. That left one option.

Tonight, they would follow the mages and figure out where they were staying, so they could intercept Amil during the transfer. Their powerful magic had discouraged idle gossip, and their inn was somewhere in the wealthy quarter where details were scarce. However, if they could find a good lookout nearby, they could free Amil during the distraction of the mages joining up with the candidates.

Pax narrowed his gaze, attempting to make out details of the four figures who probably had enough power between them to take on an entire regiment of soldiers, not to mention probably all the city's wall mages combined. These were capital mages, one of each element, with the power to use an ancient artifact to permanently awaken the youth of the Astan Empire's cities.

From a distance, their arm markings appeared to be nothing more than colorful scrawls. Still, their clothing made them stand out like nobility among dowdy peasants. Their rich fabric announced their magical elements to everyone as it glistened in the stage's light.

As the flame mage moved to his chair, he shimmered like a six-foot bonfire. The air mage, with the tall willowy shape of an elf, wore a wispy outfit and didn't even touch the floor as she flitted to hers. Pax could almost hear water flowing as the blue water mage slid with an uncanny grace to settle into her chair. The earth mage was the only one who could be called unattractive. He moved with the grace of a tumbling boulder, a solid and relatively tall dwarf. His weight and strength made his chair strain to hold him when he sank into it.

Even from where he hid, the hair on the back of Pax's neck rose, an instinctive warning of danger. He could evade the guardsmen and, given enough luck, break free from one. Sure, members of the guard had leveled abilities, but Pax and his Vipers had long practice countering them.

But a mage? With elemental spells? Pax had no illusions that if the city really wanted to root out the homeless, a handful of mages could accomplish it much more effectively than the guard or even the soldiers.

Thankfully, the ever-increasing monster hordes kept both mages and warriors too occupied on the city walls to bother themselves much with inner city business.

Except once a year. At the Awakening. Every class needed more bodies for their ranks and fought over numbers. Each new recruit was valuable, whether a willing citizen or one of the coerced shirkers who survived the process.

Pax pursed his lips, anger at the injustice swelling inside him. He'd never submit and swore to make sure none of his Vipers did either.

"They're moving," Tomis whispered in his ear.

Pax focused on the stage. After adjusting controls on their complex chairs, the mages had stood and were now moving again.

Around the square, the crowds had grown. Pax realized they would have a harder time slipping away without attracting notice.

"Quick," Pax hissed. "No running. We're strolling this time. Look natural and stay close. To the alley and then to the back of the buildings on the far side of the square. We need to get there in time to follow them."

Tomis nodded without speaking and pulled his legs in to let Pax clamber over him.

After checking both directions and finding no one paying the area close attention, Pax slipped one hand out. He raised his palm in question toward the alley where Jules, their lookout, should be able to see it and give them a response.

Nothing. The shadowed opening stood still and empty.

Impatience swelled, but Pax kept his hand steady. Small, quick motions would catch the eye, which was the last thing he wanted.

Come on, Jules, Pax silently urged the young girl to pay attention and respond. The mages would be climbing down from the stage by now.

Then a small grimy fist appeared from the shadows of the alley, close to the ground and hard to see.

Safe! The triumphant thought filled Pax. He'd worried Jules would give them the open-handed stop sign for danger, or no sign at all.

But Jules was safe, and the alley was, too.

Time to look like an average kid trying to get a glimpse of the festivities. Pax stood slowly, as if he'd just been fixing his shoe, and took a step toward the alley.

Tomis stood behind him. Or tried to. His legs must have gone numb from the cramped position. With a stifled cry, he stumbled and landed hard on hands and knees before Pax could catch him. His face twisted in sudden pain, but he thankfully bit back another cry.

"Relax," Pax whispered as he leaned down and pulled Tomis to his feet. "I've got you."

"Do your parents know you're out here drinking?" a thin and reedy voice demanded from behind them.

Pax controlled his flinch and quickly ducked his head, looking as penitent as possible before he turned.

An older lady dressed in multiple layers, including a pretentious hat with too many feathers that flickered in the lamplight, glared at them with disapproval. A younger man supported her elbow and made an impatient noise, his eyes flicking back toward the festivities.

"Sorry, ma'am," Pax said. "We're heading home now."

She sniffed, eyes narrowing. "Perhaps we should take your names to make sure your parents hear of your behavior."

"Mother!" the man said, pulling on her arm and barely giving the two street rats a glance.

Pax snuck a few steps toward the alley when the woman turned to swat at the man. He froze when she whirled back toward them, mouth turned down in a frown.

"Wait," she said, only to pause when her eyes drifted down to the arm Pax had wrapped around Tomis' waist. The position had pulled his sleeve up, exposing his left forearm.

Her eyes widened, and she choked off the words she'd been about to say. Pax watched her silently mouth the two words that had haunted him his whole life. *Monster-touched*. Instead of the usual disgust, though, a just-as-unwelcome sympathy made her eyes soften.

Pax barely controlled his expression and pulled his sleeve back into place before she could say anything. He turned his back and pulled Tomis toward the safety of the alley. His shoulders tensed the entire time, expecting her to stop them.

But she didn't.

And when he shot a glance back, he only saw the woman aiming a look over her shoulder as the man pulled her into the crowd.

Pax hurried into the cool shadows with relief. Beside him, Tomis straightened and blew out a happy breath. Impatient now, Pax motioned for Tomis to hurry as he strode along the wall, scanning the alley for Jules. Where was she?

The new knot of worry loosened when he spotted her dirt-streaked face peek out from behind a pile of construction refuse. He was already striding toward her when a sense of unease warned him something wasn't right. She stood stiff and tense instead of returning his smile. And was that remorse in her eyes?

Too late, he spun, mouth open to warn Tomis.

"Two more for the pot, right, Jonson?" A guard had stepped into the opening of the alley behind them, his nightstick out and ready. He was tall and lithe, with hard, active eyes full of experience that told Pax he'd be hard to dodge past. He likely had a high-level capture skill. "I knew this alley was too quiet tonight."

Pax reacted instantly, spinning to race back into the alley, his shoes slipping and scrambling on debris. But a second guard stepped out from behind Jules, clamping one hand down on her shoulder while raising the other, fist clenched, to her head. Pax's step stuttered, and he froze in place.

The new guard looked not much older than Pax. His guard blues were unfaded with the creases still sharp. The silver piping flashing in the alley's shadows. But he stood a head taller than Pax, and his broad weight was proof of a much better diet.

"Right, sir," the burly youth said, a cruel smile of anticipation lighting his face as he stepped farther out, dragging Jules' slight form with him. "I need to level up my Punch and Grip tonight."

"Don't just blab your abilities to the rats like that, Jonson!" snapped the older guard. "They can't use Identify yet or have it high enough to see your stuff."

Jonson's face flushed for a moment before he glared at Pax and Tomis. He gave Jules a shake that made her whimper.

Tomis shot Pax a helpless look, his eyes begging for direction.

"Listen up," snapped Jonson, still looking angry about his superior's correction. "You two are going to hold still while Guardsman Spalder restrains you. Otherwise, we'll have to force you to comply.

And it's going to hurt. A lot. Starting with this one here." He hefted Jules until her feet left the ground with an ease that suggested he'd already increased his Strength and leveled his Grip, a favorite path of brawler-focused guardsmen.

Pax hesitated. The eager look in Jonson's eyes made his stomach twist. He caught Jules' desperate gaze, and the girl's eyes brimmed with unshed tears as she mouthed the word, *Sorry*.

Pax didn't want to imagine what they'd threatened her with so she would betray them. Not that he blamed her.

The number one rule on the streets was survival.

And he was failing miserably tonight.

2

FIGHT THE GOOD FIGHT

PAX HADN'T SURVIVED on the street by being slow. Any action, even the wrong one, often made the difference between capture and freedom. Though Pax wasn't particularly strong, he was fast and agile.

And determined.

He'd rather end up a bleeding mess curled in a dark corner of the city than give up.

He possessed two weapons, slender forearm-lengths of scavenged earth-monster bone, which he had etched to a midnight dullness, making them almost invisible in even the slightest bit of shadow. A smart rat avoided using knives, which drew blood and could cause permanent injuries or even death, increasing the likelihood of a manhunt.

His cudgels proved significantly better, able to deliver a swift blow to a skull or joint to cause enough pain and distraction to escape most situations.

Pain. Right now, he needed to inflict a lot of pain on the young guardsman holding Jules, or they would all be joining Amil in lockup that night.

"Please," Pax said in a defeated voice, letting his shoulders slump and hands drop to his side, where they were closer to his weapon hilts. "Just let Jules go, and we'll come with you."

Jonson's grin widened as he straightened and let his free hand relax. He twisted the top of Jules' shirt and shook her like a small ragdoll. "No deal. This little rat is useful. She helped us easily trap you, all so we would leave the other littles alone. They're too young for tomorrow, so it's a good trade all around."

Pax heard movement behind him. He wrapped his hands around the grips of his slim sticks strapped tightly to his legs beneath his pants.

"She's our golden ticket to rooting out the rest of the older shirkers in your crew," Spalder agreed from behind Pax, satisfaction clear in his voice. "By morning, I bet we'll have the record."

"And even some gold," Jonson said, his grin widening as his eyes filled with greed.

Sharp regret swelled in Pax's throat. He'd known risking their entire crew to save Amil was a bad idea.

But a reckless abandon had raged through him ever since Amil had let the guards take him to save Tomis. The hot ember of rage burning in Pax's center flared, aimed at Jonson standing in front of him, full of confidence and swagger.

With Jules being threatened into giving up all their secrets, Pax had nothing left to lose.

The sensation was freeing.

Pax's eyes flicked to Tomis and then Jules as he twisted two fingers in the ready signal against his leg. Tomis startled and then looked down at the ground, his posture mimicking Pax's defeated one.

"That's it," Spalder said behind them. "Hands behind your backs and hold still."

Pax was proud to see Tomis bend his knees slightly and shift his feet to get a more stable stance as he moved his arms behind his back. The brief flicker of surprise and gratitude he saw in Jules' eyes was quickly cloaked.

It was time.

Pax jerked his head up and to the left, letting his eyes go wide and his mouth drop open in shock and fear. Like an idiot, Jonson's gaze lurched to the side, looking for danger.

The three street rats exploded into action.

Spalder let out a surprised curse behind them, and Pax heard his boots lurching forward.

In front of Pax, Jules squirmed to the ground, both hands raised high in a move perfected by toddlers insisting their mothers put them down. Jonson's attention jerked back to the slippery street urchin. He fought to control her, only to end up holding a ragged and completely empty tunic. Jules scrambled away into the shadows.

Off to Pax's side, Tomis spun and darted away in the opposite direction. He threw a fistful of sand from his pocket in Spalder's face as Pax had trained him. When the older guard jerked his hands to his face with an oath, Tomis jumped sideways and raced toward the alley's entrance.

Pax hadn't wasted the time either. He kicked off the alley's gravel surface and launched his wiry body across the intervening space straight at the young guard. While in motion, he shoved his hands into slitted openings in his pants. He grabbed his leather-wrapped clubs and whipped them free with the ease of long practice. He'd even learned to compensate for the stiffness in his left arm, keeping its motions shorter and closer to his body.

He didn't have to beat the guard, just get past him and make it to the sewer entrance. The man's large frame could never follow him down the narrow shaft.

Too focused on losing Jules, Jonson still hadn't seen Pax's charge. Face twisted with anger, Jonson ripped Jules' tunic into two pieces with a shout of frustration. He scanned the back of the alley for the young girl.

Pax's elbows bent, the ends of his bone clubs whipping around with a quiet whistle in the evening air. Two more steps.

Some instinct made Jonson jerk around just in time, eyes widening at Pax's figure rushing through the shadows. The young guard raised both arms into a defensive posture, hands protecting his face and elbows pulled in close to his ribs, a classic brawler's stance.

It didn't really matter.

Pax wasn't aiming for his face or ribs.

With a sharp crack, Pax slammed his first club into Jonson's leading knee, followed by a solid blow to his elbow with the other.

Jonson yelled in pain, his front leg buckling suddenly which caused his bulk to topple forward and down onto one knee as he tucked his injured arm instinctively against his body.

A cry followed by sounds of a scuffle rang out behind him. Pax couldn't spare any attention to help Tomis. Jules had broken free. Now both boys needed to scatter in different directions to give them all the best chance of getting away safely.

Pax's sticks flashed again, striking a shoulder and wrist as he tried to dodge safely past Jonson's bulk through the narrow space left between him and the pile of construction debris.

Jonson growled, struggling to get to his feet. He whipped a meaty hand from his half-kneeling position with more speed than Pax had expected.

Pax jumped up, just in time, jerking midair in an acrobatic twist to clear the man's arm. Jonson's hand whizzed beneath him, only for his other flailing arm to catch the trailing toe of Pax's shoe.

It was only a small impact, but midair, it disrupted Pax's movement, making him land with feet half-tangled as he nearly slipped.

His practiced speed and agility came to his rescue. He stabbed one club into a wall to stay upright and scrabbled for purchase on the ground. His lucky earth-skin soles on his otherwise worthless shoes proved their worth once again. They gained traction and kept him upright when a lesser material would have slipped.

Thank you, brother, he thought, remembering who'd given him the shoes so long ago, telling him to save them for when he was big enough. Still on his feet and almost free, Pax bolted for the sliver of space between the brick and an old leaning gate. A triumphant grin spread across his face. Just a few more steps.

A heavy hand clamped around his ankle with the feel of an iron chain and jerked him to a stop so abruptly it threw the rest of him forward, slamming him to the hard ground.

The pain, sudden and shocking, stabbed through his hands and knees and knocked the air out of him. But it was hardly the first time someone had hurt Pax. His survival instincts had him kicking with his free foot as he twisted over to his back to fight his way free.

Jonson, grinning widely, pushed himself to his feet. He squeezed Pax's ankle with his powered Grip.

Pax clenched his jaw and fought, jerking the captured leg back while simultaneously kicking forward with his free foot, aiming for Jonson's hand. It was like kicking a brick wall and just as ineffective.

Jonson laughed, but it was an angry laugh promising retribution.

Panic flared. Pax pulled his torso up and forward, bent almost double, and whipped his clubs forward to slam into the hand trapping his ankle, feet still scissoring as he tried to break free.

Two solid blows hit the knuckles and back of Jonson's hand. The young guard let out a harsh growl but didn't let go. Instead, he tightened his grip and gave Pax's leg a savage jerk. The powerful motion threw Pax's upper body backwards, his clubs flailing. He barely had time to tuck his chin so his head wouldn't crack down onto the alley floor.

"I'll teach you—" Jonson growled as he laced his other hand around Pax's ankle and shook it two-handed. The ankle bones ground against each other.

A stifled scream made it past Pax's lips as he arched back, desperate to free himself.

"Shut him up, Jonson," the first guard snapped. "Besides, we're not dragging him by his foot to lockup. Switch your grip to the kid's wrist already, so we can turn these two in and earn more bounties tonight."

Jonson gave Pax's leg one last shake. The pain was so intense, Pax felt his vision dim and nausea rise in his throat. He let himself sag back, barely noticing the rocks and other trash digging into his back. He needed to save his strength. There would be another chance later. He just needed a moment of inattention.

Moving more cautiously than before, Jonson stepped up beside him and kicked both of Pax's clubs free. They clanged off into the darkness. Pax wondered if he'd ever get them back.

Still keeping hold of his ankle with one hand, Jonson reached down to grab Pax's wrist with the other. Once he had secured a grip, he peeled his fingers away from Pax's throbbing ankle and let his foot flop to the ground.

"Get up," he said, jerking on Pax's wrist.

Pax bit his lip, refusing to cry out in pain as he stumbled up to his feet and tried to stand properly. Jonson gave him another shake, but Pax ignored him and hurried to scan the front of the alley.

His heart sank. He'd heard Spalder say two of them and saw the truth he'd feared. Tomis hadn't escaped either. Flat on his face, Tomis didn't struggle as Spalder held him down with a knee and wrenched his hands together behind his back. The guard pulled leather bindings free from a pouch at his side.

When Spalder looked back over his shoulder and saw the junior guard dragging Pax closer, his expression turned impatient. "Get bindings on him already. We don't have all night."

The moment's inattention was all Tomis needed. He bucked hard and pushed both arms straight out from his side. The unexpected move broke Tomis' hands free and made the guard's head lurch forward, only to meet the back of Tomis' head with a painful crack that echoed through the alley.

All of Spalder's muscles seemed to sag, and Tomis scrambled to untangle himself from the guard's limbs so he could get to his feet. Spalder sat back from the boy, eyes out of focus as his unsteady hands reached for his face. Pax could see a dark streak of blood smeared across his mouth and lips.

"You little piece of—" Jonson roared, dropping Pax's wrist and lunging toward Tomis. In two swift strides, he was close enough to aim a powerful kick at Tomis, who still fought to rise from his hands and knees.

For the shortest of moments, time seemed to slow. Pax contemplated a fast spin to escape out the back of the alley. It was the smart thing to do. If they captured him, he'd lose any chance of breaking Amil or Tomis free.

Jules was the smarter one.

But Pax was sick of being smart. And he knew exactly how much damage the brawler-leveled kick would do to Tomis. It'd cripple his friend, if not worse.

Decision made, Pax leaped toward Jonson's back, jabbing punches into the man's kidneys with a flurry of rage-fueled strikes. One after another sank into the man's uniformed back, low and to either side of his spine.

Muscles could protect the abdomen, and ribs, but the kidneys? Not so much.

The unexpected pain and attack was enough to throw Jonson's aim off. His kick caught Tomis along one flank instead of square under his torso where it would have broken ribs and important parts underneath.

Tomis flew back with a cry and crumpled into a limp pile. Jonson twisted around, roaring, his beefy arms and hands swinging and reaching for Pax.

Now was the time to escape. Pax had done all he could for Tomis, and if he couldn't outrun one clumsy guard, he deserved to be caught. Backpedaling, Pax ducked to evade a powerful punch, feet churning as he twisted to race away.

Only to trip as something wrapped around his ankles, a cord or rope. It felled him into a tangled heap of limbs in the middle of the alley.

He jerked, trying to get up, just in time to see Jonson's heavy boot racing toward him. With a skill he'd learned much too young, Pax curled himself into a ball, tucking his head and wrapping his hands to either side for extra protection.

The kick slammed into his shoulder and side. Pax bit down on a scream.

"Don't kill him," he heard Spalder snap. "If he needs too much healing, we won't get as much."

"I don't care," Jonson growled, landing another kick into Pax's torso that made nausea rise in his throat. "It's worth gettin' a smaller bounty to teach this flick a lesson."

Another kick.

Pax stifled a groan.

"That's enough," Spalder snapped. "I said stop. That's an order!"

"Yes, sir," said Jonson, his tone reluctant as he lowered his leg and settled back.

"Listen," Spalder said, sounding more conciliatory now that the junior guardsman had complied. "We both want the bounty. And I earned it. Without my Bolo skill, he'd have escaped."

The wonderful break allowed Pax to suck in short, careful breaths and try not to cough on the fluids filling his mouth. He was grateful the brute had obeyed his trainer.

"I understand," Jonson said, still breathing heavily with a background of rage in his voice.

The gravel crunched as he stepped toward Pax again, who tensed into a tighter ball.

"Shirking flick," he snarled and then spat.

Pax barely noticed the warm liquid hitting the back of his hand and cheek, just glad it wasn't another kick.

"And you might want to invest in a weapon skill like my Bolo," he heard Spalder add, as his lighter footsteps moved closer. "You won't always be near enough to rely on only your brawler skills, got it?"

"Yes, sir," Jonson said, sounding calmer.

Pax didn't dare uncurl from his position to see.

"And since you're the one who laid both of them out, you get to carry them to the prison."

Prison. Where Amil was. Where they'd hold them and force them to go through the Awakening tomorrow, if they couldn't find a way free before then.

Nauseating pain swirled with Pax's jumbled thoughts. His future had just changed completely.

Would he disappear like his brother? Or find himself an indentured laborer shipped off to an unknown city? Amidst the depressing voices, a curious thought arose, a youthful one that he usually suppressed.

What class would he be, and what would a full menu look like?

At the thought, his juvenile menu manifested again. Pax stopped it with a harsh mental command. Somehow, he had to escape before the morning came.

Someone grabbed him around the waist and hefted him into the air. The agony took his breath away, so he couldn't even cry out. A dark funnel pushed in from the edges of his mind. When his head jolted repeatedly against the guard's back, he finally passed out.

3

THERE'S ALWAYS A CHANCE

ANXIETY GREW in Pax as he slumped back on the thin pallet and glared sightlessly into the thick darkness of the cell. He'd explored the entirety of the cramped space to find that rough stone surrounded him on all sides except for a door made of iron bars too close together to squeeze through.

And he'd tried. After waking up alone and in darkness, he'd been surprised to find most of the pain from the evening's beating had faded. Someone had spent a minor heal on him, something he'd only experienced once before, as a child before his parents had disappeared.

Feeling good, he'd been determined to escape, doing his best to squeeze his skinny, malnourished body through the bars. He'd even gotten most of the way through, but not his head. He'd scraped the skin above his ears on either side bloody from trying.

He wondered how many prisoners had died in this exact cell. The idea brought back a recent memory that made him shiver. Tomis had been leading them through a new set of tunnels, and they'd stumbled upon a body. Not that it was the first body Pax had seen, but never one like this one.

Something had sucked the very life out of the poor man, leaving his skin shrunken like parchment around his bones and his clothes looking many sizes too big. And his face. Ugh. The skull still haunted him, its sunken eyes and gaping mouth covered by a thin layer of pale skin pulled tight over the bone, ragged hair in disarray still attached to the scalp.

Strangest of all, the body hadn't smelled. At all. If there was one thing Pax knew very well about the dead, animals and people alike, it was that they quickly smelled before turning into a rotten mess that eventually degraded into the dirt. But this corpse? Pax shuddered again, suspecting it was still sitting there, watching and waiting to scare another street rat to death. Pax didn't know what kind of magic would kill like that and never wanted to know.

Not sure if he was more afraid of the Awakening or being forgotten and left to die, Pax had switched to digging at the rusty pins holding the hinges of the door in place. That just left him with bloody fingertips and broken nails.

When he'd checked his inventory for something that might help, he found they'd only left him the two trinkets from his mom and brother. Not a scrap of food, a copper or extra bedding. Some high-level guard in the prison must have used an ability to empty it. At least his two sentimental items had looked worthless enough to let him keep. Pax rubbed at his eyes and clenched his jaw. He hated feeling so helpless, but levels and strength trumped anything he could do.

And he still didn't know where Tomis or Amil were. He'd yelled out in the darkness, but the only response had been a stab of light from the hallway, followed by an angry guard jabbing a hard stick through the bars and threatening to do more if he didn't shut up.

Letting out a frustrated breath, Pax racked his brain for a new idea. The tiny cell was too small and empty to offer anything. When he stood and stretched, Pax could almost touch both sides of the cell. Besides the thin pallet and scratchy blanket, he'd felt a smelly waste hole in the corner covered by an embedded grate which left one of his hands stinking. It was big enough for rats to get through, but not much else.

Out of ideas, Pax lifted the pallet and explored its length with sore fingers, squeezing along the edges, careful not to miss any sections. Maybe a previous prisoner had hidden something useful inside.

It didn't take long for him to explore the meager bedding and find absolutely nothing. Discouraged and with the oppressive darkness pressing down on him, Pax gave in and turned to the one indulgence that had always lifted his spirits: his secret spark.

He scooted to the door, pushed his face between the bars and cast a furtive glance down the dark hallway, where he could see a thin line of light under the door at the far end.

Quiet and still.

Reassured, Pax moved to the far corner of his cell and sat down with his back to the door. He curled around his cupped hands and, with the ease of long familiarity, he freed the knot inside him that released his spark. At least that's what he'd always called it. It had been his dangerous secret for so long that he'd never dared ask others if they knew what it was.

Letting out a slow breath, Pax relaxed as he felt it travel out of his center. With the feel of cool water dribbling down his chin, clean and pure, until it popped out of his palm. Staring, he let himself forget his situation and just enjoy the cool ball of light. Not much bigger than the tip of his thumb, it shimmered and awaited his instructions. Its small size only lit the area within his palms, but the dim light seemed all the brighter in the cloying darkness of his cell.

Pax's shoulders relaxed, and he smiled for the first time that night. "Hello there," he whispered, making the spark dance from finger to finger with the barest touch of mental effort. Pax let himself sink into the bright relaxation that always accompanied the manifestation of his spark. His fear and confusion eased just a touch, and the muscles in his chest loosened, letting his breathing come easier.

"I've missed you," he said with a wistful gaze, realizing the nasty cell had one benefit: no curious eyes to see his spark.

A sudden memory made the edges of his smile fade. The first time he'd discovered his spark, he'd run to show his mother. Instead of matching his excitement, Ma had hissed at him to make it go away before snatching him up and hurrying him home. She'd shut him in his room before leaving to drag Da from his leatherworking. The worried tones of their muffled discussion outside in the hall had knotted Pax's belly with worry or fear.

Their stern faces when they entered the room had made it even worse. There'd been a lot of lecturing about dangers and threats that he didn't remember now. His parents had forbidden him from ever lighting his spark again.

He'd cried. Ma had explained that the spark was something special that might make others want to hurt him or try to steal it. But it was their fear, more than anything, that had scared him into keeping the promise they'd made him swear.

Until the night the Guard dragged them away, and they never came back. The oppressive confines of his cell made flashes of that night come back with a vengeance. The hidden closet at the back of Da's room had been small and pitch dark too. Just before the guards came, their mother had stuffed the two brothers inside and told them not to come out until morning, no matter what they heard.

Listening to the scary sounds that night, Pax had shaken and stifled sobs. Only Titus' arms wrapped around him and his hand over Pax's mouth had kept them from being discovered. It was hours after the last yells and screams had faded before they dared leave. They grabbed a few supplies before fleeing to the slums. They'd never gone back or seen their parents again.

Pax remembered little about those first years with his brother on the streets. But, adrift and afraid, he'd needed something, anything, to help keep him from falling apart. So, he'd broken his promise to his parents. In stolen moments of rare privacy, he'd brought out his spark and let its soothing presence ground and anchor him. He'd only ever shown it to Titus, who'd also had no explanation for its danger or importance either. Titus had advised Pax to keep it secret, like their parents had told him. And so, he had.

Fighting to push back the dark memories, Pax focused on his spark, moving it up and down his arms and across his chest, letting the peace that always accompanied it soak into him.

The problem with a little light was that it made his surroundings somewhat visible. Stains covered the pallet. Pax was sure he saw the slight movements of bedbugs. The blanket wasn't much better, so threadbare that the edges had partially unraveled, and multiple holes dotted its surface.

But it gave him a desperate idea. Pax ignored the stabbing pain in his fingers as he tore the blanket into the thinnest strips he could, directing his spark to light his work where he most needed it. With each set of strips, Pax stopped tearing and twisted. Holding the ends between his feet, he forced his abused hands to twist them one way and then combine multiple lengths together.

After what seemed like hours, Pax finally sat back in satisfaction. He had two thin, but strong, pieces of cord the length of his arm. He didn't think his mother would have ever imagined that he would use her tailoring instruction like this. They weren't really weapons unless he could get five minutes alone with a guard to choke him out. Even so, it made him feel better than having nothing at all.

A loud clang from down the hall made Pax's head jerk around and instinctively snuff his spark. Hands suddenly shaking, he wrapped the two cords into tight rounds he slid carefully into the inside edges of his slip-on shoes.

Light poured down the hallway just as Pax adjusted the edges of the cord to a spot where he could easily grab them and pull the lengths out in a single, smooth movement.

Wiping his nervous and sweaty hands on his pants, Pax stood and turned to face the iron door that had bested him through the night.

"Time to get up, shirkers!" yelled a voice, followed by a harsh clanging down the hall. More yelling and the noise moved closer.

Pax shifted to the back wall of the stone cell, not wanting to take another blow through the bars of the door.

A bulky figure appeared suddenly, his nightstick slamming hard into Pax's door as he continued to yell for everyone to wake up. He didn't pause, and Pax couldn't stifle a relieved sigh when the man continued his cacophonous rousing down the hall.

A few minutes later, Pax heard a commotion back toward the front of the hall. A dull crack sounded, followed by someone crying out and more yelling.

4

CHAIN GANG

PAX TOOK A STEP FORWARD, wanting to sneak a quick look through the bars so he could prepare for whatever was happening out there. Just as he got close, another guard appeared, pulling a cart behind him. Pax flinched back when he stopped at Pax's door.

"Back against the wall." This guard was smaller, his eyes angry and narrowed over a beak of a nose. "Hands where I can see them."

Pax complied quickly.

Producing a ring of keys, the guard had Pax's door open in no time.

"Don't even think about it," barked the man as he grabbed a small bucket from the bottom of his cart and set it just inside the cell, water slopping over the lip. Next, he tossed a stack of clothing on the floor beside the bucket.

Before Pax could think of trying anything, the guard had shut the door with a hefty clunk.

He eyed Pax, face twisted with distaste as he rattled off instructions. "Strip everything off. Use the rag and water to wash yourself. Put on the clean clothes. Do *not* keep any of your own dirty rags. You have five minutes to finish or one of us will come in and do it for you."

His grin turned nasty. "And you really don't want one of us to come in and wash you. Got it?"

Pax clenched his jaw and gave the man the smallest of nods. The guard had already grabbed his cart and pulled it noisily to the next cell. Pax sprang into motion, hoping to finish before anyone else came to stare at him through the cell bars.

He took a quick sniff of the water, surprised at how clean it seemed. After a cautious sip, he took a handful of deep swallows before getting busy following instructions.

When he was done, he had to admit that despite being scratchy, the tunic and pants weren't half bad, made of a thick material that wouldn't tear easily. They'd even dyed the fringes of the sleeves and pant legs in Thanhil's traditional blue.

Pax had just finished pulling his shoes back on and secreting the two lengths of cords when a third guard appeared at his cell door, a ring of keys in one hand and a set of manacles in the other. A large man, he moved slower than the other guards. The buttons of his uniform strained to contain his bulk.

"Hands out through the bars," the man barked impatiently. "Now!"

Pax jerked into motion, clambering to his feet, even though the last thing he wanted to do was approach the door.

"Through the same gap, idiot," yelled the guard as he lifted one manacle and clamped it tightly around Pax's left hand.

Pax hurried to move his right hand into the same space as his left before his eyes stared down at the soft glow that was already fading from the manacle on his left wrist.

Horror filled him as he realized the significance. The manacles were powered, likely by tiny earth cores, which meant there would be no escape without the control stone.

Pax tried to jerk his right hand back, but despite his size, the guard was fast. His hand clamped down, immediately followed by the rough surface of the second manacle closing around Pax's other wrist.

"This one's done," the guard called to his left before flipping through his keys and using one to open Pax's door. Then, without another word, he moved further down the hallway to the next cell.

Before Pax could consider making a run for it, another guard appeared in the doorway and extended a long baton toward Pax's manacles. The end of the baton snapped into contact with the center chain attaching the two manacles, jerking Pax's hands forward. With the baton now connected and keeping Pax at a safe distance, the guard didn't even look at him. He simply turned and walked back the way he'd come so suddenly that Pax was almost pulled off his feet.

Scrambling to stay upright, he followed the man who led him down the hallway lined on one side by identical cells, all standing empty now. Pax looked for Tomis and Amil, but they'd already emptied this part of the prison.

Stepping through the far doorway, they emerged into a larger room with doorways leading to multiple hallways; obviously a room for the guards. Chairs and tables sat with remnants of meals and card games strewn about, now left unattended.

A weapons rack stood mostly empty against the far wall, only a few worn nightsticks and a single cracked helmet still sat on it. An alcove to the left held racks of uniforms and other clothing hung in a haphazard array. Pax realized that even if he'd squeezed through the bars of his door, he'd never have made it past this room unseen.

Other guards emerged from adjoining hallways, dragging their own prisoners along with the same callousness as Pax. But he still didn't see either of his friends.

In moments, Pax was being pulled up the stone stairs at the end of the breakroom and out into a walled courtyard. Drizzling rain filled the predawn dimness, while shadows flickered from the lit sconces arrayed along the walls. No one was wasting flame stones here. And above the walls, Pax could see just the faintest hint of the coming dawn.

Other young prisoners stood shivering, looking miserable, chained together in multiple lines. Up at the front of the courtyard, he saw the guards had attached their guide chains to a row of stone posts anchored in the ground. Behind them, two sides of a large wooden gate banded with strips of dark iron loomed ominously.

With efficient movements, the guard pulled Pax to the end of one of the prisoner lines. He grabbed the trailing end of the chain and, with a quick manipulation of the control baton, attached Pax just behind a young girl with tear-streaked cheeks who wouldn't meet his eyes.

Pax ignored her, turning his head to search among the shadowed crowd for some sign of his two friends. Was that Amil? Pax squinted. Another figure seemed to have Tomis' bulk.

"Amil! Tomis!" Pax couldn't stop himself from yelling out as he craned to see over the other heads.

Two rows over, a tow-headed figure jerked around. Pax glimpsed familiar features just before something smacked into the back of his head, reigniting last night's headache. Pax tried to jerk his hands to his head, only to pull against the manacles.

A guard raised what looked like a padded nightstick in warning. Pax spared a moment to be grateful they weren't striking with their usual iron-hard sticks.

"Quiet, or you'll get more," the guard growled.

Pax quickly shifted to the submissive posture he'd often used to pacify authority figures. It worked. The guard moved back to patrolling the other captives. As soon as he'd moved to another row, Pax strained to look in Amil's direction again . . . and found him staring back.

They exchanged tight smiles and something loosened inside Pax, even though he could tell Amil's captivity hadn't been pleasant. Reminding himself not to yell out again, Pax mouthed the name *Tomis* with his brows raised in question to Amil. His friend's expression sank, and Pax felt even worse. He should have left the younger boy safe with the rest of the crew.

Together, he and Amil scanned the growing crowd for Tomis. Pax thought he'd found him, only to have the other boy turn, revealing an unfamiliar face. Pax felt his panic grow the longer he went, unable to spot Tomis' bulky figure anywhere.

"This is the last of them," a guard called out from behind them.

Pax spun his head to look back. His heart leapt to see Tomis being pulled up the stairs by a scrawny guard barely bigger than the boy himself. Tomis had his head down and shuffled along with none of his usual exuberance. Pax tried to catch his eye, but Tomis never looked up as the guard fastened his manacles to the end of another line.

Then it was time to move.

At a yelled order, guards levered open the two sides of the heavy gate and led the lines of prisoners out into the back streets of the city. Anyone making noise or drifting out of line got a swift whack. Pax glanced at the darkened homes and businesses as they passed, and knew most of them were probably excited about the coming day's festivities.

When they finally reached the main square, Pax saw the crafters had finished the stage. Though they'd turned down the lights, it was easy to see all the work others had done to prepare for the Awakening.

Polished benches stood in neat rows facing the stage. Along the sides, crafters had assembled more extravagant booths with luxurious seating for the more important audience members.

There was even activity at the ceremonial altar that loomed in front of the inner keep. Usually, the city kept it cordoned off, posting guards to ensure no one climbed the steps leading up to the large altar.

But today, workers swarmed over the seamless rectangle of dark stone that rose to the height of a man's head, cleaning and polishing. It was easily visible from any position in the main square. Pax wondered if the rumors were true about it absorbing life essence and that it had magical controls hidden somewhere in the heavy base, accessible only by the city's governor.

The prisoner in front of him turned. The chain tugged at Pax's manacles, forcing his attention back to the guard leading them toward a roped-off area. A painted sign with cheerful letters read, "Candidates Only." Rows of folding chairs sat festooned with colorful ribbons that fluttered in the pre-dawn breeze.

Moving past, they came to a rectangular area cordoned off with heavy metal barricades made of bars anchored on each side to heavy stones. On either end of the space stood a row of heavy posts with embedded, stout metal hooks.

Pax gave a quick jerk on his manacles, testing for any give. All he did was make the chain rattle and draw the attention of a patrolling guard, who glared in his direction. Pax watched the row of prisoners in front of him being led into the space. Guards instructed them to sit down in a line on the hard ground before they fastened both ends of the chain to the heavy weights at the front and back.

There is no way out, Pax thought as guards led his group into the area and forced them to sit on the cobblestones before locking them into place.

The cold stone penetrated the fabric of his pants. Pax couldn't help the shudder that ran through him. In a few hours, he would be Awakened, and he couldn't think of a way to stop it.

5

MONSTERS AND SACRIFICES

OUT OF THE corner of his eye, Pax caught another stone thrown in his direction. He twisted and hunched, letting it hit his back with a sharp pain and then clatter to the ground. A father's scolding voice followed the giggles, shooing the children away, though there wasn't much heart in it.

The guards had been pointedly ignoring the little cretins all morning, dressed up in their celebration best and using the immobile captives as target practice. Pax was pretty sure the whole point of them sitting locked up in full view was to warn others about what happened to anyone who refused to conform.

"Can't you stop them?" Full of pent-up frustration, a boy a couple of rows over blurted the question out, glaring at the guard nearest him.

The bored man looked startled for a moment before letting out a derisive laugh. He stepped forward, letting his smile fade, replacing it with a look of cold contempt that made the objecting boy flinch back and hunch his shoulders.

"Yeah," the guard growled. "That's what I thought. Shirking coward." He stopped and raked over the others with angry eyes. "All of you! No more living behind safe walls that others die to protect. It's about time you learn how much it really costs."

"Sorry, sir," said a small elven boy, his entire body in a submissive posture. "I'm sure he didn't mean anything disrespectful. We're glad to have the chance to contribute today. Don't worry. We'll behave."

A few of the other prisoners scowled at the bootlicker, but none of them spoke. Even the clinking of manacles and shifting of positions had stopped under the guard's censure. The man looked pleased at how cowed they were, but still spat onto the ground toward the elf before turning and stalking back to his post.

"Why bother even Awakening them?" called out an arrogant voice.

Pax glanced up under hooded lids to see another elven boy standing from his fancy chair to peer in their direction. But this boy was so different from the other that he might as well be a different race. He had the pale features of a near purebred with almost white hair, a slender nose and pale green eyes full of contempt.

"Just put them to work in the mines for as long as they last," he said, making a dismissive motion with his hand.

Sounds of approval and laughter greeted his words.

The guard's demeanor instantly changed. "I agree with you, Scion Galen," he said with a respectful nod. "But they'll be more useful and probably last longer with a class. And I'm sure you know how bad things are getting out there." He glanced in the direction of the main gate. "We need all the bodies we can get, even if they are scum like this."

The well-to-do elven boy preened under the guard's respect and gave him a slow nod of agreement before sitting back down. His friends immediately chatted and laughed with him.

Pax did his best to ignore the candidate section, sitting there with families who supported them and would help them get the most out of their new classes. He tried not to think about how he might have sat happily among them if the guards had left his parents to run their tailoring business undisturbed.

A wave of weariness crashed over Pax. He'd been up most of the night and had nothing to eat or drink since the few mouthfuls of water in his cell. The main square had been filling up all morning, the festive atmosphere swelling in stark contrast to the gloom hovering over the prisoners.

"Let's get this over already," muttered a bitter girl's voice from behind him.

Pax nodded in agreement without looking in her direction before forcing himself to scan his surroundings once again. At some point, they'd have to be unfastened and led up to the stage. He wanted to be prepared if even a sliver of a chance to escape presented itself.

The bursting barrage of a bugle's notes cut across the square, slicing through the dull roar of the milling crowd and catching everyone's attention. The mood of the crowd changed. People hurried toward the benches. Parents herded children to find their seats. An excited din of conversation filled the main square.

"Finally." The same girl's mutter was just loud enough to be heard.

This time, Pax glanced back to see a sullen girl who looked about his age. Her raven black hair hung jagged, cut off at chin level, probably by her own belt knife, and while she kept her head tipped down, Pax glimpsed distinctive green eyes that were alert and watching.

Her gaze caught his, and he almost flushed and looked away. Instead, he met her eyes until she finally gave him a curt nod before turning around. The encounter lifted his spirits. He wasn't the only one still defiant and ready to fight back if given the chance.

The bugle blared in a sharp staccato a second time, and conversations hushed as a final few people slid into their seats. A quiet descended on the square until the only sounds were squawks from birds and the rustle of leaves from a breeze blowing through the landscaped trees.

It was uncanny, some prearranged signal that everyone else knew about. Pax wished he had Tomis by his side again to explain what was happening. Street rats hid during events like these when the guards were out and vigilant. Maybe he should have paid more attention to city business before this.

The bugle played again. This time a slow, drawn-out hymn full of mournful tones that tugged at Pax, though he wasn't sure why. On the far side of the square, a procession emerged, a column of four men abreast, their dark blue uniforms trimmed in the red of empire soldiers, much more striking than the silver of the Thanhil Guard.

Pax glanced at the guard who'd yelled at them moments ago, surprised to see the respect and envy on his face as he watched the incoming procession. A collective gasp broke the silence of the square. Pax turned back to see what had happened.

The soldiers wound their way through the aisles of the audience. Pax saw that toward the middle of the line, groups of them were carrying long skinny burdens about the size of a . . .

Pax swallowed hard as he realized there were bodies on the platforms the soldiers carried. The still forms were shrouded in ornate cloths, draped and tucked, but still with enough shape to make it obvious what they hid.

It was only when his eyes moved further along the column that he sucked in his breath in a mix of surprise and fear that mirrored the crowd's response. It was one thing to know that the soles of his shoes had come from the hide of an earth-based monster, but another entirely to see the severed head of one hoisted high on pylons. The massive trophy was so big it took four soldiers to handle it.

Pax gaped. It looked similar to the rats in the city, if a rat were the size of a small bedroom and had jutting teeth as long as a man's hand. The beady eyes were large black orbs that sent a shiver through Pax despite being lifeless.

The column of soldiers marched slowly past, giving everyone a chance to pay respects to the bodies and gape open-mouthed at the monster heads on prominent display.

Pax stared at another parading past, its slimy skin glistening and rounded snout propped open to display multiple rows of teeth that more than made up for their small size with quantity.

"Holy . . ." the whispered exclamation made Pax flick a glance over toward the black-haired girl to find her looking as amazed as he felt.

The final note of the bugle's mournful tribute held for a long heartbeat before fading. Pax turned back to see the soldiers had arrayed themselves in front of the inner keep's altar on the left side of the square.

Two groups of soldiers stepped out, carrying the shrouded bodies up the stone steps with solemn care. The crowd hushed further as the monster heads were propped up on a lip of the altar just below the main surface.

Pax couldn't help being fascinated as the scene played out in front of him. There were so many pieces of city life he'd missed by living on the fringes. If he were about to be shipped off somewhere else as a servant then he would enjoy the show while he could.

A troop of three figures climbed up to the altar as the soldiers retreated, finally relieved of their grisly burdens. Pax thought the center, white-haired man must be the governor because of his fine clothing. The two behind him were busy watching the crowd, with the air of soldiers, though they didn't wear uniforms. The distinguished man stepped forward and held up both hands for attention.

"Hello, my people. As your governor, I am pleased to greet all of you on this day." His deep voice spoke out over the square with confidence and a volume that had to be aided by magic for everyone to hear him. "On this day that we celebrate the new lives of our youth, it is only appropriate that we start with a tribute to those who have given their lives to protect us all."

He paused for a moment. The crowd filled the space with soft murmurs of agreement. Even Pax found himself nodding his head and had to wonder what level the governor's Charisma was.

"Bound to our city, their service in life has kept us safe. In death their life energy will strengthen our defenses."

Pax moved his gaze to watch the two shrouded bodies, not wanting to miss anything.

"City Flame Mage Llewel Asari," the governor intoned, both hands moving toward one of the shrouded bodies. "The city of Thanhil accepts your sacrifice."

Pax's eyes widened as one of the shrouds suddenly sagged to the altar, the cloth fluttering and empty. A flicker of light shot from the altar to the front of the glistening ebony wall of the keep. The ball of energy sunk into the wall and then left a glistening trail as it shot upward toward the massive crenellations and disappeared.

Pax stared, slack-jawed, at the evidence that the improbable rumors were true. Something from the mage's body had just poured into the inner keep and apparently strengthened it.

The governor had turned to watch the path of the energy and, now that it had disappeared, turned back to the waiting crowd. "Her life given that we may live," he said with emphasis on each word as he bowed his head. "Thank you."

A rolling murmur swept across the crowd as everyone repeated his words.

"Show some respect," a guard hissed at them.

Pax hurried to join in. And he thought he might even mean it. The woman had died protecting his city, after all.

As the murmuring quieted down, the governor held up his hands for attention again.

"Private First Class Gog Modir," the governor spoke again, his hands moving toward the second body. "The city of Thanhil accepts your sacrifice."

As everyone followed him through a repeat of the first ritual, the reality of what his future might bring struck Pax. More than anything, he wanted to escape and return to the familiar tasks of feeding and protecting his Viper crew.

The thrum of renewed conversations grew as the governor descended from the altar and made his way to the Awakening stage. The soldiers formed up in crisp lines only to be given a barked dismissal. Shoulders relaxed and heads turned as they moved to join friends and family in the crowd.

A group of laborers hoisted the monster heads onto carts. Pax watched as they took them down a side street, likely for processing. The teeth alone would make valuable spearheads or knife blades.

"Now for the celebration we've all been waiting for," boomed the governor's voice in a much more cheerful tone. "The Awakening of the best and brightest our future holds!" He swept his arms toward the candidate section.

As the crowd clapped and cheered, the candidates straightened with smiles, a combination of both excitement and trepidation scattered across their expressions.

Pax turned and shot a worried glance toward Tomis and Amil who were locked up too far away to call out to. Another cheer, and Pax looked up to see an assistant leading the first row of candidates up onto the stage to sit in a row of ornate chairs. The cut of their clothing and the confidence of their demeanors told everyone watching that these were the cream of the city's families.

The assistant then motioned for the first boy, a tall and handsome elf with a confident smile, to follow him to the pedestal placed at the center of the four mages.

Pax was gratified to see the boy's step falter under the gazes of the capital mages. Around the square, quiet had descended again as spectators leaned forward to get a good glimpse of the first Awakening of the year.

Looking almost bored, the four mages placed hands on the armrests of their chairs and with no warning, magic flared to life along their arms. Bright flame shot toward gusting wind and plodding earth in streams as thick as the mages' arms. Across from flame, water did the same sputtering into the wind and being engulfed by the spear of earth.

Pax sucked in a breath and braced for an explosion as the magic burst free in an incredible display of power. But none came. Instead, the mages' four elements merged together into a ring of multi-colored power pulsing above their heads. Pax could barely make out the boy on the pedestal at the center and had to credit him with the bravery not to bolt.

The mages moved again, and the ring closed in, tightening over the boy until it had coalesced into a swirling ball twice the size of the boy's head. After snatching a furtive glance above, the boy looked straight ahead, visibly working to straighten his shoulders and stay calm.

When it touched down gently on his head, the results were rather anticlimactic. The boy stiffened, and his eyes rolled back. The ball of flame lifted into the air, leaving him free to get up. Two assistants moved quickly to either side of him, and helped him gently to his feet. He staggered a bit as they led him out of the way, making space for another candidate to take their place beneath the sphere of magical elements.

The first boy was led up to stand next to the governor. His eyes kept blinking, and his knees wobbled, as a city mage whispered into the governor's ear.

A smile spread across the governor's face as he turned back to the podium to call out with enthusiasm, "A mage! Our first candidate is now a mage."

The main square erupted in cheers, and Pax saw a proud, but shaky smile gleam on the new mage's face.

"A promising omen for our city and wonderful start to this year's Awakening," proclaimed the governor.

One of the capital mages made an impatient gesture for the attendants escorting a well-dressed dwarven girl to the pedestal to hurry. On the other side of the stage, the first boy stepped down into the arms of his smiling family for hugs, back-slaps and proud smiles.

Pax glanced at the seated candidates waiting their turn and then to the other shackled youth near him. He was pretty sure his turn would be a lot different.

6

AWAKENING DAY

AND IT WAS, though not in any way he could have imagined.

The day had dragged on, the initial excitement fading as the young scions were replaced by the children of local merchants and eventually laborers and the offspring of the commoner families. Pax had exchanged the occasional worried glance with his two friends and the dark-haired girl. They were all helpless and could do nothing but watch the event play out.

Some of it was unexpected. Pax finally realized who the people sitting at the tables on the far side of the stage were: recruiters. They'd been mostly silent as the governor had worked his way through the high-class candidates whose families whisked them away almost immediately. But as the process got to the middle-class candidates, people in various sections would perk up as the governor announced the Awakened's class. They did their best to attract the attention of the candidates. They left the mages and soldiers alone, though, and Pax didn't know why. Also, while the interest of the crowd waned as the wealthy candidates finished, the recruiters increased their activity, jockeying for position to entice recruits.

The square itself turned into a milling mass of people mixed with food vendors yelling to be heard above the noise. Earlier, someone had wheeled over a cart trailing mouth-watering smells and dispensed lunches to the guards who seemed to delight in eating them in front of the hungry captives.

Pax kept his head down so he wouldn't be tempted to lose his temper. The petty cruelty made his blood boil, despite how often he'd seen it. At least someone had the decency to send two boys around with buckets of water and ladles to give them drinks. Having captives pass out from the heat would probably put a crimp in their plans.

Pax watched the crowds thin. Everyone still paused for just a beat to listen when the governor leaned forward to announce the latest class. Mage classes had received a decent cheer with warriors a close second. But now, the crafters, merchants and laborers barely caused a ripple, spectators turning quickly back to their conversations.

As the afternoon sun beat down on the stone-lined square, the city's elite had mostly disappeared. Pax figured they were probably off to parties or to cram what advantages they could into their newly-awakened children before sending them off to academies and apprenticeships in the morning.

Even most of the middle-class families had packed up and left, leaving small groups of poorly dressed family and friends who exchanged nervous waves of encouragement with their candidates still waiting their turn.

The governor's voice had long since turned to a droning monotone, though his Charisma still made it sound friendly even if his expression looked bored. Assistants on stage rushed the candidates through the process, looking tired themselves. The unhappy expressions on the capital mages' faces would have made Pax want to hurry, too.

A twinge of anxiety grew inside Pax as he watched the second to last line of candidates being led to the stage. The recruiters on the other side of the stage were busier than the spectator section, which had mostly emptied by this point.

Pax closed his eyes and shifted his hands in his manacles, wishing he could summon his spark right now to help stay calm and watch for a chance to escape.

Equipment jangled, and boots stomped nearby. Pax looked up sharply to see the guards standing from their stools and reaching for their padded nightsticks. He glanced back and tried to see his friends, but with the other prisoners suddenly shifting, eyes wide and worried, he couldn't. Pax gave his manacles one last tug, knowing he couldn't break free, but needing to do something.

"Up!" said the head guard. "All of you."

Other guards moved to unlock the front of the chains, joining in the haranguing to get the prisoners to stand and line up.

Chains jangled, and muttered groans filled the small space as the teens forced their cramped legs and bodies into action. By the time the rows of captives were standing and in order, Pax saw that the last candidate had left the stage.

The four capital mages stood and stretched, the sphere of elemental magic nowhere to be seen. The stocky earth mage glanced in their direction, distaste clear to read on his powerful features.

The square was mostly empty now. City work crews had moved in to stack up the benches while others stabbed litter with trash pickers. The food vendors packed up their carts. Only the recruiters' section still showed activity, the last of the candidates and their families arranging deals.

One hard-faced dwarf looked across toward the captives, his gaze intense. Scanning that area, Pax realized the dwarf wasn't the only one regarding the large group of prisoners. And many of them had one expression in common: greed.

Pax swallowed hard and clenched his fists.

The guards jerked on the line of prisoners next to him and pulled them up toward the stage.

With some muttering, the four mages took their places again. They used their special chairs and powers to rebuild the elemental sphere in moments. By the time the guards had unfastened the first prisoner from the chain and pulled him forward, the ball hung again between the mages, gleaming in the air above the pedestal.

The human girl stared up at it, eyes wide and fearful as two guards pulled her forward.

"No," she suddenly screamed, pushing back and flailing her elbows to free herself from the guards.

To Pax's delight, the girl actually broke free for just a moment, scrambling toward the edge of the stage, hands still handcuffed in front of her.

She didn't make it far.

Two guards had already sprung to intercept her as soon as she screamed. With a lazy reach, one of them latched a heavy hand onto her tunic collar and wrenched her back, feet dangling briefly over the edge of the stage.

With casual brutality, his partner slammed his padded stick repeatedly into the muscle of one thigh and then the other as she cried out in pain. They held her up so she couldn't crumple to the ground.

Everyone watching seemed to have frozen, some in shock and others enjoying the spectacle.

The second guard stepped back from the sobbing girl and looked up at the other prisoners, satisfaction plain to see on his face. "And double that punishment to the next one of you who tries to shirk their duty. Understand?"

A shocked silence greeted his question.

"Understand?" he barked at the stunned captives, spittle flying from his mouth as he lunged toward them, his club held high.

Heads bobbed immediately, and eyes dropped to the ground amid an uneven chorus of yessir's.

"Now let's try this again," the man said to the girl in his grip, his voice suddenly normal again, which made his performance even more scary.

Unresisting, the girl stayed on her feet long enough for the magic to descend and touch her. Then she crumpled to the ground. No one bothered to catch her.

"Crafter," called out an assistant, prompting a muttering of voices from the recruiter section. The guards dragged her off the stage and attached her manacles to a new chain, but kept the recruiters back.

Things moved fast after that, even faster than with the last of the poorer candidates. The guards made sure the next prisoner stood ready to step up on the pedestal as soon as the magic finished awakening the one ahead.

It was the fourth boy, a skinny, malnourished kid, that made the danger of the process suddenly real. He collapsed as others had when the ball of mana descended on him. But when the guards tried to pull him up afterward, he didn't respond, head and arms hanging with a limpness that was brutally final.

The guard closest to Pax raised his cudgel when chains rattled and worried whispers spread through the prisoners. Pax stared with numb disbelief as the guards made the boy's body quickly disappear. They returned as if nothing of significance had happened. And maybe to them, nothing had.

As the process continued, the guards dragged newly awakened prisoners away, sorted by class, onto new chains. Recruiters next to the stage circled and jotted down notes on the results.

Watching the death and greed play out filled Pax with angry knots of fear. He decided he'd rather face the monsters from earlier than the magic on the stage, followed by the circle of predators that saw him as an asset to be bought and sold.

In only a handful of minutes, the guards pulled him up on the stage with the second row of prisoners. He glanced back over the edge of the stage, and a quick flash of vertigo caught him, making his heart race and breath quicken. He grimaced, hating how heights made him feel.

Pax searched for Tomis and Amil and focused in on their faces as soon as he spotted them, his concentration helping ease the flash of panic. Calming, he was glad to be facing the danger first. Maybe it would help his friends.

Straightening his shoulders, Pax turned back and examined the busy space now that he stood on the platform he'd been watching from a distance all day.

Close up, it all looked even more dangerous. The four mages sat controlling the elemental sphere with a casual power Pax couldn't hope to fight. And the guards were all on high alert, no doubt knowing that this was the time they could lose one of their captives if they weren't vigilant.

Pax couldn't stop staring at the sphere of swirling elements floating in the air. The mages and their special chairs forced flame, water, earth and air to coexist together in a writhing ball that didn't look stable. The elements surging and struggling together in constant motion like a monster just waiting to consume its prey.

Pax watched the boys and girls ahead of him, doing his best to stay calm and prepare for his turn. During the Awakening, for the briefest of moments, the various elements in the sphere all seemed to flicker and freeze. Pax couldn't be sure, but the smallest flare of magic seemed to shoot down into the candidate before the sphere returned to its normal appearance a heartbeat later.

His mind spun with all the potential dangers of direct contact with elemental magic. When they finally led him up to the stage, Pax forced himself to control his breathing. It was almost his turn.

The mixed-dwarf in front of him sagged when the sphere made contact and took a staggering step off the pedestal a moment later.

A hard jab into his back made Pax dig in his heels and glare at the guard behind him defiantly. It was Jonson. Pax had been so preoccupied that he hadn't noticed the young man take up the post.

"You need more of this?" Jonson asked, pulling his stick back for another jab with a vicious smile. "I'm happy to oblige."

Pax spun around completely, letting his eyes harden and his desperation rise to the surface as he faked a lunge toward the young guardsman.

Jonson flinched back, eyes wide in alarm as he jerked his hands up protectively and almost hit himself in the face with his nightstick.

"That's what I thought," growled Pax with satisfaction.

Snickers rose, and not just from the other prisoners.

Jonson's face flushed with rage. He tensed, pulling his stick back into position.

But Pax had already turned and stepped up onto the pedestal, half hoping Jonson might try to hit him during the ritual. Surely that would cause trouble, even if it was just for the obnoxious idiot.

"Jonson!" came a barked order from off to Pax's left.

Pax didn't have any attention to spare for the bully anymore. For the first time in his life, he stood close to elemental magic, and he didn't like how it felt one bit.

7

MAGIC BURNS

PAX HAD BEEN CAUGHT out in the weather plenty in his brief life, the metallic tang in the air, the whip of the wind and ominous clouds that swooped in, heavy and angry. The sphere of elemental magic felt ten times worse. It was a raging swirl of power that wanted to escape and would forge a path of destruction as soon as it could. The last thing Pax wanted was for the thing to touch his head.

But he didn't have a choice.

He felt its approach like the fall of a building rushing straight down to smash him to a pulp. Pax clenched his fists and only stayed in place by the barest margin of control. When the elemental sphere finally touched the top of his head, it was worse than he could have imagined.

The raging magic stabbed into his mind and rushed right through, its burning power scorching along muscles and nerves. It was a shocking invasion by a power that felt so wrong and foreign that Pax couldn't catch his breath.

And the pain. It made all his nerves scream in agony and burned his bones from the inside out. It rampaged heedlessly through his body, riding to a crescendo that made Pax long for oblivion.

Pax fought to oust the invader, pushing and shoving with everything in him, but to no avail. And then a heartbeat later, the magic found the small, central core where his spark slept. His entire world seemed to detonate.

Pax had once seen a drunk man blow a mouthful of alcohol at a bonfire, only to have the flame race back to engulf his entire body.

This was worse.

His spark objected to the invasion, and in an instant, both powers flared into a raging battle with his body as the battlefield.

Every muscle in Pax's body seized up, and he barely noticed when his face hit the polished wood of the stage's floor with a dull crack. His scream ripped out past clenched teeth as his muscles convulsed in frantic surges of reaction. His spark burned with a white-hot flame, scorching him from the inside as its small size fought vainly to push back the melded inrush of elements.

Pax could barely sense the sudden flurry of activity that erupted around him. Guards leapt back, and captives cried out, some in horror and others demanding that someone help him and make the mages stop.

A barked order from the governor finally got results.

Almost insensate, Pax barely noticed the foreign magic recede with a rush that let him slump limply to the floor, a puppet with its strings cut. Shuddering tremors shook through him, and his breath came in jerky gasps as he blinked his eyes and tried to dispel the pained fog wrapped around his thoughts.

"What the blast did you do to him?" yelled a voice. "How many of us are you going to kill?"

It sounded like the dark-haired girl.

"Quiet," barked a deeper voice, followed by the sound of a dull strike. The background muttering of the other captives quickly subsided.

Still halfway stunned, Pax wiped at his eyes as he tried to sit up, only to blink at the bright red that streaked across his hands. Blood?

"What's wrong with the boy? Were you able to awaken him?"

Pax blinked as he turned to see the governor striding toward them, his voice respectful as he spoke to the capital mages.

"Reactions to the Awakening can vary, some dangerous if the light of life isn't strong enough in a candidate," the earth mage answered in a terse and masculine voice as he stood from his chair before glancing down at Pax. "Though I haven't seen one as violent as this before,"

Pax saw the annoyance in his expression and knew he wouldn't find any sympathy there. He looked impatient to get started again. Only the flame and water mages looked the least bit interested in what had happened.

His hair salt-and-peppered by age, the flame mage took a step forward and crouched down to study him. Propped up in a half-seated position, Pax froze, not daring to move or look directly at the man as he reached out to touch Pax's shoulder.

A brief pulse brushed across his nerves and was gone just as quickly.

"No," said the man over his shoulder as he stood back up. "It didn't take."

Surprised, Pax looked up at the man and caught a flicker of interest in his expression with maybe a touch of pity before the mage moved back to his chair.

Pax cleared his throat and asked, "If you can't awaken me, then I'm useless, right? Does that mean you can let me go?"

Everyone standing close, guards and captives alike, gasped.

The mage paused and turned slowly back to give Pax a considering look. A nearby guard had raised his nightstick, but didn't move without permission.

For just a moment, Pax thought the man might actually agree. And if he did, everyone here, including the governor, would be obliged to obey.

But the mage's expression turned sad as he shook his head. "No. None of us can hide from what is coming. We can't afford to discard even the lowliest tool in the empire. There's still a chance we can awaken you with a second try. If not, then . . ." He didn't finish his sentence.

It was obvious to Pax that they wouldn't stop the magic this time. If his body couldn't accept it, it would likely kill him. Pax blew out a breath as his eyes stung at the loss of hope, regardless of how brief it was. And then the memory of the pain he'd just suffered flashed back, reminding him that the horror would start up again in a moment. Suddenly frantic, Pax tried to push himself up, only to fall back to the floor. It was no use. He couldn't even fight back.

"Pick him up and put him back on the pedestal," the flame mage said with a weary voice as he and the others prepared again.

"No," Pax screamed as he felt arms reach under his to haul him back to the pedestal. He couldn't survive another encounter with that chaotic magic. A second try wasn't likely to be any more successful than the first.

He wasn't strong enough to break free, so Pax went limp, letting his body sag to the ground. He refused to make this easy for the guards. They cursed and shifted to get a better grip on him.

Pax's thoughts whirled as he sifted through and discarded increasingly crazy ideas to defeat the magical storm. He had no magic, and the meager strength of his spark had only made things worse.

When they got him to the pedestal, Pax refused to stand, sagging like a rag doll and crumpling to fall half off the pedestal when the guards let go.

A few captives suppressed snorts of laughter, which made Pax aim a red-tinged grin in that direction. It sounded a bit like Tomis, which cheered Pax. While he hadn't wanted his friends to be captured, at least he had two friends here to stand as witness to his death.

"Stand up, scum," hissed the guard on his left, giving his shoulder a painful shake and looking like he would start kicking Pax if there weren't witnesses.

"Grab the chair," the governor said dismissively. "We knew we'd need it eventually with the shirkers, anyway."

The guards dragged Pax off the pedestal while other workers maneuvered a heavy straight-backed wooden chair into place. It didn't take long before they'd hauled his limp body into the chair and locked him into place with a heavy leather strap around his chest. They attached his wrist manacles into a metal loop built into the seat of the chair between his legs.

Feeling a dull resignation fall over him, Pax was glad he'd inconvenienced the entire group of powerful people here. It had been more effective than trying to go toe-to-toe with an individual guard.

His thoughts stuttered, grasping at the seed of an idea in that thought.

Maybe. Just maybe.

He was concentrating so hard, he didn't even flinch when the elemental ring flared back into existence.

Maybe he had a chance of surviving this.

8

CAMOUFLAGE

THE CHAOTIC MAGIC ring swirled in the air. Pax knew it would only be moments before it coalesced into the sphere again. His breathing sped up as echoes of the recent pain threatened to panic him. If only he could pull his spark out and let its calm and clarity center him.

Instead, he had to control it within his center instead of bringing it out to his hand, something he'd never thought to attempt. Knowing he only had moments left, Pax forced his gaze away from the incoming magic and closed his eyes. He had to focus.

First, he shifted his awareness toward the small kernel in his center where his spark normally sat, tucked in and quiet until summoned.

There. He found it, calm as usual, as if it hadn't just raged in a power struggle against the elements of four capital mages. An ominous buzz of power loomed over Pax with a palpable pressure and urged him to hurry.

Swallowing hard, Pax pulled on his spark. Except this time, he tried to intercept its usual rush toward his hands and direct it toward his head instead. It didn't work. Grasping with imaginary hands, it felt like trying to herd a slippery worm moving as fast as light. Pax's heart raced as it slipped past him in a headlong rush along its usual path down his right arm.

No!

Pax bore down with all the concentration he could muster, his mind shaking as much as his muscles. His spark finally responded and slowed. He pulled harder.

Finally, he halted the spark just before it emerged from the skin of his palm. Pax let out a huff of relieved breath as he fought to control it. It hovered, trembling and eager. Another pull, and this time it reluctantly moved back the way it came, drifting slowly toward his head.

When the spark moved up behind his eyes, Pax could feel its aura of calm, not very powerful, but noticeable. Tingling on his scalp warned him the elemental sphere was close.

With urgency, Pax pushed at the spark so it would spread out and disperse into smaller particles, ones that he hoped wouldn't clash with the incoming magic and would give Pax's mind the strength it needed to survive the Awakening process.

His spark ignored his instructions. It bounced around his skull like a single copper in an otherwise empty piggy bank, a stubbornly solid ball of energy.

Then the elemental magic hit. With just as much strength as before, it surged into his mind. Only this time, it collided with his spark.

The explosion of pain and clashing magic burst inside with so much force, Pax couldn't manage a single coherent thought for the longest second of his life. He stopped breathing for a moment, and part of him wanted to give in and fall into the dark if the pain would just stop.

But his scrapper's instinct took over, well-trained to keep fighting when he was stunned or in pain. It forced him to suck in air with a pained gasp as his muscles seized again, spasming against the leather strap holding him in place.

The sharp pain of his wrists jerking against the manacles broke through the haze in his mind and gave him a split second of clarity. Pax took advantage of it.

Relax. Don't fight. Spread out. He jabbered a crazed list of mental commands as he tried to force the spark to do what he wanted. It stilled for a moment, but the elemental magic just flared with more power in response.

Desperate now, Pax tried to lead by example. *Like this*, he thought, and then let go of everything. Copying the way he'd let his muscles go limp with the guards earlier, he did the same now mentally, desperately hoping he could force his spark to follow suit.

Pax opened himself up to the magic and the pain, dropping his resistance and letting the mages' power have unfettered access to everything that was him. For the briefest moment, he could feel his spark still resisting, pushing and fighting back.

Then it succumbed, falling back and bursting into a fine mist of calm that doused his mind just enough for his tattered sanity to cling to control.

The sudden absence of resistance made the elemental magic stutter briefly before it rushed through his body like a powerful summer storm, unopposed, searching, prodding and changing. The pain escalated as it jammed hard fingers of power into the deepest recesses of Pax's self.

A continuous keen he was unaware of making emerged from Pax's throat. Tears of blood leaked from his eyes and ears, and his muscles and nerves burned with tense pain.

Time stretched into forever until, with the same suddenness of its intrusion, the foreign magic pulled back, up and out with a sudden jerk that made Pax gasp.

The surrounding sounds intruded again. Pax sagged against the chest strap. Raised voices argued, some angry and others confused. He worked to open his eyes, but couldn't. He couldn't even raise his manacled hands to wipe at the tears drying in itchy streaks on his face.

Pax opened his mouth, wanting to ask if it had worked, but only managed a dry croak that no one paid any mind to. He could feel exhaustion pulling him under and fought it, trying again to ask about the result.

A hand fell on his shoulder, heavy and warm as it squeezed with a comforting grip.

He heard words. Perhaps the flame mage was speaking? Pax's sluggish thoughts worked to parse out his words and failed until one word came through loud and clear as the man repeated it close to his ear.

". . . mage," said the voice filled with equal parts disbelief and curiosity.

Pax couldn't believe it either, the word hovering in his thoughts, impossible and possibly a trick of his tired mind.

"You're a mage, son." The words repeated as the hand patted at his shoulder again. "A mage."

Pax let out an exhausted breath. His shoulders sagged in relief that he'd survived the Awakening. Then the words finally penetrated.

A mage!

No. He couldn't help trying to reject the result. Mage initiates were rare and valued by the wealthy citizens. But he knew authorities whisked them off to the capital right after the Awakening. No one saw the poorer ones again, likely sent to fight beasts on a distant city wall until they died.

He couldn't help thinking of his Vipers without a leader, easy prey for other crews. Why couldn't he have received a lower class, one that let him stay in Thanhil, even if it was under the thumb of a hard master?

Pax had been dreading the laborer class, but now they'd tear him away from everything he knew. Is this what happened to Titus? The rattle of chains pulled his attention to the other shirkers still waiting to be processed.

A sudden hope flared inside him. He craned his head to find his friends. There. "Take care of the Vipers!" he yelled at Amil and Tomis.

"Shut up." A clout to the side of his head made his eyes cross in pain, but not before he saw Amil nod in acknowledgement.

Pax clung to the hope that Amil would survive the Awakening.

Then he'd be able to watch out for their crew while Pax was gone. His thoughts twisted with worry and pain, all too much to handle. He forced his mind to quiet so he could focus on his immediate survival instead.

It took two guards hauling him under his arms to get him out of the chair to make room for the next prisoner. Pax did his best to make his feet keep up, knowing the guards would love nothing better than to let him drop flat on his face as soon as they got him out of the spotlight.

"Put him right there," a bored voice directed.

Pax blinked to clear his blurry vision. The guards dropped him roughly into a chair placed at one of the desks arrayed at the back of the large stage.

A narrow-faced woman glanced up at him before dropping her eyes back to the ledger in front of her. Her ink-stained fingers scribbled words his rudimentary reading skills probably couldn't have read even if they hadn't been upside down.

Moments passed, and Pax's thoughts seemed to go even fuzzier as his reaction to the Awakening made him sway in his seat.

"Hey." The woman snapped her fingers, drawing his eyes and attention back to her. She had produced a handkerchief from somewhere and held it out to him. "Take this and clean yourself up. Don't pass out until I'm finished here."

He took the cloth, surprised that she'd dampened it, too. The coolness felt good as he cleaned the tacky blood from his eyes and face.

"Now, I just need to finalize your name and age, and then you're done."

He thought he saw a flash of sympathy in her expression, but she just waited, pencil poised to write.

"You can't Identify that from my menu?" he asked, his thoughts too confused to figure out what was happening.

"Listen, kid," the woman said, frustration creeping into her tone. "As Vitur's clerk, my job is to confirm your name, age and class and make any corrections needed. What happened before being awakened doesn't matter anymore. Understand?"

All the things Pax wanted to keep secret suddenly flashed through his mind, and he had a hard time keeping a straight face.

She must have noticed, because her features softened, and she leaned forward and lowered her voice. "Don't worry so much," she said. "Probably no one told you, but for your first month, all anyone can get from Identify is your name, class and level. The rest of your details are protected. It's Vitur's way of shielding the fledglings from exploitation. Now just tell me your name and age."

"Pax," he said. "Sixteen."

Looking all business again, she wrote the information down. "Family name?" she asked when she looked up again.

Pax couldn't tell her the truth. His reaction to the Awakening was already unusual enough. That, combined with his mother's insistence that he always hide his spark, made him leery. Not to mention, unknown forces had taken both his parents and brother. Pax needed to stay as hidden as possible.

"Don't bother lying," the clerk said with a frown. "My Truthtell isn't that high of a level, but you're newly awakened, so everyone outlevels you."

"I don't have a family name," Pax tried lying anyway.

She shook her head and let out a sigh before raising her eyebrows, waiting.

Pax swallowed and leaned his head into his hands. Then he had an idea. "What if I lost my family when I was young?"

The clerk looked nonplussed and then thoughtful for a moment before answering. "Well, technically, Vitur will accept a name that you honestly consider your family. It just has to be the truth."

With a smile, Pax suddenly knew exactly what to tell her.

"Vipersworn. Pax Vipersworn."

She looked at him, brows drawn together as she held his gaze.

"Are you sure?" she asked quietly. "This will be your name from now on. The only way to change it is joining a new family, like through marriage or being adopted into a clan. Even high-level rogue spells and skills only disguise your name, not change it."

Pax thought of his Viper crew and their constant fight for survival. He nodded.

With a curt motion, she looked down at her ledger and scrawled his new name into the entry before closing her eyes and pursing her lips for a long moment.

"Congratulations Pax Vipersworn," she said when she opened her eyes. "You are officially a mage initiate and headed to Shieldwall Academy for training. You're dismissed."

Her attention had already moved behind him as he stood from his chair and walked toward the guard motioning him forward.

A sliver of nerves stabbed through his tired body as he turned his attention inward and pulled up his menu to see what had changed. Words flickered in his vision and without warning, his head spun, and for the second day in a row, Pax blacked out.

9

FULL MENU

HIS OLDER BROTHER, Titus, shoved Pax into the dark and narrow channel behind the open sewer grate with enough force to send his smaller body flying head first into the noxious muck at the bottom. Pax threw out his arms to keep from face planting into the mess, but his left, with its monster-touched scales didn't move fast enough, and Pax tumbled to his side with a hard splash.

Behind him, Titus slammed the grate closed and whispered the last words Pax ever heard him say, "Run for it, Pax, while I draw them away!"

And then he spun and ran. Pax flipped around frantically in the narrow space, hands grasping for the grate to get back out and help his brother.

Hampered by his left arm, he took too long to manage the feat. Thundering boots made him freeze mid-motion and stare, mouth dry, as two guards came hurtling into the narrow alley from the left. One shouted in triumph, hardly slowing as he pointed towards Titus' disappearing figure to the right.

Trapped, injured and helpless, Pax couldn't breathe as he blinked his eyes, hoping somehow the world in front of him would change. He couldn't do anything to help his brother. Shudders racked his thin body, shaking him to the bone. He couldn't breathe.

Shaking.

"Wake up, Pax. Breathe," hissed a familiar voice in his ear, right before something hit his chest, interrupting the spasms.

Pax gasped, the air wonderful as it filled his chest. He could barely move, still in the nightmare's grip.

"That's it," the voice crooned as powerful arms lifted him to a seated position. "Easy now. Just breathe."

The simple task was much harder than it should have been, and Pax forced his way through the muddled memories, blinking and trying to take in his surroundings. He glanced at the person holding him and gasped in surprise.

"Amil?" he asked with a throat dry and cracking. "Where did you come from? Am I still dreaming?"

They sat on an oval carpet, richly patterned and soft. It lay on a gleaming wood floor polished to a sheen, reflecting the faint light of the lantern by the door. The suite was obviously expensive, with an unlit chandelier hanging above them and walls festooned with wainscoting, paintings and rich tapestries.

"No, not dreaming, boss," his buddy said with a relieved smile. A faint flicker of lantern light cast shadows across his familiar features. "Somehow, by Vitur's will, we ended up in the same place."

"What?" The events of the Awakening were coming back to Pax, and he still couldn't believe it.

"Um—" Amil hesitated, and finally blurted out, "I'm a mage, too."

Pax couldn't summon an answer to the preposterous words. Amil was supposed to stay in Thanhil and watch out for their Vipers. "That's impossible. There are hardly any mages each year from the entire city."

"Yeah, six of us from all the street rats and about twelve of the citizens and 'crats. I am a mixed elf. Maybe I had an ancestor who was a mage. I guess it's no crazier than you being one, right?"

Pax took a good look at his friend, still baffled by the whole mess. Amil beat Pax by at least a head and his lean, ropy muscles would have been even stronger if he hadn't had to subsist on their crew's meager diet. His mix of mostly elven heritage was obvious. Maybe it had contributed to him awakening as a mage? Under the dirt, he had the refined features and piercing blue eyes that girls seemed to swoon over.

In fact, back when his brother had disappeared, Pax had tried to turn the crew over to Amil, since he was older by half a year. But Amil had insisted that he was much better at following orders and had absolutely no interest in running the crew. True to that first day, Amil had been the perfect Second, unfailing in his support.

"We're both mages." Pax said the words slowly, testing out the concept. "Maybe we'll get to die on a wall together, at least."

"Don't be like that, Pax." Amil scooted closer, excitement in his features. "We're going to learn magic. You felt that power, right?"

Pax had to nod.

"They're going to regret giving us power, because we won't do what they tell us to with it, right? You'll figure out a plan like you always do. Then we'll use it for ourselves and our crew. You know you will. And I'll help you."

The future Amil's words built helped reframe what Pax had imagined, prompting a tentative smile to spread across his face. "Both mages." This time, the words held potential instead of threat.

Amil sat back on his heels and grinned as he ran his hand through his jaggedly-cut blond hair. "Yep. Though I didn't end up flailing around screaming during my Awakening like you did. Wimp."

Pax let out a snort. "That just means I'll have more magic. Now bring me up to speed. Where exactly are we?"

"So, they've got us all locked up in some fancy inn, and the food is really good. They fitted all the mages with these elemental suppression bracelets, including the 'crats. We can still use our mana for non-mage skills, but not any elemental or spell stuff."

Pax just stared at him, the huge changes to their lives still sinking in.

Amil held up his arms where thin strips of a shining metal wrapped seamlessly around his wrists, not much different from the manacles, though they weren't connected to each other. "And they said we're leaving for the capital in the morning. We're the last city for this caravan, so we'll be at the Shieldwall Academy in a couple of days. Then we can get started learning magic." He said the last with a determination that encouraged Pax to do the same.

Looking down at the slender bracelets on his wrists, Pax thought he should have noticed them before now, especially with how chilly they felt. Of course, metal usually felt cold, but it should warm up with body heat. But not these. What powered them? How did they work?

Pax's anger returned at the sign of just another way they were controlling him and Amil against their will. Still a little shaken, Pax scanned their surroundings as he ruminated on everything Amil had told him.

The room had recently held furniture, if the marks on the floors and rubbing against the walls were any sign. Now, though, the entire space was made up of various carpets strewn around the area filled with a host of other sleeping youth. Soft snores and snuffling noises seemed to indicate they were all asleep.

After the day's activities, Pax didn't blame them. He reached up to rub at his eyes and sore head and found once again, things didn't hurt as much as he'd expected. He looked up and aimed a questioning look toward Amil, who nodded.

"That fancy flame mage used a healing spell on you after you passed out." He leaned close to whisper. "Just a little spark of flame that flashed around your head for a few seconds."

Pax nodded, not sure he wanted to feel even a flicker of gratitude for the mages who had ruined his life. His breathing had finally evened out and, more than anything, he wanted to go back to sleep . . . after getting something to eat. His stomach felt hollow and painful, but he couldn't ignore the opportunity to escape while the others all slept.

"The window," he whispered to Amil, tipping his head toward the floor-to-ceiling drapery on the far wall. It looked almost black in the dim light.

Amil shook his head. "Barred. The door, too. And believe me, others tried for a few hours before giving up. Most of the initiates in here with us are from the previous cities, and they said the mages and guards never give them a chance to escape. But they still check, even if there isn't anywhere to go with these things on and how valuable we are to them." Amil shook his wrist again.

Pax sighed as he realized Amil was right. The mages would be skilled at controlling street rats turned to new initiate mages.

Tomis. Startled by the thought and feeling more than a little guilty that he'd forgotten his friend, Pax turned back to Amil. "Tomis?"

"He's a crafter," Amil answered, his gaze falling. "One of the others here said only shirker mages get taken to the capital for training. I guess because we're too dangerous or valuable." He gave a helpless shrug. "There will be merchants, warriors and crafters in the caravan going to train in the capital, but only the fancy, rich kids. Street kids like Tomis were pretty much sold off for commissions to the recruiters right after they awaken."

"But—" Pax objected, feeling cheated by everything he'd missed.

"I know," Amil said. "I didn't get to say goodbye either. But since he's staying local, he might be able to watch out for our crew. He just needs to finagle a bit of freedom from his new crafting master."

Pax sagged back, feeling sick, imagining Jules and the other kids trying to survive without them. He couldn't do anything about it now, but in the dark room, Pax resolved to make it back to Thanhil someday to help his crew, despite how impossible it seemed. They were both mages. Together, Pax vowed they'd figure out how to break free someday.

Then he swallowed hard and wondered if Titus had made a similar vow three years ago. Had he been awakened as a mage, too? It would explain his disappearance. If he'd stayed in the city as another class, Pax knew he'd have made contact. Warriors were the only other class that he'd heard of being sent to fight in other cities.

"Dawn is probably coming soon," Amil said in a quiet voice. "You should eat something, and then we need to sleep. Tomorrow won't be fun."

"Food?" Pax asked, perking up.

"We left you one of the boxed dinners on the tray by the door. Let me grab it." Amil jumped up and slipped among the sleeping forms toward the door.

Pax watched him go, having seen some of the same trepidation and worry he felt in Amil's eyes, but knowing there wasn't anything they could do.

When Amil returned with the box, Pax tucked into the cold sandwich and grinned at the sight of a small apple. The tart juice exploded in his mouth with the first bite, and he couldn't help grinning with his mouth full. He couldn't remember the last time he'd had a piece of unbruised fresh fruit.

When he finished, Pax gave Amil a thankful nod, and lay back on the carpet, surprised to find he had a pillow. A soft one that felt like a cloud cupping his head in luxury. The blanket Amil tucked over him was just as wonderful, softer than anything he'd ever felt. Maybe this mage thing wouldn't be all bad.

Mage.

On the edge of sleep already, the thought had Pax's eyes popping open. How could he have forgotten about his full menu?

A giddy feeling swept away the cobwebs of sleep as he closed his eyes again and focused.

Menu.

He couldn't help smiling as he saw the new format, his basic info on the first page with tabs arrayed across the top, waiting to be explored.

～

NAME: *Pax Vipersworn*
  Race: *Mixed Human (monster-touched)*
  Age: *16*
  Bound Location: *none*
  Class: *Mage*
  Element: *Light (locked)*

Specialization: Locked
Level: 1
Mage Leveling Points: 0/5
Health: 22/28
Mana: 24/24 *(elemental use locked)*
Attributes:
Strength: 2
Agility: 7
Endurance: 3
Intelligence: 7
Insight: 6
Charisma: 3
Skills: None
Spells: None (locked)
Inventory: 18/20 available
Assignments: None
Misc.: None

~

HIS EYE CAUGHT on the element for a moment, nonplussed as he barely noticed the rest of the menu. Everyone knew there were only four elemental magics, and light was definitely not one of them. "Amil," he whispered.

His friend turned to face him, blinking bleary eyes at him in question.

"Sorry, just checking out my new menu," Pax apologized. "What element did you get?"

Amil's brows drew together in confusion. "They told us we won't know that until we go through something called the Crucible at Shieldwall. Yours should just say locked, right?"

Pax swallowed and nodded, not willing to mention that it also said 'Light'.

"Besides, our mage powers are suppressed right now, remember?"

Amil held up one wrist and gave it a little shake. "They don't want us messing things up with our class build before the academy."

Pax gave him a nod, a long-held sense of caution keeping him from saying anything about the light element mentioned in his menu.

But Amil had been friends with him for years and narrowed his eyes. "Why? What does your menu say?"

Pax shook his head. "I'm not sure. I think something is wrong with it."

"Tell me," Amil said, scooting closer and looking interested.

"Not yet. I haven't finished going through the tabs. Give me some time to figure it out, and then I'll discuss it with you, alright?"

Amil hesitated and then gave Pax an agreeable shrug. "We were all discussing the changes earlier. It seems the average on attributes is around five and did you see your inventory? It's bigger and not restricted with the time lag when moving things in and out."

Pax felt the first tug of happiness since his capture. He might only have his mother's ring and the medallion from his brother left, but the unrestricted access and additional slots opened a lot of possibilities.

"We deserve a little good news, don't we?" Amil said with a wry grin, before he snuggled back under his blanket without waiting for an answer.

Feeling a shaky mix of excitement and worry, Pax laid back down, closed his eyes and explored the different aspects of his menu.

ATTRIBUTES: As the newly awakened trains and practices, attributes will level up with effort. Initial levels are based on life experience previous to awakening.

SKILLS: None. As the newly awakened unlock skills, the initial level will be based on life experience previous to awakening.

. . .

SPELLS: *None. Seek guidance from an experienced mage before selecting new spells, as choices are permanent.*

ASSIGNMENTS: *None. You haven't agreed to do any yet, have you?*

MISC.: *Nothing to see here.*

～

PAX BLINKED at the empty tabs with snarky comments before ignoring them and moving back to the wide range of numbers Vitur had assigned him for his attributes. He was glad to see some of his numbers were higher than five, but not pleased with how low his Strength was. Amil's was probably much higher. And the Charisma? Was that just from being a street rat at the bottom of society, or, as he suspected, did his monster-touched arm contribute to it?

Pax forced himself to stop brooding and ran through his higher attributes. He let himself indulge in a moment of pride at his high Agility and Intelligence. He'd worked hard to leverage his speed against bigger and stronger opponents his whole life. And keeping his crew fed and safe had required more mental smarts than some of his crew gave him credit for.

It also looked as if whatever healing the flame mage had done hadn't completely restored his health. Hopefully by morning, it would improve. He made a mental note to calculate how long it took to recover.

His thoughts slowed as the quiet room and exhaustion tugged him back into sleep. He quickly opened his inventory, excited to see what Amil had described. There were four rows of five, instead of just two. Pax tested it by popping his mother's ring into his hand. He grinned when it appeared immediately with no delay. It went back in just as quickly.

If only he hadn't lost his two cudgels. They'd be so much more useful now that he had an unrestricted inventory. He scanned the empty slots and didn't even mind that he only had two possessions to his name and his coin count was still pitiful. He'd be working on fixing both as soon as possible.

He figured they had to give them some freedom once it was time to learn magic. Working together with Amil, he planned to use their street smarts to milk every potential advantage out of Shieldwall Academy. Together, Pax resolved they'd turn this entire mess into the best thing that ever happened in their lives.

THE START OF A NEW LIFE

IN THE COOL of the early morning, Pax was happy to see he'd recovered another two health points in the night. He trudged behind Amil in a row of captive initiate mages. A guard led them into the inn's expansive courtyard, their hands in manacles again and attached to a chain. The suppressor bracelets shone in sleek contrast to manacles looking crude and unrefined next to them on their wrists. Too bad the glow of the embedded cores ensured they were still unbreakable.

When they'd been woken this morning, the guards had given them breakfast trays and waited impatiently for them to finish. As soon as they were done, the manacles had come back out, disabusing them of any notion that their fortunes had changed now that they were initiate mages.

At least Amil had lined up together on the same chain as Pax. They brought up the rear of their line. Two guards led them out of the inn and through the lobby after the other initiates, who didn't need to be restrained.

The few well-dressed guests that were up at the early hour gave the initiates congratulations and pleasant nods . . . until the guards paraded Pax's group past them. Scowls and curses followed them out into the chill of the early fall morning, making it harder for Pax to keep his spirits up. His resolve last night had faded a bit with the reality of the chilly morning with its chains and guards. How was this any different from being in prison?

At least Amil's belief in him helped him stay positive. That and his memory of how powerful the magic used in the Awakening had been. As that memory flashed through his mind, Pax felt his determination return. He and Amil would fight to get some of that power for themselves. Sulking at the unfairness of life wouldn't help either of them.

Walking behind his friend, Pax focused on mimicking him, head up and shoulders back. Looking confident was an essential skill when leading a street crew, regardless of how unsure you felt.

"Right here," the guard in the lead snapped, pointing to an area at the back of the other initiate mages. "Spread out and line up here. Keep your mouths shut, do what you're told and you won't have any trouble. Got it?"

Everyone bobbed their heads in agreement except the raven-haired girl, though she kept her head down where the guards couldn't see her glare. Her defiance lifted Pax's spirits. He decided he'd get to know her at the first opportunity. He and Amil could use new allies as they headed into the unknown.

Pax stopped in the spot the guard pointed to. Looking forward, he glimpsed Galen, the nasty kid from the main square. He stood in the front row, his head at an arrogant tilt as he chatted with the initiate next to him. Scanning the other groups nearby, Pax realized his was the only one with a row of prisoners in the back. That meant the other three groups must be the wealthy and connected warrior, merchant and crafter initiates. Pax frowned with distaste. Just his luck that Galen was a mage, too.

Pax couldn't help shaking his head at the smug postures and expensive outfits of the initiates around him. The warriors were destined for officer positions while the crafters and merchants would have their pick of prime spots once they graduated from the training at the capital.

Pax hated how unfair it all was. The elite companies and recruiters had snapped up the bulk of yesterday's non-mage initiates for trainee spots in Thanhil. The work varied from indentured slavery to apprenticeships with bright futures if you had connections and influence. And Tomis had neither.

Pax pushed his thoughts of Thanhil aside and blinked his tired eyes to focus on his current surroundings. He needed to find every advantage possible. He didn't plan on being at the bottom of the pile any longer than necessary.

The initiates shifted in their rows and whispered quietly to each other, an impatience building the longer it took for the mages to appear. A clinking of buckles and animals grunting drew Pax's attention to the line of wagons that were being prepared along the far edge of the courtyard.

The two lead vehicles were incredible, looking like they could withstand a flame attack from a legendary dragon. The armored walls were sleek, with no edges to offer weak points. And the weapon slits were small, with sliders blocking them at the moment. The crafters who'd built the vehicles had veiled the supporting platforms with metal skirts that concealed the inner workings of the vehicles. But if the large air engines on the backs were any indication, they probably ran off air cores to give them the speed and maneuverability required to battle monsters out in the Wilds.

The rest of the wagons were all manual affairs, hooked up to large animals, with rugged wheels and enclosed quarters for the passengers. It was obvious there were different classes of wagons. The one in the center looked opulent enough to rival a governor's mansion and was likely designed to carry the mages.

Pax's heart sank when he saw the last two wagons, knowing by the barred windows and heavy locks on the sides that they were just what they looked like, prison wagons. He, Amil and the other captives were in for an entirely unpleasant trip to the capital.

At least the wagons all looked sturdy enough to withstand the journey. And he was pretty sure the beasts pulling them were yugruts. They looked strong and a bit scary, which was good. Drivers scurried up and down the line, checking tack and murmuring comforting words as they finished yoking the animals in sets of two to the wagons. As they were used almost exclusively for travel between cities, Pax peered closer, having never seen one in person.

The four-legged beasts of burden stood as high as Pax's shoulder, their skin covered in a thick patchwork of leathery, overlapping plates, providing them with a natural armor that would be very helpful against monsters once they left the city walls. Their heads were flat and wide, with eyes sitting half-lidded on either side and massive jaws that could probably chomp a person in half. The ones still waiting to be hooked up chewed roots and chunks of meat in baskets placed on the ground in front of them.

They looked placid at that early hour, until Pax saw one snap at a handler with sharp teeth that glinted in the early morning light. The leather-clad woman dodged with casual practice, landing a fast blow to the creature's nose that had it backing off and returning to its breakfast. Pax made a mental note not to walk too close.

A soft ping made him jerk and look around for the source. When menu text popped up in the lower half of his vision, Pax almost bit his tongue in surprise before looking down at it.

The text immediately rose in response and scrolled as he scanned it.

*General Skill Unlocked: **Identify** Level 1*

This common active skill allows one to identify names, levels, abilities and other information about nearby people, monsters and items. More information is available as the skill progresses, though Identify may fail against a defensive skill or spell, or when trying to Identify someone or something far higher in level than the skill or user.

Distance: 10 yards

Level Differential: 2 levels

Mana cost: 5

Identify attempt failed. Level difference is too significant.

*Skill Boost: +2 to **Identify** Level 1 - 2/100*

PAX KNEW his mouth had sagged open in surprise, but he didn't care.

A skill!

He had his first skill, and even if it hadn't worked on the yugrut, it had advanced by a few points. Getting feedback on what he was learning and how fast it advanced was amazing after being locked out of his menu his whole life.

Pax still hated being controlled by the authorities, but he couldn't suppress his excitement as his mind spun with plans for gaining new skills and levels. Someday, he'd become strong enough that no one could control him.

Ignoring the chit-chat around him, Pax picked another yugrut and tried to identify it, determined to move down the entire line of animals to level up the skill as much as possible.

IDENTIFY ATTEMPT FAILED. Level differential too significant.
*Skill Boost: +1 to **Identify** Level 1 - 3/100*

IDENTIFY ATTEMPT FAILED. Level differential too significant.

IDENTIFY ATTEMPT FAILED. Subject is too far away.

PAX QUICKLY REALIZED that the skill only advanced twice using it on the same type of animal before he received no more gains. Plus, ten yards wasn't very far at all. He looked around and then smiled. He was surrounded by initiates who were a lot closer than the yugruts and should be his same level.

A blinding headache slammed into him, making his knees weak. He instinctively tried to bring his hands to his head, but the chains prevented him. When he flicked open the flashing notification, he saw the problem.

~

YOU ARE MANA DRAINED! *Unable to use active skills or spells until mana has regenerated.*

~

"WHAT'S WRONG?" Amil hissed next to him as he grabbed Pax's upper arm to support him.

Pax couldn't answer, his throat too dry as he scanned his menu for the information he needed.

There.

~

MANA: *1/24 (elemental use locked)*

GENERAL SKILL UNLOCKED: **Identify** *Level 1*
    Mana cost: 5

~

SOME QUICK MATH, and Pax resolved to never use Identify more than four times in a row.

"Pax?" Amil asked again, his grip tightening as his voice sounded more worried.

Pax swallowed so he could answer, glad the headache was receding. "I accidentally used all my mana," he said in a dry whisper.

Amil's eyes widened in surprise, followed by relief. "Wow," he said quietly, with a shake of his head. "Guess I'll make sure not to do that. Thanks for testing it out for me."

Pax snorted a laugh and elbowed his friend, drawing a glare from an initiate in the row in front of them.

For the next few minutes, Pax kept a careful eye on his mana level, watching as it climbed up fairly quickly, taking around a handful of minutes to refill. He'd need to find a clock tower to measure it exactly. While moving around the menu, he was happy to discover he could toggle small mana and health bars to appear in the corner of his vision when he wanted. They would come in handy to prevent mana drain in the future, not to mention seeing how hurt he was when he had to fight.

MAGE AMIL FAJOR - *Level 1*
> *Increase* **Identify** *Skill for more information.*
> *Skill Boost: +2 to* **Identify** *Level 1 - 5/100*

Mage Rin Esta - Level 1
> *Increase* **Identify** *Skill for more information.*
> *Skill Boost: +1 to* **Identify** *Level 1 - 6/100*

PAX GRINNED as he realized he wouldn't have to work so hard to remember names now. He had just turned toward the group of warrior initiates when the surrounding sound changed. Voices hushed and shoulders straightened. Pax stopped using Identify and glanced over to see the capital mages exiting the front of the inn. Servants milled around the elite group, looking eager to jump at any order. Two servants ran ahead carrying a blocky stand that they placed in front of the initiates.

Pax recognized the air mage as she stepped onto the stand without the least acknowledgement to the servants who'd set it up for her. Her expression was a mix of boredom and impatience as she held up her hands for silence. Two girls in the merchant section kept chatting in low voices as the rest of the crowd fell silent.

The mage flicked a hand toward the pair, and Pax had his first, up close, glimpse of a spell being cast. The intricate tattoos on the mage's wrist flared with a brief flicker of light-blue, and her lips moved in a silent command. An invisible force shot from her hand toward the girls and wrapped them up in a swirling cyclone of air that lifted them into the air.

Two matching shrieks of surprise and fear filled the now silent courtyard. Even the yugruts' attention snapped toward the display of power, some baring teeth. But no one objected as the air mage held the two initiates in a column of air while small pebbles and leaves swept up from the ground battered them.

Pax did his best not to attract her attention.

MAGIC UP CLOSE

PAX HAD NEVER BEEN this close to magic and was both fascinated and horrified at the same time. With power like that, how could anyone stop the woman from doing whatever she wanted?

Keeping one arm stretched out to hold the girls mid-air, the mage turned her stony gaze in their direction. "I guess we're starting lessons early, then." She paused to let the words sink in. "You have two jobs as initiates, whether a mage, crafter, merchant or warrior: to obey and to learn. And since the learning doesn't start until we reach the academies, your job on this journey is to obey. Immediately. And without question." She paused again, raking her gaze over the completely silent initiates.

The girls had mostly stifled their cries, which seemed to appease the woman.

"Does everyone understand?"

A chorus of ragged assents rang out. The mage gave a disappointed sigh as she shook her head and pulled her arm back, letting the two girls fall to the ground in a crumpled heap. "The correct answer is, 'Yes, Mage Eldan.' Is that understood?"

This time, the much more uniform answer seemed to satisfy her.

"Good enough for now," she said before clapping her hands

together. "Now, you'll board the wagons assigned to you and follow all instructions from the guards. As this is our final city assignment, we will travel in a direct line to the capital instead of skipping back and forth like we have been. We'll stay overnight at a caravan waypoint and use boosted travel spells to arrive in the capital before dark tomorrow. We're all tired of this and eager to be done."

Pax scanned the surrounding groups, realizing that many of them weren't from Thanhil, just like the unfamiliar faces he'd noticed among the captured mages who'd spent the night with him and Amil.

"Questions?" Mage Eldan asked as she started to turn away.

When a boy in the front row of the mages raised a hand, she paused and glared at him. Pax felt a touch of glee to see it was Galen.

But he didn't flinch under Mage Eldan's gaze, and Pax had to give him credit for being brave enough to speak up.

"Will we encounter beasts outside the city walls, and will we need our magic to fight them?"

Mage Eldan stared at the tall boy. His arrogant posture made him look ready to leap into battle if she gave the word. She shook her head. "Well, you have guts. I have to give you that."

Galen straightened further, almost preening.

"If you weren't such an idiot, it would be endearing," she said in the same tone of voice.

Galen hesitated a beat. Pax saw an angry red flush up the back of his neck as a few initiated chuckled.

"You can't talk to me like—" he began angrily, only to bite down on further words when Mage Eldan's hand moved in his direction.

She waited a beat and then nodded with satisfaction when he stayed quiet. Turning back to scan the rest of the initiates, she continued. "First, all mage initiates are prohibited from doing any magic until you go through the Crucible at the academy and unlock your element. And because we know how hard it is for children to follow orders, you're wearing suppressors to make sure you obey."

She pointed a finger toward the warriors. "And before you ask, the same goes for you. You will not mess up your builds by fighting with weapons that may not be optimal for your abilities. That is for your trainers to decide." She raised both hands again. "Again, your job is to sit in your wagons quietly until we reach the capital. We'll be traveling during daylight and at most will encounter a single beast or two. We have plenty of caravan guards who are well trained to handle them. You are not to get involved. Understood?"

"Yes, Mage Eldan," came the chorus, almost in sync this time.

"Then load up, and let's get out of this backwater place," she said, before she stepped down and headed toward the mages' wagon.

Her departure released everyone from the need to stay rigidly in place, and the courtyard quickly turned into a milling mass of confusion. On impulse, Pax cast a quick Identify at her as she walked toward the massive wagon in the center of the line.

∿

IDENTIFY ATTEMPT FAILED. Level differential too significant.
*Skill Boost: +4 to **Identify** Level 1 - 10/100*

∿

MAGE ELDAN WHIPPED AROUND IMMEDIATELY, face furious. "Next one who tries to Identify me will spend the trip with the yugruts!"

The activity and sound in the courtyard died in an instant as everyone looked at the air mage with varying degrees of bewilderment or trepidation.

"Another lesson for you all today: At my level, Identify is easily sensed, and it's considered rude to use it without permission. This is your one and only warning." Without waiting for a response, she spun around and stormed off toward the other mages.

"Sheesh," Amil whispered beside him. "Someone has guts."

Pax swallowed and did his best to mimic the looks of surprise and confusion he saw around him. He let out a relieved breath when it didn't take long for everyone to get busy and move again.

The head mages had already disappeared into their luxurious wagon, where they would likely be enjoying themselves for the rest of the trip. Pax tried not to imagine what the prison wagons would be like on the inside.

Caravan guards stood at the door to each wagon with lists clipped to boards, calling out names and checking before allowing anyone on board. Pax could easily pick out the initiates from other cities, as they headed straight to the correct wagons while the new Thanhil recruits milled around with uncertainty.

The chain attached to his manacles jerked, and Pax turned to walk quickly after Amil toward one of the prison wagons. He'd been right. The one at the end of the line was theirs.

Their guard pulling both rows of captives stopped at the heavy, iron-banded door and consulted with the caravan guard and his list. A few moments later, he handed one chain off to another guard before climbing up the two steps and pulled them inside after him. Behind him, Pax saw extra guards move to surround their wagon and the next one, hands on nightsticks and looking alert. They weren't taking any chances.

Inside, the wagon was as sparse as Pax had feared, a large space, longer than it was wide with a scarred wooden floor. The single small windows on each wall were too small for a body to make it through, even without the iron bars anchored over them. He scanned the space, dubious that all of them were going to even fit when it came time to sleep.

The guard stomped across to the far end and pulled open two simple closets to reveal bedrolls with the distinctive gray color of fabric that had been washed often.

"Use these when you want to sleep. You've got drinking water and cups here," he said, opening a second, shorter closet to reveal a squat barrel with cups stacked on a shelf above it. "And there's the necessary," he added, pointing to the corner where a flimsy wooden panel had been built out from the sidewall. "Wait until we're outside the city to use it. The inn don't need any of your crap dirtying up their courtyard. We'll bring you your meals when we stop at mid-day."

Pax peered around the panel and frowned when he saw the small hole covered by a grate, just like in the prison. Except here it meant their waste would drop onto the ground below the wagon.

"Hands up," the guard said as he moved toward them, his controller in hand.

The door guard stepped in, his nightstick out, as he eyed them warily.

"There's no escape from here," the first guard cautioned. "Even if you get past the two of us, the guards out there will stop you. So don't give us any trouble now, or we'll leave you locked up the whole trip. Got it?"

Pax nodded along with the others, eager to get the hated manacles off as soon as possible. In moments, all of them were free, and the heavy wagon door slammed shut behind the guards. A moment later, they heard the lock thunk into place.

They eyed each other with caution. No one spoke as the noises out in the courtyard diminished. They heard the yugruts snorting and shifting as they prepared to move out.

"Maybe we should introduce ourselves, since we're going to be stuck together for the next two days," Amil said, finally breaking the silence. "I'm Amil, mixed-elf and dwarf, and this is my friend Pax, obviously mixed-human."

A shorter boy with dark features and a pronounced dwarven jaw narrowed his eyes and gave them a suspicious look. "How did two friends, and shirkers at that, both awaken as mages?"

Pax and Amil exchanged a look before Pax looked back at the boy and shrugged. "I don't know. The Awakening almost killed me, so maybe Vitur blessed me with a friend to help me through."

"Killed you?" The boy scoffed, disbelief easy to read on his face.

"Yep," came a blunt voice. "All screaming and flopping around on the ground with blood coming out of his eyes. They had to do it twice, and the flame mage didn't think he'd make it. So, he deserved a bit of luck, I'd say."

Pax flashed a grateful look toward the dark-haired girl, who seemed to have bravery in spades.

"I'm Rin, obviously mixed-human, and I'm tired," she rattled off the info before turning toward the cupboards at the back of the wagon. "Dibs on the best pallet that's not taken. I'm going back to sleep."

The rest of the group stared for a slow heartbeat before someone chuckled. It broke the tension and others spoke, introducing themselves and helping Rin empty the closet and divvy up the pallets.

It turned out there was even a bit of extra space once they were all spread out. They left a bit of cleared area beneath each of the windows and next to the necessary. Pax joined a few others, clasping the bars to see out as the wagons jolted into movement.

A confusing swirl of emotions churned inside him as he watched his city pass by until the massive gates creaked open to let them through. He peered back to watch them swing shut behind the caravan.

Pax surveyed the Wilds, eyes wide and curious as he rode outside his city walls for the first time in his life. The rocky land stretched out into the distance, hills and scrubby plants standing in clusters that broke up the horizon. Pax let out a disappointed huff as he saw not a single thing moving in the view through the small, barred window.

"What?" Amil asked, moving close and peering out the window with him.

"I thought we'd see at least a monster or two," Pax said. "Everyone is always so afraid of the Wilds."

"Because it's daytime, idiot," Amil said, elbowing Pax before a touch of worry entered his voice. "And if we're lucky, we'll be behind walls by that time and never have to see a beast during the trip. Remember the heads from Awakening Day?"

Pax turned back to the window as a shiver ran through him, unsure if it was fear or just a touch of excitement.

1 2

THE WILDS

IT TURNED out that traveling through the wilds during the day just wasn't all that exciting. Pax stepped away from the increasingly boring scenery to give someone else a turn at the window as he looked for Amil in the crowded wagon.

He spotted him reclining, eyes closed, on a pallet set up a few feet from the cupboard holding the water barrel. Pax smiled when he saw an empty pallet arranged beside him. He said a quick thanks to Vitur that he had a friend with him as he threaded his way across the wagon floor.

Most of the other initiates had grabbed their own pallets, relaxing on them or chatting quietly with neighbors. A few eyed him as he passed, but no one spoke to him. Pax didn't mind. He needed to get some rest.

"See anything interesting?" Amil opened one eye and propped himself up on his elbow as Pax settled down on the pallet next to him.

"No," Pax said, unable to keep the disappointment out of his voice. "Just a bit of movement in the distance now and again, but nothing I could make out." He paused before asking his real question. "So, where do all the beasts go during the day?"

"How should I know?" Amil said as he laid back and closed his eyes again. "Just be glad there aren't any nearby while we're packed into this little wagon like a stack of monster treats."

Pax let out a short laugh and shifted back to get comfortable on his mattress.

"They're all still out there."

Pax turned to the pallet just a few feet from him. Earlier, his eyes had passed over the still form under a thin blanket. The black-haired girl, Rin, turned to face him, propping her head up on her palm and looking at him with eyes full of secrets.

"How do you know?" he asked.

She lifted one shoulder in a small shrug. "I hear things and pay attention. It's like the nobles don't think we have ears or something."

"Hi, Rin. If you know things, maybe we can team up?"

Pax turned with a touch of irritation to see that Amil had popped up behind him and was aiming one of his interested smiles at the girl.

When Pax turned back to the girl, he was sort of glad to see her eyes narrowed in suspicion.

"Why are you so friendly?" she asked.

Amil's smile fell, and he looked at Pax for help.

"To balance out my temper," Pax said with a shrug. "I get us in all kinds of trouble, and Amil charms our way out of it."

Rin seemed to think about that before flicking her eyes to the inside of the prison wagon and giving him a significant look.

Pax felt a blush creep up his neck. "Yeah, it didn't work so well this time."

She seemed to relax a bit at the admission. "Fine," she said with a quick nod. "Where we're going, I think we're all going to need someone to watch our backs. So, how about we share information and do our best to help each other out, alright?" She stopped before adding, "Well, after ourselves first, of course. But then it's the three of us next. Deal?" She lifted one hand and closed her fist, brows raised in question.

Pax looked back to Amil, a bit taken aback by the sudden offer of an alliance and not sure of the implications. Amil gave him an eager nod, but Pax knew he'd leave the decision up to him.

A scowl formed on Rin's face as Pax hesitated. She'd been a bit of a troublemaker since he'd first noticed her, but he couldn't fault her courage. And with his own trouble with his temper, who was he to judge?

"Deal," he said in a quiet tone, leaning closer to tap her fist with his own where others couldn't see.

He saw just a flicker of relief in her eyes before her confident expression was back.

"Alright, I'll tell you what I know about the beasts," she said, dropping her voice and shifting her pallet so it was closer to Pax's.

Amil shifted over to Pax's and leaned in to hear.

"They are all still out there during the day, but they're just tired, worn out from the night's surge and fighting. So, they usually hide in nests or burrows to sleep, digest their meals and recover strength until it's dark again. It's the surge of magic from the elemental wells at night that drives them all crazy into attack mode. Once the surge stops at sunrise, the beasts are tired and less aggressive, so they go into hiding." She hesitated, looking unsure. "This is just stuff I've heard in rumors, but it could be stories kids like to scare each other with. It's not like I've ever fought on the walls or anything."

Pax gave her an encouraging look. "It's more than either of us knows, and the daytime part seems to be true, at least. There's hardly anything moving out there." He waved a hand toward the window.

A distant order in a harsh voice rang out clearly from outside the windows, followed, a heartbeat later, by three penetrating clangs of an alarm bell.

Pax barely had a chance to glance at his friends in surprise before their wagon jolted forward, throwing the standing initiates to the floor and stopping all conversations as heads turned in alarm.

Pax's instincts took over, and he lunged toward the closest window before anyone else reacted. Hand braced on the bars, he pressed his face against them, trying to see what was happening.

Their wagon had been the last in line except for the rearguard one. Now their driver had turned them around to bounce and jostle over the rough ground along the side of the road in a scramble to overtake the other wagons.

"I think they're circling the wagons together," Pax called over his shoulder, only to be surprised that some of the initiates had simply laid back down on their pallets.

"Of course they are, newb," said a stocky girl with obvious dwarven blood. "They do it every time a beast makes a run at the caravan. It's pretty exciting to watch . . . the first time or two."

Nods greeted her words, and Pax realized that only the initiates from Thanhil were on edge. To the ones from previous cities who'd been on the road for a while, it must be all routine by now.

"Feel free to take the window spots," said an older elven-looking boy, who Pax thought had introduced himself as Dahni. "We've all seen plenty, and it is pretty interesting the first time. Well, as long as you're on the outside window of the attack. Otherwise, you'll have to use your imagination since you'll only hear sounds. Happy to answer questions. Just ask."

Feeling reassured, Pax let his excitement rein free as he turned back to the window. Amil joined him, followed by Rin. Pax caught a spark of interest in her usually impassive expression.

"Oh," Dahni called out. "And if the beast gets close enough, let us know so we can all get a few points in Identify. Some of us have quite a few points after practicing on the low-level monsters that have been dumb enough to mess with the caravan during the daytime."

Pax shot him a grateful look and saw that some of the other new initiates looked interested now. They clambered to their feet and headed toward the other windows.

"Just don't forget, using any elemental magic is against the rules," a high-pitched voice piped up from the other side of the wagon. "So, don't even try."

"We know, Kurt," Rin snapped back at him before moving after Pax and Amil to one of the side windows.

When Pax shot her a questioning look, she just gave him an irritated shrug before whispering under her breath, "He's one of those, you know, always angling to get on the good side of the flicks with power."

Pax nodded his understanding as they made it to one of the side windows. He frowned as he remembered Kurt had been the kid to act all submissive to the guard back before the Awakening. Even so, everyone did what they had to in order to survive.

The wagon jostled again under their feet, and they grabbed for the bars in the window to steady themselves before looking out. Outside, noise filled the fast-forming circle of vehicles. The yugruts objected with grunts and roars to the fast maneuvering of the wagons. They quieted down some as their drivers finished the circle, unhitched them and pushed them together toward the safety of the center.

Looking through their center-facing window, Pax watched, fascinated, as caravan guards and mages leaped from their vehicles, armed and dressed in tough-looking armor. He even saw an occasional flicker of magic light up when someone activated a core-powered item. It all played out in front of him like a well-rehearsed and professional routine.

When he glanced at Amil, he saw a matching grin of excitement from his friend. Rin's face was expressionless, though her eyes were intent, as if she could memorize everything that was happening for later analysis.

The fighters climbed sturdy ladders to man platforms on top of the wagons. Pax marveled at the cleverness of the crafters who'd designed the mobile parapets that sprung up between the defenders and whatever threatened them from outside the circle.

Suddenly realizing that he might be missing the entire attack, Pax nudged his friends before threading his way across the wagon to the opposite window, only to find a metal shutter had fallen down over it.

His shoulders slumped, and both Amil and Rin looked disappointed, too. But Pax couldn't argue that it was probably safer that way. And it looked as if the two front and back windows, now facing sideways, hadn't been blocked. They might face the ends of the other wagons in the circle, but perhaps they'd be able to glimpse some of the action.

He'd just taken a step in that direction when the dwarven girl extended her hand, holding out a skinny stick as long as her forearm. "Use this. They rarely bother to batten down the shutters on the prison wagon. If you're careful, you can prop it up enough to see out."

Pax grinned and took the stick.

"Just don't let anything nasty get in here. Got it?" the girl warned.

"Promise," Pax said over his shoulder as he moved in close, slid the stick between the narrow bars and gently pushed. Excitement filled him. A street rat who'd never even been to the top of the walls and now, he might actually see warriors and mages battling actual beasts.

LIZARDS OF UNUSUAL SIZE

Sure enough, Pax could push the shutter up easily. They'd built the hinges above the window to make it easy to drop into place for a fight. He and his friends pressed their faces in close, scanning the wilderness outside the circled wagons through the narrow horizontal slit.

Disappointment made his shoulders sag. Nothing of interest. A berm of rocky dirt rose about a hundred yards from the edge of the road, with short knee-high shrubs and leaves that shifted with the occasional gust of wind. The fall weather had tempered the heat of summer, but everything outside still looked dusty and deserted, in desperate need of a good rain.

Behind them, the sounds of the guards and yugruts had also quieted down, like the calm before a storm. Amil let out an impatient breath, and Pax could feel Rin shifting on his other side. Pax kept his eyes peeled, moving from one possible hiding place to the other.

"If someone saw a beast, you'd think it would have attacked by now," Amil grumbled.

"Some of the caravan mages have sensing spells, so they're forewarned," an irritated voice chimed in from behind them. "And just be glad we're not being attacked. This isn't a game."

Amil flushed, but didn't argue. Pax remembered the still bodies of the soldier and mage he'd seen placed on the keep's altar and felt sheepish, too. He had just turned to apologize when a loud crack reverberated outside, destroying the quiet. Yells and the clanging of weapons followed. Looking alarmed, a handful of the other initiates jumped up to peer out the other windows.

Pax turned back and peered under the metal shutter, but still couldn't see anything.

"There," a girl behind him cried out. She leaned close to the inside-facing window and pointed across the center of the circle. "It's hitting the third wagon from us."

Pax peered across the wagon and tried to make out details through the sliver of window he could see. The backs of agitated yugruts moved in and out of view, and Pax could see the edge of one of the nicer wagons shaking. A blast of flame flared into view, followed immediately by a rumble from beneath their feet.

Were those earth spells? The sudden chaos sobered Pax, and his smile faded.

And then, as suddenly as they had started, the sounds of battle died away, replaced by a chorus of congratulations and calls between the fighters.

Pax heard sighs of relief and saw shoulders slump as the tension bled out of the surrounding initiates.

"Wasn't much to see, and it was too far away to Identify," Amil grumbled, but kept his voice low so only Pax and Rin could hear him.

"What?" Rin asked, the reprimand clear in her voice. "Do you want one of those things to introduce themselves face to face?"

"You're right," Amil gave the scowling girl a self-deprecating chuckle. "But you can't blame me for wanting a better view, from a safe distance."

When she didn't soften, he tried again.

"At some point, we're going to be fighting these things, and getting details now could help in the future, right?"

"True," she relented, as they both turned from the window to head back to their pallets.

Some tickle along the back of Pax's neck, curiosity or warning, made him push the shutter up for a last look at the barren landscape outside. His breath caught, and he leaned forward, squinting.

Had that dark boulder just moved?

Just at the low rise about three wagon-lengths away from him, stood a cluster of dark rocks, cracked and rough, protruding unevenly from the ground. Nothing moved now, though he could have sworn one of them had shifted sideways, instead of a normal tumble along the downward slope.

As Pax stared, the air shimmered above the rocks with waves of heat that he could just make out against the backdrop of the distant landscape. Maybe that's what had created the movement he'd seen. Pax had noticed objects seemed to shimmer like that during the heat of the summer, even in the city, especially when he'd hidden close to ground level and stared down a long, empty cobblestone road.

"What are you still looking at?" Amil called out. "Better come sit down before the wagon jolts around again to get back on the road."

Sure enough, Pax heard the complaints of the yugruts and glanced over his shoulder through the inside window to see the drivers busy preparing them to hitch back to the wagons.

Pax had just begun to relax, turning back to let the shutter fall back into place, when a thought that had niggled at him finally pushed to the forefront.

It wasn't summer anymore. Heat shimmering in the air didn't happen in the fall, at least not on a cool day like today.

Heart suddenly hammering, he shoved the shutter open again and searched for the cluster of boulders. His mouth went dry at the sight that greeted him, his thoughts gibbering in a panic that held him frozen.

The ground out at the rise bulged and heaved like a soup pot boiling over. The dark stones pushed against each other as some of them rose out of the ground. What he had mistaken for jagged boulders were simply ridges along the head and spine of enormous creatures that tore out of their camouflage with scary speed.

One turned its long maw toward their wagon as it kicked itself free from the ground with wide, clawed feet. Its wide body surged with muscle under the black, rocky skin, four legs spread out to keep its form low and close to the ground like a mutant lizard the size of their wagon.

What in the world?

～

IDENTIFY ATTEMPT FAILED. *Level differential too significant and too far away.*

*Skill Boost: +4 to **Identify** Level 1 - 14/100*

～

IMPATIENT, Pax shoved the notification out of his vision and mentally told his menu to stop bothering him unless he asked. He blinked in surprise but was grateful when it responded instantly, reducing to a small, blinking box in the bottom corner of his vision. Then the significance of the points hit him. An extra four points to Identify made his stomach twist with worry. How high-leveled were the creatures?

"Pax?" Amil called out and out of the corner of his eye, Pax caught the sudden motion of Rin surging to her feet.

It was just enough to jar Pax out of his stupor.

"Beasts!" he yelled, pointing frantically. "More of them!"

Eyes around him widened in alarm. A few of the initiates called out questions. Pax could hear the growing sounds of clattering boulders and cascading soil behind him as everyone took much too long to respond.

He dashed across the wagon to the inside window, heedless of who he stepped on. Pressing his face against the iron bars of the window, he yelled, "More beasts! A whole nest of them behind our wagon! Hurry! They're coming!"

He saw heads snap around, fighters and mages instantly alert again. They'd let their guard down after the easy victory. At least there was no hesitation or confusion at his yelled warning.

With a surge of movement that was impressive, fighters raced toward his wagon, drawing weapons as mages followed, tattoos flaring with elemental magic. Cries of alarm behind him told him other initiates had seen the coming danger. Faint shouts from the neighboring wagons joined the alarm.

He felt a gush of relief at the fast response by their guards, only to have a thunderous roar drown everything out, deep and bellowing with a body-shaking boom.

Pax jerked around to stare at the outside window, only to sigh with relief when he saw the metal shutter had fallen back down to cover it. It couldn't be much protection against the enormous beasts he'd seen, but it was better than nothing.

He felt their wagon rock as guards and mages clambered to the fighting positions on top and to either side. Their footfalls drummed on the roofs as orders snapped into the quiet that followed the beast's cry.

"A Blaze Lizard nest!" came the muffled cry of alarm from over-head, followed by the yelled orders to archers and mages.

The initiates in the wagon with him barely hesitated after the monster's roar. They were street kids and scurrying for cover from danger was a survival skill. Pax felt their wagon shift as everyone scrambled toward him and the inner wall. He saw two initiates tugging on the door handle while another did his best to kick it open, to no avail.

The twang of bowstrings could be heard from above and a raging gust of wind rattled the wagon as an air mage cast spells. More roars, some of pain, filled the air with a cacophony of battle that drummed up everyone's adrenaline.

Pax stared at the far wall and the window with its rattling metal shutter, his imagination inadequate for what was happening on the other side of the thin wall. The wooden wall banded by iron had seemed so solid just moments ago, but not compared to the size and strength of the beasts he'd seen out there.

"Get out your weapons," Rin said, steel in her voice despite the tremble Pax saw in her hands. "The ones you've been hiding outside your inventory for an emergency. Now!"

Her orders snapped through the noise and gave their group something to do.

Pax watched initiates producing shivs, sticks, and even a knife or two from hidden places. All he had were two pieces of cordage he'd made from the prison blanket. He was pretty sure they were completely useless right now. That just left his fists, which weren't much better.

He forced himself to think, looking around the wagon for anything that might help. Nothing. Except the one thing they had forbidden him from using.

His magic.

He glanced down at the sleek metal of the suppressors on his wrists. There had to be a way to get past them.

IMPOSSIBLE MAGIC

Pax hadn't tried to touch his spark since the torture of his Awakening. Only the growing sounds of battle and screams outside allowed him to power past his instinctive flinch as he turned his focus inward.

The wooden floor beneath him trembled, making Pax sway on his feet. His attention faltered. A powerful thump outside was followed by a wash of heat from one of the windows on the side.

"We're all going to die," whispered someone nearby.

Pax could hardly believe how fast their wagon had turned into a chaotic madhouse.

"You have an idea," said a determined voice next to him. "How can I help?"

Pax turned to see Rin had moved in beside him, eyes edged with panic but ready to act. Amil looked just as determined. It was exactly what Pax needed to marshal his own emotions.

"It's not much," he said quickly, dropping to the floor and crossing his legs. "But maybe we can get our magic to work. What's the point of being mages if we can't fight with magic?"

Rin shook her head before he'd even finished speaking. She dropped next to him, disappointment clear on her face. "No go. We've already tried that. Only the privileged got to mess with theirs under supervision for a few hours before they got these, too." She held up her wrists and tapped the suppressor bracelets together.

Amil's head bobbed in agreement.

"But—" Pax choked on the words and swallowed hard, torn about how much to reveal.

Something large and heavy slammed into the outside wall of the wagon, followed by a mix of gasps and shrieks around them. The sounds of fighting above surged.

Urgency swamping his caution, Pax made his decision and leaned in close. "My magic might be different." He held up a finger and talked over Rin, who had immediately opened her mouth to ask questions. "No time. I have to focus completely. If you want to help, keep people away from me, so I can concentrate."

Without waiting to see their response, Pax tucked his right hand in close, hopefully out of view, and dove toward his center. He speared through the darkness and pulled on the one thing that had never abandoned him.

Pax couldn't deny the relief he felt when his spark leaped to life and lit his center with its usual enthusiastic response. At least the Awakening hadn't broken everything.

He quickly pushed it toward his arm and right hand with all the mental force he could muster. A flicker of color suddenly popped up in the small notification box, blinking with a faster urgency. The distraction made Pax's thoughts stutter.

Later, he insisted before jerking his attention back to his spark which had slowed at his shoulder. *Fast!* he commanded it as he gathered the small ball of energy and shoved it toward his hand with a burst of will.

. . . only to have it screech to a halt at his wrist, its momentum snuffed in an instant. Pax stared at the ball of energy held at a standstill and felt his hopes sag.

Ignoring the bracelet's power, he drew in a breath and pushed with his mind, fighting to break past the invisible barrier. He needed more power. Sweat broke out on his forehead as he leaned over his arm and shoved with everything he could muster.

Nothing.

Desperate, he pulled back and tried to punch through, pushing his spark back and forth in mental jabs. The back of his eyes burned. He could feel a headache growing at the effort. He flailed at the blockage with effort that grew wilder as he tired.

He might as well try to walk through a brick wall. He could push and shove with every bit of his strength and still only end up with scraped skin and an uncaring wall that didn't even notice his struggle.

"If you're going to do something, you better hurry." Amil's hiss brought him back to the present.

Pax let his mental muscles sag back. He blew out a harsh breath and opened his eyes. Around him, he only heard desperate and panicked sounds, no screaming or talking. And then he saw the reason.

Light stabbed into their wagon through a gaping hole in the corner of the roof. Beneath the damage lay a crumpled body amid scattered chunks of ragged wood.

Pax had seen plenty of blood before. Beatings were more than common in a street rat's life. But the glistening white of bone shards stabbing up from the woman's torso caught the light and made a macabre statement he had a hard time comprehending.

He looked up and felt bile rise in his throat when he saw more bone, this time dripping with gore from the arm wedged in the wreckage above them. He hadn't even noticed she was missing an arm.

"It chomped through a piece of the wagon before the guards could push it back," Rin reported in a fast voice with just a touch of controlled frenzy behind it. "I think they've killed three or four of the monsters, but there are more."

"And this wagon is *not* a city wall," Amil added from where he crouched next to Pax. He looked determined to fight back even if it was hopeless. In one hand, he clutched a metal spoon that had been sharpened into a point with fabric wrapped tightly around the handle. "Hurry up, Pax. Whatever your plan is, we need it now."

"How about we break through the door?" Rin asked. "We'll have a better chance if we can get to the center of the wagon circle."

Pax didn't want to admit his failure, but it had been a long shot. He knew his spark might have been useless in the fight, but he hadn't even had a chance to use it. His anger flaring, he glared down at the bracelets as he opened his mouth to give his friends the bad news . . . only to stop and stare.

The bracelets that had only gleamed with smooth workmanship before seemed to flicker with threads of an internal light now.

"What is it?" Rin demanded.

Amil shushed her.

Pax barely noticed as he pulled the right bracelet closer and stared as if he could see past the surface into the inner workings of the device. For a moment, nothing happened, and he worried that the mental strain was making him see things. He squinted and focused even harder, as if he could force his way inside the stupid thing.

"Relax," whispered Rin's voice. "I've heard the privileged initiates talk about letting the magic come instead of trying to force it."

Pax felt a warm hand squeeze his shoulder and push it down, making him realize how tense he was. Rin's advice went against every instinct he had. Normally, when fighting for his life, he'd be running and punching, putting all the adrenaline to good use. But now, he was trying to wrangle magic with his mind and all his pent-up frustration and fear was gathering in tense muscles that made his head throb.

He consciously dropped his shoulders and blew out a breath as he relaxed his eyes, letting his vision go soft. It seemed to work no better than his early glaring until a flash of light squirmed just under the surface of the chilly bracelet. He almost tensed up again and only a stern reminder to himself kept him relaxed.

With his eyes half out of focus, he kept watch in the same area, trying to let the magic come to him. And then, with a snap, his vision shifted. He saw two threads pulsing in the bracelet, swirling in twin rivers of blue around and around the devices. One thread was a light, airy blue, while the other was deep and dark with a touch of green. Twisting together, they gave off a cold, stagnant energy.

He had a moment of wonder to realize he was actually seeing magic, probably air and water, before he found himself at a loss again.

Now what?

His only ability lay with manipulating his spark. Brute force hadn't worked earlier, but perhaps there was another way. He had little time for attempts.

"Grab him!" Amil's voice snapped just before the wagon rocked with the most violent tremor yet.

Pax felt his friends grabbing his upper arms and shoulders, pushing him lower to the floor that heaved up at a sharp angle. His eyes snapped open to see the outside wall shoved so high in the air that it almost reached the level the ceiling had been at. Other initiates flew into the air, a tangle of arms and legs struck by flying pallets and other debris. Voices yelled in alarm from inside and outside the wagon just as Pax saw the water barrel crash down on his left to strike an elven girl in the back of the head.

Pax saw immediately what needed to be done. "Help me!" he yelled, lunging toward the outside wall that loomed above him. He climbed the floor like a slanted ladder as he fought to add his weight where they needed it.

When he looked over his shoulder, only Amil and Rin had followed him, clinging to the floorboards and struggling not to slide back toward the inner wall. The Blaze Lizard attacking the wall just outside was moments from tipping the entire wagon over. The rest of the beasts could then stream into the inner circle through the opening.

"Hurry!" Pax yelled at the other initiates who stared up at him as if he were crazy. "We need your weight to get the wagon back down."

Panic and fear looked back at him, but the realization spreading across a few faces heartened him.

"He's right." yelled Dahni, gesturing to the initiates near him. "If we tip over, we'll lose the fighters on our roof. The beasts will swarm us, and we'll die in here."

Just as a few initiates joined him in climbing toward Pax and his friends, a blast of water shot past the opening in the roof. A monstrous shriek of pain sounded on the other side of the wall and the entire wagon dropped a foot back toward level.

"Faster," Rin yelled, beckoning with one hand while holding onto a bar in the window with the other. "While we have a chance! Everyone get over here and start jumping."

Then, in an act of bravery that made Pax proud to be a street rat, the other initiates poured across the width of the wagon, swarming to add their weight to the outside edge, yelling and stomping with frantic abandon.

The wagon seemed to shudder at the different forces tearing at it. Arrows hissed overhead. With a groan that made everyone inside cheer, the wagon toppled back into place and bounced with a hard shudder.

Through the hole in the roof's corner, Pax could see the fighters above regain their feet, raising weapons and spells again. As the initiates celebrated their success, he slid back to the floor. There had to be something he could do with his spark. He was so close, he could feel it.

Pax slid back to the ground and slowed his breathing, hoping his heart rate would follow. He closed his eyes. After finding his spark still clumped near the bracelet's barrier, he reached out for the foreign magic with his mind.

At first, he could only sense the smooth surface of the device on his right arm. But he forced himself to be patient and tune out the yells and sounds of fighting that battered at his ears. Then, with a snap that came even faster this time, he saw the streams of magic powering the bracelet again.

He had one last idea to try. Amil was constantly reminding him that he caught many more of the good things in life with finesse than force. He normally referred to the girls he liked, but maybe it would work here, too.

Resisting his instinctive urge to smash at the foreign magic until it broke, Pax pulled his spark into a long thin thread, his best approximation of the size and length of the bracelet's own streams of magic.

Pax forced himself to ignore an escalation in the surrounding noise. He manhandled his spark into a crude, uneven rope of magic that pulsed with energy. With a last push, Pax sent his ring spinning around the inside of his wrist into a clumsy copy of the smooth movement of the foreign magic.

Holding his breath, Pax brought his ring of magic closer to the bracelet, expecting a painful reaction at any moment. But it didn't happen. He pushed it even closer, until it spun just beneath the bracelet, its white glow almost merging in his sight with the two shades of blue.

Holding his breath, Pax gave the spinning ring a last nudge. With an ease that seemed natural, the bracelet's magic absorbed his spark the way freshly turned garden dirt did water.

Pax sucked in a breath, amazed that it had worked. He immediately tried to push his spark past the bracelet and out of his hand. The pain flared in his wrist and head with a suddenness that made him stop immediately. The streams of merged magic went back to merrily spinning around his wrist.

Pax wanted to give up and rage at the whole situation. He was just a street rat with no idea how magic worked. He hadn't had wealthy tutors training him in all the nuances of the different classes from a young age.

And then he felt the hands holding him steady and remembered Rin's advice to let the magic come, instead of forcing it. With as gentle a touch as he could manage, he reached inside the swirling bracelet for his spark magic, and when he found it entwined with the other strands, he did his best to slow its movement, a little at a time. *Slow down and stop*, he whispered, desperately hoping the foreign magics would follow his spark. *Please slow down.*

And they did.

As his ring of spark magic slowed, the air and water magic followed suit. He stared in amazement as, finally, the three entwined strands fell still. The bracelet's bright magic faded, and the colors went dim and inert, making his spark glow even brighter in contrast.

One more time, shoulder hunched as he anticipated the pain, Pax pushed his spark past the bracelet and held his breath.

With an ease, in stark contrast to everything he'd tried earlier, his spark shot to his palm, bursting free into its usual ball of energy. Pax's eyes opened in astonishment. He stared, dumbfounded.

A flush of energy rushed through his mind, turning his thoughts clear, allowing them to flow more easily. A quick glance at his right wrist showed the bracelet still in place. But now, it had a dormant, inactive feel as it lost its chill and warmed against his skin.

The soft gasp next to him jerked Pax back to the present.

"What in Vitur's name is that?" Rin asked. "And how are you working magic with the suppressors still on?"

Thankfully, Rin had leaned in close and, together with Amil, shielded Pax's spark from prying eyes.

"Later. I promise," Pax said tersely as he closed his right fist and pulled his spark back inside, so it hovered out of sight just beneath the skin of his palm.

A loud groan of wood made them all jerk and stare. Amil jumped to a crouch, shiv in hand as they heard harsh gouging sounds and splintering wood from the right corner of the wagon, opposite the hole in the roof. Rin produced a short stick with a sharpened end, blackened by fire.

They exchanged looks. No words were needed.

Time had just run out.

A POWERFUL SPARK

WITH ALARMED CRIES, initiates scrambled back from the outer wall as fighters above could be heard barking out orders.

Mind frantic as he bent his knees and prepared to fight, Pax couldn't think of a way that his spark could hurt the monster. Maybe he could blind it, giving the fighters an easier chance of taking it down? What about sending it through the wall before the monster broke through?

Too pumped full of adrenaline and fear to second-guess his instincts, Pax launched himself forward and shoved his right palm against the wood, a few feet from the trembling and shaking corner.

"What are you doing?" he heard Rin's startled cry behind him.

"Help him," Amil yelled over the din.

As soon as his hand landed on the rough wall, Pax shoved his spark into the wood and beyond. To his surprise, it shot into the wall with just a little more effort than he usually needed to move it through his body. Another roar sounded as the wood bucked and heaved under Pax's hand, sharp splinters stinging his palm. He ignored it all and pushed his spark with a blind shove toward the monster on the other side of the wall.

He had a moment to wonder what would happen when it made

contact, before the wall in front of him ripped free with a screech of shattered wood and bent iron.

Hand still pressed to the splintered edge of the gaping hole, Pax froze, stunned as he watched the beast fling the chunk of wall back over its shoulder before jerking its gaping maw back toward the wagon. A rush of fetid breath and oven-hot heat blew past vicious teeth and washed over Pax, drying his sweaty face in an instant.

His spark fluttered as he almost lost control of it. Only a quick mental clench kept its brightness intact as he shoved it through the wood again and into the monster's jaw where it touched the broken wall. He felt a sudden connection, followed immediately by a tugging that pulled at his center.

Impossibly, the monster paused a heartbeat and closed its mouth without a sound. It shifted its snout to the side so one of its fist-sized eyes on the side of its head could focus on Pax. Dark-red and swirling with a maddened rage, the Blaze Lizard stared directly at Pax, its vertical pupil a black gash down the center.

Actually, not at Pax.

At his right hand.

And then, with a speed that was impossible to follow, it snapped its maw forward and chomped down on Pax's arm, wall and all. Sizzling teeth stabbed into his arm, cauterizing as they penetrated. Only the iron-banded wall kept the monster from biting completely through.

Pax screamed at the sheer agony of it, his instinctive jerk tearing his arm even more. Bone grated and muscles spasmed. He barely noticed the yells around him as his breath hiccupped with over-whelming fear and pain.

He flailed with his left hand, pounding futilely at the creature's black and steaming snout, only burning his knuckles for his effort. Barely coherent, Pax shifted to slam his forearm into the lizard's maw, his monster-touched scales coming in useful for once as they kept him from getting burnt worse. His arm rose and fell with futile rage, sobbing as he smashed it again and again into the snout, the lips, the teeth, anything, to make the blasted thing let go.

Just as he was ready to give up, Pax felt a rush of just enough strength to keep going. The pittance of extra energy kept him conscious and fighting.

Around him, the wagon had exploded into chaos, most scrambling back from the beast. But some of the initiates surged forward to attack. A slight girl hurled her knife at the Blaze Lizard's head. It bounced off and fell with a clank to the wooden floor. Dahni spun a sling around his head, letting sharp rocks fly almost too fast to follow as a girl next to him kept handing him more. Pax felt a shudder go through the monster as a rock hit its eye.

"The eye," he yelled out in a raspy croak. "Hit it with everything you've got! Make it let go!"

The initiates gained confidence when it became obvious the lizard wouldn't let go of Pax's arm to retaliate. Pax bit back a whimper, doing his best to block off the sensations screaming in his arm as the teeth shifted and grated.

A ragtag crowd, the initiates lashed out with every makeshift weapon they had. Someone even grabbed a chunk of splintered wood from the remains of the wall and tried to stab and bludgeon the lizard's head, looking like a child attacking a dragon with a heavy toothpick. Most of the weapons pelted the crackly, black skin with no visible effect. Thankfully, a few of them actually struck the eye, making the lizard shift and jerk its head as much as it could without letting go of its bite.

On the roof, boots could be heard scrambling as fighters fought for better positions, the swish of arrows and blasts from spells welcome sounds that made hope flicker in Pax.

The Blaze Lizard roared out its frustration and pain through clenched teeth as it fought harder to pull the chunk of iron-banded wall, along with Pax's arm, free. A blast of hot, angry breath burned at his mouth and face cutting any screams short.

With a surge of desperation, Pax fought past the cobwebs of pain fuzzing his thoughts. His spark. It might do nothing, but it was all he had. He drove his thoughts to his center and jerked his spark back into action just as a movement flashed to his right and a familiar yell rang out close to him.

Amil's grubby hand slammed a shiv into the swirling heat of the creature's eye, hitting just off of center and burying all the way to the hilt.

Pax felt a bone-deep tremor shudder through the creature when, a split second later, Rin's primitive spear slammed into the eye right next to Amil's shiv. It sank almost a foot deep with a sickening squelch.

Time seemed to slow as the lizard's body spasmed in response, and Pax realized that the Blaze Lizard would likely take his arm off when it bucked in pain. Frantic to make the jaw open, Pax boosted his spark with all the mental energy he could summon and shoved the energy along the connection through his palm and into the lizard's mouth a split second after his friends' strikes.

The lizard's deep bellow of pain choked and sputtered. Pax's spark slammed into its throat and snuffed it out with the ease of pinching out a flaming wick. Suddenly silent, unbelievably, the lizard's jaw sagged.

All the rage seemed to drain from the beast. Pax felt his spark sucked further inside it, leaving what felt like a thin tether connecting it back to his center. It tugged at his insides, draining his energy like a thirsty man guzzling at a water skin through a narrow opening. A growing weakness spread through Pax.

With movements oddly passive, the lizard's jaw finished opening, its teeth ripping free from Pax's arm and the wall. The bent iron reinforcing the wall screeched. Pax stifled another scream and pushed back weakly. He clutched his bloody arm with its tattered skin to himself as his chest heaved with uneven breaths.

His vision going fuzzy, Pax barely noticed when Rin, still clinging to the stick embedded in the monster's eye, was jerked from her feet when it slumped back from the gaping hole in a slow, confused motion.

Amil shouted and lunged forward, grabbed her waist before throwing his weight back to keep her inside the wagon. The lizard let out a pained keening sound, face not far from the gaping hole as it swung its snout side-to-side.

Pax knew something was terribly wrong. His spark had disappeared inside the Blaze Lizard. Somehow, the beast continued to suck at him, draining him further with every passing second. Desperation flared again. Pax closed his eyes and let himself fall back, muscles limp and his injured arm resting on his chest. He needed to focus all his efforts on his spark.

His attention quickly found the thin tether of energy stretching between him and the Blaze Lizard, easy to distinguish now that he was looking for it. It pulsed sending slow surges of energy from him to the beast.

A burst of adrenaline snapped Pax's thoughts into focus. He had to break the link before he was too weak, or passed out entirely. With a desperate urgency, he strained with all the mental energy he had, pulling and tearing at the surprisingly tough connection. It resisted, like twisted strands of hair, thin but resilient. His head ached with an intense pressure that stabbed behind his eyes as more of his energy trickled away.

He felt a sick sense of tiredness that eroded at his will and knew he was in serious trouble.

THE BIGGER THEY ARE

PAX DUG DEEP for the stubbornness that had always saved him on the streets. You didn't live long there if you gave up easily. Clenching his jaw, Pax envisioned two hands wrapping around the thread connecting to the lizard, dug in his heels and jerked back with an effort that ate through the last vestiges of his mental strength.

Finally, with a suddenness that made him mentally stagger, the thread snapped. It sent a sharp pain rebounding through his mind and into his core. He cried out and went limp with exhaustion. With the mental battle over, the agony in his arm flooded back over him and made him want to retch.

"Grab him."

"Is he alright?"

"What did he do to the Blaze Lizard?"

"Did you see how they stabbed the eye?"

"Everyone, back away from the hole."

The shouted questions and commands flew unheeded around Pax as his dull thoughts marveled at his survival.

"Loose again!"

The barked command came a moment before the twang of multiple bowstrings sounded from above them and the nearby wagons. The screech of bellowed pain was still close, but not right next to the hole in their wagon anymore.

"Together now. Water attacks!"

Eyes still closed, Pax relaxed further as the battle sounds changed. They might finally have the upper hand. The roars were much diminished and had shifted to pained growls, mostly drowned out by sounds of the guards' attacks.

A shudder rippled through the wagon's floor again as something heavy landed against the part of the far wall that was still intact. Too exhausted, Pax didn't stir.

His center felt drained, and a panicked thought made his heart leap with worry. He sent a probe plunging to his center. When he couldn't immediately sense his spark in its usual place, his fear grew. Stifling his reaction, Pax forced himself to stay calm and search more carefully. As soon as he relaxed, he found it, much smaller and deeper, but still with the familiar energy that had always anchored him.

Whatever had connected his spark to the blaze monster, Pax was just relieved it hadn't ruined something permanently. Letting out a relieved breath, Pax noticed the sounds of battle had diminished again. He was just about to open his eyes and try to get help for his throbbing arm when the flickering light in the bottom of his vision caught his attention. Lights, actually. What had started as a single slow flashing box in the corner had now ballooned into overlapping colors that visually clamored for attention.

What—?

He'd barely aimed the mental query toward the flashing lights when they exploded into a flurry of notifications that scrolled through his vision, each one moving as soon as his eyes finished reading it.

MAGE SKILL UNLOCKED: **Light Mana Manipulation** Level 1

This epic skill comes from dedication to understanding and manipulating the essence of light magic itself within a mage's body. As a mage's under-

standing grows, they can also manipulate other types of mana. The possibilities of this skill will become clear with practice and is dependent on the path a mage chooses.

SKILL BOOST: +2 to **Light Mana Manipulation** *Level 1 - 2/100*

MAGE SKILL UNLOCKED: **Light Mana Sight** *Level 1*
With enough focus and concentration, this rare skill allows a mage to see the organization and flow patterns of light magic itself and other forms once the mage understands them.

SKILL BOOST: +2 to **Light Mana Sight** *Level 1 - 2/100*

SKILL BOOST: +2 to **Light Mana Manipulation** *Level 1 - 4/100*

SKILL BOOST: +3 to **Light Mana Sight** *Level 1 - 5/100*

SKILL BOOST: +4 to **Light Mana Manipulation** *Level 1 - 8/100*

CONGRATULATIONS! You have increased **Insight** *from 6 to 7*

CONGRATULATIONS! You have increased **Strength** *from 2 to 3*

CONGRATULATIONS! You have increased **Endurance** *from 3 to 4*

PAX BLINKED HIS EYES OPEN, stunned by the flurry of messages. He had no clue what his two new magical skills were, only that something he'd done with his spark had unlocked them. The growing pain in his arm pulsed and screamed for attention, making it clear how he'd earned a new point in Endurance.

Looking back, he remembered the small pulses of extra Strength and clear thoughts during the battle. Those moments had to be when he'd improved his attributes.

The flutter of excitement helped him ignore the pain as he thought, *Menu.*

❧

NAME: Pax Vipersworn
   Race: *Mixed Human (monster-touched)*
   Age: *16*
   Bound Location: *none*
   Class: *Mage*
   Element: *Light (locked)*
   Specialization: *Locked*
   Level: *1*
   Mage Leveling Points: *0/5*
   Health: *7/31 (+3)*
   Mana: *3/24 (elemental use locked)*
   Attributes:
   Strength: 3 (+1)
   Agility: 7
   Endurance: 4 (+1)
   Intelligence: 7
   Insight: 7 (+1)
   Charisma: 3
   Skills:
   General - Active:
   Identify Level 1 (Common) - 14/100
   Mage:

Light Mana Manipulation Level 1 (Epic) - 8/100
Light Mana Sight Level 1 (Rare) - 5/100
Spells: *none (locked)*
Inventory: *18/20 available.*
Assignments: *none*
Misc.: *none*

~

APPALLED at losing half of his health to a bite from the powerful beast, plus a bunch of his mana to the strange draining experience, Pax resolved to be much better prepared next time. He knew his health would take much longer to recover than his mana, maybe only around five a day if last night's two points were a good measure. Pax clenched his jaw against the pain, resolving to learn more about how this all worked and get stronger, much stronger.

He was just about to expand his skill menu to see if there was more information on the mana thing, when an intrusive clanking sound behind him made him stop and open his eyes. Heads turned as they all heard the lock click open, followed by the door slamming against the inside wall of the wagon.

Still on his back, Pax turned his head and forced his eyes to focus on the three figures that pushed their way inside.

"Well, at least most of ye look alive," proclaimed the deep, raspy voice of the stocky dwarf at the front.

Pax recognized the earth mage from the Awakening as he turned to the two men who came in after him.

"Help the initiates out of here and see that any injured receive healing," he said before moving forward to help hurry the shell-shocked initiates toward the opening.

Pax let his eyes close and sagged back onto the floor of the wagon, doing his best to ignore the pain now that help had arrived.

A few minutes later, a harsh tug on the shoulder of his tunic surprised a yelp of pain out of him. He looked up as one of the earth mage's assistants pulled him up with another painful jolt.

"Be careful with him," he heard Amil cry out. "He's the one that saved us from that beast."

Pax grimaced when he saw the earth mage turn at Amil's words. He looked in Pax's direction, interest in his eyes. Pax knew Amil was just trying to help, but the last thing Pax needed was the attention of a high-level mage. He knew instinctively that if anyone discovered the unusual light aspect of his magic, things wouldn't go well for him. The flare of worry and fear on his mother's face the first time he'd shown her his spark as a child flashed in his mind.

"What have we here?" the mage asked as he looked down at Pax.

"Just my arm, Mage," Pax answered, fighting to keep his voice from trembling as he did his best to deflect questions about his role in the fight. "The beast got me good, and I'd love some help."

"It's Mage Bitterborn," said an assistant from behind Pax.

"Sorry, Mage Bitterborn," Pax corrected himself through gritted teeth.

The dwarf didn't acknowledge the apology, instead crouching down to take Pax's arm at the wrist and elbow with a firm but careful grip. To Pax's surprise, he leaned in close and smelled the still oozing puncture wounds.

After a few tense moments, during which the wagon continued to empty of initiates, the mage sat back on his heels and spoke. "I can heal most of this, but if you want full function of your hand and arm, you'll need a water-based healing spell to counter the flame damage." He looked at Pax and waited, brows raised.

"Yes, yes," Pax hurried to stammer the answer he thought should be obvious. "I'd like the full function of my arm."

Mage Bitterborn gave him an abrupt nod before carefully placing Pax's injured arm on his chest and moving to stand . . . only to freeze mid-motion and focus sharply on Pax's wrist.

A knot formed in Pax's stomach. He moved his left hand to cradle and hide the injured arm. Bitterborn intercepted the motion, taking his hand and peered more closely at the wrist.

"Your bracelet isn't functioning, and your mage tattoo has started," he pronounced with a frown.

His words caused a hush in the wagon as everyone turned to look. Pax had been avoiding looking at his arm, not wanting to see the deep, jagged wounds. But now, he couldn't help staring at his wrist where the lifeless bracelet still sat.

Mage Bitterborn shifted the bracelet aside, and Pax wasn't the only one to suck in a surprised breath. A thin line, the beginnings of a circular, curling pattern, shone steadily with a soft white light as if someone had begun to etch a pattern on his wrist with glowing paint.

Pax did his best to look as confused as everyone else, while his mind scrambled frantically for what to say during the interrogation he knew would follow.

"Bring him," Bitterborn snapped to his two assistants.

Amil moved toward Pax, hand out protectively, when Rin grabbed the back of his tunic and jerked him back. Pax gave her an approving nod just as rough hands grabbed him under the arms and others by the feet before hoisting him into the air.

The stabbing flood of pain from his arm drove out all thoughts and he bit back a scream.

"Don't jostle his injured arms, you flicks," Bitterborn said over his shoulder before marching out of the wagon, clearly expecting the assistants to follow with Pax.

Pax just hoped whatever interrogation was coming would start with a healing.

HIDING IN PLAIN SIGHT

PAX SIGHED in relief and relaxed into the bed in the healing tent as the pain-blocking liquid Bitterborn's assistants had poured onto his arm finally kicked in. The mage had stomped off to talk to someone, giving Pax stern instructions not to move while he found the water mage to heal his arm.

The murmur of an approaching argument caught his attention now that he wasn't so focused on his pain.

"We're losing too much time, Master Kruse, and you know it!" a stern and familiar voice said, slightly muffled by the canvas tent walls.

The words were loud and offered a welcome distraction for Pax. He was pretty sure the irritated voice was the flame mage. But why would he be arguing near the healing tent?

"I apologize, Mage Incedis," a placating voice answered. "But these monster parts are too important to leave behind, and we don't have enough cold storage space to just take the entire corpses."

"And your butchering team can't go faster?"

"They are going fast. Keeping the skin intact makes it much more valuable for crafting armor sections with innate flame resistance. And don't get me started on how long it takes to strip the bones after they've butchered the best cuts of meat. If we were just taking the cores, we'd be done already."

"Valuable? We're delaying the delivery of the next generation of mages for coin?" The chilly tone of the question made Pax glad he wasn't on the receiving end.

"No, it's not just about the money," Master Kruse corrected hastily as the two appeared in the opening to the healing tent. "The war effort desperately needs more supplies for better gear. And those beasts killed two of my crew. We'll need the proceeds to pay the blood debt to their families."

A thoughtful silence followed his words and Pax lay still, careful not to move or attract attention as he listened and watched them out of the corner of his eye. The two figures stood to his left, highlighted from behind by the bright afternoon sunlight shining in through a propped open tent flap. He recognized the flame-red robes of the man on the right, but hadn't seen the elf facing him before.

"Understandable, Master Kruse," Mage Incedis conceded with an abrupt nod. "I'll give you two more hours, and then we're leaving so we can make it to the way station before dark. Dismissed."

Pax saw the stiffening of the elf's shoulders as Incedis turned to step into the tent. The other man had the slender facial features common to the elves, but his broad shoulders suggested a bit of dwarf in his heritage, or simply a very physical day job.

"A small request, Mage Incedis?" the caravan master hastily said, raising a bronzed hand, the skin looking scarred and toughened by weather. His little finger was missing, giving the hand a lopsided appearance.

Incedis let out a short sigh before turning back, one brow raised.

"It would speed things along if you'd let us use the initiates?"

"I thought you said the butchering was a skilled business that required your trained crew?"

"Much of the fine processing is," conceded Kruse with a nod. "But there's a lot of bulk processing that an initiate can help with. They might even unlock a skill or two."

Pax watched with interest as the mage considered the request. It sounded like it would be brutal work, but part of him would love to get a close-up view of the beasts that had almost killed them all. Besides, he was no stranger to butchering, even if it was usually on a much smaller scale. The slums of Thanhil had plenty of vermin they'd all learned to catch and cook for the gamey, but filling, morsels of meat. His mouth watered as he suddenly wondered what a piece of Blaze Lizard might taste like.

"Fine," Mage Incedis said. "I'll give you the shirker group. And then you may request help from the other initiates. I expect you'll need to offer them an incentive, as I won't force them to help." Incedis made a dismissive gesture with one hand. "Now let me check on the injured, so they'll be ready to move by the time you finish up."

Pax didn't have time to close his eyes as the mage spun on his heel and strode in his direction.

"Good. You're awake," the sharp-eyed flame mage said as he stopped by the bed and looked down at Pax. "How is his arm, Isabel?"

Pax startled when he realized a woman now sat on his other side, having moved soundlessly into the area. She held his wrist and elbow in a soft grip that he couldn't feel at all. Not even the dull pain that the earlier numbing liquid had left behind.

"Peace, youngling," she said in a smooth, melodious voice. "You don't want to undo all my work, do you?"

Pax froze, his head cocked up at a painful angle, as he stared at the arm he couldn't feel and the woman holding in a firm grip that hadn't shifted at all when he'd jerked. She was a petite woman with long, flowing hair pulled back with a leather tie. But it was the swirling magic that made Pax's eyes widen in a mix of amazement and shock.

He blinked, but the sight didn't change. A thin sheet of swirling water he couldn't feel encased his entire lower arm and flowed in a mesmerizing pattern back and forth between her two hands.

Pax squinted, trying to peer through the water to see how bad the ragged bite wounds were. And why couldn't he feel his arm? Sure, he was glad the throbbing pain was gone, but the lost sensation was disorienting. He could see her holding his arm, but could only feel as far down as his upper arm. After that, nothing.

Worry flared to life. Was he going to lose his arm? The earth mage had said the water mage could save it, hadn't he?

She must have seen the growing panic in his eyes, because she met his gaze and spoke in a calming voice. "I used a sensation blocking spell at your elbow so the pain wouldn't interfere while I worked. And Bitterborn was right to get me so I could rehydrate the burned tissue and speed up the flow of healing fluids as everything knits back together. Give me a few minutes to work on the deeper layers. Then, it's just the skin layer, and I'll be done. It looks like I'll also need to do a touch of bone repair, so don't do anything strenuous with the arm for the rest of the day, and you'll be good as new."

He gave her a mute nod, unable to articulate the flush of relief that filled him, especially when a glance at his health showed it ticking back up to full. He moved healing to the top of his list of things to learn about.

"Any questions?" she asked before glancing up at Mage Incedis to include him in the query.

"Not about the healing," Incedis said as he pulled up a chair and sat, focusing his intense gaze on Pax.

Pax's worry returned as the mage's expression brought the day's events with its dangerous secrets back. Pax pretended to ignore Incedis, shifting to get a better look at his arm and speaking to the water mage. "Thank you so much for saving my arm," he said to her. "Can I watch the last bit of healing, uh Mage—?"

"It's Mage Janus. And, of course, you may," she answered with a smile. "Though you won't be able to learn much while you still have a suppression bracelet on, not to mention having air magic instead of water, like me."

Pax couldn't help his eyes widening in surprise. *Air magic? What was she talking about?*

When she noticed his surprise, he immediately cursed himself for letting his thoughts be so transparent. He knew better than that, but her friendliness had disarmed him.

"Don't worry," she said with a sympathetic smile before flicking a glance to the deep blue whorls of color that flared around her wrists in beautiful, slender patterns hinting of crashing waves in a storm. "Many initiates think air and water magic aren't as powerful as flame and earth, but that's just ignorance speaking. Air magic has just as many branches as the others, so I'm sure you will find something that works for you." She stopped for a minute and looked down at his wrist.

The water over his wrist stilled, and he could see the short beginning of his tattoo gleaming through the liquid. "And don't let anyone make fun of how pale your tattoo is. It's common knowledge that colors can vary by quite a lot and aren't related to mana strength."

Pax just kept nodding as she spoke, his mind furiously stitching together a believable story based on her mistaken assumption he'd unlocked air magic.

"You're not in trouble," she reassured him with a comforting glance. "Though we do our best to keep new mages from unlocking their element before the academy, you aren't the first one who's managed it."

"Yes," came Incedis' voice, almost making him jump. "Explain to us exactly how you could manifest magic despite the bracelets? And if reports are correct, how were you able to use it against the Blaze Lizard? Did you unlock a spell or a skill? Which one?"

"Aedin, he's barely awake," Mage Janus chided. "Let me finish healing him at least before you quiz him about his magic. It'll just take a minute."

Pax flashed her a grateful look as she focused back on his arm. Incedis sat back with an impatient huff. The water encasing Pax's forearm swirled into activity, and he almost wished he could feel what was happening as he saw it push and dive around the pink and gaping wound edges from the lizard's damage to his arm.

A flashback to his Awakening made him tense. The weak ball of his spark flaring as much as it could in his chest at the idea of a foreign magic invading his body again. A completely unexpected stab of pain jolted from Mage Janus' left hand and up into Pax's upper arm. He couldn't keep from flinching.

Janus froze, her eyes snapping to his. "You felt that?"

Unsure how to answer, Pax just gave her a shoulder shrug and a tentative answer. "I think so?"

When he saw Incedis perk up with interest, Pax kicked himself. He needed to have better answers ready if he wanted to avoid attention.

18

I AM NOT THE MAGE YOU'RE LOOKING FOR

"He had an adverse reaction to the magic of the Awakening, too," mused Incedis. He leaned in closer. "Try again and let me see what I can feel."

To Pax's horror, the flame mage reached across the bed and placed his hands on top of Janus's.

"Sensing only," Janus instructed sternly. "I don't want your flame messing up the healing when I'm almost done."

Incedis nodded, his expression still thoughtful. Pax, however, had already reached out to his spark, surprised to find its energy had slipped down his arm to push at his elbow, as if to break through whatever Janus had done to numb his arm.

To his surprise, now that he was looking, he could see the lines of her magic moving deep inside his arm, even though he had no sensation. They blurred beneath the water, hard to focus on as they shifted in what looked to him like random patterns instead of the orderly motion of the bracelet.

No, he instructed sternly, pulling his spark back before he did something she could detect. *Don't fight the healing*, he tried to direct it. *Let it pass into our arm. It's a good thing. Accept it.* He kept chanting the last line as he saw Janus leaning over his arm again. Pax took a slow breath and concentrated on staying relaxed instead of tensing up.

After a few long, tense moments, the feeling of his lower arm returned briefly, a pushing sensation all along the line of the bite marks on the back of his forearm. Thankfully, he kept from flinching this time. Using only his eyes, instead of watching the swirling magic, Pax watched the wound edges pull close and meld together, much like the way fingers interlaced when two hands came together. A moment later, he saw a ripple of motion move along the last of the wound edges, smoothing them flush with the surrounding skin.

"All done," Janus said softly. In a flash, she sucked the water around his arm back into her hands, leaving smooth skin instead of a gory, mangled arm. His sensation returned in a wave right behind the disappearing water.

He stared at his arm, dry and intact, as if the horrible injury had never happened.

"Go ahead. It's alright to touch it," Janus said.

Pax did, unable to hide his marvel as he wiggled his fingers and prodded at the forearm. Small pink lines were all that marked where the lizard's teeth had torn into him.

"Well done, as usual," Incedis said, sitting back and tipping his head respectfully to Janus. "And I felt nothing unusual this time." His gaze shifted to Pax. "Time for some answers from you, child. Start at the beginning and tell me everything you remember."

Pax licked his lips and organized his thoughts so the tale would come out as seamless as he could manage. He told Incedis about the Flame Lizard encounter, sticking to the truth as much as possible. Whenever his spark was involved, he gave a vague description of what he guessed air magic might feel like, mixing in descriptions of how confused he had been about what was happening. He skipped the disabling of the bracelet entirely, simply saying his magic suddenly worked after the lizard had chomped down on his arm. Hopefully, that bite would provide enough of a reason for the failure.

When he finished, he held his breath, left hand subconsciously massaging his right forearm, reassuring himself that it was intact.

"And the bright flare of magic one of your colleagues described?" Without waiting for an answer, Incedis fired more questions at him. "Why did you race to the wall and place your hand on it in the first place? How could you expect to do anything against a beast like that with the air magic you just described as confusing and hard to understand?"

Pax blurted out the first answer that came to mind. "Because I had to do something, or we'd have all died. I didn't have a choice."

Both mages stilled and looked at him. Incedis' gaze scanned his face with an unnerving intensity. Pax held his tongue and did his best to look sincere, because on some level he meant the words. While he didn't consider himself a selfless hero, like his words might make him out to be, that didn't mean he couldn't take credit for acting like one . . . even if he'd been trapped in the wagon with the others, too.

The others. As he waited for the mages' response, Pax resolved to figure out who had blabbed about the details of the fight to Mage Incedis, specifically about Pax's role. Talebearers were common on the street, and it was vital to figure out who they were as quickly as possible.

"May I see the non-functioning bracelet, Isabel?" Incedis asked, holding out a hand to the other mage.

She turned and scanned a small tray of supplies next to the foot of the bed before grabbing an object. When she passed it to the flame mage, Pax strained to see how intact it looked.

Incedis lifted it up to the light and turned it as he inspected it.

Pax kept his expression calm and sincere, letting none of his relief show as he saw the previously smooth bracelet had jagged edges now. Maybe there was a silver lining to the lizard's attack if it had damaged the device enough to disguise Pax's tinkering.

Incedis said nothing and just slid the bracelet into an ornate bag with one hand as he held out the other to Pax. "Give me your wrist," he said.

Pax hesitated, unable to read the man's intentions.

Incedis gestured impatiently, and Pax swallowed hard and complied. The mage's hand was warmer than usual, the skin much rougher and more calloused than Pax had expected. Before he could object, Incedis had pulled out another bracelet, this one intact, and slipped it onto Pax's wrist. He had just enough time to rein in his spark so it wouldn't object. Incedis' hand flared with a brief light before he placed Pax's arm back onto his stomach, the new bracelet chilly and gleaming in sync with the one on his left wrist.

"The repairs to your wagon should be complete before we get underway again. You can rest up from your ordeal on the mats set up outside," Incedis said as he stood, his gaze turning stern as he looked down. "And don't speak of unlocking your element to anyone, understood? We don't need more problems."

"What about when we get to the Academy?" Pax asked, hoping the man had a plan that would help him stay unnoticed.

Incedis paused and reached down to shift the bracelet minutely so it covered Pax's small tattoo. "Only if asked directly. Keep it out of sight until after the Crucible and maybe we can all avoid further scrutiny."

Without another word, Incedis turned toward the other beds lined up in the healing room.

Pax was still thinking anything called the Crucible couldn't be good, when he realized he was missing an opportunity. He called out, "Mage Incedis?"

He turned and gave Pax a suspicious look over his shoulder.

"Can I help with butchering the beasts? So I can learn a new skill and maybe help us get going faster?" Pax asked, hoping to sound reasonable.

Incedis didn't look pleased, but gave Pax a nod and a shrug before shooting a look toward Janus.

"If Mage Janus clears you, it's fine by me."

Pax turned to look at the smaller woman as he swung his legs over the edge of the bed and did his best to look strong and healthy. She let out a soft laugh and gave him an approving look.

"Oh, to be young and eager again," she said in a quiet voice. "Thank you for your willingness to help. Find Master Kruse and tell him I sent you, but"—she held up a warning finger—"he isn't to have you do anything taxing with that right arm. Got it?"

Pax nodded eagerly, hoping he'd be able to glimpse one of the beast's powerful cores as they harvested it. They would probably keep the initiates from getting too close, but he'd never seen anything bigger than a level 2 core. And besides, the more he learned about butchering a monster like that and what parts were valuable, the better. He had plans, and they didn't involve staying poor and under the foot of well-born mages forever.

After lacing up his sandals, Pax slipped out through the door and stepped into the clearing at the center of the wagon's circle.

A brutal slaughterhouse greeted him, making his step stumble. Massive bodies lay like shoulder-high hills. Knives flashed, and yelling orders flew across the space. The noxious reek of copper blood and burst innards made the hairs in his nose curl and his breath choke in the back of his throat.

"Pax!" a call rang out off to his right, and he saw Amil pop up from behind a massive pile of steaming meat. His white teeth shone brightly from a face splattered with blood. "Over here!"

Taking shallow breaths, Pax ducked his head and moved to join his friend.

19

BLOOD AND GUTS

P<small>AX SWATTED</small> at a buzzing fly with the knife in his hand as he straightened his back and let out a soft groan. On either side of him, Amil and Rin had also slowed in the arduous work, their fascination with the job long since faded to drudgery.

Maybe this hadn't been the best idea, after all. Pax could have easily played on his injury in order to get a pass from the work. Then he thought of his crew back home and Tomis being crushed in a backbreaking crafting position. His parents and his brother, all missing, intruded into his thoughts, too. As a future mage, he might actually have power to do something.

Pax pulled up his notifications and reread the advancements that gave him a grim smile of satisfaction. One thing every street rat learned: grab hold of anything that could possibly be useful in the future. And working on such a high-level beast was advancing his new skills quickly.

～

G<small>ENERAL</small> S<small>KILL</small> U<small>NLOCKED</small>: **Skinning** Level 1
This common passive skill allows one to remove the hide of beasts and

animals while keeping them intact for use in clothing, shelter, weapon and armor crafting. Improved quality skins obtained with practice and skill level.
  *Skill Boost: +3 to **Skinning** Level 1 - 3/100*

General Skill Unlocked: ***Butchering** Level 1*
  This common passive skill allows one to separate the inner parts of an animal for food, alchemy, weapon and armor components. Improved results with practice and skill level.
  *Skill Boost: +4 to **Butchering** Level 1 - 4/100*

As Pax grabbed another fistful of dark red muscle and hacked it free, he whispered out of the side of his mouth to Rin, "What exactly does the butchering skill description mean by alchemy?"

She glanced over at him and then down at the hunk of meat he was chopping free. "I don't know about the meat, but I've heard the blood can make potions." She gestured with her chin toward the glass jug propped up under the hole drilled in the table's corner. A shallow trough carved around the edges of their butchering block funneled the blood into the hole. "Since it's a Blaze Lizard, maybe flame resistance?" she said with a shrug.

Pax nodded thoughtfully, even more determined not to waste any chance for advancement. Leveling his Skinning and Butchering would come in handy if the future of monster killing was anything like the rumors. Pax wouldn't fast forget how lack of coin had dragged down his life. He added selling monster parts to his plans.

A burst of mocking laughter behind him made them all flinch.

"At least they have the rejects doing something useful for once," a grating voice said in a loud tone that made heads around the clearing turn.

Pax knew exactly who was speaking and knew it was useless to object. A head-to-head confrontation in front of an audience would only favor the influential idiot, especially based on some of the hostile looks thrown their way. They were shirking prisoners, after all.

Amil shot a sidelong glance his way, and Pax gave him a subtle shake of his head, hopefully communicating the plan to ignore the flick until he gave up and went away.

"What do you think, Kurt?" the cultured voice continued with an undercurrent of glee. "Maybe we should explain simple concepts like alchemy to the cowards, so they aren't completely hopeless when we get to the academy?"

"That'd be a great idea, Galen," a whiny voice piped up eagerly.

Pax didn't like the light of interest he saw sparking among some spectators at the possibility of a confrontation. Beside him, Amil clenched his jaw but kept quiet as he hacked at another piece of meat.

"How about you join us instead?" Rin's voice snapped out. "You know? Help out? So we can get back on the road faster and get safe behind walls before dark?"

Surprise and a sudden hush followed her outburst. Pax couldn't decide whether to laugh or hiss a warning at Rin to keep quiet when he saw Galen sputter for words, his face turning red. Rin should have known better.

But then Pax saw heads nodding among some of the butchering crew at Rin's words. He suppressed a smile when he saw some of the early hostility had faded. There was nothing like the shared contempt for arrogant privilege to unite strangers.

"I'm injured," Kurt said defensively, motioning to one arm in a sling. "The healer told me I couldn't help, even if I wanted to."

"Shut up, Kurt," Galen snapped. "No one cares."

"Oh, did you get a boo-boo? And now you can't help?" Pax asked over his shoulder before he could stop himself. "Good thing the Blaze Lizard tearing my arm to pieces didn't keep me from helping these fine folk out." He quickly added the last part and gestured to the rest of the butchers hard at work.

It was the perfect thing to say. He got a few snickers as well as the occasional nod of respect.

When Pax snuck a look back at Kurt, he was scowling, unable to summon a response. The ringleader wasn't too pleased, either. Glowering at the shorter boy, Galen still stood well clear of the butchering activities. He wore cream-colored linens and an expensive-looking cloak that fluttered in the fall breeze. He'd even managed to keep his leather boots clean despite the well-trafficked area within the wagon circle. His footwear had a shimmering surface that suggested maybe magic or beast components helped with that. Everything about the arrogant elven boy exuded wealth and privilege.

The other elves who accompanied him seemed content to follow his lead. However, the girl looked somewhat uncomfortable at Galen's words and stayed a step back from her comrades, while the other well-dressed boy looked more than eager to join in Galen's fun. Tall and well-muscled, he looked to be Galen's equal, though he let his friend take the lead.

Kurt, the second boy, was obviously a mixed breed. His hair hung lanky and dark. His clothing was worn, and he favored one arm in a sling. He looked like a square, awkward peg, doing his best to fit in among a group of sleek round ones.

Pax recognized him. He was the boy who'd reminded everyone of the rules back in the wagon, a fellow street rat. No wonder he didn't look like he fit in with the wealthy boys. Pax put Kurt's name on a short list of who might be the talebearer keeping the mages informed.

With a move full of speed and danger, Rin uncoiled from her seat at the butcher's table and turned to face the haughty group. Blood splattered across her apron and dripped from the knife she held loosely in one hand. "Well? Are you going to help or not?"

To Pax's delight, Galen flinched back a step from the small girl's grim appearance, only to flush angrily once he realized what he'd done. He pursed his lips, a vengeful expression Pax recognized flitting across his face.

Amil was on his feet before Pax could stop him. His eyes narrowed, and he held his own knife in a firm grip.

Praying there was a way to defuse the escalating situation, Pax also stood. He didn't speak, taking a position next to Rin and Amil, his own knife held low.

Kurt's eyes flickering from one person to another. He took a few steps back, obviously evaluating threats and mapping out a quick exit route. The elven girl looked just as worried.

Galen, on the other hand, didn't react well to the obvious threat the three of them presented. He sucked in a breath, his chest puffing out as he pointed a finger toward them.

Pax let his knees bend slightly and gripped the rough ground with his toes through the thin soles of his sandals.

"You have no idea—" Galen said, jabbing his finger at them as he took a step forward.

To Pax's surprise, he heard movement behind him. In his peripheral vision, he saw other workers putting down their butchering work and climbing to their feet.

"—who you're messing with," Galen finished, seeming not to even notice the reaction of the others.

His friend beside him, however, did. Eyes widening, he reached out and put a hand on Galen's shoulder. "They're not worth it, Galen," he said, before a cruel light entered his eyes. "Besides, the Crucible weeds out weaklings like them, so we don't have to bother. Let's head back to the wagons and enjoy the break."

Galen resisted at first until he glanced around at the situation that had suddenly escalated into a spectacle. He would know as well as Pax that this kind of confrontation could bring the mages' attention at any moment.

"He's right," Galen finally said, letting a casual smile return to his face, though his eyes stayed hard. "You're not worth my time. I don't expect any of you to last long in the academy, so why bother? Too bad I can't watch the Crucible crush you and—"

"So that's a no to helping us finish so everyone here can reach safety sooner?" Rin interrupted his monologue.

Galen sputtered, his mouth opening and closing in outrage.

"Fine," Rin said. "We'll get back to work without you selfish flicks, then."

A few sputtered laughs broke out behind them, and it took all of

Pax's control to keep a smirk off his face. He didn't need to antagonize Galen any more when he was backing down.

"It's laborer work," Galen finally spat out. "Mages have more important things to do."

That prompted angry mutters around the clearing. Pax couldn't believe how oblivious Galen was to the changing mood around him. The other workers hadn't been favorably inclined toward the shirkers initially. But now, the arrogant group of elves had supplanted them as a much easier group to hate.

"Not true." A firm voice cut through the growing clamor filling the clearing.

Looking startled and then angry, Galen spun to confront the inter-loper . . . only to hesitate when he saw an unhappy Master Kruse stalking toward them.

"Did I hear you disparaging the hard-earned skills of my highly leveled crafters?" the caravan master demanded as he stopped in front of Galen, his height allowing him to look down on the initiate.

Galen clamped his mouth shut and shook his head back and forth in what looked like an ingrained response to an authority figure over him.

"Good," Kruse snapped. "Either join in and help like these fine initiates here are"—he waved a hand in Rin's direction—"or take your petty posturing to your wagon and don't come out again."

Galen aimed a helpless look at the rest of his friends.

"Now!" snapped Kruse in a voice that made even the yugruts quiet for a moment and pay attention.

"Yes, sir," Galen answered in a respectful voice before he turned on his heel and headed back toward their well-appointed wagon, his cronies on his heels.

Kruse turned back toward his workers, only to find everyone hard at work. He raised an eyebrow at the three initiates still standing. Pax gulped and turned back to his spot, but not before he caught an angry glare aimed back at him from Galen.

Great. Now he'd attracted the ire of a well-connected group of elven initiates. Plus, when Amil and then Mage Eldan had mentioned the Crucible, it hadn't sounded ominous.

As if reading his thoughts, Rin spoke softly. "I didn't think the Crucible was something dangerous."

"It can be," said a voice behind them, much quieter now, but still with the undercurrent of someone used to giving orders. "And check in with the quartermaster for a small share of today's harvest. If any of you think you'll have a flame affinity, make sure to eat a small finger-sized portion of the meat before the Crucible. If not, check with our caravan shop to exchange it for a different elemental boost. It's the least we can do in exchange for your help."

And with that cryptic advice, Master Kruse turned and left them to finish their bloody work.

LIFE IN THE BIG CITY

PAX HAD NEVER FELT SO OVERWHELMED in his life and struggled to keep his eyes forward instead of jerking from side to side to gape at the incredible sights of Salman, the Astan Empire's capital city.

He'd always heard travelers speak about his home, Thanhil, as a rural city, but it had been plenty big for Pax. There were even sections he'd never visited.

But this? This was a city on a completely different scale, or more accurately, a bunch of vast cities mashed into one sprawling metropolis that made Pax feel no more significant than an ant in a teeming mass of people. Buildings towered over the bustling street with many more stories than Pax had ever imagined crafters could build without toppling over.

His earlier amazement at seeing his first yugrut paled compared to all the outlandish animals he'd seen during their drive through the capital. Beasts of burden with horns, claws and even multiple humps were attached to a variety of vehicles. Exotic pets, squat, winged and even some that seemed to be made entirely of magic, sat on an owner's shoulder or were caged in a stall for sale. And then there were the beast parts on display, which made Pax realize he'd only seen the tiniest sample of the creatures in his world.

And the people. There'd obviously been plenty of the usual mixed races, but he'd even seen some aristocratic purebreds with entire entourages clearing the way ahead of them. Their obvious wealth had been staggering.

He'd even seen other races, too, ones he'd only heard whispered rumors about. Rin had pointed out a Cordu and Gryon to him, but even she'd had to guess about a group of smaller beings that darted through gaps in traffic so fast, neither of them got a good look.

Pax had been relieved when their caravan had moved through a section filled with clanging metal and the stench of bellows fires. There, at least, the storefronts were full of somewhat familiar armor and weapons, though many were made from unfamiliar material.

He'd kicked himself halfway through the drive when he'd remembered Identify and quickly got to work. Despite the short ten-yard casting distance, the city streets were so busy, he had plenty of opportunities to bottom out his mana. He could almost use it five times before being out.

After doing his best to target high-level creatures and people, Pax had quickly realized that appearances were deceiving and not necessarily indicative of high levels. Instead, he focused on diversity, aiming to Identify the largest variety of targets with the time and mana he had. He also brought up his mana bar and monitored it, remembering to always leave himself a few points so he didn't get a repeat of the mana drained penalty he'd experienced last time.

He clued in his two friends, too. But when angry glares and shouts rose around the wagons following their clumsy Identify attempts on higher-level passersby, they had to duck down and stop for a bit.

Once the complaints were swallowed up in the surrounding cacophony, with no reprisal from their driver, they exchanged grins and continued. They took turns that time and staggered their attempts better.

Thankfully, Master Kruse and his caravan drivers were old hands at navigating the busy streets and didn't stop for anything. After their uneventful night at a walled caravan stop and hours of navigating Salman's busy streets through the early afternoon, Pax was sure the wagons would take the shortest, fastest route to the academy and only stop for an emergency.

With his mana bar almost empty, Pax sagged back in relief when he saw the imposing gates of Shieldwall Mage Academy appear ahead of them. He checked his most recent notification and grinned, almost giddy with the progress he'd made on his first skill.

∿

IDENTIFY ATTEMPT FAILED. *Level differential too significant.*
Skill Boost: +3 to **Identify** *Level 1 - 38/100*

∿

HE ASSUMED GETTING to a hundred points would level the skill, which had to be a good thing. He didn't want to ask and look even more ignorant than he already did. Hopefully, there would be some kind of tutorial in the beginning classes to fill in his knowledge gaps.

"Wow," Rin said softly, staring up at the open wrought-iron gates. They stood almost two stories tall, attached by hinges the size of a man's head to thick red brick walls that gleamed in the afternoon sun.

Pax had to agree as their wagon rolled into a vast circular driveway teeming with people, vehicles and the bellow of unhappy beasts of burden.

A harried-looking man waved their caravan wagons into slots just wide enough for the side doors to open without hitting their neighbors. At least the wagons full of crafting, merchant and warrior initiates had already peeled off toward their own Academy grounds, which made their group much smaller and more manageable.

As soon as they shuddered to a stop, orders and directions filled the air, urging everyone to get out quickly so the next group could pull in.

Rin put a hand on his shoulder and leaned in to whisper softly, "This is the end of the road."

Pax exchanged a concerned look with Amil, but his larger friend just gave him a shrug and straightened his tunic before turning to watch the door. Through the bars of the open window, Pax could see other wagons emptying, excited voices filling the air as the mage initiates disembarked. No one around Pax looked surprised when their door remained firmly locked for a handful of long minutes.

The hubbub in front of them had subsided as the wagons emptied and new initiates were led away. Whips cracked and empty wagons departed out of the gates, replaced by new ones. Pax pressed his face to the window, knowing it had to be their turn soon.

"I don't see anyone else chained up," Amil said, from his position right beside Pax. "That's a good thing, right?"

"Maybe they're done with the manacles," Pax said dubiously, knowing life wasn't likely to suddenly be kind to them.

"Line up!" came a yell. The wagon door jerked open and a frazzled Master Kruse poked his head in. "Exit two at a time and don't cause any trouble for my helpers here as they fasten you to the chain. Got it?"

Amil gave Pax a sour look as Kruse ducked back out without waiting for a response. The buzz of voices in the wagon had an unhappy undertone, but people moved into a ragged semblance of a line.

"I guess we've all learned there isn't much point in resisting," Rin muttered under her breath as she moved to join the line.

Pax and Amil hurried to follow her. A few moments later, they stood in the cobblestone courtyard, each with a wrist fastened again to the chain held by one of Master Kruse's assistants.

Pax relaxed a tad when he saw Mage Incedis next to the assistant. He didn't trust the flame mage, but at least the man seemed to be fair.

"Do you have to chain us like this?" Pax heard a voice up front asking in a plaintive tone. "It's not like we have anywhere to escape, now that we're in the capital."

The other initiates quieted, and Pax knew he wasn't the only one waiting to hear the answer. Mage Incedis turned at the question, looking over the line of initiates with a thoughtful expression.

For a moment, Pax thought he might actually remove their bindings, but then he gave a reluctant shake of his head. "If it were up to me—" He turned his hands over and shrugged. "But don't worry. In a few minutes, we'll be at the Shieldwall altar. Once you've bound yourselves, there'll be no need for those anymore." He made a dismissive gesture toward their manacles before turning and heading across the still busy courtyard. The assistant hurried to jerk on the chain and pull them in his wake.

Heads turned, and Pax heard smothered laughter mixed with nasty comments aimed in their direction. So much for keeping a low profile.

"Binding to an altar?" Amil hissed the question from the side of his mouth. The disdainful looks didn't seem to faze him.

Pax kept his head down and tried to reassure his friend. "If they're making all the initiates do it, it can't be too dangerous," he said, despite his own misgivings. His stomach churned with worry as he wondered how much personal information the altar would have access to. Would it uncover his light magic affinity? Or would the Awakening grace period hide that detail?

Distracted, his foot caught as their group stepped up onto a stone walkway from the courtyard. He almost fell, giving the chain a tug that jerked the other initiates near him.

"Watch it," snapped the elven boy in front of him over his shoulder.

Pax was about to apologize when he recognized Kurt and gave the ingratiating weasel a glare instead. The smaller boy didn't back down, narrowing his eyes to give Pax a dirty look in return.

"Where does he get off, being so uppity?" Amil whispered, scowling at the back of Kurt's head. "He's a street rat, just like the rest of us, even if he's figured out how to suck up to the noble kids."

Pax nodded thoughtfully as they traversed sidewalks through vast lawns of green and carefully tended gardens full of flowers he didn't recognize. Large buildings dotted the space, towering over the busy foot traffic, with stone columns and glass windows glinting in the early afternoon sun. Before spending the last three hours goggling at even more impressive sights in the capital city, all the open space and greenery would've astonished Pax.

"Actually, getting on the good side of that flick, Galen, shows some skills," Pax whispered back. "Kurt might be useful. Plus, we need to do better at keeping a low profile and stop making enemies, alright?"

Amil nodded back, not looking convinced, but keeping his mouth shut as Mage Incedis led them up the steps of the most imposing building they'd seen yet. Someone had pulled open the massive double doors, plated with intricately carved bronze plates. They looked wide enough for four yugruts to pass through without brushing shoulders. Two guards stood blocking the doorway, dressed in fancy armor with spears held upright in one hand and swords belted on their sides.

Their impassive faces barely flickered as Mage Incedis spoke to the one on the right. With a curt nod, the two guards stepped aside, one of them motioning with the tip of his spear for them to enter.

Before going in, the mage turned to face the initiates arrayed behind him. "This is the Shieldwall Academy administration building. The headmaster and Academy Council run the entire academy from here. You're likely to encounter many of the senior staff. You'll be on your best behavior and not speak unless spoken to. Understand?"

Heads bobbed nervously as their group looked up at the imposing edifice before following Incedis when he stepped into the cool shadow of the entryway. Lofted ceilings and arches filled the echoing hall, making mundane hallways look like entrances to a noble's mansion.

Pax knew instantly he didn't belong there.

THE START OF A DIFFERENT LIFE

PAX DID his best not to gape at the unfamiliar sights and instead focused on ridding himself of his manacles soon. He needed to focus on his freedom instead of the imposing halls and network of confusing passages Incedis led them through. Soon, he'd be free to learn magic, to gain power and coin. He just needed to survive long enough and figure out this new world he found himself in.

They attracted a few scowls as they walked for what seemed like forever, but it was probably only a quarter hour. When Incedis finally stopped in front of another set of guarded double doors, Pax wasn't the only one to sigh in relief.

A man and a woman seated at a desk along the wall stood and approached the fire mage. They wore white robes and moved with the calm disinterest of people doing a routine job, some kind of clerks.

"Name, position and collection assignment," the woman asked Incedis when she came to a stop, barely looking up from the clipboard in her hands.

"Mage Incedis, collector and flame trainer, Northwest Second Quadrant," Incedis rattled off without hesitation.

The other clerk walked up to the assistant holding the chain.

"Release the first three," he said. "And then send in a new one each time one comes out."

The caravan assistant hurried to obey. Much faster than Pax expected, the clerk had led the first three initiates through the right-hand door and pulled it shut behind them. The clang echoed throughout the hallway as every initiate stayed silent, eyes wide.

The woman in white motioned for them to sit on a row of benches against the opposite wall, which they did, many looking visibly nervous.

They couldn't hear a sound through the doors, only distant foot-steps echoing from the hallway they'd entered. Pax felt his nerves twist again a few minutes later when the door opened just enough to let out the first initiate. A relieved sigh fluttered through their group when the boy flashed them a grin and looked completely fine.

The male clerk asked the boy a few questions and took notes before placing his hand on the boy's forehead and closing his eyes for a moment. Then he stepped back and after an abrupt nod motioned for the initiate to move over to Mage Incedis.

He had him sit on the empty bench on the other side of the hall-way, where no one could pester him with questions. This was obvi-ously not the mage's first time at this duty.

Having spent his entire life dodging authorities and any type of control, Pax desperately wanted to avoid whatever was involved in the upcoming binding. He couldn't understand how he'd arrived in this situation, manacled to a chain, with magic canceling bracelets on both wrists and about to be bound to an altar he didn't understand at all.

He had so many questions and no way to find answers. Somehow, he knew being bound would likely be even worse than the chain or manacles. It was kind of understood in the word *bound*. The Academy would control him in just a few minutes, and there was nothing he could do about it.

Frustration mixed with a sick sensation in the back of his throat as the assistant moved to him. It was his turn. The assistant didn't take long to remove both the manacle and the suppression bracelets. He frowned when he saw the monster-touched scales and looked away quickly with disgust. Pax was glad of the chance to tug his sleeves down to cover the tendril of his small mage tattoo.

"You got this," Amil whispered from the bench beside him.

Pax stifled a wild urge to make a break for it before flashing Amil a grateful smile. Conscious of the eyes on him, Pax stood and forced his spine to straighten as he followed the man to the doors. The world had thrown blows at him all his life, so why did he expect this to be any different? He'd handled them all before, so he could handle this too. He was a Viper.

As he stepped through the door, Pax stopped and stared, barely noticing the assistant staying in the hall and closing the door behind him.

The altar room was dim, lit only by flame core lanterns set in recessed alcoves spaced around the circular, windowless room. The walls were made of a dark, shiny stone that reflected the light in haphazard streaks. Thousands of tiny colored tiles inset into the floor created a beautiful mural circling toward the center of the room.

The female clerk silently motioned him to sit in one of the two wooden high-backed chairs against the wall. Pax didn't meet the eyes of the nervous-looking girl waiting her turn.

Pax couldn't help casting a quick glance at the dim figure of another initiate standing stock still, eyes closed, and both hands pressed to the large altar at the center of the room. Pax took his seat and looked down, deciding to use the mural to distract himself.

Art wasn't something Pax saw frequently, and in a few moments, he found the elegant scene built into the floor distracting him. Magic in a kaleidoscope of colors flew from the hands of mages who fought fantastical beasts with bared teeth, claws and wings in a chaotic battle. His eye moved from a spear of flame to a tornado spell and on to an immense beast rampaging through the sky toward a beleaguered wall manned by defenders.

All too soon, the clerk tapped on Pax's shoulder and pointed toward the altar. "Your turn," she whispered with an underlying impatience, already moving toward the door to signal for another initiate.

Pax forced his eyes toward the edifice at the center of the room he'd been avoiding. It was a low, wide rectangle of shiny black rock, similar to what made up the walls. Much smaller than the one in Thanhil's main square, a body would still fit when laid atop this one, but just barely. Next to the center stood a smaller column of rock, waist high and about the size of a man's leg.

"Place your hand on the pedestal," the clerk instructed impatiently when he stopped a few feet from the altar and stared.

Before his nerves could take over, Pax took three quick strides, slapped his hand on top of it and held his breath.

The pedestal felt surprisingly warm and almost alive, more like a tough hide than a rock. Without warning, a prompt filled his vision.

∼

YOU HAVE CONNECTED to the Shieldwall Mage Academy Altar.

Binding to this altar will allow Academy officials to monitor your menu as you progress and also locate you at all times to keep you safe from harm.

Should you die, your life energy will return to this altar to strengthen the academy's inner keep and protect your fellow students, instructors and administrators.

Would you like to bind yourself and your life energy to this Altar for the next one-year time period?

Yes/No

∼

PAX TOOK HIS TIME, parsing each word and liking them less and less. He'd been looking forward to freedom, a chance for a better future, anything better than the words that suggested the Academy would be his new master and he, their slave.

∼

INTERLUDE:

The new nest was perfect. Master would be pleased. Fortysecond Spawn gently nudged the eggs closer to each other, careful to keep his claws retracted so as not to damage the next generation, their colony's new hope. He'd dug the nest deep underground where the temperature didn't fluctuate and no light or flickers of magic could warp the gestation of the new generation. Here, he could slowly release the harvested soul energy at the exact and steady rate that would produce the intelligent spawn needed to further his mission.

Fortysecond Spawn carefully positioned the drained livestock bodies where the newly emerged spawn would find their first meal to aid them after the struggle of emerging. Circumstances had forced him to leave the first body he'd harvested behind when a group of young livestock had almost stumbled upon him deep in the passages beneath their home.

The abandoned body would have been an irreplaceable loss of food for hatchlings back home and likely forced the culling of a few eggs so that others could survive on the reduced food. But here, Fortysecond Spawn had been able to just select another one of the plentiful livestock, being careful to choose one isolated from the rest of its hive.

Pushing back from the clutch, he took a moment to survey the nest and preparations. Everything was perfect. Eagerness born from perfect obedience filled him as he scrambled back up the tunnel to seal it and remove all traces of his presence.

Once back in the nest, the tunnel above now closed to intrusion, Fortysecond Spawn moved to his position at the center of the clutch. His black lips pulled back from sharpened teeth that were impossible to see in the darkness.

It was time to cultivate.

Fortysecond Spawn focused inside for the tiny nodule of soul energy that would hopefully be enough for the small clutch of eggs waiting eagerly for him to cultivate them. If only he had enough for more eggs. The brief possibility of disobeying his orders made a quick pain stab behind his eyes.

Not feasting in this land of plenty after generations of famine had been the most difficult of Master's orders to follow. Even in the deserted slums of this tiny hive, the glowing energy of available souls fairly overwhelmed him. They were everywhere, ripe for the plucking and protected only by a wall easily tunneled under.

But no. Fortysecond Spawn had to stay hidden. His orders were to only harvest souls that other livestock wouldn't miss. Ones isolated far from their hive. Alone. And never two in the same section of the hive. And he had to stop once he'd drained five of them. Well, technically, he'd drained six, but the Master's instructions were to start the nest with five drained bodies.

Only five miserable souls when there were hundreds practically offering themselves to him. But it was a start.

Fortysecond Spawn would do nothing to jeopardize the plan to harvest and eventually control this new paradise. Slow and steady would save the colony and see Master finally triumph over their enemy back home.

THE BINDING ALTAR

DEEP in the bowels of the academy administration building, Pax scanned the words hovering in front of him:

∾

WOULD you like to bind yourself and your life energy to this Altar for the next one-year time period?
   Yes/No

∾

NO.

Pax just answered the altar's question instinctively. No, he didn't want to bind to it for an entire year. He wanted to go home. He wanted his life back. Yes, it had sucked, but at least he'd been free.

Ignoring all his internal turmoil, the altar's question disappeared as soon as he'd answered, replaced by a new one.

∾

Confirm you would like to disengage from the Shieldwall Academy altar:
   Yes/No

~

THE NEW QUESTION made his throat tighten, and he froze, appalled at his stupidity. Not binding with the altar was about as idiotic as making a run for it in the hallway earlier. The officials would know immediately that he'd failed to follow instructions, and he was sure they had plenty of ways to deal with disobedient initiates, especially street rat conscripts.

No. No. He mentally stabbed at the choice over and over, trying to fix his mistake. He didn't want to come back another time. He needed to bind to the dumb thing now. Holding his breath, he waited for the first message to reappear.

Nothing.

Heart sinking, Pax kept his hand unmoving on the altar as he tried to decide what to do. Should he have said yes to the disengage question to get it to reset? Maybe if he lifted his hand quickly and placed it down again it would start over, and he could answer correctly this time?

He slit his eyes open the tiniest bit and peered through the gloom to see if the clerk was watching him.

His heart sank.

Not only had she already got a new initiate settled in the empty chair, but she was eyeing him with an obviously impatient look on her face.

Pax swallowed quietly, shut his eyes tightly and braced himself to try a quick move, anyway.

Before he could, he felt a tickle of something in his hand that spread to his wrist before stopping.

What?

He glanced down and when he didn't see anything, he knew it had to be some kind of magic. Pushing down the panic at what the altar was doing to him, he flicked his spark toward his wrist as quickly as possible and tried to reach the state of relaxation that had helped him see the magic in the suppression bracelets before. A quick glance through his menu reminding him that the mage skill was called light mana sight.

Nothing happened for a moment. Pax forced his breathing to slow and did his best to get rid of outside thoughts and only focus on his wrist, hand and the connection to the altar.

To his surprise, it actually worked. Much faster and easier than before. A flicker of white energy swirled all around the altar in thick bands that wrapped around and through his hand and wrist.

Before he could examine it further, a new script appeared in front of him, breaking his concentration and disrupting his vision of the altar's magic.

~

WOULD *you like to access Shieldwall Mage Academy Altar's light mage custom menu?*
Yes/No

~

PAX SUCKED in a breath and would have blinked in surprise if his eyes hadn't already been closed. He hesitated for the briefest of moments, but he wasn't an idiot.

Somehow, his early refusal had lucked him into another option. Based on the light mage part of the question, it was something unusual. Every street rat knew to grab something valuable before it disappeared.

Yes, he mentally answered, holding his breath as the message vanished.

~

WELCOME TO SHIELDWALL ACADEMY, *Light Mage. We are honored that you have chosen us for your education. As a new student, please choose from the following binding options:*
    1. Full binding for one year.
    2. Provisional binding for one year.
    3. Full binding renewing monthly for one year.
    4. Provisional binding renewing monthly for one year.

~

PROVISIONAL? Pax didn't know what that entailed, but it sure sounded better than the full binding option. Sending a quick entreaty to Vitur for luck, Pax chose number four.

~

THANK YOU, *Light Mage. You have selected a provisional binding with a monthly renewal. Changes can be made up to the day of each new month, otherwise your current selection will renew automatically.*
    We are committed to creating the best learning environment for you and will do our best to ensure that administrators and instructors interact with you in the way that you'd like. Choose from the following provisional options to customize your education with us:

KNOWLEDGE: *Who can access the details of your custom binding?*
    1. The Academy Director.(Recommended)
    2. The Academy Council.(Recommended)
    3. My instructors.
    4. All instructors.
    5. No one but myself. My binding will appear identical to other students until I apply for graduation.

. . .

MENU DETAILS: As a perk of attending the premier Shieldwall Mage Academy, our altar can offer light mages who are active students up to a four-year extension of the one-month Identify privacy settings afforded the newly awakened. Note: Identify skill rules based on user's and target's levels still apply. Choose from the following:

1. Reveal only name, class and level to the Identify spell regardless of the user's level. (Note: This may rouse suspicion from high level Identify users after your first month)

2. Add a show/hide toggle to each menu item that activates when an Identify spell is used on you. (Recommended)

3. Add a show/hide toggle as well as an option to show an artificially lower value (not higher) for the items that you choose to show.

Note: Deception isn't encouraged, but we want our light mages to feel safe. We know the difficulty of advancing your element may result in a slower start at the academy. We offer these options to help you fit in better.

∾

A LIGHT MAGE?

From the long wall of scrolling text, Pax couldn't get past the phrase that kept cropping up. If a light mage was really a thing, then why hadn't he ever heard of it?

And the barrage of information was more than he'd ever seen from a menu. Ever. Instead of the abrupt, bare minimum of information, the words were flowery and flattering, the way a servant spoke to convince a noble to make a specific choice, not the way the guards spoke to the street rats they'd dragged to the academy in manacles.

"Just select yes and step away from the altar!" An irritated voice disrupted his thoughts and reminded him he had an impatient audience.

The clerks and Mage Incedis would want to know what was taking him so long, and he didn't know what to tell them.

Heart racing, Pax focused on the words again, knowing he couldn't mess this up. Whatever weird circumstances had given him this menu, he had to take full advantage of it, and quickly. The hints that there was something special about being a light mage made Pax even more convinced that it was a dangerous secret. The menu also implied there were other academies he could have attended, but Shieldwall was the only one in the empire. How old was this menu?

He pushed all the questions aside and made his choices. *Knowledge. Who can access the details of my custom binding? Number 5. No one but myself.* Having his binding look like everyone else's was an easy decision. He moved to the next section.

"Step away, or I'll get Mage Incedis to break your connection," the clerk said, no longer trying to keep her voice down. "We have plenty of effective ways of handling troublemaking shirkers like yourself."

Pax felt his mouth go dry, and he forced his rudimentary reading skills to fumble more quickly through the words. He heard the creak of the heavy door to the altar room being opened.

The mention of deception, rather than warning him away, made the choice for him. The last option was the ability he'd been praying for. With it, he could hopefully hide his secrets and blend in with the rest of the initiates while he figured out exactly what a light mage was. And if it had taken light mages a long time to grow in power in the past, then he'd really need the extra protection.

Menu Details. Number 3. Add a show/hide toggle as well as an option to show an artificially lower value (not higher) for the items that you choose to show.

Finished with his selections, he held his breath to see what happened next.

THE ALTAR HAS REGISTERED *your selections. The chosen options will now appear on your menu. In addition, Shieldwall Academy provides beginning light mages with extra instruction. Visit one of the light workshops in the*

lower, protected levels of the academy to choose a mentor and receive special-
ized instruction.

Please let your instructors or the director know if there is anything else
we can do to improve your educational experience here. And thank you, once
again, for choosing Shieldwall Mage Academy!

CONFIRM *you would like to disengage from the Shieldwall Academy altar:*
Yes/No

∾

"PAX VIPERSWORN," Mage Incedis' voice echoed in the altar chamber.
"Stop this foolishness. Finish your binding and disengage from the
altar."

Pax almost obeyed, glad he'd been able to finish his custom selections. But an idea made him freeze and hold as still as possible.

He couldn't disengage voluntarily. He'd taken so much time, there
would be consequences. Instead, he needed to convince everyone that
something had gone wrong with the altar, so they wouldn't hold him
responsible. Street rats were skilled at deflecting blame.

"Go pull him off, already," he heard Incedis snap.

"You do it," the woman shot back. "You're the mage, and your
constitution has to be higher than mine. Besides, the last shock from
the altar laid me out for half a day. If I pull him free, who's going to
handle the rest of today's bindings?"

"Fine," Incedis said in a curt tone.

Pax kept still, even though the idea of being shocked hard enough
to lose half a day sure didn't sound fun. But he'd made his choice. Pain
was an old friend he expected to see often in the foreseeable future.

The sound of heavy footsteps approached, and Pax heard a heavy
sigh just behind his right shoulder.

"You can't help causing trouble, can you?" Incedis said in a low
voice that Pax could just make out. "Brace yourself. This is going to
hurt."

A heavy hand grabbed his right shoulder and jerked him backward in a swift move that made his head snap forward.

Pax barely noticed it as pain shot up from the altar, stabbing through his hand just as Incedis pulled it free. The shock traveled up his arm, out his shoulder and into Incedis' hand with a scorching heat. Pax's heart skipped a beat and his breath coughed out in a harsh gasp.

Incedis let out an angry curse, jerking his arm back and grabbing it with the other hand when it twitched uncontrollably.

Every muscle in Pax's body stiffened and jerked in a series of harsh spasms before going completely limp. He barely kept conscious, as he crumpled to the floor, catching himself just before smacking into the tiles. Pax blinked his eyes, focusing on the vibrant colors beneath him as he fought to stop his head from spinning.

The reason for the disengaging message was crystal clear now. The altar's magic had established a connection that an initiate needed to disengage correctly before letting go. Pax was just glad he hadn't just pulled his hand free earlier when he'd been trying to reset the first binding question.

A firm hand grabbed his shoulder again and pulled him to his feet. Pax tried his best to stand, but swayed like he'd been drinking.

"I've got him," Incedis said, his tone grim.

"What happened?" Pax got out past a dry mouth and sore tongue he must have bitten at some point. He didn't need to pretend to be stunned and weak to sell the act. "I was frozen. Couldn't move."

The mage stopped and looked down at him. "Frozen? Explain."

Pax gave a weak cough to clear his throat and give him time to organize his words. "After I clicked yes to the binding, the words disappeared, and I couldn't move. There wasn't anything else to choose and when I tried to move, I couldn't."

"Impossible," said the clerk as she motioned toward the next initiate to step up to the altar.

The girl just shook her head, eyeing the altar with fear in her eyes.

"Oh, for Vitur's sake. There's nothing wrong with the altar. Watch me." The clerk stomped over to the altar.

Pax saw the briefest of stutters in her motion as she placed her hand on the podium and closed her eyes. Her shoulders immediately relaxed and, just a moment later, she opened her eyes and removed her hand.

"Like I said," she said, shooting a smug look at Pax. "It just confirmed my binding. Working perfectly."

"I only know what happened to me," Pax said, beginning to panic about how bad his story was.

Incedis cut him off with a quick shake of his head, disappointment easy to read in his expression as he grabbed Pax's sleeve and pulled him toward the door again.

"Wait," the clerk said, voice suddenly sharp. "What's that on his wrist? A mage tattoo? Initiates aren't supposed to go through the Crucible before they've been bound."

"He hasn't." Incedis' voice was calm while Pax's pulse sped up.

"Then why does he have his tattoo?"

Mage Incedis turned and focused all his attention on the clerk before speaking. "Why would a binding clerk ask a mage to do her duty and intervene when an initiate had trouble with the altar?"

"Uh—" the woman stuttered, her suspicious look instantly replaced with a worried one.

"This is a mage matter," Incedis said in a decisive voice. "How about we leave it at that? Just like you're in charge of the altar matters, agreed?"

She barely took time to think about it before giving him a jerky nod.

Pax shifted his sleeves back into place and focused on trying to walk without stumbling as Incedis pulled him toward the door.

Once they exited the altar chamber, the male clerk stepped up and took down his basic information before reaching his hand out to Pax's forehead. Pax didn't dare flinch back, but his whole body tensed, ready to fight and flee if things went sideways.

"He's bound," the clerk said with a nod to Incedis before he turned to move back to his desk.

Pax evidently wasn't able to keep all of his surprise hidden, because he saw Incedis' eyes narrow and examine him more closely. Pax tried to ignore him and ducked his head before moving to take a seat with the others who had finished.

"Clerk," Incedis said abruptly, calling out to the man now seated back at his desk.

The clerk looked up, brows raised in question.

"Can you move this group up to the next available Crucible slot?"

The clerk looked down at his papers, shuffling through them until he found the one he was looking for. "They're due for a meal, followed by one of the newcomer orientation sessions. Do you really want to change?" There was obvious reluctance in the clerk's tone.

"Yes." Incedis' gaze shifted to look directly at Pax as he spoke.

Pax knew he should look away, but he couldn't decide if the mage was helping or hurting him by insisting they go immediately to the Crucible. It would definitely help keep his tattoo from being discovered, but now he and his friends would have no chance to gather info and prepare.

A stubborn anger rose in him, insisting that it didn't matter. He'd stand up to whatever they threw at him. He was a mage now, not a street rat, and he was done backing down. Mouth set in a grim line, he held Mage Incedis' gaze as he continued speaking.

"I think it would be in everyone's best interest to evaluate the potential of these initiates before we give them any more freedom or access to our fine academy."

Around them, the others, who'd been silently watching the spectacle, stirred, trading worried looks with each other. The clerk didn't quite stifle an irritated harrumph before he gathered a few papers, stood and hurried off down the hall.

"Did you have anything else to say?" Mage Incedis finally asked Pax.

Pax gave a slight shake of his head, stayed quiet, but didn't look away. There might have been a flicker of surprise or respect in the mage's gaze at that, but Pax couldn't be sure.

"Well," Incedis finally said. "If you survive the Crucible, then you'll be the academy's responsibility, not mine."

Pax clenched his jaw against the fresh surge of anxiety but held the taller man's gaze.

The mage was the first one to look away this time.

HOW MAGES ARE MADE

WITHOUT THEIR MANACLES, Pax had shifted positions, so he walked next to Amil as Mage Incedis led them across the amazing campus. Rin was just behind them, next to another girl as everyone walked two abreast toward the mysterious Crucible.

Pax couldn't decide if he should cram the chunk of roasted Blaze Lizard meat into his mouth or not as they approached an imposing circular building made from ivy-encrusted brick. Master Kruse had said it might help with the Crucible, but only for flame mages. He'd had no chance to exchange it as recommended, not like they would have any beast meat for light magic, anyway. He decided to hold back on eating the meat until he knew more.

With no visible roof, the Crucible looked like it might be an arena. Pax examined the stone structure that towered to the height of three men. Thick vines added green accents, the only bit of color on the aged structure. There were no windows affording a glimpse inside, only a single gate with attentive guards watching their approach.

Maybe the Crucible was some kind of tournament with only the winners earning a spot in the academy. But based on what they'd heard, it also unlocked a student's element. Other mages had been very close-lipped about answering the initiates' questions.

Mage Incedis approached the guards and handed them some papers. The woman took her time inspecting them before handing one of them to her partner. They both walked down the line and carefully matched names to the list.

A muffled roar drifted out from the top of the structure, followed by what sounded suspiciously like a scream. Pax wasn't the only one to stiffen and eye the wall with misgivings.

By that time, the guards had finished, returning to the front of the line and opening the gate.

"The last group should be about done," the man said, motioning for them to move in. "Take a seat and wait your turn."

Pax couldn't help feeling like this was a repeat of his altar experience. But he had to remind himself that for everyone else, it had been an answer to a simple question. He was the only one who'd been flopping around getting shocked.

As they entered at the top of the stone arena seating, Pax saw it was open to the sky as suspected. Arranged in a large semicircle, the rows of seating descended at an angle to a stone floor taken up almost entirely by a massive columnar structure built from old white brick with streaks of moss and smatterings of more hardy ivy in the crevasses.

At the bottom edge of the column's wall stood a door, manned by a dwarf with a long white beard and wrinkles that pulled his face into something halfway between a grimace and a smile. He called out something that Pax couldn't hear from where they were. The lone figure seated on the front bench stood and strode directly to the door with only the slightest hesitation.

Pax tried to glimpse what was inside the structure, but could only make out a dark shadow before the dwarf pulled the door shut again and looked up to their group.

"Come on down," he called up to them, his cheer making him sound a lot younger than he looked. "I am Master Grimfall and responsible for officiating over your Crucible testing. Closer, closer. I don't bite."

Kurt was the first to respond, calling out, "Yes, sir," as he moved down the steps to the bottom of the arena.

Amil turned to Pax and Rin, rolling his eyes. "That idiot is finally doing something useful and testing the waters for the rest of us," he said out of the side of his mouth as they joined the other initiates moving down the steps.

Their entire group looked tired and ragged as they finished taking their seats. Pax was looking forward to a meal, any meal, and a place to sleep. Plus, he'd like a little time to examine his menu after the whole encounter with the altar.

A muffled roar boomed from the white brick structure, making everyone freeze. Crashing water and heavy thumps joined the noise, none of it distinct or easy to make out. Pax exchanged looks with his friends, noticing how nervous the other initiates looked. Kurt looked suddenly unhappy about volunteering to be first. Pax saw a sheen of sweat flush on his brow.

Then they heard the screams. Not loud enough to be heard clearly, but definitely the sounds of someone in anguish.

"No worries, my new initiates," Master Grimfall said cheerfully. "Magic will give you great power to protect our people. The Crucible must forge each of you if you are to attain the power you desire."

Pax wasn't the only one scanning the arena for exits. But where would they go? The altar could track them down anywhere in the city, and there was no way they'd survive on their own in the Wilds. At least not yet.

The noises inside the structure finally subsided. In the quiet, Pax heard the nervous fidgeting of the others in their group. Street rats, all of them, and none of them pleased at being forced into an unknown danger.

Pax could only think of two things that might help him, with escaping off the table. The Blaze Lizard meat and his spark.

"Remind Rin about the meat," he whispered to Amil.

"Didn't the caravan master, Kruse, say that would only help if we're flame mages, though?" Amil asked back. "Are you going to eat any?"

Pax considered his options before answering, not willing to tell Amil that he already knew he was a light mage, not flame. "Let's see what the people coming out look like. Maybe just eating a bite will help without hurting. We just don't know."

Amil gave him a worried nod before leaning over to pass the info on to Rin.

The sound of a door opening came from the far right of the structure and was out of sight. Master Grimfall gave them all a big smile, spread his hands wide and said, "See? A new water power mage is born to join the ranks protecting our great empire."

Everyone craned to see the initiate emerging from the Crucible. Pax's eyes widened as he saw the boy, barely able to walk. Two assistants helped him across the arena floor to an exit. As the woman there waved them through, Pax saw that the boy was wearing a gold, almost yellow uniform with blue and black trim.

Whispers filled the space around him as Grimfall turned to Kurt and beckoned him forward. "Come now, young mage. It's time to discover your element and your strength."

Pax had to give Kurt credit, as the boy only hesitated for a moment before standing and making his way down to the dwarf who held the door open. Once he stood in the opening, Kurt stopped long enough to suck in a big breath before stepping inside.

Master Grimfall closed the door behind him with another of his cheerful smiles. The clang made a palpable tension fill the air, only to ratchet up again when the noises began.

It was hard to sit still, knowing that they would all have to endure whatever awful trial was happening on the other side of the white brick. A few long minutes later, Pax heard two piercing shrieks under the racket before they were choked off and not heard again.

"This isn't supposed to kill us, right?" Amil whispered.

Pax shook his head silently to reassure his friend, but wasn't so certain himself.

When the roars and thumping finally subsided, it felt as if their entire group held their breath until they heard a side door, on the left this time, clang open.

When two workers emerged carrying a stretcher between them, a collective gasp rose from the other street rats. They caught the barest glimpse of Kurt lying prone, eyes shut as the attendants carried him swiftly toward a rear door. He wore a new uniform too, but his trim was brown and white this time.

"Now don't worry yourselves so, young initiates," Master Grimfall said as he stood and clapped his hands exuberantly. "Let's welcome the first earth support mage of your group. Come on. Join in."

As a few of his fellow initiates clapped weakly, Pax knew he wasn't the only one staring back at the dwarf and feeling appalled instead of reassured. He even felt a touch of worry and sympathy for the disagreeable Kurt after seeing the shape he was in.

"Now, you may have noticed our young mage came out of the left door. He is now classified as a support mage, not as strong as a power mage, of course, but he will still be a vital part of defending the empire against the beast hordes, just like all of you. With a bit of healing, he'll be on his feet again in no time."

Soft muttering around him made Pax glad to be among fellow street rats. Simple platitudes didn't reassure them. They would fight and scrabble, grabbing onto whatever it took to survive. Pax resolved to keep track of as many as he could going forward. He would need allies if he wanted to not only survive, but excel in this place.

Master Grimfall glanced down at his papers before looking back up. "Initiate Amil Fajor. You're next. Please come down."

Pax felt his friend stiffen next to him and go still. He didn't stand.

"Amil? Please don't make me send the guards to bring you down," the dwarf said, his voice just as pleasant despite the threat in his words.

Making a hasty decision, Pax pulled his lizard meat out of his inventory and pressed it discreetly into Amil's hand. "Quick, eat this while I distract him."

Amil blinked at him in surprise. Pax gave him a pointed look before leaping to his feet and standing in front of Amil to shield him from Grimfall's view. "I'm sorry. Did you say Pax Vipersworn? Is it my turn?" he asked in a loud voice full of the exaggerated eagerness of a bootlicker.

A few snickers told him he'd pulled off the subtle mocking. The steely-eyed look from the dwarf told him it wasn't appreciated.

"Please sit down, Initiate Vipersworn and send your friend down here," he said before adding in his usual pleasant voice, "And since you are so eager to be tested, we'll have you go next."

Pax gulped as Grimfall's words quashed any mirth around him. Still, he was glad to see Amil swallow and shove another chunk of meat into his mouth before Pax moved to sit back down.

"You got this," Pax said, getting a worried nod from his friend as he chewed quickly.

Rin reached over and gave Pax's arm a squeeze as they watched their friend descend the steps and approach the Crucible's door. With the dwarf's nudge, Amil shot a last glance in their direction before stepping inside.

Knowing his time was short, Pax hurried to scan his menu to see if anything new had popped up that could help him. He groaned a bit when he saw his health had taken a hit from the altar he couldn't really afford. Pax focused on searching his menu for ideas. Maybe some fancy new light mage ability?

~

NAME: *Pax Vipersworn*

Race: *Mixed Human (monster-touched)*

Age: *16*

Bound Location: *Shieldwall Mage Academy (provisional monthly)*

Class: *Mage*

Element: *Light*

Specialization: *none*

Level: *1*

Mage Leveling Points: *0/5*

Health: *26/31*

Mana: 24/24
Attributes:
Strength: 3
Agility: 7
Endurance: 4
Intelligence: 7
Insight: 7
Charisma: 3
Skills:
General Active:
Identify Level 1 (Common) - 38/100 (+24)
General Passive:
Skinning Level 1 (Common) - 18/100 (+15)
Butchering Level 1 (Common) - 22/100 (+18)
Mage:
Light Mana Manipulation Level 1 (Epic) - 8/100
Light Mana Sight Level 1 (Rare) - 9/100 (+4)
Spells: none
Inventory: 17/20 available.
Assignments: none
Misc.: none

∾

NEXT to each item was a simple toggle, all of which currently read "Shown". He smiled with relief when he tested one and saw it instantly change to "Hidden". Next, he focused on his Intelligence and tried to change it to 6 as a test.

∾

ATTRIBUTES:
Intelligence: 7 (Shown: 6)

∾

HE QUICKLY CHANGED IT BACK, clamping down on a joyful whoop at his lucky gift that would allow him to keep his menu details secret. Hoping it would work, he moved to his element and focused on changing it to air instead of light. He only had minutes until he went through the Crucible. He couldn't let whatever was inside discover his magic type.

Nothing.

He tried again, concentrating harder, only to see a message pop up. Disappointment filled him, even before he read it. He knew it wouldn't be good news.

∼

APOLOGIES, Light Mage. You can only change numerical values to show a lower value. Your element can be toggled to 'Shown' or 'Hidden'.

∼

THE MESSAGE SUCKED most of the giddy glee out of him as he clicked the toggle to hide his element. Even looking like he had no element would be better than revealing his secret. At least until he could learn more about what was going on.

Pax scanned over the rest of the menu, unable to help a quick smile when he saw how much his general skills had gone up. And it looked like he'd even added a few points to mana sight with his experience at the altar.

The rumbling sound from the Crucible escalated and a bellow of pain rang out, jarring Pax's concentration and filling him with a mix of anger and urgency.

He needed something to help him now. Scanning through his menu again, he noticed all mentions of being locked were gone. Including his spells.

With a quick flicker of excitement, he selected his spells and held his breath, hoping.

~

WELCOME TO YOUR SPELL MENU, *Light Mage*

You have three level-1 light spell slots currently open. Would you like to select a spell now?

~

YES, he answered eagerly.

FIRST SPELL

~

Would you like to choose one of the default level 1 light spells?
   Yes/No

~

Torn by his ticking time but not wanting to throw away a chance to get something more valuable, Pax mentally stabbed at the 'No'.

~

Would you like to learn a specialized level 1 light spell?
   Yes/No

~

Yes. That sounded like a much better option. A specialized spell had to be more powerful than the default choices.

～

PLEASE OPEN the specialized spell scroll for your new level 1 light spell now.

～

SCROLL? No, no, no, Pax chanted in his mind, panicking as he realized this must be the option that allowed the noble or wealthy initiates to get an advantage by unlocking better spells right from the start.

I don't have a scroll. Go back. Start over. Pax mentally jabbed at the menu, urging it to hurry and give him another chance to pick something.

An unexpected roar from the Crucible made Pax flinch as he waited impatiently for the menu to respond. Finally, a new choice appeared in front of him.

～

WOULD you like to exit the spell selection menu and return later?
Yes/No

～

YES, he demanded, angry at himself for getting greedy when he could have already chosen a spell by now.

The sudden cessation of noise from the Crucible forced Pax to hurry and open the menu again. He wouldn't make the same mistake twice. With quick answers, he finally got out of the spell menu and dove back in a second time, this time indicating that, yes, he wanted to choose a default spell.

～

CHOOSE from the following level 1 light spells:
Illuminate

Haste
Blind
Examine
Bend

~

NEXT TO HIM, Rin gasped and grabbed his leg.

Out of time, Pax ignored the rest of the list, too desperate to even read the descriptions. *Haste.* The only decent option that might help him survive his upcoming Crucible fight. He really wanted Blind instead, but it would be too obvious if he used it. Moving faster would be much easier to explain away as an air power instead of light.

~

CONGRATULATIONS!

Light Spell Unlocked: **Haste** *Level 1*

This common spell allows a light mage to more quickly process the sensory input in their environment. The activities within the mage's senses seem to slow, allowing the mage more time to consider responses before reacting. Unlike the air spell Haste, this spell doesn't actually increase the mage's movement speed. Duration and effect increases with levels.

Mana cost: 5 mana to initiate. Variable mana to maintain, based on complexity and area of sensory input

Weakness: Requires light to work. Weaker in dim light and unusable in complete darkness.

~

PAX SKIMMED THE WORDS QUICKLY, his heart sinking the more he read. It didn't make him move fast like the title promised. He clenched his fist and let out a low growl of frustration. He'd wasted a spell on something that took a chunk of his mana to cast and then drained it away the longer he kept it active.

A roar of surprised voices around Pax forced him to jerk free of his menu and open his eyes. Worry choking at his throat, he scanned both sides of the Crucible for a glimpse of his friend. The left side was empty, which made hope suddenly flare to life inside him. Could Amil really . . .?

"Congratulations to the first power mage of your group," Grimfall called out, voice full of excitement and pride as if he were responsible. "Let's hear it for Shieldwall Academy's newest flame power mage!"

This time, the response was exuberant as the rest of the conscripts took heart at Amil's success. Pax and Rin were the only ones quiet, eyes focused on the figure of their friend as he limped across the back of the arena, hanging onto the two attendants that supported him. He also wore a new uniform that looked to be in much better shape than he did. His hair was wet and a small section looked scorched, though it was hard to see from the distance. But there was no missing the red and black trim along his tunic and pant legs. Red for flame and black for power.

Pax let out a relieved breath when Amil finally looked up, eyes searching the stands. Despite the grimace of pain on his face, his eyes lit up when he found Pax and Rin. Pax let out a cheer and pumped his fist in the air, which prompted a weary grin and wave from Amil before he turned back and let the attendants lead him out.

"If he did it, so can you," Rin whispered. "The 'crats can't keep us down now that they let us get magic."

Pax shot her a grateful look before he stood and moved down toward the dwarf before he could call his name out. It wasn't much, but taking back a small piece of control, plus the flicker of surprise on the dwarf's face, heartened him.

"It is good to see a new initiate eager to face a challenge and strengthen himself, Initiate Vipersworn," Grimfall said quietly, holding the door open once Pax had reached him.

Pax's step stuttered as he stopped in front of the doorway, shrouded completely by darkness. Squinting, Pax could only see another wall just a few feet inside and likely part of whatever construction that kept the inside of the Crucible a secret from outside observers.

Steeling his nerves, Pax forced himself to walk inside before he could second guess the decision. He stopped as he encountered the dark inner wall. Glancing to either side, he could barely make out that both sides were also blocked. He had just spun around to call out to Grimfall when the door clanged shut, dousing every bit of light and covering him with an eerie blackness that made him blink to make sure his eyes were actually open.

He quickly reached for his spark, splitting its energy and pushing it to sit just behind the palms of both hands. Next, he readied himself to activate his Haste spell as soon as the first attack came. He'd have half a minute to beat whatever opponent popped out at him.

His breathing quickened as nothing happened, the darkness thick with a dampness that reminded him of the lower sewer levels back home.

Pax had just opened his mouth to yell out a challenge when a groaning creak to his left made him turn, both hands coming up in a defensive posture. He had no clue how to use his new magic, but he was ready to do his best.

With a ponderous movement, the wall slid open, letting in a sudden light that made him blink and move one of his hands to shield his eyes.

"Well, come on in, and let's get started," an impatient voice said. "We don't have all day, and we've got most of your group of shirkers still to get through."

"Uh," Pax stuttered past a dry mouth as his vision cleared, and he caught his first glimpse of the inside of the Crucible. It was nothing like the battle he'd imagined.

Unlike the dark box built to shield the entrance, the rest of the open space was bright. The white brick reflected the sunlight from above with a fervor that made Pax think of the white sands covering the scorching deserts he'd heard about up north.

At the center of the circular area, on a wide dais, stood a transparent column about as wide as a man with both arms held outstretched. It seemed to be made of glass, but was very smooth and clear, lacking the typical whorls and distortions of the cheap glass Pax was used to.

The flat platform supporting the expensive-looking glass structure gleamed with a metallic shine, extending a foot past the edge of the enclosure all around. Equidistant from the metallic dais, four rods of similar metal protruded straight out, just above floor level, before bending up to about waist high where each angled again into a handle shape, about the size you'd see on the end of a wheelbarrow or dolly.

The four mages sitting in comfortable chairs, each holding one of the handles, immediately set Pax's hair on edge. All too similar to his Awakening, it looked as if a mage of each element was ready to do something directed at the enclosure.

"Well, step on inside," the voice called out again, impatiently.

Pax looked around, finally spotting a woman seated in a chair high above the center of the enclosure. She looked as if she'd never missed a meal and might actually be planning ahead for a famine. The rolls of her neck obscuring the collar of her shirt, and the underarms of her embroidered tunic had turned dark with sweat.

"Don't worry, Initiate," she said in what she probably thought was a reassuring tone, but just sounded impatient. "Everyone has to step into the Crucible to unlock their power. We all did it too," she said with a wave toward herself and the four mages who were barely paying attention to him. "I'm Healer Zayne. It's my job to make sure you survive. I'll have you know I'm very good at my job."

Pax couldn't help his instinctive step back.

She shook her head before turning to call out an order, "Staff, get him inside, please." As soon as she finished speaking, her attention shifted to look down inside the enclosure.

Pax stiffened as workers he hadn't noticed moved quickly toward him from the other side of the chamber. He scanned the space and saw a row of alcoves against the wall standing open behind a long wooden counter.

The gleam of yellow cloth on racks in the alcoves made it obvious where the new uniforms came from. The counter itself had stacks of what looked like patches or badges, along with tools and supplies Pax couldn't identify from where he stood.

The three assistants dressed in plain tunics and pants strode toward him, eyes full of a mix of boredom and impatience.

Pax had finally had enough. Logic fled, and his fighting blood rose. "Stay back," he snapped, his hands coming back up. He had his spark and an untried Haste spell to defend himself this time. If they were dumb enough to remove his manacles and give him a chance, they were going to find out how well a desperate street rat could fight.

"Hold," the large healer said sharply.

The three assistants froze, hands open and ready, eyes fixed warily on Pax.

"So, you've got some fighting spirit," Healer Zayne drawled. "How about you save that courage for the walls fighting the hordes? Right now, you have one choice. Survive the Crucible to unlock your element or go back where you came from."

"I can go home?" he asked, the sudden hope almost painful.

This got the attention of the other mages. One of them laughed, while one just gave him a sympathetic look as he shook his head. Pax clenched his fists and looked back up to the woman above, waiting for her answer.

"Sure," she said, looking completely uncaring. "If you don't mind having your magic permanently burned out and returning home as a manual worker. The empire can't have untrained mages running around, now can it?"

Pax felt his face flush. He wanted nothing more than to give into his rage and somehow wipe the smug look off her face. But his pragmatic side had had plenty of experience with living to fight another day when confronted with injustice.

Besides, she couldn't know that he'd already unlocked his element. Maybe he'd unlock another. Whatever happened, he'd remember Mage Zayne and how she'd treated him.

He jerked his head in an abrupt nod, not trusting himself to speak.

Zayne gave him a satisfied smile. "Let him step in himself," she directed the assistants.

They didn't seem to mind, one of them shrugging before she turned toward the enclosure while the other two returned to the supply counter in front of the uniforms.

As Pax followed the woman, he watched in surprise as she opened a slender door that had been sliced out of the glass so perfectly, and fastened with clear hinges, that it was hard to see until opened. He couldn't believe crafters could build something like it.

She stepped back, and Pax just kept walking, afraid that he might change his mind if he didn't.

"Careful of the partitions. Place your feet in the indents," the assistant instructed him as she swung the glass door shut with a quiet *snick*. "Head up. Look straight ahead and keep your hands down by your side."

Pax flinched as he almost ran into the clear walls poking in from the sides of the enclosure. A quick glance showed there were four of them, separating the interior space into quadrants except for a small, open section in the center. There, Pax saw two oblong depressions on the polished stone floor.

It was obvious where they intended for him to stand. Ignoring his uneasiness, he followed directions, placing his feet in the indentations and standing at the center of the four sectioned spaces. He let his hands fall to his sides and looked back up, only to jerk when he felt something cool move around his ankles. A quick glance down showed a silvery liquid wrapping tentacles around both of his feet and legs, moving much like the healing water Mage Janus had used to fix his arm.

"Head up," Healer Zayne called down.

Pax forced himself to comply as he felt the cool substance wrap around his legs before reaching his wrists and clamping them fast against his thighs. He winced as the liquid tried to pull his left arm fully straight and the monster-touched scales on his inner elbow stretched painfully. Once his arms were tight, the snaking bonds fell still and solidified, not budging at all when he tried to shift against them.

Above him, he heard the healer clear her throat. When she spoke again, her voice had taken on the practiced cadence of someone reciting a formalized ritual.

"Initiate Pax Vipersworn, the gift of magic during your Awakening showed the world that Vitur has chosen you to spend your life serving His empire as a mage. Today, in the Crucible, your struggle to live will burn away all weaknesses to reveal the power of your magic."

Pax swallowed hard and closed his eyes, reaching for his divided spark that still swirled just under his palms. He quickly pulled them back into his core, pushing them to disperse into the mist that had helped him during his Awakening. But he held himself ready to adapt quickly, in case he needed to fight back this time.

He couldn't help feeling disappointed that he'd wasted the choice of his first spell. While Haste might have been useful in a battle against real opponents, he didn't think it would be very useful now, immobilized as he was.

The four mages around him leaned forward, each of them settling their hands on the metal handles in front of them.

"Initiate Pax Vipersworn," Healer Zayne intoned above him. "May Vitur give you the strength to survive the Crucible and emerge stronger." She paused and then gave the order, "Commence."

25

FORGED BY THE CRUCIBLE

PAX COULDN'T HELP TUGGING against the bonds holding his hands and feet. It was hard not to panic while being held immobile against a coming attack. A gurgle behind his right side made him jerk his head and look. At least they'd left him that little bit of freedom.

His eyes widened in surprise as he saw a flash of water spurt from the rod where it merged with the enclosure. It sputtered for a minute before a stream burst out and hit him hard enough in the face to rock his head back.

Pax jerked away, choking and coughing as the cold water continued to blast into the back of his head, dripping down and soaking his tunic, pants and back of his right side. A soft whump ahead and to his left was followed by a rush of heat as a column of flame climbed up the inside wall of the enclosure opposite the water.

The heat stung his face and body while the air in the quadrant to his right whirled so fast that it tugged at his clothes and stole his breath. Desperate for a refuge, Pax turned his head to face the quadrant behind and to his left. Gratefully, he gasped in a lungful of air that wasn't super-heated, full of water or tugged away from him.

Then his eyes widened as a steam of dirt and small rocks poured into the earth section. Still, at least this section gave him a chance to breathe for the moment.

"Let me out of here," he yelled through the glass at the earth mage on the other side. The woman didn't react to his words, her eyes glazed over with a look of concentration.

His panic and anger grew as he struggled against his bonds. Why couldn't they just let him fight something instead of sticking him in this torture chamber?

He spun to glare at the other mages and yelled, "What am I supposed to do?"

Or tried to. Heat stabbed down his throat and cut his words off. Turning his head, the air just stole his breath before he made it to the water, trying not to choke while it soothed the heat.

Pax jerked his face back to the earth section to catch his breath. At least his flailing had spread some of the water and air over to combat the heat that reddened his skin and made his tunic steam.

Seeing the dirt had already filled up to his knees, Pax had to assume the water was at a similar level. His breathing quickened as he envisioned what would happen when they both reached his mouth and nose. Unless the heat roasted him or the air tore him apart by then. It was obvious they'd designed the Crucible to force initiates to unlock one of the four elements. Only he didn't have access to the standard elemental magic.

Heart racing, Pax closed his eyes, his head still held back at an awkward angle so he could breathe. He had to calm down and figure out how to survive with light magic and still keep it hidden.

But his skin and clothing were burning hot. Pax couldn't focus past the pain. First things first. With an awkward move, Pax twisted and jerked as much of his upper torso as he could over into the water section. A familiar rush of energy helped him dodge the powerful spray of water, keeping his mouth clear until he found the perfect spot to keep his head down and tuck his face safely out of the deluge. Was that his Agility increasing? The spray shifted to follow his head, but he found it easier to keep ahead of it, maintaining a small pocket of air to breathe. The cold relief was heavenly, as Pax was more than happy to shiver instead of burn. He couldn't do anything about the side of his leg that felt on fire, but some relief was better than none.

"Clever," Healer Zayne's voice called down from above, just loud enough to be heard over the roaring and rumbling elements. "But you're only delaying the inevitable. Use your magic, Initiate. It's the only way to survive."

A sudden inspiration had him aiming an Identify at the nasty woman, followed by one at each of the four mages for good measure. Her gasp of outrage made him smile as he ignored more notifications.

The small revenge energized him. Pax reached inside for his spark, pulling it back into a solid shape before sending it down to where the now-solid liquid held him prisoner. If he could break free, maybe he could make it into one section and face a single element to survive without too much damage.

As his spark sped through his body, around his waist and then out to his captured wrists, Pax fought to ignore the water rising with an occasional slosh just below his face.

The substance holding him captive looked like nothing to his inner sight. Nothing at all.

It held him trapped, impervious and solid, as if it were inert stone. Pax couldn't see any of the streams of elemental magic flowing through it, as he had with the suppression bracelets.

"Time to stand up," Zayne's voice called out with a nasty glee in it.

To Pax's horror, the arms of the imprisoning liquid moved again, flowing up his waist, forcing him to straighten and face all four elements again. It stopped halfway up his chest, leaving only his head free with limited movement. The water level followed right behind, lapping up to his elbow while the dirt and stone behind him pressed in with its weight. His cheek flamed with heat while he felt slight cuts tearing at his clothing and stinging his exposed skin as the whirlwind screamed with fury.

After a quick tip of his head toward the water side to cool off, Pax tucked his chin to his chest and took shallow breaths through his nose only. Desperation growing, he pulled his spark up to his face. It was bigger now than it had been before his Awakening. About half the size of his fist, it pulsed with a soothing energy just behind his eyes while every other part of Pax's body made him want to cry out in pain. How could he counter the attack of four elements at once? Or even just one?

His focus faltering from the pain, Pax still had enough sense to choose the front of his left shoulder still covered by his steaming tunic for his attempt. His skin screamed with heat making Pax desperate to soothe the burn. He pushed the small ball and tried to soothe his left shoulder.

Nothing. The burning pain continued to pulse insistently.

Water lapped closer behind his right shoulder as dirt cascaded on his left. It was hard to get a full breath of air against the pressure. Pax caught the noxious odor of burning hair and let out a scream of pain and outrage.

His heart raced faster. His shallow breathing couldn't keep up, leaving him lightheaded and nauseous. He forced himself to dig deep and felt an answering rush of energy that gave him the smallest increase in strength, taking the edge off his pain and panic.

The extra power gave him just enough to stay awake. Holding on, Pax pushed the edge of his spark just outside his skin, hoping that the tunic and the bright flame would disguise any evidence of his magic.

The barest edge of pain abated, but hardly enough to notice. In a brief flash, his spark drew his attention to the heat and its pulsing waves. But the pain quickly overwhelmed any curiosity. Pax would have sagged back in despair if the bindings hadn't held him up.

He barely noticed the flash of more notifications accumulating in his lower vision. The encroaching water and dirt fell against the back of his neck, forcing him to lift his head and hold his breath. He had a hard time reconciling the cool pressure behind him with the heat slamming full force into his face and the air whipping his hair into a frenzy.

Now that the elements had reached his head, they moved past the dividers, combining into a steaming, liquid slurry of mud that whipped around his face, parts being baked into hard patches that pulled at his skin and offered a moment of protection before they heated further. Squeezing his eyes tightly closed as well as his lips, Pax pinned his hopes on one last frantic gamble.

The need to breathe stabbed with urgency through the blanket of pain that smothered his body. As his lungs burned, Pax held onto his concentration by a bare thread and pulled his spark up to his face, forcing it to spread out into a new shape, a concave shield just large enough to cover his mouth and nose.

It resisted for a moment, a stubborn refusal to do something unfamiliar. With a frantic push, Pax slammed his will into the energy from both sides. Finally, with a snap, his spark flattened into a disc. Pax shoved it out in front of his face, giving it a slight cupping shape at the last moment, so the edges stayed flush with his head.

More notifications blurred across his vision, only to be dismissed immediately. He felt the new shape of his spark as it contacted the hot, swirling muck, trying to smother him. With his eyes closed, Pax focused desperately on the disk of magic he'd pushed in front of his mouth and nose.

Inexplicably, a kaleidoscope of color flashed into his mental vision, bright colors of the four elements entwined in a roiling mass, fighting to get past his magic. His attention bored into the phenomenon, trying to disentangle the inexplicable sight of all the elements . . . until he sucked in his first frantic breath and scalded his lungs.

Heat. Pain. Fire.

Fighting to stay conscious, all thoughts of magic shattered as Pax pursed his lips and sucked in the barest amount of the blistering steam with each shallow breath.

At least it's air, Pax reassured himself, his body torn between rebelling and craving the noxious stuff.

Hot sludge slopped against his ears and eyelids. A desperate panic rose from under the pain, an instinctual fear of being buried alive. Pax felt the inexorable creep on the skin of his forehead a moment before the sludge closed over the top of his head with a finality that made his will crack.

He whipped his head from side to side, fighting as he felt the heat bake the substance into something thicker and thicker. His arms and legs strained against his binds and a crazy scream burst free from him. Almost incoherent, he grabbed at the disc of his spark and pushed out with all the power he could summon. Just as he felt his power flail and sputter, a flare of resolve bolstered his sagging reserves.

With burning lungs starved for too long, Pax drew on his new Endurance and roared. Air! He needed air.

Something cracked in front of him, a smidgen of space that let a swirl of air reach his parched lips.

"Cease!" The muffled order was barely perceptible through the layers encasing his head.

Still fighting for breath, darkness encroached on his vision even as Pax felt the world around him still. The pressure behind him fell as the water drained and dirt disappeared. His flayed and burnt skin still throbbed, but the attack had ceased. The hardening sludge encasing his head sagged, but still kept him confined.

On an instinctive level, however, he knew he'd survived. That helped him push back the panic and relax his cramping muscles. The surge of relief almost made him pass out, but he fought to stay conscious, still sucking quick breaths through the small passage his spark had made. It took all his focus to keep the panic from over-whelming him again. He wanted nothing more than to fight and rail against his bonds.

Hurry, he urged the mages. *Out. Get me out.*

"Release him. Quickly," said Zayne's voice, sounding irritated.

Movement and noises made Pax gasp with relief. When the substance encasing his head cracked and fell away, he didn't mind the bright light. He sucked in a full breath of cool air with a promise to never take it for granted again. His lungs felt burned on the inside, making him cough weakly even as he tried to calm his breathing.

"Hold still and keep your eyes closed while they finish," Healer Zayne said. "They'll get you out and onto a stretcher in a minute."

The water, mud and bindings disappeared somehow, the mess gone. His injuries remained, throbbing insistently and making him flinch as hands moved him to a stretcher before stripping his ruined clothes from him. He almost opened his eyes at that, but decided he couldn't be bothered, too focused on not whimpering at the pain.

At the edges of his attention, he could hear the mages behind him in a murmured discussion. Something about which element he had manifested. Suddenly alarmed, he strained to focus on their words.

"Definitely no flame," he heard an unfamiliar voice say.

"So, the only element anyone sensed was possibly air?"

That was Zayne, he thought.

"Maybe?" a gruff voice answered. "It was right at the end, before you called it."

"Well, he's an awakened mage, so he has to have an element," snapped Zayne with impatience.

"Not much of one, if any," a third voice muttered. "I never thought the Awakening made mistakes, but now?"

"I'll hear no blasphemy out of you," Zayne said, her irritation making her easy to hear now. "You're the official Crucible mages. One of you, decide, so we can tell them how to dress him. I'm going to heal him."

Pax tensed as the bad-tempered woman stomped toward him. His eyes popped open when he realized he was lying on the stretcher, naked. Looking down he saw the reddened blisters peppering his left side with multiple weeping cuts and abrasions on his right.

He only caught a single appalling glance before two of the workers shook out a thin sheet over him. He was grateful for the covering until it brushed against his injuries, making him bite back a cry of pain, turning it into a quiet groan.

"Quit bawling. I'm going as fast as I can," said Zayne, her frowning face appearing as she leaned over him and clamped both of her hands down onto his shoulders.

Her grip shot more pain into his body, but he bit down tightly and kept quiet, refusing to give her the satisfaction.

Her eyes narrowed just before the intricate mage tattoos on both of her wrists flared to life. "There just might be something to you, weakling."

When he met her eyes and glared, she just laughed.

When a rush of heat washed into his body, forcing it to mend with the brutality of a sledgehammer, Pax finally let go. He'd survived and kept his light magic a secret. That was more than enough for the day.

As he quit fighting, he heard one of the Crucible mages call out, "We've agreed. He's an air support mage."

The breath of relief Pax sucked in didn't burn for the first time, and that was all he cared about. Eyes closed, he did his best to ignore Zayne as she finished her heavy-handed healing.

Dried mud tugged at his face when he let a small smile spread across his face. He'd survived everything they'd thrown at him, and they'd officially declared him an air mage. Now that was something.

26

ORIENTATION

Pax shoved another meat roll into his mouth, chewing as little as necessary so he could swallow another bite, chasing it down with another gulp of a chilled, purple juice that was so delicious he wouldn't mind living on it the rest of his life. Apparently, using magic, followed by torture and being brought back with extensive healing, required lots of fuel to recover.

"Please eat your fill and restore your strength as much as possible from the Crucible before leaving for orientation," the motherly-looking worker called out from the head of the food tables, her voice cutting through the muted conversations in the small hall as she repeated her instructions for the latest haggard looking arrivals. "Generally, we don't allow you to take extra food without permission during mealtimes, but today is a special day for all of you. Your bodies need extra nourishment, so please take an extra snack or two for later. Finally, after discussing your new magic with your advisor, you'll also be able to receive portions of elemental beast meat during regular meal times to support your growth."

Pax tuned out the announcement he'd already heard earlier. He snuck two of the rolls into his inventory, planning to grab a few more to add to the stack in his inventory if he could get away with it. The array of food and drink on the tables against the wall had floored him when he'd finally had the strength to stand from his stretcher in the recovery area at the back of the hall.

And it was all free. As much as he wanted to eat. He'd even seen some initiates making faces at the food or throwing away plates half full. It hurt him to see the waste. A sudden pang of sadness made his eyes sting as he thought of how long his Vipers could have lived on the bounty discarded here.

"Sorry," Amil mumbled again from his spot at the table beside them, his face flushed and eyes fixed firmly on his plate.

Pax swallowed hard before shaking his head and holding up a hand toward his friend. "Stop saying that," he said in a quiet voice so others wouldn't overhear. "You making power mage is a good thing for us."

"But you gave me your lizard meat," Amil said miserably. "Maybe if—"

"He's air, you big lug," Rin said, flicking a grape at Amil. "The meat probably would have ruined the tiny bit of air magic he managed, anyway."

Amil's head snapped up, eyes wide, and Pax aimed a glare at her.

"What?" she asked, grinning as she waved one wrist at them, the start of her deep blue tattoo obvious against her pale skin. "I'm support too. And you know I'm right. Now isn't the time to be gloomy. We're mages, guys. We can do magic. Look." Rin plopped her finger into her glass of juice and when she pulled it out, the berry juice had wrapped around her finger like a baby garden snake.

She gave the boys a triumphant look, only to flinch back when the juice lost its form and splashed over the food on her plate.

"Oops," she said, giving them a sheepish grin before shrugging. "Well, I like the taste of juice, anyway. Maybe if I practice a lot, I can be as strong as a big power mage like you, Amil."

Pax couldn't help laughing at her antics and was glad when Amil joined in. It eased the remaining tension between them, though Pax couldn't help the sting of jealousy when he saw her ability to control water. How was she so good at it when he'd had his whole life to work with his spark to get that good?

And she was right about the impossible reality of them being mages. They even looked the part. The Crucible had destroyed their ragged clothing. Now they were all dressed in the crisp, new mage uniforms with the various colored trim denoting their positions: red and black for Amil, dark blue and white for Rin and light blue and white for him. Affixed to their left breast, they each sported a wooden first-year badge. Amil's had a flame and fist symbol stamped into the center while Pax and Rin had hammers with their elemental symbols.

For the first time in his life, Pax might actually fit in with the people around him, regardless of their social station. His plan to grow in power and get back to rescue Tomis and the other Vipers might be more than a daydream. As a powerful mage, he could even track down his family, or at least find out what happened to them.

He gave himself a mental shake, knowing he was getting ahead of himself. It was only his first day, and he needed to focus on the basics first. The thought brought back his curiosity about what the Crucible had been like for the rest of the students with a normal elemental power.

"So, uh," he started, not sure how to word what he wanted to know. "Are any of us going to talk about what happened in there?" He tipped his head toward the Crucible exit door where they could still hear muffled, but disturbing noises, during lulls in the surrounding conversations.

Rin and Amil exchanged an uncomfortable look, which Pax understood. He flashed back to almost being smothered and burned at the same time. "Never mind," he said with a shake of his head. "Sorry I asked."

"No," Rin said. "We're the new kids here, and one way we can get up to speed is by sharing information with each other—" She shot a glare in the Crucible's direction before turning back and continuing, "—even if it sucks."

Amil didn't take too long to nod his agreement, and Pax didn't feel so bad about asking.

"So, I figure the torture is the same for all of us," Rin said quietly as she leaned in and lowered her voice. "They pour all four elements into the Crucible while holding us trapped. Somehow, this is supposed to be a good thing and force our magic to wake up. Mine was already working pretty decently, but I could only handle some of the water, not that huge, crazy amount. Even though I could keep it away from my mouth and nose, it didn't take long before I passed out. And boom. I'm a support water mage." She looked at the two of them. "Any different for you two?"

"Same, but I actually snuffed out the flame in mine, barely," Amil said, looking sheepish. "It took so much out of me, I almost passed out anyway, but I didn't, so that earned me the black trim."

They turned to Pax, and he debated how to answer. "I didn't manage even close to what you two did. I barely pushed away a little section of the hardening goop before they called it. And my magic wasn't even—" He stopped himself, suddenly remembering where they were.

"Wasn't what?" Rin asked. "Does this have anything to do with what happened on the caravan?"

Amil looked really curious, too, but stayed silent, waiting.

"Can we talk about this later?" Pax asked, feeling torn.

"If that's what you want," Rin said, sitting back, movements stiff as she picked up her fork to eat again.

"This isn't a good place," Pax tried to explain. "And I don't understand much myself. So, how am I supposed to tell you guys?"

Rin relented a bit, looking at him. "But you will?"

"Yes. I promise," he said, suddenly sure that he would need the help of his friends if he wanted to unlock the puzzle of his light magic and survive.

"Good," she said with satisfaction before aiming a significant look toward the rest of the new mage students seated in the hall. "And, Amil, I think it's going to be more important than you know that we've got both power and support."

Pax glanced at the room and saw what she meant. Even though they'd barely emerged from the Crucible, the power and support mages had already separated from each other naturally, the power differential creating an obvious divide.

"Next group leaving for orientation in five minutes," a willowy girl called out from the doorway. Dressed in plain, well-worn clothes, she was obviously another of the messengers that had been showing up every quarter hour.

"Only go if you're feeling recovered and take some extra food for later," the kitchen worker called out.

Pax gave the others a look and assessed how stuffed he felt. His mind said eat more while his stomach insisted it needed time to digest. Rin gave him a nod that he returned. The three of them stood, moving to the food table to stock up before leaving.

"NEXT MAGE TALIA will go over your daily schedule," the officious-looking man running the orientation said, waving toward a younger mage who had already caught the eye of many of the initiates.

Dressed in form fitting-leathers with a cape trimmed in the deepest blue, the water mage stood and walked toward the podium. She was tall and moved with the grace of an experienced fighter. But it was her hourglass figure and almost perfect features that turned heads.

Pax nudged his friends and whispered to Rin and Amil, "Check out her tattoos."

Rin nodded impatiently, likely having already noticed the complex whorls of water-themed blue lines snaking halfway up Mage Talia's forearm. But Amil's eyes widened in surprise when he moved his gaze from her chest to her wrists.

"Bunch of perverts," Rin muttered.

Pax frowned, looking around and finally paying attention to the words in the undercurrent of whispers that had spread through the large room. Mage Talia must have heard some of them, too, because her cheeks flushed, and she scowled.

"First, I'd like to add my welcome to the academy and congratulations on attaining your elements in the Crucible," she said in a clear, no-nonsense tone of voice. "And second, I'd like to remind you that magic is all about power, not looks." She said the last two words slowly with emphasis, letting them hang in the following silence for a moment.

Pax heard a snicker off to his right and glanced over to see Galen still leering at the mage, while one of his friends rolled his eyes at her warning. Pax just hoped he would be around if the noble brat ever ran afoul of Mage Talia.

"And now, I'm sure all of you would like to know what you'll be doing every day here at Shieldwall Academy," she continued, her tone brisk and businesslike again.

That got everyone's attention, and the room went silent.

"You will have three morning classes on Monday, Wednesday and Friday as well as another three on opposite days. There will be no classes on Sunday. Starting at 8 o'clock, classes will last one hour, with a thirty-minute break you may use to recover, heal or study."

A startled murmur swept through the crowd. Pax exchanged an alarmed look with his friends. A thirty-minute break to *heal*?

"Yes, young mages," Mage Talia snapped. "You are here to fight and grow stronger, which means you will suffer. Injuries and pain will strengthen you. Every night, the beast waves are getting larger and more powerful. Mages and warriors are dying on the walls of our empire, and it's up to you to reinforce them. If we don't make this training as hard as possible, then you're useless to the empire. We might as well just kill you now." She paused and scanned the crowd, all silent again. "Any volunteers?"

Pax heard Amil gulp beside him as no one answered Talia's challenge.

"I like her," Rin whispered.

"Alright, then." Talia said as she glanced back down at her notes. "Your required morning classes are Meditative Healing, Advisor Meeting with a weekly seminar, Basic Spells, and Beast Identification. You have two electives. For our support mages, we have collaborative classes with the crafting and warrior academies like enchanting, empowering, weapons, armor, etc. Power mages can choose from electives like element manifestation, dueling, and beast combat. And, in case you were curious, the merchant academy rarely collaborates with the rest of us. "

The titles of the power classes sent murmurs of excitement through the group. Pax, however, glanced over at Rin before rubbing his fingers together in the sign for money. Rin grinned back, and Pax knew she'd be on board to gain wealth and advantages with him as quickly as possible.

"After lunch, you are all required to attend a conditioning course for students of the three academies."

A collective groan swept through the students, but Talia just raised her voice and spoke over them. "We are at war!"

That shut everyone up.

"A weak body will get you killed on the walls as fast as weak magic," Talia said, her glare daring anyone to argue with her. "Conditioning class is on all six days. Besides keeping you alive by increasing your physical attributes, it will also allow you to incorporate the energy from the elemental meat you'll be eating at lunch, which will strengthen your magic."

Amil made an approving sound, and Pax reminded himself to quiz his friend on what the lizard meat had done to him.

"Once conditioning is over, your afternoons are your own for practical training," Talia said. "You will need to arrange your own schedule and get your advisor's approval. We give you a lot of latitude to train in a way that fits you best. Using your magic will always advance your levels faster than sitting in a classroom and learning about it."

Pax couldn't believe the amount of freedom they were being offered and could hardly wait to get a few schemes going to churn out experience and coppers for him.

"You can vary your practical training as needed. We have an extensive obstacle course complex organized by element and level, with a combined one at the center. For those who are still lacking the funds for tuition, there is a board filled with posted assignments in the dining hall that offer both coin and Academy Points as rewards. Instructors also award points for exemplary performance."

Someone's hand shot up in the front, and Pax thought he recognized the back of Kurt's head.

"Save your questions for your advisor," Talia instructed severely, and the hand went right back down. "You can use Academy Points to buy better spells, abilities and gear in the Academy Store on the levels reserved for students."

An older mage on the podium behind Talia cleared his throat. She glanced back before speaking faster.

"Finally, at night, one of the most valuable opportunities here at the academy is to take a shift on the tri-academy wall with other crafter and warrior students. Again, the merchant students obviously don't participate. Now, this section of Salman's wall has ancient magical filters that sort the beasts into leveled areas. Students are able to combine all their training in a real test against swarming beasts close to your own level. Be warned, shifts are valuable. Upper-classmen get first pick. Any other questions, ask your advisors."

Before anyone could raise a hand or ask a question, Mage Talia turned on her heel and marched back to her seat, leaving a speechless audience staring at the podium.

"Now no one is staring at her looks," Rin whispered with a laugh.

Pax smiled at her comment until Amil leaned in and, in a worried voice, asked, "What did she mean by tuition?"

With a sinking feeling, Pax knew the answer wouldn't be good.

27

INITIATION

WEARING a new backpack dragging at his shoulders, Pax hurried to keep up with the group of other new students assigned with him to the Solaris boys' dorm for support mages. He hadn't wanted to fill his inventory with the large variety of items he'd received today. With how full his backpack was, though, he was more than ready to dump some of the stuff in his room.

Once the orientation was over, assistants had shepherded them through a whirlwind of processing, sorting by gender and power into groups assigned to various dorm rooms. Clerks had pushed them through a dizzying array of tables and counters where they'd measured the students and given Pax more new clothing than he'd ever owned in his life. They'd also assured them that the armory would now have their measurements on file for the basic armor provided to students when they needed it.

Then there were the school supplies. The array of notebooks and writing supplies they'd each stuffed into their new backpacks or inventories had started a knot of worry growing in Pax. His mother had taught him his basic letters when he was young, but there had been little chance to improve the skill on the streets. At least he seemed to read the system messages easily. Now that he gave it some thought, Pax realized that Vitur's system was helping his reading skills.

"This is your dorm," the young messenger boy yelled out in a penetrating voice as he jogged up a stone pathway that curved up to an elegant house.

Built of a mix of gray and patterned stone outlined with dark wooden support beams that accented the walls and roof, it looked a bit like Pax would imagine a noble's vacation home would. Not sprawling enough to be a mansion, but with three full stories and large banks of windows on either side of the ornate door, it would house plenty of people.

The messenger ran right up to the door as the rest of the students slowed to look at their new home.

"This is for us?"

Pax glanced over to see Dahni, the elven kid who'd treated him pretty decently while with the caravan. He looked as shell-shocked as Pax felt.

"I know," Pax whispered back. "I'm not sure what I expected life as a mage to be like, but it sure wasn't this."

"Of course you didn't," a sour voice broke in behind them. "You can take a kid out of the street, but for some of them, you can't take the street out of the kid."

Pax's smile faded, and Dahni shot an irritated look behind him. Dahni being assigned to Pax's same dorm had been a welcome surprise, but Kurt, too?

"You know you're included in that group, right?" Dahni asked, his tone much more level than Pax's would have been if he'd replied.

"Not hardly," Kurt snapped back. "I've got noble blood, and I'll become a powerful mage that proves it."

"So, you're accidentally grouped here with us support mages instead of the power ones?" someone in the group asked, voice dripping with sarcasm.

Others snickered. Kurt's face flushed, and he stormed up to the front of the group just as the messenger gave three solid knocks on the door.

"Head inside," he called out to their group. "The dorm attendants are waiting to help you get settled."

Kurt shouldered his way past the boy, making him stumble on a step. The boy glared at Kurt before spitting in disgust off to the side and running back toward central campus.

"Follow me, everyone," Kurt said with a smug look over his shoulder before pushing the door open.

Pax followed the group of students as they entered a dimly lit, but very spacious, entrance hall. He could barely see the lofted ceilings in the minimal light that made it past the heavy curtains drawn closed over all the windows. Pax wasn't the only one to stop and stare, only moving when others pushed in from behind to enter.

The entrance hall might have once been an airy space arrayed with comfortable furniture for lounging, but now, someone had stacked the couches and chairs to form a low wall that bisected the space. On the other side of the wall, an assembly of shadowy figures with disturbing outlines stared at them in an ominous silence.

A clang behind them made a few of the students startle as the door slammed shut. Pax turned to see the closed door had cut off their only real light source.

"Welcome to Solaris Dorm, first-years!"

A raucous cheer from the other side of the unstable wall rang out at the words. Pax turned back to see a figure had clambered to the top of the unstable wall and now pumped a stick-like weapon into the air. His eyes adjusting, Pax could now see he wore some kind of beast mask on his head, an evil-looking snout full of bright sharp teeth. He had everyone's attention.

"We represent the beasts you must learn to overcome if you want to fight on our Empire's walls. Your rooms are in the basement. Through that door." He swung his stick to point toward an arched doorway on the far side of the entrance hall. A mage light hung just inside, beckoning in contrast to the rest of the dimness. "The strongest and most determined of you will get downstairs first and pick from the best rooms. Consider this your first trial as a mage."

A few excited murmurs cropped up around Pax.

"Two rules," the leader called out, making everyone hush again. "No magic. And no injuries that we can't heal ourselves. Got it?"

The other figures arrayed behind the wall roared their approval, looking more than a little horrifying in their disguises.

"Crew initiation?" Pax whispered to Dahni, getting a toothy grin from the other boy.

"Don't be first and don't be last," Dahni whispered back, making Pax return his grin.

Finally, something his time on the streets could help him with at the mage academy. For a moment, Pax considered using his Haste spell, knowing it would be invisible to observers. But he understood how initiations worked. The point was to challenge new joins, not to destroy them. Besides, he could really use a straightforward, non-magical challenge right now.

"Beasts versus firsties," the central figure roared out. "Fight!"

Chaos ensued as new students rushed forward, scattering and scrambling for any gaps in the wall and defenders. They ducked heads and raised hands to fend off the beasts' clubs.

Kurt, as expected, sprang forward first, darting off to the side toward what looked like a lower section of the improvised wall. Pax smirked when he saw two beasts leap out, one sweeping Kurt's feet out from under him while another batted him across the shoulders.

"After them," Pax hissed to Dahni, pointing to a group of first-years who had banded together and were attempting to bulldoze their way through the opposition.

The elven boy was quick on the uptake, joining Pax in doing their best to take shelter in the bit of calm behind the large group pushing forward in front of him.

A blow hit Pax from behind, making him stumble. Dahni jerked him forward, and the two of them turned on the attacker, lashing out with feet and fists until the beast leaped back and gave them a fist pump before disappearing back into the melee.

"They're padded training clubs," Pax called out to Dahni.

His friend shot him a fierce smile that Pax returned. This battle had all the thrill of a good brawl with none of the danger. Even the tone of the battle had changed, shouts and cries filled with excitement and challenge.

"There." Dahni pointed to a gap underneath a couch propped up across two chairs.

Pax, being closer, dove for the opening. As soon as he crawled through the tight spot, he turned and jerked Dahni through. He did his best to monitor the surrounding madness.

A crowing victory shout drew the attention of many of the fighters to a first-year pumping both arms high in the alcove before spinning and disappearing down the dark stairs. Pax and Dahni took advantage of the distraction to sprint for the wall far to the left of the alcove. In moments, they had reached it. After a straight shot along the back wall, they joined the others who'd made it.

"I hope they don't make us clean all that up," Dahni said through panting breaths as they hurried down the stairs to the lower floor.

Pax groaned and thumped a hand on the wall next to him. "Hand-to-wall. Don't jinx us."

"Sorry." Dahni looked sheepish as they reached a landing with a cozy open area and hallways leading off from either end.

While not as gloomy as they had made the upstairs for the initiation, the common room was still dim. Underground without windows, weak-looking mage lights set into the walls provided some light. A musty smell with a damp tinge reminded Pax of his crew's hideouts in Thanhil's underground system.

A worker sitting behind a desk against one wall pointed a hand to his right. "The necessaries and practice rooms are down that hall. The rooms down the other. Claim any bed that doesn't have something on the bed. Then come let me know, and I'll write your assignment in the book."

Still pumped on adrenaline from the brawl, Pax took off toward the rooms, Dahni on his heels. Students stood in the closest doorways and waved them off as they hurried to find one unclaimed. About halfway down the hall, they found a still-darkened doorway and hurried inside.

A recessed mage light in the center of the ceiling flashed on as they entered, revealing their new quarters. Pax's first thought was that it was big enough for half of his crew to fit comfortably, followed immediately by the idea that the nobles among his fellow students would likely complain about it. He smiled as he imagined Galen's reaction, happy to know that, at least in one detail, the academy would force the arrogant 'crats to be equal to everyone else.

The walls were made of rectangular blocks of stone fitted together rather crookedly, with signs of workers adding extra mortar on a regular basis to repair things. However, a fresh coat of bright white paint covered most of the imperfections and left the faint scent of chemicals in the air. The fresh smell helped dispel the damp scent and whiffs of mold that filled the basement floor.

To either side of the door stood two identical desks with what looked like mage powered lamps on each. The desks gleamed, their wood thick with slight depressions in the center, likely from years of student elbows and books. Rows of drawers ran up both sides of the desks with identical wooden chairs pushed flush into each.

On each side of the room, two narrow beds sat flush against the walls, covered with thick muslin mattresses that looked to be stuffed completely full under the sheets and blankets tucked tightly around them. And at the head of each bed lay a pillow covered by a smooth white linen.

Across from the door and on the far side of the room stood a sturdy stone table with various hooks along the wall and ceiling above it. Large empty shelves beneath it looked sturdy.

The last features were two inset closets to either side of the table, a rod running through the middle with wooden shelving along both sides and hooks along the back wall.

Pax looked at Dahni and saw a look of wonder on the fellow street rat's face.

"Is this all for us?" he asked, looking more unsure than Pax had ever seen him.

Pax couldn't help the smile that widened across his face. "Yes, I'm pretty sure it is. Do you care which one?"

Dahni shook his head and Pax tossed his backpack on the desk to the left before turning and throwing himself back onto the bed with a delighted whoop. He let out a groan of pleasure as he sank into the mattress and his head landed on what felt like a soft cloud. His first pillow ever.

In no time at all, both boys had unloaded their backpacks, ate another meal from their stashes and were bouncing on their mattresses with a childlike glee.

"Back to work, firsties!" The faint call could be heard drifting down the hallway. "Playtime is over. Advisor time. Classes start tomorrow."

"Well," Dahni said with a pragmatic shrug as he swallowed the last of his sandwich and stood from his bed. "The break was nice while it lasted, right?"

Coming to a sudden conclusion, Pax stood and extended his hand to Dahni. "Want to help each other out if we can?"

Dahni looked suddenly apprehensive. Every street rat was familiar with infiltration followed by betrayal. "What's the catch? And the terms?"

Pax wasn't about to trust the mixed-elf as much as he did Amil or even Rin, at least not yet. He just knew they would need all the allies they could gather. "Just allies to start. Share information and help each other out, but nothing that hurts ourselves. We can agree to more if that works out. Deal?"

Dahni looked much more pleased at the general terms and, after a sharp nod, shook Pax's hand.

"Look alive, firsties! You have five minutes to get back upstairs. Make sure you stop by the table to register your room number." Pax barely glimpsed the young man who poked his head into the doorway briefly before moving further down the hallway and repeating the instructions.

He and Dahni joined the stream of new students streaming up the stairs, happy to see that the older students had transformed the entrance hall back into something much more normal looking. They'd pulled back the drapes on the floor-to-ceiling windows, and the late afternoon light poured into the now-inviting space full of patterned throw rugs, couches, soft chairs and a smattering of study desks.

"Line up and see these three to get your advisor assignments," a squat but powerful-looking dwarf called out in the familiar voice of the lead 'beast' from earlier. A filigreed whorl of brown tattoo lines twisted around his wrists, evidence that he was much further along in his magical training than they were. "In ten minutes, all of you will leave to meet your advisors. We'll have four errand kids to guide you to the different elemental instructor buildings. But don't get used to being shown everywhere." He held up a hand in warning. "After today, we expect you to have memorized your campus map and get where you need to go on time."

The students nodded as they moved to split into lines. They moved quickly as the older students behind the tables found their names and gave them slips of paper.

"My name is Dulmot Mudmace, a fourth-year earth mage and in charge of Solaris Dorm," the leader continued over the quiet voices of those handing out assignments. "I'm the one you see if you are having any trouble with your living situation. Don't come to me with class or magic trouble. That's for your instructors and advisors. That being said, we all want you to succeed, so if we can help, we'd rather you speak up than not. Understand?"

Heads bobbed in agreement, with a few verbal answers, which made Pax think he wasn't the only one feeling overwhelmed. Once at the head of the line, he gave his name, only to freeze in place as he stared at the name on the slip of paper handed to him.

Mage Incedis.

"But I'm an air mage," he tried to protest to the older student, only to have him wave impatiently for Pax to move.

"Take it up with him," he said, leaving Pax to wonder how much trouble he was in and how he would ever keep his secret under the sharp eyes of the perceptive flame mage.

MAGICAL ADVICE

"You. I forgot they added you to my list," Mage Incedis said with annoyance when he looked up and saw Pax was the next student to walk into his office. "I bet you didn't think you'd be seeing me again. Well, me either."

Pax was too tired to get angry and just gave the man a nod before walking forward and plopping down into the comfortable chair in front of the mage's desk. "If you'd just help me put together my class schedule for tomorrow, I'll get out of your hair as fast as possible. I really just want a meal and a bed right now."

Incedis' arched eyebrow made Pax flush and straighten in his chair as he realized how disrespectful his casual words might come across. "I'm sorry, Mage Incedis. I just—"

"No, no," Incedis interrupted, waving a hand to cut off Pax's apology before he leaned back into his high-backed leather chair and let out his own weary smile. "I'm just feeling my own frustration at the start of this year. No sense taking it out on you."

Pax relaxed and let out a relieved breath.

"Let's get you set up for this week at least," Incedis said, as he picked up a pencil and scanned the stacks of paper on his desk before pulling one out. "Then we can adjust things as we go if something isn't working. Sound good?"

When Pax nodded, Incedis waved at him to approach.

"Scoot your chair closer, and we'll pencil things in until we get something that works."

The conundrum had been bothering him ever since leaving his dorm, and Pax decided to risk asking about the topic, praying it didn't endanger any of his secrets. "Um. Can I ask a question?" he said as he pulled his chair closer to the mage's desk.

Incedis cocked his brow at him again, and Pax flushed. "In addition to that one, I mean?"

"Well, at least you're not stupid," Incedis muttered before making a go-ahead gesture. "But just one. You're not the only first-year they've roped me into advising this term, and I would like to eat sometime this evening myself."

Pax blinked, suddenly struck by the thought of the all-powerful mages he looked up to and feared having the same needs as regular people.

"Well?" Incedis asked.

"Sorry," Pax hurried to say, scrambling for the best way to phrase his question. "If I'm an air mage, why would they assign me to a flame mage like you?" He gave a hesitant wave of his arm, briefly exposing the small but bright tattoo on his wrist before pulling his uniform sleeve back down.

Most of the other first-years were wearing the short-sleeved version, proud to display their new tattoos. Pax hoped as the weather got colder, his choosing differently wouldn't make him stand out so much.

For the first time, Incedis looked hesitant, before he shrugged and said, "I'm too old to dance around the truth. You are the weakest mage to survive the Crucible in as long as anyone can remember. Combined with the growing desperation for more mages to man the walls in the empire, we're short the normal cadre of lower-level instructors. That means not enough advisors, particularly air ones this year. So, they're drafting senior instructors like me into helping with menial tasks like this. The short answer is we both got stuck with each other."

Pax's mouth had sagged open at the explanation, and he quickly clamped it shut.

"Don't worry, Vipersworn," Incedis said as he opened a booklet and pushed it across the desk toward Pax. "You'll find that I have quite the well-rounded knowledge about all four elements, though the powers that be would rather we all stay confined to our own little boxes and never stray outside the lines." He paused and glanced out the window before muttering. "We can only hope they get desperate enough to listen to reason."

Pax held his tongue, not understanding what Incedis was talking about, but sensing that he'd likely not intended to speak like that in front of a new student. Pax quickly buried his head in the pamphlet, diligently turning the pages and doing his best to sound out the class choices he found there.

"Oh, just give me that," Incedis snapped, "or we'll be here all evening. Let me go over the basic information, and then I'll pick your classes for you. You understand how to level up, right?"

More than anything, Pax wanted to answer that he did, but he couldn't let pride interfere with the chance to learn the ropes. He gave a quick shake of his head. The instant irritation on Incedis' expression made Pax's face flush in embarrassment.

Then the mage looked suddenly chagrined. "It's nothing to be ashamed of. You were living on the streets just days ago, and I bet becoming a mage wasn't something you'd ever given thought to."

"Never," Pax muttered in agreement.

"Alright. Pay attention, because I'm not repeating myself." Incedis let out a breath and spoke in a precise tone. "Everyone starts at level 1 when awakened, regardless of their class, though infant beasts can start at level 0. First, anything you learn and unlock that isn't part of your class goes under the general category in your menu. These don't count toward your next class level. Skills and spells that do not require mana to work are passive. Your menu lists the ones that do under your active one. Make sense?"

"Why improve the general ones if they don't help you level up?" Pax asked without thinking.

Incedis stopped speaking and cocked an eyebrow at Pax. "Why do you think?"

Pax thought about his non-magical skills like Identify and Skinning. He felt like an idiot, because the answer was obvious. "Because higher levels will improve my results like getting more information with Identify or better hides with Skinning."

Incedis gave him a sharp nod. "So, you can think after all. Now let me finish. To reach level two as a mage, you will need five leveling points. Now, you could earn five single points by leveling up five separate mage skills or abilities from one to two. Or, since each new level of a mage skill earns you more leveling points, you could focus on one skill to get all five of your points."

"How many do you earn for each level?" Pax asked, numbers and possibilities already filling his mind.

"You'll earn a single leveling point for improving a mage skill from one to two. And then four when you level it again to three, followed by nine when you get the skill to level four."

Pax nodded, doing the math in his head. He'd always been better with numbers than letters. "So, leveling a skill up to level three would already get me the five points I need for second-level mage? That seems much easier than getting five different skills up to level two for a point each."

"Yes." Incedis looked happy he understood the first time around. "And you're right. That is the easier path at the start, which most students follow, advancing a single skill or ability at the start of their training. But your mage level requirements also increase quickly, too. It'll take twenty leveling points to reach level three and forty-five to reach level four." He gave the numbers a moment to sink in. "Do you see the problem?"

"So—" Pax drew out the word as he ran through the calculations. The problem wasn't difficult to figure out. "If I focus on one skill, I'll earn big bonuses as I get it higher, but at some point, I'll end up slowing down a lot when I have to level up other skills back at level one that give hardly any points in the beginning."

"Yes!" Incedis clapped one hand on his desk and smiled. "As is true for most things in life, more work now will save you work in the future and better prepare you for the dangerous life of a mage. Those who take the easy route usually live to regret it."

Pax nodded, his mind churning with workable plans as he thought about his menu, finally feeling a little more in control as he understood the system better. Only one thing didn't make sense. "You keep saying skill and abilities. What about spells? Do those count too?"

"Of course. Abilities and spells are the same thing." Incedis waved an impatient hand. "Mages have to be special, so we call our active abilities 'spells' while the other classes just call them abilities. Basically, if you can generate a discrete result with a standard mana cost and duration, it's a spell for mages and an ability for the other classes, like Shield Bash for a warrior. Skills, on the other hand, are usually innate knowledge that is always active, though you can funnel various amounts of mana through some of them, like enchanting or rune crafting. So, when you level either skills or abilities that are part of your class, the leveling points you earn will count toward your class level."

"So, if I learn a club skill, it just goes under my general stuff?" Pax asked, disappointed that he couldn't use that skill to help reach his next mage level.

"Exactly. And to give you an idea of the overall pace of advancement, the average student levels once or twice a year, usually faster at the start and slower by the time they graduate. At that point, they'll need to be facing stronger beasts, which is why those who qualify to finish all four years hope for a tower ring assignment to take on the biggest beasts. They help remove the biggest dangers to our cities while also facing enough challenges to level faster. Got it?"

Pax nodded and hurried to squeeze in another question that had been bugging him. "And my health and mana totals? Those go up with some of my attributes, right?"

"Yes." Incedis' tone was turning impatient, but he still explained. "Everyone starts with a base value and then health goes up by two for each point in Strength and by one for an Endurance increase. A point in Intelligence increases your total mana by two. There are also boosts from gear and temporary buffs."

Pax tried to memorize all the new information to think about later. It seemed the more Incedis taught him, the more questions he had. He opened his mouth to ask another, but Incedis held up his hand to stop him.

"That's enough for now. Write your questions down and try to answer them on your own before our meetings instead of wasting my time. We have a library full of this type of beginner's information. Let's move on to your schedule so we can finish here. Write these down too."

The next few minutes were a whirlwind of instructions as Pax did his best to pencil the class titles in the correct slots under the pressure of the flame mage's impatient gaze.

He'd wrangled for enchanting in one of his elective slots and let Incedis decide everything else, which left him with a six-class schedule including: Meditative Healing, Advisor Meeting, Basic Spells, Beast Identification, Enchanting and Magical Harvesting.

"And I can't have armor crafting instead of magical harvesting?" Pax tried one more time, envisioning being able to protect himself against attack and selling off the extras he would learn to make for piles of copper and silver.

Incedis let out an impatient snort. "Learn to crawl before you try to walk, child. Enchanting will give you plenty of difficulty and with your limited financial means, harvesting is one of the few avenues that might keep you from spending all of your afternoon training time working to earn your tuition."

Incedis' statement cut off Pax's objections mid-sentence. His visions of wealth and power stalled so suddenly, it made him blanch.

Incedis let out an irritated huff. "I can't believe they still get away with doing this to you lot every year. Listen." He leaned forward and met Pax's gaze with a serious expression. "You're going to hear a lot of blah blah blah about how we're all fighting to protect the empire's walls from the beast hordes. And I won't say that's wrong. But there is a hierarchy of power that is motivated to stay in power and to make sure they aren't the ones whose bodies are carried to the altars at the end of the day. So, they'll train you just enough to put you up on a wall to fight, but not enough to threaten their positions, ever. Understand?"

Pax swallowed hard and nodded.

"They do that by requiring you to earn your tuition during your afternoons and evenings. The assignments and work keep you from having anywhere close to the amount of training time their pampered offspring have."

Pax clenched his fists and wanted to crumple up the class schedule that had looked so promising moments ago.

"I'm surprised I need to explain something like this to a street rat like you." Impatience was back in Incedis' voice. "It had to be the first lesson you learned to stay alive. Am I wrong?"

"No. You're not wrong." Pax shook his head, turning his gaze down to his schedule to disguise the anger that burned at the back of his eyes.

"Then tell them to blast off," Incedis growled back at him, making Pax look back up in surprise. "Take the assignments that let you train your skills and earn money at the same time. Fight for spots on the wall regardless of what hours of the night they are. Harvesting will teach you how to gather the most valuable beast parts and even plants, if you figure a way to get outside the walls at night. For that matter, once you're a little stronger, find an entrance to the catacombs, and you can find plenty of valuable training and maybe even ancient items down there."

Pax just stared at the surprising rant by the older instructor, doing his best to memorize every tip he had just shared. "Catacombs?" he couldn't help parroting back with stunned curiosity.

"Oh, I forgot you're so new. I'm used to working with upperclassmen," he said, looking impatient with himself. "Forget that for now.

You're too weak. So don't even try exploring them without a good handle on both an offensive and a defensive spell. I know how tempting exploring a mystery with potential treasures can be, but I don't want to be responsible for your death. Understand?"

Pax bobbed his head while already planning to share the information with his friends.

"I mean it," Incedis snapped. "Stay out of the catacombs."

Pax squirmed, but had to nod under the older man's steely gaze.

"Now, I'll get you registered for your classes while you get started on the following assignments: First, register for two or more paid assignments. Search through what's posted at the student hall. Grab the ones that pay the best and give you a chance to practice your magic. If you have to choose, pick the magic-heavy ones over the better paying. You have a while before your first tuition payment is due."

Pax pulled a small notepad from his backpack and hurried to scribble notes so fast he hoped he'd be able to read it later. Incedis finished speaking and gave Pax an impatient look as he finished up. Pax distracted the mage from looking too closely at his poor penmanship by blurting out the question that had been bothering him since Incedis had mentioned the topic.

"How much is the tuition?"

Incedis waved a dismissive hand. "No reason to worry about that yet."

"But how can I pick assignments if I don't know how much I need to earn?"

Incedis gave him a serious look. "Are you sure you want to know? It's usually better to discuss this in the second or third week so things don't get too overwhelming."

Incedis' warning made the knot of worry inside Pax even bigger. Besides, how bad could it be? "Tell me."

"Five gold."

Pax sucked in a shocked gasp.

"Per term. So, ten for the year."

The amount sucked away all his dreams of power and wealth in an instant. He struggled to comprehend how anyone outside a noble or merchant house could earn such an enormous sum.

Incedis scrutinized him in the ensuing silence, waiting for him to respond.

"And if I don't earn enough?"

The mage smiled, looking satisfied. "Smart boy. They send the students who can't to the walls after their first year of training to spend the next few years paying off their debt in service to the empire."

"And if I don't want their expensive training?" Pax couldn't help the anger that made him spit out the question.

Incedis let out a short, but bitter laugh. "Mages are required to be trained for a year at the academy. Untrained mages are a danger to society and have to have their talent extinguished before being consigned to life as a laborer."

Pax sat back, shocked. His anger deflated as he realized how complete the Empire's trap was. It was genius, in a sick sort of way, if they wanted to produce indentured mages as fast as possible to man the walls of all the small towns and cities within its borders.

"Yes. Like I said earlier. As a street kid, you should already understand this type of thing."

Pax met Incedis' gaze and saw that the mage seemed to expect something from him. Then he realized how much he'd let his inner despair grow and felt his anger struggle to fight back. Just because powerful people stacked the odds at Shieldwall Academy against him didn't mean he would give up. He never had before and wasn't about to start now.

"Then I'll beat their system." His determination pushed back against the doubt brought on by the overwhelming flood of new information.

Incedis just looked at him, seeming to evaluate him without speaking.

Pax pushed aside his exhaustion and added in a more courteous voice, "With your help, of course."

"Good," Incedis said with a pleased nod, looking thoughtful. "Practical and spirited. Maybe this advising business won't be as onerous as I expected."

Too tired to laugh or glare, Pax just waited silently, hoping the mage would hurry and finish.

"Right, then. I'll finish your list of tasks, go over your build, and we'll be done."

29

A DECENT PLAN

"Ready?" Incedis gave Pax's notebook a pointed look. "You might want to add penmanship practice to that list."

Pax held his pencil still and just looked at Incedis expectantly.

"Fine." The mage chuckled. "Once you have your paid assignments scheduled, you'll need to squeeze in at least three obstacle course training sessions weekly around your assignments. And a week from today, on Sunday morning, as soon as they open the wall schedule to first-years, you will be at the front of the line and get your name on at least one slot, even if you have to fight a few other students to get one."

Pax nodded, the focus and determination in Incedis' gaze speaking to him, despite how little faith the mage seemed to have in him. He'd seen something similar in his brother's eyes when he'd fought to take care of Pax and the other Vipers during the early years. Maybe he should send a quick prayer of thanks to Vitur for helping him land here with this advisor.

"What else?" Incedis tapped his chin, thinking. "Oh right. Your build." He looked a bit embarrassed and shrugged. "Sorry. It's been a while since I've worked with a first-year. Not to mention a street kid who doesn't even know the basics."

Pax suddenly didn't feel so enamored with his advisor, and aimed a glare at the older man.

"Save that anger for the beasts and your opponents," Incedis said with a chuckle, which didn't help. "Remember, I'm here to help. And you'll need to learn to swallow that pride if you want to survive here. Or at least not let it show so easily."

Ducking his head, Pax blew out a quick breath to calm down again before looking back up. He knew that and had plenty of practice keeping his head down back home. So many new things being thrown at him had disoriented him, making him forget his survival skills.

"So, three spell slots per level until you reach level five, but that's many years away. That doesn't include learning to manipulate your element itself, which some mages can use like its own versatile spell. But usually only for melee range work, since at range, without the structure of a spell, your element will quickly lose power." He stopped and shook his head with impatience. "I keep getting distracted. So, what you need to do right now is read off your list of choices of common air spells. We'll pick the best all-around one. Then you're going to see how much silver and Academy points you'll be able to earn so we can help you buy better uncommon spell scrolls for the other two slots. Plus, that will give you time to decide on your preferred style of support magic so we can get you ones that fit. The worst thing a new mage can do is waste their spell slots. Once chosen, they're permanent."

Pax couldn't help blanching.

Noticing his expression, Incedis made a reassuring motion with one hand. "It's not the worst thing, as long as you're careful. And at high levels, there may be an opportunity to combine spells to free up a slot. Plus, I've heard of some mages deleting a spell, but no clan is ever going to share those kinds of secrets with outsiders."

Mind scrambling for what to say, Pax stayed silent.

"Well, come on, boy," Incedis demanded. "Read me your spell choices already. It's not like I remember what level-one air mages have access to. Flame mage here, remember?"

"I already chose one." Pax just blurted it out and then held his breath for the reaction.

It didn't take long.

Incedis looked surprised at first, followed immediately by incredulous with furious fast on its heels. "Then why in Vitur's name are you even bothering with an advisor, if you're so smart? You already know exactly what spell is perfect for your build. And what?" He pushed up from his chair, making it skitter back from him and almost topple over. "You already have a plan to train your attributes, too?" Incedis leaned forward, both hands on the desk as he spoke in a cold tone, staring directly at Pax. "Why didn't you just say so at the beginning, and I wouldn't have had to waste my time. Do you have any idea how much I get paid to consult? Do you, child? More than your tuition you're so worried about!"

Pax shook his head back and forth, mute and frozen on the spot by the threatening aura that emanated from the angry mage, the bright red tattoos looking ominous along his forearms.

Incedis glared at him in taut silence for long, tense moments. Finally, he let out a long breath, shook his head and turned to pull his chair back. When he slumped into it, he rubbed at his face with his hands.

Pax relaxed just a fraction when it looked as if the storm had passed.

"I apologize for losing my temper after just instructing you to be better at managing yours. I am tired, hungry and your reckless behavior may have just handicapped the start of a mage career I'd hoped might actually exceed expectations," Incedis said in an almost normal voice. "So, tell me quickly. What spell did you choose?"

"Haste," Pax answered, glad that his voice didn't sound as shaky as he felt and even more grateful that there was an air spell similar to his light one.

"Not the worst one," Incedis said with a bit of surprise. "Maybe my anger was ill-considered. It'll likely aid you in your paid assignments, allowing you to level it while completing work faster. Plus, considering all you're going to be up against at the start, running away might come in handier than you'd think." Then Incedis raised a finger, his eyes narrowing again. "Just don't even think about adding another spell without my express approval, understand?"

Pax nodded again, not trusting himself to speak.

"Getting something powerful in your two remaining slots is likely your only chance to make it through the Northern Purge alive, much less the tournament at the end of the school year."

Pax frowned, suddenly worried again as he gave Incedis a questioning look.

"Never mind all that," Incedis said impatiently. "You have enough to focus on surviving your first week. Now, conditioning will help train your physical attributes. Make sure you give everything you can in that class, since time is going to be something you have little of. Then, pay attention in your Meditation and Healing class. Pick some exercises you learn there and practice them every spare moment of the day. While waiting in line, walking across campus, as you fall asleep. Every spare moment!"

Taking mental notes again, Pax groaned inwardly at how long his list was getting.

"Your mental attributes are the foundation of your power as a mage, especially with how little power you're starting with. Despite how hard you work, even with my help, you may never catch up with those who are more naturally gifted."

The casual disparagement of his abilities only made Pax more determined to prove everyone wrong.

"I have one last question," Incedis said. "And it's a mere curiosity. Don't answer if it's too personal."

Pax shifted in his seat and couldn't help glancing out at the fast-fading light through the window. He nodded anyway. He couldn't refuse the mage who was working so hard to help him.

"Don't worry," Incedis said, following Pax's gaze out the window. "I'll make it fast. I'd just like to take a look at your arm."

"My arm?" Pax looked down, confused and a little worried. He'd rather the mage didn't take too close a look at how white his tattoo was instead of the light blue it should be for an air mage.

"The scales," Incedis motioned impatiently toward Pax's left arm.

"Oh, sure," Pax said, relieved and a little weirded out that the man wanted to look at the monster-touched defect that usually repelled anyone who saw it. He scooted forward and pulled up his sleeve, turning his wrist so the small line of his tattoo faced down.

"Were you born with it? Did it grow at the same pace as your arm? Or is it expanding or shrinking? Do you have any control over the growth? What advantages does it have? Is it resistant to heat? Cold? Injury? Does it cause you any problems?"

The questions poured out in a barrage as Incedis took Pax's wrist in a firm grip that felt hot and unbreakable. Pax didn't know where to start.

"Sorry," Incedis said in a distracted tone as he opened a wooden box with his free hand. "The monster-touched phenomenon is a pet area of study for me, as it has grown in time with the increase in monster waves. Just pick the easiest of those questions to answer. We can discuss the others during another session, since we'll be spending a lot of time together this term."

"Uh, I was born with it," Pax said in a hesitant voice, taken aback by the first genuine interest in what he'd always considered a disability. Even his brother had teased him about it. "It's always been on the inside of my arm like that and since it's not as flexible as normal skin, it makes it painful to straighten my arm all the way which interferes with things like fighting with my sticks or reaching for something."

Incedis listened while leaning in close and running a thin metal probe along and under some of the scales.

Pax jerked back.

"Sorry, did that hurt?"

"No, just a mix of ticklish and irritating, like scratching your fingers across a chalkboard."

"Mind if I test cold and hot?"

"You're going to burn me?" Pax couldn't help the yelp in his voice.

"No, just test the different response between this and your other skin to heat. May I?" Incedis had put down the probe and had his index finger poised over Pax's forearm.

"Oh, it protects me from heat," Pax blurted out, suddenly remembering. "I used it in a fight against that Blaze Lizard, switching to my forearm when my hand got too hot."

"You didn't tell me that before. Interesting." Even more interest popped into Incedis' eyes before he gave his head a quick shake. "I'll start low and build up. Say stop at any time or when it becomes painful. May I?"

The mage's curiosity was a bit contagious, especially since it made Pax see his shameful secret in a new light. The disfiguring scales might actually have some value. "Go ahead."

Incedis' finger glowed as he touched it gently to Pax's forearm.

Almost immediately, Pax's spark flared to life at his center, rushing toward his forearm with an eager energy. Closing his eyes in sudden panic, Pax caught his magic just as it entered his arm, berating himself for not anticipating this, especially after his experience in the Crucible.

"Did that hurt?"

Surprised, Pax realized he could see the power of Incedis' flame pull back. And the flame wasn't a simple magical energy like he'd been able to see before. Instead, it had color, various hues of red that twisted and flickered around the mage's finger.

"No," Pax answered, suddenly eager to uncover more pieces of the puzzle of what kind of magic he had. "I just focus better with my eyes closed. Please go ahead."

"Sparring practice will break you of that pretty quickly," Incedis muttered under his breath.

Pax watched the flame magic swell again and push at his scaly skin. It was beautiful. The power of the magic tantalized him. Understanding the flames hung just out of reach like a name he couldn't quite remember. He was so fascinated that he yelped in surprise when pain from the growing heat finally made him jump. The fascinating show quenched suddenly, leaving Pax blinking and trying to organize his muddled thoughts. The cluster of flashing notifications at the corner of his vision blinked even faster and more insistent, making him resolve to get home as soon as he'd eaten something and spend some time with his menu.

"You were supposed to speak up before it hurt," Incedis accused him with a frown. "I'm not like some power mages who take pleasure in hurting those weaker than myself."

"No, of course you aren't," Pax hurried to reassure his advisor. "It was just so gradual that it took me a moment to notice. How did it go?"

The mollified look on Incedis' face was quickly replaced by enthusiasm. "Your scales can handle at least twice the amount of heat that normal human skin can. Even a bit more than a young Cordu."

An unbidden smile spread across Pax's face, though he was trying to remember exactly what a Cordu looked like. It was just nice to hear his scales were actually useful.

"Now go," Incedis said impatiently, already bent over a notebook and taking careful notes in a handwriting that looked loads better than Pax's.

He scrambled to his feet, eager to escape before the mage came up with something else to dump on him.

"Run, don't walk," Incedis' voice called out just as Pax had opened the office door. "Hopefully you'll beat out the lazy and ignorant students to the best of the paid assignments."

With a burst of energy Pax dug from his almost empty reserves, he raced out of the building and across the lawns toward the student hall. Between breaths, he muttered at Incedis for delaying him so long.

JOB INTERVIEW

HOLDING the map of campus he'd tried to memorize in his head, Pax only made one wrong turn before finding the right path to the student hall. He slowed from a run down to a fast walk as he approached the sprawling, well-lit building from the side. Around him, the trickle of students heading in the same direction had grown. He could easily tell the first-years apart from the upper-class students by their lost, over-whelmed demeanor. The older students looked a lot more confident, with a patronizing look or just a distracted focus on other things.

"Pax!"

Pax turned to see Rin hurrying toward him from a side path, one hand in the air as she waved at him. He slowed but didn't stop, impa-tient to get to the assignment board. The impossible tuition amount loomed over him despite Incedis' reassurances.

"What's the rush?" she asked, as he picked up his pace as soon as she pulled alongside him.

"We need to get some of the good assignments before they're all gone," he said between breaths, a little tired himself.

"Assignments? For classes? I thought those didn't start until tomorrow."

"I mean the paid ones. Didn't your advisor tell you about them?"

"She mentioned something about them, but said not to worry about them until after I got settled in my classes." Her confused look changed as her eyes narrowed. "I knew it. I had to sit and wait in a huge line for my time slot with her and when I finally sat down with her, she rattled off a bunch of stuff, handed me the schedule she'd set up for me and sent me to get some dinner."

"Uh—" Pax was suddenly less irritated with Incedis. At least the mage had spent a reasonable time with him and did his best to help him with a good start.

"I knew it!" Rin grimaced. "My advisor spent way more time with the arrogant idiots assigned to her. It was obvious she didn't care about what happened to me. So, spill it. What are we doing?"

Knowing a practical street kid would want to hear the bad news first to figure out how to deal with it, Pax summarized their precarious situation as best as possible in a low tone as they hurried up the stone steps into a side door.

Rin's expression turned hard and determined by the time he finished, eyes up and helping him spot the assignment boards. The bulk of the students were streaming through the entrance toward brightly lit, open double doors. Delicious smells wafted out, with the clatter of dishes and the cheerful thrum of conversations overlapping each other.

"Take the left," Rin instructed as they stepped out of the traffic and looked at the hallways leading to either side of the entrance lobby.

Another student walked quickly ahead of them down the wide hall with polished stone floors. Mage lights embedded in the ceiling made it as bright as mid-day while outside the evening twilight moved in.

"Hey," Rin called.

The stocky figure paused and turned with an irritated expression on his face, the iron badge on his tunic announcing he was a second-year.

Pax froze and stared, never having seen a Cordu up close like this before.

"Sorry," Rin said in a cheerful but subservient tone Pax wished he could pull off. "Just wanted to ask if this is the way to the assignment boards?"

The student's gaze narrowed. Pax couldn't help staring at the scales that ran down along the side of his face and covered his neck before disappearing underneath the collar of his tunic. They reflected the light in such a way that Pax had a hard time deciding what color they were, other than an ebony mixed with silver highlights.

"Are you done staring?" the Cordu asked, his tone biting. "Or maybe you'd like to stare at my teeth and claws, too?"

With a sudden violence that was shocking, the Cordu feinted forward, teeth bared with a scary hiss and both hands raking forward as sharp claws extended.

Both Pax and Rin flinched back, instinctively pushing off to either side, hands raised and ready to attack from both flanks if needed.

To their surprise, a throaty chuckle emerged from the scary Cordu as he dropped his arms and laughed so hard he had trouble breathing.

"Whatever," Rin spat back. "Just because we're new doesn't mean we're helpless."

She moved to push past the still chuckling Cordu, motioning that Pax should stick close and follow her.

"Wait," the Cordu blew out a breath, still smiling as he held up both hands in a palm-up placating gesture. "Your response to my threat was well done for firsties. And as it seems you weren't deliberately mocking my race, I owe you a small favor for my little joke. How can I help you?"

"We're just trying to find the appointment board?" Rin said, still looking suspicious as she pulled Pax along to edge past the Cordu.

"Well, you're going the right—"

"Wait," Pax interrupted. "Would a small favor include helping us choose the assignments best suited for us?"

Rin looked abashed, like she wished she'd thought to ask that herself.

The Cordu looked thoughtful before giving them an abrupt nod. "I'm that way myself, and helping a couple of working students is something not against my creeds. I am called Kelshilrirth of the Vutrionic Clan. Or Kelshi, which is easier for the other races to pronounce."

"I'm Pax, and she's Rin," Pax answered when Kelshi looked at them expectantly.

"Those are very simple names," Kelshi said with a nod that left Pax unsure if he'd just insulted them.

Kelshi spun on his heels and hurried down the hallway, leaving Pax and Rin to exchange puzzled looks before moving after him.

From behind, Pax could indulge his curiosity further, trying to see his claws. How did he write? And the shifting scales running up the back of his neck made Pax think of his own, though his were nowhere near as fine and uniform. Something flickered on the back of Kelshi's head.

"Did you see that?" Pax whispered to Rin. "His hair just moved."

"It's not hair, dunder," she hissed back. "Just really thin scales that poke out like hair."

"Here we are," Kelshi said, slowing as he turned to gesture as the hallway opened up into a large foyer before continuing on the far side. "And yes, what you call my hair is actually made from scales, a trait of the Cordu, like our exceptional hearing."

Rin elbowed Pax, and he could feel his cheeks heat. "Sorry. You're just the first Cordu I've met."

"I have no issues with your comment," Kelshi said, his expression calm and difficult to read, "as it stems from natural curiosity instead of scorn or contempt."

Pax opened his mouth to reassure Kelshi, but the Cordu had already turned and walked into the spacious lobby, moving around a small seating area and toward the far wall where other students congregated.

"Here are the first-year paid assignments with hourly jobs on the left and one-time tasks on the right. The other boards to the right are for years two, three and four." Kelshi stopped a few feet from a large corkboard that ran from knee-level up to head height. Someone had attached small square papers in what had likely been an orderly arrangement before students began browsing and reattaching them haphazardly.

The multiple empty spots made Pax grind his teeth, irritated again that Incedis had kept him for so long. He wished, now, that he'd known enough to run over here first before visiting his advisor.

"So many are already gone," Rin echoed Pax's thoughts, her tone a mix of discouragement and anger.

"Only the ones that look the most valuable," Kelshi's voice interrupted, low and quiet for the first time, though Pax saw a couple of heads turn in their direction. "Not the ones that actually are."

He had both of their attention and seeing it, his lips parted into what probably passed for a smile, but looked more like a hungry predator to Pax. He forced himself not to take a step back.

Unfazed, Rin stepped in close. "Which ones should we take?"

"How much time are you planning to allocate daily to working?" Kelshi asked.

Rin looked back at Pax.

"As much as possible," Pax said quietly. "Not only do we need to earn our tuition, but we need enough Academy points to buy at least one uncommon spell scroll from the store."

What might have been a look of approval crossed Kelshi's face, and he stepped up to the board, removing squares of paper with no regard for the other students trying to decide. Someone complained, but a direct stare from the second-year Cordu made the student back down.

He finished quickly and stepped back, motioning for Rin and Pax to step aside with him for some privacy. "Here." He handed a small stack of cards to each of them. "Two tasks appropriate for your levels that will allow you to gain Academy Points while training your attributes. As well as these two regular shift assignments that will earn a reasonable rate of copper and provide extra income if you can endure the work and keep an eye out for opportunities. If you agree to take them, see the registrars over there and officially claim them." He waved a hand toward a long table with two clerks bent over their work and a line of students waiting in front of each one.

"Thanks," Pax said, eager to see what their new friend had chosen for them.

"**Academy Workshop Trainee**: Two-hour afternoon shift. MWF from 3pm - 5pm. Magical item preparation for Academy Workshop #3. Starting pay: 40 coppers and 1 Academy Point per hour. Complete 30 hours and earn approval from your supervisor to advance to Intern. Rewards for advancement are variable and based on performance."

"**Charity Clinic Trainee**: Two-hour evening shift TThS from 6pm - 8pm. Help healers at Salman Charity Clinic #9. Starting pay: 35 coppers and 1 Academy Point per hour. Complete 30 hours and earn approval from your supervisor to advance to Intern. Rewards for advancement are variable and based on performance."

"**Maintenance Trainee**: Within the next ten days, clear at least three blockages in the Academy sewage system that are causing trouble under the Air magic building. See maintenance office #2 for specific instructions. Pay: 20 coppers and 1 Academy Point per cleared blockage. Clear 21 blockages, or the equivalent, and earn approval from your supervisor to advance to Intern. Rewards for advancement are variable and based on performance."

"**Exterminator Trainee**: Within the next three days, report to the Academy kitchen head manager and kill the vermin assigned. Starting pay: Base of 15 coppers and 1 Academy Point for the session (2-hour minimum) with a bonus of 3 coppers per kill and 1 Academy Point for every 10 kills. Kill 100 vermin, or the equivalent, and earn approval from your supervisor to advance to Intern. Rewards for advancement are variable and based on performance."

By the time he looked up, Pax had more questions than answers. He couldn't help grinning at the wages offered, more coppers in a week than all his Vipers had ever had together. Though he frowned, trying to do the math to apply it to the impossible tuition goal. His tired brain couldn't figure it out and he left it until he had some quiet time in his room with a pencil and paper.

All Pax wanted was some hot food and his bed, but Rin had moved back up to the board, reaching for more cards. Kelshi turned from his perusal of the neighboring second-year jobs and moved toward her at the same time Pax did.

"What are you doing?" Pax leaned in close to whisper, seeing that she'd grabbed another two assignments.

"What I chose for you will already be a stretch for a new first-year to manage," Kelshi said as he stopped on her other side. "Be careful of underestimating the assignment difficulty and overestimating your abilities."

"I'm trying to find ones similar to ours for Amil, our friend. He's a power mage friend," Rin explained to Kelshi before aiming a disappointed look at Pax.

He flushed, knowing she was right. He should have been thinking of Amil himself.

Kelshi nodded. "Looking out for your wyer is admirable. Make sure he registers the assignments within the hour or you need to put them back on the board. And, as he is a power mage, I'd recommend at least one defense job and a shift on the enchanting line instead of the magical prep room."

Rin glanced down at the ones she'd selected and back up at the board, suddenly looking unsure.

"Here," Kelshi said abruptly, taking the cards out of her hands. "I'll extend my small favor to your wyermate." He hardly seemed to read the cards as he put the ones Rin had chosen back and pulled another four from the board.

"Clear away from the first-year board," a familiar, arrogant voice called from behind them, cutting through and silencing the hum of conversation in the room.

Pax stifled a groan as everyone turned to see who had made the loud demand. Sure enough, Galen Larhorn stood at the head of a group of obvious nobles, even though they wore the same uniform as the rest of the students. To Pax's dismay, the trim of the group was universally black and red threaded through Galen, the same as Amil's.

"Step back from the registrar, in case we need to choose from your selections for ourselves," Galen said, before moving aside and motioning for the group behind him to enter.

Pax expected the students around him to object to the heavy-handed bullying. But, to his surprise, they just obeyed, only a few grumbling quietly enough not to be singled out.

Pax looked up at Kelshi, sure the second-year wouldn't accept this kind of behavior from first-years. But the Cordu gave a regretful shrug before joining the others in stepping back from the boards.

"It's got to be Aymer Wynrel," Rin hissed, pulling at Pax, who'd frozen to stare at the whole spectacle. "The tall, gloomy-looking elf. I heard the heir to the Oakhouse Consortium and his twin sister were in our year."

Pax didn't know who she was talking about, but realized this was far outside his experience, and he should fall in with the others. He moved just a moment too late.

"Pax Vipersworn," Galen called out, drawing out the name as he stepped forward with a nasty smile on his face. "How nice to run into you again. I'm surprised you survived the Crucible, though I hear you have the least magic of any mage student in history. That's not surprising."

Pax met the striking green eyes of the noble boy as every eye turned to look at them.

OLD ENEMIES

"I DON'T WANT any trouble, Galen," Pax said, taking a step back and annoyed with himself for letting his tiredness dull his reactions. His street instincts to scatter and hide at the first sign of trouble should have kicked in much sooner.

Galen let out an ugly laugh, obviously enjoying holding center stage. "You can't even get that right, can you? Don't you know that trouble is how mages grow? Danger accelerates growth, right, Aymer?" He looked back for support from the group behind him, only to find the tall one in charge looking impatient.

"Let's just grab the best assignments, so we can get to dinner," Aymer snapped, striding toward the now-deserted first-year boards. "I've had enough of all the games today."

"Fine," Galen said with a quick nod of agreement before turning to glare at the first-years grouped up against the wall. His eyes narrowed, and his cheeks flushed with anger. "I'll just grab the assignments from these students while you check the board."

Aymer didn't answer. He and the rest of his group were already scanning the board. Pax noticed they weren't even glancing toward the more distasteful jobs that he and Rin had grabbed.

"Give me those." Galen snatched the cards out of the hands of a dwarven girl. "Hand them over. Hurry up."

Pax tried to push back into the group and tuck his cards behind his back, wondering where he could stash them. Sure, there were more cards with the harder work available, but he and Rin had chosen a set of three for some of them, so they could all work together. Who knew if they'd be able to get another matching set?

"Don't even think about putting those in your inventory," Galen growled, honing in on Pax.

Kicking himself for forgetting his new inventory was instant, Pax immediately made the cards disappear. "Sorry," he said, holding up his hands and plastering on the most innocent look he could manage. "I didn't choose any cards yet."

Galen growled, glancing between him and Rin, who was also holding up empty hands. Smart girl.

"I can help you read some assignments on the board, if that would help," Pax said, unable to help himself.

Rin's elbow in the ribs hurt, even as the stifled snickers made Pax grin. He knew he shouldn't antagonize the flick, but since all this had started, he'd found himself tired of always taking abuse from jerks.

Galen's fist moved so fast, Pax barely saw it. Pain exploded in his stomach as Galen's punch drove all the air from Pax's lungs in a single blow. His body crumpled around the heavy fist before he sagged back and fell to the ground, curled around his center. He couldn't even cry out, his lungs spasming in a demand for his core muscles to work and let him breathe again.

Pax felt Rin's arms sliding under his arms from behind, pulling him up. "Let me straighten you out, so you can breathe. Push in and out with your stomach to help things along," she whispered in his ear.

Pax's eyes watered, and a claustrophobic panic grew as his lungs still refused to inflate. He pushed past the pain and panic, focused on following Rin's instructions. Finally, he sucked in a small, but sweet breath.

Galen's laugh made Pax glare up at the boy's triumphant gaze. He'd expected more bluster and posturing, not the surprise punch. And how could the elven boy hit that hard and fast?

"Now, are you going to give me your cards, or do you need more encouragement?" He stepped closer, holding his hand out in a demanding gesture, arrogant in his assurance that Pax would comply.

For the briefest moment, Pax considered launching his own surprise attack. A head butt to the groin would be fast from his position, and devastating.

Rin's hand squeezed his shoulder in warning. Pax knew she was right. People easily ignored a noble punching a commoner in public. The commoner fighting back in front of noble witnesses? Not so much. They might all be wearing the same uniforms, but that didn't make them equals.

"Yes, I'm so sorry, Mage Galen," Pax said in a loud voice as he pushed himself to his feet and summoned his cards. "I'm not sure why you think Mage Wynrel wants my assignments to unblock the sewers and clean out basement vermin, but you know him best. Here. Please take them."

Galen's smirk vanished completely as his eyes widened, and he stepped back, waving off the cards Pax pushed toward him. "I didn't. He doesn't."

"Sewers, Galen? Really?" Aymer spoke with distaste as he turned and aimed an impatient glance over his shoulder.

"No, Aymer," Galen hurried toward his friends, his tone both apologetic and submissive. "I was just trying to—"

"Shut up and grab an assignment that requires noble training. They pay the most Academy Points. We left a couple for you to choose from."

"Please, Galen," Pax called out in his best submissive tone, unable to resist one more dig. "If you don't want the sewer or vermin jobs, I've got one for healing in a Salmon charity home. It pays an Academy Point, like you want."

Galen spun around and growled, "Shut up!"

"Of course," Pax said, ducking his head to hide his grin. "I was just trying to help."

"I might be interested," a soft voice spoke up from Aymer's group, drawing everyone's attention from the spectacle of Pax and Galen.

"Kali, no," Aymer said, turning to an elven girl who stood by his side.

"No, Aymer," Kali said, walking toward Pax. "It will allow me to train both my elemental control and healing."

"You're a power mage," Aymer hissed. "You can give up on the useless healing now."

She stopped and turned slowly. Pax was impressed with how much strength radiated from her, despite her smaller stature and lack of any anger. "I rather think if your life is on the line, you might prefer a healer with the strength of a power mage rather than a support mage?"

Aymer's jaw worked before his face relaxed into resignation. "Fine. Do what you want. You've always cared about others before the family. Why should anything change now?"

Kali had a touch of hurt in her eyes as she turned back toward Pax, but covered it up so quickly that Pax thought he might have imagined it.

"Here," he said respectfully as he handed her the card. She had faced down her entire group without hesitating. Pax had to admire that.

"Thank you," she said, looking down at the card. "It is admirable that you chose this assignment, not to mention the other more distasteful ones."

Rin made a surprised sound behind Pax, and he could feel the attention of the other first-years nearby.

Kali glanced once over her shoulder where the others in her group had already moved to the registration tables. "I have a feeling that the day will come," she said with a touch of resignation, "that we'll be fighting and dying on the walls together. When that happens, I hope to have someone by my side willing to do the hard and necessary work, not someone who relies on artifacts from their family to be strong and hit hard."

Pax nodded his thanks, not sure he deserved the compliment, but glad to know Galen wasn't that fast on his own.

"Thank you," Kali said as she handed his card back to him.

He tried to refuse, but she shook her head. "There are more of these still on the board. I'll just grab the same one you have."

"Why are you all even here?" Pax couldn't help asking. "You obviously don't need the copper."

She gave him a sharp look. "Oh," she said, face relaxing. "You really don't know. Everyone needs Academy Points. For enchanted equipment, better spells and especially the ranking board with its rewards."

Pax pursed his lips, noting even more important information he'd missed out on.

"Two pieces of advice, because I don't like how the odds are always stacked against your type," Kali leaned in and whispered. "Learn all you can as quickly as possible about how the academy works. And second, watch out for Galen. He might have harassed you for fun before, but tonight, you made him your enemy."

She'd turned on her heel and returned to the board before Pax could respond.

"Close your mouth," Rin said a bit sharply and scoffed. "*Our type.* I'm not sure I really want to spend our working shifts with a noble."

"She seems almost decent compared to the others," Pax mused. "For a noble 'crat."

"Whatever." Rin waved him off, cutting short any further words. "Tell me her being beautiful isn't messing with your opinion."

Pax flushed and tried to object. Rin just raised her brows, meeting his gaze.

"Fine," he said, too tired to deal with much more right now other than getting some food followed by sleep. "At least she's better than her brother or Galen."

Rin shook her head and pushed past him to the end of the line that had formed at the registration tables again now that the nobles had left.

32

CORNUCOPIA

Pax felt as if he had died and gone to heaven. His mouth watered, and his hands shook with eagerness, making his tray tremble as he and Rin moved closer to the buffet tables. Dishes steamed with an array of delicious aromas, set out on three long stone counters built along the far wall of the hall. A shimmer of heat under the pots of soup arrayed at the start of the food line made Pax momentarily curious what magic was being used to keep things hot.

And then they had reached the head of the line. He noticed Rin casting a surreptitious look at the students in front of him, too. Neither of them knew the appropriate etiquette here. Following the examples ahead of them, they each grabbed a bowl, plate and cup, as well as silverware and a cloth napkin.

Staring down at his tray, Pax hesitated for a moment, his previous life of only days ago in such stark contrast to what he saw now that he couldn't move. Food was meant to be shoved into the mouth as quickly as possible. End of story. What use did he have for all this equipment just to eat?

"Pax," Rin hissed, jarring him out of his daze. "Come on and get some food."

Seeing her standing in front of a colorful array of so many foods he didn't recognize, Pax couldn't help grinning. Maybe he'd be willing to let the noble flicks beat him daily and go into debt with the empire if it meant he got to spend the next year eating like this.

He maneuvered his way along the line, doing his best to try as many of the dishes as he could and despairing at how fast his plate filled up.

"Slow down, sir," a quiet voice said as Pax tried to squeeze one last roll thing between his roll and glass of juice. "You're welcome to come back through the line as often as you like."

Pax's head snapped up in surprise at the information. He saw a dwarven boy younger than him dressed in a crisp white uniform, standing poised with a pair of gleaming metal tongs at the last section of the food tables.

"Really?" he asked, unsure if he'd heard correctly. If they let hungry teens have unlimited food, maybe the steep tuition wasn't without cause.

The boy cracked a smile and nodded before turning serious again. "Would you like your beast meat, sir? Normally, first-years get theirs once a day at lunch, but your Crucible Day is different."

"Beast meat?" Pax asked, suddenly interested.

"Yes sir," the boy said, reaching with his tongs over a large array of small containers steaming with a variety of tidbits that gave off a tantalizing smell brimming with more power than the previous selection of food. "This is Level 2 Skrien leg, today's portion for a first-year air support mage."

The boy put a chunk of dark meat about as big as his thumb on his tray. Looking at it, Pax felt a bit let down.

"I know it doesn't look like much, sir," the boy hurried to reassure him. "But make sure to take small bites spread out through your meal. And if you have a meditation technique, you'll want to use it a bit afterwards. Got it?"

"Keep the line moving," a woman's voice barked out through the long window cut into the wall where refilled food dishes and emptied ones moved at a dizzying speed to and from the kitchen.

Pax realized he was attracting impatient glares from the students behind him and gave the boy a grateful nod. "Thank you. I'm Pax. What's your name?"

"Who cares?" a girl behind him said.

Pax gave her a sharp glare that made her flinch back. He turned back to the boy and waited.

The boy looked even more uncomfortable, but mumbled, "Krasig, sir."

"Well, thank you for the help, Krasig," Pax said and aimed a last annoyed look at the students behind him before turning to find somewhere to sit.

The delicious smells wafting up from his plate distracted him from his irritation. It was all he could do to keep from grabbing something off his plate and eating it right where he was standing.

"Pax, over here." Amil's deep voice penetrated the din of conversation and silverware that filled the eating hall.

Pax scanned the crowded tables made from solid, but well-worn, wood, lined with chairs full of busy students talking and eating. A quick glance at badges and uniform trim made him realize it wasn't as chaotic as it appeared at first glance. Similar years, elements and powers had grouped themselves together with very little intermixing.

At a back table far to the right, Pax saw Amil's bulky shape stand up and wave at him. He recognized Rin pulling out a chair next to his friend, and Pax's smile returned. Regardless of everything looming over him, he was a mage with two friends to watch his back and all the food he could eat.

It was something he'd have never dreamed was possible just a week ago. As he reached his table, he gave in and snatched a bite from the fluffy pastry on his tray that had been calling his name. He moaned in pleasure to find it contained a tart, fruit filling so tasty he didn't mind that it burned his tongue.

"Good, isn't it?" Amil asked around a mouthful of food, looking delirious with pleasure himself. "Wait until you take a bite of the beast meat."

Pax settled his tray and reached for the small bit of Skrien leg, as Krasig had called it.

"Fork," Rin hissed, giving him an elbow to the ribs.

Still enamored with the fruit-filled pastry, Pax didn't mind complying. He grabbed the fork and just treated it like a knife, spearing the beast meat and remembering at the last moment to take just a small bite before moving to other bites of deliciousness and shoveling them into his mouth with a wide grin on his face.

Just as he swallowed again, a sudden flush of eye-watering spice shot up the back of his throat and made his nose itch.

"Your first taste of beast meat?" a student across from Rin asked.

Coughing and blinking rapidly, Pax gave her a suspicious look, taking note of her wooden badge and the deep blue and black trim on her uniform. But instead of a mocking expression, she looked like she was trying to be helpful.

"She's alright," Amil jumped in to reassure Pax as soon as he finished swallowing. "Her advice helped me a couple of minutes ago when my flame kind of started spreading down my arm."

Both Pax and Rin shot alarmed looks at Amil. Pax could only imagine how much trouble his friend would be in if he started a fire in the crowded eating hall.

"The beast meat kind of supercharges your element, right, Tansa?" Amil hurried to explain. "But it's not too hard to control. Explain it to them, too, please?"

Tansa flushed a bit, but jumped right in. "If you don't have a meditation technique yet, just close your eyes for a second and try to spread the energy throughout your body. Kind of diluting it, you know? It strengthens the elements in your muscles and organs. Or at least that's what I've been told."

"Can anyone eat it?" Pax asked, visions of bringing some back home to his crew and boosting their strength.

"Not really." Tansa looked worried. "And don't eat any that isn't from your element, either. If you don't have a way to merge the energy with your body, it can hurt you. You'd need to get a mage of the correct element to help drain it off then."

Pax swallowed nervously. It was one thing to pretend to be an air mage, but another to eat something full of a bunch of air magic energy.

Under the guise of following Tansa's directions, he quickly closed his eyes and went searching for the energy he'd just ingested. He found a gust of something swirling out from his center, thin tendrils of energy flailing around and making his stomach churn uneasily.

Hoping it would work, Pax reached out to the energy, urging it to relax and dissipate into a cloud or mist, like he'd done in the past with the energy of his spark. It didn't respond at all.

The pressure in his stomach built, like the uncomfortable fullness of an enormous meal scarfed down after too many days of nothing. With one last idea, Pax reached for his spark and manipulated it into its cloud form before pushing it to blanket the roiling air energy at his center.

To his surprise, the cloud of his magic sucked at the air magic, engulfing it into a mix of both. Quickly, before he lost his concentration, he pushed at the combined magic to burst and spread out in all directions, hoping dilution would work like the new girl had said.

A rush of extra energy filled him wherever the cloud of dual magic touched. A few moments later, it seemed to run out of steam, leaving behind only the familiar energy of his eager spark.

He opened his eyes, surprised, only to see another notification blur past his sight to join the host of others flashing for attention at the bottom of his vision.

"See," Amil said with a grin as he elbowed Pax. "Told you it wasn't hard. It's a rush, though, isn't it?"

Pax smiled back and even thanked Tansa for her help. But as soon as he was able, he sent the rest of the Skrien leg into his inventory. He and his friends just didn't know enough, and they needed to step up their information gathering fast.

Just glad he'd avoided another pitfall, Pax focused on something both simple and enjoyable. He had an entire tray of new dishes to sample. He promised himself he'd look at all the notifications that had piled up . . . as soon as he finished eating.

NOTIFICATIONS!

AFTER AGREEING to meet his friends early, before breakfast, Pax finally staggered back to his basement dorm room, almost asleep on his feet. He found Dahni already in their room, changing into different clothes, his hair wet as he toweled it off.

Confused for a moment, Pax wondered how he'd gotten wet, since it wasn't raining outside, and he was an earth mage, not water. Seeing his look, Dahni looked hesitant.

"What?" Pax asked.

"I was going to offer you the quick tour that one of the second-years gave me before you got here. He started as a street kid like us and realizes there's a bunch of stuff about normal life we don't know." He shrugged. "But only if you want."

Pax glanced at his bed, where he'd been about to flop down and go to sleep. But if there was one thing this day had taught him, it was how woefully uninformed he was of important things everyone else knew.

Instead of feeling downtrodden, Pax drew on the hard core of resolve that had kept him alive on Thanhil's streets. He was going to figure out how this academy worked, and then he was going to beat it. "Thanks," he said, giving Dahni a grateful smile. "Show me."

It didn't take long. It turned out that among the clothing they'd been given was an extra outfit that was just for sleeping in. Also, the bathrooms contained showers that sprayed heated water down from above at the turn of a knob. Dahni explained that there was still a communal bathhouse for a true soaking, but that the shower allowed them to more easily remove the grime of the day.

This, combined with the sleep clothes, would keep their beds and linens relatively clean, though Dahni said any linens or clothing they put in the linen basket outside their door would be returned clean by evening.

All the obsession with cleanliness had made the tour tedious, with one exception. Opposite the bathrooms at the end of the hall were practice rooms. Four of them. And though small, they were specially reinforced against each of the elements, with well-used practice dummies similarly protected.

Dahni had pointed out an hourly sign-up sheet outside the door that aided in scheduling future practice, but explained the second-year said it was only really busy in the evenings.

Finally, clad in his own set of sleep clothes, Pax flopped into his bed, having barely enough energy to pull his covers over him. He distantly worried that his damp hair might damage the amazing pillow, as the fresh scent of the bed linens reminded him of the cleansing breeze after a storm. With his body clean and tingling from the harsh soap, he decided that maybe the whole obsession with cleanliness wasn't half bad after all.

Sighing tiredly, Pax expected to be asleep in moments. Except, the flashing notifications he'd ignored all day were extremely bright against the darkness of his closed eyes.

It was the first time he'd felt he had a break to look at them. Besides, Pax couldn't help a sudden flush of excitement as he wondered what his first day at the academy had done for him.

Preparing himself for an inundation, he mentally tapped the stack of urgent flashes. He almost jerked back into the pillow as a wall of text scrolled past his eyes.

When it finally stopped, he had to go through it again, more slowly this time, so he didn't miss anything.

He felt a thrill at the new points he'd earned in Strength, Endurance and Agility, but fervently hoped he wouldn't have to resort to being tortured again to improve them further. The increases also explained how he'd been able to finish a full day of activity instead of simply collapsing to recover after the Crucible and being healed.

Pax smiled at the familiar increases to Identify when he remembered how he'd earned those. Sure, Mage Zayne had healed him, but he couldn't deny the pleasure he had taken in tweaking the Crucible mages who'd treated him as if he were nothing.

Another smattering of notifications let him know both his Mana Manipulation and Sight had increased. He wouldn't be forgetting the torture in the Crucible soon and knew exactly where the points had come from. The increases in Sight would be from probing the structure of the snake-like bindings, and the Manipulation points had to be from the new shapes he'd forced his spark to take and breaking the sliver of a hole he'd used to breathe at the end.

Done with the familiar notifications, Pax just stared at the new ones. He had to reread them twice as he tried to understand exactly what they meant. Could they really mean what he thought they did?

～

*NEW PATH of Elemental Understanding Unlocked: **Flame***
Congratulations. You have used your light magic to contemplate the structure and element of flame in contact with your body. Continue to ponder on its characteristics and attributes, its strengths and weaknesses to reach a more complete understanding. Each level will open an additional spell slot.

*INCREASED UNDERSTANDING OF **FLAME**: +3. Level 1 - 3/100*

. . .

New Path of Elemental Understanding Unlocked: **Air**

Congratulations. You have used your light magic to contemplate the structure and element of air in contact with your body. Continue to ponder on its characteristics and attributes, its strengths and weaknesses to reach a more complete understanding. Each level will open an additional spell slot.

New Path of Elemental Understanding Unlocked: **Water**

Congratulations. You have used your light magic to contemplate the structure and element of water in contact with your body. Continue to ponder on its characteristics and attributes, its strengths and weaknesses to reach a more complete understanding. Each level will open an additional spell slot.

New Path of Elemental Understanding Unlocked: **Earth**

Congratulations. You have used your light magic to contemplate the structure and element of earth in contact with your body. Continue to ponder on its characteristics and attributes, its strengths and weaknesses to reach a more complete understanding. Each level will open an additional spell slot.

Increased understanding of **Flame:** *+1. Level 1 - 4/100*
   Increased understanding of **Air:** *+2. Level 1 - 2/100*
   Increased understanding of **Water:** *+2. Level 1 - 2/100*
   Increased understanding of **Earth:** *+2. Level 1 - 2/100*
   Increased understanding of **Air:** *+1. Level 1 - 3/100*
   Increased understanding of **Flame:** *+5. Level 1 - 9/100*

Pax's pulse raced as he read over the notifications one more time. Had he really unlocked all four standard elements in the Crucible? But what did it mean by understanding? And in contact with his body? Did that mean he needed to get burned a bunch more to reach a level 1 understanding?

He shuddered at the memories from the Crucible. But at the same time, excitement raced through him at the possibility that he could learn more types of spells. *Each level will open an additional spell slot.* Visions of throwing a fireball in Galen's face made him grin in excitement. He could see all the students cheering him on.

The scene materialized in his mind, and Pax savored the imaginary spectacle. He added in an earth spell that opened a hole under the bully's feet, followed by a deluge of water from above that left the 'crat choking and sputtering.

"What are you laughing about over there?" Dahni's quiet question pulled Pax out of his thoughts.

"Just imagining getting even with a 'crat student who has made it his mission to ruin my life."

"Oh," Dahni said, sounding doubtful. "Isn't it better to avoid people like that?"

"Yeah," Pax admitted with a sigh. "But it's really nice to imagine throwing a fireball at the flick."

"As long as you keep it to your imagination," Dahni said. "The only way to handle people like that is to avoid them or kill them."

Pax turned a surprised gaze toward his roommate, who was looking back at him, face serious in the dim light.

"What?" Dahni asked. "Being pragmatic has saved my life a lot more than trying to pretend the truth is prettier than it is. Tell me I'm wrong."

Pax nodded slowly, seeing his roommate in a new light.

"Besides," Dahni said with a barely visible frown. "Aren't you an air mage, not flame?"

Pax froze, his scene of revenge against Galen suddenly popped by reality. He was a light mage masquerading as an air mage. Of course, he couldn't just flaunt a bunch of elemental spells when anything hinting at the combination of different elements would get him kicked out, or worse. His fantasy of suddenly becoming the most powerful first-year student mage was just that, a fantasy.

A sudden stab of nerves replaced his earlier glee. How was he supposed to improve any of his new magic options while under the eyes of instructors all day? He suppressed a groan before answering Dahni with something he hoped sounded reasonable. "Um, I just always fantasized about getting flame instead of air."

"Yeah," Dahni said with his own sigh. "I like earth and all, but probably wouldn't have picked it first either. But hey, magic is magic, right? Much better than awakening as a laborer."

"Exactly," Pax answered, relieved that he hadn't aroused any suspicions. "Thanks for the help tonight. Good night."

"No problem. Good night," Dahni said before letting out a wide yawn that Pax couldn't help but copy. "We street kids gotta watch out for each other," Dahni added as he laid back and closed his eyes. "Who else do we have?"

"Truth," Pax agreed, lying back and closing his eyes too.

But his mind was still busy, running through how to keep from being caught practicing his new skills. He couldn't risk drawing the attention of the powers that be. Whatever they did to him, it would be bad. A street kid with access to all four elements plus a new one? Yeah, right. He'd disappear as soon as even a hint came to light.

He'd have to train in secret. But once he had all three light spells, along with four more elemental ones . . .

A feral grin returned as Pax envisioned possible plans. His new abilities might be dangerous to him if discovered, but they were also a real chance to become so powerful no one could control him or the people he cared about ever again.

Starting tomorrow, he was going to push the limits of his new options and grab for power with both hands.

Determination filling him, he closed his eyes to sleep before remembering that he had forgotten to check the final tally in his menu. A sleepy scan made him smile at the changes.

∾

NAME: *Pax Vipersworn*

Race: Mixed Human (monster-touched)

Age: 16

Bound Location: Shieldwall Mage Academy (provisional monthly)

Class: Mage

Element: Light (Hidden)

Specialization: none

Paths of Understanding:

Flame: Level 1 - 9/100

Air: Level 1 - 3/100

Water: Level 1 - 2/100

Earth: Level 1 - 2/100

Level: *1*

Mage Leveling Points: *0/5*

Health: *34/34 (+3)*

Mana: *24/24*

Attributes:

Strength: 4 (+1)

Agility: 8 (+1)

Endurance: 5 (+1)

Intelligence: 7

Insight: 7

Charisma: 3

Skills:

General Active:

Identify Level 1 (Common) - 44/100 (+6)

General Passive:

Skinning Level 1 (Common) - 18/100

Butchering Level 1 (Common) - 22/100

Mage:

Light Mana Manipulation Level 1 (Epic) - 20/100 (+12)

Light Mana Sight Level 1 (Rare) - 12/100 (+3)

Spells:

Light (1/3):

Haste Level 1 (Common) - 0/100

Inventory: *15/20 available.*

Assignments:
Academy Workshop Trainee
0/30 hours
0/1 Supervisor approval
Charity Clinic Trainee
0/30 hours
0/1 Supervisor approval
Maintenance Trainee
0/21 Cleared blockages
0/1 Supervisor approval
Exterminator Trainee
0/100 Vermin killed
0/1 Supervisor approval
Misc.: none

IT HAD BEEN incredible progress for a single day. Even the extra three inventory slots filled with food and drink reassured him, adding a sense of security that no magic spell ever could. The one holding the fruit pastries he loved let him start his sleep with pleasant dreams.

He'd only been here a day. Tomorrow would be even better.

Just as his thoughts drifted, a stab of alarm swept away his drowsiness, and he opened his menu again. He hurried to mark everything to do with his light magic, including the mana skills, to be hidden from anyone casting Identify on him.

A cold sweat popped on his brow as he imagined what would have happened if a higher-level mage with some special ability had taken the time to focus on him. Sure, the clerk at the Awakening had told him he had a one-month protection from detailed Identify, but Pax knew better than to rely on something like that.

Besides, he didn't have to rely on that with his perks from the binding altar. From now on, he would hide any unusual bonuses he gained as soon as possible.

Wide awake now, Pax needed something to help calm and anchor him. Glancing over to confirm Dahni's eyes were closed, he summoned the only two personal items he still owned, the ring his mother had given him and the medallion from his brother. Rubbing the smooth surface of the ring, he was glad it didn't look valuable enough for the guards to have confiscated.

The metal looked like old bronze, but mixed with some streaks of black and gray that just made it look dirty. But he'd never been able to scratch it, despite how worn the coloring made it look. Besides, it was completely plain, without a single embellishment, except for the unreadable symbols stamped along the inside. Pax had memorized them after so long, but despite keeping an eye out, never seen them anywhere else. Maybe someday.

For now, he just let his fingers slip in comforting circles around the ring as it warmed in his hand. Warmth. A weary smile emerged on his face. His mother had always had a moment to wrap him up in a hug, her love warm and comforting. A pang of loss intruded, and he sent the ring back to his inventory, focusing on his brother's medallion instead. Titus had been full of strength and defiance, which Pax suspected would come in much handier at the academy than his mother's love.

The medallion was made from cheap pewter, stamped with an interesting symbol made of lines and curves entwined together in an unbroken pattern. In letters mostly worn, "Salvation through Innovation" had been stamped around the edges of the medallion. It had taken Pax a long time to read the long words, and he still didn't know what they meant. But knowing Titus, it would be something rebellious, anything that upset the status quo.

A sudden thought made him focus on the medallion and before he could think better of it, he cast Identify.

∾

Item: Pewter medallion
   Rarity: Common
   This medallion is made of pewter, approximately two inches in diameter,

with an unknown design etched into the surface. It appears to have been hand-carved and adorned with a leather cord for wearing.

~

DISAPPOINTED, Pax sagged back into his bed, realizing that the first level of Identify wouldn't tell him much, even if his brother's medallion had some hidden secret. And he hadn't even earned a point in the skill. Giving it some thought, he realized it made sense. It would have been quite the exploit, if he could have walked around using Identify on common household items every time he had enough mana.

And in the end, it was a good thing. If Identify had shown some value, the Thanhil guards would surely have taken it. Still, Pax couldn't resist swapping the medallion out for his mother's ring and trying again.

~

ITEM: *Simple Ring*
  Rarity: Common
  This ring is made from a mix of unknown metals, approximately three-quarters of an inch in diameter, with an unknown design etched into the inner surface. It is heavily worn and old.

~

PAX SAGGED BACK into his bed and pressed the ring to his heart for a moment before sending it back to his inventory. Maybe once he had Identify leveled higher, he'd be able to learn more.

Closing his eyes, he let himself sink into happier times with his family before the world tore them apart. Thoughts of family entwined with magic spells and the taste of fruit pastries. Together, they kept the nightmares at bay as he fell asleep.

ECCENTRIC INSTRUCTOR

"COME IN. Be seated. We have a lot to cover." A woman's demanding voice drifted out of the propped-open classroom door as Pax ran down the hallway. His backpack was much heavier with the Beast Compendium from his last class. He'd gotten turned around multiple times on the long trek from his Beast Identification class on the far side of campus, close to the academy's section of the wall. Finally, he'd asked for directions and took off running to make it. He really needed to memorize the campus map.

Breathing hard, Pax was the last one to step through the door of the large classroom for his Meditative Healing class, just behind another boy who'd been in his Beast class, too.

Pax stopped and stared when he didn't see the rows of chairs or desks he expected. Instead, the students were all sitting, scattered, on a polished wooden floor, some shifting in discomfort. Up front, a harried-looking elven woman stood looking at them, dressed in, of all things, leather armor over loose linen clothes. Her skin was darkened by the sun, which only made the ropy scar running down from below her ear and disappearing beneath her collar much more obvious. She looked nothing like he'd expected a meditation or healing instructor to.

Behind her, a man stood holding a stack of notebooks, poised at attention with his hair carefully combed and, overall, looking much more put together than the woman who seemed to be in charge.

Behind them, and along the walls, stood multiple tables draped in white cloth over an assortment of strange shapes. The shrouded forms looked somewhat ominous. One even looked a bit like a body. A limbless one. Pax shuddered and told himself to stop imagining things.

"Shut the door behind you and take a seat," the teacher ordered, her words sharp and expecting obedience.

Jarred into motion, Pax pulled the door shut before scanning the other students for Amil, who should be in this class with him. To his relief, he saw his friend on the far left, doing his best to get Pax's attention without drawing the teacher's.

"Thanks for saving me a spot," Pax said quietly as he lowered himself to the floor, taking off his backpack with a quiet grunt of relief.

"No problem," Amil said, looking so excited he might burst before leaning closer and whispering in a rapid torrent. "I hit my target with Flame Blast. Actually hit it. And only two other powers did it with their spells. That earned me an academy point for third place in class. The instructor said I'm doing really well. Really well, Pax. As a mage!"

Pax gave his friend a punch to the shoulder in congratulation, grin wide and giving no hint of worry about how he himself would perform when he got to Basic Spells today. And he hadn't come close to a top spot for points in his beast class.

Amil flushed with pride at Pax's recognition, so he couldn't help but push away his own doubts and be happy for his friend.

"Settle down. Quiet," their teacher said from the front, silencing any remaining whispers. "Welcome to Meditative Healing. My name is Mage Liara Lorkranna. Yes, my parents enjoy alliterations. You may address me as Mage, teacher, or Mage Lorkranna if you're feeling formal. My element is air."

With a shocking suddenness, she waved her hands and a veritable tornado exploded underneath her and lifted her three feet in the air without even disturbing her hair. As fast as she'd summoned the power, she dismissed it, sinking back to the floor with perfect control.

"Just a brief demonstration for those of you who think meditation isn't necessary." She stopped and slowly enunciated each word. "You'll never reach your full power without it."

Many of the students just stared at her in open-mouthed astonishment. Pax was pretty sure he wasn't the only one suddenly reevaluating his opinion of the class.

"Good," she said with pleased satisfaction. "Now, your starting goals for this class are to unlock and then improve elemental healing, elemental manipulation and elemental meditation." Mage Lorkranna held up one finger, ticking off a list. "To do this, you will first gain a basic understanding of anatomy and, therefore, your own bodies. Second, you will experiment with various meditation techniques until you find one that fits you. This will help you gain more control." Another finger. "And third, you'll learn to manipulate your element within and close to your body without the aid of spells. Understand?"

Before anyone could answer, she held up another finger. "Oh, and finally, Crux here will cut each of you at the beginning of every class, with the goal of healing the minor injury by the end of class. First one to do it gets a prize. Any questions?"

"Cut?" Amil whispered to Pax as most of the students just stared at the crazy teacher.

"Excellent." She clapped her hands and turned to the man behind her. "Crux, we're ready to start. Start cutting them while I begin the anatomy lesson."

That got a reaction. A collective gasp ran through the group while those closest to the front scooted back. Pax was just glad he and Amil were in the back.

"Excuse me, Mage Lorkranna," a stern voice interrupted, with only a slight, underlying quaver. "I don't think the academy allows instructors to injure students on purpose."

Lorkranna turned back and met the eyes of the girl who'd objected. The student straightened her already perfect posture and did her best not to quail under the teacher's glare.

"Miss—?"

Crux leaned in and whispered in Lorkranna's ear.

"—Gedoss. Do you realize where you are? What is happening every night on walls across the empire? The carnage at our tower ring that shields us all from the true horrors?" The look on Lorkranna's face was impatient with an underlying turmoil that Pax recognized. Violence always left a mark.

"Uh—" the girl stammered, glancing at the students around her for support.

Some of them were stirring, even surreptitiously gathering their book bags and casting glances back toward the door.

"Oh, for Vitur's sake," Lorkranna spat out, charging back toward the students as her hands moved skillfully to the buckles along the side of her cuirass. "I thought you were training to be mages. You know, powerful fighters able to go toe-to-toe with vicious beasts on the empire's walls." She jerked the cuirass off her head and tossed it in Crux's direction.

The man moved silently, making the catch of the awkward piece of armor look easy.

"So, you're all scared about a little test cut while sitting here safe in class," she ranted, her fingers undoing the ties at her side that kept the two crossed sections of her linen top closed.

Pax wasn't the only one staring in shock. Was she really going to? She did.

Grabbing either side of her shirt, she jerked the front open, exposing herself to the class.

Amil's gasp mixed with everyone else's as they stared at their instructor's whipcord, lean torso. The chest band that protected her modesty might have otherwise caught every boy in the room's attention.

If not for the scars.

The one visible on her neck was just the thin tip of a central scar, a healed diagonal wound that had ripped from her right shoulder down and across to the opposite hip. As thick as three fingers at the center, it was accompanied by matching ones to either side that, though long healed, looked just as grotesque. Something massive with three claws had almost torn her body in two.

"Now that's a cut, students," she said into the gaping silence. "Three of them all at once. Don't worry, though. Yours won't be quite this deep."

Pax gaped at her. Had she just made a joke?

Done with her point, Lorkranna pulled her clothing back together, thrusting an impatient hand out for Crux to hand back her cuirass. "We'll wait until at least next week for something like that."

Pax couldn't help the snicker that slipped out at the unexpected macabre humor. Her eyes shot to him, and he went still, wondering if he was imagining a connection. She was no pampered 'crat and, more than anything, he wanted to learn to wield power as easily as she did. Despite how strange her teaching methods were, she was right. There would be a lot more violence in their futures than a simple cut.

A few nervous chuckles joined in, but Mage Lorkranna had already turned back to Crux for an item that she showed to the students.

"A multipurpose air blade," she announced, holding it aloft. It looked more like a thick writing utensil, but with a small core slotted in one end and a narrow tip at the other. "Crux will cut you like this." Without a single sign that it hurt, she drew the tool across the back of her other forearm.

Blood welled immediately.

"And you'll heal it like this." In front of their rapt attention, the cut sealed, almost as if time had reversed itself. She held her arm out to Crux, who had a damp cloth ready to wipe it clean.

Holding her forearm up to the class, the only sign of the cut was a pink line, so thin, Pax wasn't sure it was even there.

"Now tell me that skill won't be valuable not only when you reach the walls, but how about today, when you cut yourself during a stumble in conditioning class?"

That got a few excited murmurs, and the students who had been looking to escape were suddenly leaning forward with interest.

"Didn't anyone tell you why there is a half hour between your classes?" she asked, continuing without waiting for an answer. "That's to heal up, so you're not too broken for the next class. By the end of my class this term, you'll be able to heal any minor injuries in that amount of time. Understand?"

Heads bobbed in reflexive agreement. Pax was already calculating how much faster her healing ability was compared to the paltry amount of health he regained in a day. Hopefully, once he improved his attributes, that would improve, too.

"Your empire and your people don't have time for injuries, for slacking, for recovering in bed. We'd throw you on the walls today if we could do it without getting all of you killed. That's how bad it is out there!"

With a last glance across the students that seemed to pin each under her glare, Lorkranna turned and stalked back to the table behind her. She pulled off the sheet with a dramatic flair and turned back to the students with a big smile.

It was a body.

FREDDY

THE BODY WAS SO LIFELIKE and grotesque, it made Pax suck in a startled breath. He heard gasps nearby and was glad not to be the only one taken by surprise. Once the shock wore off, it was obviously not a real body, but it still looked very creepy.

Half the face was gone, revealing bone and gaping sockets that would definitely look better covered up. The arms and legs were also missing, leaving a life-sized torso mounted to a pedestal on the table where Mage Lorkranna patted it with a proud smile. Pax still couldn't get over how realistic it looked and almost expected to see blood dripping from the amputated limbs.

"Class, say hi to Freddy," Mage Lorkranna said in an almost cheerful tone. She reached for a series of latches fastened along the side of the dummy's rib cage and with a move eerily similar to her earlier disrobing, she removed the flesh-colored panel from the front of poor Freddy.

"Freddy is the product of master crafters who have made him as accurate and life-like as possible with one goal in mind." She smiled at the class as Pax stared in fascination at what had been revealed. "By understanding his body, you'll be able to understand and heal your own and others under your care. This knowledge will also aid you as you learn control over your elements and use them to strengthen your muscles and organs."

Amil made a gagging sound next to him as Lorkranna reached into Freddy's chest and pulled out two elongated, triangular structures with rounded corners that had been painted a mottled pink. Holding one up in each hand, she continued.

"These are your lungs. You use them to breathe. We only have time for a quick run-through of the major organs today since everyone also needs to leave class today with a good meditation technique, so you won't bleed all over the place every class period. For today, just focus on moving your element to the wound as best you can and see what happens. Now, pay attention."

She proceeded to pull out various strangely-shaped objects, slowly emptying Freddy's chest cavity while Crux moved quietly among the students leaving blood and flinches behind him.

Pax barely noticed when it was his turn, ignoring the minor cut in favor of studying a large bundle of flexible tubing that Lorkranna explained would absorb the substances necessary for life from food. The intestines, she called them. A stab or arrow that hit the organ would result in a wound that would fester if not healed quickly.

All too soon, the anatomy lesson was over, and Lorkranna asked for a volunteer to help her put Freddy back together while the others spaced themselves out for the start of their meditation lesson.

"I will, Mage Lorkranna," Pax called out, already on his feet and moving forward before anyone else could respond.

She eyed him for a minute before giving him a curt nod and motioning him forward.

"Pay attention to the names and functions of each organ as we put Freddy back together, class," she said before turning back to the now empty torso of the life-like dummy. She proceeded to hand Pax each organ and indicate where he should place it.

It was a complex puzzle and more than once she had to help him wedge some of the fabricated organs into tight spaces where a handful had to be placed together perfectly for them to fit.

Like anyone, he'd heard of his stomach and heart, but a liver or spleen? And the mass of red and blue ropey snake-looking things that were called arteries and veins. Who knew the path of blood in the body was so complicated.

By the time he helped the mage fasten the bony plate of ribs and plate of fake skin over the front of Freddy, Pax's head was spinning with new information. He'd been flooded with so many new concepts in such a short amount of time, it felt as if it would explode. He forced himself to pull it all together, doing his best to organize it visually and conceptually. A pulse of energy pushed through the mass of information, aiding him and making many of the difficult concepts suddenly clearer. He smiled as a notification blinked in his lower vision. That had to be a point in Intelligence.

"Pay attention," Mage Lorkranna said with another clap of her hands.

Pax hurried back to the empty spot Amil had saved for him as everyone stilled and waited for the next surprise their eccentric teacher would throw at them.

"Don't worry. This next part will help you consolidate everything you've learned today and hopefully leave you in a calm and confident state for your next class."

Someone nearby scoffed in disbelief which made Pax stifle a grin. The class was growing on him.

"Meditation is crucial for your development as a mage. Ignore my advice at your own peril." She paused to aim a serious look across all the students before continuing. "I will teach you four basic methods. You will try each of them for five minutes and then spend the little bit left of class attempting to use the one you choose to fix your minor injury. Ready?"

Everyone nodded, though some were a bit reluctant. Pax could empathize. Despite how fascinating Mage Lorkranna's class had been, he couldn't help the low thrum of excitement he felt for his next class, Basic Spells.

"I will teach you two simple breathing meditations and two focus ones. The first breathing one uses a linear, in-and-out pattern where you focus on breathing in the good and breathing out the bad. The second uses a circular pattern pulling and concentrating the good inside you while the things you don't want are expelled with an outward spiral."

A hand shot up near the front. Mage Lorkranna ignored it.

"The first focus method is external. Crux will distribute and light candles so you'll be ready when we get to this one. You'll keep your eyes open and focus on the flame until your eyes water, learning to let go of all distracting thoughts and develop a singular focus. This is often a favorite of power mages." Her eyes lost their focus with what looked like painful memories. "It's easy to get distracted and lose control of your spell in the middle of the chaos of battle."

Pax couldn't help but feel a bit of the chill of past battles enter the room.

Crux gave a quiet cough behind her when the silence dragged on, and students shifted uncomfortably.

"Yes," Mage Lorkranna said, clearing her throat. "And the final focus technique is to focus inward. You pick something simple, similar to a candle flame to focus on to the exclusion of everything else. Some examples are a gold coin, an apple, or a blade of grass. Avoid using something as complex as a person's face for now and choose a single-colored simple object. If none of these work for you, please see me after class and I have a couple of others you can try. Alright, everyone ready? Close your eyes."

Pax did so, though he couldn't help the bit of nerves that moved through him at not being able to keep an eye on his unpredictable teacher.

The last half of class passed in a blur and none of the meditation techniques did much more than relax him until they got to the internal focus one. After thinking of things as simple as coins or pieces of fruit, Pax took a risk and decided to try using his spark as his focus. It was small and, to his mental eyes, glowed with a mono-chrome bright energy.

It only took a few breaths before he got a measurable response, his spark pulsing and growing just a bit in size. Pax was so surprised he almost lost control of the feeling, but just managed to keep his focus on the spark and pushed all intruding thoughts far enough away that they didn't interfere.

It was the first time he'd really examined the little ball of energy that had been his only steady companion since childhood. Focusing in on it, he saw it wasn't truly a single color as he'd always thought.

It reminded him of a violent stormy sky he'd stared up at, so many shades of gray twisted together in a roiling energy, moments from exploding. This was a complex mix of whites and off-whites, some blinding shades and others soothing. The longer he focused, the more he felt his connection and understanding of his magic grow. And were those other shades of color he saw?

Keeping his breathing even, Pax slowly pushed his focus closer, not wanting to disturb the careful balance he'd achieved.

There.

The blinding, swirling energy of his spark was so bright, it was hard to see details, but the longer he allowed his mental vision to adjust, the more details emerged. After another few moments, he was sure. The smallest tendrils of color appeared as quick dips and swoops among the white, appearing and then gone so fast, it was hard to follow them. Crimson, walnut brown, and traces of indigo.

His pulse quickened as he realized the implications of finding traces of three other elements in the energy of his spark. Holding onto the calm of his trance, he kept up his scrutiny, knowing, or hoping to find the fourth. The icy blue was hard to distinguish from the bright white of his light magic, but he finally caught the barest glimpse of it before it dove back into the small ball of energy. He barely held onto his control, wanting to cry out in celebration.

The new path of understanding in his menu had made it clear he had somehow activated something with the other elements, but it was still hard to believe.

A mage had one element. One. It was a fact that no one ever questioned. How could he not only have an unheard of one like light, but now access to all four of the normal ones?

But now, confirming the entries in his menu, he watched the four fleeting colors of magic, though weak, entwined with the light magic of his spark.

Pax still had a hard time believing it. He had five magic elements!

THE COMPLEXITIES OF AIR

Mage Skill Unlocked: Elemental Meditation Level 1
   This common skill aids mages in the mental aspects of learning to wield magic. The following can improve with diligent practice: understanding of magic flow within their bodies, consolidation of new learning to higher levels, greater control and an increase in the power of elemental manipulation and spells. This skill is crucial for every well-rounded mage and will unlock more specific paths as a mage specializes.

*Skill Boost: +3 to **Elemental Meditation** Level 1 - 3/100*

*Skill Boost: +2 to **Mana Sight** Level 1 - 14/100*

*Improvement to your Path of Understanding **Flame:** +2 Level 1 - 11/100*

*Improvement to your Path of Understanding **Earth:** +2 Level 1 - 4/100*

. . .

*IMPROVEMENT to your Path of Understanding **Water:** +2 Level 1 - 4/100*

*IMPROVEMENT to your Path of Understanding **Air:** +2 Level 1 - 5/100*

*CONGRATULATIONS! You have increased **Intelligence** from 7 to 8*

JOGGING DOWN THE SLATE PATH, Pax's step stumbled a bit as he did his best to read his new notifications without slowing. It was a bit of a challenge to split his focus between the semi-transparent words and the path ahead of him. But he'd learned his lesson about ignoring the notifications for too long, especially after the unusual things he'd seen during his meditation.

His mouth moved as he reread the words of his new skill. A wide grin spread across his face as he felt the extensive collection of new knowledge settle more comfortably in his mind from both the anatomy and meditation he'd learned. Even the small glimpse of the four elements inside his spark had boosted his understanding by a couple of points.

Mage Lorkranna had let any students who wanted to stay through part of the break continue their meditating. Crux had tapped him on the shoulder after what seemed like a minute or two later to tell him he only had ten minutes left to get to his next class. As he'd left, Lorkranna had even mentioned that if he continued to be so diligent, he might make it into the top three to earn a few academy points at the end of class.

Pax's steps slowed as other paths joined his to make a much wider one ending at two large iron gates up ahead. They stood open, an entrance in the man-high wall that extended many yards to either side.

They were on the far west side of campus, past most of the class-rooms and office buildings, and not too far from one of their neighbors, the warrior academy. From what Rin had said this morning during their info-sharing session before breakfast, the two academies shared the arena complex here, having built it to straddle the border between the two properties and allowing them to split both the use and maintenance.

Pax joined the growing group of students pouring through the gates and soon found himself in a central courtyard with an array of more gates set into the circular wall of dark stone enclosing the busy, teeming space.

"First-year?" a voice behind him asked, making Pax realize that he'd just stopped in the middle of the mayhem and had been staring. "Find out which arena your class is in at the posted board over there."

The student, a third-year based on his silver badge, pointed toward large sheets of paper posted neatly on an enormous board affixed to a wall on the far left. Before Pax could thank him, he disappeared back into the crowd.

By the time Pax found he'd been assigned to arena seven for his Basic Spells class, the crowd had thinned out significantly, making him hustle, so he wasn't late.

"Welcome to Basic Spells for Air Mages," bellowed a bear of a man who was either pure dwarf or close to it. "My name is Mage Gray-brew, and this is the class you've been waiting your whole lives for. I'm going to finally teach you how to do magic."

That got a bit of a cheer from the students arrayed on the grass in front of him, while Pax froze in recognition of the name. His hasty use of Identify during the Crucible had given him the names of the mages running it, and Graybrew had been the air mage.

Pax stifled a groan, remembering the man's disparaging comments about Pax's lackluster amount of air magic. If anyone was going to notice something wrong with Pax, it would be this teacher. He glanced around the arena, looking for suitable spots to stay in the background.

Arena seven seemed small to be called an arena, the grassy space the size of a small meadow surrounded by a wall made of more of the dark stone. Only a few benches sat along one side, empty now. A sheltered structure in the corner looked like it might be for storing gear. It was obviously a place to train, not compete.

"The goal for this week is to learn to manifest your element, if you haven't already done so," Graybrew continued. "If you have, then we'll work on your focus and control."

Pax swallowed nervously, hoping he could keep up the pretense that he was too weak to manifest his air yet. Around him, a few of the power mages groaned, which made Graybrew wave a hand and smile.

"Don't worry. During the second half of class, we will have you use your first spell. Your advisor should have helped you select at least one so far that fits your preferred build. Remember that you'll need your second spell by the end of this month and all three before we all head out for the purge in just over two and a half months' time.

He'd mentioned the purge again. With a quick glance around, Pax saw that no one else looked confused by the reference. He clenched his jaw, hating how ignorant he was. Hopefully, by pooling their knowledge together, he, Rin and Amil could catch up fast.

"You'll practice your offensive spells against the dummies we have stored in the shed. My assistants will help by starting with low-level attacks for those who need to practice defensive spells."

Eager smiles appeared again.

"Finally, we will work with our partner class of first-year warrior students every Wednesday, occasionally joined by a crafting student or two who are interested in battle teams. This will be good practice for your own future team, which you'll also need to have joined in time for the purge."

Students glanced around, evaluating their fellows. Some looked arrogant in their strength, and others looked like the kids who always got picked last and hoped someone would invite them to join.

"I'd advise you to work hard in and out of class," Graybrew admonished them. "There is no slow buildup here. Sparring bouts are Friday and like all instructors, I'll be awarding Academy Points every class period to the top three students."

That got a reaction. Some of the power mages students looking smug, while other students looked surprised.

"But—" one of the support mages raised his hand.

"Don't worry," Mage Graybrew said with an impatient wave. "I take into account the differences between power and support mages and award accordingly. With enough hard work and skill, everyone has an equal shot. Now, we'll separate into two power groups and two support groups and spread out into the four corners of our practice space. My assistant will help you get organized. Get to work!"

The students shifted and looked around. Pax was careful to stay out of Graybrew's line of sight.

The four assistants had spread out to each of the corners of the training yard, two with white in their trim and two with black. Pax picked the support mage with the fewest people heading his way and quickly joined a few students moving toward him.

When Pax drew closer, he couldn't help staring at the assistant teacher's angular features and bony figure that towered a good foot above the other students. His lightweight clothing looked like a single piece of fabric strategically tucked and wrapped in a way that clung to his body while still allowing him freedom of movement. His clothing didn't shroud his legs and arms enough to keep their unusual length hidden. A Gryon!

"I'm Mage Reekit Zanneth," he said in a sharp voice, the words coming out fast and staccato. "I don't care if you call me Mage Zanneth, Reekit, or whatever, as long as you do what I say and work hard in my class." Ignoring the surprised looks and stares, he made an impatient gesture at their group of five mages. "Spread out in a circle around me."

The students sorted themselves quickly, the rapid-fire orders instilling a sense of urgency in them. Pax just wanted to keep out of reach of the Gryon's long arms if he decided one of them wasn't moving fast enough.

"Good. At least you can follow instructions," he said with a satisfied smile that looked predatory. "First test. Hold out one hand. Summon your air *and* contain it to a ball no bigger than the size of your head. Go."

Pax stuck his right hand out with the rest of the students and lowered his lids, as if closing his eyes to concentrate. Instead, he did his best to sneak glimpses of what the other students were doing.

He heard a few grunts of effort, and a sudden curse followed by a surprised yelp.

"Contained, I said," Mage Zanneth snapped, hurrying toward a panicked-looking mage who wrestled with a fist-sized swirling ball of air floating skyward, panic in his eyes.

Others stopped to stare.

"Focus on your own work," Zanneth said as he did something to the student's uncontrolled magic that made the ball calm before he siphoned it away into his hand like a chastened puppy. "Do you think you can stop and stare in the middle of a battle without getting your-self and others killed?"

Pax wasn't the only one who looked quickly back to his own hand.

"I usually wait a bit before I train my new students on resisting distractions, but you lot obviously need extra help."

Pax swallowed at the gleam in his new instructor's eyes and got serious about the exercise. He didn't think he could do anything with the few points he had of air magic understanding. But that didn't mean he couldn't try.

He pulled at his spark and in moments had it pulsing just under his palm, much faster and more obedient than it had ever responded in the past. He did his best to dampen its power and keep it just under the skin, not wanting to attract attention with a glowing palm.

A rush of wind tore past his right side, tugging at his clothes and whipping his hair across his face. His eyes snapped back open, and his spark dissipated, drifting around inside his hand and arm without control.

"Focus!" called out Mage Zanneth, sending another gust that slammed into Pax's stomach and made him lose his breath.

He straightened himself, suppressing the glare he wanted to aim at the assistant teacher, but Zanneth had already turned to torment another student. "Don't let anything," he said, emphasizing the word before continuing, "distract you from your magic if you want to stay alive."

The next few minutes felt like getting caught in a particularly vindictive dust storm. But Pax and the other students quickly figured out how to hold still and ignore Zanneth's poking and prodding if they didn't want to be subjected to even stronger attacks.

"Still nothing?"

Pax opened his eyes, but didn't flinch as he met Zanneth's probing look before giving the slightest shake of his head.

"I heard you barely made it out of the Crucible alive. Mage Graybrew isn't pleased you ended up in his class."

Pax held the instructor's gaze, not saying a word as he fought to push his anger down. Besides, Zanneth hadn't asked him a question, had he?

"Good." Zanneth said after a moment of staring at him. "You're going to need that will to survive."

Before Pax could respond to the sideways compliment, Zanneth had reached out and gripped Pax's hand tightly in both of his. The teacher's skin felt cool and fragile, like thin parchment, but the strength of his grip was just shy of painful.

"I'll push and pull some of my air magic through your hand. Focus on how it feels and memorize it. It should help."

With no more warning than that, a powerful pulse of magic flooded his hand only to wash back out with a rush in the next second.

He bit back a painful scream as the dissipated energy of his spark flared in reaction to the intrusion.

"Wait." The magic disappeared, and Zanneth leaned in close with the curious look of a bird right before it eats a worm. "That hurt you?"

"No," Pax tried to bluff. "Just surprised me. I wasn't ready. Try again."

Zanneth frowned but didn't object before looking back down at his long hands wrapped around Pax's smaller one.

"Please." Pax tried what he hoped looked like the smile of a student eager to learn.

Zanneth gave a small shrug and complied. This time Pax was

ready, shifting the cloud of his magic to the accepting mode he'd first discovered during his awakening.

Just accept the magic, the energy. Let it in. Let it pass.

The rush entered his hand again, a veritable storm of energy that didn't hurt this time, though it stretched and pushed. Just as his hand felt as if it would burst, the magic flowed back out.

Still focusing on keeping his light magic relaxed, Pax reached out with small tendrils, doing his best to analyze and sample what he could from the inrush of air magic. His own magic threaded around the stranger's with tentative stealth.

Zanneth's magic felt so light and insubstantial, but at the same time, full of power. The contrast was striking as the magic, colored by a swirling mix of azure shades, pushed through the muscles, bones and nerves of his hand.

He didn't even notice the new notifications at the edge of his vision.

In and out, forward and back. The hypnotic pattern continued, and Pax's understanding of the essence of air grew. True knowledge hovered just out of reach as he made tiny steps of progress.

The loss of the magic, when it came, was so sudden, it made him mentally stumble and blink his eyes in confusion at Zanneth.

"That's enough," his teacher said. "Now you try on your own, so I can help the others."

Pax nodded, but Zanneth didn't leave, obviously waiting to see the results of his assistance.

Knowing it was hopeless, Pax still closed his eyes and tried to access the air magic swirling together with his spark. He could see it more easily now, the sky-blue color stronger than the faint colors of the other elements. It had obviously grown, but he had no clue how to separate it out and give Zanneth the results he wanted. He reached for the blue, trying his best to grab a hold of the elusive thread with absolutely no luck.

Reluctantly, he opened his eyes and gave his instructor a defeated shake of his head. All Pax's earlier excitement deflated. What did a special element or extra menu items matter when he couldn't complete the simplest of exercises in his spell class?

But Zanneth didn't frown or even show disappointment. He just gave Pax an emotionless nod. "Keep practicing. The only way to fail is to quit."

As his instructor walked away, it didn't help that Pax could see every other student had achieved some success. Even the dwarven girl to his left, with her face scrunched up in effort, had managed a walnut-sized ball of swirling air.

Pax groaned quietly. They still had the second half of class left where he had to pretend his haste spell actually did something.

~

SKILL BOOST: +12 to **Mana Sight** Level 1 - 26/100
    *Improvement to your Path of Understanding **Air:** +24 Level 1 - 29/100*

~

HIS EYES WIDENED IN SURPRISE, the jump in points dispelling some of his discouragement. His new progress had to mean something, didn't it?

HASTE NOT

LIGHT'S HASTE spell was *not* the same as air's.

The words kept running over and over in Pax's mind as he did his best to dodge another scything air blade that slashed across his right arm despite his leap sideways. Thankfully, Mage Zanneth was skilled enough to blunt the edge of his weapon, which meant it left behind bruises and welts, instead of slicing clothing and flesh.

Sure, when Pax had first activated the spell, he'd thought it would be useful. The other students with defensive air spells had spread out around Mage Zanneth and waited for him to attack. Pax had reached for his spark of light magic and then held the idea of Haste central in his mind. It was as simple as the Identify spell, requiring mainly intent, focus and enough mana, of course.

Mage Zanneth had given a single command to prepare before he leaped into action, swinging what he had called a practice-level air blade at the students one by one.

Pax's Haste had engaged just as the instructor spun toward him. As soon as Pax felt the internal tug on his mana, the world around him slowed just enough to be noticeable, but wasn't anything spectacular. At least it made Zanneth's movements appear slow enough that Pax could see the incoming attack begin.

It was only when he tried to dart out of the way that he realized he was in trouble. His foot took a longer moment to move than expected. With a sinking feeling, he realized Haste had reduced his speed, too, leaving him still slower than Zanneth.

Pax quickly learned that being able to see and predict a blow didn't actually help much when he couldn't move faster. The first blow hit with a broad slap against Pax's face, which was only made worse by being able to see it coming. Zanneth's Agility must have far exceeded Pax's, because the blows had been easy to see but impossible to dodge.

And now, Pax tried his best to glimpse the first flicker of the next air blade so he could dodge in time. Zanneth spun, taking turns attacking the other students with languid but elegant movements. A moment later, his speed suddenly jumped. Pax's eyes widened as he realized he'd lost the minor advantage of Haste. He didn't come even close to blocking the next flurry of attacks.

"A poor but reasonable start." Zanneth stepped back and waved a hand at them. "Take a five-minute break."

Out of breath, Pax bent his knees and dug his boots into the grass. He monitored his mana, hoping it would regenerate enough for more Haste before Zanneth came around to him again.

It did. But Haste made little difference. It helped him better see the attack, but not move fast enough to stop it. Pax failed . . . again and again.

Head ringing and bruises aching, Pax resorted to making fast, jerky movements in as unpredictable directions as he could manage, keeping his fists in tight to protect his face as much as possible. It felt the same as enduring a trouncing by a stronger bully. Being a mage hadn't changed things one bit.

Pax watched his mana recover once more, surprised to see it higher than he'd thought until he remembered the extra point in Intelligence he'd earned earlier. He clenched his muscles before blowing out a breath and relaxing his entire body, feeling the hum of elastic readiness he'd used many times to generate enough speed to evade the guards back home.

He wasn't strong like Amil. It was his speed that had always gotten him out of tight situations. The last of the other students gasped out and yielded, obviously out of mana. Zanneth spun to face him, both hands moving in a fast weave together, making it difficult to tell where the attack would come from.

Haste. One last time, Pax cast the spell, ignoring the headache that let him know he'd used almost all his mana. He focused on Zanneth's lanky body moving in.

There.

Pax had been using the previous casts of Haste to examine every tiny move of his opponent. He'd seen that distinctive twist of the wrist before. Pulling on his muscles to jerk as fast as he could in his slower state, Pax dove to the left, aiming to dodge just under the incoming attack.

It was disconcerting to see the ripple of Zanneth's air blade extend out from his arm as Pax strained to tuck his head and torso down in time. When a whoosh of air tugged at his hair instead of a blow to the side of his head, a grin burst across Pax's face. He tucked and rolled, dropping his spell as the world around him jerked forward to normal speed.

"I yield!" he called out quickly, coming to his feet and aiming a triumphant look at Zanneth. Grim satisfaction filled him at not only enduring longer than the other students, but finally moving fast enough to dodge one of Zanneth's strikes, even if he was going easy on the first-years.

Zanneth straightened back to a natural stance, letting his hands drop, his face expressionless, though he gave Pax a nod. "Meditate to practice recouping your mana and healing your minor injuries for the last few minutes of class."

"That's it?" Pax couldn't suppress his frustration completely. "You're just going to pound on us without teaching anything?"

Zanneth paused, gaze moving back to meet Pax's.

"At the early stages, only the mages themselves can unlock and develop the best path to their power. My assignment is to motivate you. Did you need more motivation?" Zanneth raised one brow in question before he cast a glance around the training yard at the other groups of mages practicing against rows of dummies or defending themselves against the other assistants. "You dodged my last attack. Are you saying you'd like to try again instead of meditating?"

Pax gulped and waved a hand as he shook his head. "No, thank you. I'm out of mana. Meditation is a good idea."

Zanneth just nodded. "Hopefully, you will make a breakthrough with your element before training becomes more dangerous." With those ominous words, the assistant instructor stepped back and motioned for the group to sit and meditate.

Pax took a few shaky steps off to the side and sank down to the cool grass. Meditation sounded like it might actually be helpful right now. Not only did he need to level up his weird collection of skills fast, but he needed his new meditation pattern to ease his injuries before the last class of the day.

Letting a quiet groan escape, Pax closed his eyes. Conditioning class would not be fun. As his breathing settled, and he focused on the energy pulsing at his center, Pax found flashes from the fight playing out in his mind. He saw the fast rush of Zanneth's air magic, the textures of the air blade rippling as it moved.

He peered closer at the memories, reaching to grasp at the elusive insights. Air was invisible, insubstantial, only seen when moving fast enough to cause a disturbance. Full of life when sucked into desperate lungs. Angry enough to rip through trees and homes when it became a powerful storm. The playful breeze that carried with it the scent of new blossoms.

So simple and complex at the same time. Pieces of understanding clicked into place while others eluded him. How could he control something as ephemeral as air?

"Clean up your practice gear and everyone back to the center. Quickly now!" Graybrew's commanding voice startled Pax out of his meditation, making some of the concepts he'd been trying to hold slip away.

Around him, the other students hurried to obey the head instructor.

"Don't forget to practice what you've learned today during your afternoon schedules. The obstacle courses are a good place to start. And students can book the smaller arenas to practice with each other. Remember, though, first-years may not use magic on each other without supervision. Unless you want to be sent to work the walls early." Despite the ominous warning, Graybrew gave them all a broad smile and continued. "Enjoy your lunch. A word of advice. Don't eat too much before your first conditioning class, except for your portion of beast meat. Eat all of that if you want to survive."

Pax hurried to join the rest of the students as they left the arena.

"Vipersworn," Mage Graybrew called out. "A word, please."

Heart sinking, Pax turned around and did his best to straighten his shoulders as he walked back. "Yes, Mage Graybrew?"

The dwarf glared at him while Zanneth stood behind his right shoulder, eyes forward and expression indifferent, as usual.

"If you want to stay in this class, I expect more improvement from you than anyone else, Vipersworn," Graybrew said in a sinister tone. "I'm only allowing you on a probationary basis because this is a required class for first-years. Come with less than a complete effort or mess up, and you're gone. Am I understood?"

Pax clenched his jaw, but managed a stiff nod.

"Zanneth said you can't manifest any air magic at all. I expect more from you by the end of the week. Don't make me pay you more attention than I already have. Now get out of here."

Pax drew on the control he'd developed as a street rat to not just give in and throw a punch at the shorter man's smug mouth. Stifling his humiliation, Pax forced himself to turn on his heel and march out of the arena. He let out a shuddering breath as soon as he made it to the central gathering area, doing his best to calm down as he navigated through the other students to exit the arena complex.

Pax didn't feel steadier until he'd made it far enough from the arenas for the crowds to thin. He looked through his recent notifications to help distract him from the angry thoughts swirling inside him.

~

*Spell Boost: +16 to **Haste** Level 1 - 16/100*
  *Improvement to your Path of Understanding **Air**: +14 Level 1 - 43/100*

THOSE CHEERED HIM UP IMMENSELY. Pax grinned, even though it tugged painfully at his bruised cheek. His air magic performance might have looked subpar to anyone watching, but the significant strain against a higher-leveled opponent seemed to have given his numbers quite the boost. He was almost halfway to leveling his air path. If it meant what he hoped it did, he'd be able to learn to control air and even get a genuine air spell. That would hopefully be enough to satisfy Graybrew, so he'd turn his attention elsewhere.

What Pax really needed was access to more information. He felt as if he were a blind man stumbling through a room of treasures with no idea what any of them were. He couldn't ask for help without revealing himself. Maybe there would be something in the library?

With a sigh, Pax added a library visit to his ever-growing list as he hurried to lunch. He was starving and not only did he have conditioning class, but his first shift at the Academy workshop was this afternoon, followed by reporting in for the vermin killing job this evening. At least on that one, he'd have Amil and Rin joining him.

A feral grin emerged on his face as he picked up his pace. After a day filled with challenges he had little clue how to handle, he'd end the day hunting vermin. Now that was something he was good at. Excellent at, really. And maybe he'd even level up some of his magic.

TOUGHENING UP

PAX WISHED he'd taken a nap for lunch instead of meeting with Amil and Rin, regardless of how good the food was. Today's beast meat had been something called Osuth breast, mostly white but with streaks of red through it. Pax thought about looking up these beasts in his new Compendium to see what he was eating, only to decide maybe he didn't really want to know.

While the flush of air energy had done nothing to perk up his exhausted mind, the jittery pulsing through his body was the only reason he hadn't just collapsed somewhere and taken his chances with missing class.

Well, his two friends had helped him too. Amil and Rin stood beside him in the back of the crowd gathered for their conditioning class. Their teacher hadn't arrived yet, but the class wasn't supposed to start for another five minutes. Advice from Tansa, their new eating hall friend, had ensured they arrived early. Apparently, conditioning teachers were known for vindictive punishments for even perceived tardiness.

By the number of other students already here this early, Tansa's information had been good. This minor success gave Pax hope that he and his friends might actually catch up soon and stop being penalized for not knowing things that were common knowledge to everyone else.

At lunch, both of his friends had been wide-eyed with excitement about their gains for the day, Amil especially. He'd gone on and on with more details about landing his Fire Blast spell on a dummy when plenty of other students had failed. Rin hadn't been nearly as boastful, but did mention she'd had some success getting her Water Snake to solidify enough to pull over a test post.

Pax heard a disturbance to his left and turned with the other mage students around him to see what the problem was. A girl and boy in a group of warrior students were almost nose-to-nose, fists clenched and glaring daggers at each other. Most of their fellows dressed in warrior red had stepped back, making it clear they wanted to have nothing to do with the conflict, while a handful had shifted to back one or the other.

"Now, my little warriors, if you have enough energy for nonsense like that, we're not doing our jobs." The booming voice was so loud it felt like the man was yelling right next to Pax.

Heads snapped around, and all the warriors, including the two having the disagreement, were instantly at rigid attention, heads up and arms tight by their side. This sudden shift sent a worried reaction through the mage students and the small contingent of crafter students dressed in green on their other side. They shifted with uncertainty before doing their best to attempt a passable imitation of the warriors.

A man, shorter than some of the teens in front of him, marched across the paved gathering area. He'd sheared his hair short enough to make him almost look bald, and his dark tan uniform gleamed with a perfect fit and crisp creases. A twisted white scar pulled at the skin above his left eye, giving him half of a permanent scowl on a face with skin weathered and tough. His eyes gleamed with a sharp blue that seemed to miss nothing as he scanned over the students.

Behind him, another four figures followed, obviously under his command. They all moved with a predatory grace that made the instinctual part of Pax's mind sit up and worry. These were dangerous people.

"I am Sergeant Necos Iglis, currently assigned to hone the future fighters of our empire into weapons to protect us all. As some of you have a bit too much energy, let's get rid of a bit before I explain further. You can thank your two friends there." He motioned at the two warriors who had been arguing earlier, and the ire of the group focused on them. Iglis didn't give it time to settle. "One lap around the track, now. Move it!"

The order boomed over them, and Pax wasn't the only one looking frantically for more direction. What were they supposed to do? What was a track?

The four assistants leapt into action, swarming toward the students in what looked like an attack. The result was a disjointed stampede away from them, because standing still wasn't an option.

Luckily, a handful of the warrior students seemed to figure out what to do and, in moments, the students were running along a raked dirt path laid out in an oval around the large, grassy training area.

An all-out sprint ensued, and Pax's lungs burnt as he forced his tired and bruised legs to push hard. He fought to stay clear of the screaming instructors and not fall into last place, as that seemed to attract the most attention. Up front, the leaders, a mix of all three uniform types, ran at a fast pace while hardly breaking a sweat.

"Guess things haven't changed much from back home," Rin gasped the words out between panting breaths. "Some people still have all the luck."

About a minute later, the first runners arrived back at the gathering plaza, looking hardly winded as the rest of the class straggled in after them. Sergeant Iglis stood at stiff attention and waited silently for the last student to make her way, breath heaving, to join them.

His four assistants fell in behind him and stood at ease, their arms clasped behind them in identical stances. They looked as fresh as the leaders of the run, not even breathing fast.

"I have a question for you," Sergeant Iglis finally spoke into the silence broken only by students struggling to get their breathing under control. "Do you think our three venerable academies would hire *me*," he emphasized the last word, his voice getting louder as he continued, "to train the lot of *you*, only to allow the use of attribute boosting accessories in this class?" He yelled the end of the question so loudly that Pax was very glad to be three rows back. Seeing the sudden discomfort of the students in the front row who had just been preening, Pax wasn't the only one to stifle a grin.

"Anyone who just used an artificial aid in my class will immediately remove any and all such aids and run to your backpacks. Do not put them into your inventories where you can sneak them back on. Deposit them in your packs in a tidy fashion and run back here. You will run, not walk. Now, I said," he bellowed, prompting many up front to scatter toward the sheltered array of cubbies provided for students' extra equipment during class.

The sturdy stone cubicles took up one entire wall along the outside of the large changing rooms attached to a shared wall with the neighboring obstacle course.

A single student in the front row hadn't moved, calmly looking at the sergeant and waiting. Only seeing him from behind, Pax wasn't sure, but it looked like the snooty elven heir, Aymer Wynrel, from their confrontation at the assignment board last night.

"Were my instructions unclear, student mage? Or are you going to convince me you achieved your little performance under your own well-trained power? I'd hate for you to ruin our new relationship by trying to cheat. I will keep any attribute boosting devices I find on you after this, a nice boost to my meager pay."

"No sir," the boy answered in a bored but still polite voice. "I am using attribute boosters, as is my usual habit. But I would appreciate it if, as my instructor, you would make your expectations clear beforehand instead of playing games like this. I'm more than happy to comply, sir."

The snooty elven heir then gave the sergeant a respectful nod before turning on his heels and walking, not running, toward the cubicles as he removed rings from his fingers.

"He said he'd comply," the sergeant said with a slight turn of his head to one of his assistants. "How about we make sure he knows what I meant when I say to run."

The assistants exploded from a standing start like a pack of hunting hounds already yelling at the boy to run as they charged toward him.

Aymer gave a startled look over his shoulder, and Pax saw the indecision on his face.

"How do you expect to get any stronger without all those baubles?" Iglis yelled over the shouted orders of his underlings. "Run, little mage. Run!"

Aymer broke into a run, just ahead of the assistants, who, seeing his compliance, spread out to harangue everyone else to finish and return as fast as possible.

"Let's see how fast you do the run this time without your cheats," Sergeant Iglis said as soon as the last had returned from removing their boosters. "Go! Now! Last one gets to spend extra time with us during the class break."

As the now visibly sweating students took off at a sprint, followed by two of the assistants nipping at their heels, the sergeant turned back to the rest.

"As for you," he said, waving an assistant forward. "You can all wipe those smiles off your faces, because she's going to scan you with her very high leveled Identify and anyone showing an attribute boost in their menu is in lots of trouble."

A boy in crafting green to Pax's left broke from the crowd and ran back toward the cubicles, yelling something out about a misunderstanding.

"Grab him," he told one of his assistants, before smiling at the remaining students. "There's always one. Going forward, you'll understand that I don't tolerate lying and cheating. Low physical abilities are acceptable, as long as you work hard to improve them. We all start with unique gifts. But don't insult me by lying."

The students finishing up a lap without their boost came running in, now huffing and panting like the others had with the assistants on their heels, driving them to go faster.

Iglis gave them a dismissive glimpse before turning back to the rest of the students. Every eye snapped to him.

"I find fighters work harder in groups they choose themselves. And picking teams is its own form of social fighting." He paused and let his words sink in for a brief moment before clearing his throat and speaking rapid fire. "Alright, as we have an unusually mage-heavy class for once, make teams of six. Three mages, two warriors and one crafter. You have one minute. Go."

While other students stared in confusion or called out questions, Pax turned immediately and motioned Rin and Amil to move in close. "We're agreed it's the three of us, right?" he asked to get it out of the way first.

Amil gave him an impatient nod, but Rin looked thoughtful. "The only reason I see to split up is if we want to gather more information about other first-years. But I think it's too early for that. We need to get stronger first."

Pax gave her a grin and nodded. "My thoughts exactly. So, do any of the warriors or crafters catch your eye?"

As one, the three friends turned to survey the chaos that had broken out around them. Some of the wealthy students were just arriving back from their run and yelled at others when they realized what they were missing out on. Many of the powers and supports grouped together instead of intermixing. Some warriors had paired off, looking for a likely group of mages to join. Most of the crafters just looked on, only a few approaching groups.

Pax skimmed over the crowd, looking for suitable candidates.

"I see a crafter I like the looks of," Rin said in a low voice to him.

"Nice," he said. "Me and Amil will try to grab some warriors. Hurry."

"Those two," Amil said, pointing to two warrior students moving through the crowd with none of the worry or panic on many of the surrounding faces.

One was a stocky dwarf with determined eyes as she pushed through the crowds, eyes locked on some destination. Beside her, an elven boy followed silently, eyes alert and constantly scanning the surrounding crowd.

"Looking for a group to join?" Pax asked as he stepped in front of them.

The dwarf almost stumbled, startled, as she stopped to avoid colliding with him. The elf beside her narrowed his eyes in suspicion.

"We're joining a different group," the girl said, pointing over Pax's shoulder to a trio of power mages, one with a heaving chest and a scowl on his face. "Move out of the way."

"Thirty seconds left," Sergeant Iglis called out. "My assistants will take care of anyone not in a properly balanced group." This prompted a sudden flurry of frantic activity.

"Looks like your people already have warriors," Amil said with a droll voice, tipping his head toward the far group.

The dwarf groaned as her eyes landed on the trio of mages exchanging handshakes with two tall, athletic warrior students.

"Why should we join you?" she asked, eying Pax's white trim of a support mage with distaste. "And where is your third?"

"She's grabbing a decent crafter and will join us in a second. Join us because we're not with the flicks that tried to cheat. We'll work hard and smart to survive, because we don't have wealthy families supporting us. We support each other and will make sure the entire team makes it, or none of us do."

The elf's eyes had been growing less suspicious as Pax rattled off his spiel as fast as possible.

"And you need to decide now, or Iglis will throw you to the assistants."

That got a worried glance over their shoulders where the Sergeant was looking down at a time-keeping device in his hand.

"Hi guys," Rin said out of breath, pulling a stocky boy along behind her who didn't meet their eyes.

His broad shoulders suggested a bit of dwarf in his ancestry and would hopefully make him sturdy enough to join them without falling behind.

"This is Tyrodon," Rin continued. "He's really shy, but very smart.

Are these our warriors?" She looked the two up and down, obviously evaluating them.

"Another support mage?" the dwarf almost spat out the words. "I should have known. Tasar, let's find a different group."

"Bryn, we're out of time," Tasar said, glancing around the area where more and more students had formed groups, the remaining solitary individuals looking desperate as they hurried to find someone to join. "It's just a group in conditioning class. Not like we're deciding on a purge team."

"Fine," Bryn snapped, turning back and pushing her hand out to Amil. "You do right by us, and we'll do the same for you. Deal?"

"Deal," Amil said happily, shaking her hand vigorously. "I'm just glad to avoid a run-in with the assistants."

"Since you're the warriors and know a lot more about this type of training, does one of you want to lead us?" Pax asked, blurting out the idea that had just occurred to him. He figured it would be an excellent test, especially since Bryn seemed predisposed to look down on support mages.

Bryn and Tasar exchanged a surprised look and, after some unspoken communication, Bryn turned back and gave them a sharp nod.

"Thank you," she said, sounding a bit mollified. "You won't regret this. I've been training to fight since I was young, since our city puts everyone on the walls. We can't afford a civilian class. Stick with me, and I'll make sure you're some of the strongest mages in your year." She cast a considering look over the group and grimaced. "Even if we don't win a top spot for academy points, we'll still get stronger and faster."

Pax gulped, unsure if he should smile or worry. Rin shot him a look, and he hoped he hadn't just made a bad decision.

VERMIN HUNTING

THE FAINT CHITTERING ECHOED along the dank walls of the tunnel. Pax held up a hand, motioning for Amil and Rin to stop while he peeked around the corner. A sliver of light from Rin's lantern behind him reflected just enough to reveal a dark opening up ahead on the left, with indistinct shadowy vermin milling around.

"It's a nest," he said, after ducking back to rejoin his friends.

Amil's face lit up with an excited grin while Rin's nose wrinkled with disgust as she brushed at a tendril of stringy moss that hung near her shoulder.

Pax adjusted his grip on his new set of clubs and tried not to wince as his shoulders and forearms twinged. Bryn had been true to her word, pushing them to excel when matched against other teams and to keep going, even if it meant carrying each other or crawling on hands and knees. When he'd felt the familiar rush of a new point in both Strength and Endurance, the brutal conditioning class had been totally worth it.

And on top of his attribute gains, he'd scrounged materials in his workshop shift to make new weapons. The bone white of his clubs gleamed in the flicker of the light from the lantern Rin carried. They looked mismatched but felt lightweight and strong. He'd made them from leftover monster bones crudely sanded to be mostly smooth and wrapped with air-based rawhide that was still curing around the handles.

His workshop supervisor had come through on the promise of a bonus if he worked diligently through his entire shift, letting him pick through the scrap pile and use one of the idle sanders to rig his new weapons. The blood and gore from processing monster parts in the huge workshop had left multiple colors of dried blood under Pax's nails, along with an awe at the number of monsters killed on the capital's walls and delivered for processing daily.

The job had quickly become mind-numbing, and Pax had turned to using his spark to keep himself focused. Running his power into hooves, bones, blood and tissue for two hours had helped train his mana sight to activate more easily. The practice had even bumped up each of his elemental understandings a few points.

When he'd finished his crude weapons after his shift and pushed his light magic through them, he'd been excited to feel the faintest hum of mana. By the traces of heat and crimson flecks of power, he figured the bones came from a flame-based beast. With the touch of mana, weak though it was, the bones were lightweight, a perfect mix of flexible and solid, the best clubs he'd ever owned.

"Everyone ready?" Pax asked, as he stepped back and gave his clubs a whirl to warm up. He whipped them through a quick figure eight, feeling the aches in his arms and shoulders loosen. A sharp hum sounded at the fastest part of the arc, making him smile. Magic was amazing, but holding familiar weapons built stronger and lighter than the discarded wood he usually had access to was even better.

Rin reached up to hang their lantern on one of the series of hooks embedded in the catacomb walls. They would need all of their hands free. "Depending on the size and strength of the rat nest, they'll either scatter or attack us. Rin, you stay behind us, trapping as many in your nets as possible, while Amil and I do our best to kill them and funnel the runners in your direction."

Amil was fairly hopping from foot to foot with excitement. He carried a worn double-sided hammer in one hand that Pax would have trouble handling with both. Amil had his right free to use Flame Blast, a light shimmer of heat already swirling. Together, with the glow of his fledgling tattoos, they lit his face from below in the dim tunnel.

Rin leaned the extra nets against the wall, stepping back to the center of the tunnel to spread her first one out. She propped the mouth of the net open at about knee level with the skinny wooden handle.

The kitchen staff had supplied the nets for the job, showing everyone how to lock down a full net with a lever on the handle to trap the critters inside. With this method, they could quickly switch to an empty net if needed, leaving the killing of the entrapped vermin for after they finished swarming.

"You both will do the killing, like you promised. I'm just trapping them, right?" she asked, still looking unhappy about the whole idea.

"Yep," Amil said. "Just use your Water Snake to funnel them into the nets. The faster we gain points in our spells, the better. Copper for tuition and Academy Points for better spells. Bring on the rats!" Amil chanted the last phrase, giving his hammer an exuberant flourish that made even Rin smile.

"Uh-oh," Pax whispered as he realized the noise up ahead had stopped. They'd been too loud, a rookie mistake. "Go. Go," he said, sprinting forward, glad of how well his new boots gripped the stone floor despite the slime and damp.

Amil charged right beside him. The narrow tunnel, about the width of three men, left just enough room to run side by side and swing their weapons without hitting each other or the ceiling, if they were careful.

Amil let his flame flare brighter as they rounded the corner, feet scrambling for purchase. Pax sucked in a surprised breath and dropped to a fighting crouch, clubs held high as he stared at the mess they'd landed themselves in.

"Those aren't rats," Amil whispered out of the side of his mouth.

"And there are too many to count," Pax replied in a low tone, a sudden frisson of fear making the hairs on the back of his neck rise.

Multiple sets of eyes shifted to focus on them, flickering rainbow reflections in them from Amil's flames. The creatures were at least twice the size of rats, more like small dogs. A pair of mottled tusks rose from their lower jaws as they peeled lips back and hissed at the newcomers from snouts that were wide and oddly flattened at the front. Some kind of whiskers or quills with wicked points spread out in a protective array to either side of their maws.

Four legs ended in wicked claws matching the jagged teeth they bared, many badly chipped and stained with hard use. Instead of fur, the creatures sported narrow, black feathers slicked back against their skin by some kind of dark oily substance which contributed to the heavy musk hanging in the air. In the back of the tunnel, a trio of the creatures rolled in a vicious battle over a bloody hunk of something unidentifiable, paying no attention to Pax and Amil at all.

To the left, Pax saw the ragged hole gaping open in the brick-lined tunnel. An even stronger stench emanated from it, making his nose wrinkle in disgust. At the appearance of Pax and Amil, two of the creatures sprang into action, shepherding what looked like smaller or juvenile members of the mass back inside the hole.

An angry skittering filled the space around them as the front row of creatures puffed up with angry postures, their feathers suddenly pointing straight out and doubling their size. Glistening points and wicked barbs made the danger of the feathers obvious. They were being warned off, but would the creatures attack them if they ran? Something true both in nature and among street kids: Appearing weak was never a good idea.

"I think they are Bog Swarmers," Amil whispered, taking a careful step to line up on Pax's right in a practiced move that used the left tunnel wall next to Pax to anchor the two of them and prevent them from being surrounded. This wouldn't be the first time they'd fought multiple opponents together. "They're a low-level air beast we learned about in Monster class today, weak to flame. But how did they get past the wall and build a nest under the Academy?"

"Real beasts, not just vermin? Cores and parts we can sell, right?" Pax asked, shooting Amil a look of surprise. This was an amazingly lucky find or something very dangerous. Or both. "Do we fight or go back and report?"

Amil let out a chuckle mixed with nerves and eagerness. "We're not some weakling 'crats who need daddy to take care of us. Plus, these guys are little money bags asking us to kill them. Bet I kill more than you."

Pax returned his friend's grin. A good fight was just what he needed now to vent the frustrations of the day. And if it left him with more skills and coin, all the better. "You're on," he whispered to Amil, being careful to stay still, not wanting to startle the creatures into attacking first. "Start with the biggest burn you have. That hole looks like a nest, so who knows how many are in there? We'll kill as many as we can, and when it gets crazy, we retreat to hold the line with Rin. Got it?"

Amil gulped, nodded and raised his right hand. The flame surged to cover his entire fist and part of his forearm. The front row of creatures flinched back at the sight, angry sounds flaring to life. "Flame Blast." Amil voiced under his breath, jabbing his arm toward the center of the milling creatures.

To Pax's surprise, a stream of flame as wide as Amil's arm launched in an almost blinding arc to splash just over the front row of swarmers. It landed with an explosive splash in the middle of the thickest group of creatures.

The swarmers closest to the Flame Blast caught alight with exploding suddenness as whatever coated their fur acted like an accelerant. Overlapping squeals of pain and fury erupted as the fire spread, jumping from one swarmer to the next with incredible speed.

Amil swung his arm in a short arc, moving the flame across the tunnel in the next seconds before his spell sputtered and went dark.

"Wow," was all Pax could manage. He returned the grin Amil shot him as his friend sagged from the mana expenditure.

"I'm out," Amil said, looking unsteady.

"Get back to Rin," Pax said, voice firm as he moved in front of his friend, both clubs held up and ready to meet the front line of swarmers who had missed being lit on fire by charging forward. "Just give me a little light. I'll be right behind you."

As Amil backed away at a fast stagger, he kept one hand up, gleaming weakly with a flicker to illuminate the attacking beasts. The lead swarmer bunched its legs a few feet in front of Pax and launched itself into the air, turning its head and opening its mouth wide to tear into Pax's abdomen. From either side, two more creatures bulldozed ahead, feathers out in a full splay, obviously intending to ram into Pax's legs and bring him down where the swarm could overwhelm him.

But Pax had killed his first rats for food when he was only the size they were now. Speed and evasion were survival skills ingrained into his bones. With a lunge, he charged forward at an angle that let the convulsing body fly past him, feathers and all, as he raced in toward the next closest swarmer, the one now completely out of position.

Skimming the wall, Pax used his arm and hip to launch himself at the leftmost swarmer, torquing both clubs down in vicious arcs that slammed with two rapid cracks into the beast's head. The first blow ricocheted off a hard skull, ripping a strip of bloody skin off with it. The tip of his second club hit perfectly centered on the eye, shattering the vulnerable organ with a disgusting gush of something he was glad he couldn't see in the dark shadows.

With a quick flick of his wrist, Pax let his club follow the collapse of the stunned creature and then gave a savage stab through the damaged eye and into the skull. Its feathers and legs twitched and jerked, but Pax had already sprung past it to come from behind the swarmer on the far-right. It had scrambled back around much faster than the airborne creature that was just now making an awkward landing further down the tunnel.

Amil's arm swung in a desperate motion with the small bit of flame he could manage. Thankfully, it was enough to deter the lead swarmer, especially when Pax was behind it, an easier target flanked by the rest of its swarm.

Pax didn't spare Amil any more thought as he used his momentum to slam a well-placed kick square into the abdomen of the creature, the only part where the feathers still lay flat. He felt cracks and snaps through his shin as his kick lifted the creature and sent it to smash into the far wall with a pained squeal.

Pax had just enough time to take two running steps toward the returning leader, hoping it would be dumb enough to take another leap. But it had learned its lesson and just charged full speed, jaws open wide as it threw its body toward Pax's legs. He dodged to the other side this time, his sticks whirring in the fast one-two pattern that had worked before.

But this beast was smarter and faster. In a blur, it crouched, letting Pax's clubs whistle harmlessly overhead as it whipped its body sideways and bent almost in half to snatch at Pax's calf.

At first, all Pax felt was a heavy tug on his left leg, which made him stumble and almost fall. Icy pain followed, stabbing into his leg and making the muscles spasm and go weak. He bit down against the pain as desperate adrenaline flooded into him.

Twisting with as much speed and agility as he could summon, he whipped both clubs down onto the head of the swarmer. They hit with dull, fleshy impacts, followed by angry grunts of pain. But the stubborn creature just tightened down further, shaking its head back and forth and shredding Pax's pants and skin with its sharp feathers while doing its best to make Pax stumble and fall.

Again and again, Pax swung his clubs down at the awkward angle, unable to hit as hard as he wanted with the thing halfway behind him and flailing about with its whipcord strength.

"Pax, hurry," Amil called from the bend in the tunnel, waving frantically at him.

"I'm trying," Pax grunted out, switching to straight jabs down at the face of the swarmer, hoping to get a lucky shot to the eye again.

But the blasted thing lashed out with its forward claws now, digging for even more purchase on Pax's leg.

Clamping down on a scream of pain, and wishing he'd thought to use Haste before the swarmer had clamped down onto his leg, Pax did the only thing he could think of. He pulled on his spark and sent it slamming through his clubs to fill them to bursting. With as much strength as he could manage, Pax whipped them at the swarmer's jaw with two backhand strikes. The power flooded through the somewhat familiar structure of the clubs and they felt lighter, faster.

The two blows landed so close together to almost sound as one sharp crack that shot through the din of roaring flames and squealing pain filling the tunnel. The swarmer's movement slowed, and Pax thought its jaws might be relaxing.

But his spark wasn't done. As soon as his clubs made contact again, Pax felt his spark leap to the swarmer with an eagerness that made him panic.

No.

Remembering the Blaze Lizard almost draining what he now knew had to be his mana, Pax knew he couldn't let that happen again. He jerked at his spark, insisting it stay in his clubs.

It was too late. Something in the beast tugged on his spark, taking a long pull at it as Pax swung his clubs back for another set of blows. The swarmer's ferocious snarl faded. It let go of his leg, its teeth tearing painfully free. Pax's clubs landed one more time, and this time, the swarmer didn't even fight back, looking more drunk than anything.

His right club sparked with light as it slammed home just below the swarmer's eye, doing serious damage. Pax stomped down onto the creature's head, ignoring the pain in his calf and enjoying the finality of finishing the dogged creature.

Pax wearily raised his clubs again as he took a shuffling step back and hoped the other beasts were still too busy with the fire to notice him.

"What did you do?" Amil asked him.

Only then did Pax realize the swarmers had quieted, leaving only the crackle of flames and a few pained whimpers to fill the tunnel. Every one of them, still able to, had turned to focus on him, eyes intent.

DEADLY SWARM

"Run!" Amil yelled, his voice joined by Rin, who must have moved up to see what was happening.

Abandoning all dignity, Pax turned and ran in the fastest hobble he could manage. The commotion behind him made it easier to ignore the stabbing pain and warmth of blood soaking his left leg.

Turning his back and running triggered something in the odd intent of the surviving swarmers. They exploded into a boiling mass of teeth and claws, doing their best to catch him. Only the fact that many of them were half-burned or injured gave him a chance.

He raced toward the gleam of Rin's lantern that shone from around the corner, his friends no longer in view. Hopefully, they were preparing something to stop the swarm after him. Feet skidding in the muck that covered the tunnel floor, Pax made the turn and almost lost his balance as his injured leg threatened to buckle.

Amil darted forward, grabbed his arm and manhandled him a few feet back from the corner.

"Here," he said, speaking rapid fire and pushing a wooden handle into his hands. "Take this net. You have this side. Lean against the wall if you have to, but stay on your feet. We'll trap as many as we can in the nets before dropping them and reforming a new line behind them to handle any stragglers."

Pax nodded his approval. On the other side of Amil, he saw Rin's grip on her net turn white-knuckled as she looked down at his bloody pant leg.

"I'll be alright," he said, doing his best to reassure her. "They've got healers for stuff like this."

She had time for a dubious nod before the first swarmers came sliding around the corner, eyes scanning the lit tunnel and the three defenders before they honed in on Pax and charged.

"Vitur save us," Amil muttered before they all raised their nets to knee level, the three side-by-side openings almost enough to span the width of the tunnel.

Haste. Pax cast his spell, the sudden pull of mana barely noticed among his other pains. He wouldn't make another stupid mistake. Unlike his confrontation with Zanneth's high-level Agility, Pax was just as fast or faster than these creatures. And with his leg hurt, he needed every advantage he could get.

His spark burst into energy, shot up and filled his mind. With a minor wrench of his vision, the swarm of creatures filling the tunnel ahead of them slowed just enough to make their vicious scramble look less intimidating. Spittle still flew and their claws threw muck into the air, but Pax had that extra moment to think that he needed.

He could let his frantic mental pace relax and, even injured, could move his net to the perfect spot. He trapped angry creatures before they could get another bite out of him. When their traps filled, they snapped them closed, grabbed a new one and moved back with as much coordination as they could manage. Pax ran into trouble when he had three swarmers dragging his net down, the weight awkward to handle with a hurt leg.

They fought to tear through the tough cording to get to him, teeth gnashing with slower motion and madness filling their eyes. Thankfully, the handles attached to the nets were extra long for just this reason, and kept the frantic monsters at bay.

Minutes ticked by, seeming to take eons, as the trio of friends shifted tiredly in the flickering lantern light, catching one swarmer after the other. They tossed full nets to the side, the raging catches inside bucking to break free. Pax resorted to moving behind the nets of his friends, too, since the incoming swarmers kept focusing on him.

A persistent one made it past Rin. It twisted, wide-mouthed, to snap at her leg only to be jerked down to the ground by ropy snakes of water wrapping around its forelegs and stopping it mid-attack. A quick bash from Amil's hammer ended the danger.

Amil stepped up and snagged the last of the intact swarmers in his net, just as Pax felt his mana slow to a trickle. He let go of his Haste, and his knees almost buckled as the world jolted back to regular speed.

"Whoa," Amil called out, grabbing his arm again. "Shut your net before you drop it. We don't want to start all over."

With fumbling fingers, Pax triggered the closing mechanism before stumbling back a few steps and sinking to the ground. Moments later, Rin and Amil joined him as they stared at the roiling mass of trapped creatures in the nets. Even now, all of them did their best to claw their way to Pax.

"You should start killing them before they break free," Rin said in a pragmatic tone.

Amil and Pax turned and stared at her, wordless.

"What?" she asked, sounding defensive. "You said you'd do the killing. And those Bog Swarmers are definitely worse than tunnel rats. No way I'm going to get their nasty body funk all over me."

Pax turned and sniffed, realizing that he must have gotten used to the smell at some point, which made him worried about how he himself must smell. He noticed Amil sitting right beside him, while Rin had left a definite space between herself and the two boys.

"How did you know they were Bog Swarmers?" Amil asked, ignoring Rin's comments about their smell. "Did they go over them in your beast class, too?"

"No," she said, looking confused. "I just used Identify."

Pax groaned and shook his head. First, he forgot to use Haste, but Identify, too?

"It's ok," Amil said. "Identify Level 1 only gives the name and level. It doesn't mention the air affinity, which made them particularly vulnerable to fire."

"Of course," Rin said. "If we could get everything we needed from Identify, why even have a Beast Identification class?"

A sudden snapping growl made Rin flinch back, and she gave Amil's hammer a pointed look.

"I've got a hurt leg," Pax said when his friend looked at him. "Maybe Rin can help me bandage it up while you kill them. I'm mostly out of mana, too, so I've probably earned all the points I can for my Haste spell for one battle."

"I've got a bit of mana still," Rin said slowly, looking back at the lurching swarmers with conflicted interest.

"Great, use it to kill a few, so I don't have to do all of them," Amil said with a cheerful grin. "I'd use my last bit of Flame Blast for more points, but I don't want to burn the nets. I'll get some levels to my new hammer skill instead, and you can choke a few swarmers out with your Water Snake. You don't even have to get that close."

As his two friends clambered to their feet, Amil looked at Pax's leg with a considering look. "Want me to burn your wound shut? Didn't Lorkranna call that *cauterizing*?" He dragged out the sounds of the unfamiliar word. "If we're going to keep up this kind of stuff, healing abilities are important."

"No." Pax put a hand protectively on his leg and pulled it back. "I'm not letting you burn my leg and make it worse. Go practice on a swarmer first. I'm sure there are some still alive back there."

"Got you," Amil said with a broad grin before turning back to the trapped swarmers.

"Idiot," Pax muttered before looking for the biggest two swarmers to get a few more Identify points.

~

Bog Swarmer - Level 2
*Increase **Identify** Skill for more information.*

*Skill Boost: +2 to **Identify** Level 1 - 46/100*

Bog Swarmer Juvenile - Level 1
   *Increase **Identify** Skill for more information.*
   *Skill Boost: +1 to **Identify** Level 1 - 47/100*

∾

WITH WEAK HANDS, Pax slipped his lightweight pack around to his front to dig out the small first aid kit the kitchen staff had provided. The corners of his mouth turned up in a tired grin as he pulled up his pant leg and did the best he could with a jar of pungent ointment, a soft absorbent pad and a bandage roll. Amil's statement about a new hammer skill had made him notice his own cluster of flashing notifications that had piled up during the skirmish.

Once he'd finished with his leg, he leaned back against the wall, focused on his breathing and accessed his menu. If he was lucky, a bit of meditation might even help speed up the healing in his leg once he finished counting his gains.

Scanning over his gains with a smile, he appreciated the extra notes showing how much specific items had improved. His air path looked high at +40 points until he realized it was showing him his total gains from the last time he'd looked at his complete menu, regardless of the notifications he'd already read.

∾

NAME: *Pax Vipersworn*
   Race: *Mixed Human (monster-touched)*
   Age: *16*
   Bound Location: *Shieldwall Mage Academy (provisional monthly)*
   Class: *Mage*
   Element: *Light (Hidden)*
   Specialization: *none (Hidden)*

Paths of Understanding: *(Hidden)*
Flame: Level 1 - 14/100 (+5)
Air: Level 1 - 43/100 (+40)
Water: Level 1 - 7/100 (+5)
Earth: Level 1 - 7/100 (+5)
Level: *1*
Mage Leveling Points: *0/5*
Health: *21/37 (+3)*
Mana: *3/26 (+2)*
Attributes:
Strength: 5 (+1)
Agility: 8
Endurance: 6 (+1)
Intelligence: 8 (+1)
Insight: 7
Charisma: 3
Skills:
General Active:
Identify Level 1 (Common) - 47/100 (+3)
General Passive:
Skinning Level 1 (Common) - 24/100 (+6)
Butchering Level 1 (Common) - 36/100 (+14)
Clubs Level 1 (Common) - 14/100 (+14)
Mage:
Light Mana Manipulation Level 1 (Epic) - 24/100 (+4) (Hidden)
Light Mana Sight Level 1 (Rare) - 34/100 (+22) (Hidden)
Elemental Meditation Level 1 (Common) - 6/100 (+6)
Spells:
Light (1/3):
Haste Level 1 (Common) - 20/100 (+20)
Inventory: *10/20 available.*
Assignments:
Academy Workshop Trainee
2/30 hours (+2)
0/1 Supervisor approval

Charity Clinic Trainee

0/30 hours

0/1 Supervisor approval

Maintenance Trainee

0/21 Cleared blockages

0/1 Supervisor approval

Exterminator Trainee

42/100 Vermin killed (+42)

0/1 Supervisor approval

Misc.: *none*

HEALING ISN'T EASY

AFTER CHECKING out his boosts in mage skill points and the hard-earned Strength and Endurance points from conditioning class, Pax reached the bottom of the screen only to stop and stare. They'd killed 42 swarmers? Confusion quickly replaced his surprise. They were air beasts, not vermin, which meant they probably shouldn't count toward his assignment.

But the number sat there and even ticked up to 44 as he heard Amil and Rin killing more back toward the nest. His head hurt too much to calculate the earnings they'd rake in when they reported back, but it was going to be a lot. And he'd even added another few points to his Haste spell.

He wouldn't forget to use it again, already thinking of ways to practice it that might be challenging enough to earn more points. Even if he just kept casting it whenever his mana recovered, something should improve. Single points here and there would add up.

His leg throbbed insistently for attention and, now that the fight was over, Pax could feel scratches stinging on his hands and one on his neck. How had the short, nasty creatures gotten to his neck?

Pax focused on his spark with a lot more ease than just this morning in meditation class and let his thoughts and worries fade away, sinking into the glowing ball of calm and vibrant energy.

Time passed unnoticed as he felt his emotions balance. His thoughts cleared and focused. The sensations from his injuries faded into pressure instead of pain, still insistent for attention, but under his control now.

With more confidence than he'd ever had, Pax encouraged the growing ball of light energy to expand and sink down through his left leg to soothe the raging chaos he could feel there.

He followed along, curious how this would work. Pax watched as the energy moved easily through his leg, something Pax had considered something solid his whole life. Well, maybe there was bone, muscle and skin. Oh, and blood.

Expecting a simple structure, Pax let his spark flow into his leg like a lightstick, revealing the contents of a darkened room. To his surprise, his light magic illuminated an intricate system too complicated for him to do more than stare.

The bone was easy to pick out, a solid structure standing strong like a column supporting a building. Around it, though, a veritable swarm of activity shifted and moved. Long, bulging muscles pulsed with energy while around them, thick cords of vessels pumped blood in all directions, splitting over and over into fine threads too small for him to follow.

Feeling suddenly overwhelmed, Pax pulled back on his inner vision. He pushed his spark down toward his injury and then let it sink in and permeate the area nearby. Here, the activity was even more frantic, like a hive kicked over and full of angry bees.

Pax stared at his energy, waiting for it to do something, anything. He could feel that he'd summoned the power, but it still felt aimless, pooling and awaiting direction.

A vision of Freddy popped into his head, and Pax suddenly realized why Mage Lorkranna had started her class with a lesson on anatomy. Pushing his internal vision closer, Pax felt a bit of resistance, but he pushed through, looking for the structures he knew had to be there. His new point in Intelligence helped him maintain his focus and see connections.

With a sudden click, the injured area snapped into focus. The damage appalled Pax. Jagged slices disrupted the long, ordered lines of his calf muscles, a mess that oozed important fluids inside his leg and out through the ragged tears in his skin.

Unsure if he was doing it right, Pax stared at the muscle fibers just above the injury and then pulled at the light energy, encouraging it to line up with the healthy fibers and then push through the destruction down to the lower leg where things were working again. His magic stuttered when it hit the injury, but Pax pulled on more of his power and pushed it through. It finally obeyed, pulling some of the injured tissues into ordered lines before emerging through to the other side of the wounded area.

Remembering the circular meditation option, Pax swung his magic around to come back up through the injury, hoping he could connect it up above and make a path that would circulate to heal the injury.

His mind struggled to control the path of his magic until he finally attached the leading edge back to the trailing tail. The click of connection eased the drain on his mana that he hadn't realized was happening.

With a tired satisfaction, he took a mental step back and watched as the thin ellipse of light magic moved in a continuous loop down and then back up through his injured calf. He could see and feel the swollen and angry wound improving. He was actually healing himself!

He pulled up his notifications, scrolling past all the minutiae to find the new one he was hoping for.

MAGE SKILL UNLOCKED: **Light Healing** Level 1

This rare skill allows light mages to use their element to study, understand and heal their own bodies. It improves with increased practice and levels. The following will increase the mage's healing skill and decrease the mana cost: a better understanding of anatomy, a higher understanding of how to use specific elements in the healing, and an increase in mana manipulation, mana sight and elemental meditation.

Distance: touch

Mana cost: Cost over time is dependent on severity of injury.

Note: Take care to monitor mana levels. Once the mage depletes their mana, the skill will use the mage's health.

SKILL BOOST: *+4 to* **Light Healing** *Level 1 - 4/100*

~

TO HIS SURPRISE, he saw another bulky notification for a skill that made his grin widen further.

~

GENERAL SKILL UNLOCKED: **Clubs** *Level 1*

This common skill allows one to use straight, unsharpened implements as weapons to strike harder and extend the reach of a fighter. Level up to unlock further bonuses and specializations.

SKILL BOOST: *+14 to* **Clubs** *Level 1 - 14/100*

~

A QUICK LOOK back at his menu verified that his new Clubs skill was indeed listed, along with a boost in both skinning and butchering from his shift at the warehouse. The high vermin kill count had just distracted him from noticing the gains.

"If you're done with your beauty nap, you want to help us get the cores?" Rin's droll tone pulled him out of his meditative state.

He blinked at her in the dim tunnel lit by their lantern. It took a mental shift to move back to reality from the text in his crowded menu and the roiling activity he'd just been studying inside his leg.

"Oh, how bad off are you?" Rin's teasing turned to concern as she frowned at him. "Do we need to get you up to a healer first?"

"No," Pax said, waving off her concern as a huge smile split his face. "I just unlocked my healing skill. I think if I stay off my leg for a bit, I might be good to walk out of here on my own."

"No fair," Amil growled. "You should have let me burn your wound for practice if you were going to just heal it up afterward. I'm the one that's going to get hurt the most."

"And I'll practice until I learn how to heal you," Pax countered, still excited as he felt the circle of energy still swirling in his leg.

Rin scoffed. "Not for a while. I heard Healing Others is a much higher-level skill, or one you have to evolve. Definitely not level 1. If any of us want to heal up this year, we're going to have to do it ourselves, which means lots of meditation."

Amil groaned.

"Or just be randomly lucky like Pax," Rin said, throwing him a suspicious look. "Is this something to do with what happened back on the caravan? When are you going to explain that all to us?"

Pax swallowed as Amil turned and waited for an answer, too. "I'm still trying to figure out how my magic works. And it's not like there's a manual anywhere. It's still too confusing to make much sense of it all."

Rin paused and said tentatively. "Maybe you should run it by the two of us. We could help you figure it out."

Pax hesitated, thinking of the four elements swirling around with his light magic and what the insides of his leg had just looked like.

"Never mind," Rin said before he could come up with a suitable answer. She turned her back on Pax and spoke to Amil. "Let's just finish this up. Time to dig for cores. Amil, you want to drag a few over for Pax to work on? I don't know how these count as vermin, but getting double paid is going to help us out nicely."

Pax gave up trying to explain himself and promised to talk things out with his friends soon. The task in front of them was gruesome until Pax mentally translated all the monster corpses into coins. He smiled and got to work.

RULES OF HARVEST

PAX EXCHANGED a satisfied look with Rin as he put the last core into a stack in his inventory. He liked keeping empty spots available for valuables and weapons while keeping the mundane things in his pack. Despite the bloody task of harvesting them, the energy that filled them helped to slough off the gore once they removed them.

Each of the Bog Swarmers had yielded an air core the size of Pax's thumbnail and perfectly round. To his naked eye, they had a simple glow and were probably no big deal to a lot of their fellow students. But to three street kids, they felt like instant riches.

Even more fascinating, though, had been when Pax used his mana sight on one. A swirling of different shades of air blue magic writhed together, filling each of the little pearls with an energy that looked ready to burst free to his skill. He couldn't wait for some privacy and free time to examine one more closely.

"Maybe we shouldn't have sent Amil to report this and bring back help," Rin said, pulling his thoughts back.

"What?" Pax asked. "And spend the entire night harvesting all the beast parts ourselves? Didn't you get enough of that during our work-shop shift today? Plus, we have no tools, just our knives? It'd take all night, if not longer."

"You're right. I know." Rin tipped her head back and let out a soft groan. "I'm just imagining how much attention this is going to bring down on us. We found beasts in the tunnels, you know? The walls are supposed to keep them out." She turned back and held Pax's gaze. Her tone turned uncertain. "I know the hordes have been growing our whole lives, but are the walls failing, too?"

"Great," Pax complained as her words brought more implications to mind. "And now we're going to be connected to that nasty bit of news, or even blamed for it somehow."

Rin nodded, looking suddenly more vulnerable than Pax had ever seen her. "What are we doing here, Pax? Even with all the controls and hardships here, we have magic now. I was just beginning to think I might grab more out of life than the occasional full belly and handful of copper. But if even the walls of the capital can't keep out the beasts —" She swallowed, her head shaking in slight movements back and forth. "Are we even going to make it through the first year? And what about the purge coming up? Students die during that." Rin's voice filled with worry and anger. "Every year, Pax. Every year!"

"Then we'll do what we always do, Rin," he reached out to place a hand over hers, but stopped when he saw her stiffen. He let his hand fall back, unsure where his confidence was coming from, but feeling as if they both needed it right now, regardless of the reality they found themselves in.

Rin shook her head, visibly working to calm herself. Pax could see regret and worry flicker in her eyes as she realized how vulnerable she'd just made herself.

"We survive, Rin," he said, projecting as much strength as he could into his words.

"But—"

"No, it's the same as the streets, Rin. We take whatever the flicks here can teach us, and we get strong enough to survive. In their brutal classes, fighting beasts underground, on a purge team, wherever. Hey, even if the walls fail, you, me and Amil will figure out a way to survive, even if we have to live outside them. Got it?" Pax still wasn't sure where the words were coming from, but he'd just been thinking he might succeed at this mage thing. He could see the magic inside his body, for Vitur's sake. Inside him, a kernel of angry stubbornness had formed that wouldn't let anyone rip away the first decent thing he'd had in his life since losing his family.

Rin searched his eyes, looking for something before her expression firmed with her own version of resolve. "Even outside, if we have to," she agreed.

"Even outside," he confirmed, giving her hand a squeeze.

"Is that our new motto?" she asked, shifting back and suddenly looking uncomfortable at how close they were.

"No one will know what we mean by it," he said with a shrug, the corner of his mouth turning up as he considered it. "That we mean to out-survive them all."

"Even outside," Rin said in a quiet voice before giving him a smile and nodding.

Something moved through Pax, making him feel more agreeable, put together and even a touch eloquent.

～

*Congratulations! You have increased **Charisma** from 3 to 4*

～

"Sweet!" he couldn't help saying.

"What?"

"I finally got a level in Charisma."

Rin eyed him dubiously, her cocky demeanor firmly back in place. "You have charisma?"

He couldn't help his snort of laughter, in too good of a mood to take offense. "Not much," he agreed. "So, every point helps."

They shared a grin, only to freeze as they heard clomping footsteps and indistinct voices bouncing eerily off the walls of the darkened tunnel in the direction Amil had disappeared not too long ago.

"This better not be a prank." The strident voice of an older woman came through clearly as the noises grew closer.

Pax steadied himself against the wall before taking a quick glance down at himself to check his appearance. Ugh. Gore splattered his once-fine uniform and the left pant leg looked too torn to be fixed, even for the Academy laundry. What would the approaching people think of him looking like this?

He paused for a moment in confusion. Since when did he care about his appearance? Then he realized and clenched his jaw. Charisma, of course.

"Oh, Vitur protect us."

The awestruck whisper made Pax's head turn back up to see the new arrivals, who stood frozen at the edge of the remains of their battle with the swarmers.

A tall woman with angular features stared at the scene, her mouth moving with no words coming out. Dressed in a light gray uniform, her blouse looked as stiffly ironed as her slacks. A pristine, white apron kept everything well protected and tidy. She'd pulled her hair back into a tight bun that revealed severe features. She looked accustomed to bossing people around all day.

Beside her, but just a step back, Amil stood with a young boy that looked kind of familiar and held a lantern high that brought the scene into an even starker focus.

"I can explain—" Pax began, moving his hands in a pacifying motion.

"Be quiet," she barked in such a commanding voice that Pax's mouth snapped shut. "Let me see what we have here, and then I'll decide what to do."

Pax exchanged a worried look with Rin. Maybe she'd been right, and they should have kept the discovery to themselves.

Wordless, the woman walked through the remnants of their battle, the gruesome sights seeming not to bother her as her eyes scanned the space, taking in the bloody nets leaning against the wall and the pile of swarmer corpses with chest injuries from their core removal.

A moment later, she strode toward the nest, avoiding stepping in any of the puddles of blood before she disappeared around the corner, her assistant hurrying to follow with his lantern.

Pax and Rin immediately turned questioning gazes on Amil.

"That's Mistress Nymeli, the head chef of the kitchen," he said with a helpless shrug. "I tried reporting to the lady that gave us the assignment, but the mistress was there planning for tomorrow's food. At first, she got really mad at me for lying and wasting everyone's time. When I showed her the tusk and air core, she grabbed Krasig and dragged us all back here at a fast march." He shot a grateful glance at Rin. "Good idea for me to bring proof. I don't think anyone would have believed me otherwise."

Rin nodded, but still looked worried.

"And if this works out," Amil continued, looking excited, "we might find even more beasts when we explore that hole we found at the back of the nest cave."

"What hole?" Pax demanded in a harsh whisper, looking at Rin for an explanation.

"Oh," she said, looking sheepish. "I meant to tell you, but got distracted harvesting cores. There was a small hole in the back of the nest area, about knee height, big enough for a swarmer to fit and us if we're willing to crawl." She made a face. "Maybe there's a reason I forgot to mention it."

"Too bad the mistress and Krasig are going to find it now," Pax complained, shooting a look in the direction the two had disappeared.

"No," Amil said with a smug look. "We filled it in with rubble, plus a bit more around the edges, so it blends in with the rest of the mess in there."

"Good thinking," Pax congratulated him, already imagining what treasures they could find down in underground catacombs hidden beneath the academy and the capital. Even a smaller town like Thanhil had an extensive underground buried by years of successive generations.

"But these are beasts we're talking about, not rats, making it past the walls. That's not supposed to be possible," Amil whispered.

Before Pax could say anything, Rin spoke up. "Don't worry," she said, her voice fierce. "Pax and I discussed it, and we'll figure out how to survive, even if we have to live outside the walls."

"Outside?" Amil's eyes went wide as he stared at her.

Rin grinned. "Street rats never take the easy road, so that's our new motto. Even outside. Whatever it takes to survive."

Pax nodded his agreement. Obviously, he wasn't ready to give up on the academy any time soon, but every street rat knew to always keep a hidden exit or two available for emergencies.

NEGOTIATING FOR PARTS

PAX COULD SEE Amil playing with the idea in his mind before he grinned, even looking a bit excited about the challenge. In an abrupt move, he stuck his hand out, palm down, toward his two friends. Rin looked confused, but Pax placed his hand on top of Amil's, heartened by the familiar ritual their crew back home had used to encourage each other. "Go ahead," he tipped his head for Rin to add her hand.

When she did, Amil and Pax said in unison, "Even outside." Then they threw their hands up in the air and grinned at each other.

Rin just gave them a curious look, but couldn't suppress a half smile.

"If you're done with your childish behavior, I've come to a decision."

The droll words made all three spin around to see Mistress Nymeli had returned, with Krasig still holding the lantern dutifully behind her.

"One cardinal rule of our society is that a beast belongs to the ones who kill it. Even though these beasts are in a place, they have no business being, we can't break that rule. So, the cores, as well as all the beast parts, belong to you."

Pax couldn't help the smile widening across his face.

"However," Nymeli said, holding up a stern finger, "I highly doubt three first-years have the time, tools or energy to butcher this many beasts properly. Am I right?"

They exchanged nods, and Pax nudged Rin. Even with his new increase, he was sure she had a higher Charisma than he did. If anyone could help them come out ahead in an exchange with the mistress, Rin could.

Rin cast a glance back at him. At his encouraging nod, she turned back to Mistress Nymeli. "What are you proposing?"

The harsh woman unbent enough to offer Rin an approving nod. "I will bring down a crew to process these beasts properly, and we split the materials when we're done. The cores are completely yours, obviously. As for the harvested parts, I can help you negotiate a bulk sale to the factories, you can sell your items to the Quad-Academy store, or place them on consignment for other students to buy."

"Quad-Academy store?" Amil parroted, sounding confused.

Mistress Nymeli sighed, but visibly reined in her impatience. "I'll explain, but first let me know if you plan to come to an agreement with our kitchen, so I can send Krasig back for help."

Just as Pax was about to agree, Rin spoke up. "What are our other options?"

That got a look from Nymeli that almost held respect. "You can process them yourselves with the time and equipment you have. You'll also have to figure out how to preserve them so they don't spoil as well as navigate the selling process without my help. Another choice is to notify the mages, and they will probably swoop in, hand out non-negotiable orders, and you'd come out with little more than the cores you already harvested."

"Or we work with you and both of us benefit?" Rin said slowly.

Nymeli nodded and waited.

Rin glanced at Pax and Amil and, seeing their nods, turned back to Nymeli. "Deal."

Without hesitating, she turned to Krasig. "Wake the five newest apprentices. They need the skill points. Pick another five journeymen to wake, as well as Mistress Luna. Tell her we need enough equipment for three butchering and three skinning stations and four cold-transport carts. Let them know we have a deadline of dawn and a lot of work to do before then. Now, hurry."

Krasig didn't hesitate, running on his shorter legs back the way he'd come. He flashed Pax a quick grin as he passed.

"Now, a quick rundown on the things you need to know," Mistress Nymeli said to them as Krasig disappeared down the tunnel. "Pay attention. I don't enjoy repeating myself. And please think twice before wasting my time with unnecessary questions."

Pax gulped, the grin he'd flashed to Krasig fading as he turned back to face the intimidating woman. He was really glad not to be working under her.

"The Quad-Academy Store, like its name implies, is open to students and instructors from all four academies. The upper floors are often called the treasure store, because items there are more valuable, like enchanted armor, weapon and spell scrolls. Everything upstairs costs Academy Points and requires additional levels to gain admittance to each floor. This encourages students to work hard in their classes and perform services that help the academy overall."

"And helps the ones already at the top," Rin muttered, "so it's even harder for the rest of us to catch up."

Nymeli shot Rin a sharp look. "Strength matters. Don't fool yourself into thinking anyone here really cares about the weaker students. One powerhouse can make more difference on the walls than dozens of mediocre mages or warriors."

"But they're only strong because of the benefits their families and clans give them," Rin protested.

"Strength is strength," Mistress Nymeli said with a shake of her head. "And are you telling me you wouldn't do the same for your own children, should you find yourself with power in the future?"

Rin looked startled but didn't answer.

"And all of you should know better," Mistress Nymeli chided them. "Life isn't fair and never will be. You'll have to fight for every advantage you get, just like the rest of us. Now, are you done whining so we can get on with using this windfall to help us both?"

Rin nodded. Pax was just glad the mistress had decided to help them. With how they'd been floundering compared to the regular students, it was nice to find someone willing to school them on the basics so they could get ahead.

"As I was explaining," Mistress Nymeli continued, "the main floor of the Quad-Academy Store is full of basic items for sale by the store itself. But even better is the consignment section that takes up the entire back half. This is where students and instructors can sell things they've earned, harvested, crafted, traded for, etc. You can set a sale price or even run a timed auction, with the item returning to your possession if it doesn't sell."

The information dripped like liquid gold into Pax's mind as visions of building a monster part empire ran through his head.

"Now, there isn't much demand for simple Level 1 parts like these in the store, except as practice ingredients for new crafters." Nymeli waved a dismissive hand toward the pile of corpses. "So, making a bulk sale to the factory acquisitions department may be the way to go, though you can always set up a few test lots in the consignment shop, maybe the tusks and a set of skins? It may only net you a few more coppers over a bulk sale and take more time, but I'm guessing coppers are more important to you at this point."

"But the cores—" Pax argued.

"—are the most valuable part of this whole scenario," Nymeli interrupted and finished for him. "You'll make the most from selling them, though you might want to speak to your advisor about how to use some of them since you're an air mage." She nodded toward Pax.

"Then why are you negotiating so hard for the monster parts, if they're not really worth much to someone like you?" Rin interjected, her suspicion back full force.

Mistress Nymeli ticked off a finger as she answered. "One, there are a lot of them. And two—" She paused, and her voice lowered. "What makes you think this will be the only incursion? If I establish from the start that responsibility for beasts within our walls falls under the umbrella of vermin extermination, which I oversee, then you and I are in for a very profitable partnership."

"As long as we take all the risks," Rin countered.

"And you know the mages would rip it all away from you in an instant," Nymeli countered.

"And you won't?"

"Do I look like a mage?" she said with a scoff before waving at herself. "Someone who can go toe-to-toe with beasts?"

"You could find other students," Rin said, and Pax was tempted to kick her so she would stop arguing and just work something out.

"Where would I find a trio of different element mages who are desperate enough to work long hours outside of their schoolwork to kill low-level beasts in our sewers? Do you know how hard it is to get anyone to take the vermin killing assignments in the first place?" Nymeli hesitated. "Besides, this is the perfect partnership. Neither of us can do it without the other, and both of us benefit by working together and keeping others from interfering."

Rin held her gaze and finally nodded. "And the pay for the Vermin assignment? The coppers and Academy Points?"

Nymeli let out an amused scoff before tipping her head toward Rin. "All yours, of course. I can hardly claim authority over this if I don't give you credit for eliminating *vermin*."

Pax glanced at Amil and saw his friend looking just as excited as he felt. They were getting paid twice, just like they'd hoped! And if things worked out, this might be a trend.

"Fine. We're in," Rin said, smiling too. "Now we just need to negotiate the shares."

Pax and Amil groaned, but both Nymeli and Rin looked eager.

THE POWER OF RUNES

SEATED next to Rin at the second of four long workbenches in their enchanting class, Pax wasn't the only one keeping his mouth shut while keeping a worried eye on the silent man standing at the front of the classroom. Their instructor was an average-looking man, just an inch or two taller than his students. He kept his light brown hair trimmed short and combed with some substance that held it stiff and still, like his expression.

Both Pax's recovering leg and mind were aching. Mage Incedis' office wasn't close to the gardens where Magical Harvesting had spent their class period learning about a bunch of new plants on a list their teacher had given them to memorize. He'd also successfully navigated Incedis' questions about his progress without letting anything dangerous slip.

Pax had confided in his mentor about the developing 'beast as vermin' situation and hoped he hadn't made a mistake. At least Incedis had expressed confidence in Mistress Nymeli, and promised to stay hands off and let them handle it.

The fast trip all the way from the gardens to get to enchanting class on time had stressed his weak, still healing leg even more. He was glad he'd taken the time to visit healer hall last night despite how unpleasant it was. There'd been no way he could handle today's classes with only his new and slow healing at work.

It had been his bad luck to find the unpleasant Healer Zayne on duty last night. She'd made her opinion of him clear during the Crucible and hadn't changed at all. Pax was sure she'd done the minimum for his leg she could get away with.

Rin nudged him and tipped her head toward features of the unusual classroom with raised brows. With their instructor still as a stone, the students took the opportunity to look around.

To the left stood huge racks full of identical boxes with carefully written names on the fronts. Scanning a few of them, it took Pax a few minutes to puzzle out the contents.

"Air - Chinook Stinger - Pwd bone, Lvl 1-3"

"Earth - Lutum Burrower - Blood, Lvl 3-4"

"They're all full of processed beast parts," he whispered to Rin, giving the wall of boxes an impressed look. After his workshop shift yesterday, the bog swarmer butchering and today's harvesting class, he realized how much work and expense went into producing crafting products out of the raw parts.

"And tons of tools on this side," Rin responded, drawing Pax's attention to the opposite wall, where rows of labeled drawers sat beneath cork boards hanging with a dizzying array of instruments. Some were familiar, like chisels and hammers, while others only made Pax frown as he tried to imagine their uses.

The instructor up front suddenly moved, striding in a fast move-ment along the edge of the classroom toward the front door. Every student immediately fell silent, a thrum of both curiosity and worry filling the chamber.

Without a word, the man pulled the door closed and turned a deadbolt that clunked shut with a solid finality. No one was getting in that door now.

When he turned back, all the students snapped around towards the front, watching him out of the corners of their eyes as he silently moved back to stand behind his podium again.

He stood as motionless as he had earlier, the silence drawing out until it became uncomfortable. A few students shifted in their seats.

A moment later, the man reached down for something behind his podium and pulled out a . . . huge, gleaming sword!

A collective gasp filled the classroom, but the man's expression still didn't change. He held the sword aloft, capturing the eye of every student. A dark, almost black hide wrapped around the hilt. A rather simple-looking guard of sturdy bars in a curved T-shape protected the man's hand.

But it was the blade that drew Pax's attention. Something about the well-polished metal pulled at him. Squinting to focus as best as he could from the second row, he could almost make out patterns inscribed into the metal, but they kept flickering in and out of focus. His pulse picked up, and he ached to get his hands on the sword to examine it with his spark. Those had to be runes!

Something immediately spoke to him. His experience with his light magic had pulled him toward understanding the structure of things, his magic, the other elements, even his body. If he could turn his magic to understanding runes, then there was nothing he couldn't do. A fire rune on his simple knife would elevate its power significantly.

Another thought occurred to him. They had planned a visit to the Academy Store tonight after dinner. Pax had figured the first treasure floor open to them would be full of temptations far out of the reach of his paltry five Academy Points. But what if he could learn the runes himself and how to enchant? He could create his own enchanted gear for much cheaper.

"I am Mage Harding, your enchanting instructor," the man finally spoke in a monotone voice. "Follow me."

With no more explanation, he turned and walked toward the back wall, which was covered by a bank of windows and a set of double doors Pax hadn't noticed before. He carried the sword with a negligent competence that made Pax wonder what level his Strength and Agility were.

Rin nudged him hard, jolting him out of his thoughts to scramble to his feet and join her. In a moment, the entire group hurried after their disappearing instructor. Once outside, Pax glanced around at a spacious yard, obviously set up for the enchanting activities too dangerous to be done inside.

Above, a wooden awning protected the closest section from the weather. Workbenches and a storage area gleamed with the same pristine organization of the classroom. Walking out from under the overhang, they emerged into a wide-open area with various equipment lined up along the sides and what looked like targets against the far fence. The ancient stone paving under their feet looked recently swept, and as Pax was trying to take it all in, something slammed into him from behind, knocking him forward to land hard on his hands and knees.

He let out a pained yelp that drew the others' attention. Pushing up from the ground, he spun to glare angrily behind him, only to see no likely culprit.

"Over there," whispered Rin, her eyes cold and hard as she stared to the left.

Pax followed her look and saw Kurt standing relaxed with two cronies Pax recognized from the incident with Galen and the Oakhouse heir, Aymer. They must have been in the back rows for Pax to have missed them. He needed to keep a better eye out for the flick.

When a student with Kurt caught Pax looking his way, he gave him a mocking smile before shrugging and turning his attention back to their instructor, dismissing Pax.

"He's only following Galen's orders, harassing you," Rin said quietly. "You know, it's better to just avoid flicks like him."

Pax frowned, forcing his fists to relax, because as much as he hated it, Rin was right.

"No matter how good it would feel to smash in his face," she added quietly, prompting a grin from Pax.

"We'll just have to get stronger then, won't we?" he agreed, keeping his voice low as he enjoyed the fantasy of finally being able to fight back. "And richer."

"Richer?" Rin asked.

"Who says we have to take them on ourselves?" Pax mused, his mind already running through possibilities. "So, I'm thinking, with enough coin, we can make almost anything happen."

"True," Rin said slowly as her eyes turned thoughtful as her grin widened.

"Form a semicircle and pay attention," Mage Harding said as he stopped in the middle of the yard and turned back to face them.

The students froze again under the oddly uncomfortable gaze of the strange teacher.

"Now!" he barked and everyone moved, spreading out in a loose arc behind the mage, who had already turned back to face the far fence and its array of targets.

With no more warning than that, he lunged forward in a move almost too fast to follow. He jabbed his sword in a powerful strike straight toward a large metal shield fastened to a sturdy tripod across the yard. It stood a few feet in front of the other equipment.

A blast of light tore through the space between the tip of the sword and the shield in a powerful, blinding rush, followed immediately by a booming crash that slammed into Pax's ears hard enough to make them ring.

The sharp smell of ozone hung in the air as the stunned students stared at their teacher. The man simply turned back to face them and nodded, as if summoning a lightning bolt was an everyday occurrence.

"That is a demonstration of what we can achieve with enchanting. The laws may forbid mages from combining mana, but everyone loves a powerful artifact, so items are the exception. Here, the flame and air runes on this sword combine to produce lightning. Anyone with enough mana, mage or not, can activate it. Follow me if you want to learn." And then the man moved at a rapid clip back toward the classroom.

This time Pax was the first one behind him, though he had enough presence of mind to keep a careful eye on Galen's buddies this time.

～

"BLAST," Pax cursed softly as the curved chisel slipped and cut a thin line along the inside of his index finger before he could jerk away in time. He popped the finger into his mouth and stared down, discouraged, at the rectangular piece of wood on his workbench.

He'd only graduated to an actual piece of wood once he'd proven he could draw the simplest activation rune connected to an air rune on his wax tablets four times to the satisfaction of each of Mage Harding's assistants. His initial fascination with the starburst pattern and circular curls of the two runes had long since faded with how difficult it was to get the distance and angles between the lines and loops precisely correct.

It had taken another four pieces of wood before he'd inked the rune well enough to be granted access to the next step of carving the actual runes. At least he'd unlocked the Runes skill. It was also a mage skill that would count toward his leveling points, once he improved it. He scanned the message again to encourage himself to keep working.

～

MAGE SKILL UNLOCKED: **Runes** *Level 1*

This uncommon skill is an essential tool for a mage with skilled mana control to empower non-living items with magic properties and powered by outside sources of mana. The eventual results are only limited by power and imagination. Creation of more complex and stronger runes will increase the level of this skill.

Mana cost: None for rune creation before activation. Amount of mana needed to imbue for activation varies and requires the Mana Infusion skill or a more advanced version of it. Warning: Failed activation can cause destruction of objects and injury to the mage.

～

PAX LET himself focus on the imagination part, playing with fanciful ideas of powerful items he might make in the future to distract him from how much work it was to engrave the two simple runes correctly at the moment.

"This is crafter work, not mage work," a voice grumbled from a row behind him.

Agreeing murmurs responded. Pax heard a chisel being dropped to the workbench, followed by a clatter of wooden blocks, wax ones and even a few styluses.

This drew the attention of the elven assistant who was currently supervising their portion of the classroom. "Without a basic under-standing of the entire process, you can't succeed when it comes time to imbue mana and enchant a rune," she chided the group two tables behind Pax.

Pax glanced up, and when he saw her face, he was more than happy she wasn't talking to him. Her displeasure didn't bode well for the complaining students.

45

STUDENTS AREN'T IN CHARGE

AROUND THE CLASSROOM, others looked up to watch the unfolding spectacle. Pax noticed a handful actually looking hopeful. They probably wanted to skip ahead past the tedious crafting part, too. They were all mages and likely excited about the fun magic part of runework coming up.

Pax felt the same, already daydreaming about infusing the rune with magic and watching it come alive during the last step of the enchanting process. But he knew better than to tick off an assistant teacher, despite how much difficulty he was having making progress.

Besides, with only access to light magic at the moment, Pax wasn't in too much of a hurry to expose his inability to control air mana. Though, if he could figure out the path of understanding air magic sometime soon, he was sure there had to be something they could build with all the air-affinity supplies and cores they'd gained last night.

The few long, bloody hours of processing had left them with two large cold boxes worth of harvested parts. Part of their agreement with Nymeli gave them the use of the boxes for one week and even let them keep them in the kitchen storage area. They'd agreed Nymeli would sell one box to the bulk factory acquisitions to earn them some quick coin.

Pax had been inclined to keep it all, considering all the potential uses they might find for the stuff. Nymeli had quickly educated them on all the costs of processing the raw parts. Their own cold box, even a small one, was very expensive. Then there were bottles for the blood, paying crafters to process the organs and bones and to cure the hides.

For someone who had started this mage thing with 52 coppers to his name—just barely more than half a silver—the expenses were a dizzying prospect. Pax couldn't help smiling, though. The potential earnings were just as staggering.

He couldn't help another giddy glance at his current wealth. Only once in his life had he actually gained the hundred coppers needed for a silver, much less two.

~

COIN COUNT: 0 Gold, 2 Silver, 11 copper (+1 Silver, +59 Copper)
 Academy Points: 5 (+5)

~

AND THAT WAS JUST for the partially finished vermin quest. Once they decided how to best turn the rest of their acquisitions into coin, there'd be even more.

"My father is a very skilled enchanter," a haughty voice drew Pax's attention back to the brewing discontent behind them. "He lets me observe and learn from him all the time. His crafters and servants have everything perfectly prepared so that when he arrives, he can focus all his attention on the important part, filling the runes with magic."

Pax glanced back, seeing one of the two students who'd been with Kurt arguing with the impassive assistant. On the other side of the room, Mage Harding didn't even glance up from the student's work he was checking.

When the assistant didn't respond, the idiot kept going. "Now, I demand that you allow us to move on to practicing magic infusion. I'm sure, with my head start, I'll be able to learn it quickly, as soon as you stop wasting our time with this busy work."

The elven assistant still hadn't said a word, but a growing aura around her made many of the nearby students turn back to their work.

Even Kurt and the second friend looked nervous, scooting their chairs slightly away as they reached for their work again.

"Are you done?" the assistant asked coldly.

The boy nodded as he sat back and folded his arms with a haughty tilt to his head.

"Name?" she asked, reaching into a pocket on her leather apron for a small notebook.

"Student Mage Sid Torneau," he enunciated with pride. "You've probably heard of my father, Mage Ingram Torneau."

She silently wrote his name in the book and carefully put it away before looking back up. "Student Mage Sid Torneau, get out. I have dismissed you from Mage Harding's Enchanting class."

Sid stared at her stupidly, his cheeks flushing red. "What? You can't do that," he almost yelled, a tinge of panic in his voice. "My father specifically told me Mage Harding is the best enchanting instructor. I just want to learn actual enchanting, not this—" he sputtered, waving a dismissive hand at his discarded tools.

"Maybe your father should have taught you that Mage Harding likes to see hard work and respect from the students in his class."

"Um. No," Sid said, his bluster fading as he looked around and didn't find any support.

The nearby students had all returned to their work, hands diligent and eyes focused.

"This isn't necessary." Sid pleaded, looking helplessly at the elf's implacable expression. "Please, I'll do better. This is just a misunderstanding."

"The only way back into this class is a direct request from the head of the academy. Maybe your father has the pull for that?"

Sid's mouth opened and closed wordlessly while every other student in the class became even more industrious.

"You have to the count of five or even that avenue will be lost," she said, unyielding as she walked over to unlock the door.

Realization sunk in, and Sid quickly stuffed his belongings into his bag as she counted, barely making it to the door and out before she got to five. Any desire Pax had to snicker at the boy was squelched by the possibility of drawing the assistant's attention.

The rest of the class period passed in relative silence, only the industrious sounds of chisels and the scritch of inking pens filling the classroom.

When class was close to finished, Mage Harding walked to stand in front of a large, freestanding board at the front of the room. "Attention up here, please."

Every eye snapped up to watch him. Pax wondered how he would top the lightning sword he'd pulled out at the beginning of class.

"I will now demonstrate the goal of the exercises you have been working on today. Watch for clues on how to improve, as you will not move on to learn anything else until you can successfully do this yourselves."

Pax watched with fascination as Harding lifted a rectangle of wood identical to what they'd all been working with. He pressed it to the demonstration board where it clicked and somehow stayed attached in a vertical position so they could all see the surface.

Next, he took an inking pen and with a grace and ease that was too fast to really appreciate, he sketched the starburst shaped activation rune, followed by the perfect swirls of an air rune. Pax was still staring at how even and perfect the lines of the runes were when the mage switched to a slender, curved chisel and with quick but delicate taps of his hammer carved perfect grooves into the coarse wooden surface. Finally, he picked up what looked like a stone pen with an etched, rounded end and smoothed the already perfect-looking grooves.

"I think this is as far as any of you made it in today's class, correct?"

Heads bobbed in answer as the dumbfounded class stared at what their instructor had done in just a few moments.

"Should I finish it and show you the result you are working toward?"

Heads bobbed with excitement. He cocked one brow at them.

"Yes, Mage Harding," came in a ragged chorus from multiple students.

With a sharp nod, he turned back to the work, pulling it from the board with a snap so he could hold it horizontal. "Gravity won't allow me to do this next step on the vertical board, so I'll describe it as I go. This is powdered bone from a level 1 Osuth beast, air affinity," he said as he raised a thin straw like device and moved it along the surface of the wooden board in his hand.

Pax craned up in his seat, doing his best to see what was happening without actually standing up.

"The trick is to use enough bone to cover the surface of the groove and to keep the amount even along the entire rune," he said in a precise voice. "You can use any affinity of powdered bone in the activation rune, but the elemental runes require components that match."

Pax wasn't the only one leaning forward to hear every word.

"There," Harding said with satisfaction in his tone, the first bit of emotion Pax had heard during the entire class. "For beginners, the next step would be to use the correctly sized smoother to run along the rune channels to ensure even thickness and coverage of the powder. I'll skip ahead to the infusing."

Pax exchanged an excited glance with Rin as Mage Harding placed the wooden block down on his demonstration table at the head of the classroom. Without even the slightest pause, his wrist tattoos flared to life and the palest blue magic enveloped just the tip of his index finger. He touched the wood for all of three seconds before lifting his finger again and swiftly pulling the block up for the class to see.

Magic had filled the perfectly drawn runes and danced along the lines with the playful energy of a fall breeze. Every student watched in rapt attention as the magic slowed, thickened, and then finally settled, seeming to soak into the wood before it disappeared. It left behind a faintly glittering rune in a rather plain piece of wood.

"I hope you paid careful attention and learned from my demonstration," Harding said, lowering the block. "I expect at least a couple of you to complete your runes next class. Dismissed."

A collective sigh of disappointment had no impact on the instructor, who had already turned away, his attention having moved on.

"Mage Harding, would you like me to demonstrate the activation of the rune to the students?" The elven assistant spoke up from Harding's left in a deferential tone.

"What?" Harding asked, obviously startled out of other thoughts.

"The rune," she said, pointing to the block. "I think some of the new students may not be as familiar with runes as others and would learn from a demonstration."

"Of course," he agreed with a distracted voice. "Go ahead." And with that, he walked toward a small office door in the far corner of the room and disappeared inside.

"I know this is redundant for some of you, but with enchanting, it is important that everyone understands exactly what is going on, understand?" The assistant had turned back to them and waited for students to answer before continuing. "A rune needs mana or a core to be powered." She held up the wooden block. "The correct element is required to create a specific rune, like air, for this one. A matching beast core is also required to power something that needs to operate continuously. However, mana from any awakened person can power this simple activation rune. Like this."

Rin elbowed Pax with excitement as they watched the assistant touch the rune, followed by a gentle breeze that blew out toward the students from the enchanted surface of the wood.

"A simple fan, though it blows everywhere," she said with a smile. "Being etched in wood means it's too unstable to hold a beast core permanently. And it will wear out with a few uses from the mana moving through it. But this is the concept that sits at the core of your role as support mages." Her tone turned serious. "Enchanting allows you to use your magic to strengthen weapons, armor and devices to make those fighting on the walls stronger, faster and more deadly. Our role is just as important in keeping our cities and families alive."

Her words settled over the quiet students. Even the wealthy ones looked thoughtful about the new potential of their magic.

Pax's mind swirled with possibilities.

SHOPPING OR HAGGLING

"WE'LL BE CLOSING for the day in an hour," an impatient voice called from behind some shelves as Pax stepped inside the Quad-Academy Store with Rin and Amil.

"Wow," Amil whispered, echoing Pax's sentiments as the three friends came to a halt and stared at the impressive sight just inside the large double doors.

Pax had known the store would be massive as soon as they'd walked past the front of their own academy to enter the gate to the store grounds. Expensive core-powered street lamps lined the manicured lawn with tasteful flower beds that must look amazing during the day. Three crushed gravel paths coming in from each gate met together in front of two double wooden doors that looked sturdy enough to stop a siege engine.

From the outside, the massive building looked large enough to fit an entire arena inside its chiseled stone walls. Bright green ivy reflected the lamplight as it wound its way up and around the tall windows. Pax got a crick in his neck looking up and trying to count the stories that faded into the sky above him, shrouded by dark clouds in the early evening sky.

Standing inside now, Pax found his expectations exceeded by more than he could have imagined. Instead of a crowded collection of boxes and shelves he would normally find in a town shop, this was as cavernous as he imagined a castle's main hall would be.

In front of the door, rows and rows of waist-high display tables spread into the distance of a large open space big enough to fit their whole caravan, and then some. An entire section to the right seemed to be full of various types of armor, some affixed to sturdy display boards, while they'd hung others on the blank-faced mannequins arrayed in a stationary battle line.

The left section looked a bit like Mage Harding's workshop, only bigger. Rows and rows of drawers and cubbies stood next to carefully organized tools and shelves containing bigger devices whose function Pax could hardly guess at. With all four academies shopping here, he was sure there'd be plenty of items he wouldn't recognize.

There was another section at the far back that looked more disorganized and had a half wall sectioning it off. Most of the scattering of other shoppers browsed back there, the colors of their uniforms showing a few from each academy doing some last-minute shopping.

"Pull the door shut," a man carrying a small box said impatiently as he stepped out from behind two mannequins dressed in matching pieces of leather armor. "And wipe your feet. What are you? A bunch of savages?"

Looking down, Pax quickly scrubbed his boots on the large mat and gave them a couple of stomps for good measure. If this man was the gatekeeper to the contents of this amazing store, the last thing he wanted to do was annoy him.

The portly man of average height moved to set the box down on a well-polished counter. The ropey muscles visible on his forearms suggested he wasn't as soft as he looked at first glance.

"We're here to—" Pax began as the shopkeeper moved behind the counter and carefully unpacked small glass bottles from the box.

"I know," he interrupted, "You want to window shop for when you earn more coin and academy points and would I please reserve a bunch of items for you?" He looked up and raised a sharp finger. "The answer is no. And I don't care who your parents are."

Pax stared at the man, nonplussed. The idea of them being arrogant 'crats made a snicker slip free before he could stop it.

The man's head snapped up from his work, frowning with suspicion.

"I'm sorry," Pax said, waving one hand in apology. "But the three of us don't even have parents anymore and wouldn't dream of asking you to reserve items for us. When we want something, we'll have the coin or points to pay for it up front."

The man's demeanor relaxed, and he set down the bottle in his hand with a sigh. "I apologize. I've just been dealing with the influx of entitled brats that a new term always unloads on me. Let me start over." He gave them a cheerful smile. "I'm Crafter Jacoby, the head shopkeeper here. We sell the equipment on the first floor for coin. The treasure floors above use Academy points only and require an escort and certain levels to access. Now, how may I help you?"

Pax looked at Rin and Amil, but his two friends waved at him to continue. "We actually do want to look at what is available for our level and how much things cost, but"—he held up a hand and hurried to reassure the man—"we just need to know a goal to aim for. We've never had more than a silver or two in our whole lives, so this will all be new to us."

"Tell him about the stuff we have to sell or trade," Amil hissed.

Jacoby looked sympathetic, his head already shaking. "I'm sorry, students, but I don't buy family heirlooms or whatever it is you're planning to raise coin with. This is an academy store. We buy and sell equipment, ingredients, spell scrolls and other such things at student-only prices to help produce the best academy graduates possible. Come back when you've finished a few shifts on the academy wall and have cores to sell. Now, feel free to browse."

"But—" Pax tried to interrupt, but Jacoby just talked over him with the speech he had probably rehearsed many times.

"Just remember that the displays have anti-theft protections. So, you've been warned." He raised his finger again. "Also, the items in the displays have information cards that should answer all of your questions. Oh, and check the consignment area in the back. That's where the students and instructors can sell their extra supplies and gear to each other. You're likely to find better prices on items for your level back there. Enjoy."

He had already turned and opened the glass front to a display case behind him to fill with the small bottles.

"We have over forty level 1 air cores, plus the harvested materials from a host of Bog Swarmers. What would those be worth?"

Jacoby stilled before carefully setting down the bottle in the cupboard. He turned to look back at them, finally showing a bit of interest tinged with surprise. "Forty? Show me one." He held out a hand while reaching into a pocket on his apron with the other.

Pax pulled one from his inventory and took a step up to the counter. "There," he said triumphantly, holding it out for Jacoby to take.

With a nod of acknowledgment, he took it and leaned in close to his palm to examine it with a round device he'd placed in one eye. The three friends waited with bated breath for the verdict. Pax had just shot a nervous glance toward Rin when Jacoby cleared his throat and looked up with a smile.

"At my age, I should know better than to judge by appearances," he said with a small shake of his head. "Now, this is an uncommon level 1 air core, just one step up from the smallest size, which means it could power a small, single-rune air device for a month or two."

Pax was fascinated that the man could tell all that about the core. He couldn't wait to hear how much it was worth.

"Despite all that," Jacoby finished, looking up and popping the odd device out of his eye. "It isn't anything special or worth all that much. But what is special is how three first-years harvested so many only a day into the semester. Would you care to share the story?"

"How much is 'all that much'?" Rin countered as both Amil and Pax exchanged disappointed looks. "And maybe if you give us a good deal, we'll share the story."

"Well," Jacoby said with a chuckle. "I'll have to decide how much the story is worth. If it's something significant, you know I'll hear it soon enough, anyway. The academy's gossip mill is hale and healthy."

Rin shifted impatiently, but at least she didn't interrupt the shopkeeper.

"Yes, yes," he said, tapping a finger against his chin. "Let me see. The going rate for this type of core would be about 20 coppers, maybe a bit more or less, depending on how many hit the market from the wall harvesting on any given day."

Pax brightened, working out the math in his mind. For him, numbers had always come much easier than letters.

"So, a bulk price here would be fifteen coppers each."

Pax frowned and adjusted his numbers.

"Now don't look so ornery," Jacoby chided Rin's sudden scowl. "Any shop in town will only buy for half retail, so ten coppers, in this case. We give much better rates as the academies run this store and only take enough to cover operating costs instead of needing to make a profit like the shops in town."

"So, six silver, if we sell forty of them to you?" Pax asked, his grin reemerging at the astronomical amount for one evening's work.

"But we could make more if we sold them ourselves back in the consignment section?" Rin asked.

"Take it easy," Jacoby said, holding up his hands with a smile. "If you share the story of how you got them, I'll give you the best advice I can for you to squeeze the most copper out of your loot, alright?"

"And a ten percent discount on what we buy from you," Rin added.

Jacoby looked affronted. "Now, young mage, I don't give that large a discount to my own family."

"For a single purchase," she countered. "The first one, when we buy the basic gear and spells we need? You want to support young mages trying to grow strong enough to protect you on the wall, don't you?"

Jacoby let out a full-throated laugh before nodding. "You drive a hard bargain. Fine. I'll only agree because I admire your pluck, and you're a refreshing change from the aristocrats I've been dealing with today. But—" He held up his finger again. "It's for only a single purchase, and don't tell anyone about the discount. I don't want a bunch of begging students insisting I give them the same, you hear?"

All three quickly nodded their heads in happy agreement eager to get the advice of the man running the Quad-Academy Store.

47

BUSINESS ADVICE

"I'LL EXTEND you a bit of trust by giving you my advice first." Jacoby waved a finger at them. "But your story better be a good one, hear?"

The three bobbed their heads in agreement.

"Now, depending on how much time you have to babysit your enterprise, here are your options," Jacoby said, all business again. "Selling to me or to the academy workshops for raw materials will net you the best bulk prices. Better would be to sell in the consignment store in the back. The shop keeps a ten percent consignment fee that basically pays the wages for the apprentice shopkeepers running that section. You could price your cores at 17 or 18 coppers, for example, undercutting my price of 20 up front here and making a bit more for yourself. But selling forty to individual students would take a while. A suitable compromise I'd recommend is keeping four or five of the same items for consignment at a time while selling the rest to the academy in bulk."

Pax reached into a side pocket of his backpack, pulled out a small notebook and jotted down notes.

Jacoby gave him an approving nod before continuing. "Now, the raw materials that go along with all those cores won't sell well at all without being processed into crafting-ready materials. Past the tables back there is a crafting job board. That's where the most profit lies, but also requires the most time and effort. You can post that you'd like forty hides turned into leather, for example, with what you're willing to pay and a deadline. The crafting students are always here, because extra jobs like that are a bonanza for faster leveling, especially bigger jobs or working with more unique items. They may write a counter to your proposal, altering the pay, quantity or deadline, for example. The dickering back and forth can take time unless you catch someone in the store and work it out in person. Once they finish the leather, in this example, you can then sell it in bulk to me or individually to others."

Amil's eyes had glazed over, and Pax saw him trying to peer into the nearby display cases holding spell scrolls.

"But the best profit lies in turning whatever you have into a final product, armor, weapons, potions, etc.," Jacoby finished up. "For that, you'll need to know a lot more than you do now, even to understand what you can craft with your supplies and what has a decent market, so you don't invest a bunch of coin only to have to sell at a loss. I wouldn't recommend this route without more experience and a good relationship with a skilled crafter who will help educate you."

"Well, that won't happen for the likes of us," Rin said, discouragement easy to hear in her voice.

"I wouldn't abandon the idea so fast," Jacoby argued. "You'll find crafters care more for materials and projects than they do for pedigrees. If what you've done already is just the start, you may have to beat off the interested crafters with a stick. Loads of cores and monster parts, plus interesting jobs, are the quickest way to a crafter's heart." He grinned and tapped his chest. "Who knows? If you get high enough items, I might even throw my hat into the ring."

Pax scribbled his last notes, hoping he'd be able to read it all later. But the concepts made sense to him and caused ideas to swirl in his mind. Both his goals of growing stronger and wealthier could work together efficiently.

"Now, the story," Jacoby said, leaning forward and placing both hands on his counter. "Don't leave any of the juicy details out."

"But aren't you closing soon?" Amil protested. "We still need to look at armor and spells."

"Plus, the consignment area and the crafting job board," Pax said, casting a look in that direction, itching to get more information to fuel his half-formed schemes.

"Tell me as much as you can and, when the half-hour bell rings, I'll let you loose to browse for the last thirty minutes. Deal?"

"And you'll keep what we tell you a secret?" Pax asked, still reluctant to share their methods in case others tried to horn in on their success.

Jacoby gave him an affronted look. "You have my word. Any merchant worth their salt knows better than to burn a good supplier." He mimed sewing his mouth shut with two fingers and then gave Pax an expectant look.

Pax gave his friends a look and when they both shrugged, he started talking.

～

As soon as Jacoby let them go with smiles and congratulations about their feats, the three friends hurried into the store. Pax and Amil quickly scanned the sets of leather armor so they'd have some idea of what it would cost to upgrade their school-issued set. Rin was a few rows over, looking through the cases holding spell scrolls.

"Don't bother with those yet," Jacoby called over. "It's too expensive. The unenchanted armor the academy provides is more than adequate for your shifts on the practice wall until you face higher-level monsters. All the new crafters' practice pieces have to go somewhere."

Pax glanced at the price card hanging from the cuirass, just to see. Eyes wide, he quickly checked the rest of the pieces and gulped. Almost two gold for the entire set.

Next to him, Amil let out a groan. "At these prices, we won't be wearing anything like this for years."

"Don't forget how much we made in one night," Pax said quietly. "We won't let the lack of coin hold us back anymore." He glanced around the rest of the shop, knowing most of what he saw was totally out of reach right now. "Not anymore," he said fiercely, meeting Amil's eyes.

Amil's mouth firmed, and he nodded back.

"Let's head to the cheaper section for now, though," Pax said with a grin. "We're flush with silvers even if gold is out of reach."

With renewed excitement, Amil hurried toward the back of the store, with Pax close behind. Threading through the display cases, Pax took in what he could as he passed by. The names stirred his imagination and caught his attention.

Thin rolls of parchment tied up by pieces of plain ribbon filled glass cases. His eyes gleamed as he looked at the treasure trove of abilities and power. Any of them would have been priceless back when he'd been a street rat at the mercy of everyone around him. Pax scanned the spells, drooling and wishing there was a way to get all of them.

Wind Funnel offered the ability for an air mage to summon a tornado. Pax had to snicker at the six-inch tornado specified for level 1. It would take some creativity to use it as an effective distraction in a fight. But for pranks? He grinned and thought of Amil. It would be awesome.

Mound, the level 1 earth spell next to it, described the ability to make a specific amount of ground bulge upward. It could easily disrupt a group of small beasts or be a defensive aid to provide high ground when being swarmed. It could even come in handy as an alternative to a rope or a ladder.

Water Breathing, the next spell, proved that not all scrolls were equally useful. Pax couldn't see much use for the ability to breathe underwater unless a mage ended up far to the south fighting the colossal beasts in the lakes and oceans.

The next one caught his eye enough to go over the details on the card more closely. If his Paths of Understanding actually let him unlock spell slots for other elements like he hoped, this might be the perfect one to help disguise what his Haste spell could do and bolster his pretense of being an air mage.

"Flurry - Air

Level 1 Common

Price: 2 Silver

This common spell allows an air mage to boost attack speed by a factor of 1.125 at level 1. The speed increase does not automatically improve reflexes or effectiveness of attacks. Extensive training is required to derive maximum benefit from this spell.

Distance: self only

Mana cost: Initial cost 10 mana for the first minute, 4 mana maintenance per additional 10 seconds.

Weakness: To gain maximum use of the spell, higher Agility and Intelligence are required."

"I thought you already had Haste," Rin asked from behind, startling him as she leaned over to examine the case. "Why would you want another movement spell?"

"Um," he said, caught off guard as he tried to come up with a suitable answer. When he met her eyes, he saw immediately that she could tell he was keeping things from her. Important things.

She gave him an expectant look.

He hesitated further, trying to decide how much to share. There would be risks to both of them depending on how much he told her about his light magic. And Amil too, of course. Whatever he told Rin, he had to tell his best friend. He shot a quick glance around the sparsely populated shop. There wasn't anyone close enough to eavesdrop, but that still didn't make this a good place to share dangerous information.

"Never mind," Rin snapped. "Keep your secrets. We agreed to help each other out, not bare our souls. I get it." She strode past him at a fast march toward the consignment area, back stiff.

"Rin, wait," he called out, hurrying after her and grabbing her arm.

She turned and gave him a sharp look that had him letting go immediately.

Before she could march off again, he leaned in and whispered quickly, "Listen, I'm planning on telling you and Amil everything that's going on, but not here where anyone could overhear, alright. You two are the only family I have now."

Rin's shoulders softened, though she still gave him a suspicious sidelong look.

"I mean it. I've mostly been trying to figure out more about"—he shot a look around them to ensure no one had gotten close before leaning in close and speaking even softer—"this *crazy* magic I have and how dangerous it was, before I got you two involved."

"You mean that?" she asked, suddenly looking more vulnerable than Pax had seen her.

"That I planned on telling you, eventually? Yes, of course."

"No, not that," she said with an impatient shake of her head. "The family part?"

Pax straightened and really looked at her. An emotion he rarely felt hit him and made him blink against stinging eyes. Holding her gaze, he dropped some of his own defenses and let her see the truth as he nodded. "Yes," he said simply.

"You better not be lying," she said, her features stiff as she ran her eyes over him, looking for something.

"Because you'd kill me?" he asked with a grin. "Is that any way to treat family?"

"Don't lie to me about this," she said, still serious.

"Never," he said, letting his expression match hers. "Never. Not about this. The only way you lose me and Amil is if one of us dies."

"And we're not letting that happen any time soon," Rin said, her fierceness returning, pushing aside the vulnerability as if it hadn't existed. Then she grinned. "I'm the only one allowed to kill you."

"Hey," he said, raising his hands in protest. "You have to be nice to me. We're family now."

"Not hardly," she said as she moved past and arched a brow at him. "Family can be much more dangerous than just friends."

Grinning, Pax followed her toward where Amil browsed through weapons in the back. Now they needed a detailed plan on how to best capitalize on the items they'd reserved to sell on consignment.

48

SHARED SECRETS

"AND THAT'S REALLY ALL I know about it, even though I've had my spark since I was a little kid," Pax finished, leaning back in his chair at the outdoor table and looking at a speechless Amil and Rin.

He forced his expression to stay friendly despite the sick feeling of regret that bubbled up inside him. Had he just made a horrible mistake sharing information that could bring the Academy mages down on him and ruin his future?

The three had met an hour before breakfast to share information they'd gathered and hash out a game plan. The chilly seating area outside was deserted this early, fallen leaves scattered across the stone-paved courtyard. A few determined birds pecking between the cracks for any remnants of dropped food.

Pax had weighed the value of his friends helping him with his new magic versus how dangerous it was to share his secrets. He knew he could trust Amil, though his friend was known for letting things slip by accident.

And Rin? She was smart enough to realize the value and danger of his secret immediately. If she wanted to capitalize on it, he would be in real trouble. Pax felt his breath catch in his throat as he waited for their response and hoped he hadn't just ruined everything for himself.

"So, just to be clear, you have a different element?" Rin finally asked, leaning forward and lowering her voice. "Light, not air? But you think you'll be able to use all four elements, eventually?"

Pax blew out his breath slowly and couldn't help his shoulders slumping in relief. Rin, wanting more technical details, was so much better than the other responses he'd imagined.

"It looks like it," Pax said, doing his best to keep his tone even. "And it's something that might get me kicked out, or worse. So, we can't let even a hint slip to anyone else." He paused a moment to give Amil a pointed look. "I'm struggling with how I can both keep this a secret and still advance my magic at the same time. I really need your help."

"Of course." Rin sat back, her eyes thoughtful. "And both of us know how to keep a secret." She exchanged a nod with Amil, and Pax couldn't help smiling.

With a proud grin spread across his face, Amil nudged Rin and chuckled. "I told you he always has something amazing up his sleeve." He turned back to Pax. "So, how is this going to help us get ahead? What's the next step?"

"Well, obviously, he's got to get this understanding path thing done as quickly as possible." Rin tapped one finger on her lips, thinking. "At least for air. His spell instructor will figure something's wrong pretty fast if he doesn't get a real air spell and control a bit of air around him. They're serious about sticking to the rules here. Any experimenting with the normal elements, much less a new one, will raise suspicions, or worse, get you snapped up and questioned by inquisitors."

"Wait, by who?" Pax asked.

Amil aimed a surprised look at Rin, too. "How are we supposed to learn if we don't try different things?"

Rin looked exasperated. "Did either of you even pay attention during the Traditions and Rules lecture on the first day?"

"Um," Amil said slowly, as he ran a hand through his blonde hair looking sheepish.

"I think we both might have zoned off during that," Pax admitted. "That day is just a blur now, and that part was pretty slow and boring."

"How are we supposed to figure out this place if you don't even know the rules?" Rin asked, looking exasperated. "Obviously, I'm fine with breaking them, but being ignorant is going to get you both caught and leave me all on my own again."

"Sorry," Pax said. "You're right. Can you summarize?"

She nodded and paused, gathering her thoughts. "So, you know the Cataclysm?"

"Sure," Pax answered. "The nasty event that opened the elemental wells out past the tower rings. Those wells spew out lots of evil magic and create the monsters that come in the beast waves, right? But wasn't that hundreds of years ago? What does it matter now?"

"The cause of the Cataclysm was experimenting with magic," Rin said and paused, waiting.

"That makes no sense," Amil objected. "How could the wells and all the beasts for years and years come from trying something new with magic?"

"I don't think people know all the details," Rin said with a shrug. "The story they told us in the lecture is pretty vague. The empire back then, or multiple empires maybe, was facing some kind of powerful enemy. Mages constantly ran out of mana in battle and needed a new source if they were going to survive. A bunch of horrible, short-sighted mages got together to try something dangerous."

"Horrible? Short-sighted?" Pax asked, sounding dubious.

Rin shrugged. "If you hadn't snoozed through it, you'd have heard the official story slamming these mages at every chance, even though it seems they were just trying to survive. Anyway, the flame mages were the first to use some big, new spell that used a bunch of mages together to open up the first well. At least they did it out close to the battlefront and far from the populated areas."

"But if it spewed monsters, why would they open the other three?" Amil asked.

"That's just the thing," Rin explained. "At first, it was a stable, powerful mana well, just like they'd hoped for. The mages could draw on the well and refill their mana over and over. A mage could fight for hours without running out. The lecture glossed over this part, but it seems the success convinced the other three elemental groups to do the same thing on the remaining corners of the battlefront."

"Wow," Pax said. "I can't imagine what all that power would look like, bubbling up from a well and free for the taking. How did it go wrong?"

Rin shrugged. "That's the problem. No one really knows."

Amil let out a disappointed sound.

"Well, it happened forever ago," Rin tried to explain. "But even worse, all the best mages and students moved out to the wells, taking their equipment, manuals and spell scrolls with them. The wells became new hubs as the empire started to win the war. I'm guessing that means only the crappy mages stayed behind in the cities and capital. Of course, that's not in the official story. So, that means—" Rin paused and gave them an expectant look.

"When the wells turned dangerous, or whatever happened—" Pax said slowly, realization dawning.

"—the Cataclysm killed the best the empire had and wiped out all their stuff, leaving us with the political mages and scaredy cats who weren't brave enough to fight on the front lines." Rin finished.

"And they were the ones in charge of rebuilding and making rules, so another cataclysm never happened," Pax said, appalled.

"Which means absolutely no experimenting with new magics, ever," Rin held up a hand to tick off the rules. "And no working magic together in groups or casting spells with other mages, even if you're the same element. Though if your spells run into each other during a battle, as long as it's after casting, that's alright. The only real bit of freedom that's allowed is a mage's build and choice of spells, or a powerful artifact with a special ability. So, now the clans hold tightly to their spells, meditation techniques, etc. since there won't be anything new coming along."

"And there's nothing left of all those spell scrolls, training manuals, even the mages' journals destroyed at the wells," Pax said, sitting back and feeling dejected. "So, based on what I saw at the pedestal, they probably had light mages back then, but no one knows."

Rin's expression turned grim as she glanced around to ensure they were still alone. "Don't even say stuff like that out loud. From the tone of that lecture, the inquisitors will snap you up at even the slightest hint of something off. The last half of the lecture was just a bunch of warnings and threats to scare us into falling into line."

Pax swallowed hard, glad of his paranoid instincts. Without them, he might have already run afoul of the people in charge. "So, job number one is for all of us to keep this very quiet and not let anything slip, right?"

Rin nodded, looking serious, but Amil was still grinning and looking excited.

Rin gave him an exasperated look. "This is serious, Amil. We could all lose our magic if anyone gets wind of what we're doing."

When Amil looked suitably chastened, Pax continued, "Then I'll test to see if I'm right about my Path of Understanding for air. I had planned to see if I could do anything with the extra air cores we held back. Plus, maybe you two could help me with flame and water? It'll be even harder to keep the extra elements under wraps, but we're going to need them in the catacombs, and especially during the purge. Plus, if I can figure out a way to unlock them for others, then even crazier things become possible."

"And dangerous things," Rin muttered, but Pax could see her considering the possibilities.

Her caution dampened Pax's excitement, but he was glad to have her on his side. She'd help keep them all safer. But he still refused to settle for the safe route of being an obedient mage student.

Pax had never dreamed he'd leave the street rat life. Now that he had, he would never go back to accepting his lot in life. Not that he planned on taking stupid risks, but the glimpse of power and possibilities here filled him with more hope and excitement about his future than he'd ever had.

"And make sure you do the core work where no one can see you either." Rin was still speaking. "That was on the list of no-no's, too. Apparently, messing with beast cores is really dangerous and can burn out a mage's magic somehow? Plus—" she paused, looking hesitant.

"What?" Amil asked. "Tell us."

"Well, in the list of threats at the end, they mentioned trying to draw on the magic in beast cores might increase the chance of becoming monster-touched." She gave an anxious glance at his left arm, covered by his sleeve.

Pax snorted a short laugh, and Rin looked relieved. "First, since almost all I've done so far is figure out how to force my magic to obey me, I can't see a tiny core burning me out. And the monster-touched warning is pretty stupid, since everyone I know with one was born with it. Besides, since I already have one, I don't have much to worry about, do I?"

"Maybe I could get one," Amil broke in. "If we ever get any flame cores."

"What?" Pax stared at his friend in surprise and tapped his arm. "Why would you ever want something like this?"

"What? Tough scales that keep me from being cut? Maybe a claw that comes in handy during a fight? Are you kidding?" Amil said. "I've always been jealous of yours. Besides, it just looks so cool."

Pax broke into a tentative smile as Rin shot him a look and shrugged. "I don't think it's all that bad either."

"Thanks, guys," Pax said, suddenly in a much better mood, but ready to change the subject. "People are showing up. What have we figured out for this week?"

Amil glanced over his shoulder through the glass windows into the eating hall where they could see a few figures trickling in.

"We still have time," Rin said dismissively, pulling her cloak closer. "None of those delicate flowers will come out here until it fills up inside. Now here's what I was thinking . . ."

49

BEST-LAID PLANS

"WAIT, before the boring stuff, can we talk about the rankings?" Amil said, turning back and leaning in toward Rin and Pax with a conspiratorial glee on his face. "I can't wait to see people's faces when we go in for breakfast. If we can figure out how to keep earning points this week, we might actually make it into the top three and score some sweet gear."

Pax looked at Amil, not wanting to admit he didn't know what his friend was talking about.

Rin saw his look and laughed as she shook her head. "You've had your head in the clouds about killing monsters and selling all our loot. Why do you think everyone is so focused on earning points in classes?"

"Hey," he protested. "I've noticed. Amil even earned one in his spell class on the first day. But I just thought we'd need quite a few before we could get anything good on the treasure floors of the store."

"That's still true," Amil agreed. "But it's the weekly ranking that's a big deal. This is the first week, so, on Saturday, they hand out the prizes to the top three earners for the week during an assembly. And everyone says the first week has awesome prizes, like enchanted items or even uncommon spell scrolls."

Pax's eyes widened, and he felt his own flicker of excitement and greed. "And you get to keep the points you earn? Or do they take them in exchange for the prizes?"

"Keep them," Amil said with a smug nod. "So, you get the winning prize and can still go spend your points at the store."

"Wow," Pax said, as he resolved to pay better attention.

"Exactly," Rin said with a nod. "And sometimes they award a prize scroll good for a certain rank of item. You could choose from among spell scrolls, a piece of armor or even a weapon with one of those. And if it's a specific prize, you can always take points if the prize doesn't work for you or sell it on consignment."

"No," Pax objected. "That would be a complete waste when the three of us still need so much: better armor, spells and even a decent weapon each."

"Yes, weapons," Amil interrupted, latching onto the topic. "Thank you for being practical, Pax. I tried discussing weapons with the other power mages and got shot down hard. The idiots think that they only need a decent set of armor, their spells, and the warriors in their group to protect them. Idiots."

"Exactly," Pax agreed. "I've got my clubs, and you seem pretty comfortable with a hammer, Amil. Rin, we need to help you pick out something good. I'll add that to our list for the week. We'll take some time in the yards trying different practice weapons on the dummies to see what fits and works the best for each of us." Pax jotted a quick note in his notebook before looking up. "But back to the potential rewards. What do you think about working together on those, too?"

"To earn more points together?" Rin asked, looking puzzled. "I thought we were already doing that with our assignments and killing beasts."

"Well yes, that too. But I mean, if any of us earns a top prize. If it's something we can't use ourselves, then we see if it's something one of the other two can use before taking points or selling it."

Amil was already nodding while Rin looked interested.

"Because if we can track the source of these beasts," Pax said, already imagining the coming windfall, "we may earn more prizes than expected."

"This might all fall through, but I agree," Rin said slowly, "As long as we make sure it eventually comes out even. One of us shouldn't walk away with all the prizes just because they fit them perfectly, while the others get nothing."

"Agreed," Pax said, thinking quickly. "How about whoever gets a prize moves to last place in consideration, and if one of us ever has two more than the others, they get nothing else until the others catch up, even if we have to take points or sell it to get an item that works better?"

"Perfect." Rin gave him an impressed look, and Pax felt the now familiar wash of energy through him. He could read the unspoken respect in her body language and felt his own internal dialogue of what to say next improving. A flash in the corner of his vision told him he'd likely see a boost in Charisma next time he checked.

"So, how about we reserve either an arena or a practice field every morning around this time?" Pax continued, jotting more notes in his book. "Then we can keep up-to-date with each other before doing spell or weapon training. We could even try to get a spot in one of the obstacle courses together, too? I think if we try for the afternoon, we won't be able to get one to ourselves."

"Sure. Sounds good. So, are we done?" Amil asked, throwing a longing look over his shoulder at the filling mess hall.

"Just meet back here after dinner to do another run down into the catacombs," Rin said. "Mistress Nymeli grabbed me yesterday and said she's wrangled permission for us to do another search for more beasts. Apparently, the mages are in a bit of a tizzy about the whole thing, some fighting over whether it should be under their control, with a bunch doubtful if it even really happened."

"What?" Pax asked. "The pile of beast parts wasn't proof enough?"

"Poor Mistress Nymeli is just a kitchen worker who has no magic or experience with beast identification," Rin said in a sing-song imitation of an arrogant voice before returning to her own sardonic one. "And none of them will take a trip into the nasty underground to see for themselves. Other mages felt that a handful of measly level 1s weren't much concern as long as someone was working to get rid of them."

Pax's smile kept widening as Rin explained. "I bet the mistress did her best to encourage that attitude, didn't she?"

Rin nodded. "Which means that, for now, we have whatever beasts we can find down there all to ourselves."

The door to the mess hall opened behind them, letting out a bubble of sound and warmth as three students holding trays backed their way through before turning to look for somewhere to sit.

"Yeah," Rin said, aiming a pointed look at them as she changed the subject abruptly. "I'm hoping my advisor can help me figure out my next spell, too."

Playing along, Pax gave her an interested nod and took the hint that their private discussion was now over.

Chatting animatedly, the trio headed their direction only for the lead boy to pull up sharply when he saw them. Eyes wide, he leaned close to the others and whispered something. Both of them shot looks toward Pax and his friends before the trio veered away and found somewhere else to sit.

"What was that about?" Pax asked, not sure if he should feel insulted.

"Oh," Rin said, exchanging a knowing look with Amil. "Do you want to explain to Mr. Oblivious what's going on, or should I?"

Amil grinned. "Remember how you wanted to stay under the radar?"

Pax dropped his head and rubbed at his eyes, already guessing what was coming.

"Well, the other first-years aren't as disinterested about an unknown source of beasts under our feet, level 1 or not. I heard a bunch went looking for vermin assignments, but Mistress Nymeli had already pulled them. We're the only ones authorized for the duty until we know more about the problem. I've already had a few students approach me, asking to join us." Amil's eyes turned dreamy, making Pax groan.

"No one is joining our team right now," Pax insisted. "I don't care how cute they are."

"I know. But a guy can dream, can't he?"

"That's not all," Rin said, when Amil didn't continue. "Check out the Academy Point rankings for the week."

Pax perked up. He might not like attention, but if it turned out to be lucrative, then maybe he'd change his mind. "Where are they posted?"

Both Amil and Rin snickered at him as they stood to head in for breakfast.

"In your menu, dunder," Amil said. "Under miscellaneous."

"Oh, and don't get upset when you see which of us is on top," Rin said as she bumped Pax with an elbow.

Pax ignored their antics as he hurried to pull up his menu. There it was, under the miscellaneous section he'd always just skimmed over.

~

Week 1: Shieldwall Academy First-Year Academy Point Top 10

1. Codrun Shadowforge - 11
   2. Izoa Yelren - 9
   3. Hoset Wraithaxe - 8
   4. Aymer Wynrel - 8
   5. Orist Valdi - 7
   6. Maleth Chaosback- 7
   7. Kali Wynrel - 7
   8. Amil Fajor - 6
   9. Rin Esta - 5
   10. Pax Vipersworn - 5

~

"Top ten?" Pax stopped just before entering the eating hall and grabbed both Rin and Amil's arms in excitement.

"Keep it down," Amil said before shooting an impish grin toward the filling hall. "There might still be one or two students who don't know."

"So, not quite following your plan to avoid notice, but—" Rin added, with a pleased grin.

Pax nodded happily, only to stop. "Hey, I get Amil being up on us by one with the point he got on the first day of class. But you and I are tied. Why are you listed first?"

"The powers that be have obviously recognized my genius," Rin said with a smug look before turning to lead the way into the hall.

"I'm just keeping a low profile," he called after her with a laugh before he and Amil shrugged and followed her inside.

GEARING UP

Pax crammed an entire voca pastry into his mouth from dinner that evening as he and Amil hurried to catch up with Rin. He'd made a point of asking Krasig the name of the delicious purple fruit that filled the treats he'd fallen in love with. The kitchen baked the crusts to perfection, flakey and buttery. The voca was the same fruit that made the dark juice they'd enjoyed right after finishing the Crucible. It grew somewhere in the warm land to the north, out in flame country.

"Can you finish that thing so we can get your attention back in the real world?" Rin interrupted his musing with the half-irritated, half-amused question. "I'm still worn out from classes today, and we don't have a lot of time to get geared up and practice.

Pax blinked when he realized they'd already made it to the arena complex and were walking inside. The full day of Wednesday classes had tapped him out, and he wondered if he could get Krasig to start slipping him extra beast meat at dinner instead of just lunch.

The thought triggered an idea, and Pax kicked himself for not thinking of it earlier. Could he process some of the remaining bog swarmer meat and use that for a boost? He'd need to be careful, because there was probably a reason for the single serving a day for first-years, but it warranted looking into.

He could sure use the boost. Conditioning class, even more brutal than the first day, had only given him a single, long-awaited Agility point, but nothing to Strength or Endurance. It appeared the progress toward attribute points was cumulative and got more difficult the more they advanced. He couldn't figure out how to tell how close he was to the next ones. The first-year warriors they'd brought in to attack with padded weapons in his spell class had likely pushed his Agility up the final bit it needed.

Graybrew had been less than impressed with Pax's continued inability to summon air, but at least his light Haste spell had worked a lot better while facing the other students who didn't have Zanneth's insane Agility. He'd evaded most attacks, leaving Graybrew aiming a disgruntled look his way but not calling him back after class.

And then, he'd still had his shift in the workshop after an already long day, which made his sore muscles thrum even worse. He was really looking forward to the next bump up in Strength or Endurance.

As soon as Pax had a free moment to think, he planned to try to see if his new healing skill would do anything for his worn-out body. He couldn't help the flush of satisfaction as he remembered stopping the bleeding of his cut during meditation class. He hadn't healed the cut completely before time was up, but was making progress. A little faster, and he'd earn a top spot in class for more Academy points.

In fact, he'd paid a lot more attention in beast class this morning and almost made the top three there, too. Funny how an in-person fight with beasts made the class suddenly a lot less boring.

"Done eating yet, Pax? You with us?" Rin had stopped and turned to punch his shoulder.

"Hey," he protested, rubbing at his arm as he saw Rin had led them to the far side where a row of small practice arenas stood.

"Don't get between a man and his favorite food," Amil said, walking past the two toward an open doorway with lights and people moving about inside. "Just offer him something just as nice, like his pick of practice weapons and armor." Then he lowered his voice and said, "Or a beautiful girl for me."

Pax swallowed, wiped his hands on his pants and grinned as he followed Amil. "You know me so well."

Rin let out a disgusted snort and followed the two boys into the arena supply center where clerks stood behind a long counter, assisting a variety of students.

"Next," called out an older man in a bored tone, waving them forward when the warrior student ahead of them left the counter, intent on the bow and quiver she held in her hands.

"What can I do for you?"

Pax hesitated and looked at his friends, unsure of what they could ask for.

"First-years," the man said under his breath before plastering on a fake smile. "Alright. Mage students get a set of plain leather armor to use for the year and while not responsible for normal wear and tear, they *are* responsible for any damage done to said armor. The crafter academy has a repair shop set up next door where you can either learn how to fix things yourself, or pay one of their students to do it for you."

Pax grinned at Amil, not at all put off by the warnings. If he'd had something to protect his legs, he would have done much better against the swarmers.

"What about weapons?" Amil asked, looking eager.

The man stirred at that, giving Amil a curious look. "Most mages don't carry anything more than a knife, especially once they can afford enchanted staffs and such."

"What about when their mana runs out in a battle?" Rin asked the question they'd all been wondering about.

"They sit down in a protected area and meditate to get it back faster," the man said as if it were the most obvious answer. "If they spend time fighting instead, it'll only take longer before they can use their spells again."

"Oh," Amil said, the logic seeming to have burst his idea of fighting like a warrior in between spell uses.

"But, as mage students, you are entitled to check out a single weapon to train with," the man said as if expecting them to refuse.

"That would be perfect," Pax answered brightly. "Can I take a look at your clubs? Amil here would like a good hammer and Rin?" He turned to look at her.

"A bow," she said, surprising Pax and Amil.

"Are you sure?" the clerk asked, doubt obvious on his face. "That isn't an easy skill to learn, even for warriors who have access to class abilities that help them."

"I'm sure," Rin said, a stubborn set to her jaw.

"Fine," the man said, making notes on a handheld chalkboard. "The same rule applies to the weapons, you are responsible to fix any damage before turning them in or exchanging them."

The three of them nodded their heads in agreement, waiting for the man to finish.

"Alright. One of you can step into the back room for your armor fitting while I bring out the weapon choices for the other two.

"We've got less than an hour left before we agreed to report to Mistress Nymeli," Rin said as they jogged across the hall to the practice arenas they'd reserved. "I got us an arena with both targets and practice dummies so we can work on whatever we think we'll need tonight."

Pax and Amil were right behind her, grinning in their new-to-them leather armor; weapons in hand. Pax had found the basic clubs no better than his own bone ones, though he'd convinced the man to let him look at more advanced versions and had some ideas for improving his when he had time. Amil had found a much sturdier version of the hammer he'd borrowed from the kitchen and had taken some time to give it a good polish with the provided supplies while they waited for Rin to finish. It had taken a bit more time for her to get fitted with a bow that matched her size and strength, but they were finally done and ready to break all the new gear in.

Rin pushed open the wooden door. "After you mages," she said in a snooty voice, waving them in with an extravagant gesture.

It didn't take long for them to get busy. Amil quickly got the feel of his new hammer with happy grunts while Rin did her best to figure out her bow. Pax heard occasional curses from her direction until she finally moved close enough to the target to see some success.

Already very familiar with his clubs, Pax focused on practicing the technique he'd stumbled upon with the swarmers, filling them with his mana while fighting. Choosing a good position in front of the practice dummy, he took a cleansing breath and settled into a loose combat stance, clubs raised and ready.

Reaching for his spark, Pax split the energy and sent it rushing up both hands into his clubs. It moved easier than ever, filling the clubs only to wash back like a wave returning after hitting the shore.

Frowning, Pax pushed again. The mana seemed willing to go where he sent it, but as soon as he stopped pushing, it left on its own, naturally flowing back to his body. As he tested the effect, Pax realized he needed to keep a constant mental pressure on the mana to ensure it stayed in the clubs. He'd probably done that instinctively during the adrenaline-fueled fight, but that was another reason he was practicing. He needed to understand exactly what he'd done so he could reliably reproduce it.

A few moments later, he used some of his simpler strikes against the dummy, reveling in how light and responsive his clubs were when filled with his mana. Once warmed up, his muscle aches fading to the background, Pax knew he needed to figure out a way to affix the mana to his clubs so it would stay without his constant monitoring. Fights already required a lot of focus and once he had more spells, he'd definitely need fewer things pulling at his attention.

Considering the best way to proceed, Pax looked down at his clubs, thinking.

"One thing at a time works best," Rin called out.

Pax looked up to see her rueful look as she motioned toward the target that now stood only a handful of yards in front of her. "Don't try to do it all at once like I just did. It's working much better now that I'm up close. I'm working on just one thing right now, a gentle release while holding everything else steady. I'll worry about hitting the target from farther away once I get the other stuff down."

Pax gave her a grateful nod and turned back to his dummy wondering if he should have taken up the clerk on his offer of a short club lesson to help him get started. Next time, he resolved to take the time to see if he could pick up any useful pointers.

Setting himself up again, Pax took Rin's advice. He'd do as much by routine as possible so he could focus on the mana in his clubs. Moving at a relaxed speed, he began a simple, repeating movement with his clubs. Right slashing in, left in, right out, left out, a basic figure eight, the first pattern he'd learned when he'd added a second club to his fighting technique.

Once he fell into a comfortable pattern with the thuds against the dummy reverberating up his clubs, Pax let his body run on autopilot while he turned his focus to the mana in his weapons. It had already ebbed in strength just from the little bit of distraction.

For a moment, the whole thing was a bit too much to keep in control, not just moving his arms correctly, but trying to focus on his mana with his eyes open. Pax hadn't realized how much it had been helping to close his eyes and practice with his mana in a still, quiet environment.

Wanting to tense and force his mana wasn't going to help, so Pax took a moment to regulate his breathing, slowing his inhale to a four beat that coincided with one set of strikes before exhaling for the next set. It took another few minutes and a couple of out-of-sequence breaths before he felt himself settle into the pattern.

Holding onto the fluid state he'd found, Pax completed a few more cycles until he felt he could continue both the strikes and the breathing without giving it much thought. Forcing himself to keep his eyes open, Pax let the focus of his eyes soften a bit so his clubs and the edges of the dummy blurred. He pushed, and his mana responded eagerly under his command, filling the clubs at his insistence.

He kept pushing until he felt resistance push back, as if the clubs had reached their capacity for mana. His pattern stuttered a moment, but he quickly got it back under control, his breathing and the *rat-a-tat* of his clubs back to their regular pattern a minute later.

Finally, Pax felt as if he'd achieved an equilibrium and while the drain on his mana was continuous, it was much smaller than when he had healed his leg. He regenerated mana faster, which would allow him to almost keep his clubs infused indefinitely. But now what? How could he keep the mana from leaking out as soon as his attention was needed elsewhere?

His first idea was that he could block the end of the clubs with some kind of mental cork, like a bottle once you'd filled it. The next few minutes were a fruitless exercise in trying to turn his slippery magic into a solid shape that would plug the end of the clubs.

Pushing the frustration aside, Pax let his mind search for a new idea. He ran through everything he'd done and learned with his strange magic. For some reason, learning to heal his leg came to mind. The cycle he'd been able to establish there didn't seem to have anything to do with creating a blockage. More the opposite, really.

Then why had his subconscious brought it to mind? What else had he done to heal his leg?

With sudden clarity, Pax understood what his mind had been trying to tell him.

BREAKTHROUGH

UNDERSTANDING.

His magic was all about delving into the world around him and understanding its inner structure and functions: magic bracelets, attacking beasts, and even his own body. Excited by his new idea, Pax pushed his mana sight closer into the clubs, trying to understand them like he had his leg. Keeping his eyes open while continuing the figure-eight pattern and steady breathing made the entire thing much more difficult than studying his leg had been.

Pax was tempted to give up and sit down with the clubs to examine them in a quiet meditation position instead. But he could sense he was close. His stubborn side plus his practical fighter insisted he keep going. It wasn't like a swarm of beasts was going to wait politely for him to close his eyes and focus when he needed to. His magic skills had to be trained to work in combat, not a calm classroom.

Slowly, amidst the regular thudding against the dummy, Pax followed his mana as it flowed through the inner structure of his bone clubs. Time fell away, a much stronger effect than his Haste spell, as he delved deeper and deeper. The solid outer shell of bone, he expected. But to his surprise, Pax found the center of the structure made of a fine matrix of thin crisscrossing strands and chaotic air pockets, as if a mass of bubbles had suddenly frozen solid.

His mana raced along the inner latticework, seeming to add both strength and flexibility to the inner structure. Fascinated, Pax felt as if he'd discovered an entirely new world invisible to the naked eye. He would have to ask Mage Lorkranna if Freddy had a bone he could examine next time he was in class.

Now to get the mana to stay. Over the next few minutes, Pax tried everything he could come up with. Pushing it, pulling it, even squeezing it together with individual parts of the bone. Long frustrating minutes passed, and Pax could feel the muscles in his arms and upper back burning despite trying to stay as relaxed and strike as lightly as possible.

Just as he was about to give up, he remembered the flicker of flame magic he'd felt in the bone clubs when he'd first pulled them from the scrap pile at the workshop. His success with the bracelets had been when he'd merged his magic with the mana he'd seen. With renewed energy, he pushed his mana sight to look for the echo of flame mana left from the beast's life.

It turned out to be very simple once he found the flickers of heat still rooted to the structure of the bone. They provided the anchors he needed. Pulling on both his light mana and the threads of flame he could find in his own energy, Pax forced it to bend to his will and affix itself to the bone's mana. He held the pressure for another few ticks of time before holding his breath and letting go. It held. With no extra effort, his mana stayed in the clubs. When a notification flickered below, he expanded it with excitement.

～

MAGE SKILL UNLOCKED: **Mana Merge** Level 1

This epic skill is a more advanced version of Mana Infusion, which is used only to empower runes for enchanting purposes. Merge gives a mage more flexibility to merge their mana with the innate mana in either objects or people. With more control, the mage can change or enhance the attributes of the object or innate mana depending on the elements of mana used and their relative strengths. The better a mage understands the structure and magic of the target for the skill, the more effective the merge, and the more possibilities are available. This skill replaces Mana Infusion and works in concert with mana manipulation, mana sight and element meditation.

Distance: Touch. Distance merging is possible at higher levels, depending on the advancement path.

Mana cost: The amount of mana merged will be lost if the merge is made permanent or recovered if not.

*Skill Boost: +3 to **Mana Merge** Level 1 - 3/100*

∽

"Yes!" he yelled out, hitting the dummy with two last strikes full of all his excitement and energy.

Amil stopped mid hammer swing and glanced over at him in question.

"What?" Rin called out, lowering her bow and looking interested.

"Let me check my menu first and I'll explain," Pax said, and closed his eyes before they could object.

∽

Name: Pax Vipersworn

    Race: Mixed Human (monster-touched)

    Age: 16

    Bound Location: Shieldwall Mage Academy (provisional monthly)

    Class: Mage

    Element: Light (Hidden)

    Specialization: none (Hidden)

    Paths of Understanding: (Hidden)

    Flame: Level 1 - 21/100 (+7)

    Air: Level 1 - 51/100 (+8)

    Water: Level 1 - 9/100 (+2)

    Earth: Level 1 - 10/100 (+3)

Level: 1
Mage Leveling Points: 0/5
Health: 40/40 (+3)
Mana: 21/26
Attributes:
Strength: 6 (+1)
Agility: 9 (+1)
Endurance: 7 (+1)
Intelligence: 8
Insight: 7
Charisma: 5 (+2)
Skills:
General Active:
Identify Level 1 (Common) - 59/100 (+12)
General Passive:
Skinning Level 1 (Common) - 36/100 (+12)
Butchering Level 1 (Common) - 49/100 (+13)
Clubs Level 1 (Common) - 16/100 (+2)
Mage:
Light Mana Manipulation Level 1 (Epic) - 32/100 (+8) (Hidden)
Light Mana Sight Level 1 (Rare) - 40/100 (+6) (Hidden)
Elemental Meditation Level 1 (Common) - 8/100 (+2)
Light Healing Level 1 (Rare) - 4/100 (+4) (Hidden)
Runes Level 1 (Uncommon) - 4/100 (+4)
Mana Merge Level 1 (Epic) - 3/100 (+3)
Spells:
Light (1/3):
Haste Level 1 (Common) - 22/100 (+2)
Inventory: 6/20 available.
Assignments:
Academy Workshop Trainee
4/30 hours (+2)
0/1 Supervisor approval
Charity Clinic Trainee
2/30 hours (+2)

0/1 Supervisor approval
Maintenance Trainee
0/21 Cleared blockages
0/1 Supervisor approval
Exterminator Trainee
48/100 Vermin killed (+6)
0/1 Supervisor approval
Misc.: *First-year Point Ranking (expand)*

THE HOST of increased points spread out over almost all his skills and abilities made him smile. The combination of classwork, along with his shifts in the workshop and clinic, had boosted almost everything. Plus, the potential in the new mana merge skill filled him with excitement. He toggled it to (Hidden) and resolved to spend more time exploring its uses and reading carefully over the description.

Grinning, he opened his eyes to share his new breakthrough, only to find both his friends had turned to face the entrance, postures stiff.

The familiar voice made Pax's heart drop.

"Why were his clubs glowing?" The grating voice, full of suspicion, made all three friends turn to the entrance of their arena.

Kurt stood in front of the opened door and glared at them. "I knew the three of you were up to something. Good thing I followed you after dinner and cracked open the door to keep an eye on you. That's not air magic."

Pax opened his mouth to explain, a jumble of crazy excuses trying to coalesce into something logical but failing.

"Are you spying on us?" Rin lowered her bow, an arrow in the other hand as she strode toward Kurt, going on the attack before Pax could get a word out.

Kurt looked startled at her censure, as if he'd expected the three of them to be cowed.

With a pull that was becoming more practiced every day, Pax jerked his mana back into the clubs, returning them to their natural glistening white bone in the evening light. Moving to join Rin, he let a disdainful sneer fill his face, adopting Rin's instinct to attack, which was a much better idea when dealing with Kurt.

"The arenas are public," Kurt argued. "Students can observe if they want."

"Hmm," Pax said, adopting a dubious look. "How about we all go together to the scheduling clerk and ask if another student has permission to open a closed door to a private practice arena that was officially scheduled? We've got a few minutes to sort this out, don't we guys?" He gave Rin and Amil an exaggerated questioning look.

"Well," Kurt stuttered as he backed out of the doorway.

The three walked closer, weapons lowered but still in hand. Pax let a predatory grin emerge on his face as he realized he liked being on the more powerful side for once.

"And just because you're too weak to afford enchanted gear and equipment," Amil drawled with scorn heavy in his voice, "doesn't mean the rest of us can't."

Sudden doubt flashed across the elven boy's face as he glanced at Pax's lowered clubs and hands.

"Scurry on back to Galen now," Pax ordered, flicking one club and trying not to enjoy Kurt's flinch.

"That's exactly what I'm going to do," Kurt retorted, suddenly stiffening with strength again. "You're going to regret treating me like this, when I tell him what I saw."

Pax kept his face impassive, doing his best to disguise the flash of worry he felt at Kurt's words. With Graybrew already keeping a close eye on him, the last thing he needed was more suspicion to fuel Galen's already burning hatred. The 'crat could bring an investigation down on him if he got the idea in his head.

Rin's full-throated laughter caught him by surprise, and only after Amil followed suit did he hurry to join in.

"What?" Kurt asked, looking flustered. "It's not funny. Galen is going to mess with you. All of you."

"Sorry, guys," Rin said, stifling her laughter and waving an apologetic hand at Pax and Amil. "I couldn't keep it together when I saw his face. I almost made it."

"No worries," Pax said, picking up on her game immediately and grinning at the beauty of it. "We'll put on a better show next time."

"What?" Kurt shook his head, looking confused.

"Nothing," Pax said. "Just head on back to your buddy and tell him all about my *glowing* sticks." He held up his clubs with a face of exaggerated horror, prompting snickers from Rin and Amil.

"Just face it, Kurt," Rin said, her humor suddenly replaced by a chilly look that made Pax glad she wasn't aiming it his way. "We're ahead of you every step of the way, and that goes for the idiot you're sucking up to. Now scram!" She barked the last part out while jamming the arrow in her hand toward Kurt's face.

He let out an involuntary squeak and almost tripped, scrambling out through the door.

Rin pushed it shut with a resounding thud behind him. Turning, she sagged back against it, her face suddenly full of doubt and worry as she met the others' gazes. "Do you think he bought it?"

CATACOMB DISCOVERIES

"Maybe we should have picked an entirely new tunnel to explore," Rin said, pointing her small fire-core lightstick at the jagged hole as Pax and Amil finished pulling the last bits of debris out of the way. "With the big nest of swarmers we killed here, there aren't likely to be more beasts down there, right?"

"You just don't want to crawl down a dark tunnel," Amil said with a mocking grin.

"Because I'm smart," Rin countered. "Or did you not realize you can't use your hammer at all in there? And if you use your flame blast, we'll likely get cooked along with any beasts."

Amil's smile faded as he looked at Rin, obviously having not thought it through.

"And it's nasty," Rin added triumphantly. "So, go find another tunnel?"

"No. Because—" Pax said, immediately lifting a hand to fend off Rin's objections when she whirled on him "—the swarmers were the only beasts anyone has seen down here, right? And since we're not the only ones with maintenance assignments, that means the swarmers were likely an unusual case. And where did they come from?" He pointed triumphantly down at the forbidding hole.

"In there," Rin said dejectedly.

"In there," Amil crowed, looking excited again.

"Did you not get enough exploring nasty sewers back home?" Rin asked with irritation.

"Nope." Amil didn't look at all fazed by her disapproval as he vanished his hammer into his inventory and pulled out a pair of leather gloves and a knife. "And we always found the best stuff in the places no one else would go, didn't we, Pax?"

Pax gave Rin a sheepish shrug and nodded. "He's right. And I've got a feeling it might happen here, too. Really, where do you think this leads to, and how did the swarmers make it through the wall protections? The answer is in there." He pointed at the knee-high hole, gaping at them like a monster frozen in mid-bite, waiting to swallow anyone who entered.

"In there," Rin agreed reluctantly. She shook her head and inventoried her bow and quiver, following Amil's example by donning gloves and equipping a knife. "Fine. But you're going to help me get my equipment and clothes clean after this. Deal?"

"Deal." Pax nodded happily. "Now, let's put anything we think we'll need into our inventories, but leave spots open in case we find anything good. I'm leaving my pack over behind those rocks once I get what I need out of it. We can't wear anything that'll get caught if the tunnel gets even smaller."

Rin frowned at that, but followed his example. The next few minutes passed as they shifted supplies around, pulling out a lot of the gear Amil had used their funds to pick up from the Academy Store. Ropes, twine, canteens, hatchets, utility knives, fire starters and even a fire-core lightstick for each of them.

The last had been a bit of a splurge and made him look glumly at the diminishing number of coppers in his total, but with all the work they had planned down here, he figured they'd pay for themselves. Good light could make the difference in seeing beasts in time to defend themselves. Plus, they'd be useful for their sewer blockage assignment, too.

"I think one length of rope is plenty." Rin stopped packing up when she saw both Pax and Amil holding rope.

The two boys exchanged a surprised look before they laughed.

"Not only is it not enough," Pax said with a shake of his head, "but you better take some, too. Never go exploring without rope. If we get separated and you fall into some kind of hole, how long do you want to sit there and wait?"

Rin's eyes widened, and she held out a hand. "Gimme."

Pax grinned and reached into his pack for another. Finally, they were ready.

"I'll go first. My clubs might help hold something at bay. But I'm sure the tunnel will widen before we run into anything nasty."

"Pax!" Amil chastened him. "You know better."

"Sorry," Pax said. "Didn't mean to jinx us."

"Just get in already," Rin said with an impatient look at their antics. "Let's get this over with."

With a piece of twine, Pax fastened his lightstick to one of his armor straps and tightened it down so that it pointed almost face up, which meant it would point straight ahead as he crawled. Forcing himself not to make a face, he crouched down in the damp muck and rocks at the bottom of the hole and began crawling.

Pax did his best to ignore the occasional drips from the ceiling. The smell, though, was harder. It crawled into his nose and demanded his attention. Wet mustiness and a pervading waft of rot combined with a bitter stench that reminded Pax of how his shoe smelled after squashing the beetles that got into their food back home. He couldn't help coughing, which only sucked in more of the funk and made his nose and throat sting.

"You're going soft," Amil teased in a low voice from behind him. "This would be a walk in the park for us back home."

"Shut it," Pax said, giving a light kick back with his foot. "You're supposed to help me listen."

Amil let out a surprised yelp, and Pax felt him swat his boot back down. A few moments later, Pax's light highlighted a smaller hole leading off to his right, another tunnel that looked smaller and even more crude than the one they were in.

"Do we ignore this and stay in the main tunnel?" he asked back, in as quiet a voice as he could manage.

"Keep straight. There's a breeze from that direction every now and then," Amil said. "Besides, I'm barely fitting in this tunnel."

Pax turned his shoulder to aim his light into the offshoot, just in case it opened up right away. Just more darkness and the walls and ceiling glistening with dampness. Amil was right, so he moved on.

As Pax's knees hurt, he worked harder to take some of the weight on the tips of his boots. The last thing he wanted to do was ruin his leather armor on his first day wearing it.

"Go faster," Rin hissed, her warning tone prompting worried glances back from both boys. "Something's wrong in the tunnel behind us."

Pax couldn't see much, but picking up on Rin's worry, moved faster. There was a discernible breeze ahead of them. If something was on their tail, they'd need more room to fight. Rin wouldn't be able to hold off everything by herself.

"Guys, there are a lot of them." Rin's words came fast, with a sharp edge to them.

"Amil, you try Identifying them without stopping so Rin can save her mana," Pax snapped, moving forward as fast as he could despite the burning desire to stop and look behind him. "Rin, tell us when they're close, and we'll stop and squeeze together to fight if we have to."

"Will do." Rin's breath was quick.

"Venomous Nerodai level 1." Amil rattled out the information. "They are slithering like snakes, but some have legs and maybe claws? Probably water-based."

"Where is an earth mage when we need one?" Pax muttered under his breath, cursing when his hand landed on a sharp rock that shot out from under it.

He ignored the minor pain, scrambling as fast as he could while behind them, a soft, rustling noise grew louder than the sounds of their frantic passage. A quick glance over his shoulder showed fingers of water, Rin's magic, almost black in the gloom, fighting a defensive battle to hold back a writhing mass of shapes pouring after them out of the dark and covering the walls and ceiling.

"A few more seconds, and there'll be too many," Rin yelled at them.

"Count of ten, then?" Pax asked.

"Yes!" Rin answered, her relief easy to hear.

"Here's the plan when I hit ten. Everyone, put your best weapons in your right hands." Pax fired off the ideas as fast as they came to him, planning the best way the three of them could fight together in the narrow confines. "Spells ready. Amil, you'll lie flat. Rin, take the left side facing back. I have the right. We'll be on top of each other and plug the tunnel. Only so many of them can get to us."

He called out the countdown, eyes squinting ahead for the end of the tunnel. If they could get out soon, the entire battle would be different. As if answering his wishes, another breeze swept toward them, and Pax thought there might be a dim glow up ahead. The sound of running water echoed faintly off the walls.

But the count was done. Rin was out of time.

"Ten," Pax finished with a loud yell. Tucking into a ball, he spun around and dove to his right over the top of Amil, who had already turned and flattened himself on the floor of the tunnel. Rin wriggled herself backward and squirmed into the spot on Pax's left over the top of Amil, face glistening with sweat and effort.

Elbows and knees collided. Pax almost couldn't believe it worked when they settled into the tunnel like a three-headed snake plugging the entire passageway and facing the oncoming beasts.

Below him, he felt, more than saw, Amil's flame hiss out along his blade. With Pax's left arm too pinned against the others to move, he was down to his right arm and the one club. Hastily, he thrust his club into the passageway, pushing his mana into it with a frantic rush. This time, he was more than happy it glowed. Until he saw what was coming.

Big snakes as thick as Pax's arm. Their jaws flared twice as wide, revealing pairs of fangs glistening with what was surely something venomous. Small retractable flippers tipped with vicious claws stabbed out from their sides as they fought with each other to get at the humans who had invaded their space. The handful in the front filled most of the tunnel, but in the light from his club, it was easy to see more of the Nerodai pushing and shoving from behind.

"Down to half my mana," Rin got out between breaths. "My Water Snake can hold a few at a time, but they're too tough for me to strangle."

"We'll take care of that part," Amil growled, shifting under Pax and pushing his knife further forward.

"Just hold them still for us to smash, and don't let them get too close," Pax said, shuddering at the thought of a wriggling snake making it close enough to squeeze between them and bite.

Rin thrust her arm out, sending out a bolt of water that separated into tendrils, hooking with unexpected accuracy just behind the beasts' heads and slowing their headlong rush.

"Hurry," she said through gritted teeth as the writhing muscles of the Nerodai struggled to break free.

Amil's single blade stabbed out like his own version of a snake's tongue, avoiding the fangs and cutting up from below to slice necks. The hissing and burning flesh added another layer of stench to the tunnel.

Pax's first few strikes were completely ineffective, the narrow tunnel giving him almost no way to strike powerfully with his club, despite the mana he'd filled it with.

Bodies fell with the slackness of death in front of Amil as Rin pushed her Water Snake toward the new beasts jockeying to the fore-front. Pax shoved his club into the gaping jaws of a beast, giving Rin an extra moment to trap it. The beast immediately attempted to suck down his light mana, but his better mana control helped Pax prevent it. When he had a chance, he really needed to figure out the strange phenomena. But now, he needed to kill the blasted things.

He quickly activated Haste to give him more time to come up with a better strategy. The extra bit of breathing room gave him a chance to get a handle on what was going on around him. It was obvious jabbing wasn't effective enough, so he flicked his wrist to snap the end of his club from the ceiling down to the floor with as much speed as possible. Up and down. Again and again.

The satisfying cracks and occasional limp body told him he was onto something. His lips pulled back with fierce effort as Pax whipped his club up and down as rapidly as possible, smashing through squirming bodies in a macabre imitation of a drummer with his arm stuck in a pipe. Once his Haste wore off, he didn't cast it again. He'd likely need the mana to feed into his club.

"Try to scoot back," he called out to the others as the dead and injured Nerodai bodies partially blocked the tunnel in front of them, giving them some breathing space. "A bit at a time. I think the tunnel exit is close."

Grunts of effort filled the next few moments, along with some of the most uncomfortable maneuvering Pax had ever engaged in. As they fought a retreating battle all jammed together on top of each other, the attack slowed to one or two Nerodai at a time, who pushed their way through the other bodies to attack them. Pax cringed as he realized they'd likely need to push their way back through this gruesome tunnel to return later.

Behind him, his feet scrabbled over a lip, and he felt the space below them. "Rin, you're the smallest," he said, panting. "Scoot back and see if we're finally out."

She didn't argue, just waited until Amil's blade finished the Nerodai writhing in front of them before absorbing her Water Snake and wriggling backward into the dark.

"Finally. Now get off me," Amil said, squirming to the left into the space Rin had vacated. "You're no lightweight."

Pax had to stifle his retort as one of the largest Nerodai they'd seen shoved its way through the bodies with a burst of viscera and body parts. After the long running fight, Pax barely flinched, his club quickly flipping up and down again.

But they didn't have Rin to stop the gigantic snake, and this monster writhed with an uncanny agility, avoiding most of Pax's strikes to lunge directly at his face.

Pax yelped in panic, scooting back as he tried to bring the edge of his club back into play. Amil's knife flashed out, but the Nerodai curled its body mid-air, somehow avoiding the blade.

The charging beast slammed into his left shoulder as Pax jerked his face to the side just in time. White hot pain exploded as the beast buried fangs into Pax, at least one penetrating where his armor didn't cover.

"Get it off me," he yelled, using the short end of his club to pound frantically at the melon-sized head latched onto him.

Amil's knife flashed into the beast's body, and Pax felt the Nerodai's muscles flinch, but the jaws didn't loosen. Burning filled his shoulder, and he could feel the effect of the bite moving to his arm and up his neck.

∼

STATUS: Poisoned. -0.1 HP per second until venom is negated.

53

CLOSE CALL

PAX COULDN'T THINK STRAIGHT, but knew he was in trouble. Serious trouble. Acting on instinct, he jammed the short end of his club into the side of the Nerodai's head and with an internal flex slammed his mana into the beast, wishing he could form it into a blade somehow.

The blade thing didn't happen. As his spark jabbed into the Nerodai, it gave him a glimpse of the swirling mana inside the beast. Pax recognized the indigo of water as his spark highlighted the internal structure of the creature for a moment before the monster suddenly stilled. Its jaws relaxed, and it slid to the floor of the tunnel in a limp slump. Before Pax could figure out more, Amil had wrenched himself around and slammed his knife through the Nerodai's eye and into its brain.

Pax's mana returned with a rush through his club that he'd let sag against the now-dead beast. His head felt dizzy and his mouth dry. "Poisoned," he whispered to Amil as he tried his best to move out of the tunnel with his weakening muscles.

Amil's eyes widened in panic, and he latched onto Pax's armor, scrambling backwards and dragging Pax roughly with him. "Rin," Amil yelled. "Pax got bit. He's poisoned. Help!"

Checking his health showed the venom was quickly draining him.

∽

Health: 22/31

∽

PAX DIDN'T NEED math to know he only had minutes left. Closing his eyes and trying to ignore his body jolting over the rough ground, Pax did his best to breathe through the pain spreading outward from his shoulder so he could gather his spark.

It took a few long moments to push past the distractions and find the concentration needed to activate his mana sight. When he pulled his spark toward his shoulder, he blanched at the sickly green tinge to the indigo energy spreading from the bite.

Why hadn't he spent more time advancing his water path of understanding? And all the other mana types? He knew better than to face unknown dangers without being as prepared as possible. He'd let the easy victory and loot of their first fight tempt him into another before they were ready. Without Amil's flame eliminating so many at once, the bog swarmers might have overwhelmed them that time, too.

Someone pulled at his body and straightened him out on his back.

"What's wrong with him?" Amil's panicked voice sounded muffled.

"I've got him. Just kill the beasts as they come out of the tunnel. We can't afford another bite." Rin's practical-as-always words faded as Pax pushed everything he had into his spark.

Emulating his success with his leg, he pushed his energy to encircle the angry mana pulsing outward from his shoulder. If he could do something about the source, maybe his body could handle the remnants of the venom on its own.

His breathing tried to quicken, struggling against his control as he finally connected the two ends and got a cycle of his mana circling just inside his shoulder. He pushed his sight closer, trying to under-stand the foreign magic so he could merge with some of it and gain control over it.

It felt slippery, evading his attention with ease and spreading out into tendrils that slipped past his circle, diving eagerly into his body. Pax felt a scary numbness spreading down his arm and up into his jaw as his mana bound with a negligible amount of the Nerodai's.

The small piece of the foreign mana's angry chaos calmed significantly once his magic merged with it. With a quick shove, he forced it out of his body.

But when he tried to grin at the minor triumph, he couldn't move his lips and knew he wasn't going fast enough. He couldn't even grit his teeth as he forced himself to keep fighting, trying to analyze the overwhelming amount of chaotic mana spreading through him.

A sudden rush of more indigo magic flooded into his shoulder, making him almost quit. There was no way he could handle all of it.

His shoulder shook. A muffled voice got louder. And louder.

The words finally broke through, being yelled right in his ear. "Let my mana in! Let me help!"

And then he saw the difference. The new mana, while similar, was less chaotic and definitely missing the corrupt, greenish tinge of the venom. Immediately, he disassembled his circling mana and sent it in a rush to join with Rin's water mana . . . only to have it rebound with a painful jolt.

Pushing aside his desperation, he focused his mana sight to see the underlying patterns of Rin's magic. It was pure water and resonated with the liquid everywhere in his body. Ignoring his growing pain, he let his awareness meld with it and almost gasped as a vista unfolded in his sight, spreading out to encompass everything inside him.

There was so much water in his body. He saw a dizzying array of tributaries of liquid that pulsed in a complex array crisscrossing every inch of his body. Liquid carried air, fuel and even waste products back and forth throughout his body, even permeating all the space in between the vessels. It was all water.

While he knew the sudden clarity had to have increased his water path, it would all be for nothing if he didn't link into Rin's mana somehow to drive out the venom, and fast. Pulling the indigo streaks in his spark to the forefront, he matched his mana to Rin's as best he could and gently nudged them together.

A strong shield repulsed him, one that pulsed with Rin's indomitable will and powerful defenses. Desperate, he forced his eyes open and licked his lips, looking wildly for Rin in the dim glow of the cavern.

"Pax, tell me what to do," she begged, her face inches from him and desperate.

"Open up your magic to me," he got out.

"How?" she shot back. "I don't know what to do. I'm pushing all the mana I can into your shoulder, and it's doing nothing." Her words came out rapidly and on the edge of panic.

"Let down your walls. Just try. Let me have your magic." Pax's eyes sagged shut, and he knew he only had enough energy for another minute or two of effort.

"Here. It's yours."

The whispered words gave him the smallest boost of hope as he returned his attention to his shoulder. Rin's mana swirled with a beauty only made more dazzling by the contrast of the sickly venom oozing all around it.

Merge. Pax gave the mental command and pushed one more time.

And this time, his mana slid into Rin's with the ease of a hand into a well-fitted glove, followed by a breathless moment where they blended together. His order pulled at her offered strength until they merged into one.

Pax paused a beat in astonishment before he hurried to exert his control over the combined magic, so much larger and more powerful than his alone. It fought him for a minute and somehow, Pax knew Rin hadn't given up all her control. In fact, Rin seemed to move the newly combined mana around the inside of his shoulder, like someone trying to feel their way around a dark room.

"Give me control. I can see," he whispered without opening his eyes and hoping she was paying attention.

She must have heard because the entire mass of power suddenly went still, swirling but waiting. Holding his breath, Pax attempted to shift just a small section.

It responded with an ease that almost made him mentally stumble.

Yes! He would have crowed in triumph if he'd had any energy to spare. With the vast indigo mana under his control, he slammed a chunk into the nearest section of sickly green magic where it stuck fast, allowing him to do whatever he wanted with it. A thrust with his mind, and he'd shoved the venom out toward his skin, pushing it through the myriad of tiny holes he found there, like running water through a cloth.

More notifications joined the ones he'd ignored from the fight, but Pax barely noticed.

More. He had to hurry. First, he put the largest portion of the mana to work clearing up the venomous mess at his shoulder. He had a distant sense of Rin's attention following his work. Maybe she could see better now?

When his shoulder suddenly burned with pain again, it heartened Pax. Any sensation was better than the scary numbness. Next, Pax split the remaining mana into thread after thread, sending them scurrying out into the rest of his body, following the trails of damage left in the vessels by the venom's passage.

His concentration wavered as he split his attention again and again, wishing he could give the mana a task and leave it to work without him babysitting. Moving up his neck and into his jaw, he pushed more and more of the miasma out through his skin, giving barely a thought to what it would look like to his friends to see all the nastiness oozing out everywhere.

"I understand now. I think I can do some." Rin's voice still seemed to come from far away, but Pax felt her actions immediately as some of their combined mana shifted down toward his lower body and chest.

"Thanks," he mouthed, hoping she could see it as he raced his mana through smaller and smaller vessels in his head and neck, chasing down every speck of the greenish-tinged Nerodai venom. The stuff was insidious and had already spread so fast.

Time seemed to slow as Pax and Rin fought to remove the venom, and his body worked to heal the damage left behind. His breathing evened out, and the numbness receded as he felt the balance finally tip in his favor. The rest was clean-up and regardless of his exhaustion, Pax leaned on the power of Rin's mana as he diligently scoured every corner of his body for the last remnants of the venom.

"It's done," he whispered as he opened his eyes and moved his mouth, extremely glad things were working normally again. He raised his hands slowly and glanced down at his body, not surprised to see his sleeve and tunic under the edge of his armor wet with the venomous sludge he'd dispelled. He restrained himself from rubbing at his face, not wanting to get anything in his mouth or eyes.

"Wow. I don't even—" Rin's words trailed off as she sat back on her heels and let her hands fall limply into her lap. Meeting his eyes, she shook her head. "What was that? What did you do?"

"I'm not sure," he said weakly, feeling as astonished as she looked. "I didn't even know my light mana could combine with yours, much less let me control some of it." He paused, remembering how much mana she'd had and how powerful it felt. "And wow, you have tons more than I do. Are you sure you're not a power mage?"

"But yours is so much more controlled," Rin said, her eyes turning thoughtful. "Plus, I think some of it rubbed off on me. I feel like I can —" She broke off and lifted one hand, instantly summoning a ball of roiling blue water. Eyes narrowed in concentration, tendrils emerged from the water, one after another. Two. Four. She kept splitting them until she had at least a dozen moving like an eerie head of hair at her command.

"Wow," was all Pax managed when Rin let out a gasp, and they all collapsed back into her hand with a splash.

"Oh, let me help you with that," Rin said, eyes moving over his face.

Before he could ask what she meant, a blast of water sprayed across his face. He barely got his eyes closed in time, sputtering as the water stopped a moment later.

"It's important to get stuff like that off your skin as soon as possible," Rin said, her stifled grin belying the instructional tone to her voice.

"Fine," he said, still feeling weak and relieved. "I'll give you a free shot, since you just helped save my life."

A flicker of worry in her eyes let him know she knew just how close he'd come. He was more than happy to let her enjoy a little joke.

Then he noticed his notifications again, flashing with a crazy demand for attention. "I need a sec to see what changed with me." He quickly scanned his notifications, glad his menu consolidated his gains by skill instead of the barrage of individual notifications that had probably flooded in during the fight and subsequent healing.

Skill Boost: +12 to **Clubs** *Level 1 - 28/100*

Spell Boost: +2 to **Haste** *Level 1 - 24/100*

Skill Boost: +4 to **Mana Manipulation** *Level 1 - 36/100*

Skill Boost: +8 to **Mana Sight** *Level 1 - 48/100*

Skill Boost: +16 to **Mana Merge** *Level 1 - 19/100*

Skill Boost: +13 to **Light Healing** *Level 1 - 17/100*

Skill Boost: +3 to **Elemental Meditation** *Level 1 - 11/100*

Improvement to your Path of Understanding **Water:** *+78 Level 1 - 84/100*

Congratulations! You have increased **Endurance** *from 7 to 8*

Congratulations! You have increased **Insight** *from 7 to 8*

PAX FELT STUNNED by the increases. Apparently, almost dying boosted any skills used to stay alive. And his Water Path? He was closer to leveling it than he was to finishing his Air Path. But if it gave him access to a water spell like he suspected it did, it would be just one more thing he had to keep hidden.

"Pax, You're better!"

Pax's eyes popped open to see a large, hammer-carrying form running out of the darkness toward the two of them. Rin barely got an arm up to slow Amil down.

"Careful with him," she said, and Pax was happy Amil landed with a thud next to him, instead of on top of him.

"The venom?" he blurted out, face anxious as he ran his light up and down over Pax, looking for problems.

"All on the outside of me now. Thanks to Rin's help," Pax said weakly, deciding to keep quiet about his new progress until he had time to consider it more. They didn't have time for long discussions here.

Amil sagged back in relief before shaking his head. "Don't scare me like that."

"And the rest of the Nerodai?" Rin asked, making Pax shoot an anxious look back toward the tunnel exit.

"All dead," Amil said. "It almost felt like cheating, hammering the heads right as they poked out. I thought about sending a flame blast up the tunnel, but didn't want to make a big scene just in case there were more nasties out here. Besides, it got me more points in my hammer skill."

Pax pushed himself up to a sitting position as Rin turned to scan their surroundings, eyes suddenly worried as she swept the area with her own light. Neither of them had been paying much attention to where they were.

Her light was tiny, quickly swallowed up by the vast cavern they found themselves in. Shadows danced among a jagged array of protruding rocks above them, the ceiling too high to make out details as her light disappeared off into the darkness. Pax's brows rose as he saw that the rocky shelf they were on dropped off, out of sight, twenty yards from where they'd exited the tunnel.

Past that loomed a huge dark space with boundaries they couldn't see from where they were. What disturbed Pax was the faint echoes of a myriad of noises, shuffling, grunts and the occasional distant screech. Just what exactly had they discovered?

OVERWHELMING ODDS

"I GUESS we need to get closer to see what's over there," Rin said, her voice reluctant as she turned back, giving a disappointed look at her lightstick. It had done little to penetrate the vast gloom behind them. "Unless you're not feeling up to it, and we need to get you back as soon as possible." She aimed a hopeful look at him.

"I wish," Pax said with a harsh laugh as he struggled with one of his clubs to lever himself to his feet. "If there are more beasts like those Nerodai waiting to come bursting out and swarm the campus, we need to find out."

She made a disgruntled noise as Amil reached out a hand to help Pax.

"Thanks," Pax said, holding still and waiting for his head to stop spinning. Seeing Amil's brow crease with concern, Pax said, "Just to see what we're dealing with. Then we'll leave. You know we have to."

Amil nodded reluctantly, giving him a concerned once-over before letting go. "But no fighting. If we see anything this time, we run. You're in no shape to take on a single rat, much less another beast swarm."

"Oh, I know. Believe me, I'm heading straight to bed when we get back," Pax said before he shot a quick glance down at himself and made a face at the remains of his battle with the venom. "After a quick shower, to get the rest of this gunk off first."

"Then, let's get this over with," Rin said, brushing her hands off on her leather leggings and fastening her lightstick on her shoulder again. She aimed a scowl at Pax. "And we're just looking. I am *not* climbing down into whatever mess is in the dark down there."

"But you have rope," Amil said, holding back a snicker.

Rin backhanded him with a solid thunk to his arm. He yelped and scooted back, giving her an aggrieved look that made both Rin and Pax laugh. Feeling better and steadier, Pax followed his friends as they moved cautiously toward the rocky edge that disappeared into the darkness.

Their mood sobered as they shifted their grips on their weapons, eyes intent as they scanned their surroundings and got closer to the lip. Luckily, it seemed the stony plateau was deserted except for their group, though they could see shadows and alcoves in the distance where rocky walls appeared again, shooting up to the ceiling.

Ahead of them, however, didn't sound deserted at all. As they neared the drop-off, the noises that had been mostly in the background became louder and more distinct. All Pax could tell for sure was that the noises came from beasts, not people. He heard rustles and scrabbling claws along with the snuffling and deep grunts that brought enormous creatures to mind.

A sudden screech answered by an equally angry roar made all three friends stiffen. Pax could almost see over the lip ahead and through the vast darkness beyond. An unwelcome surge of fear stabbed into him, making his breath quicken and his heart hit hard into his chest. Heights. They'd bothered him since he was a kid and he hated them.

"That didn't sound good," Rin said as she slowed and gave them another worried look.

Pax wanted to just forget the whole thing and report back to someone else who could come down and figure this mess out.

"Let me take the lead," Amil said. "I've got the most health and can probably take a hit better than the two of you if something comes up from below."

Rin opened her mouth to protest when Pax interrupted. The three of them were here and needed to bring back some kind of information on how bad the threat was. He didn't want to wake up one night to a campus swarming with beasts. But that didn't mean they needed to take unnecessary risks. "True, you're the biggest, but getting information safely is what's most important. Forget Strength. Let's go stealth. Do our best to stay unnoticed, get information on what's down there, and get out just as quietly."

Rin looked at the debris-strewn rock at their feet with distaste, but didn't hesitate to follow Pax's example as he lowered himself to the ground. "Just like the tunnel, guys," he encouraged them, moving forward and trying to ignore how shaky his muscles felt. At least he'd be down low when they got to the lip, probably the best position to help himself keep calm when he saw the drop-off.

"Lights off," he whispered as they crept the last few yards forward. "Just a bit of flame from you, Amil, so we know when to stop. Just don't let it shine over the edge."

The sudden darkness felt better and worse at the same time. Without being able to see, Pax could imagine he was in a small room, safe and enclosed. Only he knew better, and his mind imagined a variety of encroaching horrors sneaking toward them unseen from the vast cavern. The growing noises of a battle below them only made it worse.

When the fingers of Amil's hand glowed, Pax couldn't help letting out a relieved breath. Together, the three of them belly-crawled the last few feet to the edge. Forcing his sick fear down, Pax shifted forward just enough for his eyes to look over the abrupt drop-off.

Pax's air stuck in his chest as he heard quiet gasps from both Rin and Amil on either side of him. On a ledge only ten yards below them, two shadowy forms fought in a desperate struggle. Claws and paws slammed into each other. Flames flickered from the claws of one, lighting up the violent scene.

Past the battling duo, the cavern fell away into more darkness, where the sporadic bits of dim light highlighted ominous patches of movement.

Identify. Pax quickly reached for the information close enough to gather.

Ashen Phantom - Level 1
   *Increase **Identify** Skill for more information.*
   *Skill Boost: +1 to **Identify** Level 1 - 60/100*

Abronia Terror - Level 1
   *Increase **Identify** Skill for more information.*
   *Skill Boost: +1 to **Identify** Level 1 - 61/100*

IDENTIFY *ATTEMPT FAILED. Subject is too far away.*

PAX STIFLED HIS DISAPPOINTMENT. He'd known anything further down was likely too far away to Identify, but he'd still hoped. At least they had something to report. Besides the nerodai from earlier, he expected their news of three different beasts, even if only level 1, would get a reaction from the academy's leadership.

Pax forced himself to stay still as the phantom let out an anguished screech below them when the abronia's jaws slammed shut on the side of its neck. The two beasts might only be level one and barely the size of a medium dog, but Pax had no desire to draw their attention. Besides, they didn't know what else hid in the spread of the huge cavern below them.

Rin's hand tapped on his shoulder, and he could just make out a silent motion with her head back toward the way they'd come. After a few tense moments, they reconvened back by the tunnel exit with the grisly pile of Nerodai bodies with smashed heads.

"All I know is that all that back there is bad," Amil whispered, shooting worried looks back toward the lip.

Rin nodded her agreement, looking more shaken than Pax felt.

"We have to get word back to someone in charge fast," Pax said. "This can't have been going on long, or others would have seen beast incursions. Someone needs to figure out how they're getting in here and plug the hole."

"As long as it's not us," Rin said. "This is way beyond our little money-making plans."

"It wasn't going to be little," Pax grumped, feeling a pang as his inner greed made a case for keeping the whole thing secret and setting up some kind of funneling ambush so they could harvest to their heart's content. "There's got to be enough beasts there to pay for all of our tuition, and then some."

Rin's gaze snapped to him with a glare.

Pax hurried to speak first. "I know. We need to warn the academy. Just let me imagine it for a second, alright?"

"Imagine it while you help harvest the Nerodai cores and clear enough out of the tunnel so we can get back home," Rin grumbled, pulling her knife out of its sheath and moving toward the pile. "We don't want to be around when that abronia finishes the phantom and comes looking for more to eat."

Her warning spurred them on, and it didn't take long before they'd figured out exactly the quickest way to dig the nerodai cores out. Not long after they'd started the messy work, they had cleared the first section of the tunnel back and had set up a system. Rin, the smallest, moved at the front, using her whipcord strength and occasional Water Snake to send the bodies back to Pax and Amil, who took turns pulling them out of the tunnel mouth and harvesting the cores.

"Enjoy ripping the core out of this one," Rin's voice echoed out of the tunnel, followed by the body of the huge Nerodai that had bitten Pax.

He took great pleasure in dragging the body back out of the tunnel and plunging his knife into the monster's belly to rip out his prize. He held up the core with a grin to Amil, only to hear a sudden, sharp hiss behind them, cutting through the blend of background noise from the beasts below the drop-off.

Pax spun around fast enough to send droplets of blood flying from his knife. In the dim light of the lightstick on his shoulder, Pax saw the Abronia Terror emerge from the shadows, its body low to the ground and shifting side to side as it stalked them. Beady eyes moved between him and Amil as something gruesome hung from the row of jagged teeth lining its long, leathery snout. Flickers of flame popped in and out of view from the finger-long, black claws that clicked on the stone floor.

THERE ARE MORE

"RIN, INCOMING," Pax hissed back toward the tunnel as he switched out his knife for both of his clubs, making a mental note to figure a way to affix some kind of sharp blade to the ends without making them as long as a full spear.

"As soon as my flame ends, you come in from your side and hit it while it's hurt and blinded," Amil said under his breath, a rope of flame springing up along his hands, bright in the thick darkness.

Pax had just shifted to the side and bent his knees, ready to jump in when more movement in the shadows behind the flame-based monster caught his attention. "Amil. More of them," Pax said, backing up and scanning the area around the tunnel entrance for any shelter besides the rock face. They needed to keep from being swarmed.

Nothing but a heap of Nerodai corpses slumped on top of each other like a giant pile of gruesome noodles.

Pax latched onto the idea that popped into his head, already running toward the bodies as he sent his clubs into inventory. "No flame yet," he blurted at Amil. "Quick. Grab the Nerodai and throw them."

Amil hesitated a fraction of a moment before following Pax, despite the question clear in his expression.

"Stuff the hungry monsters," Pax said with a grunt as he slung a limp beast body toward the advancing Abronia. "And maybe they won't follow us."

The beast bared its jaws wide as the Nerodai flew toward it, catching it with an audible snap as its teeth slammed together so hard it almost bit the thing in half. Another rough chomp simultaneous with a vicious shake of its head had the Nerodai falling into two halves on either side of its snout.

"Vitur," Amil whispered as he hurried to hurl two more nerodai bodies at the abronia. "No wonder they're called terrors. This won't hold them for long."

Pax didn't bother answering, moving as fast as he could, aiming a few bodies to either side of the lead beast and hoping their delaying tactic gave them the time they needed.

"Into the tunnel," he hissed to Amil when they'd flung most of the pile ahead of them, resulting in a feeding frenzy just yards away. "Hurry."

"You first," Amil insisted, when Pax stepped back to take the rear position.

Pax tried to object, but Amil grabbed him and pushed him forward. "I'm not the one who almost died. And if the worst happens, I can send flame behind us and do my best to keep it from broiling you two ahead of me. Now go."

Pax couldn't argue, despite how much it grated on him. He dove into the tunnel and scrambled forward as fast as he could, almost running into Rin.

"Abronia swarm," he gasped out. "We fed them the nerodai to slow them down. Hurry."

Her eyes went wide, but she didn't waste time with words. Using flexibility Pax knew he couldn't emulate, she curled in on herself to turn around and scuttle back the way they'd come, squeezing past the remaining nerodai bodies.

Pax spared a glance back to ensure Amil was on his tail before tucking his chin and focusing on what strength he had left, very glad for the boost the extra point in Endurance had given him.

His light bounced off the remains from their running battle against the nerodai, his hands landing in dark puddles of nastiness. He was very glad he'd worn gloves. It wasn't long before Pax heard growls and scuffles echoing off the tunnel walls behind them.

"They're in the tunnel," Amil said unnecessarily, his words coming between panting breaths.

Ahead of Pax, Rin twisted to the side, disappearing from view so fast his movements stuttered in surprise.

"In here, dummy," her voice came from a dark hole to his left.

The side tunnel!

Pax didn't waste time second guessing her. As his shoulders brushed the narrower opening, he hoped Amil could make it inside.

Claustrophobia threatened to engulf him as the ceiling lowered even further. They crawled forward, ducking even lower. All he could imagine was the three of them getting stuck with their backs to the abronia, who could pull them out one by one at their leisure.

"Yes," Rin whispered in a voice full of relief.

Hope flared as Pax scrambled after her to find a pocket of space had opened up to the left of the narrow tunnel. The irregular space looked like a handful of bubbles formed in the dark stone. At least it had room enough to fit them easily, as long as they didn't stand up.

Pax joined her and couldn't help a brief pause to enjoy nothing pressing down on his body.

"Move it," Amil grumbled, pushing Pax's legs out of the way as he emerged from the tunnel like an infant after a difficult birth.

Angry hissing boiled out louder behind him now that his body wasn't blocking the sounds.

"Quick, time for your flame, Amil," Pax said, mind jumping to the only idea he thought might work. "Lie down and aim just your hand back down the tunnel."

Amil obeyed with a trust that Pax vowed to thank him for later. If they survived.

"Rin. Right next to him. Fill the narrow tunnel just behind his flame hand with your Water Snakes to keep the heat away from us. I'll try to merge my mana with you, but this time, you take control and use our power together. Got it?"

Rin nodded, already moving as the tunnel filled with the noise of claws and grunting movement. Pax couldn't help the pride that swelled inside him at his small team, and how well they faced challenges that should be well beyond their skills. If they could survive long enough, they would be a powerful force together.

Water flared from Rin's hands, the Snakes thinning and joining to fill the small opening above Amil's hand, facing back the way they'd come. A moment later, a soft *whump* of fire almost blinded Pax as Amil sent his flame back the way they'd come.

Ear-splitting shrieks filled the small space, tearing at Pax's ears as he saw the writhing shapes of burning terrors through the distortion of Rin's Snakes.

"Pax," she grunted at him, voice strained with effort.

He jolted and placed both his hands on her shoulders from behind, and reached for his spark. Keeping his eyes open made it harder, but if nothing else tonight, he'd learned that closing his eyes was a luxury he wouldn't always have.

As soon as his magic pushed into Rin, he realized why she was already struggling. Being a support mage meant she could manage the small tendrils of her Water Snake for a lot longer than manifesting an entire shield of them, even with the tunnel being as small as it was.

He threaded his mana into hers and activated merge. The ease at which it happened surprised him. With a stretch, he followed her mana to the Snakes and felt along their structure, doing his best to strengthen her efforts as he simultaneously worked to understand them.

The water's power felt so much more familiar now, and he saw its ability to adjust its form into almost any shape.

"Thinner. And move it in a pattern," he said to Rin. "Like this." As he reached for control, he felt Rin pull back to let him work with her Snakes.

Except, he couldn't. Her mana resisted his control with an immovable obstinacy. With no one at the helm, it quickly began to fail. The heat from Amil's rapid blasts just under Rin's Snakes suddenly radiated hot steam back into their faces, making Pax and Rin flinch.

"Quick, get them back up. I can't stop for long," Amil said as he turned to look up at them from where he lay at their feet.

Seeing movement already scrambling in the shadows ahead of them, Pax focused back on his light, leaving Rin to manage her water. "Just make your magic follow my light."

As Rin scrambled to form her shield of Snakes again, Pax did his best to show her the way. Giving his spark a deft twist, Pax pushed it into a pattern of circular movement like the way storm water would circle a drain. Rin's chaotic clump of water responded sluggishly at first, but quickly fell into line as she fine-tuned her control and followed Pax's example.

"Now make it thin," Pax said through teeth clenched in effort. "To make your mana last."

When the now-rotating disk of Snakes decreased in thickness and the amount of water mana leaving Rin decreased significantly, Pax let out a relieved breath. Amil didn't need to be told to start up his flame blasts again. Stabbing his hand back under the lip of Rin's Snakes, he lit up the tunnel. Squeals of pain sounded as he drove the beasts back again.

"Thanks," Rin said as Pax felt her shoulder muscles under his hands relax.

Together, his friends shielded them from the swarm and drove it back. Amil's flames filled the tunnel with blinding light again while Rin's spinning disc of Snakes kept them from roasting. An added benefit was a hot steam just in front of Rin's shield that also helped protect them.

Pax wasn't sure how long it took, but eventually the shrieking of the monsters dropped off significantly, only the occasional scrabbling noise making it through the roar of the slowing Flame Blast.

Pax waited another few heartbeats, not wanting to run both of his friends completely dry, but also afraid to stop too soon.

"Stop. Let them drop," he said finally, feeling how much Rin had drained. "I think they're gone."

Both Amil and Rin grunted as they cut power to their magic, dropping the alcove into a sudden darkness.

Pax clicked on his lightstick and pointed it back down the tunnel while blinking and trying to see any suspicious flickers of flame from the claws of the Terrors.

Nothing.

"I think we did it," he said with a grin and sagged back against the near wall. He finally let himself hope they might make it safely back to campus.

"What a team!" Amil crowed, still keeping his voice low but aiming an exultant grin at the two of them and holding up a hand for high fives.

Rin let out a weak laugh but looked just as happy as she returned the gesture.

Pax clapped his hand to Amil's. "Amazing Flame Blast and wall of Snakes, guys." He aimed another grin at Rin. "As soon as you're up for cooling the tunnel off . . .?"

"Give me a second to recover," she said, aiming a weak backhand his way. "Besides, you know enough about my water magic now. Shouldn't you be able to do it yourself?"

Pax stopped, struck by the idea.

"Wait," Amil said, eyes wide as he looked at Pax. "You unlocked your water path by working with Rin?"

"Not all the way, yet," Pax said, a quick check showing that although he'd received another eight points for helping with her Snakes, putting him at 92. So close, but not quite there.

He wanted to grab Rin and do whatever it took to push him over the edge. But with the exhaustion on her face and the proven danger of the tunnels, he couldn't justify it.

"Well, next training session, let's get you there," Amil said before a sly smile moved across his face. "And I'm happy to burn you as much as it takes to get your flame path unlocked, too."

Pax had just opened his mouth to needle Amil when Rin stiffened and pushed back against him, her focus on something at the back of their cramped alcove. Something moved in the shadows. Pax jerked his lightstick toward it, equipping a knife and a club by instinct.

"What is that?" Amil asked, horrified fascination in his voice but not sounding alarmed.

"Ugh," Rin voiced her opinion in a tone full of disgust.

"Wait." Pax held out his hand to stop Rin's impulsive move to kill the weird but small beast. There was something he really needed to test, and he didn't think he'd get another chance like this.

ITTY-BITTY BEAST

"Pax," Rin almost whined his name as she gave him a tired look. "We don't have the time or energy for anything but getting back. Let's just kill the little beast and get out of here. Please."

Amil, holding his hammer out in case the small thing tried to attack, gave Pax a shrug and a look that suggested he agreed with her.

"Just listen for a second." Pax held up his hands defensively. "Every single beast I've run into seems to be drawn to my light magic like crazy. Remember the blaze lizard? And what about the bog swarmers? Even when they were in the nets, they kept fighting to get to me, right?"

Rin's expression turned thoughtful, and Pax hurried to finish.

"Not only that, but when a beast comes into contact with my light magic, they seem to somehow"—he stopped and tried to come up with a way to describe it, but only thought of one word—"try to *eat* it."

Both Amil and Rin frowned.

"I know it sounds wacky, but it's happened more than once. Beasts suck down my magic, draining me like they're starving." He held up a hand. "And not only that. It changes them."

"Changes them how?" Amil aimed a skeptical look at him.

Pax hesitated, knowing how crazy his theory would sound if he said it out loud.

"Just spit it out," Rin said, impatient. "We've heard all kinds of weird things from you and are still your friends. Go ahead. What does your light magic do to the beasts?"

"It seems to calm them." Pax just blurted it out and then tucked his thumbs into his cuirass straps while he waited and hoped they didn't laugh.

Both of his friends looked at him, expressions inscrutable.

"So." Rin drew out the word, looking thoughtful. "Are you saying you're merging with their mana like you did with mine? When you did that, it made my magic feel more structured and gave me better control over it." She tapped a finger on her chin thinking before she said, "I guess I could call it calmer."

"Wait," Amil said, an excited grin spreading across his face. "So, you're some kind of monster tamer? How many can you do? If you could make a bubble of calming magic in front of us, we'd be unstoppable against swarms." His voice got louder as his eyes lost focus, imagining the scene. "Can you imagine? Just knocking them down while they're frozen in front of us?" He gave his hammer a mini swing in the small space.

"Not quite," Pax said, unable to suppress a laugh at his antics and noticing Rin wasn't able to curb her own smile completely, either. "It's only happened one on one with a beast and took a lot out of me. That's why I need a chance to test it when we're not in the middle of trying to stay alive."

It seemed his words had convinced them. They turned to look at the object of their discussion. The beast, only the size of one of Pax's hands, had backed into a small nook where it must have hidden during the fight. A fine layer of shadow-gray scales covered the thing. But what drew the eye, and probably Rin's disgust, was its snout.

Instead of a simple animal nose, a host of pink, worm-like things wriggled in a tight, circular shape. They waved toward them in a disturbing impression of a nest of tiny snakes. Beneath the strange

organ, it pulled its lips back in a soundless snarl as it shifted frantically, snuffling in their direction.

Identify.

~

Baby Talpasauria Shade - Level 0
*Increase **Identify** Skill for more information.*
*Skill Boost: +1 to **Identify** Level 1 - 62/100*

~

"THAT'S QUITE a big name for such a little guy," Pax said as he filled his
club with mana, the glow filling the space and highlighting the strange
creature. Long claws flexed on large, pad-shaped paws. Pax caught
motion behind it, surprised to see a bony knob flicking nervously on
the end of a scale-covered tail.

The talpasauria's snout jerked immediately, homing in on Pax's
club with intense interest. Pax gave his friends a pointed look. Rin's
eyes widened in acknowledgement, while Amil nodded as if he'd
always known Pax was right.

"You want some of this?" Turning back to the baby beast, Pax
crooned in the soothing voice he usually saved for the youngest
members of his crew back home. He crept forward in a slow, steady
movement, nudging his mana to bulge out at the end of his club. "Just
hold still, and I'll share."

The creature became more agitated, shifting back and forth, the
snout tentacles in constant motion. Rin made a groan of disgust
behind him.

"Here you go," Pax said quietly, moving his club the last few inches
toward the talpasauria's snout. "Take all you want."

"That thing is strange, Pax. Are you sure?" Rin whispered. "Didn't
you say beasts drain your mana?"

"Sure, but I've gotten better at cutting it off. Besides, how much
could this little guy take, anyway?"

When the talpasauria moved, Pax barely saw it, despite the light from his club. In a blink, the little guy had lunged forward, opened a wide, tooth-filled mouth to chomp on the end of his club. The tentacles latched onto the club while its claws wrapped around the middle.

Pax barely kept a hold on his club as the creature jerked at it with unexpected strength. He felt the mana drain start immediately, glad it was just a thin stream, as expected.

Amil's hammer twitched forward, and Pax shook his head quickly. "It's ok. I got it. I think it's working."

As his friends eyed the talpasauria with suspicion, Pax moved his attention to his mana, following it through his club and into the small beast. With Rin's suggestion that it was similar to the merge he'd done with her, he could feel it now. His mana was a thin stream of soothing power, small but built of careful structure.

The beast, in contrast, was filled with a maelstrom of various shades of brown mana twisting and raging inside it. It seemed as eager to tear the insides of the beast apart as it did to attack anything nearby.

It was the first time Pax had felt any kind of empathy for a beast. Were all the beasts tormented like this every night? No wonder they went crazy and attacked everything.

Forcing himself to pay attention to the experiment, he felt his light mana calming the storm as the beast absorbed it. The raging mana inside it slowed, shades of brown sorting themselves and settling into the muscles, bones, pelt and other body systems.

The creature's agitation visibly faded, and a few moments later, it flopped to the ground with a sigh of exhaustion.

"What happened?" Amil asked as Pax cut off the mana flow and pulled his club back. A quick glance showed he was down to only a fifth of his mana, but couldn't be sure how much the experiment had cost because he'd been down quite a bit at the start.

"I'm still not sure," Pax said, unable to take his eyes off the little thing. "But this guy was full of a crazy, raging mana. And my light mana kind of fixed it."

"So, you can actually tame beasts?" Amil asked, looking excited again, his eyes flashing and full of ideas. "Can you tame me a good riding beast? Oh, wait. What about something with wings? Can you see me flying? Swooping down on a battle with my hammer?"

"Hold on," Pax said, smiling and shaking his head. "I'm pretty sure it's not that easy. I don't know if what I did will fade. What if the thing goes nuts again tomorrow night? Plus, I burned through a lot of my mana with just a baby here. I can't imagine trying much more than a quick pulse of mana on anything bigger. I know that blaze lizard almost drained me dry in no time at all."

Amil's face fell as he gave Pax a sheepish nod. "I get it. We'll need to test it more. But just promise me an awesome mount if you ever get to that point, alright?"

"Of course," Pax agreed before turning back to the talpasauria, whose only sign of life was the subtle shift of its chest moving up and down with each breath. "Now, what do we do with this little guy?"

"Leave him, of course," Rin said.

"Take him with us," Amil said at the same time.

"Amil," Rin snapped, turning to him. "We can't take a beast with us. Anyone who sees it would freak out and rightly so. Where would Pax keep it? And don't forget, it could go crazy at any moment and start attacking students. What would he do then?"

Pax ignored the two of them as he scooted forward and carefully picked up the little guy, cupping the limp ball of strangeness in both hands. He ran his spark through his palms and found it interesting that even unconscious the talpasauria still absorbed a thread of his mana, snuggling into his palms like one would a warm nest of blankets on a frosty night.

"Pax," Rin hissed a warning at him.

"I've got gloves on," he reassured her, looking up and hoping she would understand. "It's level zero. It shouldn't be able to do much to hurt me."

"Shouldn't?" she asked skeptically, but she still scooted in to take a closer look.

Pax let some of his spark glow from his palms so she could see better. "Look how cute. His little tentacle nose looks kind of like your Water Snakes."

"I guess he doesn't look so strange once you get used to it," she said, sounding dubious as she shifted so Amil could get a look, too.

"Well, I have to keep him. Besides merging mana with you two, he's the only other way I have to learn about what my light magic can do. It's not like I can ask the instructors for help."

"Well, just don't come crying to us if he attacks you while you're sleeping," Rin grumbled as she moved back toward the tunnel. "You know beasts are nocturnal and get riled up at night."

Pax pushed aside the second thoughts that tried to intrude as he pulled a piece of spare leather wrapping and twine to fashion a simple carrier for the talpasauria. He kept probing the small creature with his magic, feeding it small bursts of light mana as he followed his friends back through the narrow tunnels.

Despite how tired they were, they still took the extra few minutes needed to harvest the handful of Abronia flame cores before rejoining the main tunnel. By the time they made it back to where the Bog Swarmers had nested, Pax was ready to concede all the beast remains they'd slain in the tunnel to Mistress Nymeli as long as she didn't ask them to help with any of the butchering.

Then he shook his head at the idiotic thought. They couldn't let the kitchen staff anywhere near the dangers in the tunnel.

"Remind me never to take standing up straight for granted again," Rin said, cracking her back with a groan as they finally emerged into the regular tunnels and could stand straight again.

"You're telling me," Amil said as he bounced on his feet and swung both of his arms in big wide circles before clapping them back and forth against his chestplate. As they grabbed their packs and headed back, he grumbled. "All the tight tunnels back home never really bothered me. But we didn't have to fight beasts in them."

Pax gave them both a weary grin as he used slow and regular breathing to regain his stamina and strength as they walked back, a lot slower than they'd come.

"See," a whiny voice suddenly echoed from the tunnel walls. "Didn't I tell you they came this way?"

Still on edge, Pax leapt back, his clubs popping into his hands as he crouched, ready to fight. Beside him, Amil had his hammer raised. Rin had taken a step back, an arrow already nocked in her bow as four figures stepped out from the shadows and moved to block their way forward. Kurt grinned at them as he scampered around the other three, lit two torches and placed them in sconces to light up the scene.

"Maybe you aren't as useless as I thought," Galen said with a dismissive look.

"But—" Kurt tried to object, his face sagging with disappointment.

"You did what I asked, and I'll give you what I promised. Now shut up," Galen cut him off with an impatient flick of his hand before he turned to face Pax and his friends. A cruel smirk spread across his face as he stepped forward, his two buddies a step behind him. "Viper-sworn, you've had all the warnings you're going to get. Your time pretending to be a mage ends tonight."

STAND-OFF

"YOU'LL GET KICKED out for using magic against other students," Rin said, voice cold and strong in a way that made Pax doubly glad she was on his side.

"Who's going to report me?" Galen raised both hands and scanned his surroundings with an exaggerated motion. "It's the word of three scions against street rat weaklings no one cares about."

"Amil's a power mage," Pax countered. "The mage college won't take it lightly when you mess with people they need to fight on the walls." He let his disdain for the flick drip from his voice. "Or didn't you realize we have a war going on and need every mage we can get?"

Galen let out an angry growl, lifted his hand and, with a sudden flare, lit the tunnel with a flame brighter than anything Pax had seen Amil manifest.

"Galen!" The girl next to him grabbed at his shoulder before leaning in to whisper something to him.

For a moment, it seemed as if Galen would ignore her, pushing her back with a scowl on his face. But he let his flame subside and shook out his hands before a dagger appeared in each hand. He shot a significant look at the boy and girl on either side of him, and they followed his example, equipping their own knives.

"As my friend here has reminded me," he said, as he turned back toward them. "You came down here to fight supposed beasts, so when they tragically overwhelm you, your injuries will need to look like a mauling, not magic. So, no watching you dance to my flame for fun. But I'll take what I can get."

"You're actually going to try to kill us?" Pax couldn't keep the astonishment out of his voice. He'd been expecting some kind of beating, a hazing to put them into their place. But murder?

"Not try." Galen's mouth twisted into a snarl tinged with a sick excitement. "While everyone is going nuts responding to the recent surge, no one will miss a handful of the weakest students."

"You said nothing about—" Kurt spoke up from his hiding spot back in the shadows behind Galen's crew.

"Shut up," Galen snarled over his shoulder. "Unless you want to join them?"

"No." Kurt's voice squeaked up an octave before he hastily retreated, the echo of his racing footsteps fading back down the passageway.

"Now, that's a street rat who knows his place," Galen said with a satisfied nod. "Too bad the three of you couldn't follow his example."

"Do we fight?" Rin's quiet question was just loud enough for Pax to hear.

"Against three powers?" Amil sounded worried. "I'm still only at half mana."

"Distract them on my signal with everything you have left," Pax said under his breath, deciding for them as he took a careful step back. They had no chance against the three, especially not in the shape they were in now. "Then run until we lose them."

"You can run, but we'll find you," Galen said, his grin widened. "But feel free to try. We enjoy a good fight, don't we, guys?" His friends echoed his chuckle.

Pax glimpsed a slight glow in his peripheral vision. Amil was getting ready.

"Now," Galen called out and rushed forward in a straight tackle, one knife high and the other low.

Both of his crew followed hard on his heels.

Rin's arrow hissed past Pax's shoulder, close enough to feel the brush of air as he clenched his clubs, planning to disarm Galen if possible before they ran. To his left, two short bursts of flame shot to either side of Galen, one each aimed at his two cronies' center mass.

Rin's hands were already nocking another arrow when her first one hit, only to stop midair a few inches from Galen's neck. Pax watched in horror as both of Amil's flame blasts fizzled against invisible barriers, too.

"Back," Rin yelled, switching out to knives with practiced speed. "They've got barriers."

"Now you stupid street rats finally understand." Galen's victorious laugh rebounded off the tunnel walls. "We are better than you in every way, but it's even more obvious in equipment."

Pax backpedaled, striking out with his clubs at Galen's incoming knives. His first strike rebounded, doing nothing to block the first stab, making Pax wrench his torso aside. The knife stabbed through the air, a hairsbreadth from piercing Pax's leather chestplate. Pax whipped his left club around, even as he fought to get back into a stable fighting position.

To his surprise, Galen couldn't dodge fast enough. The end of the club slammed Galen's gauntlet with a powerful thud. He yelped in pain, dropped his knife and shook his left hand.

Pax couldn't believe the idiot had been so disrupted by a single hit to the wrist, regardless of how much he knew it hurt to take a hit to the bones there. And even though Pax now knew their shields had limited power, to be safe, they needed solutions that would work regardless of the scion's protections.

"Get ready to run," Pax hissed as he kept his clubs flashing in a fast pattern to keep the other two at bay. He needn't have worried, because the two had no idea how to handle their leader's injury, minor though it was. They froze and gave each other helpless looks.

"Quick!" Pax hissed, realizing this was their chance. "Run as fast as you can. We need some distance."

His two friends didn't hesitate, turning on their heels and

sprinting back the way they had come. That got an instinctive response from their attackers.

"You're going to pay for that," Galen growled and broke into a run after them with only one knife. "Get them!"

Ignoring the sounds of pursuit behind them, Pax planned the best ambush he could come up with. After rounding the third corner, his breath coming fast and his strength ebbing, Pax finally saw what he'd been looking for. A dark offshoot from the main tunnel.

"In here," he said and rattled off instructions before they'd all made it into cover. "Amil, flame the floor just this side of the turn. Let's hope they're stupid enough to take the corner at full speed."

Rin's white teeth gleamed as she smiled and nodded. "And I'll use my Water Snake to trip them onto the burning floor. Genius!"

Pax gave her a smiling nod. "Exactly. Even with shields, your Snake should be able to trip them. And whatever energy their shields have left shouldn't hold up to the continuous damage from face planting onto glowing hot stone."

Amil let out a breath, his face a study of concentration as he focused back on the main tunnel. "I'll give it all I can and then we run, right?"

Pax glanced over his shoulder at the new tunnel and shrugged. It wasn't like they had much of a choice. "At least we don't have to crawl down this one. Next time we need a better map of the tunnels so we can plan multiple routes out of here."

"They're 'crats. They'll give up before we do," Rin said simply, joining Amil just out of sight of the main tunnel.

"I'll scout ahead," Pax said, angry at himself for not unlocking at least one offensive spell so he could help. "Follow me as fast as you can. If there are branches, I'll always take the one furthest left. Got it?"

They nodded silently, and he turned on his heels, clicking on his lightstick as he headed down what he hoped would be his last tunnel for the night.

FAINT YELLS FOLLOWED by at least one person screaming echoed through the tunnels behind him, spurring Pax to move even faster. He still kept a careful look at all four sides of the tunnel. The last thing he needed was to sprain an ankle or fall into a hole at this point. And the nerodai had taught him how beasts could easily drop from the ceiling.

After two junctions where he took the left turns, Pax stepped out into a large stone-lined space with a channel running through it and splitting off into more tunnels.

The stench hit him with palpable force, making him choke on his next breath and reminding him of the blocked sewage quest. The sling holding his talpasauria stirred as the smell even disrupted the little creature's sleep. Apparently, unblocking the sewers was a true necessity, but he immediately understood why it didn't have many takers.

Scanning his choices, he didn't like any of them. The leftmost branch was the nastiest, without even a basic ledge along the side to walk along. He knew they'd all be paying for replacement boots if they had to step down into that stuff. And with the darkness of the slow-moving sludge, there was no way to tell how deep it was. The other two branches at least had narrow walkways along the edge, but if he didn't take the left, how would he let Amil and Rin know which one he took without it also being obvious to their followers?

He glanced again at the left tunnel, knowing instinctively that no 'crat would ever step foot in it. It was really their best option.

"We're going to kill you!" Distance muted the roaring voice, but it was still easy to distinguish over the random drips and whistling breezes that filled the tunnels. An echo of thudding footsteps grew in volume behind him. The scions hadn't given up after all, and Pax and his friends would need a good place to hide if they wanted to remain undiscovered.

Pax had just stiffened his resolve and pulled out a club to plumb how deep the oozing sludge was when his light caught a slight irregularity in the stone to the left of the tunnel. Eager for even the tiniest possibility of another option, he turned and shined his light-stick at the wall, only to find nothing unusual. Second-guessing whether he'd actually seen something, he moved back and positioned his lightstick how it had been when something caught his eye.

There. He saw a collection of small reflections that needed a glancing angle of light to appear. Holding his light steady, Pax turned his head and examined the wall. His eyes widened as he followed the fine lines that reflected the light, some faint, while others were wider and stronger.

He'd seen plenty of similar shapes before . . . in enchanting class. Somehow, someone had embedded a rune right into a rather plain and grungy rock wall next to a sewage line.

Torn and knowing time was running out, Pax reached out, running his hands along the lines, keeping his lightstick angled just right so he could see the rune. It wasn't one of the four basic elements they'd studied so far, and Pax was kicking himself for not reading ahead in the enchanting textbook. He pushed and prodded at it, but got no results. He checked for an activation rune or a spot he could slot one of their harvested cores in, but came up empty.

"Check all the tunnels," he heard Galen's distinctive voice snapping out orders somewhere far away. "Look for footprints. No one's been down here for a while."

Pax groaned in dismay as he looked behind him. His scuffling footprints stood out easily in the debris strewn across the dirty floor and led directly to him. Even if he took the plunge into the sewage tunnel, it would be obvious which way he'd gone. They'd just have to hope the scions would balk at the nasty chore of following them.

Giving up on the rune, Pax scrambled down the ledge lining the central tunnel, dragging his feet and making an obvious trail before he skidded to a stop fifteen feet in, letting his footsteps end right against the lip before dropping off into the canal. Without hesitating, he plunged his club into the thinner stream of muck in this tunnel and flung some in what he hoped would look like splashes from a person jumping down.

Spinning on his heels, he raced back and repeated the subterfuge with the far-right tunnel, varying the distance he raced into the tunnel. He grimaced as he flung clods of dark gunk in a spray against the walls at the point his footsteps stopped, praying the scions would choose either of the decoy tunnels instead of the one he'd actually chosen.

Returning to the junction, Pax could hear footsteps echoing louder. They were close. Racing toward the left tunnel, Pax steeled himself to jump down into the channel, just hoping Amil and Rin wouldn't hesitate to follow him to the left, despite needing to wade through the nastiness.

He froze just before jumping, a sudden idea stopping him mid-move. Reaching his left hand out to touch the edge of the rune, Pax shoved a quick burst of his spark into the shape, prepared to jump into the muck once nothing happened.

But something did happen.

58

A CLOSE ONE

THE WALL practically jerked his spark inside, spreading like a stream of water in a rush through the lines of the rune. The pattern that had been so hard to make out sprang into bright relief against the drab stone of the wall. Pax stared in slack-jawed amazement before he shifted his gaze, trying to take in the details of the fascinating formation. He was too overwhelmed to even notice the steady drain on his mana until it stopped, leaving him light-headed. Stumbling a step back and pulling his hand free from the wall, Pax was just glad the old structure hadn't completely drained him.

And then the wall moved.

Startled, Pax jumped another few feet back and watched in amazement as the section of the wall covered by the rune slid into a hidden side pocket with a low rumble, much too quiet for what he was seeing. As it revealed an opening wide enough for two people to walk in side by side, Pax saw a set of stone stairs that ascended into an unknown darkness. As soon as the wall stopped moving, the rune embedded in it flashed, its brightness slowly fading.

When the rune was dark again, Pax suspected the door would close. Galvanized, he held his breath and forced himself to poke his head inside and aim his lightstick up the stairs. When his actions didn't trigger some trap, he blew out a relieved breath. Ditto to the fact that the stairwell seemed to be free of any beasts or other dangers.

Now he just needed to get Rin and Amil inside before their pursuers caught up. With no time to think of another plan, Pax turned on his heel and raced back into the tunnel he'd come from.

Running and scrambling sounds bounced off the walls of the dark tunnel. Pax was just glad he didn't hear sounds of fighting. Running noises meant his friends were still in the lead.

Coming to a small fork in the tunnel, Pax's boots slid in debris as he reminded himself to take the one on the right. He dug deep to go faster, only to feel some mass coming out of the darkness to his left.

He ducked, both of his clubs suddenly bursting with glowing mana as he lashed out . . . only to pull his strikes hard at the last second when he recognized Amil's surprised face in their glow.

"Amil," he hissed, too rushed to be patient. "It's me, dunder. Where's Rin? We have to hurry."

"Behind you," Rin whispered, tapping his shoulder and making him almost jump out of his skin.

But he didn't have time to chew her out. "Hurry," he said, dousing the light in his clubs. "I found a hiding place for us." Without bothering to wait for a response, he spun on his heel and raced back the way he had come, hoping the door still had enough of his mana to stay open. Obviously, he could use more mana to open it again, but would they have time?

As if his worries had summoned Galen, he heard a loud laugh echoing behind him. "Found you, little rats!" Galen's triumphant voice chased after them.

Pax tucked his head and ran faster, his palm over the end of his lightstick, letting the barest bit of light escape so he could see the ground ahead. Relief filled him as he recognized the opening into the junction ahead. He took the corner at almost full speed, boots scrabbling on the floor as his eyes shot to the wall with the door.

It was closing. The runes were barely visible now, and the opening narrowed at a snail's pace. "Follow me," he hissed back to Rin, who was right on his tail. To Pax's dismay, he saw Amil had fallen further behind, his movements tired and lumbering.

"Quick, in the doorway before it closes," Pax told Rin as he stepped out of the way and took the risk of calling back to Amil. "Hurry! It's closing," he whisper-shouted.

He was too loud.

"Hah! We've got you now." The shouts echoed down the tunnel, and Pax could see a trio of lights bobbing in the distance. They were close.

The threats gave Amil a last burst of energy. He picked up his pace for the final few steps, following Pax around the corner and looking ready to collapse. Pax could see Rin on the stairs, waving toward them frantically as the opening narrowed enough that Pax knew he'd have to turn sideways to fit.

One glance at Amil's fallen expression, and Pax knew his friend was too big to fit.

"Get ready to squeeze through," Pax whispered, hurrying forward and placing his hand on the rune for the second time. This time, he tried to moderate the amount of mana he used. They just needed to nudge the door open by the barest amount.

It didn't matter. The mechanism tied to the rune seemed to be automated. To Pax's horror, it latched onto his mana, drawing out a steady stream and lighting up the entire rune again. The door stopped closing and opened instead.

Frantic, Pax jerked his hand free, but it was too late. The apparatus had enough power, and the door slid all the way open, allowing Amil easy access. While Amil smiled in relief, Pax looked past him and met Rin's gaze. She obviously realized how much trouble they were in.

Pax hurried to join them anyway, standing in the stairwell landing in front of a wide-open doorway with a bright rune that was just beginning to fade again. They might as well have painted a target on themselves.

Thinking desperately, Pax wondered if he should try to lead Galen down one of the other tunnels until the doorway closed. He immediately dismissed the idea, knowing he might as well seal his friends into a tomb, as they would have no way to open the door again. A glance up the dark stairwell seemed to be their only hope. Maybe they could find another way to barricade themselves up there?

Running boots and laughter got louder, echoing around the stone junction space.

"Hurry," Rin grabbed his arm and shook him. "Shut the door!"

"I can't," he hissed. "I only know how to open it."

"Well, do the opposite of whatever you did to open it," she growled impatiently. "They're almost here."

Pax froze, kicking himself for not thinking of the idea himself. "Thanks," he whispered as he placed both of his hands on the back of the door and reached for the mana infusing the rune. For a moment, it seemed to stick to the rune, reluctant to let go. Glad of his practice merging with Rin's mana, Pax shoved his magic into the rune's power without an ounce of finesse. As soon as he felt it merge, he pulled back, tearing the power out as fast as he could.

The glow of the rune blinked and almost went out completely. Suddenly worried, Pax jerked his hands off the door, leaving the tiniest thread of power still in the rune. For a moment, nothing happened. Had he broken it? Next to him, both of his friends were barely breathing.

"They're just up ahead!"

"Knives ready, guys."

"I'm going to enjoy this."

The voices were close, maybe only a few yards down the tunnel.

Then the door shifted, sliding closed in a smooth movement, faster than Pax had seen the door move yet. The last remnants of the rune's light faded fast, blinking out just as the last sliver of an opening closed in front of three relieved faces.

"Which way did they go?" The stone door muffled confused voices, though they were still easy to understand.

Pax stood stock-still in complete darkness, afraid to turn on his lightstick or make any kind of noise that their pursuers might hear. He reached out and briefly touched Rin to his left and Amil to his right to make sure they stood still and quiet. He needn't have worried, as his two friends barely breathed, making Pax almost feel alone in the dark tomb.

"Yuck!" someone complained. "All three of these are sewage channels. I didn't sign up to go wading in that."

"Oh, so you'll help me kill a few street rats, but can't handle a little crap?" Galen's distinctive voice was easy to make out despite the muted quality.

"That's not a little crap," a third voice said, this one with a feminine quality.

"It doesn't matter. We have to take care of them. We don't want them getting back to report us."

The feminine voice scoffed. "So, what if they do? I know how clever you are, getting friends to rent a study room and pretend to be us. No one will believe street rats over us, anyway. Let's just get out of this nasty place. Unlike dunderhead here, I won't go along with anything just for a chance to hurt people."

"Hey," the first voice objected.

"Shut up, both of you." That was Galen again. "You're right. I'm the clever one, which means you'll do as I say if you don't want to suddenly have your own problems."

A tense silence greeted his words.

"Good," he said. "Since their tracks lead here, we know they didn't get past us. There are three passages and three of us."

He paused, and Pax could just imagine his face as he surveyed the three disgusting choices. Pax put a hand over his mouth to keep from letting any sound escape.

"I'll take the center one, and since you were smart enough to keep tabs on my plans, you can take the other one with a walkway. You get the one without."

"Aw, Galen," the first voice complained, followed by a gagging sound. "That'll ruin my boots and leggings."

"When do we turn back?" the woman asked, ignoring the complaints.

Pax heard a brief pause as Galen obviously thought it through before answering. "We all continue until our passage splits again, or for 500 paces, whichever comes first. Understood?"

A few murmurs followed, and then Pax could hear them moving out. A large splash from the left made him pinch back a snicker, imagining the larger crony jumping down into the sewage that Pax had recently been steeling himself to enter. Seeing how Galen had covered all three passageways made Pax even happier that he'd found an alternative.

Pax waited an extra minute after the sounds and voices had faded before clicking on his lightstick. "Well, should we see what's up these stairs?" he asked Rin and Amil with a grin.

Amil gave him a smile, but Rin just looked tired and shook her head.

"We don't know where that leads," Rin countered. "We only have a brief window before they come back. If we leave now, they won't know we slipped out behind them."

Her words deflated his excitement, compounded because they were logical and accurate. Pax shot a look up toward the bottom of the door he could just see at the top of the stairwell. "I have to look. Even if it means spending the night trapped here until Galen and his buddies give up completely."

"Splitting up isn't safe," Rin objected. "We can come back later."

"I know," Pax said. "But you heard them about the additional troubles on the wall, and we were helpless against those guys. The only way I'm going to survive is to figure out my magic, and fast."

She didn't look convinced.

"Rin, my light magic controlled the rune on the door. Light magic," he repeated for emphasis. "It's the only clue I've been able to find. How about I just take a quick look up there, so I have an idea if it's even worth coming back? Really fast and then we leave."

"Promise?" she asked.

He nodded and turned to race up the stairs. To his relief, the wooden door at the top of the stairs, despite its obvious quality and banded metal, had a simple door knob. For a moment, he thought someone had locked it, but with an extra hard twist, it turned. The door opened with a drawn-out squeal that suggested no one had opened it in a very long time.

Pax stepped inside, ignoring Rin's cautioning hand, and blinked at the sudden light that sprang from the expansive ceiling, almost blinding after the darkness of the tunnels. Knowing he only had moments, Pax tried to scan the room as fast as he could.

Before he could see much, someone spoke, the voice deep and gravely like a grandfather who'd spent too long in the mines or smoking his pipe for years.

"Welcome to my workshop, young light mage."

59

ANCIENT SECRETS

PAX FLINCHED and looked around for the source of the voice. The space was much bigger than a regular room, more like five or six spacious ones with the walls removed. A polished wood floor gleamed with use, slight depressions worn into the common paths by years of traffic. With the ancient, abandoned feel to the place, Pax thought there should be a layer of dust over everything, but the surfaces were tidy.

Sturdy wooden workbenches stood in a square pattern, all facing a central desk piled high with strange equipment. A small bookshelf stood next to the desk, stuffed with books and papers. Bookshelves that reached from floor to ceiling covered the entire right side of the room. A ladder leaned against the far end, ready to help reach the higher shelves.

At the back of the room, a counter with rows of beakers sat next to a large ceramic-looking vat. Above, a large cork board held lots of strange instruments Pax had never seen. Further along the back wall, another huge wooden section covered the wall with small cubbies stuffed with a variety of scrolls that made Pax want to run over and start grabbing. Finally, a door on the far side of the back wall meant there was even more to explore down here.

Before he could take a step forward, a sudden glow to his right made him glance over at the end of the railing leading into the workshop. A smooth crystal sat at waist level on top of a dark stone pedestal covered with ornate engravings that looked kind of like runes. The rest of the amazing workshop had distracted him too much to notice it until it lit up.

"Young light mage, please place your hand on the crystal, and then we can proceed." The voice spoke again, filling the workshop and seeming to come from everywhere.

"Whoa," Amil whispered from behind him on the stairs, his hammer out as he shot Pax a glance filled with worry.

"Don't do it," Rin whispered, already half-turned to head back down. Then she resumed the soft mumbling she'd been doing since they came up the stairs.

Listening closer, Pax realized she was counting and had reached somewhere in the three hundreds. *The paces!* he realized. Once Rin reached 500, Galen and his two followers would likely head back in their direction.

Before she could stop him, Pax reached for the crystal and held his breath. To his surprise, the surface was cool like glass, instead of warm as he'd expected. Shifting his spark toward his hand, Pax could feel the tiniest fluctuation of foreign mana, but it was gone before he got more than a sense.

The voice let out a disappointed sigh before speaking again. "I'm not sure how you figured out the altar's clues to find the workshop, but you haven't learned to control your light magic enough to qualify for entrance. Please return when you have developed better control."

"But—" Pax objected as the lights on the ceiling flashed out one by one.

"Leave," the voice insisted, as a dark barrier rose between them and the rest of the workshop. After a pause, the voice added with a wistful tone, "I will be eagerly awaiting your return. It has been too long since I've been able to instruct a new mage."

Grasping for ideas, Pax called out, "There are no light mages left to instruct me. Can't you give me something? A beginning book? Anything?"

The barrier slowed and stopped. Pax held his breath.

"You don't have a beginning class or manual?"

"No," Pax confirmed. "No one I've been able to talk to even knows what a light mage is. I truly just want to learn." Pax tried to sound as earnest as possible.

The barrier had stopped at shoulder level, and only two squares on the ceiling right above them still glowed.

"That makes no sense. No one? That might explain—" The voice trailed off to a mumble Pax could no longer make out.

"Um, sir?" Pax finally had to interrupt when it seemed the voice had forgotten him.

"Yes, right." The voice came back strong and confident again. "Have you received a beginner's manual for light mages?"

"No," Pax said, pulling back and aiming a pleading look at Rin as she tugged at his arm urgently. "Do you have one?"

Pax held his breath, despite wanting to urge the voice to hurry.

"Can I trust you to protect the information of our class of mages? Only light mages may read the manuals. The information can be very dangerous to others. Not to mention the unscrupulous who try to exploit the information for their own benefit."

"Yes." Pax hurried to assure the voice. "I promise I will keep whatever you share with me safe and allow no one else to look at it."

"Agreed then. But you may only have beginner material until you return and prove yourself worthy for more. To your left, on the second shelf just past the barrier, are satchels containing the starter manuals. You may take one, but then leave. Agreed?"

"Thank you so much. I will. Promise," Pax called out, already leaping forward to pull himself up on the smooth surface of the barrier as it lowered too slowly for him. He saw a row of leather wrapped satchels and strained to reach them.

"I got you," Amil said behind him just as Pax felt a strong hand wrap around his ankles and give him a nudge forward.

Heart racing, Pax snatched the bundle like the lifeline he hoped it was. "Got it," he called back and winced as Amil jerked him roughly back over the barrier.

"410," Rin barked at them, before she turned and raced back down the stairs, her lightstick dim compared to whatever had lit up the workshop.

"Thank you very much," Pax called over his shoulder as he put the satchel in his inventory and ran after his friends. "I'll be back."

Rin slid through the runed door as soon as it opened a sliver and alternated between fidgeting and aiming worried looks at the three sewage tunnels as Pax repeated his earlier feat of drawing back his light mana to drain and close the door.

"Go, go," Pax waved at them as soon as the door slid shut.

The sound of an irritated curse drifted to them from the center tunnel, spurring them to draw on their flagging energy and run back the way they'd come. After traversing more of the same tunnels, Pax wondered if he'd ever be free of the dank and smelly darkness again.

As they walked back, Pax's impatience grew until he finally gave in. He pulled out the satchel as they walked and tucked it under his arm once he had the book out. His friends walked closer, curiosity piqued by the ornate leather tome covered in intricate patterns. Grinning, he pulled on the front cover to see what it could teach him. It didn't open.

"Quit fooling around and show us," Amil said, leaning closer.

Pax stopped and used a better angle to pull on the book. He groaned and gave his friends a helpless look. "It won't open."

Amil reached over and gave the cover a tug, too, before scowling. With a disappointed grumble, Pax sent it back to his inventory and started walking again.

"I'm sure you'll figure it out when you have a little time," Rin said with an encouraging look.

He gave her a grateful nod and focused on making it back to the surface as quickly as possible. It was with a sigh of relief that he saw the familiar stairs leading up to the kitchen's back door. Pax couldn't wait to report the beast infestation and turn it over to someone else's capable hands.

"Mistress Nymeli—" he called as he pushed the kitchen door open, expecting to find a skeleton staff prepping for the coming morning.

A wave of light, steam and clanking dishes greeted him. The kitchen was full of workers weaving in and out, carrying dishes, trays and pots.

"What—?" Amil asked quietly behind him.

Rin just rubbed at her eyes, gaze moving back and forth as if things would change if she took another look.

"Krasig," Pax called out, waving a hand toward a smaller figure diligently placing cheese on a host of bread slices laid in neat rows across a gleaming metal table.

The dwarven boy's gaze popped up, looking for who had called to him. His eyes lit up when he saw the trio by the door. After a quick, furtive glance around for anyone watching him, Krasig put down the stack of cheese slices and scurried over.

"What is going on?" Pax asked as soon as he was close.

"The alarm bell went off," Krasig answered, looking puzzled. "Didn't you hear it?"

Pax swallowed, disheartened by another important piece of information they had no clue about. "Alarm?" he asked.

"Oh right," Krasig said, ducking his head as he flushed. "The alarm drill for first-years is usually after the first week of classes. Well," he gave them a shrug, his expression a mix of fear tinged with the excitement any boy feels at the possibility of danger. "I guess you get to practice early. The waves tonight have been getting worse and worse. And about thirty minutes ago, they rang the *third* alarm." He said the last with somber emphasis, as if they knew what he meant.

Pax glanced at Amil and Rin, but they looked just as clueless as he was.

At their confused looks, Krasig hurried to explain. "The first bell rings across the city for five minutes straight to summon the warriors and mages on call. Those are the ones who have their stuff ready to go and can respond quickly. Most of the time, that's enough, but it's a warning to everyone else in the city, just in case. Once those reinforcements arrive, the wall commanders decide if it's enough. Once every year or so, they ring the second alarm, and that's for the back-up warriors and mages who aren't on call."

"And the third alarm?" Pax asked, appalled as he eyed the activity around him and suspected the answer.

"That's for everyone with any kind of training to respond and all the support people like us"—he waved at the busy kitchen—"to get ready for a long night. We're preparing supplies to keep everyone strong and fed on the walls. It's exhausting to fight for hours. We'll include beast components to help, too."

The four of them paused for a moment and looked at the organized chaos around them and the gravity of the situation sunk in for Pax. This went far beyond an incursion of level 1 beasts below the academy. This was an assault on the safety of the entire capital.

"Is there a fourth alarm?" Rin asked the question Pax hadn't wanted to say out loud.

Krasig's expression sobered as he nodded. "That means everyone who can walk or even crawl needs to get to the wall . . . because we're being overrun."

"Krasig!" an overweight man barked out, his glare across the kitchen making Pax take a step back, even though he wasn't the object.

Krasig flinched, but aimed a grin in their direction. "Got to get back to work. And you're supposed to report to the eating hall for instructions. Good luck!"

And with that, he dove back into his work, head down and focused, as his hands flew.

Pax exchanged a resigned look with his friends before skirting along the edge of the kitchen toward the eating hall exit. They pushed through double doors into a chaos nowhere near as orderly as the kitchen they'd just left.

A handful of senior students stood scattered around, standing on tables and yelling out instructions to the students milling around them. Only some seemed to know what they were doing while many just ambled around; a mix of scared and confused.

At the far wall near the doors, things looked more organized as

Pax watched a group arranged in neat lines march out of the door with purpose to their movements.

"Who are we supposed to report to?" Rin asked, a dubious look on her face at the lack of organization nearby. "Besides, we haven't even done a shift on the student walls yet."

"But we've probably fought more beasts than any of the other first-years," Amil said with enough pride in his voice that Pax had to smile and nod in acknowledgement.

"So, what do we do?" Rin asked.

It took Pax a moment to realize she was asking him. His surprise must have been obvious, because she chuckled quietly. "I think you've done pretty well by us so far tonight, so why mess with it?"

Pax swallowed hard, and when Amil nodded in agreement, he didn't object. Straightening, Pax turned and looked over the busy space to pick the best group to join, only to remember what they'd seen down below. He stepped back into the shadows of an alcove holding kitchen supplies and waved for his friends to join him.

"What is it?" Rin asked.

"We can't join the other students yet," Pax said. "We'll get assigned to some supervisor and won't be able to leave until the emergency is over."

"I'm tired, too," Amil said, looking dubious. "But I want to help. This is our home now, and we need to protect it."

"All of it," Pax agreed. "Including what's below us."

"But the surge against the walls is much more powerful than the level 1 swarms we found below," Rin said. "The people in charge won't divert people from the walls to take care of them."

"And when all the mages and warriors are on the walls, who is going to protect the support staff when those beasts come boiling out of the tunnels?" Pax asked.

He saw when both of his friends realized the problem. On any normal night, there would be plenty of people available to handle a horde of low-level beasts on the Academy grounds, especially once someone raised the alarm. But not tonight.

"Follow my lead," he whispered. "And look like you have somewhere to be. It's the best way to keep from attracting notice."

They nodded and stepped out after him as he strode with a confident urgency for the doors on the far left. A fourth-year flame support mage looked up from the clipboard he held. "Do you have your assignments?" he asked, giving their group a dubious look.

Pax suddenly realized that no amount of confident posture would make up for them being three first-year students who looked extremely ragged. Pax barely prevented himself from glancing down at his scratched armor and ripped clothes, not to mention the reek he'd grown so used to. No wonder the other students hadn't minded giving them a wide berth.

"Just a minute," the fourth-year said, standing and looking for someone back in the hall. "You can't leave."

60

RECRUITING HELP

PAX KNEW they'd lose their chance if he followed orders. "Mistress Nymeli insisted we go help Mage Incedis immediately. Would you like one of us to go back to the kitchen and bring her here?" Pax adopted an extremely reluctant expression and threw a fearful look over his shoulder.

The student blanched at Mistress Nymeli's name, looking unsure for the first time.

"Quick," Pax injected impatience into his voice as he turned to Rin. "Go tell the Mistress that Student Mage—" he paused and looked back at the young man expectantly.

"Student Mage Sidur," he said reluctantly.

"—Student Mage Sidur needs her approval to let us leave on the mission she gave us," Pax finished, injecting a bit of the authoritative tone he'd learned from the Mistress herself.

"You go ask her," Rin said, taking an immediate step back and shaking her head. Her act was so perfect that Pax almost lost his own composure and grinned.

"No, no," Sidur interrupted, waving a hand at them. "I'll just write your names down and put you under assignment to Mage Incedis. Does that work?"

"If you're sure," Pax said. "I know the Mistress wouldn't want us violating any rules."

"No," Sidur assured them, already flipping to a new page and getting ready to write before he looked back up. "Names, please?"

"MAGE INCEDIS?" Pax asked, trying to project his voice through the hubbub of the busy lobby on the ground floor of the instructor office building. Unlike the chaos of the students back in the eating hall, here, experienced mages with grim faces worked in small groups, some intent as they discussed plans, while others packed up supplies arrayed in neat rows on tables. A steady trickle of mages exited the building, determined expressions on their faces.

Outside, Pax and his friends had navigated a campus very different from the one they'd grown used to. Someone had turned every light to maximum, lighting the paths to almost daylight levels and shining from windows in every building as the entire campus came awake like an angry anthill someone had kicked over.

Pax and his friends had helped two kitchen workers struggling to carry heavy boxes of supplies inside and wound their way around to where Mage Incedis was in an intense discussion with two other mages.

"Excuse me," Pax tried again, when there was a break in their conversation.

"What?" Incedis snapped as he turned and glared at Pax with so much irritation it made Pax's next words dry up in his mouth.

Incedis' eyes widened as he took in Pax, his two friends, and the state they were in. Pax groaned internally, resisted an urge to smell himself as he rubbed his hands on his leggings.

With a sigh, Incedis ran a tired hand over his face before speaking again. "I'm sorry, Pax. You're obviously having trouble tonight. What do you need?" Then he frowned. "Why aren't you at the eating hall where the first-year students are being organized? And who are these two with you?"

"Can you give us just a few minutes to explain?" Pax asked.

Mage Incedis narrowed his eyes and aimed a questioning look at Pax.

"It's important," Pax assured him, hoping his advisor would believe him.

"Mage Incedis?" The tall woman with a robe patterned in swirls of light blue asked in an impatient voice.

"Just a minute," Incedis said under his breath to Pax before he straightened and turned to face the other two mages. "Araal, you work on organizing the teams we're sending to reinforce the city wall sections. Boddux, you make sure we have an experienced mage, minimum level 5, to reinforce each section of our practice wall, even the beginner section."

"The beginner section?" The dour man questioned, raising one bushy eyebrow. "With only level 1 and 2 monsters there?"

Incedis shook his head and pinched the bridge of his nose. "We have reports that there are so many beasts, they are overwhelming some of the ancients' sorting devices. We may get much more powerful beasts than we should at the different sections."

The man's face blanched, and he nodded in agreement before turning to wave over more mages. His response worried Pax, even though he didn't understand the details about the Academy wall they had mentioned. All he knew was that the situation was bad. Really bad. Maybe their report was actually insignificant in comparison, after all.

"Now," Incedis turned toward them before glancing around and heading toward a small table nestled in a nook off to the side of the huge fireplace against the wall.

Pax and his friends exchanged an anxious look before following him and sitting in the chairs he motioned them toward.

"Now, tell me exactly how you ended up in this state," Incedis ordered. "And make it fast."

Pax did as told, and all three of them did their best to answer the questions Incedis fired at them for more and more details.

～

"I WOULD ASK if you were making this all up or lying to me," Incedis said, leaning back into his chair when they finished. "But your appearance speaks for itself, and you're too smart to do that on a night like tonight. Regardless, every beast you encountered was level 1 and logic would suggest they all are, so I'm inclined to just forget the whole thing until tomorrow, when we'll have the resources to deal with this easily and quickly."

"But—" Pax protested.

"If—" Incedis interrupted him with an imperious hand. "If you weren't right about the risk to our most vulnerable people. Within the next two hours, the campus will be almost completely empty of anyone with power, and even a small swarm of level 1 beasts would cause more bloodshed than is acceptable."

The idea of an acceptable amount of bloodshed struck Pax as a concept that just sounded wrong, but he didn't object as Incedis continued.

"Here's what we're going to do," Incedis said as he placed both hands on the table and leaned forward. "You have one hour to eat, resupply and gear up. Then recruit any first-year students you can to join us. Your lot is not much use on the walls anyway, but even a beginner's spell will work against level 1 beasts. I'll see if I can find two or three mages or upper-class students who will join me, because honestly, even that is more than we can spare on the capital's walls tonight. But even with all my power, I still can't handle an entire cavern of the size you described on my own. And I'll grab potions from my personal stock."

"The Academy council mages won't send more help?" Rin asked.

Incedis paused and took a moment to examine her. She stiffened and held the old mage's gaze without flinching.

"Have you heard of the expression that it's better to ask for forgiveness than permission?" he asked quietly.

Amil shot a glance at Pax and the relief Pax had felt at turning the whole mess over to the authorities soured. They might not be on their own, but it wasn't looking much better.

"The council of mages takes days to come to any kind of consensus under normal circumstances. During a third alarm, it would take a direct act of Vitur for them to overrule the response protocols."

Now Rin was giving Pax an uneasy look.

"You aren't children," Incedis snapped impatiently. "You are mages, and this is a danger you brought to me. I can easily go either way. Let the authorities handle this tomorrow night or do something now. You decide. Now."

Thinking of Krasig, Mistress Nymeli and the other non-mages they'd gotten to know in their various assignments, Pax knew there was only one decision he could make. A quick glance toward his two friends showed they agreed. "We do something now," he said, his voice firm.

"Good," Incedis said, approval in his gaze as he pulled out a piece of parchment with a symbol stamped in wax. "This is a stamped order from me, so people don't mess with you."

Pax looked down in surprise at the note when Incedis handed it to him.

"You have one hour, and we'll meet you in the eating hall," Incedis said as he put away his pen and stood. "Go, already!"

They ran back to leave word at the eating hall for the available first-years to gather and only after long, wasted moments of examining the stamped order did the older students reluctantly agree to have the first-years gather and wait for Mage Incedis.

"If we hurry, I think we'll have time for a quick strategy planning session," Pax said as they ran back out of the eating hall. "Round up any first-years at your dorms and then get over to mine as fast as you can. We'll use one of the training rooms."

Rin opened her mouth to ask a question, but Pax just ran, noticing that the campus was already a lot less busy than it had been on their trip over just a few minutes ago.

As Pax raced along the paths back to his dorm, he pulled food from his inventory and chewed as he ran. The knot of worry in his gut ruined even his favorite pastry's taste.

At his dorm, he found it deserted except for a handful of first-years, including Dahni, fast asleep in their dorm rooms, impervious to the clanging alarms and activity. It took precious moments to wake them and explain enough to get them moving to the eating hall.

Finally finished, Pax stood at the front door, peering into the night for a glimpse of Rin and Amil. Nothing. Besides the retreating backs of the students he'd just hustled off, nothing else moved. The emptiness was so eerie after all the chaotic bustle of the evening.

Knowing they couldn't have more than a half hour left at most, Pax was torn between staying and waiting for his friends or just heading back to the eating hall. Then he realized if he wanted to make plans for the coming fight, he needed to check over the details of his menu first.

He sat on the cold stone of the front stoop, closed his eyes and focused.

~

NAME: *Pax Vipersworn*

    Race: *Mixed Human (monster-touched)*

    Age: *16*

    Bound Location: *Shieldwall Mage Academy (provisional monthly)*

    Class: *Mage*

    Element: Light (Hidden)

    Specialization: none (Hidden)

    Paths of Understanding: *(Hidden)*

    Flame: Level 1 - 21/100

    Air: Level 1 - 51/100

    Water: Level 1 - 92/100 (+83)

    Earth: Level 1 - 10/100

    Level: *1*

    Mage Leveling Points: *0/5*

Health: *42/42 (+2)*

Mana: *21/26*

Attributes:

Strength: 6

Agility: 9

Endurance: 8 (+1)

Intelligence: 8

Insight: 8 (+1)

Charisma: 5

Skills:

General Active:

Identify Level 1 (Common) - 62/100 (+3)

General Passive:

Skinning Level 1 (Common) - 38/100 (+2)

Butchering Level 1 (Common) - 54/100 (+5)

Clubs Level 1 (Common) - 28/100 (+12)

Mage:

Light Mana Manipulation Level 1 (Epic) - 39/100 (+7) (Hidden)

Light Mana Sight Level 1 (Rare) - 48/100 (+8) (Hidden)

Elemental Meditation Level 1 (Common) - 11/100 (+3)

Light Healing Level 1 (Rare) - 17/100 (+13) (Hidden)

Runes Level 1 (Uncommon) - 11/100 (+7)

Mana Merge Level 1 (Epic) - 30/100 (+27) (Hidden)

Spells:

Light (1/3):

Haste Level 1 (Common) - 24/100 (+2)

Inventory: *14/20 available.*

Assignments:

Academy Workshop Trainee

4/30 hours

0/1 Supervisor approval

Charity Clinic Trainee

2/30 hours

0/1 Supervisor approval

Maintenance Trainee

0/21 Cleared blockages
0/1 Supervisor approval
Exterminator Trainee
102/100 Vermin killed (+54)
0/1 Supervisor approval
Misc.: *First-year Point Ranking (expand)*

PAX COULDN'T HELP SMILING when he saw all the advancements accumulated from his first merge with Rin's water mana, cleansing his body of the venom, and merging again to help her with the water shield to protect them while Amil flamed the Abronia. He was so close to completing his Water Path.

That and the handful of points in his mage skills from figuring out the door rune solidified his resolve to grab his friends and do what they could to get stronger before they headed back into the tunnels again.

He almost missed the change at the end of his menu. Fifty-four vermin killed? He couldn't help the broad grin as he realized their active assignment was still counting the beasts toward his vermin count. And the total was enough to hit the requirement, his first completion.

A quick scan of the vermin assignment's specifics verified that the assignment would show completed and advance to intern as soon as he got his supervisor's approval. Thinking of the number of 'vermin' they were likely to encounter tonight made Pax resolve to get Nymeli's approval as soon as possible. Hopefully, it would give them an even better per kill bonus.

With a burst of excitement, Pax pulled up his coin total, pushing it to merge with his menu so it would show up automatically from now on.

COIN COUNT: 0 Gold, 3 Silver, 88 copper (+1 Silver, +77 Copper)
   Academy Points: *12 (+7)*

~

ALMOST GIDDY AT his new wealth, he couldn't help pulling up the
Academy Point standings.

~

Week 1: Shieldwall Academy First-Year Academy Point Top 10

1. Codrun Shadowforge - 14
   2. Amil Fajor - 13
   3. Rin Esta - 12
   4. Pax Vipersworn - 12
   5. Izoa Yelren - 10
   6. Aymer Wynrel - 9
   7. Hoset Wraithaxe - 8
   8. Orist Valdi - 7
   9. Maleth Chaosback - 7
   10. Kali Wynrel - 7

~

HE OPENED his eyes and was chuckling when Rin and Amil ran up, out
of breath.

"I don't think there's much to laugh about right now," Rin scolded
him.

"You're right," Pax said, hopping up and heading inside quickly.
"We don't have long to get ready."

"You're not telling us what you were laughing about?" Amil asked
as he jogged after him.

"Look at the Academy Point ranking," he said, unable to keep the
glee out of his voice as he hurried down the stairs.

His grin widened as he heard his friends' delight behind him. Pax pushed open the heavy door to one of the medium-sized practice rooms.

Now they just needed to see how strong they could get in the little time they had left.

61

LAST-MINUTE SPELLS

PAX JERKED the practice room door shut behind them with a clang and turned to face his two friends, who were still catching their breath.

Rough stone lined the boxy, medium-sized room, reinforcing it, but still showing scratches and pockmarks from years of student use. A row of three even sadder looking dummies were standing in a ragged row on the far side. Metal had been used to build one, which had kept it in better shape. The floor had a barely noticeable slope leading to a large drain in the left corner. Finally, just inside the door stood a wide wooden table to hold student possessions. Otherwise, the space was empty and open, perfect for their needs.

"I think we each need to unlock a new spell before we head back down with Incedis," he blurted out in a rush, feeling each second ticking away.

"A new spell," Rin objected. "We don't have enough time and besides, I thought we were saving up to fill our other two slots with uncommon spells, at least. Didn't your advisor give you the big warning about not deciding without approval? Besides, the two of us don't have chances for bonus spells like you might."

"I know," he said, trying to summarize his thoughts as succinctly as possible. "But saving the spot for a future emergency might leave you hurt or even killed in tonight's fighting. Just hear me out, since we're running out of time."

Rin nodded reluctantly.

Amil just looked excited at the idea of another spell. "Incedis said to ask for forgiveness instead of permission in an emergency."

Pax nodded. "We're splitting the difference. Saving one empty spot for something powerful we find or earn, while using the other to keep us alive tonight. And who knows, with all the new magic stuff we're discovering, maybe we can improve your common choices in the future. Plus, remember all those books and scrolls in that library. Once I get access to that stuff, I'll do everything to build both of you up. But we need to survive tonight. Rin, you need a defensive or an area spell. Amil, a good defensive spell could make all the difference if we get swarmed."

"You said our common choices," Rin shot back. "You're not using up one of your spell slots, too?"

Pax looked sheepish and raised a defensive hand when Rin's frown deepened. "Yes, I want to use a spell slot, too, just not one of my light ones." He hesitated, but didn't have time to delay. "I'm hoping to use a water slot if I can complete my Water Path. I'll need your help for that."

Understanding dawned on her face, and she gave a decisive nod. "You haven't led us wrong tonight, so I'll stop delaying us. Tell us what to do."

"Both of you quickly pull up your choices and call them out, starting with Amil, since he's looking for something defensive. We'll put our heads together to pick the best one. Go, Amil."

With a nod and an intent look, Amil closed his eyes and called out the name of a spell every few seconds. Then opened his eyes and looked at them. "Those are the only defensive ones."

"Both of you tell me which one caught your attention the most and we'll see if we agree. We'll have Amil read the descriptions and then decide."

"Flame Wall," Rin said at almost the same time as Amil.

The two exchanged a pleased grin.

"Can we take a quick look at Flame Shield, too?" Pax said, hesitant to take the time, but knowing Amil would be stuck with this spell for a long time. "Mobility is an issue," he explained. "Does that wall stay in one place? And how often would you be able to absorb and recast it? I'm just thinking of swarms charging us. A wall would be perfect to funnel them or protect our rear, but not if you can't recast it or move it in a reasonable amount of time. The Flame Shield wouldn't be as useful, since it would just protect Amil instead of helping all of us, but since it'll form on Amil's arm, it'll always be with him regardless of where the battle moves."

Amil's eyes shut as he took a moment to check the descriptions, and Rin raised her brows at Pax, looking impressed.

"What?" he whispered with a grin. "Staying alive gets my complete focus." Then he made a hurry-up motion toward her. "Choose your top ones, so you're ready when we're done with Amil."

She flushed, looking embarrassed at needing the nudge, and closed her eyes. After a rapid back-and-forth, Amil chose Flame Wall with the plan to keep them as small as possible to preserve mana and allow faster recasts. The option to funnel large numbers of beasts to prevent them from being overwhelmed was too valuable for what they expected to face that night.

Rin was stuck between Wave and Water Spear. Wave was the obvious choice with the swarms in the cavern, but the Spear was much more appealing to Rin's desire to be sneaky in a battle and kill with a decisive attack.

"I promise I'll help you find an awesome attack spell after this if you take the Wave," Pax said. "And maybe even make Wave work more the way you prefer."

"Thanks," she said grumpily. "I know what I need to choose. Just let me be a little upset about it, ok? Compared to my wave knocking my opponent down once or twice in spell class, jabbing him with a spear or two is just so much better."

"Thanks," Pax said, giving her a helpless shrug and not sure what else to say.

She closed her eyes, her head still shaking as she frowned. "Done. Now, how do we get your water path finished?"

"First," he paused and turned to Amil. "Can you take the right side and practice your Flame Wall, just small ones to measure what you can sustain with your rate of mana regeneration?"

Amil nodded and moved over with a grin on his face and a spring in his step.

Pax turned back to Rin. "You need to attack me," he said, stepping toward the center of the room and taking a breath to prepare himself. "I've already gained points twice from merging with your water and a third repeat never seems to advance skills. I think the fastest option is to fight your water magic."

Her smile was much more dangerous-looking than Amil's.

"Don't hurt me," Pax hurried to caution her. "I still have to be in shape to fight tonight. If it doesn't work, I'll unlock a second light spell, but I really don't want to do that." Worry pushed at him. "With everyone down there, I won't even be able to use it without being seen. I really need a water one that will blend in or that they'll attribute to you instead of me."

She nodded, the understanding on her face easing his nerves, before it turned thoughtful. "What about trying to get the last few points from one of the water cores instead?"

Pax hesitated. "They're supposed to be dangerous, and I want to take my time when I mess with cores. Besides, working directly with your mana got me this far already, so—" He shrugged and gave her an expectant look.

She gave him an abrupt nod and raised her hands, cords of water swirling around her wrists. He suddenly felt an entirely different type of nervousness.

When the Snakes shot out and wrapped around both of his arms, their feel, solid but mobile, surprised him.

Focus, he told himself, and allowed himself to close his eyes since they didn't have time to waste. First, though, he needed to monitor his progress. With a quick push at his menu, he pulled at the line item for his Water Path and sent it to the lower left of his vision, opposite where his notifications were almost always blinking at him.

~

PATHS OF UNDERSTANDING: (Hidden)
   Water: Level 1 - 92/100

~

READY NOW, Pax split his growing spark in two and shot it to both wrists, swirling just under the skin where Rin's dark blue magic tightened and pulled his arms out to the side.

He tried to merge with her mana, but found it resisted this time, repelling him back with a sharp pain that reverberated back up to his chest. Concentrating on the feel of her water repelling him, he got a sense of the solid nature of the ever-changing water and its inability to be compressed. A flicker of numbers in his lower vision made him grin.

~

PATHS OF UNDERSTANDING: (Hidden)
   Water: Level 1 - 94/100 (+2)

~

ENJOYING THE CHALLENGE, Pax focused on the thick thread of dark blue he had in his own mana. Pushing it to the forefront, closest to Rin's mana, he tried again, easing it closer and attempting to maneuver his mana to merge with hers so he could assert control.

A sudden pain in both of his shoulders disrupted his concentration, as the Water Snake jerked his arms straight out from his body in a sharp, painful move.

"Hey," he protested, his eyes opening and glaring at Rin.

Her face was a study of concentration, sweat beading on her forehead as she returned his glare. "I'm a support mage, not power, and we're out of time," she said through gritted teeth. "Do you want a decent fight so you can earn the last few points or not?"

"You're right. Sorry," he said, shame flushing through him. "And I've already got two. Just six more to go."

Her glare narrowed further.

"Sorry," he repeated. "I'll call out the points as I earn them, so you know what's working." Closing his eyes, he said, "Do whatever it takes. I have to do this."

Her Snakes tightened further, pulling at his arms, just enough to hurt. Pax ignored the pain and kept trying to match the water component of his mana with hers. With little success. A moment later, the pressure eased, and the Snakes shot up his arms and then his chest.

Following them and desperately trying to penetrate the mystery of water's power, it took Pax a moment to realize they were winding around his neck, interlocking into a broad collar that tightened with power around the entire length of his neck.

They squeezed, cutting off most of his air. Panic drove all thoughts of careful study out of Pax's mind. His eyes popped open as both hands shot up to his neck, scratching futilely at the thick bands of water clamping down.

"Rin," he tried to yell in alarm, but only a harsh whistle came out as he fought to breathe.

"Figure out my water," she barked at him, no sympathy at all. "Use your magic to stop it!"

"Rin!" Amil said, alarm in his voice as he dropped his Flame Wall and lurched toward them.

"No," she shook her head firmly toward Amil. "He said to do whatever it takes. And everything else was going too slow." She looked back toward Pax, holding his gaze. "Whatever it takes, Pax. Fight me!"

Lightheaded from the shallow gasps he could manage, Pax could see she wouldn't back down. And she was probably right. That didn't mean he wouldn't get her back as soon as this was over.

But for now, he closed his eyes and summoned all his power to figure out her water mana and break it from his neck. With none of the finesse of earlier, Pax gathered his spark and, using all his strength, smashed it into her mana. He fought to break free and breathe. Only to rebound right back, the solid attribute of her water mana manifesting strongly.

It took a force of will to push the panic back and keep some coherency to his thoughts. Tentative merging wasn't the answer, and brute force didn't do a thing. Maybe he could combine the two? With a thought, Pax spread his spark into its mist form and gathered it into his chest, only to have another thought.

It was called the Path of Understanding, not domination. His magical strength came from understanding the underlying structure of the world around him and bringing order to it. With a quick rearrangement that took more mental effort than he expected, Pax had separated the dark blue mana from his mass of mostly light mana.

The ball of water mana looked pitiful, smaller even than he remembered his spark being as a child. But Pax focused on the aspects of magic he'd already gained understanding of, its ability to cleanse poison, to flow and adapt to any container, and finally the resistance to being deformed when it wanted to. So many contradictions.

Feeling darkness lurking in the wings as his breathing narrowed further, Pax pushed all his energy into the little ball, bursting it into a fine mist of mana. Sending it racing to his neck with the strength he still had left, Pax kept the essence of water's nature at the forefront of his mind.

When the mist slammed into Rin's barrier, it penetrated so easily that Pax's thoughts stumbled. His mist swirled among Rin's much larger energy, at a loss for a moment.

Mist, a fine mist, Pax pushed the concept out from his mana, sending the image of this form of water into Rin's mana with all the power he had left. For a moment, he felt Rin's magic fluctuate before it turned solid again. His little cloud of water mana just didn't have the power to force Rin's to change form.

Desperate, Pax dissipated his light magic into the mist form and pushed it along the same path his water mana had taken. It didn't penetrate anywhere as easily, but he kept pushing. The energy spread out and attacked on every front instead of focusing on specific areas. With a pop that made his hopes flare, his light magic finally made it through, the fine fog invigorating his bit of water mana with the power it needed.

"Mist," he whispered, or tried to with the bit of breath he could muster as his legs sagged.

Again. *Mist!*

With a suddenness that made him stumble forward to his hands and knees, the collar of death around his neck exploded into a fine mist of water that dampened his face and chest. The full breath he sucked in immediately afterward was more delicious than one of his voca pastries.

As soon as he caught his breath, he pointed a shaky finger at Rin and a shamefaced Amil. "You're both going to pay for that."

"Yeah, yeah," she said. "But did it work? Did you get the points?"

When he didn't answer, she gave him a sheepish shrug and added, "Danger accelerates growth, right?"

He gave her a pained smile, but couldn't argue when he saw the notifications flashing and opened them.

～

Paths of Understanding: (Hidden)
  Water: Level 1 - 101/100 (+7)

Congratulations Light Mage! You have completed Level 1 of the Water Path of Understanding!

Through dedicated study of the element of Water, you have gained a beginning comprehension of its properties and powers and have unlocked one Water spell slot and increased your mana capacity. Continue studying the magical elements of your world to better enlighten those around you, unlock more spell slots and continue to increase your mana capacity.

. . .

PATHS OF UNDERSTANDING: (Hidden)
    Water: Level 2 - 1/200
    Mana: *11/31 (+5)*

~

PAX COULDN'T HELP the stupid grin that split his face as he finished reading. He'd not only earned a water spell slot, exactly as he'd hoped, but also bumped up his mana total. Gaining more mana, plus spells in all the other elements, filled him with a giddy excitement, despite how much work he knew it would be.

When he glanced at Rin, she nodded with satisfaction. She could obviously read his success from his expression.

"Well," Rin said, putting her hands on her hips. "Now it's our turn to help you pick a spell."

SPELL CHOICES

EXCITED BUT, at the same time, scared his choices would disappoint him, Pax closed his eyes. Holding his breath, he pulled up his spell menu.

WELCOME TO YOUR SPELL MENU, *Light Mage*
    You have two level-1 light spell slots and one level-1 water spell slot currently open. Would you like to select a spell now?

YES! Pax couldn't help a quick fist pump.

"It worked?" Both Rin and Amil asked at almost the same time.

Grinning, he opened his eyes and nodded. "Quick, Rin, what are the basic water options?"

"Water Snake, Wave, Water Spear, Water Blade and Shape Water," she said, ticking off her fingers.

"We don't want duplicates, so give me a quick rundown on what you know about the other three from watching in spell class," he said, heading toward the door. "I'll pick one on the way and try to get a practice cast or two in while we walk. And you do the same with your Wave, since I took up all your practice time," he added with an apologetic shrug.

"Spear starts with small, hand-sized bolts of water, but it takes a lot of concentration to keep that solid and sharp enough to do significant damage. Plus, they don't fly far at the start," Rin said as she and Amil fell in behind him, heading toward the stairwell.

"Oh, no." Pax stopped and made an abrupt turn to run toward his room.

"What?" Amil said, moving to race after him, his hammer already in his hand.

"Sorry." Pax waved him off and called over his shoulder, "My talpasauria. I can't risk it down in the tunnels."

Their tension relaxed at his explanation. He raced down the hallway, ignoring his tiredness. Skidding into his room, he snatched one of his dirty tunics out of the laundry basket. He crouched by the far end of his bed as he swung his pack around and carefully pulled out the sleeping beast. He sent a pulse of light mana into the little guy, glad that it only stirred a little and didn't wake. Wrapping the shirt around the improvised satchel, Pax slid it into the shadows against the wall under his bed. He pulled a piece of Bog Swarmer meat from the stack he still had in his inventory and placed it next to the small bundle.

A momentary surprise at how fresh the meat still looked made him wonder how long perishable items would last in his inventory. He needed to remember to ask Rin. She probably knew. Hopefully, the snack would keep the beast happy if he woke up before Pax returned.

"Sorry," Pax said, barely pausing as he ran past his friends and up the stairs.

Rin growled at him, but Amil just grinned. "Flying pet for me. Don't forget."

"Will do," Pax said before motioning for Rin to continue explaining as they pushed open the dorm door and exited into an almost deserted campus. At least all the lights were still on, making it easy to find their way.

"Water Blade is kind of self-explanatory, just like the spear. Its advantage over a real blade is that you can form and absorb it instantly. With practice and strength, you can make it bigger and sturdier."

"Can you manifest it on any part of your body, or does it need to be held in your hand like a sword or knife?" Pax asked as they ran, his mind working on how he could use it without it being obvious.

Rin shot him a thoughtful look. "I don't see why not, but I haven't paid enough attention to see anyone do it."

"And Shape Water?" Amil asked, looking more interested in the discussion than Pax had thought he'd be.

But it made sense, as the three of them had spent the last few days depending on each other to survive. Knowing what your team could do would be crucial. Pax made a mental note that they needed to plan some team practices to coordinate their skills after they survived the night.

"Everyone can control their mana inside their bodies without a spell, but Shape Water pushes that further, giving you a lot more control and also letting you control water around you if it's nearby. With more levels, you can work at a further distance."

They ran in silence for a few moments as Pax considered his options, visualizing the cavern full of beasts they'd seen and imagining how the coming battle might play out.

A sudden rush of water startled him until he saw Rin's grin and the small wave that bent a two-foot section of bushes to the side.

"That's great," Amil said, his eyes on the effects of Rin's new spell. "If you call out left or right when you use that down below, I'll head in that direction while you're casting and be ready to clear the beasts you knock down."

"You do the same so we know where you're casting your wall, and we'll do much better against the next swarm," Rin agreed with a cheerful smile.

Meanwhile, Pax could really only see one choice for his new spell.

Observers could trace Spears directly back to him and Shape would be even more obvious. "So, Blade for me? Unless I'm missing something?"

They both nodded, and it gave Pax a bit more confidence to have their agreement. As they turned the last corner and saw the eating hall in the distance, he made his choice.

~

CONGRATULATIONS!

Water Spell Unlocked: **Water Blade** *Level 1*

This common spell allows a water mage to summon an edged weapon made from water or even add an edge to any part of their body or object they are holding. At the beginning level, the mage will have limited size, time, sharpness and durability of the blade. Practice against new and stronger challenges will improve these and level the skill. Manifesting blades at a distance is possible with increased level and evolution.

Distance: Touch

Mana cost: Initial and maintenance cost varies by size and structure of blade.

Note: Both Intelligence and Insight help with stronger blade structure and quality.

~

FULL OF EXCITEMENT at a spell he could actually fight with, Pax didn't waste any time summoning the blade. He focused his mana on the edge of his right hand as he ran. For a moment, nothing happened, and he pushed his awareness into the mana swirling and full of energy in his hand.

He couldn't help the stab of disappointment and worry he felt. After all he'd done and the help and risks his friends had taken, it didn't work.

Water Blade. He gave the mental command with even more force, staring down at his hand while doing his best to watch the path in

SPELL CHOICES | 443

front of him as they ran. Something in his mana flickered, trying to respond, but the bulk of his magical energy seemed unaffected.

He ran through ideas, trying to diagnose the problem in the few minutes he had left. Only some of his mana was responding. Acting on instinct, he dove into his energy, searching out the cords of indigo mana threading through his light and pulling, doing his best to bring them close to the surface toward the edge of his hand, where he wanted the blade to manifest. Distracted, his foot caught on a loose stone, and he stumbled.

Amil reached out to keep him from falling, and Pax shot his friend a grateful look before going back to his efforts to get the new spell to work. His friends hadn't seemed to have trouble with their new spells, but he had more than one type of mana, so maybe it took some sorting and more practice.

His stumble had disrupted him, and it took another moment to balance his running and split off enough concentration to manipulate his water mana again. It felt like trying to listen to two conversations, but he quickly found the precarious mental balance that let him try again.

"Water Blade," he whispered, this time focusing his attention on the gathered water mana that kept trying to slip out of his control.

With a distinctive rush, he felt something both cool and hard flash along the edge of his hand. Eyes wide and eager, he pulled up his hand and stared in wonder at the thin edge of water, a blue so dark it looked almost black in the shadows of the night.

Unable to stop himself, he reached up to touch it with his other hand, only to snatch his finger back and pop it into his mouth to suck on the minor cut.

"You did it!" Amil crowed, punching Pax in the shoulder in excitement.

"Let me see," Rin said, her voice huffing on his other side. She grinned when he held his new bladed hand up, though he saw a touch of jealousy in her gaze.

"We'll get you an awesome fighting spell for your third slot, I promise," he reassured her. "With everything we're earning, we'll be able to buy something good."

She nodded, looking mollified.

"And wait until we see what our Academy Point ranking gets us at the end of the week," Amil added with even more excitement.

He was still grinning when they arrived at the eating hall and pulled open the door.

"Wait a second," Pax said before entering. He stepped off into the bushes and pulled out one of the Nerodai bodies. With a fast slash, he sliced through the skin and into the thick muscle of the snake-like creature and laid out two filets onto a mostly clean rock in the landscaping.

"What—" Amil was staring.

"Just cook it with your flame. Quick," Pax said. "And Rin, give Amil your Blaze Lizard meat from Master Kruse. You and I will have this water meat in case of an emergency."

Understanding flashed in his friends' eyes, and they followed his instructions. Moments later, they burst into the eating hall, a host of eyes turning to see who had come in.

"Cutting it close, aren't you?" Incedis' distinctive drawl was easy to make out over the nervous sound of multiple voices in the eating hall. "You're just in time to hear the plan. Any later, and you'd have missed the entire thing."

Letting out a relieved breath, Pax hurried across the empty half of the hall with his friends to find out how Incedis planned to cleanse out the infestation below.

INTO THE DARK

AMIL USED his bulk to push past some of the other first-years. They had gathered around two tables that someone had pushed together in front of Incedis, who'd climbed up on another table so everyone could see him.

Rin pulled over a bench so the three friends could climb up and see better. Incedis had spread three detailed maps on the table he stood on. A host of about thirty first-year students crowded in to see it all. Most were mage students, but there were a handful of warriors mixed in, and Pax saw the distinctive green of a few crafter uniforms.

The students wore everything from fancy armor to just their student-issued leathers. Some carried weapons, while others just had sheathed knives. Pax saw a couple of shields that would come in pretty handy against a big swarm.

Dahni was one of them, and Pax exchanged a nod with his roommate. Tansa, the power water mage that had helped them with advice, stood next to him and smiled, too. Pax abruptly realized that his association with Galen might have kept him from realizing he was gaining more good relationships than bad among the first-years.

Pax's eyes widened when, along the edge of the group, he glimpsed

Aymer, the wealthy scion who'd been in charge of the fiasco at the Assignment Board. He looked pretty angry, and Pax had to snicker, despite the sudden sour feeling that tainted his good mood. The 'crat had probably insisted that they needed him on the wall. Incedis would have shut that down pretty fast. At least he only had one of his cronies with him, a lanky girl scowling as much as he was.

Behind them, a student ducked his head when Pax's eyes scanned that direction. Recognizing Kurt, Pax clenched his fists and nudged Amil. "Kurt and that flick, Aymer, over there. Keep an eye out for Galen and his buddies. They're probably back up here somewhere by now."

Amil's eyes followed Pax's, and he nodded before a sudden smile lit up his face. "Maybe they're still down there, and the beasts killed them."

Rin snorted. "We're not that lucky."

Incedis cleared his throat, drawing their attention back. Everyone quieted down. To Incedis' left stood a fourth-year water student that looked to be helping run things. Then the boy moved, and Pax saw Zanneth, the assistant from his air spell class. Pax groaned quietly. One more thing to worry about. Zanneth might carry tales back to Graybrew if he noticed Pax doing water magic.

"Here's the route we'll be taking," Incedis lifted a map and pointed with a stylus, tracing a path as he explained. "Students Pax, Rin and Amil discovered the infestation, but our party can't make it through the same narrow tunnels as they did. We'll start our descent through this abandoned facility before moving over to the section of mainte-nance tunnels here." He lifted a second map. "We should come out along one of these two paths. One should lead to the cavern they described. We'll look for signs of the beasts when we get to the fork and may have to divide into two groups, depending on what we find."

That got a nervous murmur from the other students, who had been straining to see the map details as Incedis outlined the plan.

"Don't worry," Incedis said, his voice impatient. "Air Mage Zanneth and Fourth-year Turgan here will help lead the other group if we need to split up. And neither group will engage with any beasts until we're able to join back up again." He paused, and his expression turned serious. "I'm treating you like mages and giving you all the facts that I know. This won't be easy and is not something we would usually throw a bunch of first-years into during their first week. But we're the only ones that those fighting on the walls tonight can spare." His gaze pulled at theirs with an almost palpable purpose. "And like all the people fighting tonight, we're going to step up and save the people who can't save themselves."

Pax felt a mix of fear and pride rush through him. Seeing other students standing straighter, he knew he wasn't the only one.

Incedis gave them a stern nod of approval before continuing. "I'm splitting you into teams. Let's have each of the six warriors step up here and spread out. The rest of you mages divide up equally between them while we get the supplies set up to distribute to you." He turned with his two assistants, waving toward the kitchen as he produced racks of potions from his inventory to spread out on the nearby tables.

Rin grabbed Pax and Amil, tugging them off to the left before many other students, besides the warriors, had even started moving.

"Wha—?" Pax said, only to stop when he saw Bryn, the dwarf from their conditioning class taking a position up front while casting a disgruntled look at Tasar, her elven friend, who moved to stand a few feet away from her.

"Dahni, Tansa, over here." Pax waved toward the two, who were looking a little lost as groups formed.

Bryn's frown softened when they hurried to stand with her.

"Are you fine if we group up with you again?" Rin asked politely.

"If Tasar and I have to be separated, then I guess you are the best I can hope for," she grumbled, but looked happy to have familiar faces joining her. "But one of you needs to be in charge." She paused, looking hesitant. "I'm a good choice to run a more balanced group, but with all of you mages, I won't know how to use all your spells effectively."

"Pax does," Amil said without hesitating.

Pax opened his mouth to object, part of him not wanting the responsibility. What if he messed up and some of them got hurt or even killed?

"I agree," Rin said, her gaze challenging him. "You kept us alive the whole time we were down below tonight, so why mess with a good thing?"

Pax glanced at the others and saw them nodding. "Fine. But only if all of you speak up when you have an idea or see something dangerous or suspicious. I'm just as new to this as all of you."

"Guess I'm with you guys," a tentative voice said behind them.

Turning, Pax saw Tyrodon standing there and struggling to meet everyone's gaze.

"We're glad to have you," Pax said, hoping to encourage the shy boy. "Those on the wall are missing out."

Tyrodon looked up and gave them a smile. "I missed the group of crafting students heading to the practice wall, so when I got here, the fire mage told me to join up. I don't know how much I can help, but I'm pretty decent with tripwires and basic traps. Plus, I've got lots of supplies in my inventory." The flood of words suddenly stopped, leaving Tyrodon looking surprised, and a bit embarrassed, at himself.

"Traps are great!" Amil said, clapping the smaller boy on the shoulders.

Pax grinned, too, knowing Amil was thinking of the warrens back home. They had both loved setting traps back home. All the rewards with very little risk. "Whatever you can set up that works against swarms would be great, you know, like nets, pit traps, splash damage, stuff like that."

"Oh, I have a few more things that might work." Tyrodon's eyes lit up, and his words came out with a lot more confidence now that he was talking about his area of expertise. He opened his mouth to add more, but Mage Incedis, up front, clapped his hands for attention.

"We have time for one practice formation. Then we'll gear up and get going. Time is short, everyone." Incedis arranged the five groups into a loose star, with his group at the head of the formation and the two groups led by his assistants forming up to either side of him. He assigned Pax's group, and the one led by Aymer, to the two rear slots side by side at the back.

"This is our formation once we're out in the open," Incedis explained. "Warriors, you and your shields will face outward, absorbing as much damage as possible so the mages can attack at range from protection. Each group also needs to designate one or two of the mages to join your warrior with a barrier spell, while those with the strongest ranged attacks will kill as many beasts as possible. Anyone with an area attack will focus on disrupting the swarm just in front of our shields and barriers. As soon as you're done, head over to the tables to gear up. Everyone, take one set of potions, one portion of beast meat, and a basic first aid pouch."

Everyone exchanged excited looks mixed with worry as the teams sorted themselves out. A murmur of questions and answers filled the space as the students figured out their team dynamics.

After asking a few questions, Pax had a rough plan. "Bryn's our shield and we'll have Dahni start with his Earthen Barrier to supplement it. When he's tired, Amil will take his place with his Flame Wall, so save a bit of your mana for that."

Both Dahni and Amil nodded, looking more serious than he'd ever seen his friends. The sudden weight of responsibility made Pax swallow hard before continuing.

"Rin will use her Wave to disrupt the beasts that are closest to us, while Tansa uses her Spear and Amil his Blast to attack over the protection." Pax paused, and when Tyrodon's gaze dropped, he hurried to include the shy crafting student. "Tyrodon will set up traps whenever we prepare a position in advance, and we'll get him a spear to stab past Bryn. He'll also be in charge of taking out any beasts that make it past our defenses."

Tyrodon smiled at the last part, looking toward the extra student armor and weapons piled haphazardly on a nearby table.

Pax looked at the others, trying to think of anything he'd missed.

"And you?" Bryn asked after a few seconds of silence.

Pax felt like an idiot and suddenly worried as he struggled to find a significant contribution he could make with their current turtle formation. He didn't have any kind of barrier or ranged attack. Even the water blade he didn't dare use in sight of the others was restricted to touch distance at his new level.

"His Haste spell will let him move pretty fast," Rin piped up. "He'll be able to take out the beasts that get close to us with his clubs and still monitor the whole situation so he can change things up if needed." She said it so matter of fact that Pax only caught how unsure she was because he knew her well enough to read her tells. She waited to see how he would take her speaking up when he was supposed to be in charge.

"Thanks," he said with a grin.

Her shoulder relaxed.

"This is exactly why I need you guys to help me tonight. We're in this together and will help make up for each other's mistakes. Just behind the shields with Tyrodon and his spear is the perfect place for me. We'll do our best to turn the area in front of us into a meat grinder for the beasts."

"Two minutes," said Turgan, the fourth-year water mage assisting Incedis. "Hurry up!"

"Dahni and Tansa, can you grab stuff for the three of us?" Pax asked as their group turned toward the crowded supply tables. "We need to have a quick talk with Mistress Nymeli."

"Sure," Dahni said.

Pax was grateful he moved to follow the request without voicing his obvious questions.

"We need to get the mistress to approve our trainee exterminator assignment," Pax said under his breath to Amil and Rin as they hurried after him toward the kitchen.

Luckily, Mistress Nymeli noticed them before they got too far. She didn't hesitate to pass off their assignment. Before Pax could scan the new notification flashing in the corner, she waved three boys forward, sturdy packs on their backs and each carrying a short spear. Krasig stood among them, trying his best to look serious, with a flickering grin ruining the effect.

"Against my better judgment, these three are going with you," she said. "They will follow orders and support you. They know the tunnels better than any of you and will also be your fastest way to summon more help if the worst happens."

"But—" Pax tried to object, casting a worried glance back through the window of the kitchen door to where Incedis was barking out orders.

"I have an agreement with the good mage," she said, brushing off his objection before he could speak, her gaze turning solemn. "Don't think we don't understand the risk all of you are taking to protect us when you aren't required to."

Pax snapped his mouth shut and had to nod in acknowledgment.

"These tunnels are our backyard and, besides supplying you, the least we can do is offer you a few guides to help as much as possible."

"Thank you," was all Pax could say.

"Mistress, we need to go," Krasig said, shifting from foot to foot with impatience and eagerness. "We don't want to be left behind."

She snapped around to the three lanky boys, who flinched back and straightened immediately. "The three of you will do as you're told and will not take any foolish risks, or I will kill you myself. Am I understood?"

All three heads bobbed immediately in agreement, and Pax had to stop himself from joining in, even though she hadn't aimed the admonition at him.

"Then hurry," she said with a wave. "Go clean out the beasts and protect your families."

All of them turned on their heels, and Pax didn't think he was the only one happy to get out from under Mistress Nymeli's powerful eye.

"And don't let the mages claim all the beast parts," she called out as the door swung shut behind them.

Rin turned and gave her a nod through the window in the door with a grin. Pax couldn't help but agree. Their alliance with Mistress Nymeli had already paid off, big time.

As Mage Incedis led them down into the tunnels, Pax finally opened his new notification.

～

Congratulations! You have completed the **Exterminator Trainee** *assignment and your supervisor has rewarded you with the maximum reward of 1 Silver and 3 Academy Points and wishes to continue employing you in the position of Intern.*

Accept: **Yes/No**

～

Pax gleefully selected yes, anticipating what the extra points would do to their rankings. Depending on how many points the other students won for their efforts tonight, Pax and his friends would have a fantastic chance at taking the top spots.

"Make sure you accept the new position from Mistress Nymeli," he said to his friends as they tramped behind the long train of students in the tunnel.

Amil grinned as Rin scoffed. "We already did, dunder."

Pax hoped his flush wasn't visible in the dim light as he quickly scanned the details of his new assignment.

～

Exterminator Intern: You are on call to the Academy kitchen head manager to aid with vermin infestations as needed. Base pay: 15 coppers and 1 Academy Point per week when on call. 20 coppers and 1.5 Academy points for each session (2-hour minimum) with a bonus of 5 coppers per kill and 1.5 Academy Point for every 10 kills. Kill 300 vermin, or the equivalent, and

earn approval from your supervisor to advance to Apprentice. Rewards for
advancement are variable and are based on performance.

A FIERCE GRIN of anticipation filled Pax as he continued down the
tunnel, refueling his body by working his way through two of the
savory wraps provided by the kitchen crew.

Tonight was going to change everything for him and his friends.

THE GRIND

THE CLAWED PAW ricocheted off Bryn's shield to his right, and Pax jerked his head back just in time to avoid a slash to his face. His left club jabbed out instinctively, landing with a solid thump into a dark body that jarred the tired muscles of his arm. Without hesitating, he whipped his right club down with fresh energy fueled by the shot of adrenaline. He gave his new water mana spell a push to form a blade along the striking edge of his club at the last moment, where it was impossible to see in the busy fighting around him.

A pained yelp followed as something steaming splashed his leg. The beast slumped to the ground, joining other bodies in their own gruesome version of a barrier. But the next beast with charred spots still smoking from Amil's narrow flame barrier had already clambered at him, jaws snapping wildly.

After only a single use of his mana-draining Haste spell, Pax had switched to his new routine, rationing out small bits of mana for the almost invisible blades. It worked much better for continuous fighting. Increasing the speed of his mana regeneration was now high on his list of things to investigate as soon as he had a chance. Maybe Crafter Jacoby at the Academy Store would help him find a scroll or training manual to buy on the topic.

Around Pax, their star formation fought on all sides in a wild display of magic, punctuated by yells, roars and shrieks. Thankfully, Incedis had cast some kind of advanced flame spell of floating balls of light overhead to illuminate the battle scene and occasionally flash bursts of light to blind the dark-dwelling beasts.

It hadn't taken long for the beasts to fixate on them, and their forward progress across the cavern floor had quickly stalled as wave after wave of different beasts crashed over them, with only a few breaks.

Thankfully, they all seemed to be small level 1 beasts. Whatever breach had let them in was size or level limited. Pax's hands lashed out on autopilot with his clubs, knocking the next beast to the side where Tansa skewered it with one of her Water Spears.

"Switch," Dahni clapped him on the shoulder, and Pax gave him a grateful nod as he took two steps back into safety to recover his strength and mana. Dahni's Earthen Barrier immediately knocked back the closest beasts, highlighted by the flickering flames of Amil's barrier.

Oh right. Now that he was recovering his mana, he could afford it. *Identify.* Pax had been wanting the name for the new creatures swiping at him, claws gleaming with sharp points.

∼

Midnight Pardur - Level 1
*Increase **Identify** Skill for more information.*
*Skill Boost: +1 to **Identify** Level 1 - 69/100*

∼

Even at only a point each because they were his same level, it still added up, getting ever closer to advancing his first skill. Then Pax shuddered, thinking about what it would take to level his Identify skill. No, he would rather not meet another thirty or more different varieties of beasts tonight.

Breath whistled through his teeth as Pax's muscles trembled from effort now that he wasn't on the front line. Without time to second guess himself, he pulled a piece of Nerodai meat out and popped it into his mouth. He only had one healing and one mana potion. They hadn't even found the breach yet, so he needed to save them.

As he chewed and swallowed, he focused on his spark, its new size and complexity still surprising him. It had already grown from the size of a small fist to the size of his head. No longer pure white, threads of water mana were the easiest to see, but the other three were there too, if he looked hard enough.

The glow of water mana growing from his stomach was wild, filled with chaos, just like the beast the meat had come from. Pulsing, it shot out in all directions with no order, leaving energy and a burning pain in equal portions wherever it touched.

Pushing his spark into action, Pax did his best to encompass what he could, forcing his own water magic to surround and merge with the wild strands. To his surprise, the process was much easier than he'd expected it to be and, with a burst of energy that made his muscles buzz, the wild water mana blended with his own, taking on ordered lines and eventually responding to his will.

He shook his head, grinning at the rush, and considered eating more. But the energy of his spark instinctively objected, an almost overwhelmed feeling insisting he could only take in so much.

"Help her!"

Pax's head snapped up and next to him, Amil straightened despite the strain clear on his sweaty face.

"I got this," Pax assured his friend as he turned toward the cry for help. "You can't let your barrier drop." He could see the frustration on Amil's face as he gripped his hammer uselessly and focused back on his Flame Wall.

As Pax reached the next group over, it was obvious they were in trouble. An elven mage had hit the ground in front of the battle line. The jaws of a Pardur clamped on her calf and dragged her back into the dark.

Obviously out of mana, she frantically punched at the snout of the impervious animal while kicking with her free leg too. The group's warrior blocked two more beasts lunging to get past his shield, unable to help her. Aymer, a fancy sword in his hand, fended off two beasts as he tried to force his way forward toward his friend. Beasts, both living and dead, prevented him.

"Naexi!" Aymer screamed out, his boots slipping on bodies as he lunged forward.

Pax raced to join him, knowing if the Pardur dragged Aymer's friend much further, they'd lose her. Flush with the extra energy from the Nerodai meat, Pax moved up on Aymer's left and with a swift blow, slashed the beast's incoming limb.

When the Pardur turned on him and lunged in too close for his clubs, Pax jumped into the air just in time to avoid the gnashing teeth. He landed with a hard stomp on the back of the creature's neck. The sharp crack cut the growl off abruptly. Aymer shot a surprised glance at him. Agility had been coming in handy for him all night.

"Let's go," Pax urged, already pushing forward. "Get her."

Gratitude quickly replaced the suspicious look that had formed on Aymer's face. He turned and impaled the oncoming beasts by alternating between his Earth Spears and his fancy sword. Apparently, he'd already tapped out whatever expensive mana aids he'd brought with him. Though the practical realist inside Pax countered, Aymer might still have something in reserve for his own emergencies. They still had the rest of the night ahead of them.

"Follow my Wave," a voice barked out from behind, breaking through the surrounding din.

A quick glance back showed Turgan, the fourth-year leader, with both raised hands roiling with water, face twisted in concentration.

Pax spun back around as water streamed past him, Aymer and the other students before it combined into a waist high deluge. The mini-wave, just wider than their group's front line, smashed into the beasts between them and Naexi. She fought on the ground, a knife in each hand now as she battled to keep more Pardurs from taking advantage.

The wave lifted beasts, dead and alive, throwing them out of the way. Pax let out a yell and charged forward, Aymer only a beat behind him. Turgan's wave sagged to the ground just as it reached Naexi, the water melting away into the shadows between paws and legs.

"Protect us," Aymer said as he skidded to a stop, shooting another Earthen Spear toward the torso of the Pardur dragging Naexi further from the fighters.

When Aymer didn't even wait for Pax to acknowledge his order, Pax couldn't help feeling a bit miffed at the typical 'crat attitude. But away from the safety of their formation wasn't the place to argue, so he swung out with his club. He tightened the muscles of his center, focused on making his blade pop into existence only when needed. He spent his energy with abandon in a flurry of fast impacts and thuds.

Despite the flickering shadows, the squelching mess under his boots, and the never-ending flood of beasts that did their best to get a piece of him, Pax felt the hint of something incredible. The possibility of the melding of body, mind and mana seemed just out of reach.

"Come on, kid!" a weak, but feminine voice shouted, pulling Pax out of the strange state he'd been reaching for.

With a start, Pax realized it wasn't the first time she'd called out. Beasts had almost surrounded him, while the other two were already halfway back to safety without him. He met the desperate gaze of the injured elf, who waved at him to hurry. Aymer didn't even look back, just pumping with his powerful legs as more Pardur closed in.

A flush of rage destroyed the feeling of whatever achievement he'd been about to make. With a roar, Pax flung himself after the pair, his clubs moving with more brute strength than finesse now. Kicking bodies out of his way, he fought in a frenzied rush to make it back. Pain stabbed into his left arm. Still running, he pounded the butt of his other club until he broke the grip of the gnashing jaws. Feeling sudden warmth along his wrist, he hoped the combination of his monster-touched scales and his leather vambrace had minimized the injury. He couldn't afford to lose the use of one of his arms.

Just as he made it within two strides of the other team's warrior, something heavy slammed into his upper back, throwing him forward face first toward the solid shield in front of him.

Luckily, the warrior's reflexes weren't so tired he couldn't jerk his shield out of the way at the last second. Pax skidded back into the formation on his hands and knees, something vicious scrabbling at his back and streaking lines of pain along the back of his scalp.

"Get it off me," Pax yelled out, his clubs completely ineffective at striking the beast on his back. Out of the corner of his eye, he caught sight of a boot kicking at the beast, which just made the thing go even crazier. More than anything, Pax wanted to stab the thing with a Water Blade jabbing right out of his back. He didn't think it would be much harder than doing the same through the end of his clubs.

But on the ground with so many people watching him? Impossible.

Desperate, he lunged up to his feet and jumped as high as he could into the air before throwing himself back. Tucking his chin down and his knees up to his chest, Pax did his best to land with all his weight concentrated on the beast. The thing had to be injured. It shouldn't take much more to finish it.

Just before he hit the ground, Pax had second thoughts. This was an uneven, rocky floor, after all. He just prayed that his improved Endurance and other attributes would protect him.

The impact was worse than he'd imagined. His back wasn't really intended to bend in that direction, and the force tried to fling his head back. His neck muscles protested, straining to keep his head from cracking against the ground. He felt a squirming spasm beneath him. Something scratched at the back of his armor before the thing went limp beneath him.

Feeling battered, Pax accepted a hand to his feet, giving the student mage a nod of thanks. But the boy had already gone back to flinging some kind of air attacks out into the swarm. Pax turned wearily to head back to his own group when a hand on his shoulder stopped him.

"I just wanted to say thanks." Naexi stood beside him, favoring her injured leg as she gave him a grateful look.

"Come on," Aymer said from behind her, completely ignoring Pax. "We need to get you to the kitchen guys who have more healing potions."

"Without this guy here, I wouldn't have made it," she said, her voice turning flat. "Give me a second to thank him."

"Technically, I'm the one who brought you back," Aymer said, folding his arms.

She just held his gaze in a silence that quickly made Pax uncomfortable, and he wasn't even the one she was focusing on.

Aymer didn't flinch, instead giving her a shrug. "Then should I go get a healing potion and bring it back for you?"

"Or you could give me one of yours," she countered, still keeping her tone even.

Aymer looked uncomfortable for the first time. "You know I need to save that one."

"Just like you saved your emergency port when you could have used it to"—she paused and lowered her voice to a hiss, enunciating the next three words—"save . . . my . . . life?"

Aymer flinched, but then immediately straightened and cleared his throat. His eyes had gone as flat as her tone. "I'm just glad you're alright and hope they'll have healing supplies to help you. I'm needed back in the fight."

Pax held absolutely still, enthralled by the drama playing out, but definitely not wanting to attract anyone's attention.

But when Naexi turned back toward him, she gave him a sheepish look and smiled. "Sorry about that. Sometimes he means well, but in his family, everything is so calculated. He made it very clear how much my life and friendship are worth to him."

"Um—" Pax hesitated, giving her a generic nod and backing up toward his group. "I'm glad I could help?"

"Sorry again to drag you into all that," Naexi said with a shake of her head. "Just keep me in mind if you ever find yourself in trouble. I'll try to do the same as you did. Ignore danger to help."

When he saw she meant what she said, Pax gave her a grateful nod. "Thank you. Really."

She gave him a half-smile before limping toward the center where they kept the supplies. As he hurried back to his group, Pax pulled off his left vambrace, relieved to see the blood already slowing from the crush injury just where his scales ended. Having already had more practice than he really wanted tonight, he quickly applied ointment, gauze and had the injury wrapped in clean bindings from his first aid kit.

He had just pulled his tunic sleeve back down and reattached his vambrace when he heard the order ring out from the front of their formation.

"Turtle Formation! Prepare to charge!"

Amil grinned as he ran up. Rin had moved back too, as all five groups pulled in closer to each other, shields and walls popping up along all sides.

"Is this another push?" Pax asked as he moved into his spot, trying to make out what everyone around him was saying. "Or have we found the source?"

"Incedis can see the far wall," Bryn called over her shoulder with a grin, her shield shuddering with repeated impacts. "He thinks he found the breach."

Cheers rang out among the tired students around him, and Pax joined them. It had been a brutally long night, and he was more than ready to stop these beast swarms for good.

INTO THE BREACH

THE NEXT FEW minutes felt like pushing through a brutal storm, assailed on all sides. Everyone pushed together, shoulder to shoulder as they navigated the uneven cavern floor. A mishmash of elemental walls appeared to either side just wide enough to repel the waves of attackers as they fought past in their turtle formation.

Pax jogged in step just behind Bryn. The stocky dwarf shook her head wearily, but her shield didn't waver, tucked in close to her left shoulder. Every fourth step, she'd jab her spear over the top of her shield at whatever had gotten close. Pax supplemented her attacks, jabbing his clubs tipped with Water Blades at the last minute in the downtime between her strikes.

He'd almost grown numb to the feeling of the Water Blade sinking into muscle or skittering across bone and chitin. Honestly, the beasts were blurring together into a continuous horror of teeth, claws and tentacles around them. Above, Incedis' lights kept pace, casting just enough light to highlight the surrounding nightmare.

"Halt. Fuel up." The command came from up front when they reached one of the all too rare pockets of calm.

Stretching up on his toes, Pax peered at the dark cavern wall, climbing up to disappear into the darkness overhead. His pulse picked up a beat as he saw three areas that bulged with writhing movement, the distance too far to make out more details. His heart sank as he realized there might be more than one breach. It would be a challenge to fend off the beasts while Incedis and his assistants sealed the holes with whatever fancy spells they had prepared.

Around Pax, hands moved quickly, stuffing food and beast meat into mouths and tipping back drinks of water or potions. Pax still had all three of his potions because he couldn't shake the feeling that they would be crucial later. But he felt so exhausted, he knew simple food and water wouldn't be enough as they fought through the last stretch.

Checking his inventory, he popped out another serving of Nerodai meat, only to look at the stack of water cores in the slot next to it. He took one out and just held it in his closed fists, letting a finger of his spark probe at the edges.

Much more familiar with water mana now, he could immediately sense the roiling strength in the small sphere. But unlike his own dark blue energy, this radiated an almost rabid power, the mana seeming to battle with itself as much as it fought to break free.

Reluctantly, he returned it to his inventory. Testing one of those would have to be done when he could take his time and proceed carefully, ideally with Rin nearby to help, if things got out of control. If that happened, he'd probably need to expel the chaotic water mana as fast as possible. He scoffed and shook his head, imagining how badly that would go for him right now, if he spewed out water in front of everyone.

With that disturbing vision in mind, he let out a breath and shoved his second piece of Nerodai meat into his mouth and chewed. The surge of energy from his center was the same strength as before, but this time his ability to control it was much more sluggish, his mana exuding reluctance to engage with the wild energy that quickly shot out through his body.

Pax harnessed only about a third of it, sending the merged power to fuel his muscles as he felt his body react to the rest of the rampaging mana that had escaped. The wild mana burned as it passed, stabbing randomly and making it hard for him to keep from jerking uncontrollably.

Desperate, he glanced around, gasping in relief when he saw a puddle in a depression nearby that was empty since no one wanted to sit in the water. It was exactly what he needed.

Plopping down into the puddle, he closed his eyes and placed both palms down just under the surface. Gritting his teeth, he turned his attention inward to the mess he'd made. He might be a light mage, but apparently that didn't mean he could flout the rules about how much beast meat was safe to take. At least not easily.

His mana resisted his directions, but he powered through, forcing it to reach out and herd the chaotic strings of mana into a single direction. *Down. Down and out.* It seemed to take forever, but finally he felt the water bubble around his hands, despite the shooting pains everywhere else. He immediately noticed the strength of the wild mana diminishing, so he pushed harder.

Down. Down and out. He chanted the mantra in his mind until he felt the last vestiges of the excess mana expelled. Letting out a long breath, Pax took a last moment to pull on the small amount of merged mana he'd salvaged.

In a matter of moments, he spread it through as many of his muscles as possible. The infusion of strength was refreshing, but nowhere near as much as he'd achieved the first time and not even enough to erase the shadows of pain left behind by the wild mana's frenzy.

"Are you alright?" Rin said through a mouthful of food as she sat down next to him. "You're all wet." She looked down at the puddle he sat in with a quizzical expression.

"I was hot," he replied and then lowered his voice. "Don't try a second piece of beast meat. You have to expel what you can't use. It's hard, and it hurts."

She looked startled and gave the puddle of water a second look before nodding. "Got it. And we should join the others. The break'll be over any second."

He nodded, retrieving another pastry from his inventory as he stood. At least he could rely on the simple pleasure the treat brought him, even if it didn't fill him with power.

"Two minutes!" Turgan's voice called out from the front just as Pax heard the scuffling of claws on stone and grunting breaths, letting them know the beasts had gathered another wave again. "Gather close for orders."

"We're racing for the wall," Incedis said as he stood tall, his voice easily reaching out to the group, but low enough that he hopefully didn't attract more attention from nearby beasts. "We'll set up just before it and turtle again, doing everything to dig in and bolster our defensive position. Warriors will keep employing their shields. The rest of you will use whatever defensive spells you have left and your mundane weapons when you run out of mana. Wounded stay in the center and heal, unless you have mana to spare for defensive measures. The three of us need enough time to purge the breaches of beasts and once they're empty, seal them."

Pax wasn't the only one to groan in disappointment at the mention of multiple breaches.

"In the worst case, if I order a retreat, we will do the moving turtle again, doing our best to make sure all of us make it out of here alive. Anyone who's used their potions already, grab more from our supply helpers. They won't do anyone any good in the packs."

A few students shifted toward the center, eyes looking for the boys from the kitchen.

"One last thing," Incedis said in a low voice that drew their attention back. "I'm proud of what you've done tonight and proud to be fighting side by side with you warriors and mages."

"And crafters," Turgan added with a grin toward Tyrodon. The boy dropped his gaze immediately to the ground, but Pax caught the edge of a smile before he did.

"And crafters," Incedis agreed with a smile.

Around Pax, students straightened and more than a few smiles replaced tired features.

～

"ABOVE YOU," Rin yelled.

Pax leapt to the side, barely avoiding a hissing ball of angry beast whose tiny legs were more than compensated for by the vicious spikes protruding from every surface. They glistened with some kind of liquid that couldn't be good.

Two quick strikes from his clubs landed just before Rin wrapped a Water Snake around a handful of its spikes and launched it out of their defensive position. It flew off with an enraged squeal.

Incedis had set up their formation a mere twenty feet from the towering wall that loomed over them. While the students held the line against the attacks from around them, barely, the beasts emerging from the three small tunnels above seemed to enjoy launching themselves through the air as soon as they discovered the mass of mana radiating up from below.

Without a barrier or ranged spell, Pax had placed himself on air duty, using his clubs to defend against the living bombs as Incedis and his assistants finished summoning their spells. Pax even managed the occasional lucky blow, catching a beast in mid-air and sending it flying off before it even landed.

"Now," Incedis cried out, hands thrust upward toward the far-left breach. "And watch your strength." The last he directed at Zanneth while Turgan stood alert on his other side, but with his arms down.

Pax snuck a glance toward the breach when he didn't see any type of flame gush from the mage's hands, like Amil's spell. To his surprise, about a foot of rock above the hole began to glow, a deep red, almost hard to see in the darkness. It brightened quickly, turning to a bright, cherry red in only moments.

Pax thought he could see the rock sag as the emerging beasts screamed in rage and pain. The pungent stench of burning fur drifting down below. Was Incedis actually going to melt the rock?

"Tighten your beam," Incedis said to Zanneth, his voice strained. "Push the heat further down the tunnel."

Staring in awe at the powerful magic, Pax almost missed batting away a writhing, snake-like creature as he realized Zanneth was using an air spell to direct the intense heat from Incedis' flame spell deeper into the breach. Instead of just melting the opening, this would seal a solid section of the tunnel. As the glow intensified, the beasts stopped emerging from the tunnel.

Beside him, he heard the twang of Rin's arrows. On his other side, he saw Amil had joined him with his hammer. He forced his eyes away from the magic above to focus on protecting everyone around him.

"Out of mana for my Flame Wall," Amil said with a grin, shaking his hammer in the air when he saw Pax looking his way. "About time I get to smash something."

Pax smiled back, moving closer so they could cover each other, eyes trained on the moving shadows above them. He fell back into a rhythm, slamming the smaller beasts, or ones shot by Rin, out of the sky and knocking the bulkier ones within reach of Amil's hammer. Now and then, he'd hear a cry of pain or curse nearby and could only hope everyone's rudimentary healing skills, potions and first aid kits were enough to keep them alive.

A sudden cheer caught his attention and a quick glance showed the glow of the leftmost breach quickly fading, leaving behind solid stone, empty of beasts.

"He closed it!" Pax's cheer joined the others.

"One down," Amil said in triumph, pumping his hammer in the air. "Two to go."

Pax grinned and, more than anything, wanted to dismiss his clubs and take a breather. But instead of tapering off, it seemed the flood of beasts from the two remaining breaches just intensified, squirming bodies pushing against each other to get through.

A stab of alarm made Pax inspect the jagged wall between the breaches. A few of the lines that he'd taken for normal uneven features of the craggy wall had suddenly shifted. He blinked his eyes to clear them, unsure but worried at the same time.

They looked like cracks. And that would definitely not be good.

VICTORY IN SIGHT

"Rin." Pax nudged her urgently and pointed. "Look up there. Are those cracks? Please tell me I'm seeing things."

"What?" Looking surprised, she lowered her bow and squinted up at the wall.

Next to her, Amil did the same, peering up into the darkness.

Watching with them, Pax held his breath, hoping the only movement up on the wall would be the beasts, not the stone itself. Instead, a sharp crack rang out, just loud enough to be heard through the din of battle.

Not only did one of the suspected cracks shift, the dark line widening, but Pax could swear he saw something move in it, a tip of something pushing and writhing from inside. The hole to the right already glowed as Incedis and Zanneth had shifted their attention to it. Roars and squeals of pain erupted as the mass of beasts pushing out of that breach went crazy.

Another crack sounded, and this time, Pax definitely saw the tip of a dark tentacle jabbing out before vanishing. To his horror, he saw it reappear in another crack, joined by a second, as something did its best to widen the new breach.

"It's breaking through the stone," Rin said, shock filling her voice.

"And there's no way that's a level 1." Amil's earlier glee had disappeared. He shot a worried look between the tiring mages and the new threat. "Anyone got mana for an Identify?"

"In a minute," Pax answered before swallowing hard, his friend's words making him realize something even worse. "If that crack makes a bigger breach, it won't just be the tentacle thing that makes it through. What if the swarms hitting the walls tonight flood in after?"

Rin punched him in the shoulder, hard. When he stared at her in surprise, she jabbed the tip of her bow toward Incedis.

"We need to warn him. You're the one who knows him the best. Hurry!"

"Stick with me," Pax countered, jolting into action. "We might need to protect them." Without waiting for their answer, he spun to shove through the tight crowd, past those recovering in the center. By the time they reached the mages, a quick glance confirmed the situation was worsening fast.

"Incedis, the crack," Pax blurted out, having to yell past Zanneth because there was no way he wanted to walk in front of the actively casting mage. "Something big is breaking through!"

"Obviously," Incedis growled through gritted teeth without looking in Pax's direction. "Do your job and stop interrupting us while we do ours."

Pax flinched back, but the mage paid him no more attention, all his focus on the breach where the stone visibly melted. Being this close, Pax could see the strain on the mage's face and the sweat beading on his brow. A quick glance showed Zanneth in even worse shape, eyes narrowed and body stiff, as if forcing himself to stay erect. On the far side, Turgan stood, looking helpless, but antsy, as if waiting for a chance to do something.

A similar, helpless feeling rolled through him as Pax turned back to his friends. He wanted to rage and do something to fight back, anything.

But what? His Haste and small Water Blades, much less his clubs, couldn't do anything to help fight the danger threatening them overhead. A shower of small stones and rock dust clattered to the ground between them and the wall. Pax jerked around and looked up to see a jabbing tentacle as big as his forearm, now shoving out through the wider crack, joined by two smaller ones along the edge.

"Protect the mages," he said, the only idea he could come up with. "I've got this side. Rin, you take behind and Amil, get over on the other side of Turgan."

They moved with an alacrity that made him both proud and worried that he would mess this leadership thing up.

He caught a mumble from Incedis that sounded like, "Stubborn boy." But when he glanced back toward the mage, he had, along with Zanneth, thrust both of his hands up to the breach.

Another beast fell from overhead, eight legs splayed out in dark shadows. The fiery patch of wall highlighted the alarming details from behind. Pax had no more time to spend in thought. He got back to fighting, stealing a quick glance now and then at the mages. He forced himself to trust them.

"Done," the mage finally grunted a few moments later.

Another murmur of excitement spread through their group. Pax glanced up to see they had finally sealed the second breach, leaving just the center one with the ominous cracks radiating out from it.

Two more had joined the original fissure. Pax couldn't get a good count of the tentacles that kept jabbing in and out in a tireless effort to break through. The battle on the ground, at least, seemed to have finally ebbed. The bodies had been piling up, even though beasts had dragged away a few of their unfortunate brethren for a quick snack. Hopefully, it wouldn't be enough to level any of them.

The students had even used the growing pile of bodies to boost the height of their rotating barrier spells. This denied the incoming beasts a ramp to charge up. As long as mana held out, they couldn't use the extra height to fling themselves over the tops of the warriors' shields.

The ones that forced their way through all the obstacles arrived smoking or half drowned, depending on which element they'd forced themselves through. With only one breach fully open, the reinforcements had slowed considerably. A small ember of hope filled Pax. He imagined their triumphant return to campus, a group of brand-new first-years who had saved the academy.

The only sour note in his hope was the growing size of the injured group being protected in their center. Only a bare minimum protected the perimeter now, their bodies and weapons sagging with tired determination.

"Time to finish this," Incedis said, drawing Pax's attention back. "It's time, Turgan."

"Finally," the younger mage said, raising his hands with an eagerness and energy that everyone around him had already spent.

"One more, Zanneth. And then we'll help Turgan," Incedis said, raising his hands.

Zanneth gave the mage a nod, obviously tired, but his face was as implacable as always. Pax's estimation of the man jumped again. He hadn't thought the mild-mannered assistant in his spell class would have stayed so strong during the hours of a continuous running battle.

"All together now," Incedis called out.

Pax couldn't help holding his breath for a beat as he watched the big finale, keeping one eye out for any beasts that might threaten the mages. But instead of anything new and flashy, Incedis and Zanneth engaged in another repeat to seal the final breach, ignoring the new tentacled monster fighting to emerge through the cracks.

Turgan, however, did not. He thrust both arms upward toward it. He whispered something under his breath, but Pax couldn't see any evidence of his water magic.

An enraged screech, muffled through layers of rocks, made Pax snap his gaze up. The tentacles had gone berserk, jabbing and flailing with a frenzy even worse than before. The surrounding cavern rumbled and stones clattered to the ground in front of them as the entire wall shivered from a powerful blow somewhere on the other side.

"Drain," Turgan said, audibly this time, his voice strained and the veins standing out on his neck.

And then Pax saw it. The largest tentacle was visibly shrinking, wrinkles hard to see but still obvious on the surface of the menacing limb as fluids dripped out of it. A black viscous stuff fell down into the darkness. Sagging, it looked weak for the first time Pax had seen.

"Go, Turgan!" Amil's cheer called out, echoing Pax's sentiments. If the fourth-year water mage could weaken the monster enough, the other two mages could help finish it as soon as they closed the final breach.

Around them, the faces of other students looked upward with new hope. Their first true battle might finally be over. Pax couldn't help sagging down to a crouch to recoup some of his strength, his hope-filled gaze joining others looking above.

To his dismay, Turgan's weakening of the main tentacle only seemed to infuse the smaller ones with renewed energy, their rapid jamming in and out of the cracks picking up speed. Another snap of sound, followed by a shower of gravel, heralded a sudden widening of the largest crack. The dark gap had split in two, adding new routes splitting off from the original. A new crop of small tentacles immediately emerged along both of the new sections, invigorated like some kind of evil plant being fed magical fertilizer.

"It's in the breach now, too." Rin's worried warning drew his attention back to the final breach, already glowing with heat that made the stone sag.

He immediately saw what Rin meant as another tentacle stabbed out through the frantic beasts trying to escape. With an alarming speed, the thing wrapped around the middle of a squat, muscular beast and jerked it back through the tight tunnel, sending other beasts flailing away from the powerful tug. In the light, Pax thought the heat of the tunnel hurt it, but obviously not enough to dissuade it.

"What's it doing? It can't be eating them." Pax tried to figure out what was going on, looking back at Rin and Amil. They had moved to join him now that the flood of beasts had slowed to a trickle. "There have to be lots of them on the other side of the wall."

His friends looked just as confused, but Pax could tell they were all feeling the pressure of something bad closing in. An instinctive sense of danger was crucial on the streets, and his was screaming at him to run away while he still could.

DEADLY BREAKTHROUGH

ANOTHER BEAST TRIED to escape the tunnel above, only to disappear the next instant. Its head jerked back out of sight, leaving the opening clear. It was suddenly obvious why the tentacles had been going after the smaller beasts.

"The tentacles are clearing the tunnel, so they can get in," Pax blurted out, suddenly alarmed at how many of the things could fit through the breach once it was clear. The jagged entrance wasn't huge, but a two-foot circumference could fit a lot more of the tentacle things compared to the long, narrow crack they tried to widen at the same time.

Hurry and seal it, Pax silently urged the two mages on. Turgan was working on another tentacle. The original one he'd attacked was nowhere to be seen.

"It's all one beast," Incedis said, his voice strained. "A Zophos Hydra. If it breaks through, we'll be lucky if anyone survives." He shook his head, looking torn before he raised his voice. "Turgan, enough. Time to evacuate. You're in charge of the students now. Get everyone out of here."

"But I can still—" Turgan protested, splitting his hands in what looked like an attempt to Drain multiple tentacles at once.

Pax noticed his mana had recovered enough to do a quick Identify, appalled at what they were dealing with if all the tentacles had a single source.

~

IDENTIFY ATTEMPT FAILED. *Level difference is too significant.*
Skill Boost: +5 to **Identify** *Level 1 - 74/100*

~

PAX CLENCHED HIS JAW, realizing the thing was at least level 4 if his Identify didn't work.

"Evacuate plan," Turgan yelled out, taking charge, though it was obvious he didn't like it. "Tighten up, help the wounded and use as little mana as possible on your defensive walls, so we have enough to make it back."

Questions and objections broke out, and a palpable panic threaded through the bedraggled group.

"Quiet!" Turgan roared before continuing in a calmer voice once everyone subsided. "We are moving out. Every one of you will get back alive, understand?"

Heads bobbed, looking a little reassured by his words.

"One minute, and we move out." Without another word, he hopped down from his rock and got to work.

Pax had just turned to lend a hand with the wounded when a tremendous crack reverberated through the entire cavern, followed by an outcry of fear and surprise. He jerked back around to see two huge tentacles stabbing down toward them. A smattering of wall chunks tumbled down end over end.

Behind them, in the faded glow of the rapidly cooling stone, Pax could see tentacles emerging and elongating with an ease that was terrifying. They shot from the last breach and out of every crack.

"Shields up and back away," Incedis roared, his hands moving in a circular pattern, a flat shield of flame bursting into existence, just a split second before the descending threats impacted.

Stones bounced as Incedis tilted his flame shield and yelled something at Zanneth. Some of the smaller stones made it through, one slamming into a boy next to Pax, making him yelp in pain and slap at the sudden flame that burst to life on his sleeve.

The tentacles held Pax's focus as he moved backward in formation with everyone around him, his clubs out, but feeling pretty useless.

Despite the sudden panic, the students still followed orders and stayed together in a decent formation as they moved back. A full night of battling together had forged them into a cohesive unit. The never-ending beast attacks had curbed anyone's instinct to race away on their own.

Behind Pax, a tentacle hit Incedis' shield with a thundering force that made it bow as the students scrambled to get away even faster.

Pax didn't even see the second tentacle that swept in from the side under the flame shield. Multiple screams filled the air as a solid limb of darkness ripped through their formation, scattering students like bowling pins. Pax grunted in pain as Rin's head slammed into his chest and Amil's full body swept through his legs. They all flew sideways as Incedis' shield blinked out of existence. Only the handful of flame lights still above them kept the darkness from completely swallowing them.

Pandemonium erupted as everyone scrambled to dodge the gleaming tentacles that flexed and stabbed out like a cat chasing mice after scattering their nest.

Pax landed in a slippery pile of beast bodies. His breath whooshed out in a gush when one of Amil's legs landed across his chest.

"Up, up," Rin yelled, grabbing Amil's shoulder and Pax's arm to hoist them up. Her gaze swiveled to take in the surrounding danger.

Scrambling up, Pax ignored the acrid reek around him and kicked his way free until he found solid rock to stand on. He wiped both eyes clean with the back of his upper arm as he held both clubs up and scanned for danger.

Amil staggered into position behind him just as Pax saw eyes glistening in the darkness, back the way they'd come. Just because the beast hordes had slowed, didn't mean they wouldn't take advantage of the disruption to the previously impregnable turtle formation.

"Down," Rin cried.

Both Pax and Amil dropped immediately to the muck on the floor. The whoosh of another tentacle was close enough to feel the breeze.

A scream of rage rang out to their right, closer to the wall. The tentacle they'd just avoided stabbed toward a figure bracing himself with a familiar, fancy sword. Aymer had positioned himself between two pillars of earth he raised from the ground to either side of him. Behind him, more students climbed unsteadily to their feet, some armed, while others fought to summon their magic. Pax recognized one of them as Bryn, her shield an easy silhouette to identify.

"Hurry, let's help," Pax said to Rin and Amil, racing ahead and trusting them to follow.

Aymer's pillars of earth finished forming just in time to meet the tentacle. Behind him, Pax caught glimpses of a host of smaller tentacles stretching in their direction. Just how many of those things were there? And how could they even target the students if the main body with the eyes was presumably still behind the wall? If Pax could figure that out, they could camouflage themselves enough to get to safety.

Aymer's pillars crashed together in a skillful pincer movement as he stepped back and used them to trap the tentacle attacking him. Or at least they did their best. With a powerful spasm, the tentacle struggled to free itself, but not fast enough to avoid Aymer's sword all together. Dirt sprayed everywhere, but the pillars held long enough for Aymer's strike to land with a thunk, loud enough to hear from a distance. A dark purple ichor sprayed as his sword almost sliced completely through before getting stuck.

Another roar sounded, muffled but still powerful despite the rock it had to travel through. Aymer fought to free his sword as the tentacle spasmed, almost jerking his weapon free.

"Group up and get out," Turgan's voice called from behind them.

"Don't cut the tentacles," Incedis said, from somewhere off to the right. "Burn them if you do!"

Around Pax, fellow students stood, grabbing to help others as they fought to get further from the wall and the tentacles lashing out from it.

"Don't." Pax raised his voice when he saw Aymer's sword slashing back to finish the job.

He was too late, and a three-foot section of the huge tentacle fell to the floor, squirming with a repellant movement as more of the ichor sprayed from the live end. It lashed around like a cut water hose.

Pax found Amil in the chaos. "Burn the end!"

Amil's hands went up, but he shook his head after looking back over his shoulder while still running forward. "Too far." He struggled to catch his breath.

The group behind Aymer, while on their feet, could barely dodge the flailing tentacle as they did their best to help each other get past Aymer and to safety.

The scion let out a victorious yell, looking like he wanted to take on the beast single-handedly. He held his sword high as he tracked the injured limb and tried to get in another shot. A yell of surprise replaced his battle roar as the blood from the injured tentacle dried up a moment later and birthed a horror.

Three new tentacles popped from the cut end. Growing with surprising speed, they reached out as if tasting the air before homing in on the remnants of Aymer's pillars. One bent to the side, seeming to probe toward Incedis, where he clashed with the other main tentacle.

A moment of insight filled Pax, and he immediately called out. "They're attracted to mana! Don't use your spells unless you have to."

Aymer had stared too long at the mesmerizing sight of the Hydra's transformation. Two of the new tentacles jabbed forward with insane speed.

A split second before impact, Bryn shoved her shield in front of Aymer, knocking him to the side. The two tentacles impacted with rapid-fire clangs, pushing her back. Her braced feet skidded back along the ground as she leaned into the impact.

Too busy fending off the two-pronged attack, Bryn didn't even notice the third tentacle shooting in from the darkness. Pax and Amil cried out as they watched it wrap around her throat with inhuman speed before they could do anything to save her.

Bryn's eyes widened in fear, but instead of fighting the tentacle around her throat, she kept fighting smart. She slammed the edge of her shield up into the tentacle and lashed at it with the short sword in her right hand.

Pax realized how stupid it was to avoid using magic as he fought to get to Bryn in time. "Flare up your mana to distract them." His voice felt raw from yelling to be heard. "Switch back and forth. Only a second or two at a time."

It was so chaotic that Pax wasn't sure who heard him, but at least a few students' spells popped on and off from various directions as they ran. The movement of the incoming tentacles seemed more chaotic than before. Their efforts distracted the two other tentacles near Bryn.

Rin's arrows hissed past him. The ones that landed true made the tentacles spasm. Pax ran harder.

Bryn's struggles had kept the tentacle from dragging her away, blood splattering her armor from the wounds she'd made with her short sword. Her face had turned purple. Both her shield and sword movements slowed, turning weak. The tentacle choking her didn't have the strength to keep her aloft, but it still fought to drag her back toward the wall.

Pax and Amil were almost in range when a flurry of motion closer to the wall gave them hope. A slight figure leaped from the shadows with a high-pitched scream, stabbing down into the tentacle holding Bryn with a spear.

"Yes!" Pax managed a breathless cheer for Tyrodon, who had apparently stayed behind to help.

A narrow wall of earth shot up and over the tentacle at almost the same time, as Dahni did his best to pin it. Tansa shot out both hands, sending needle-sharp spears of water toward the two loose tentacles, keeping them distracted so they couldn't latch onto Bryn, too.

Pax saw Naexi join in, her whirring blades of air slashing out. She threw an angry order over her shoulder at someone and when the gleam of a blade flashed, Pax realized she'd even enlisted Aymer's help, too. Together, they damaged the tentacles enough to send blood spurting everywhere without actually cutting through any of them.

Finally in range, Rin's Water Snakes wrapped around Bryn's waist and jerked her to a stop, fighting against the tentacle's pull. Stretched out on the ground between the two forces, Bryn's shield sagged to the floor, and her short sword fell out of limp fingers.

"No." Desperation in his tone, Pax skidded to a stop. He torqued his clubs with all the power he could summon, slamming them down in a rapid two-beat pattern over and over into the section just past Bryn's neck. Blood and chunks of meat flew as he spent mana to add Water Blades to the end of each club.

"Burn it as soon as I'm through," he said to Amil.

His friend arrived, panting, his hammer already raised to join in. Amil nodded, not wasting breath on answering as he slammed his heavy hammer into the tentacle just past the deepening gouges from the damage Pax did. It seemed to take forever to cut through. Bryn's limp body jerked with every spasm of the tentacle. But finally, the vicious thing parted with a last tear of skin, the cut end snapping back toward the other group of students fighting all three of them.

"Burn—" Pax yelled at Amil as he threw himself down to help Bryn. He hadn't finished the order when a blinding flame lashed out toward the retreating stump.

"Hold it still," Pax heard Amil yell, followed by another flash. Burning a flailing stump couldn't be easy, and Pax had to hope the rest of them handled the problem while he and Rin took care of Bryn.

They both clawed at the length of the tentacle still wrapped tightly around her neck despite being limp. As Pax grew more frantic, Rin slipped a thin Water Snake under one edge and with a quick flex of her mana, expanded it to pop the thing loose.

"Bryn." Desperate, Pax leaned in close.

She wasn't breathing.

HARSH REALITY

"Move over," an urgent voice said from behind him. "Let me."

A flare of new hope filled him when Pax saw Naexi running toward them. Trying not to second guess himself, he scooted out of the way just in time for her to drop beside the unconscious dwarf.

When Naexi placed her hands over Bryn's mouth and nose, both Rin and Pax objected.

However, in the next moment, a gush of air filled Bryn's lungs, her chest rising in a stunningly normal movement. Another breath moved in and out, and Pax smiled.

By the third one, though, his hope sagged again. Naexi glanced over at him with a worry-filled gaze, and he pushed close again.

Even worse, the surrounding battle had picked up. Rin had dashed over to help. Others had helped Amil cauterize the severed tentacle. But the small group now struggled to pin down and chop off the main branch while still protecting themselves from the other tentacles, stumpy one and all.

In the other direction, it looked as if Turgan had organized the students to form a battle line just out of reach of the tentacles. A few kept watch, but the bulk faced away, focused on repelling the occasional rush of beasts from the shadows.

Pax could barely make out Incedis and Zanneth in the storm of dust, flame and spraying blood as they fought back to back against the flurry of tentacles. The myriad of smaller ones looked like more trouble than the huge one smashing at them with ground-shaking force.

"I'm sorry," Naexi said, sitting back on her heels and giving a helpless shrug of her shoulders.

"But you had her breathing?" he said. "I saw it."

"All I have is air magic. It won't start her heart."

Naexi gripped his shoulder and glanced back at where the others were fighting, obviously wanting to help.

Looking down at his friend, time seemed to slow. Everything they were doing suddenly felt heavy, more real. Bryn, alive with her indomitable spirit just a moment ago, lay unresponsive on the floor of the cursed cavern. Only a week into her warrior training; and somehow, her life was over in an instant.

Pax had known what they were doing was dangerous, even deadly. But it still felt like some grand adventure, learning magic, slaying beasts and reaping the rewards.

Until now. Now? It just felt wrong. Sad. His mind insisted he rewind the day and make different choices. Even just a small one that would have him arriving a moment sooner to save Bryn. His eyes stung with a mix of outrage and pure fury that drowned out the sadness.

Naexi's last words struck him suddenly, and Pax lunged for Bryn, slapping his hand onto her chest.

"Keep her breathing," he said before he closed his eyes and shoved his spark into her chest, aiming just a little to the left of center, where he'd seen Freddy's heart, the model in Mage Lorkranna's class.

Diving deep, Pax found himself inside an environment sluggish and fading compared to his own body. Desperate, he pushed his energy into the fist-sized lump of still muscle that should power Bryn's body.

Nothing. Not even a flicker.

He despaired. Why couldn't he have something more powerful

than light to jumpstart her heart? Water! He'd forgotten about his recently unlocked water mana. With renewed energy, he reached for the blood that sat stagnant in her vessels. It stirred in response to his touch, but he didn't know what to do from there.

Which direction did it need to go? While he had a spell helping him form his new Water Blades, he had little to no talent manipulating liquids on his own, yet. He could probably move a bunch of her blood around her body with his inexperienced ability, but pushing small amounts in the right direction along a complex highway of vessels? Impossible.

Rapidly cycling through other possibilities, the only one he came up with was a burst of energy from a flame healer, but Amil was the nearest source and had made little progress with his own healing, much less someone else's heart. Incedis was battling to keep them all alive, so he was out, too.

Just as Pax was about to give up, a wisp of a light gray energy wavered across his view, barely bright enough to make out. What? Was that Bryn's native mana? He knew warriors used their mana for their specialized fighting skills, in addition to active skills like Identify that everyone could access.

Without an element of focus, it must lack the color of a mage's mana. Gray or something with little color seemed logical. Holding his breath for a moment, he concentrated on reaching out for it, pushing his bright mana to wrap around it and try to sync with its energy.

It was slippery, weak and fading. His hands trembled on Bryn's chest as he fought for the elusive merging he'd managed with Rin. It seemed so long ago, even though it had only been at the start of this endless night.

So close. He focused his mana sight on the gray energy, noticing its solid nature, despite how faint it was. Force. Might. A warrior's power. He pushed the concepts toward his own mana, trying to match the feel of Bryn's power. Finally, with a snap that made him suck in a hopeful breath, his mana clicked into place with hers, interlocking like two puzzle pieces.

Knowing he was out of time, Pax shoved a burst of energy through the merged mana on a path directly to Bryn's heart. He felt a tug on his mana and pushed even harder.

Was that a flutter?

Again. A glance showed more mana ticking away.

"Come on, Bryn." Summoning everything he could manage, he pushed another, even stronger surge. It felt so close to working, Pax scrambled for something else he could do to tip the process over the edge and restart her heart.

A vision of Amil and his hammer popped into his mind. Sometimes power really was the answer. Pax clenched his free hand and timed a final pulse of his mana with a solid blow to Bryn's chest, hitting her so hard it made her body jump.

He opened his eyes, hopeful and scared at the same time. Waiting.

Then something happened. Something visceral and amazing.

Bryn flexed up off the ground and sucked in a strident breath, followed by a round of violent coughing that pushed both Pax and Naexi back.

Pax couldn't decide if he wanted to cheer or cry, and Naexi looked just as astonished.

"Wha—" Bryn tried to speak through a raw throat. Even disoriented, her hands patted at the floor around her.

Pax realized, like a true warrior, she was searching for her shield and short sword. It reminded him that regardless of the miracle; they were all in genuine danger.

"We need to get you to the others." Naexi tipped her head toward Turgan's group, who continued to defy Incedis' order to evacuate.

They stayed just out of range, obviously waiting to help the other fighters if they survived.

Pax felt torn. He wanted to get Bryn to safety, but needed to join his friends as quickly as possible. How could he justify letting them get hurt to save Bryn?

"I'll take her," an imperious voice butted in.

Before either of them could object, Aymer had crouched down and lifted Bryn under her arms.

"My sword," she objected, the croak barely understandable as she held her shield close and reached out.

Pax glanced around, swept up her sword and took two quick steps after the already retreating Aymer to place it into her hand.

"Thanks," she said, her gaze full of questions about what he'd done to bring her back.

Pax just nodded and spun on his heels before she could ask any of them. Naexi, frowning at Aymer, spat off to the side before joining Pax as he raced back toward the battle. He didn't mind. If Aymer wanted to use Bryn as an excuse to avoid battle, at least he was helping get her to safety.

Their friends had done a number on the single large tentacle with its three offshoots. The main trunk moved sluggishly, purple blood dripping from too many cuts to count and arrows protruding every-where. The branching tentacles were even worse off, both pulverized by Amil's hammer, and shot through with gaping wounds from spears and swords.

The sight would have filled Pax with pride, except he saw the bulk of the other tentacles focused on the powerful display of mana put on by Incedis and Zanneth, who struggled to manage the onslaught.

"What now?" Rin asked him as he and Naexi ran up. "We can cut this one off and flame it, or a few more smashes should put it out of commission."

"We've got to help Incedis," Amil said, not pausing the powerful swings of his hammer that pounded the weakening main tentacle.

"No. We need to get to safety. They can't leave until we do," Tyrodon piped up from where he crouched a few steps away, securing what looked like anchors to the ground.

Now that Pax was closer, he could see the crafter had somehow tangled the tentacles in ropes that kept them from evading the group's attacks. Now, he was tightening them and, as injured as they were, Tyrodon's ropes should keep them captive.

"If we hurry and leave now, then I'm sure they'll follow," Tyrodon said, his voice emboldened by urgency. He waved a small hammer toward the two embattled mages. "This mess is too big for our little group."

Naexi nodded, and it seemed everyone but Rin and Amil agreed. Pax hesitated, the sight of the defeated tentacles offering hope that they could still pull off a complete victory somehow.

While Amil's flame had prevented the smaller tentacle from forming new ones, it had still been plenty strong, just missing some of its length.

But together, the group had pummeled all the hydra tentacles so thoroughly that they'd lost a ton of blood and structure. They'd accidentally discovered a method of defeating the powerful monster while negating the hydra's power of replication. Their method didn't destroy the tentacles, but still took them out of the fight, twitching weakly against Tyrodon's ropes.

A new solution occurred to him. Depending on Tyrodon's abilities and some creative use of their non-magic fighting skills, they might pull it off. The worrisome part would be the role of his light magic and how beasts responded to it. Irrational fear tried to veto his plan, but Pax did his best to push it back down and consider the actual issues.

Would it be enough to overpower the creature's innate defense against invading mana? Plus, it would be difficult to hide his involvement. Maybe he could disguise it as simply working together, attacks with two mana types that just happened to land close to each other. And what about his Water Blades? If things turned bad, and he needed them, someone could notice that, too.

Clenching his jaw, Pax shook his head and dismissed his doubts. They had a brief window to pull this off. After only a few short days, his group almost felt like family and they needed the academy. He couldn't let these beasts rip it apart from underneath. Not if they could stop it.

"I think we all know this monster will break through the entire wall before we can get help," Pax said, trying to summarize everything in as few words as possible. "A whole flood of stronger beasts from outside will pour in here and up to kill the non-combatants. We can't let that happen."

While Amil and Rin nodded, others threw worried glances back at the tentacles still pushing through the cracks up on the wall.

"We have to weaken or kill it, drive it back where it came from to contain it long enough to get help."

Dubious looks made Pax hurry and turn to Tyrodon. "Do you have a non-magic way for us to climb that wall?"

The diminutive boy looked surprised, but his expression quickly turned calculating. A moment later, he nodded as he pulled a bag from his inventory, full of clanking items.

"Then here's what I think will work." Pax leaned in close and laid out his plan as fast as he could.

Eyes widened as he unfolded his plan. By the time he finished, he'd only convinced some of them.

"Are we allowed to do something like that with our magic?" Tansa asked, a dubious look on her face. "They told us combining our magic is really dangerous and can get us kicked out of school early."

"We're not combining our magic, just fighting right next to each other. It's no different from two of our spells hitting the same beast, like we've been doing all night," Rin answered, voice impatient. "And we don't have time to argue. Either help us save the Academy, or join the others over there."

"Rin's trying to say that we're both in." Amil gestured between himself and Rin with a grim smile.

"Me too," Dahni said, already equipping a spear.

"I agree. No time for questions. I'll get to work on the wall," Tyrodon said, surprising Pax. "Just distract those things if they notice me." Without another word, the boy ran toward the wall, though he still cast an occasional worried glance up at the undulating danger of the tentacles above him.

The rest of the group paused, looking floored by the bravery of the crafter. Pax let out a relieved breath when he saw the tentacles take no notice of him.

"See?" he said, relief in his voice. "They can't track us if we don't use mana. We have one chance to do something while the two mages are still keeping it distracted."

Before the others could respond, an out-of-breath voice broke in from behind them. "You've got to be kidding me. Why are any of you listening to him?"

Pax spun to see an angry Aymer glaring at everyone.

The 'crat beckoned them, looking sure they'd obey. "Come on. I'm getting you out of here safely, like Mage Incedis said. Let's go."

Tansa took a half step forward before Naexi stepped out, blocking her and getting right into Aymer's personal space. Pax saw her fists clenched tightly, and her jaw jutted out at the surprised scion.

"We are all equals here. We can make up our own minds. And we all agree his idea will work." She glanced Pax's way with an approving nod. "I'm following his lead. You can choose to run and hide or come help us save lives. Up to you."

Aymer opened his mouth to object, but Pax spoke over him. "We're out of time. Everyone who is coming, follow me. Remember. No mana!" Ignoring the red flush that raced across Aymer's pale cheeks, Pax gave everyone a quick glance. Once he saw nods, he raised his clubs and sprinted toward the cavern wall.

Tyrodon had already climbed halfway up to the crack, hard-to-see anchors of some type protruding from the wall below him. A touch of fear shot through Pax at the height of the wall he'd have to climb. Swallowing hard, he forced himself not to miss a step. He let the adrenaline rushing through him push all the fear and exhaustion into the background. He bared his teeth with a grim smile and did his best to collect the mana swirling around inside him.

They had a monster to kill.

A LONG SHOT

PAX'S BODY insisted that he hyperventilate, maybe scream, and most definitely get down off the cavern wall. Now! Heights were not something a poor kid living in the undergrounds of Thanhil ran into very often. Which meant he'd been able to keep the irrational fear from interfering for a long time.

Not so much now. Forcing himself to take slow breaths, Pax reached down to check the rope tied around his waist for the third time and reassured himself that even if he fell, it would catch him. To his side, Rin shifted over and made room for him to add to the row of anchors they placed above their group.

To his other side, Amil must have noticed his tension, because he paused for a moment and whispered, "It's always my rope that saves the day, right?"

The inside joke was just what Pax needed, the humor giving him the edge he needed to master the panic. He aimed an acknowledging grin at Amil before focusing back on their preparations for the upcoming battle. Chanting in his head to keep looking up might have helped a bit too.

Tyrodon had produced an almost unlimited number of what he called blanks from his inventory. The thin, rectangular slats of metal were the perfect size to pound into the myriad of small cracks riddled across the cavern wall. Once pushed in deeply enough, they made for stable hand and foot holds and a place to fasten their ropes.

After the crafter had shown them what to do, they'd worked in a tense silence, creating a vertical route wide enough for two of them to climb the cavern wall at a time. Pax swallowed hard now as he looked up at the menacing tentacles, so close above them.

Now that their group clung to the wall only a body length below the crack, the upcoming battle felt all too real. This close, the tentacles looked even stronger as they writhed out of the dark openings. The partial light from the balls far below created shadows that made everything look even more ominous.

The other students worked frantically to add stable footholds above their head out to either side so they would have access to the entire crack before launching their attack. The hydra might have completely focused on the two mages below, but Pax knew its tentacles would react with lightning speed as soon as their attacks caused pain.

"Do we trust him?" Rin whispered as she used a small block of wood to pound another anchor above her shoulder into the wall with short, quiet taps.

Pax followed her gaze down to where Aymer had taken up position under the sparse cover of a small, rocky outcropping about fifteen yards out from the wall and plenty of distance from the fighting mages.

Pax jerked his gaze back to the wall above them and swallowed hard, mad at himself for looking down again. "No. Obviously," he said with a scoff, doing his best to hide his discomfort. "But do you want him up here fighting beside us, even if he were willing?"

Rin grunted in agreement before adding, "He's a total flick and would probably let us fall or knock us off on purpose."

"You know he's still going to take all the credit when we pull this off." Amil's words elicited a stifled snort from someone on his other side.

Shaking his head, Pax focused back on his job, bolstered a bit by

Amil's confidence that they'd succeed. Three more anchors, and he'd be done with his section. "We just have to hope someone with Turgan's group will notice and come through if we actually need a distraction."

Nods greeted his words, but everyone stayed silent, movements short and quick as they finished up. Another few moments passed and quick glances to either side reassured Pax that the rest of the team was about done.

"Finished," Amil whispered from Pax's other side. His teeth flashed white as he grinned. "We ready to do this?"

"Yes. Get into position. Pass it down," Pax whispered, his pulse picking up.

His instructions moved down the line, and everyone climbed up to the top row of anchors. Once there, they crouched low and moved beneath the tentacles, careful not to touch them.

Pax forced himself to focus on his footing, keeping his eyes glued to the wall in front of him as he moved carefully from one anchor to another. The tough scales of the creature above him glistened with an innate moisture that gave off an unpleasant smell of musk and fish at the same time.

A near slip by Tansa made Pax's breath catch. But Dahni helped her, and within moments, they were all in position. Tansa and Naexi crouched under the furthest two tentacles with Dahni positioned between them, ready to reach out to add his earth magic to both of theirs when needed.

Rin and Amil were under the other two, and Pax had positioned himself between them. Glancing to their right, Pax saw the huge tentacle taking up the diameter of the final breach Incedis hadn't been able to seal.

The thing was as big around as Pax's torso, and he could only hope they could take out the other tentacles and eliminate them fast enough to gang up together on the final one.

Knowing Tyrodon had set himself up below gave Pax a touch of reassurance. Several of his metal blanks poked out of the wall, extra anchor points for their ropes and a safety backup in case everything else failed. Pax shuddered, forcing thoughts of falling from his mind as best he could.

An exhausted cry of effort from Zanneth below egged Pax on.

"Ready," he hissed, raising his hands to either side and preparing his magic to join theirs. Pulling his mana up, he split it to rush down each arm, the bulk of his indigo water mana going into his right arm toward Rin.

The jagged crack above them pinned the writhing, oblivious trunks of the tentacles in place, an advantage Pax was sure few opponents ever had against the hydra. They would find out if it was enough.

"Now!" he yelled, slapping a hand on both of the tentacles squeezing out of the crack above his head. Distractedly, he noticed the scaly skin was cool and damp, the powerful muscles rippling under his palms.

His spark leaped into the tentacles, a burst he hoped would be enough to stabilize the beast's rage as it had done on previous beasts. He just needed enough to make it vulnerable for a moment.

It definitely got the hydra's attention. Pax felt the tentacle jerk under his hand, only for the muscle to slump a fraction, the chaotic energy inside suddenly stilling for a moment. The power of the hydra pulled on his mana, hungry and impatient. This time, instead of resisting, he pushed deeper, but fought to keep his mana a thin thread to limit his loss. Just as he'd hoped, he felt the natural defenses of the creature lowering as it sucked at his energy with a desperate eagerness.

It was just enough. Behind his light, a host of indigo snakes came stabbing into the tentacle. A natural barrier repelled them, bowing in like a flexible shield that yielded but wouldn't break.

The stench of burning chemicals came from his other side as Amil poured his flame into the second tentacle, fighting to follow the path of Pax's light mana.

More. Pax spread the ends of his mana thread, pushing them to burst into mists of mana that changed the energy of the tentacles, taming both of them further.

"Harder. Stronger," he got out through gritted teeth, urging Rin and Amil on.

Rin's indigo snakes slammed at the tentacles in a staccato even more powerful. Pax tugged on the chaotic energy inside, distracting it. With a sudden rush, Rin's magic tore into the tentacle, churning and stabbing in a powerful storm that tore at the insides, ripping through muscles with eager abandon.

A savage grin on his face, Pax shifted his attention to focus on the tentacle Amil fought to overwhelm. Amil's heat raging across the hydra's skin, still unable to penetrate very far. Pax quickly duplicated his efforts, distracting the innate energy of the tentacle, soothing the chaos just enough for Amil's flame to burst inside.

With Pax's light mana paving the way, Amil's raging inferno blasted through the powerful muscles, scorching the tentacle from the inside out. Fluids bubbled, building up an explosive pressure that made the skin bulge and crackle, hot and painful under Pax's hands.

Both tentacles spasmed, a reawakening energy doing its best to drive out the intruders, but the damage had already been done. Together, their magic tore the powerful appendages apart from inside.

A panicked cry rang out on the other side of Rin, making Pax jerk his mana free. The others were in trouble.

Pax had hoped that attacking with two types of mana directly into the tentacles would be enough to break through. But all three of the others were fighting, without success, against the two tentacles that thrashed back and forth in a powerful frenzy.

"Go," Rin yelled at him, her face straining as water roiled over both of her hands and dove into wounds now gaping on the tentacle flailing in front of her face. Its movements were already weakening as it swelled from her internal attack.

"Start on the big one as soon as these go limp," he called back, already maneuvering around her. He focused on the rope and how strong it was as he forced himself to move quickly and hold on to the anchors.

Dahni had abandoned helping Naexi and jammed a narrow barrier of earth repeatedly up under the narrower tentacle he and Tansa wrestled together.

Just past them, Naexi wrapped her arms around the bulk of her tentacle, hair whipping in the gust of her air attacks. A primal yell poured out of her mouth as she slammed attacks over and over into the thing.

But they all hit from the outside, none of them powerful enough to penetrate and destroy the tentacles from within as planned. The beast's level was much too high.

Their plan was falling apart fast.

DESPERATE MEASURES

PAX RUSHED to help Dahni and Tansa, hoping to tip things in their favor fast enough to help Naexi too. Even though only seconds had passed since they launched their attacks, the other ends of the tentacles would shift from the mages soon to retaliate against them up on the wall.

"Send your mana attacks inside," he told the two, whose panic looked like it was fast dismantling their attacks.

"We're trying, but it's not working," Dahni said, eyes wide as he glanced down, obviously considering how to get away.

"It will. Try again." Pax snapped the words at Dahni and slammed both of his hands onto the flexing skin. "With me."

Determination returned to Dahni's eyes as he gave Pax a grim nod.

It took even less effort for Pax to stab his light mana into the hydra, ballooning it out immediately into a mist this time. The entire thing shuddered, the chaotic mana snapping its attention immediately to Pax's. As soon as it made contact, he felt the order from his energy ooze into the beast. It relaxed for a split second and let down its guard.

Dahni and Tansa attacked immediately afterward. A dark brown wave pushed inside, smothering and slowing muscles and fluids.

Tansa's indigo water spears tore through flesh and vessels alike. Pax jerked his mana back, knowing Naexi had to be in real trouble by now.

Just as he left the inside of the tentacle, he glimpsed something strange. An unusual effect happened where his two friends' earth and water overlapped. Just a flicker, but instead of repelling each other or staying separate, small areas seemed to combine into something new. And then it was gone as he pulled out. He didn't have time to wonder if he'd imagined it.

Letting out yells mixed with rage and panic, Naexi fought the last tentacle and was obviously losing. A streak of blood smeared down the side of her face from a bulging knot that split on her forehead. Her movements were slowing.

She'd wrapped both arms around the thing, one hand holding white-knuckled to the hilt of a knife plunged deep into the tentacle. Just above the knife, a two-foot-wide band of air swirled and clamped down around the entire thing, constricting while the tentacle fought to free itself.

Reaching out for Dahni's sturdy shoulders, Pax struggled past Tansa and then his roommate, doing his best to make the most of the small bits of the supports he could grip with the tips of his soft boots. Desperate to help his new friend, he barely noticed the dangerous height.

Just as he made it past Dahni, a sudden sense of looming danger made him duck. He crouched so low, so fast, he felt his balance teeter.

Something heavy slammed into the rock face just above his head, sending a shower of small stones pelting into his hair. Shielding his eyes, he glanced up and saw the deadly end of the tentacle whose base Naexi was strangling. It retracted far back from the wall, rearing up and gathering momentum for another attack.

"Hurry, Pax!" Naexi screamed at him, eyes wide and focused intently on the movement of the tip. She had her legs curled up from the supports, using the base of the writhing tentacle to support all her weight. "Shove some magic into this beast while I keep that thing off us."

The dark shadow was already stabbing back toward them, and only then did a lethal looking spear made completely of bright blue magic stab out. Gleaming and almost transparent, it looked like an impossibly long and skinny shard of perfect glass. The constricting band around the tentacle had become smaller. Naexi had obviously routed a significant portion of her air mana into the spear.

The tentacle lashed forward, feinting only to shift mid-attack to stab in from the side. Naexi's Spear shifted just as fast, landing a split second ahead of the attack and anchoring itself against the base of the tentacle. The attacking tip couldn't adjust in time and smashed into the Air Spear, the impact sending a meaty thud reverberating through the air.

The momentum of the incoming tentacle had enough force to impale itself on the Spear. With a burst of pressure, Naexi's Spear exploded into a spray of air, making Pax's breath catch. Another muffled roar of pain came through the cavern wall, and the remaining tentacles renewed their struggle.

Pax grappled for a suitable position at the thrashing base of the injured tentacle. Everything happened so fast, he could hardly keep up. His mana slid inside the injured limb with ease. The encircling band of Naexi's air mana pulsed around him, pushing and shoving to strangle the appendage.

For a moment, the tentacle seemed too distracted by pain to notice his intrusion. Pax pushed another pulse of his fast-dwindling mana into the center of the thickest part of the tentacle, bursting the light into a mist that the tentacle couldn't ignore.

Like a starving street dog, something from deep inside snapped out and grasped at his energy, sucking it down with a desperate strength.

"Hurry," he cried out to Naexi, feeling his mana draining as he fought against the pull. "Stab it from inside."

She didn't need to be told twice. Her band of air transformed into a collar of Spears aimed inward in an instant, stabbing with gleeful abandon through the diminished defenses.

Already injured, the tentacle's resistance shattered. A rush of deadly Spears broke inside in a barrage so powerful that Pax stared with his inner sight, stunned by how much mana a power mage could summon compared to a support mage.

It was only when he tried to pull back that his panic flared. Something deeper wouldn't let go of his magic, something further in the wall and back where he suspected the main body of the hydra hid.

Gritting his teeth, he used all his will and pulled, doing his best to break free. His string of mana stretched, but despite his best efforts, he couldn't break the connection. A sense of foreign glee echoed in the distance, and Pax felt more of his precious energy disappearing down the connection.

And then his face exploded in pain.

His body reacted with a flush of adrenaline. Both of his hands jerked up in defense, and just like that, he was free. He blinked his eyes at Naexi's concerned look. Between them, the tentacle, as big around as his torso, hung limp against the wall, its length disappearing into the darkness below.

"Are you alright?" Naexi asked, the words coming out fast. Her face looked flushed, and her chest heaved with exertion. "I don't know what you did there, but whatever air spell you have did wonders compared to mine."

He nodded, her curious glance making him think fast about how to deflect her questions. "Thanks for the save," he said.

"Back atcha." Her gaze flicked over his shoulder and narrowed with a savage grin. "Let's take care of the last one and get out of here, okay?"

"Yes." He gave her a smile more weary than savage and struggled to pull in a full breath. If he could calm his inner core a bit, it might boost his mana recovery. He didn't have time to actually meditate.

A sudden flash of light filled the dark cavern like a sunburst with blinding intensity. Pax's thoughts ground to an immediate halt, and everyone else froze, stunned. A sudden hush washed over the cavern, even the constant background of beast movements suddenly gone.

With his back to the cavern, Pax hadn't seen exactly what had happened. Something about the massive mana surge tugged at his mana sense. It had been so bright and hot that it had to be some major flame spell by Incedis. But the flavor that lingered in the air was not pure flame. Something about it hinted at air, but not quite?

"What was that?" Naexi demanded, distress clear on her face as her eyes blinked sightlessly.

"We're out of mana!" Pax heard Zanneth's voice yell from below. "Everyone retreat. Now! We need to go for help."

Gritting his teeth, Pax looked down, surprised to feel his usual nausea over heights wasn't as overwhelming. Down below, he saw the tiny figure of Zanneth pulling the limp form of Incedis back over the uneven cavern floor. The powerful tip of the primary tentacle wavered in the air above them, obviously stunned or injured by whatever spell Incedis had unleashed.

Zanneth took advantage of the lull, scrambling back as fast as he could with the older mage in tow. For a moment, Pax's practical side urged him to do the same, scramble down the wall with his friends and run to safety.

Killing the primary tentacle was not his job. He was a brand-new student. This wasn't really his home. He didn't need to risk his life for these people. If even the full mages had decided it was impossible, then he should follow their lead.

And then he saw the backs of his other friends as they raced across the face of the wall to fight the final tentacle ahead of him. Amil, Rin, Dahni and Tansa threw themselves forward with a bravery that made him ashamed of his second thoughts.

That's when he realized warriors and mages didn't throw themselves into battle just to protect their cities. They fought for the comrades on either side of them.

How could he do any less? Jolted into action, he grabbed Naexi's hand and guided it to the next anchor. "Follow me."

"I got it." She waved him to move ahead, urgency in her voice. "I can feel my way along. Go on ahead."

The tentacle below wouldn't stay stunned for long. Their window to take out the final limb of the hydra was closing rapidly.

"Distract it with your mana!" Rin yelled down to Aymer from her position, crouched near the final breach just a few feet from danger.

Only the shadow of a figure running away greeted her words. Aymer's footfalls echoed off the walls. Not far away, the huge tentacle's movements grew more stable. It was already recovering.

71

STRONGER TOGETHER

"FLICKING 'CRAT!" Rin said and spat over the side, the spittle disappearing into the dark.

"Three of us on either side. Quickly," Pax yelled out as he climbed as fast as he could along the wall, feeling like a vulnerable spider waiting for a large palm to come out of the darkness and squash him.

Amil had already made it to the other side, lashing his rope to an anchor behind him. He jabbed out an urgent arm, pulling Rin to his side and beckoning for Dahni to follow.

By the time Pax and Naexi made it to the cramped section of anchors by Tansa under the final tentacle, the others were in position. With three of them to either side, their anxious gazes shifted between the massive tentacle's length undulating in the cavern air behind them and the section they needed to attack right above them.

If Pax had thought the other tentacles were imposing from close-up, this one seemed monstrous. It was as wide as three people. Streaks of oozing ichor trailed down the wall below it, evidence of damage caused by the ragged and unyielding wall. Its power this close felt as if it could burst the wall wide open if it flexed hard enough.

"All together. Hurry!" Pax raised his hands, amazed as all his friends did the same, pushing past the fear he saw lurking in their eyes. "Danger accelerates growth!" he added, blurting the words as soon as they popped into his mind.

Grins spread across faces, and Amil snorted. The tension of their small group crammed beneath the high-level monster eased just a fraction.

"Now!" Pax said, forcing himself not to flinch. His hands slammed into the scaly muscle as his friends reached over each other to get close enough to do the same. He tugged at the remnants of his mana and thrust it into their last opponent with as much speed and power as he could manage.

For the briefest moment, he thought it would work as easily as it had with the others.

But that otherworldly intelligence was back, perking up and latching onto his mana like a greedy leech. Around him, Pax felt the elements of his friends fight to follow his path inside. A veritable storm of elements exploded: air, water, fire and earth . . . on the surface of the tentacle.

No. Pax tried to burst his light mana into a cloud to infuse the massive tentacle and provide a weakness for his friends to exploit. Instead, his energy battered futilely at the unyielding grip of a malevolent energy clamping down on him.

The powerful enemy flooded into the entire section of the tentacle, muscle and skin together. Somehow no longer chaotic, it had focus and purpose, deliberately fighting his efforts.

As he struggled harder, Pax heard the cries of dismay from his friends against the backdrop of the creature's greedy satisfaction. It pulled and drained the bit of light mana he had left at an alarming speed.

All Pax could think about was escape. His head pounded as his mana depleted to alarming levels. Remembering his last escape, he desperately tried to jerk his hands away, anything to break free or at least cause a spark of pain to help him.

He felt his hands come free from the hydra's skin, but the mana link only stretched without breaking. A building pressure spiked in his head as the hydra's energy thrived on what it drained from him, reveling in its consumption.

Just as Pax despaired, he felt a hand land on his left shoulder. A moment later, another gripped his right. Expecting a rush of mana from his friends, he was overwhelmed when pure pain slammed into him from both sides instead. Water rampaging on one side. Flame blazed with sizzling fire through the other.

Pax screamed, his head rocking back at the staggering attack. A split second later it stopped, and he sagged, a limp mess. He glanced at his two friends, unable to form a coherent word.

Rin grabbed the back of his armor before he could fall. "Sorry, but Naexi said only pain would break you free."

Amil had a sick look on his face as he glanced at his hand as if it had betrayed him.

"Watch out!" Tansa yelled, her voice frantic and high-pitched.

Pax sagged down to the spotty array of anchors holding them up just before an enormous mass slammed into the rock face just above them all. The boom was deafening, and the shower of sharp rocks stung.

"Pax!" Rin's cry made him jerk around.

Her right arm hung limply as her left scrambled frantically for a handhold. Pax lunged forward desperately, but knew he wouldn't be in time. Gravity's hold was faster and stronger than he was. Below, he saw Tyrodon's wide eyes looking up at them as he braced himself. Pax prayed the ropes held.

"Nope," Naexi barked out, her hand jamming under the shoulder of Rin's leather armor. "You're not getting out of this fight that easily."

Pax felt as if his heart had stopped and restarted in rapid succession.

Guttural cries from beside him made him look over and see the other three slamming their knives into the tentacle with a rapid intensity, like the sewing machine Pax's mother had used so deftly.

"Do your thing again," Naexi urged, turning and reaching up. "Our spells can't get through the skin."

"I can't—" Pax started, weak enough that he knew his light mana was completely gone.

"Then we'll just keep hitting the thing until it breaks." Rin's mouth settled in a grim line. She wrapped rope around her limp arm before reaching past him to place her good hand against the bucking tentacle above them.

The rush of her indigo magic nearby made his shoulder flare up in recognition, and Pax realized he still had one weapon. His water mana.

Though it was mostly drained too, he had a way to recharge it. A dangerous way.

Pax forced himself up on weakened legs, pushing aside the reservations in the back of his mind. He might lose his spot in the mage academy if he revealed his water mana. Plus, he knew firsthand how dangerous too much beast meat could be.

None of that mattered now. Shoving all the disturbing worries aside, Pax pulled out a handful of beast meat from his inventory. Opening his senses to it, he could feel the latent power pushing to break out.

Rin gave him a fierce grin as he placed his right hand against the ichor-slicked skin near hers. Both hot and cold, the surface of the hydra pulsed with anger and injury.

"Knives everyone," he called out. "Weaken it while I mess it up inside. Get ready with your magic when I tell you."

Shoving the handful of meat into his mouth, Pax forced his focus inward as he chewed and prepared for the deluge. He was the only one who could push his mana past the thing's defenses. He'd either destroy it himself or break open a path for the others to help.

He'd just have to survive consuming the wild mana that was about to overwhelm him. Then, if anyone noticed his light or water magic, he'd just have to deal with the fallout later.

An adrenaline-filled whoop from Amil inspired the others to move with a renewed rush of energy. Knives flashed in the shadows as they fought to inflict as much damage as they could.

Just before his last swallow, Pax saw their efforts having some effect. The end of the tentacle spasmed as it tried to smash them into the rock again. It missed by a few yards, sending a tremor through the wall, but not hurting any of his friends.

Pax could feel the flare of wild mana building in his center, roiling with energy that grew at a fast pace. Hurrying, Pax used the barest thread of light mana he'd regenerated to stab into the tentacle, fighting to gain a foothold before he had to deal with the wild mana. He immediately burst the miniscule light mana into as many small pieces as he could. Sending them jolting in random directions, Pax felt the hydra's attention split as it tried to track them. Perfect.

A moment later, the flood of power swelling in his center burst, exploding out in all directions and stunning him with its intensity. Eyes narrowed with effort, Pax fought to stay standing as he braced himself against the force surging through him like a tsunami. He'd once tried to drink water cascading from a downspout during a spring rainstorm. This was worse.

So much magic, more than he'd ever felt, even in the power students. It filled him, stunning his insides like a magic stampede.

In the background, he felt the hydra flex its own magic, countering the thin mist of his remaining light mana. But he had to survive the onslaught in his own body before he could deal with the hydra. Pax knew he was in serious trouble.

He aimed his will at the foreign magic and fought to impose some sense of order on the rampaging mess. A gnat would have had an easier time stopping an angry yugrut.

His mind in upheaval, a single idea broke through the fog. He didn't need to stop it, did he? Grasping at the concept with desperation, Pax quit trying to impose his will on the storm inside him.

He directed it instead, a gnat doing its best to herd a yugrut stampede. Pax pushed and drove with calculated angles at the wild mana, fighting desperately to push and guide it toward his arm. Up, through and out.

Once the barest lip of one wave entered his limb, it broke, tearing through with wild abandon. He screamed as indigo magic rushed through his arm and tore out his palm, punching into the hydra's tentacle.

He clenched his jaw against the pain and power surging through him, guiding as much of the mana as possible to follow the path forged by his light mana. With a clear outlet, the bulk of the wild mana was more than willing to blast along the route.

Pax held on, fighting to direct the flood and hold his concentration amidst the storm of pain. His grin turned feral, and he clenched his jaw, watching the mana tear into the tentacle, spreading destruction in its wake.

He was so close. Just one more step. One last bit of order to impose on the wild magic. Dredging up his last strength, Pax pulled on the pattern of his Water Blade spell. His constant use of it during the fight across the cavern had refined his casting just enough to be familiar.

Water Blade.

The growing ball of indigo energy invading the tentacle exploded outward in a storm of small, curved blades churning out in a maelstrom of destruction. Pax shoved mana into the spell as fast as he could, draining even the prodigious energy from the beast meat at a rapid rate. Pax pushed the blades outward, determined to do as much damage as possible before the spell ran out.

His mind screamed in pain, yelling for him to stop. His body sagged like an empty bag stretched too long and now empty. He held on for one beat longer and grinned in satisfaction as the edge of his ball of blades broke out through the skin into the dark cavern air. An explosion of blood and water splashed in a hot mess across his legs.

For the second time, Pax sagged down, his body wanting to collapse as he scrambled to find a handhold so he didn't fall.

"Mana, everyone," he called out, his voice harsh as he clung to a rope. "Through the wound!"

Pax blinked, trying to focus his eyes as knives disappeared into inventories. His friends' hands jabbed toward the gaping wound, their elements swirling with eager energy.

"Just Rin and Amil, while I make it wider." That was Naexi's voice.

Pax crouched lower, doing his best to get out of the way. He felt an angry tremor through the rough wall as the hydra went crazy on the other side.

"Got it. Dahni and Tansa. There's room right here now."

Pax glanced up, and a rush of excitement and anticipation filled him. His friends shoved hands into the ragged wound, yawning widely under their attack. The scaled skin nearby spasmed, frantic to escape. Shards of rock broke free under the onslaught of the powerful tentacle. The breach widened a fraction, giving the thing just enough room to flail side to side.

"Die already!" Amil roared out, the flicker of flame visible at his wrist much weaker than earlier.

Now that he focused, Pax could see none of them had much mana left. Forcing himself up, Pax tried to find another thread or two of mana. He ignored the savage pounding of his head. They just needed a bit more to tip the battle in their favor.

"Watch out!"

He snapped around to look at Rin's terrified eyes. But instead of looking at him, she stared behind him into the cavern.

Instantly, Pax knew what was happening. But his muscles were too exhausted and limp to respond fast enough. He twisted and saw the desperate end of the tentacle speeding toward them.

Why didn't he have a shield in his inventory? Or some kind of shield spell? Anything at all. He vowed never to be caught like this again.

Without even enough mana to cast Haste, Pax flung himself the few inches he could down against Naexi's legs.

It wasn't enough.

The tentacle slammed into his leg with so much force it ripped him free of the wall. Pain and panic tore through him as his greatest fear was realized and he fell. His reserves gone, he almost succumbed to the darkness and just gave up.

Almost.

Pax forced himself to twist as he fell, reaching back desperately for a handhold. Another thud next to his shoulder made him flinch as the tentacle stabbed again.

Then the rope around his waist went suddenly taut, making him grunt in pain just before he slammed back into the wall. Dazed, he forced himself to turn and face outward. Somehow, he needed to dodge the next attack.

The crazed tentacle burst out of the darkness once again. Pax kicked with his good leg, hoping to swing on his rope and avoid another blow.

An inarticulate scream of rage rang out above him. He glanced up to see a small shadow launch itself from the wall.

Naexi!

"No!" He wasn't the only one to scream. Horror filled the faces of his friends as they looked out at their friend flying toward the enemy.

Pax sucked in a breath when he saw the crazy elf land on the tentacle and frantically wrap her hands and legs around the thing. The glint of blades flashed. What did she think she could do against it?

Then her weight and momentum hit fully, jerking the tentacle down and off course, so it missed Pax. He didn't know if she was lucky or brilliant.

"Hurry," he yelled up at the others. "Tear up the insides before we lose Naexi."

Rin had already turned back to the fight. Amil roared, his flame flaring back to life. Dahni and Tansa closed their eyes as they bore down.

The next events happened so fast that later Pax would wonder how things would have been different if Naexi had waited to jump for just a few more seconds.

72

REALITY STRIKES

THE FURY of the hydra on the other side of the wall had almost become background noise. It may have increased just a tad when his friends above him finally overwhelmed the tentacle.

A visible wave of weakness, loss of muscular function, shot through the immense length of the tentacle. A weak chorus of cheers wafted down to Pax, sounding so minor in the cavern's immensity.

All Pax could do was stare in horror at the length of the tentacle and the shadowy lump toward the very end. The appendage had tried flailing to remove Naexi. When that didn't work, it flexed to pull her high toward the cavern ceiling. The extra height was probably an attempt to counter her weight, so it could still attack the others clinging to the cavern wall.

"Naexi!" Pax screamed out, forced to watch the inevitable happen while he hung helpless on the wall.

The sagging of muscles traveled in a ponderous wave to the tip of the tentacle. With a horrifying end, the entire thing went limp in mid-air. Pax pounded his fists against the wall, barely noticing the pain as he watched Naexi fall from an unsurvivable height.

"Naexi! Use your air magic." His voice broke on the yell, hoping she could pull off a miracle somehow. Then he remembered Turgan's distant group. "Someone help her," he screamed at them.

But they had already seen her predicament, faces upturned as distant cries of alarm rang out. Pax searched for a sign that Incedis was back on his feet, but all he saw was Aymer yelling in desperation, his hands raised and summoning an earth Spear.

"No," Pax whispered quietly, sagging against the unyielding rope tied around his waist. Was the idiot going to impale her as she fell? Pax watched Naexi and the tentacle plummet, unable to look away. His stomach roiled at the prospect of watching a friend die.

A flurry of motion suddenly knocked Aymer and his Spear aside. Pax leaned forward as if it would help him see the distant details better.

Zanneth!

The air mage pushed both hands into the air, just seconds before impact. The tentacle's fall hiccupped, slowing visibly for a brief second before it slammed down into the cavern floor. Zanneth just hadn't had enough mana to stop it.

"Help me down," Pax called out frantically to Tyrodon as he tried to convince himself that the impact was survivable.

The next few minutes were a mess of worry and chaos as Tyrodon helped them sort out their ropes and the anchors so they could safely lower themselves back down the wall. Pax suddenly noticed the height again, but forced himself to ignore the returning panic. He had to hurry.

He kept slipping and dangled in awkward spins before he could get his good leg back on the wall to hop down in short awkward movements.

Both Amil and Rin made it before him, reaching out to help him down when he got close.

"Thanks for waiting for me," he said breathlessly.

"We weren't letting you run around on your own." Rin said, pragmatic as always. "There are still beasts down here."

Her words broke into his frantic rush to find out if Naexi had survived.

"She's got the best care," Amil said quietly. "Turgan's group should have the leftover healing potions, and both Zanneth and Incedis are there. We don't have to rush."

Pax gave them a nod. A flood of grief and guilt welled up inside him. "She did that to save me," he whispered, his voice breaking.

"To save all of us," Rin answered, stepping close but not touching him. "Just like you did earlier."

Amil didn't have Rin's reservations and pulled Pax into a sideways hug, squeezing him almost painfully. "We all fought for each other. Don't mess up her sacrifice by feeling guilty."

Their words weren't anything he didn't already know, but hearing them and having them close eased the tight knot in his chest just enough that he could summon a weak smile and nod again.

Behind them, Dahni helped Tansa to the ground. Tyrodon arrived last, his slight, lanky frame looking the most skilled of all of them maneuvering along the ropes.

Amil stepped back, and Pax scrubbed at his face before facing them. The others looked away, though Tyrodon gave him a sympathetic nod.

"Orders?" Rin asked him, her tone matter-of-fact and expectant.

Pax looked at her blankly for a minute.

She cleared her throat and raised her eyebrows.

"Um, yes," he said, as he forced his thoughts back to the matter at hand. Their two powered students could each take the front and back, with the others keeping eyes out to the sides. "Weapons out, since we're all low on mana. Amil will help me at the front. Rin and Dahni keep eyes on the right and left. Tansa, you monitor our back. Avoid everything we can. Let's keep it to a fast walk. Speak up if you get tired."

Organizing their simple formation helped pull Pax's thoughts back from despair. He hobbled painfully with Amil's help and kept watch for danger, glad of anything to distract him from what they would find when they arrived.

"It's about time," Aymer's angry voice snarled when they got close.

The aristocratic elf stormed out from the crowded students, eyes flashing and homing in on Pax.

Another student tried to step in front of him, but Aymer shoved him aside.

"You're dead," he screamed as he charged. "You and your stupid plans killed her."

His anger caught Pax flat-footed, too stunned to know what to do. "She's dead?" was all he could manage, his grief rushing back full force.

His obvious distress seemed to penetrate Aymer's rage. The elf stopped in front of him, chest heaving as a matching grief briefly crossed his face, disrupting the anger.

"Enough!" The command cut through the air, making everyone snap around to see a fuming Incedis glaring in their direction. His voice rang out with much more strength than the flame mage appeared to have. Leaning against Zanneth for support, Incedis looked as if a stiff wind might knock him over.

"Save your arguments for when we get back to safety," he snapped. "Turtle formation right now. As soon as we finish with Naexi, we'll be getting back as quickly as possible."

Students hurried to obey him, many looking relieved to have someone powerful back in charge. Aymer gave Pax a hard glare before turning on his heels and walking back to the others with a wooden gait.

Pax stumbled forward with the rest of his group, only to stop when he got there. "She's not dead?" he asked no one in particular.

The students around gave him mixed looks, but no one answered, busy shuffling back into their groups and setting up with shields and weapons. He forced himself to ignore his injuries as he pushed through to the center, looking for Incedis and Zanneth. Breaking through into a small cleared area, he found both of the mages crouched down. Incedis had his hands placed to either side of Naexi's chest, while Zanneth had one on each side of her hips. Empty potion bottles lay discarded on the rocky ground near her head.

Completely motionless, Naexi was much too pale, a trickle of blood from both her nose and mouth stark against her skin. Her legs didn't look right despite someone's attempt to straighten them. He blanched at the sight of a jagged and bloody bone protruding out of her arm.

"She's alive?" he whispered the question.

Neither mage answered. The last thing Pax wanted to do was interrupt them while they fought to heal her. Instead, he moved in to kneel on an empty spot near her, wincing as his leg objected. When he gently took her limp hand in his, it felt cold and broken. He didn't dare squeeze.

A quick glance inside to his core verified he had regained some of his mana. Though his usual ball of energy had only recovered to the size of a small walnut now. Before he could second guess himself, he pulled up a tentative thread and prepared to send it into her hand.

He'd already exposed his secret by using water magic today. Dahni and Tansa would have to be blind not to have seen that. Naexi had sacrificed herself to save them all, so the least he could do was see if his unusual magic could save her.

His magic slipped into her so easily that he knew things were terrible. Without her consciously inviting him in, her natural defenses should have fought to keep him out. That they didn't . . .

She was a mess inside. It felt like traveling through the halls of a deserted town after armies had come and gone, leaving nothing intact. Where he would have expected order and life, he found only destruction. Her muscles were torn, bones shattered in pieces and organs weakly fighting to perform their functions.

As Pax pushed toward her center, he saw two glowing collections of energy. The bright red and cool blue made it obvious they represented the efforts of the two mages to put Naexi back together again.

His eyes stung as he saw how futile it was. Just as he tried to decide what to do next, a flare of interest from the air magic shifted in his direction. He hesitated just long enough for it to get close before his mana stumbled back. He couldn't help her now, and getting caught was pointless. Pax pulled out in a rush and hoped he'd escaped unseen.

A moment later, both mages sat back on their heels. Zanneth rubbed at his eyes while Incedis just shook his head sadly.

"Please don't stop." Aymer's words were full of anguish and desperation.

Pax looked up to see he'd slipped in while everyone had been busy. The aristocratic elf crouched near Naexi's head across from him and reached out to smooth her hair back from her face.

"I'm sorry. Her injuries were too severe." Incedis kept his tone calm and even, though his eyes softened with sympathy.

"My family will pay," Aymer begged.

Zanneth shook his head and straightened to rise.

Aymer grabbed his hand, his expression suddenly demanding and angry again. "Try again!"

Pax expected the air mage to teach Aymer a bit more humility, but Zanneth simply held his gaze, waiting for the boy to let go.

"Did we do it?"

The soft words made all four men freeze and stare. Pax sucked in a breath and scooted forward to meet Naexi's confused gaze.

"Yes," he said, leaning in close and blinking back tears. "You did it. You saved us all."

She looked at him for a moment, as if her mind took a few extra beats to process his words. When they did, she smiled. "Just like you did for me. Ignore danger to help, right?"

Something was wrong. Her gaze kept going out of focus. Sadness pushed aside Pax's fledgling hope. He nodded, and his voice broke as he tried to reassure her. "Yes, that's right," he said with a watery smile. "You didn't hesitate. We would have died without you."

"Naexi?" In a voice sounding more hesitant and lost than Pax had ever heard, Aymer asked for her attention.

Her eyes fluttered side to side as she turned her head in a way that made the simple movement ponderous. When her eyes met Aymer's, she let out a soft chuckle and gave him a half smile. "There you are."

"Here I am," he agreed.

The naked intimacy that shone from his eyes made Pax feel as if he were intruding. He scooted back to give them privacy, stifling a groan of pain as he pushed himself to his feet.

"Drink this," Incedis said softly, handing him what had to be one of the last healing potions.

"No," he objected, eyes wide as he looked down at Naexi. "Give it to her."

"She's past such things, boy." His voice wasn't harsh, but he spoke in a way that left no doubt that he knew what he was speaking of.

"But she's awake. Speaking." Pax grasped at hope. They had pulled Bryn back from death's door. Why not Naexi, too? If she lived, next time he'd be more prepared, stronger and better with his magic. He'd be able to save everyone next time.

"Vitur's gift."

Zanneth's words were so quiet, Pax almost didn't hear them over the sound of the others.

"What?"

The stoic mage met his gaze and explained. "Vitur often grants a momentary burst of mana and energy just before death. A gift of time for last words and emotions to be shared before the end. She's sharing her last."

His words rang true and destroyed the last vestiges of hope that Pax had been clinging to. He forced himself to stand and witness her last moments. Out of respect. Out of admiration.

The fight was suddenly more real than he'd ever wanted it to be. Rin and Amil stepped up beside him, standing in silent support. Hot tears dripped down Pax's cheeks as he watched Naexi's head sag back weakly. Her eyes closed, and Aymer let out a wail of distress.

It was obvious she was gone when some vital energy suddenly left her, leaving a limp body lying on the hard ground, the only evidence of her heroism.

"Time to wrap her up and get her home," Incedis said, reaching down to place a hand on Aymer's shoulder as he motioned for Zanneth to get busy.

For a moment, it seemed as if Aymer would crumple. But then, something fierce tore through him. He knocked Incedis' hand free and pushed up to his feet, rage filling his expression.

"The two of you let her die," he said in a low, furious voice. "And I'm going to make it my mission to make sure you pay for it."

Incedis didn't even flinch, meeting Aymer's anger with unshakeable calm. This only infuriated him more. His gaze flicked back and forth, agitated and looking for another target.

Pax swallowed when his eyes landed on him.

"And you," Aymer took an angry step toward Pax, hand raised and finger jabbing toward him.

"None of that," Incedis said, grabbing Aymer's arm and holding him back.

"Maybe if you'd used your mana to distract the hydra instead of running away like a coward, your girlfriend would still be alive." Rin's bitter words cut through the anger and emotion like a knife.

Aymer blanched, mouth moving, but nothing coming out.

"That's what I thought." Rin scoffed. "Just another 'crat blaming others for your own messes."

More red flushed through Aymer's expression. With an incoherent yell of rage, he lunged toward Rin, only to be held back again by Incedis. For a second, Pax thought he would actually fight Incedis. But even in his rage, it seemed some sense of self-preservation still worked.

Chest heaving, he settled for glaring at Pax and Rin. "You. All of you. You'll pay for dragging her into this." After growling out the threat, he turned on his heel and stormed off.

Pax stared after him, not sure how he felt. Stunned? Angry? Or both?

"Guess I didn't help much," Rin said after another few moments had passed. She shook her head tiredly. "Like we need a new enemy."

"You were amazing," Pax said in a quiet tone. "You just said what all of us were thinking, and he was going to blame us, anyway. So, thanks."

"Go, Rin," Amil said with a grin, leaning in and nudging her shoulder.

Rin looked at them and, when she saw they meant what they said, she let out a relieved breath. "Thanks, guys."

As they helped gather up the wounded and prepare to leave the cavern, Pax felt a sense of gratitude under the somber mood. He had friends who would fight by his side and stand up for him, even against powerful students. Amid everything that had changed in the few harrowing hours since they'd left, that fact reassured him.

THE WAY BACK

THE WAY back had none of the excitement of their initial delving into the cavern. A somber silence hung over their group, and even the few beasts who attacked were dispatched with a grim efficiency that would suit hardened warriors better than first-year academy students just starting out.

They'd wrapped Naexi's body in someone's cloak and carried it on a makeshift stretcher, along with three others whose injuries kept them from walking. Krasig, the eager, young kitchen assistant, had a lower leg too torn up to walk. Bryn was breathing, but still too weak to do much. The low-leveled healing potions they'd brought were fine for simple wounds, but serious ones needed both more attention and time to heal fully.

And they still needed to hurry for other reasons. They'd left the breaches in the cavern wall stuffed with the swollen and damaged tentacles. However, by the time they finally got underway, the hydra had already begun shifting and struggling to pull the appendages free. The opening and cracks wouldn't remain blocked for long.

Now that they'd been underway long enough for the adrenaline and emotion to fade, Pax realized how awful a shape he was in. Even the low-leveled healing potion he'd taken wasn't helping enough because he couldn't rest his leg. His painful hobble made him take twice as many steps as the others, just to keep up. A throbbing beat pounded in his head, berating him for how many times he'd drained his mana. And even the slowly refilling spark inside him refused to make things better until he ate, drank, and rested.

Pax couldn't decide if a hot shower, a full plate or a warm bed sounded more appealing right now. Instead, with his clubs in hand, he forced himself to plod along, one foot after the other, as he did his best to keep an alert eye on his surroundings. The incessant blinking of his notifications didn't make things better.

"You ok?" Rin asked, looking back over her shoulder.

"Yeah," he answered automatically, but not meaning it.

Rin slowed her steps and peered closer at Pax. "Is it more than losing Naexi?"

He paused before answering, because she looked as if she actually cared about his answer. "Sure, that's part of it. It's all a big mess, but right now . . ." His voice trailed off as he tried to figure out what specifically was bothering him.

She just waited, and he had to aim a half-smile in her direction. Rin always seemed to know when to be quiet and just listen.

"It's my notifications," he finally blurted out.

"What?" she asked, looking surprised. "You're not happy with what you got?"

"No," he quickly objected. "I haven't looked at them."

"Why not?"

"It just seems like . . . well, I usually get excited about all the points, levels, coppers, you know?" He gave her a helpless shrug. "It just seems wrong. That's all."

She looked forward again, giving his words some thought before she spoke. "I get it. It feels like you're making money and getting ahead from Naexi's death?"

"Yeah, but that's just part of it."

She waited again, giving him time.

He wasn't sure he could tell her what had been really bothering him. The relief, sadness and guilt had all mixed into a nasty mix that tore at his insides.

"You don't have to tell us," Rin finally said as she shifted to avoid stepping into a puddle of something unpleasant.

Amil nodded, his usual cheerful look also more shuttered than usual.

Their acceptance made it suddenly easy for Pax to unburden himself. "Is it bad that I'm glad Naexi died instead of me or one of you two?"

As soon as he said the words, he wanted to take them back. The dark guilt was almost overwhelming as both of them kept up their plodding pace but didn't answer.

Finally, Amil mumbled something, looking down.

"What?" Pax asked quietly, leaning in to hear better.

But it was Rin that answered. "He said he's the same."

Pax looked at her, surprised. "But—"

"And so am I," she interrupted him, her expression switching to mulish at his look. "The three of us, we're family now. And that comes first, understand?" Now she looked demanding, though Pax thought he saw a flicker of uncertainty in her eyes.

He glanced over to see Amil had looked up and was nodding his agreement. It didn't fix everything storming around inside him, but it eased it somehow. Pax felt the truth settle inside him. Everyone knew family came before a stranger, even a fellow student who had fought beside you.

A flicker of memory made part of him long for his parents and brother again. The thought that they'd be glad he was finding a new family was bittersweet.

"Yes," he finally said quietly. "We're family now, and that comes first."

Amil beamed at both of them, clapping them on the back while Pax saw Rin's shoulders slump slightly in relief.

"So, are you going to look at your notifications soon, then?" Rin asked. "Though I don't think there's a limit to how long you can ignore them."

He cocked his head, thoughtful. The simple acceptance of his friends had made the issue feel a lot less emotional. And then he thought of trying to go to sleep with the annoying notifications still flashing. He let out a rueful chuckle.

"What? Now it's funny?" Rin asked, half-smiling herself and looking as if she wanted him to share the joke.

"I was just imagining trying to get to sleep with my notifications still flashing for attention. I guess Vitur doesn't appreciate them being ignored forever."

It wasn't that funny, but both Amil and Rin chuckled.

"Did you get some good stuff?" Pax couldn't help asking them, his curiosity emerging now that he felt a bit better.

She nodded, and Amil's grin widened. Then a somber light filled her green eyes. "Anything you earn would only have made Naexi happier. You know that, right? She'd say you were getting stronger so you could keep ignoring danger and helping. We all need to get stronger."

He couldn't help agreeing and nodded as he thought of the beasts the stronger mages and warriors must still be facing tonight on the wall. Then there were the beasts faced on all the city walls in the empire. He gave her a nod. Yes, they all needed to get stronger.

Ahead, Incedis called for a break. Pax quickly found a wall to lean against and gave Rin a grateful look as she helped him down. Amil plopped down on his other side, handing out meat and veggie wraps to each of them. They were still warm.

"Thanks," Pax said softly to his friends as he finished eating. "Give me a minute while I see what I got." He closed his eyes and let the flood of notifications scroll by, scanning what he could, but mostly waiting to see the totals in the final menu.

∽

NAME: *Pax Viperssworn*
  Race: *Mixed Human (monster-touched)*
   Age: *16*

Bound Location: Shieldwall Mage Academy (provisional monthly)
Class: *Mage*
Element: Light (Hidden)
Specialization: none (Hidden)
Paths of Understanding: *(Hidden)*
Flame: Level 1 - 40/100 (+19)
Air: Level 1 - 69/100 (+18)
Water: Level 2 32/200 (+40)
Earth: Level 1 - 18/100 (+8)
Level: *1*
Mage Leveling Points: *1/5 (+1)*
Health: *28/43 (+1)*
Mana: *3/31 (+5)*
Attributes:
Strength: 7 (+1)
Agility: 9
Endurance: 8
Intelligence: 8
Insight: 8
Charisma: 5
Skills:
General Active:
Identify Level 1 (Common) - 74/100 (+12)
General Passive:
Skinning Level 1 (Common) - 38/100
Butchering Level 1 (Common) - 54/100
Clubs Level 1 (Common) - 49/100 (+21)
Mage:
Light Mana Manipulation Level 2 (Epic) - 3/200 (+64) (Hidden)
Light Mana Sight Level 1 (Rare) - 65/100 (+17) (Hidden)
Elemental Meditation Level 1 (Common) - 11/100
Light Healing Level 1 (Rare) - 39/100 (+22) (Hidden)
Runes Level 1 (Uncommon) - 11/100
Mana Merge Level 1 (Epic) - 55/100 (+25) (Hidden)
Spells:

Light (1/3):
Haste Level 1 (Common) - 39/100 (+15)
Water (1/1):
Water Blade Level 1 (Common) - 26/100 (+26) (Hidden)
Class Evolution Points Unused: *1 (+1)*
Inventory: *0/20 available.*
Assignments:
Academy Workshop Trainee
4/30 hours
0/1 Supervisor approval
Charity Clinic Trainee
2/30 hours
0/1 Supervisor approval
Maintenance Trainee
0/21 Cleared blockages
0/1 Supervisor approval
Exterminator Intern
80/300 Vermin killed (+78)
0/1 Supervisor approval
Misc.: *First-year Point Ranking (expand)*
Coin Count: *0 Gold, 8 Silver, 98 copper (+5 Silver, +10 Copper)*
Academy Points: *28.5 (+16.5)*

~

ON HIS FIRST LOOK, the amount of coin and academy points he'd earned distracted him. Completing the Trainee stage of the Exterminator assignment had given him a few, but the bulk came from slaughtering 'vermin' for hours on end.

Images of all the things he could buy with his new wealth flitted through his mind, not to mention dreams of winning the Academy Point ladder this week and what powerful prizes that might bring.

But something else tugged at his attention, and Pax went back over his menu. When he saw it, he sucked in a breath and stared at the tiny number, so small but so significant.

Mage Leveling Points: 1/5 (+1)

He had earned the first of five leveling points toward his next mage level! And after only a week. If he could keep that up, he'd earn a level in another month. Leveling once or twice a year was the norm, but he was on track to do much better.

How had he earned a point already? Excitement flushed through Pax, and he searched his menu again, looking for which of his mage skills or spells had done it.

And there it was: *Light Mana Manipulation Level 2.*

Shaking his head, he couldn't understand how he'd gained so many points in the mage skill. Sure, he'd had to manipulate his light mana to break into each of the tentacles, but 64 points worth?

He quickly sifted through the individual notifications again, and what he found made his eyes widen. He'd actually earned a chunk of points when he helped direct the mana of his friends during the fight to penetrate the tentacles' defense. Working with all four elements had given him an enormous boost.

However, what had tipped him over was the cascade of points he'd received for channeling the wild water mana when he'd absorbed all the beast meat. Manipulating the sheer amount of energy had required all his mental strength. Even though he'd only directed it instead of completely controlling it, it had pushed his manipulation skill to unexpected heights.

He remembered almost losing control at the end. He'd been barely able to hold on long enough. Had the level up happened then, giving him the extra strength and control to make the difference? It seemed manipulating all forms of mana would level up the skill, not just light. No wonder it was an epic skill.

And now it was level 2.

Not letting worries blunt his excitement, Pax quickly pulled up the description of his newly leveled skill, excited to see how it had improved.

UNEXPECTED SKILLS AND POINTS

MAGE SKILL LEVELED: **Light Mana Manipulation** *Level 2*

This epic skill comes from dedication to understanding and manipulating the essence of magic itself within a mage's body, though this restriction will diminish as the skill increases in level. Emerging from the ranks of a beginner, the light mage is just beginning to control various types of mana and improve their understanding and skill. Future levels will offer the ability to handle greater amounts of mana, finer control of specific varieties of mana and eventually the ability to move from internal to external control. This skill is crucial for a light mage dedicated to controlling the mana within themselves and eventually their environment.

VISIONS OF REACHING out and controlling all the magic around him made Pax grin, though he knew it wasn't something he'd be doing anytime soon. Still, he couldn't help imagining everything his mage skill might turn into.

But his mind still nagged at him. He had missed something else. *Evolution.*

The word jumped into his mind, prompting him to glance back

over the stat list he'd just skimmed. Another line he hadn't noticed popped out now that he was looking for it: **Evolution Points Unused: *1 (+1)***

Blaming his tiredness for missing so many important things, Pax did his best to focus on the new line. What were evolution points, anyway?

Frustration filled Pax as he realized that his lack of knowledge was coming back to bite him again. He thought hard, trying to remember if he'd heard the term before. If it was linked to his light magic, he couldn't just ask around. Maybe Rin or Amil had heard of them?

And then he remembered. There had been something about an evolution in the notifications, hadn't there? Eager now, Pax dug through them, scanning for the word. The lines scrolled by, seeming much more numerous now that he was trying to scan each one. It made the battle seem as if it had taken place over a week or more instead of a day.

Come on. Pax scrolled faster. The break wouldn't last forever.

There. Buried in a string of notifications, he finally found what he was looking for.

~

*SKILL BOOST: +9 to **Light Mana Manipulation** Level 1 - 101/100*
*Congratulations! **Light Mana Manipulation** is now Level 2*

*+ 1 **MAGE LEVELING POINT**. 4 more needed for next class level*
*Congratulations! **Class Evolution Points** Unlocked!*

CLASS EVOLUTION POINTS: For each leveling point gained in your class, you will earn an evolution point that you can use to further specialize a skill or spell. Using evolutions wisely is a key to the direction of a mage's special-ization. Evolution choices are permanent and will both open up new possi-bilities while closing others. As the first evolutions set the path for future ones, new mages are strongly encouraged to seek advice before making a selection.

*+ 1 **Class Evolution Point**. Total: 1*

~

PAX'S first thought was to chew out Incedis for not telling him about evolution points. And what about Rin and Amil? Did they know too?

Why had no one told him he could evolve his mage stuff? Not only did he have new spell choices filling his head with possibilities, but now they could be further specialized as evolutions. Also, maybe Rin and Amil could evolve their second common spell into something better.

His thought triggered a new menu, this one listing his current skills and spells. Two lines led from each item off into the distance, flashing for his attention. Somehow, he knew selecting these would expand into the specific choices for each of them.

Pax suddenly felt like the academy had invited him to a fancy shop and told him he could pick any item he wanted, but just one. It filled him with both delight and worry at the same time. How would he be able to choose?

With an effort of will, Pax shut down his menus and just sat for a moment with his eyes closed to gather himself. The warning at the end of the Evolution Point explanation wasn't something he could easily ignore. Choosing something that would affect what kind of mage he would be in the future wasn't something done on a whim while injured and exhausted in a cavern.

He blinked his eyes open, ignoring the urge to take just a peek at the evolution choices. Thankfully, another thought helped distract him. His tattoo should have also grown with the new point.

Amil and Rin were whispering quietly to each other and around him no one else was looking in his direction. He pulled up just the edge of one sleeve under his bracers. With a sense of both wonder and worry, he saw that the thin, filigreed band of light had etched itself further, about an inch of a graceful curve on the inside of both wrists.

Four more advancements and the tattoo would complete its first circumference.

It almost looked alive, all the energy of his spark swirling under the surface. And bright white.

White. Pax swallowed hard and pushed his sleeve back down before anyone could catch a glimpse. Only the variety in individual tattoo coloring and the assumption that there were only four elements possible would make anyone call it a variation of air's light blue color.

Could he change the color somehow? He was used to wearing long sleeves to cover his monster-touched arm scales, but even he knew he couldn't keep his tattoos hidden forever. With his water magic unlocked, maybe he could add a touch of blue? How hard would that be, and could he make it permanent? Or would it be something he'd have to maintain any time others could see his tattoos?

Pax pushed his worries aside to address later and instead focused on the insane gains he'd made. Coin, Academy Points and even another point in Strength would have been more than plenty. But now he had made a significant stride toward his next mage level with all the additional complications that entailed.

Pax was pretty confident that he and his friends had progressed faster than any students before them during their first week in the Academy. And not only them, but all the first-years who'd fought that night. He had a brief thought, wondering if Tyrodon had leveled up his crafting skills, too.

"Break's over. Time to get moving." Turgan's voice rang out from the other side of their group.

Pax couldn't help joining in the general murmur, objecting to the end of the brief break. Rin and Amil looked up and smiled with expectant looks. He couldn't help returning their smiles.

"Crazy, isn't it?" Amil leaned in to whisper. "I'm close to level 2 on my Flame Blast after all that."

"My Snake is close, too," Rin said quietly. "What about you?"

Pax really didn't want to get into details with so many others close by, so he just shook his head and mouthed, *Later.* Besides, if they'd been holding out about the evolution points, he wanted a little revenge. He couldn't help the satisfied upturn of his mouth.

Rin's eyes widened, and she leaned in. "You leveled something up, didn't you?"

His grin spread, but he didn't confirm it. He could keep a secret, too. Instead, he swung his gaze to the others, getting ready to move with a pointed look.

She pursed her lips and slugged him in the shoulder.

"Hey, injured here," Pax protested, waving at himself.

"That's your leg. Your arm's fair game." A half-beat later, a smile struggled to break through her grouchiness, and she shook her head in disbelief. "We're discussing this as soon as we have some privacy."

He held up both hands and nodded in agreement. That seemed to satisfy her, and they joined the exodus of tired students navigating their way through the dank tunnels under the academy.

Thankfully, Incedis could still maintain his hovering lights. They helped dispel the gloom and discourage any straggling beasts who glimpsed their battle-hardened group.

After an interminable series of turns and painful trudging, the tunnels dried out, the walls cleaner and in better repair.

Just as Pax recognized the area, Incedis called back from the front, "Five minutes, and we'll be home. Hold on a little longer."

The last steps of their trek went by in a blur; Mistress Nymeli's shock, followed by rattled orders that had workers racing to obey. They whisked the severely injured away, while treating milder injuries with first aid and simple potions. Pax nodded vaguely at the instructions for those less injured to inform their dorm leaders so the healers could check on them tomorrow. Apparently, they were overwhelmed already tonight.

Tired cheers greeted the announcement that they canceled classes for the rest of the week. Pax really had a hard time staying awake after that. A few days with nothing to do but recover sounded heavenly. That would give him time to figure out everything that had happened with his magic and get things prepared to stand up under scrutiny when classes started back up.

Kitchen workers dispensed hot food and drink. Warm blankets seemed to appear out of nowhere to drape over sagging and tired shoulders. Tired students answered whispered questions from the staff. Pax was too tired to notice the wide-eyed surprise of the kitchen workers scurrying around to help as best as they could.

When he finally hobbled out into the cool pre-dawn light back to his dorm, Dahni slid an arm of support around him from one side. Before he could object, another bundled-up student slipped in to help on the other.

A brain fog of tiredness and pain blurred the trip back to their dorm. Only the second helper excusing himself once they reached the hallway to their room jarred Pax awake enough to respond.

"Hey, thanks," he mumbled tiredly toward the smaller figure.

"It's nothing. And I'm sorry," the boy said with a quick wave before hurrying off in the other direction.

Pax stared open-mouthed, blinking his eyes and not sure he was seeing right. "Was that Kurt? Why would he think I'd want his help after he led Galen and his buddies to us?"

"Yes, that was him, and I don't know." Dahni asked, looking surprised. "When he first helped you, and you said nothing, I thought you were alright with it."

"I—" Pax didn't know what to say. Seeing Kurt's back disappear down the hallway was eerily similar to the way he'd left them in the tunnels, at the mercy of Galen.

But Pax's emotions couldn't summon any anger. "Let's just go to bed."

"Yeah." Dahni sounded as tired as Pax felt.

Pax just wanted this day to be over, finally. He could deal with tomorrow and all its troubles . . . well, tomorrow.

A NEW ADDITION

QUIET SCRATCHES. Snuffles nearby. Claws scrabbling.

Pax tossed in agitation, reaching for his weapons. He could hear the beasts gathering and had to prepare for the next attack. His hands came up empty, and he twisted, only to find himself tangled and unable to get up.

A hard thump jarred him the rest of the way out of sleep. He sat up from the stone floor of his dorm room, bleary-eyed. He tried to kick his legs free of the sheets, only to yelp in pain as his leg reminded him of the tentacle's vicious blow the night before.

A tired yawn behind him made him glance up.

"You alright?" Dahni asked, looking concerned as he stood in the doorway, hair damp with a towel wrapped around his waist. "I thought letting you sleep might help you heal up, but not if you're going to crash onto the floor. Need a hand?"

Pax was just about to accept the help when he heard another quiet rustle . . . from under his bed. His confusion lasted a split second before a sudden realization made him blanch.

"No," he said in an overly loud voice, shifting his blankets to disguise any further noises from beneath his bed. "I'm good. I think I'll just do a bit of meditation and see if my beginning healing skill can help. Then I can check in with the dorm leader, Dulmot, upstairs, to see if the healers gave me an appointment. Classes are going to be impossible until I get this healed." He waved a hand down toward his leg and had to wince himself when he saw how bad it looked.

His sleeping shorts rode high enough to see an enormous bruise wrapped around his entire thigh from his knee and disappearing up toward his hip. He knew it had to look even worse on the back of his leg where the hydra's tentacle had impacted. The mess on the front was just from slamming against the cavern wall.

"Want me to bring you back some breakfast?" Dahni offered as he sat on the bed and pulled his pants on, favoring his left hand. "My shoulder is messed up a bit, but at least I can still walk."

Pax looked up in question and Dahni turned so Pax could see a ragged wound across the back of his shoulder blade. Freshly showered, all the blood and dirt were gone, but it still looked puckered and raw. "Ouch. Are the healers going to help you with that, too?"

"Yeah, but I'm way down on the list." Dahni pulled a shirt on and let it settle carefully over him with a wince. "I'll check in with Dulmot upstairs and ask for both of us. Then I can let you know when I get back with some food."

"Thanks." Pax pushed himself up to his bed, shuffling his good foot a bit to keep making some cover noise.

Dahni gave him a curious look but asked nothing else before pulling on his boots and leaving.

When the door clicked shut behind him, Pax let out a relieved breath before returning to the floor. He winced in pain as he crouched down and looked under his bed with no idea what he'd find.

At first, he couldn't tell what he was looking at. It was dark underneath. The crumpled tunic and satchel he'd left his talpasauria bundled in lay spread out among the dust.

Then something moved. Something small, sinuous and enough like a tentacle that it made him flinch back in surprise. An alarmed squeak greeted his sudden movement and the form in the shadows skittered to the furthest corner of the darkness.

"Sorry, little Talpa." Pax chastised himself for scaring the thing.

Just because it had strange tentacle sensing organs on its face, didn't mean it had anything in common with the hydra. And now it was too far back for him to reach without crawling under the bed himself. "Do you mind if I call you Talpa? Are you a boy or a girl?"

He didn't get an answer, of course.

"We'll go with boy, for now. Hi there, little guy. My name is Pax, and I want to be your friend."

Pax's stomach growled, interrupting him. But then he smiled, realizing there was an easy way to befriend the little beast further. Pax pulled out a piece of the Bog Swarmer meat, hoping its water attributes wouldn't mess with the earth-based beast.

"Here you go." He pulled out one of his clubs and used it to push the meat under the bed. "You hungry?" Pax kept up a random string of reassuring words, hoping it would help or at least get the thing accustomed to his voice.

Pax almost jerked back again when the little creature shot forward, swiping a claw-tipped paw out to snatch the food with a speed at odds with Pax's expectations. He held still long enough for Pax to see him better as he worked to shove the large piece of meat into his mouth just beneath the disturbing sensing organ.

Pax stared at the fascinating thing he'd brought home and hoped to tame. Its scales were a mottled gray, the color of shadows, which explained how hard it had been to see him at first. The color had to be a boon to a creature needing to hide to survive.

The nest of worm-like appendages that made up its sensing organ was both repugnant and fascinating. A handful had wrapped around the piece of meat, probing and analyzing it, while others waved in the air in his direction, almost as if they could see or smell him somehow.

Its voracious attack of the meal, along with the fat claws almost as long as its paws, reminded Pax to be careful. Even as a baby, the thing was still a beast. The last thing Pax needed was another injury.

He set out another piece of meat right at the edge of the shadow under the bed and scooted back a foot, waiting. A moment later, Pax held his breath as the clump of agitated sensing organs emerged first, before latching onto the snack and sucking it back to its mouth.

A loud laugh out in the hallway made both Pax and Talpa flinch. Knowing he had limited time, Pax pulled at his light mana, pushing it out to his right hand.

Talpa's head lifted almost immediately, the tiny eyes beady and almost invisible along the side of his head. Diligent chewing made the strip of meat disappear, but his attention was definitely on the power Pax was working with.

Remembering the way he had latched on the first time, Pax pulled a club from his inventory and sent a thin stream of his mana along it, not willing to risk his hand yet.

Whether it was the food or the amount of light mana he had already consumed earlier, Talpa didn't attack the club this time. He finished the meat and moved tentatively forward, probing with the little worms until they touched the tip of the club and the mana glowing there.

Talpa let out his version of a squeaking sigh and the tense muscles under his scales relaxed in unison. He latched onto the end of the club like an infant on a teat, happy and content to guzzle.

"Is it ok if I hold you?" Pax asked in a low, soothing voice, as he moved closer. A few appendages moved in his direction as he approached, but didn't seem to object. Pax reached out a hand and slowly stroked from behind Talpa's head along his back. His scales were surprisingly warm.

Other than an initial flinch, Talpa kept sucking up light mana and radiating a contented aura.

"You like this here?" Pax asked, stopping to pay special attention to the junction between his head and short neck when he felt a vibrating hum under his fingers.

To Pax's surprise, he suddenly felt assent along with a delicious sense of spreading satiety.

"Is that you?" he asked, looking down at the Talpa.

～

Congratulations! You have initiated taming an earth-based Baby Talpasauria Shade - Level 0.

Requirements:

Earth magic or Universal Light mana: Fulfilled by Light Mana.

Earth or Universal Light Mana skill or spell: Fulfilled by Light Mana Manipulation.

Acquire mana sources and experience for your beast companion to increase progress and levels. Your companion can use these sources for growth and unlocking abilities.

Accept this bond: **Yes/No**

Note: Accepting this bond will unlock the rare skill, Universal Beast Tamer.

～

Pax couldn't click to accept fast enough, a wide grin splitting his face as he carefully scooped up Talpa and set him in his lap.

～

Mage Skill Unlocked: **Universal Beast Tamer** *Level 1*

This rare skill is versatile for a light mage with experience merging light mana with the innate mana of other creatures. The skill allows a light mage to create a bond with a creature as well as bring order and strength to its body and mana. The skill creates useful companions that can be customized to meet many needs. Use your companion menu to track progress and make decisions.

Mana cost: Varies depending on the size of beast being tamed. The stronger and larger the beast, the higher the requirement.

Warning: A failed taming can kill or enrage the beast and hurt the mage, making it difficult to defend themself. Take careful precautions before attempting.

Number of companions allowed at current level: 1

This skill improves with each successful bonding and by improving the strength, ability and level of a beast companion.

～

PAX'S GRIN widened as he scanned the amazing skill. Not only had he been able to bond with Talpa, but he'd be able to level the little guy up and unlock his own skills and powers.

Pets had always been the purview of the wealthy back in Thanhil. Food had to go to his fellow Vipers instead of a puppy or kitten, despite how desperately he'd longed for a pet since he'd been young.

Looking down at the odd creature curled up in his lap, Pax had to laugh. It was as far from a cute puppy as he could imagine. But the little guy was growing on him. Plus, with earth-based powers, Talpa would definitely come in useful. If he could learn to burrow reliably, he'd be the perfect spy. Or in a battle, he could dig holes to trip up and even trap enemies. With a bit of strength plus a skill or two, he would be amazing.

Pax felt a stab of disappointment at the limit of one beast, knowing Amil wouldn't be happy. But having a number there meant that he could eventually increase it. It was just a matter of time before he could get to the next level and unlock a second beast.

It didn't, however, say anything about being able to transfer control of the beast to someone else. A beast for Amil might be further away than he thought. Pax grimaced. Amil might need to unlock the skill himself. And with it being tied to his element, he'd likely have to find a flame-based beast weak enough to tame.

Pax shook his head. These were all concerns for another day. He needed to find a better solution than keeping Talpa hidden under his bed before Dahni got back with breakfast. As Pax pushed a last bit of light mana into the resting Talpa, he felt a small pulse of mental pressure from his pet. Turning his attention to it, another notice popped up.

～

MENU OF TALPA: *Earth-based Baby Talpasauria Shade - Level 0*
   Open: **Yes/No?**

$\sim$

FILLED WITH A GIDDY EXCITEMENT, Pax hoped Dahni would take just a few more minutes. He opened Talpa's menu.

$\sim$

NAME: *Talpa*
   Race: *Earth-based Talpasauria Shade*
   Master: *Pax Vipersworn*
   Age: *Baby*
   Class: *Tamed Beast*
   Level: *0*
   Energy to next level: *14/20*
   Ability Points: *0*
   Element: *Earth (Tamed by Light)*
   Available Mana: *16/16*
   Health: *13/13*
   Attributes:
   Prowess: 1
   Vitality: 1
   Cleverness: 2
   Passive Abilities: *None*
   Active Abilities: *None*

$\sim$

EVEN WITH TALPA's menu much shorter than his own, it still seemed amazing for a baby beast that he could hold in two hands. But Talpa had mana! Pax didn't understand the new attributes or exactly what kind of energy it was that Talpa used to level up. But if Pax could figure out how light magic worked, how hard could his little beast's menu be?

A thump on the door made his head jerk up.

"Open the door," Dahni's muffled voice came through. "My hands are full."

"Coming," Pax called out as he hurried to wrap Talpa back in the worn tunic. Being careful not to wake him, Pax slid him as far under the bed as he could reach before clambering painfully to his feet.

"Sorry," Dahni said as he came in with the tray piled high with food. "Didn't mean to make you get up."

"It's alright," Pax said as he hobbled back to his bed while Dahni followed him and placed two full plates on the bed next to him.

"Did your meditation help?" Dahni asked as he moved back to his own bed and quickly stuffed a forkful of food into his mouth.

"Huh?" Pax asked, distracted by how fast Dahni inhaled the food.

His friend flushed and swallowed with some difficulty. "Sorry. I waited to eat, so you wouldn't have to have breakfast alone, but it was torture smelling the food the entire way here." Then he waved a fork toward Pax's leg. "And I meant, were you able to activate your healing with some meditation while I was gone?"

"Oh. No. Not this time." Pax fumbled the answer and hoped it didn't sound suspicious.

"Well, don't worry." Dahni put on a reassuring expression. "You've done it once already, which is much better than most of us. I'm sure it will activate more regularly with practice."

"Yeah," Pax answered, relieved to escape further questioning.

Silence descended, the only sound two ex-street rat teenagers doing their best to replenish their energy stores after a brutal adventure.

Dahni was the first to finish. A few moments later, it was Pax's turn to be the object of amused scrutiny for his eating. Looking up, mouth full, Pax couldn't help a sheepish shrug.

"Oh, I almost forgot," Dahni said as he snapped his fingers. "Dulmot said your healing appointment is the hour before lunch. I'm not until tomorrow."

Pax nodded, glad he'd get some help soon. Having a leg out of commission made his danger sense itch continuously.

"And there was a message waiting when I got back." Dahni let his words trail off, adding nothing further.

When Pax looked up, his full belly twisted in a knot at his friend's expression. "What?"

"The Academy council wants to see us after lunch," he said quietly. "I'm sure they just have a few questions about what happened down there, right?"

"Yeah," Pax said without meaning it as he put his fork down. He'd lost his appetite.

UNCERTAIN PROSPECTS

PAX and his five friends sat in chairs against the austere walls of the spacious hallway outside the Academy council chamber, awaiting their turn. Mage Zanneth waited, too, sitting on his own down the hall, eyes closed and paying them no mind.

Pax shifted in his seat, wondering if he should meditate too. He'd had his appointment at the healer's hall for his leg, but it still ached. He planned to work on it more with his own healing spell when he had a chance. If his treatment by Mage Zayne earlier was any sign of how future treatment in the healer's hall would go, he would need to level his own healing as much as possible.

Pax clenched his jaw, remembering. Mage Zayne, the nasty lady from the Crucible, had been on duty again and assigned the most junior healer to his case. At least the young mage had been decently skilled, if still inexperienced and tentative.

Still, any healing was more than many others received, who were still waiting to be seen. His leg injury interfered with his abilities enough to move him up in the line. At least now he could walk with minimal pain, which was a vast improvement. He had plans for the rest of the week and it didn't include being laid up with injuries.

Glimpsing the slings both Rin and Dahni wore on opposite arms gave him a twinge of guilt. They were still on the waiting list. Pax didn't dare risk trying to help them with his own magic when real healers should be available soon. Thankfully, Amil, Tansa and Tyrodon had emerged with only minor injuries that low-leveled healing potions and a bit of rest could fix up.

And at least one decent thing had come from his visit to the healer's hall. Both Bryn and young Krasig had excellent prospects for recovery. The relief he felt at that eased his other concerns. There were plenty that were much worse off. There'd been more deaths besides Naexi last night, all on the city walls. With skilled healers, potions and spells, everyone fighting still had a much better chance of surviving. But that just meant they packed the healing halls this morning with moaning, critically injured survivors that were all in desperate need of attention.

Pax swallowed hard and tried not to think about everything he'd seen earlier. Buying better healing potions and improving his own skill had both moved up on his priority list.

And he still hadn't had a quiet moment to go through his new evolution possibilities, much less discuss them with either his friends or Incedis. He desperately needed a break, a little time to recover and figure things out. Why did they have to deal with this council nonsense?

The imposing double doors opened with a clang that echoed through the lofty marble-lined hall, startling Pax out of his thoughts. Three men walked out of the council hall, backs straight and postures proud. Pax recognized Aymer easily enough. An older man with similar features and the visible arrogance of wealth led the way. The third man dressed just as well, but his demeanor put him solidly behind the other two in terms of power.

"Mage Zanneth. You're next," a calm voice called out from the council chamber.

Pax couldn't help the knot of worry that tightened inside him as he watched the air mage stand and stride to the door without a glance in their direction. How much of Pax's magic had he seen or suspected?

"Coward," muttered Amil.

Pax realized his friend was still glaring at Aymer's group. He wasn't the only one giving disgusted looks at the boy, who had left them hanging on the wall to fight the hydra alone.

When Aymer glanced their way, their contempt didn't seem to faze him at all. In fact, he scowled, anger clouding his face. He reached out to tap the older man beside him and pointed their way.

"That has to be his dad, Master Wynrel." The disdain in Rin's voice was easy to hear, even though she kept it quiet, just loud enough for Pax to hear.

"Master Moneybags," Dahni muttered from the chair behind Pax, making Amil snigger and Pax fight back his own chuckle.

"You," Wynrel barked out, turning in their direction.

Next to him, Aymer looked smug as he followed his father.

It took all the strength Pax could summon to stiffen his back and hold the powerful man's gaze. Every street rat instinct insisted he slip away from the danger. The ingrained habit of surviving by fleeing and hiding was difficult to fight.

But in this new life of his strength, not stealth, seemed to be the key to surviving. Flashes of the beasts they'd faced through the night boosted his confidence enough to push him to his feet, despite the twinges in his still recovering leg. He wouldn't back down to this blustering fool. Master Wynrel was nothing compared to an angry hydra busting through rock walls.

Wynrel's face turned cloudy when he saw Pax stand up to him instead of cowering away. He stomped forward, jabbing a ringed finger into Pax's face. "You're done. When the council is through with you, you're going to die shivering and alone on some backwoods wall during your first beast wave. You'll regret killing Naexi for the rest of your miserable life."

Taken aback by the accusation, Pax turned to meet Aymer's gaze, ignoring his father. "That's what this is about? You didn't tell him the truth?"

Aymer's face blanched for a half beat.

"Tell me what?" His father aimed a demanding look at his son, one hand clenching into a fist and twitching.

Aymer's mouth moved, but he quailed in front of his father and said nothing. The flicker of fear in the boy's eyes and his flinch ruined Pax's glee that had sprung up at seeing Aymer getting his due. He'd seen the same fear in Tomis' eyes after he'd left his father to join the Vipers. The pain faded, but never quite disappeared.

Shaking off the memory, Pax straightened and pulled Wynrel's attention from his son. "I will." He emphasized the two words with enough strength for them to echo off the surrounding walls.

Wynrel turned slowly, looking astonished that a boy would dare interrupt him. "You will *what?*" It sounded more like a threat than a question.

Pax ignored him and turned to meet Aymer's gaze instead. "Regret *not saving* Naexi for the rest of my life."

Aymer swallowed. His gaze dropped as he took a small step back, distancing himself from the confrontation.

Pax couldn't decide how he felt about the boy who had obviously enlisted his father's power to ruin them all out of some mix of guilt and spite.

"Pay attention to me when I'm talking to you." Wynrel stepped forward and grabbed Pax's face, jerking it toward him.

Around him, his friends objected, outraged, as they stood in a staggered response. Chairs fell, pushed back, some even tipping to clatter on the marble floor behind them. Elements flared to life, fiery flame, twining water, cords of earth and gusting air, all prepared to lash out and protect their friend.

Wynrel's eyes went wide at the response. He jerked away from Pax as if scalded, stumbling two steps back out of instinct. When he realized what he'd done, his face flushed red, and he raised a hand again. "How dare you? Impudent—"

"—student mages with powerful spells they haven't quite learned to control yet," an imperious voice boomed from behind him. "You might want to be careful there."

"It's Mage Eldan," Aymer whispered to his father.

The other man with Wynrel leaned in to whisper something else in his ear. Wynrel scowled, obviously unhappy with the words.

Fascinated, Pax watched the man wrestle his temper under control and plaster on a pleasant mask. He aimed a last glare at Pax before turning to face Mage Eldan.

The elven air mage stood in the doorway to the Academy council chambers. She looked just as regal and powerful as she had that first day in the courtyard after the Awakening.

"Please tell me, I didn't just hear you threaten my academy students and disrupt our council proceedings," she continued, her tone icy and implacable. "I'm sure you know following through with that is an offense with specific and harsh sanctions by the Academy, not to mention our mage graduates everywhere. I don't think more money in Headmaster Ravalar's coffers could fix that. Do you?"

"I apologize, Mage Eldan," Wynrel said immediately, with a contrite bow of his head and a submissive slouch of his shoulders. "I was just encouraging these fine students to work harder and do better than they did last night."

Pax gaped at the radical transformation, which made him more worried about the man as an enemy.

"What a snake," Rin whispered, and Pax had to agree.

"Their performance is for us to judge, not you." Mage Eldan didn't give the man an inch.

Pax saw the flush of anger creep up the back of Wynrel's neck, but the man still bowed his head in agreement.

"I apologize for taking more of your valuable time. We'll be going." He turned and strode past the waiting students, his fine boots not quite stomping away.

Pax caught the glimpse of a hand cuffing the back of Aymer's head just before the trio disappeared around the corner. It made Pax realize that maybe those born to wealth didn't always have the amazing lives he'd imagined.

～

ZANNETH TOOK SO long to reappear from the council chamber that Pax's imagination spun with a host of scenarios, each ending worse and worse for him and his friends.

The air mage finally stepped out, his expression composed and collected, as usual. He showed the smallest bit of hesitation as he glanced down the far hallway before looking back toward where Pax and his friends sat.

Seeming to decide something, he suddenly strode toward them, his flowing robes swirling around his long legs. In his peripheral vision, Pax saw his friends straighten, a mix of worry and hope easy to read in their expressions. All morning, they'd been discussing what would happen when they faced the Academy Council.

Tansa had argued they were just first-year students following the direction of their instructors, so no one could hold them accountable for any of it. Amil's go-to argument was that they'd closed the breach. Disobeying direct orders didn't matter in the face of saving lives. Dahni and Rin had kept mostly silent. Pax wasn't sure if it was because they knew they'd be fine or they were making plans for the opposite.

No one really mentioned that Tyrodon, as the crafting student not involved directly in the fighting, had the best chance of avoiding trouble. The council had still summoned him, because the incident had happened on mage territory. His summons had an additional clause that the crafting academy would need to approve the mage council's verdict before enforcing it.

Besides, all of their worries paled compared to what Pax knew would happen if his prohibited magic came to light. A sense of irony suddenly filled him. Not long ago, he had hated even the idea of being awakened as a mage.

But now? He swallowed hard. Now, he couldn't imagine what he'd do without it.

"I apologize for this farce being forced on you younglings." The slight frown on Zanneth's angular face was more emotion than he usually showed. "Truth is something that should be simple and irrefutable. Yet somehow, the *politics*"—he almost spat the word as he threw a glance over his shoulder—"in that room are twisting the truth. Normally, I wouldn't even speak to the subjects of a hearing. If I did, it would be to instruct you to answer with the truth."

When Zanneth stopped to consider his next words, Pax wasn't the only one listening intently. It was more than he'd ever heard the Gryon say on a single occasion. That he felt obligated to give them advice was even more worrisome.

"I recommend you do the following." Zanneth raised a hand and ticked off each point on his bony fingers. "Don't volunteer information. Answer truthfully, but with as little as you can. If a truth might hint that you have broken rules or tradition, substitute another truth instead."

Pax was still trying to process the advice when Zanneth clapped his hands to his sides and bent into a deep, respectful bow.

He straightened and in a solemn voice said, "Good luck, students. Last night, you fought with fierceness to protect those weaker than you. I honor you for that." Without waiting for their response, he turned on his heels and left.

"Wow." Amil stared after the Gryon.

"Blast." Rin's curse was just as quiet.

Dahni, Tyrodon and Tansa said nothing, though each looked even more nervous.

"Students. Please enter." The sharp command made them all startle. The steward stood in the doorway to the council chambers, looking at them expectantly.

None of them stood immediately, instead exchanging worried looks with each other.

"Now." The command was just as direct, with only a touch of irritation.

Pax forced himself to his feet. There would be no running from this. The least he could do for his friends was take the lead. He paused just enough for the others to stand and follow him before he walked across the hall and stepped through the lofty doorway.

He almost missed a step as he got his first sight of the extravagant room with its lavish furnishing. Luckily, this last week had helped inure him to such intimidating sights. Five mages clad in resplendent robes sat behind a long bench of rich, polished wood. Their chairs were works of art, edges carved with animals and elements that looked almost alive, while rich velvet cushions made sure they were comfortable.

As far as Pax could tell, none of the chairs would look out of place in a throne room. In contrast, the chairs down on the floor facing them were simple wood, straight backs and no padding. Core-powered lighting hidden somewhere in the ceiling bathed the entire chamber in soft light, leaving almost no shadows. Long banners and tapestries hung from the walls full of intricate patterns and images that made Pax want to take a closer look.

Instead, Pax kept his gaze up and focused on the men and women waiting for them. With as much confidence as he could muster, he strode to the center chair and stood, waiting for the others to file in behind him. He kept his back straight and his chin up. He refused to show any of the mages that they intimidated him.

Scanning their expressionless faces, he recognized Mage Eldan on the far right. She caught his eye, and the quick wink she gave him was so unexpected he almost let his surprise show. Grappling for control of his own expression, he had to admire how fast her features returned to the same bored indifference of the others.

Pax hadn't met the three mages in the center, though the middle one with the haughty expression was familiar, Headmaster Ravalar. A stoic, dwarven woman sat on his left, while on his right sat another officious-looking mage who gave them all an impatient look.

A flicker of disgust showed on his face as his eyes passed over Pax. For a moment, Pax wasn't sure exactly how he'd angered the mage until he caught the mage's eye on his left forearm with its concealing sleeve. It took Pax a moment to realize the problem, because his friends had accepted the handicap so readily, he'd almost forgotten about it. But now, it seemed a mage on the council had something against the monster-touched.

Great. Pax had just decided this was going to be a disaster when, to his surprise, he saw Mage Incedis seated in the last spot on the left.

With an iron grip on his control, Pax didn't let his flare of hope show when he recognized his mentor on the council. Incedis did the same, not meeting his eyes or giving any acknowledgement. Pax had to hope he was acting, too.

"Sit down already, so we can finally finish with this debacle." The headmaster snapped out. What had been a mild irritation flared to angry impatience now that they had all entered the council chamber.

Heart sinking, Pax took his seat in the center of the row, his friends following his example in silence. Pax wasn't sure what a 'debacle' was, but it couldn't be good.

INTIMIDATING COUNCIL

PAX WAS MORE than pleased when the next half hour of questioning visibly frustrated Headmaster Ravalar. Following Zanneth's advice, the first-year students stayed tight-lipped, requiring repeated questions to draw out every answer.

His favorite was when it was Amil's turn to summarize the night's activities. "We killed monsters. No one didn't quit. We saved the school. It was the right thing to do." After the curt report, Amil leaned back, crossed his arms and limited further answers to a handful of monosyllabic words until the mages finally gave up.

They questioned Pax last, giving his nerves plenty of time to worsen. He did his best to follow his friends' examples. By the reactions of the council members, it seemed he was succeeding. The two mages he didn't know looked visibly impatient. Mage Eldan let out intermittent huffs and kept shuffling papers noisily in front of her, earning her glares from Ravalar.

Just as he thought Ravalar was finishing up, the headmaster looked at him and asked another question. "How did you combine different magics to subdue the hydra's tentacles?"

After the long, boring routine, the surprise question almost got a reaction out of Pax. He caught himself just in time.

The sudden hush in the room made it clear this was a serious subject. Pax had been afraid of what would happen if someone had noticed details about his magic, but the sudden mood shift of the mages on the council made him wonder if the consequences might be even worse than he'd imagined.

Pulling on his best acting skills, Pax let his brow furrow and forced the most genuine expression of confusion he could muster. "What do you mean?" Then he glanced at his friends with the same confused expression as if they might know what the headmaster was asking.

Ravalar's stare bored into Pax when he turned back, not looking fooled at all by the act. An unexpected flush of calm came out of nowhere and helped Pax keep control. In the lull, Pax could suddenly read Ravalar's expression better. He knew nothing. This was all a gambit to surprise information out of Pax. The knowledge was just what Pax needed to keep his act intact.

When a notification flashed at the bottom of his vision, he realized what must have happened. His Charisma had leveled up again and with perfect timing.

"According to your fellow students, you proposed combining different types of mana to overcome the hydra, correct?" The satisfied look in Ravalar's eyes told Pax that the man had been waiting for the perfect time to spring this question.

Out of the corner of his eye, Pax could see Incedis looking even more stone-faced than earlier. His danger sense screamed at Pax to be extremely careful here.

He spared a thought to curse Aymer for his troublemaking as he scrambled for the best way to answer. Knowing any hesitation would look bad, he relied on Zanneth's advice. Use the truth and nothing but the truth.

"I don't know what Aymer meant by that." Pax did his best to summon a bit of genuine bewilderment, so his expression would look more natural. "We never combined our mana to defeat the hydra, Headmaster Ravalar. We all fought with the magic our instructors taught us to use this week. No one ever mentioned how to do something like that. Is it even possible?"

"It's forbidden!" The man sitting next to Ravalar broke in, flushed with indignation. "It's blasphemy against Vitur to use magic that way. How do you think the Cataclysm happened?"

"Oh." Pax plastered on surprise and horror this time. "I'm sorry. I would never . . . everything I did was to save people, not hurt them."

"You only used your air magic last night?" Ravalar asked, his eyes still narrow as he watched Pax closely.

"I only used my own magic," Pax immediately responded, making his voice as earnest as possible. Then he placed a hand over his heart. "I swear by Vitur that I didn't combine my magic with any other student's." Technically, he'd only guided the mana of his friends. His light magic had merged a bit with the hydra's, but the beast was obviously not a student.

Both Ravalar and the man next to him glared at him for a long, silent moment. Pax felt his future balanced on a tightrope and desperately tried to prepare more statements that were technically true to field the next questions.

If he survived this, Pax vowed to thank Zanneth for his coaching. Pax didn't want to imagine how this would have gone if he'd come in unprepared.

"I don't think you understand how serious this subject is." The mage next to Ravalar was more flushed, his voice getting louder. "Combining magic directly flouts Vitur's laws. Dabbling in this will force us to extinguish your mana and send you back home as a laborer. Is that what you want?"

Pax couldn't keep from blanching and shaking his head. He'd expected some kind of stiff penalty, but extinguishing his magic? That was supposed to only be for mages who refused training.

"That's enough, Mage Herwin," Ravalar interjected. The glare he aimed at the mage next to him broke him out of his mini tirade.

"I apologize, Headmaster," the mage said, sitting back in his seat, his posture suddenly submissive again.

Ravalar sighed and shook his head. "While I applaud your fervor for Vitur's laws, I am still trying to get the truth from these students, understand?"

Mage Herwin bobbed his head in agreement. Pax wanted to shake the man's hand. Now Pax knew the consequences would be extreme if others discovered his secret.

The headmaster turned back to them. "Now that you realize how severe the penalty is for breaking these rules, I'm sure you'll be extremely forthcoming with the truth of what happened last night, correct?"

Pax was pretty sure he wasn't the only one nodding eagerly while planning the exact opposite.

"Now, tell me every detail about the powerful attack at the end of the battle?" Ravalar asked, his gaze fixed on Pax like a beast intent on a kill.

For a moment, Pax didn't have to fake his confusion, wondering which of their last attacks he meant. But then he saw a flicker of tension from Incedis and realized what Ravalar was asking.

Despite the odd flavor of his mentor's last blast of magic, Pax had no intention of saying anything that might throw suspicion on the only mage who had listened to him about the danger in the catacombs.

"Thank you for calling our attacks powerful," Pax said, letting a sheepish gratitude fill his voice as he bet everything on his act of an oblivious student. "We're just first-years, but by following what we've learned in just a few days of instruction here, we could fight side by side and overwhelm the hydra long enough for stronger mages to come back later and finish the job."

"I'm not talking about your attacks, you imbecile," Ravalar snapped.

It was all Pax could do to stifle his pleased reaction to successfully goading the man. Instead, he plastered a contrite expression on his face. "I'm sorry, Headmaster, sir. I thought—"

"That's just the problem. You obviously can't think. I want to know what kind of magic lit up the cavern last night at the end of the battle and—"

"Oh, enough already," Mage Eldan interrupted with a bored drawl.

"It's obvious to everyone here that these are brand new students who did the best they could."

Ravalar sputtered, almost apoplectic at being interrupted. "You will *not* interrupt—"

"Oh, get off your high horse, Zory. I changed your diapers when you were little."

Ravalar's mouth gaped open and closed. A strangled hiss made it past his throat before he finally managed to speak. "My name is Headmaster Zhorron Ravalar. You will address me with respect or else—"

"Or else what?" An icy threat suddenly replaced Eldan's bored nonchalance.

Pax shivered, glad he wasn't between the two mages.

"You have no control over my hereditary council position and the privileges it grants me." Eldan delivered the facts with a finality that no one disputed.

Ravalar must have sensed he'd taken a wrong step, because he clamped his mouth shut, looking torn. If Pax hadn't despised the man, he might have felt bad for him. Ravalar would obviously lose prestige if he backed down, but Eldan had an aura of crazy power that fairly screamed danger right now.

"Perhaps we can address the consequences for the students disobeying a direct order by their superiors during a battle?" Mage Herwin spoke calmly, carefully not meeting either Ravalar's or Eldan's eyes. The way he inserted the idea spoke of plenty of experience mediating conflicts between the two in the past.

Eldan glared at the man before folding her arms and leaning back without objecting.

"Yes, thank you, Mage Herwin. Let's move on to the clear infractions," Ravalar said eagerly, grasping at the offered lifeline. "We've heard clear testimony that all of you heard and understood the order to retreat but disobeyed it, correct?"

Pax swallowed hard as all the powerful mages' attention shifted back to them. Why couldn't they keep arguing amongst themselves a little longer?

A CLOSE CALL AND NEW ENEMIES

PAX WASN'T the only one who didn't like the way Ravalar had talked about their actions. Instead of giving them credit for risking their lives to save everyone trapped in the cavern and the vulnerable campus above, Ravalar's phrasing painted them as disobedient rebels.

When Amil opened his mouth to object, Rin elbowed him, and he clamped it shut. It took an effort of will, but Pax followed suit. With Eldan arguing on their behalf, it was probably better to say as little as possible and let her defend them instead.

Ravalar's glower strengthened as his eyes moved along the line of students. "This also led directly to the death of another first-year student, her life cut short right at the cusp of great potential. We can't just ignore this, despite how *brand new* these students are." He shot a smug look toward Mage Eldan before turning back to glare at the students. "Do you deny this?"

Amil turned and glared at Pax, expression expectant. Pax shot a look to Eldan and then to Incedis to see if either planned to speak up. Besides, how bad could the punishment be, compared to the extreme one for using forbidden magic techniques? They were only first-year students, not seasoned war veterans.

Ravalar jumped in before Pax could decide to speak, a satisfied smirk spreading across his face. "In that case, and as Headmaster of the Academy, it is my sad duty to inform you we will cut your tenure at our fine institution short to the minimum training requirement of one year—"

Pax's relief at successfully protecting his secret disappeared in a flash as Ravalar's words condemned them to something almost as bad as losing their magic. He looked at Incedis, who didn't object despite the look of regret on his face.

"But we saved everyone." Amil's yell silenced everyone in the hall as he leapt to his feet, fists clenched. "We almost died to protect everyone here, and everyone out there." He swept a hand toward the windows. "And Naexi did, too. She's a bigger hero than any of you will ever be!"

The lavish tapestries couldn't keep his outcry from echoing in the chamber. The entire mage council looked taken aback by his outburst.

Pax stood immediately, standing next to his friend in support. Rin, Dahni, Tyrodon and Tansa followed suit, closing ranks with each other as they faced the powerful mages in front of them. Pax couldn't help the surge of pride that rushed through him. Whatever happened next, they would support each other.

Eldan's gaze traveled over them, and Pax hoped it was a flicker of respect he saw in her eyes. Yet she wasn't the first to speak.

"That still doesn't excuse disobeying orders in a battle, especially when it led to a student's death." Herwin's officious voice finally broke the silence.

"This is their first year at the academy." Incedis' voice was just as officious and calm. He turned to look at them without a hint of support or friendliness. "Have any of you completed your first shift on the Academy walls and received instructions on how to handle yourselves in battle?"

It took Pax half a second to grasp the implications of the question. He immediately joined his friends in their chorus of negatives.

Incedis nodded, but it was Eldan who spoke next.

She clapped her hands as if their answers had settled the matter. "Obviously, we can't hold them responsible for something they had no training in after arriving on campus just a few days ago. In fact, continuing to fight in the face of mortal danger is an admirable quality we hope to train in our students, isn't it?"

"Yes, but—" Ravalar raised a hand in her direction, looking beleaguered now.

She ignored him. "And why were you going to restrict these talented new students full of potential to a single year of training without a vote, Headmaster?"

"It's an obvious infraction, and they confessed. There is no need for a vote."

"But I insist," she said with a purr. "I don't like the implication that you're letting Wynrel and his son lead you around by the nose with their coin. You are required to act in the best interests of our Academy, not your pet merchant. Have you forgotten our empire is in a battle for survival here, Zory? What good is coin if we've got swarms of beasts rising under our feet and need to be saved by first-years?"

"Use my proper title and name," he barked. "And they didn't save us. The mages we sent afterward killed the hydra and sealed the breaches."

"Oh, save me from your stupidity." She scoffed and stood. Her voice took on an official sing-song tone. "As the current holder of the Eldan family's hereditary position on Shieldwall Academy's council, I call for a vote on whether these fine new students have the rest of their training cut short because they risked their lives for us last night. Please vote in favor or against."

Ravalar looked appalled that she'd superseded his authority, but it was apparently something she had the power to do. "In favor," he growled, casting his vote and then looking to either side of him.

"In favor." Herwin, next to him, quickly added.

Ravalar smiled, only to have it turn to a frown as the silence lengthened with no other votes.

"Against," Eldan said in a satisfied voice, as if she already knew the outcome.

"Against." Incedis was next.

Another silence, and all eyes turned toward the fifth member of the council, a dwarven woman with skin leathered by age. She hadn't spoken the entire time, but her eyes were full of lively intelligence as she took her time to examine each of the students.

When she looked at Pax, it felt as if she could see right through him. While he had secrets, he hoped she couldn't see, he wanted her to see his determination to become a powerful mage to save not only his friends and new family, but as many innocents as he could.

With a single abrupt nod, she looked at Mage Eldan, who still stood on the left, waiting. "Against."

"Yes!" Amil let out an excited whoop that got him a stern look of disapproval from Ravalar. His friends shushed him, too, but had grins splitting their faces at the outcome.

"Then it's decided," Eldan said as she dusted off her hands. "Now let's go get something to eat and celebrate all the heroes from last night, the ones who fought on the walls and those who fought beneath them."

"Wait," Ravalar said, holding up a hand. "I can't limit them to a single year of training without a majority vote. But as headmaster, it is within my purview to dole out punishments for infractions. I hereby impose the punishment for a level four infraction, a fine of fifteen academy points and four silver."

Pax's mouth dropped open in horror at the amount.

"That's almost everything we just earned," Rin whispered.

"Really, Zory?" Eldan said, her nose wrinkled in disgust. "This is an obvious maneuver to make sure Wynrel's brat wins the points competition this week. I'll make sure news about this gets out. The academy won't forget this."

"That's not what—" Ravalar's face reddened in confirmation despite his objection.

"A level four is too high," Incedis broke in, his voice calm but firm. "You're forgetting that these students were the ones to discover the danger to the Academy. Without their warning, beasts would be overwhelming the Academy as we speak."

"But they still disobeyed a direct—" Herwin held up a hand to interrupt.

"I wasn't finished speaking." Incedis snapped back, his voice suddenly full of hot power.

Herwin flushed and clamped his mouth shut.

"You're also forgetting that of all of us here, I was the only one in that cavern last night, fighting alongside these brave children. The danger to all of us and the entire academy was real and imminent. If they hadn't disobeyed that order and fought the hydra to a standstill, it would have most likely broken through the wall, letting in a flood of all levels of beasts to attack us, not just level 1s. Take half a second to imagine what that would have looked like while all of our strongest were busy on the walls."

It heartened Pax to see Herwin's face lose some of its color while the dwarven mage's expression turned somber.

Incedis turned to meet and hold Headmaster Ravalar's gaze. "If they'd obeyed that order, and the hydra broke through, we'd have a *lot* of dead students, not just one. And that's not counting all our support staff."

Ravalar didn't answer, obviously calculating how all of this would play out when word got out to the rest of the academy. Pax held his breath, hoping Incedis' words would sway the man.

"Fine," Ravalar snapped, turning to scowl at the students. "A level three infraction. But no lower, not with the Ralodi heir dead. That's ten academy points and two silver. Now you're dismissed. You can go now."

Amil jumped up, looking more than ready to get out. And he wasn't the only one.

"Wait." The single word by the dwarven mage stopped them in their tracks. Once they all were looking back at her, she clapped a closed fist to her chest and bowed her head in respect. When she looked back up, she said, "Thank you for your bravery and sacrifice. It is exactly what our empire needs right now."

The simple words changed the mood of the entire council hall. A somber mood of respect and gratitude replaced the bickering and political maneuvering. Both Eldan and Incedis stood and silently copied the other mage's gesture of respect.

Ravalar and Herwin didn't move, but neither spoiled the moment either.

Feeling a need to acknowledge the unexpected tribute, Pax straightened and returned their bows. His friends turned and followed his example.

"Thank you," he finally said, the simple words inadequate to express everything he felt at that moment. But he didn't have any better.

PLANS AND REWARDS

STEPPING out of the administration building, Pax still couldn't believe how much a single beast surge, no matter how powerful, had changed the academy. From what he'd heard, the city beyond was just as bad or worse.

Every able-bodied person had dropped their usual tasks to join in clearing and processing the overwhelming number of beasts killed last night. He'd heard that, in some sections of the wall, they piled up so high, other beasts had used the piles as jumping platforms to reach the parapet.

Running steps from behind him made Pax and his friends glance over their shoulders and step to the side to let a group of third-year students pass. One third-year gave them a weary glance before noticing Pax and doing a double take.

Pax tensed. But the student just tapped his friends before slowing and giving his group a respectful tip of his head. "Well done last night. You did us all proud."

"Um, thanks." Pax gave an awkward wave, not sure how to respond.

The eyes of the other two students widened in recognition as they saw the rest of Pax's group. One of them chimed in her approval, but the third scowled. Before he could say anything, his friend elbowed him. He kept quiet, but Pax could hear an irritated discussion start up as they took off again.

"Killing beasts is much easier than dealing with the mess afterward," Amil muttered.

Pax had to agree as their group continued, doing their best to stay clear of all the traffic. Carts and wagons trundled everywhere, crowding the paths between the workshops and the academy section of the wall. Ones loaded to the brim moved in one direction while empty ones clattered back on the return trip. Weary faces and dirty clothes seemed universal regardless of station and magical power. No one was exempt from helping today.

"I guess losing all that silver and the academy points isn't so bad when you see this," Dahni said quietly. "We're lucky to be alive. And access to healers for kids like us? Could you ever imagine we would live like this?" He looked at his friends, all of whom, besides Tansa and Tyrodon, were former street rats.

Amil shook his head but aimed an angry look back in the direction they'd come from. "Flickin' 'crats. We earned those points and silver fair and square, fighting to save them."

"Not them," Pax said quietly, slowing his steps. "The kitchen staff. Other students. Everyone left behind when the fighters raced to the walls." He met the gazes of his friends, who had slowed to listen. "And each other. We fought to save each other."

Nods greeted his words, and Pax was glad to see some of the angry frustration in Amil fade.

"Besides." Pax let a smile spread across his face. "I'm pretty sure Headmaster Ravalar was too lazy to even check our Academy Point balances before he fined us."

"What?" Dahni blurted out. "You had more than ten? I only had six and am really glad his fine only took those instead of leaving me negative."

Pax hesitated, shooting a quick glance at both Rin and Amil for permission. They nodded, though Rin took a moment longer than

Amil. Pax gestured for the group to step off the path with him and gather closer.

"We have a vermin-killing quest that Mistress Nymeli, our supervisor, negotiated, so it counts beasts killed in the catacombs toward the total. We advanced it to intern level right before the mission with Incedis. 5 coppers per kill and 1.5 Academy Points for every 10 kills." Pax stopped speaking and just waited.

Eyes widened as the implications hit.

"You're right," Amil said with a joyful whoop, his eyes unfocused as he obviously finished checking the standings. "We're still in the top 10!"

Pax grinned as everyone else went silent and checked for themselves.

"No way," Tyrodon was the first to speak. "Can I get in on this? Is this a class-specific assignment, or do you think it would be available on our crafting board?"

"Are there still assignments available?" Dahni asked. "How do I get one?"

"Why didn't you tell us this before the mission?" Tansa cut in, frowning.

"Hold on." Pax raised his hand to stop the questions. "First, Tyrodon, come with us to help Mistress Nymeli. If anyone can figure out a way for a crafter student to join us, she could. Dahni, she took the assignment off the board, but as the supervisor, she should be able to assign you, if you'd like. And Tansa, there just wasn't time and none of us had any idea what would happen."

"But what's the point of getting the assignment now that the breach is closed?" Tansa still looked disgruntled at missing out, and Pax didn't blame her. Ravalar and his agenda had wiped out any gains she had made last night.

Pax gave her a helpless shrug. "A few beasts should still be wandering around down there, even with the breaches closed. The week isn't over. I'm sorry about what you lost, but we still have time to kill more for the Academy Points and coin."

"It's not your fault." Tansa let out a sigh and relented. "My family just isn't important enough to protect me from Ravalar's punishments. I shouldn't take it out on you. You're just doing your best."

"Thanks." Pax gave her a helpless smile before looking at the other three, who felt almost as close as Amil and Rin. "The three of us are just street rats who know even less than most about magic. We're trying our best to survive. But we know who our friends are. You had our backs against the hydra and again in the council room, sharing as little as possible about our hydra fight. That means we have your backs, too."

He paused and saw agreement in both Amil and Rin. Turning back to the others, he took a leap of faith, forcing down the paranoid thoughts that warned him about trusting so many people he'd just met. With his new level of Charisma, Pax found it much easier to find the right words.

"The three of us have an alliance already. We've agreed to help each other out, but not at the expense of our own interests. And when we get valuable items we can't use ourselves, we give first dibs to each other. Basically, we started as allies, cautious, as I'm sure you guys can understand. The streets don't really encourage trusting others."

Dahni nodded while Tansa and Tyrodon looked thoughtful.

"Now, though . . . well, we're—" He hesitated before using the word that was tied to so many complex emotions inside him. "—family. We're family now. And we want you to join us. What do you say?"

Pax held out his hand. Amil and Rin copied him, reaching out to the other three.

Tyrodon was the first to respond again, gripping Pax's hand and pumping it before moving on to the other two. "I'm in. Last night was terrifying, but one of the best things I think I've ever done."

"I've been in since last night, too," Dahni said, following Tyrodon and shaking each of their hands. "And I understand if you take a while to trust us with your secrets, including exactly how you helped us beat the hydra. But I've got my own, so I get it."

Pax forced himself not to flinch at the hint that Dahni had noticed something unusual. He'd already decided that keeping his secret safe by trusting no one wasn't the path he wanted to follow. So, he made himself meet Dahni's gaze with a smile.

When Dahni finished and stepped back, all eyes turned to Tansa.

She shifted, looking uncomfortable. "Look, you just admitted you don't know a lot about magic or the academy. Well, you've crossed some powerful people already, and I don't know if you realize how hard they're going to work against you."

"So, you're out?" Rin asked, her eyes suddenly hard.

"No," Tansa said, looking surprised at the idea. "I was just thinking I might help our group better as a secret ally. You know, not openly hang out with you, maybe even act like I don't like you guys. Just so I can keep a better eye on what flicks like Galen or Aymer are doing."

"You mean you get all the benefits of hanging with the other popular power mages and stay clean of our street rat reputation at the same time?" Rin looked even more suspicious now.

"No, that's not what I mean." Tansa's tone was hot. "I'm happy to be with you openly. I'm just saying we'd be throwing away a chance to keep tabs on our enemies. But whatever. If you think it's a stupid idea, I'm still in."

Rin subsided, finally looking as if she was considering Tansa's idea instead of just reacting.

"I guess this is a good first test," Pax said when he felt they'd had enough time to think. "Tansa as our secret agent or not?"

"We all get a vote?" Tyrodon asked in surprise.

"Of course." Pax nodded. "We're in this together. I only led us during the cavern battle because you all insisted. So, what do you think?"

Rin was the last to agree and held Tansa's gaze for a long moment. "You'll meet with us, in private, at least once a week, and let us know everything you've found out?"

"Or more often, if things come up," Tansa said, her gaze resolute.

"Fine," Rin said. "In a place like this, we're going to need information almost as much as coin and power."

"Exactly," Tansa said with a firm acknowledgement.

"Perfect." Amil gave a pleased nod before turning to look toward the dining hall. "Now can we get over to helping Mistress Nymeli before anyone else gives us different orders because we're standing here doing nothing?"

"You're just hungry," Dahni joked, clapping Amil on his shoulder.

"Hey, power mages need a lot of fuel. Tell them, Tansa."

"Don't bring me into this," Tansa said with a grin, shifting to the side with hands held up defensively.

"One last thing." Pax hurried to speak before they all got off topic. "Is it alright if I invite Bryn and her friend Tasar to join us once she recovers?"

"Of course," Amil said with a grin at the idea. "Tasar is good people, and Bryn will whip us into shape."

Pax wasn't the only one to suppress a groan, knowing Amil was right. But the others still nodded.

"Then let's go eat." Grinning, Pax got them moving again, feeling much more hopeful than he had during the stand-off with the academy council members.

"We can all use a bit of a break," Rin agreed, her expression more relaxed now as she shifted out of the way of a young messenger racing past. "But it'll probably only be a short one."

Tansa frowned and shot her a questioning look.

"Well, the beast waves should be light for a while after a surge as bad as last night. But we'll need the extra time, since you know Mistress Nymeli will have us skinning and butchering everything we left down below for days."

That got a load of groans until Rin interrupted. "Don't forget, the beasts Mistress Nymeli claims for the kitchens won't belong to the mages and won't fall under Ravalar's control. She'll give us a fair split and even help us sell them."

A wide grin spread across Tansa's face, followed by the others. Their mood improved and quickening their steps, the group of friends headed for a meal followed by work that promised to be as bloody as last night's . . . but much less dangerous.

ANTICIPATED REVENGE

"I CAN'T BELIEVE Saturday is finally here." Pax leaned in close to be heard as their group struggled to stay together in the mass of students jockeying for position. He was so exhausted after the last two days and couldn't wait for a chance to not only rest, but to go over his advancements and make some decisions.

Up ahead, the guards pulled open the gates to the Academy parade grounds, backing up quickly to let the crowd stream in.

"I know. It feels like weeks have gone by instead of days since the council ambushed us on Thursday." Rin sent him an excited smile, despite how tired she looked.

Amil, using his bulk to push through the crowd for them, shot a happy look back over his shoulder.

"Stay together." Dahni reached out to grab Pax and Rin's arms and pull them in close behind Amil.

Rin evaded his grip, but moved in, regardless.

"We're sticking close, Amil." Dahni had to almost yell to be heard over the din. "Keep pushing through the crowd and find us good seats."

Working to keep up, exhaustion tugged at Pax after the recent brutal work. They'd worked back-to-back shifts, processing all the slain beasts while also squeezing in hunting trips to clear out the left-over beasts that had scattered into the tunnels. Their unusual attraction to Pax's magic had turned into something more useful than dangerous, attracting stragglers instead of an entire horde.

On an easier note, he'd followed Mistress Nymeli's advice and returned two of his assignments: Charity Clinic and Maintenance Trainee. With all the beasts to mop up in the tunnels, he'd wanted to beg off his assignment at the Academy Workshop, too, but the potential for scrounging parts and learning how to craft items in the future wasn't something he wanted to give up. At least the shift there had given him a change of pace from the dark catacombs.

As Pax and his friends moved into the stadium, the exuberance of the academy population streaming into the celebration was contagious and helped Pax push aside his weariness. Grins and excited chatter filled the air, and Pax let it flow over him and focus on a hard job finally done.

The city and academies had finished processing the aftermath of the beast surge. Workshops and classrooms were bursting at the seams with supplies. The capital was flush too, cores and coin in abundance.

Still, families had mourned at the city-wide altar ceremony for the fallen and there were still many recovering from serious injuries. As Pax followed Amil up onto a pathway between the rows of stadium seating, a twinge of sadness tugged at his joy as he remembered how Naexi's family had barred all but a select few from her services. At least they hadn't been able to prevent him from attending her altar ceremony. Many academy students had turned out to give homage to her last act of service as the life force of her soul reinforcing the wall of the Academy she was bound to and had loved. But today was a day to celebrate. And even though Pax had only known Naexi for a short time, he thought she would agree.

They finally found a section of bench wide enough to accommodate all of them. Squeezing into their seats, Pax thought about how

Ravalar had cheated them and couldn't help a self-satisfied grin spreading across his face. Today's revenge would be very sweet.

Pax swung his backpack off and placed it carefully between his legs. With a motion that had already become a new habit, he slipped a small piece of earth meat out of his inventory and slid it under the top flap.

Talpa's appendages grabbed eagerly onto his hand in their now-familiar ticklish fashion. The happy pulse of pleasure through their bond made Pax's smile widen.

"Nice seats," Dahni congratulated Amil as they exchanged fist bumps and got comfortable.

Rin, however, noticed what he was doing. "You brought him?" She cast a quick glance around them to see if anyone was paying them attention.

Thankfully, the crowd was busy getting settled and craning for a better view of the VIP stand set up down below.

"Sorry," he shrugged. "I got used to bringing him with me during all the work in the cavern the last few days. He doesn't enjoy being left in the room anymore."

"Well, he'll have to get used to it when classes start back up next week," Rin said, sounding stern. But then she ruined it by slipping a treat into the top of Pax's bag herself.

Another pulse of pleasure from Talpa.

"He says thanks," Pax said with a soft laugh. "And we're working on developing an ability so he can hide better. Just think of what he can do once he gets that working well."

Interest sprang into Rin's eyes, and she looked down at Pax's bag with an intent expression. "We need to find one of his siblings for me."

"I'm pretty sure Amil's first in line the next time we find a beast baby to tame. Besides, you know I can't share my spell."

Rin didn't look disappointed, though, just thoughtful. "If your scheme today works, we should have more than enough for a nice spending spree with Crafter Jacoby. I bet he can help me find a path that leads to taming."

"Or maybe we could find something in the library. I've been meaning to go as soon as we have a little free time."

"Oh." Rin held up a finger. "I keep forgetting to tell you, but another student mentioned that the library has yearbooks going back for decades."

Pax frowned, confused about where this was going.

Rin glanced around at the excited crowd. When it was obvious no one was paying them any attention, she leaned in. "Your family."

"What?" Pax was so surprised he almost forgot to keep his voice down.

"I just thought—" Rin hesitated, looking uncomfortable, like the conversation wasn't going how she'd expected. "You said you don't know what happened to them. And since magic runs in your family, maybe one of them used to be a student here. If they were, they might be in the yearbooks."

Pax sat back, too stunned to say a word and feeling completely blindsided. But he couldn't stop the sudden surge of ideas. Did magic run in his family? His parents had been leatherworkers, not mages. And guards had dragged his older brother, Titus, away to the Awakening. Could he really have awakened as a mage? It seemed ludicrous, but with both Pax and Amil here, it was obviously possible. It would explain why Pax had never seen him again.

"I'm sorry I mentioned it," Rin said softly. "My family is dead, so I guess I kind of got caught up in the idea of figuring out what happened to yours. They might be alive out there and I could help you find them . . . sorry. It was a dumb idea."

"No." Pax met her eyes and tried to convey how much the gesture meant to him. "That's probably the nicest thing anyone has ever done for me. Thanks."

She flushed and smiled, looking away in embarrassment.

"How about we go to the library together? You help me look through the yearbooks, and I'll help you look for info on taming."

"Deal." She cleared her throat and looked back in control. "Because I need to buy water and stealth stuff with our coin first and probably won't be able to afford a taming scroll anytime soon." She gave him a rueful shrug. "Though I guess it depends on how much coin we end up with. Do you really think this is going to work?"

His grin widened as he looked at her. "Depending on how arrogant you think 'crats are."

A chuckle replaced her worry. "Very."

"Then, as long as Mistress Nymeli comes through for us, I think we'll be able to pull off a surprise that everyone will talk about for days."

Dahni had leaned in closer to listen and now wore a dubious look. "You're all sure about this? There's still time to call it off. You know what Tansa said. Antagonizing the 'crats and drawing more attention from them might make things worse."

"Did they leave us alone when we were completely powerless, with no way to hurt them?" Now it was Amil who leaned in, a serious expression replacing his previous grin.

Dahni sighed and had to shake his head.

Amil's voice turned low and fierce. "Then we're going to fight for as much coin and power as we can until they're the ones who are afraid of us."

Rin nodded, and Pax was glad to see Dahni's spine stiffen. They would need to be as strong as possible for the foreseeable future. He just regretted that, as non-mages, neither Tyrodon nor Bryn were here today. He missed Tansa too. She'd been true to her word over the last few days, keeping them abreast of everything Aymer and Galen had been up to. And now, she would be sitting with one of their groups, pretending to join in their antics.

"Mages, students and workers of Shieldwall Mage Academy! Welcome to our weekly assembly and award ceremony!" The boosted voice of Headmaster Ravalar boomed out over the stands, making the crowd's noise fade as people settled down. The academy leader stood at a podium set up at the center of the field. Behind him, in three rows of comfortable chairs sat other important personages.

Pax recognized the other members of the Academy council as well as a few senior instructors. He couldn't help feeling a thread of predatory anticipation when he saw Master Wynrel seated with a handful of what were likely other city dignitaries. Pax clenched one fist and, despite what he'd told his friends, fought back his doubt that everything might fall apart at the last minute.

After everything they'd fought through, today's plan just had to work.

81

SETTING THE STAGE

"Mages, students and staff, I have to say this was a very difficult and trying week to start our semester." Headmaster Ravalar's voice filled the stadium.

Even at a distance, Pax could see the empathy and concern in his expression as his gaze traveled over the gathered crowd. "I'd like to start by taking a moment of silence to pay our respects and offer our gratitude to those we lost."

If Pax hadn't seen the other side of the man, the performance might have fooled him. In the stadium, a sudden, somber silence spread through the crowd and heads bowed.

"Too many warriors and mages died on our walls to the beast hordes. And finally, one of our own, first-year Naexi Ralodi." Ravalar said her name with a solemn tone. Then he fell quiet, letting the silence stretch out.

Pax could hear the wind rustling through the stands along with the cries of a flock of birds that flew by overhead.

"We can never repay them for their ultimate sacrifice for us." Ravalar straightened and let his voice fill with strength. "They set the example we followed by coming together to survive and triumph. We have grown together as we conquered one of the biggest beast surges on record. Thank you, mages and students of Shieldwall!" He practically yelled the last, his excitement greeted by a cheering roar of the type that only comes after surviving a terrifying disaster and coming out the other side alive.

Around the stands, people stood and cheered even louder. Others quickly followed and, in moments, the entire audience was on their feet with an uproar of approval.

Pax and his friends stood to join in. For a moment, standing in such a huge press of humanity celebrating their victory, there was no room for schemes and infighting. 'Crat versus street rat. Mage, student or worker. Everyone joined in together, happy to have survived and deriving strength from each other to face whatever came next.

Ravalar looked almost swollen with pride by the time everyone calmed down and let him speak again. "Before we get to the fun part, I have a few items of business."

This would have normally received a few groans, but the crowd was in such a good mood that they settled down patiently.

"Because we finished processing the aftermath of the surge this morning, I'm declaring the rest of today a holiday, in addition to tomorrow's normal day off."

Cheers greeted the pronouncement, and Pax couldn't help smiling as he fantasized about a hot bath and a nap. He might finally get the dried blood out from under his nails and heal his leg back to full strength. Plus, he really needed to unlock his air magic so he could get a real air spell before his next basic spells class.

"Monday, however, we will be back to our usual class and work schedule," Ravalar said once everyone had quieted down again. Now the usual number of groans greeted this announcement. "However," Ravalar said, holding up one hand and waiting for everyone to quiet. "I have two exciting pieces of news for the start of this new semester."

That got everyone's attention again.

"Because of the amount of processed loot from our section of the wall, along with your diligent help in the city over the last few days, there will be two bonus offers to all current students this semester.

The academy and some of these fine citizens sitting with us are funding enough prizes for the top five instead of the usual top three of each year's Academy Point standings every week."

Excited cheers greeted that announcement, and the headmaster had to hold up a hand to get the crowd to quiet down again.

"They will also fund a program to outfit the top team from each year with elite equipment for the upcoming Northern Purge. Team Week is always an exciting start to the academic year and sets the groundwork for success during the purge and in the class tournaments at the end of the year. Do your best to find trustworthy and powerful teammates you can rely on. The Academy Council will pick out the top teams for the elite gear prize the week before the purge."

That got a response, too, but an undertone of agitation tinged the noise, especially in the first-year section where they sat. Rin gave Pax a concerned glance, and he nodded, understanding they needed more information on this team thing as soon as possible. Dahni and Amil met their gazes, looking determined and ready to get to work again, too.

Pax made a few mental notes for planning sessions, but resolved to carve out some downtime for the team, too. They'd had an exhausting first week. Still, with enemies actively working against them, they would need more work than others to make sure they not only survived the purge, but came out the other side stronger and with more resources.

"Elite armor," Amil said, with a touch of longing in his voice.

Dahni let out a short laugh. "You know there's no chance the council will let any of us even get close to that prize. Besides, with how our student armor looked after fighting in the cavern, even an uncommon set would be an upgrade for us."

Amil gave a rueful shrug. "I can still dream."

"Don't forget how rich we're about to be," Rin said, motioning toward Headmaster Ravalar, who was accepting a clipboard from an officious man seated behind him.

As he held up his hands for attention again, the stands quieted, though an excited murmur still thrummed at a low level. "Now, this is what you've all been waiting for. Our first Academy Point winners of the new school year!" He paused for a few beats, letting the cheers wash over him.

Pax sat up straighter, pulled out a small device and looked over to the staff section he'd made sure to notice earlier. The straight posture of Mistress Nymeli was easy to pick out from among her surrounding staff, even from behind. Her hair, pulled back in a tight bun, gave Pax a good view of her emotionless profile. She kept her gaze focused on the headmaster as he spoke.

Pax looked down at the small device in his hands and forced himself not to fidget with it as the headmaster read off the winners of the senior class.

"Turgan got robbed."

Startled out of his thoughts by Rin's angry mutter, Pax tuned in to see the fourth-year winners parading off the stand with wide grins and prize scrolls in hand that they would redeem at the Quad-Academy Store. Turgan wasn't among them.

"He would have had third place if Ravalar hadn't fined him, too," Rin answered his unspoken question.

Now that Pax was paying attention, he could hear a discontented muttering poisoning the cheers for the winners. Looking around, he could see a scattering of angry expressions that mirrored how he felt. Turgan had kept a lot of the first-years alive that night, and instead of being heralded as a hero, he was being penalized.

"Moving on to the cream of our third-year class," Ravalar announced with a cheerful clap of his hands before he pulled up the next list to read aloud.

Pax couldn't be sure, but the headmaster's expression seemed to have an edge of tension that hadn't been there before.

"Aren't you going to push it?" Rin sounded worried, and flicked her eyes toward the signaling device in his hand.

She was right. The plan had been to signal Nymeli once the headmaster had started the awards, to give the system plenty of time to tally things before the first-years had their turn.

"Not yet," Pax muttered under his breath.

"If you wait any longer, we might miss the whole thing." Rin leaned in, sounding worried.

He turned to meet her eyes. "But if I get the timing right, it'll be so much worse for the 'crats down there."

She looked confused for a moment, glancing down at Ravalar grinning proudly as he handed the prize certificates to the third-years parading across the stage. A moment later, she sucked in a quick breath before her expression hardened into something fierce. "Yes. Do it," she whispered, her tone savage. "In front of everyone."

Pax returned her fierce grin. He loved how fast she picked up on the implications of his plans without him having to explain everything.

A flicker of movement caught his eye, and he saw Nymeli glancing back in his direction with an expectant look.

Expression hardening, Pax gave a slight shake of his head. She just nodded calmly and turned back to the front. She probably thought he was backing out.

When he'd explained his ideas the morning after the battle, she'd listened and even helped him go through all the pros and cons. In the end, though, Mistress Nymeli had said the choice was his and his friends'. She agreed to follow through on whichever they chose.

Now, she probably thought he'd changed his mind and decided to take the easier, less confrontational route.

But she'd be wrong.

82

TOPPLING EXPECTATIONS

"A ROUND of applause for our second-year winners, please."

"Now?" Rin asked, looking nervous.

Pax just shook his head. His entire focus narrowed to the podium as he watched for a specific action.

Sure enough, a moment later, the officious man behind the headmaster leaned forward and slipped a sheet of paper onto the podium. Ravalar's glance down turned into a satisfied smile.

It was time.

Pax pressed the signal, hoping he wasn't too late. He saw Mistress Nymeli flinch slightly, so he knew she got it. Now they just had to rely on their planning and hope things worked as expected.

According to all of their information gathering over the last two days, the academy's altar tallied and distributed points and coins almost instantly when students met the requirements.

After Ravalar's penalty, Pax, Rin and Amil had dropped considerably in the ranking, but not off the chart completely. They'd all enjoyed speculating how much backlash the headmaster got for not verifying that the huge ten-point penalty wasn't enough to eliminate them from the running completely.

In the end, though, it had looked like the headmaster and Wynrel would win, anyway. After the night of the battle, Aymer, Galen and a handful of other 'crats got busy, gaining as many points as they could. It quickly became obvious that even the vermin exploit wouldn't be enough to counter the connections the 'crats had for well-paying assignments.

With classes canceled to process the aftermath of the surge, the 'crats could substitute cushy assignments like tutoring wealthy youths to earn more points while everyone else was stuck finishing the brutal processing work.

A chance comment had changed everything and hatched their current plan. Pax had stopped by to visit Krasig in the healing hall and mentioned he really wished there was a way to save up points in secret and have them all awarded at once.

The young kitchen boy had asked for more details. Pax still remembered the sly smile on his face when he'd explained a work-around. Apparently, a supervisor could require their own approval for any aspect of an assignment, allowing unrewarded points and coin to accumulate without showing on the scoreboard.

It was a common setting to use with new workers as they learned the ropes and needed someone to check that they were doing things correctly. It gave Pax the seeds of a plan to surpass the 'crats without them seeing it coming.

"And last, but not least, it is my pleasure to bring the fine first-year student mages to your attention." Ravalar's voice fairly burst with pride. "Amid the greatest challenge our empire has ever faced, Vitur has sent us stalwart youth with powers greater than we've ever seen, a boon in our time of need. As a special bonus to encourage them at the start of their learning journey, this week's top finalists will all receive a piece of elite gear, in addition to the normal prize."

Pax couldn't help the mix of excitement and worry tearing at his insides. Elite gear! Even just a piece each could make an enormous difference in their training, not to mention their assignments and shifts on the academy wall.

He scanned his menu, praying to see that the system had tallied their points.

∼

Week 1: Shieldwall Academy First-Year Academy Point Top 10

1. Aymer Wynrel - 33
  2. Codrun Shadowforge - 32
  3. Hoset Wraithaxe - 31
  4. Kali Wynrel - 26
  5. Hammon Petor - 26
  6. Izoa Yelren - 25
  7. Tobin Milter - 24
  8. Amil Fajor - 19.5
  9. Rin Esta - 18.5
  10. Pax Vipersworn - 18.5

∼

A FLUSH of sick panic filled him as he opened his eyes and glanced at his friends. Nothing had changed. They were still sitting at the bottom of the list because of the headmaster's punitive ten-point fine.

Rin looked equally worried. Both Amil and Dahni gave him helpless shrugs. Pax craned his head and tried to catch Mistress Nymeli's attention, but she stared resolutely ahead, not glancing in his direction at all.

She'd promised to approve all the tasks they'd completed over the last few days when he signaled. They'd spent every extra minute down in the caverns, clearing out all the leftover beasts they could find, plus a decent number of actual vermin. The large influx of points and coin was supposed to shoot the three of them up to the top of the chart.

Did one of the 'crats get to her and convince her to betray them? He felt guilty even thinking the thought, but couldn't help his paranoia.

"Master Wynrel, leader of the Oakhouse Consortium, has long been a patron of the Academy." Ravalar continued his grandstanding as he motioned for Wynrel to come up and join him at the podium.

"This year, we are delighted to not only have his twins as new first-year students, but to see his son set a new first-year record in Academy Points this week, taking first place while his daughter has placed fourth. "

A smattering of polite cheering began, louder up front, closer to the podium. Ravalar hadn't paid this much attention to any of the winners in the other years. Pax could tell others were also noticing the favoritism.

Ravalar waved toward the front rows, and Pax saw two familiar figures stand up and walk toward the stairs that led up to the stand. Aymer's arrogant posture was easy to recognize. Back straight and chin up, he looked as if all of this was his due. His sister, however, seemed reluctant to be in the limelight. She stayed behind her brother and, though she kept her gaze up, she didn't meet anyone's eyes. She looked ready to have the whole thing over as soon as possible.

"While they're coming up, let's bring up the other three winners," Ravalar said with a cheery smile, looking down at his list.

"The points took too long to show up." Amil's words were glum.

Pax hoped that was all that had happened, since a betrayal at this point would be even worse. He shook his head and sank down into his seat, sick at their loss. He shouldn't have delayed the signal just to humiliate the headmaster and Wynrel's family. If he'd had Nymeli tally the points at the start of the assembly, they'd be the ones being invited up to the stands now.

A murmur in the crowd caught his attention and made him look up.

Ravalar read off names, only to trail off and aim an angry look at the noisy crowd. He had just opened his mouth to deliver an admonishment when the clerk behind him popped up to his feet and placed a hand on Ravalar's shoulder. Ravalar growled at him, but the man ignored it and leaned in to whisper urgently.

Ravalar's entire demeanor changed and everyone heard an angry, "That's not possible," before his clerk turned off the sound projector.

"Yes." Amil gave a quiet cheer as he opened his eyes and looked over at Pax. "Check the stats."

Hope bloomed inside Pax. He pulled up the standings, a fine tremor of excitement making his hands shake.

∼

Week 1: Shieldwall Academy First-Year Academy Point Top 10

1. Pax Vipersworn - 51.5
   2. Amil Fajor - 49.5
   3. Rin Esta - 48.5
   4. Aymer Wynrel - 33
   5. Codrun Shadowforge - 32
   6. Hoset Wraithaxe - 31
   7. Kali Wynrel - 26
   8. Hammon Petor - 26
   9. Izoa Yelren - 25
   10. Tobin Milter - 24

∼

A SHAKY LAUGH left his lips as he opened his eyes to meet the gazes of his friends. "It worked!" He couldn't help following with a quizzical question. "I thought Amil would be in first?"

"That was our idea. We got Mistress Nymeli to give you a *leadership* bonus—three academy points." Amil laughed and pulled him into a rib-crushing hug. "You deserve it, buddy."

Letting go of his worries, Pax grinned and pounded on his back before pulling a grinning Dahni into the hug, too. When he turned to Rin, she took a quick step back.

"No hugs," she insisted with a half-smile, but she reached out to pat his chest in congratulations.

He placed his hand over hers and gave it a quick squeeze before letting go and looking at his friends. "This is all of us. We did this together. Bryn, Tasar, Tyrodon and Tansa, too. We'll use the prizes and coin to make us all stronger."

The growing commotion around them finally pulled Pax's attention back to the situation. An upwelling of excitement had filled the first-year section with opposing voices raised in arguments. Fingers pointed their direction, and heads everywhere craned toward them.

"As the headmaster's assistant, it is my pleasure to finish announcing the winners on his behalf." The tentative clerk cleared his voice and looked over his shoulder for support from the other mages. His voice barely made a dent in the rising agitation of the audience.

Pax couldn't help grinning when he saw Wynrel and Ravalar had stepped aside to argue fiercely with each other, fists clenched and visages flushed red.

A loud screech from the sound projector broke through the noise and silenced everyone for a moment. It was just long enough for the timid assistant to blurt out instructions.

"Because of an unexpected update to the first-year standings, the previous announcement was incorrect. Would the following winners please come to the stand immediately: Pax Vipersworn, Amil Fajor, Rin Esta, Aymer Wynrel and Codrun Shadowforge. You've accelerated your growth through facing danger. Congratulations to you for all your hard work!"

The assistant's last words were almost completely drowned out by the growing noise mixed with both excited cheers and angry cries.

Pax had to swallow hard, disbelief and elation filling him in equal parts as he watched the chaos he'd help create spread through the entire gathered academy population. He shook his head, overwhelmed. Maybe he hadn't really thought this through.

FINAL TRIUMPH

"Follow me again, guys." Amil had to yell the words, jerking Pax out of his daze. His friend looked almost as pleased to wade through the crowd as he was to battle beasts.

Pax had expected the anger of the headmaster and Wynrel, but he'd completely underestimated the reaction of the rest of the academy population. He felt as if he'd kicked over an anthill, only to discover a tremendous battle already taking place under the surface.

Glee and congratulations came from all sides as they made their way down to the front. But there were just as many curses hurled in their direction. For the first time, Pax wondered if Tansa's recommendation to stay under the radar might have been the better choice.

"That is enough!"

The commanding words made almost everyone freeze in place, heads snapping toward the podium.

"We are mages, not rabble." Mage Eldan stood at the podium, her air magic whipping her hair and robes in a blatant display of power. "Now sit down and let us finish this assembly with some semblance of order."

Faces flushed, and gazes dropped at her words.

"Now!" she roared, her air magic blasting the word across the open space with a power that stabbed at Pax's ears and made him jump to move faster.

With the crowd sufficiently cowed, Pax didn't dare smile like he wanted to when Eldan nodded at the clerk with a look that seemed to say, *That's how it's done.*

It only took a few moments to reach the podium, and moments later, the top five moved one by one to receive their awards from the headmaster's assistant in front of the academy population.

When it was his turn, Pax moved as directed and looked down in stunned awe at the prize scroll they'd given him. He looked up and had to search out Mistress Nymeli. Face stoic, she still gave him a discreet nod of approval. His grin widened. He was extremely glad to know she was an ally, after all.

Aymer spoiled his good mood a moment later as he walked past Pax for his turn and said under his breath, "My father will never forget this."

Pax saw Rin's eyes narrow at the words, and they both eyed the 'crat while he accepted his fourth-place prize. He maintained a stoic and emotionless expression, making it hard for Pax to interpret his words. Was he venting his anger or actually trying to give them a warning about his father?

"A piece of elite gear, plus the prize scroll!" Amil's low voice burst with excitement that he fought to keep quiet, oblivious to Aymer's warning. "How are we going to pick?"

Pax shoved aside worries about the Wynrel house, deciding he'd rather join his friend and celebrate their victory. Not only would the academy give them a piece of elite gear, but the scroll would let them pick anything from the first-year treasure floor at the store. Pax couldn't wait to see the choices. A spell scroll was his most obvious choice, but a chest plate could save his life in a battle.

The headmaster's assistant moved back to the podium and leaned in. "Thank you for your attendance at the first assembly of the school year and everyone's diligence in helping fight and process the recent beast horde. As we leave, please celebrate that all of you are winners this week." He stepped back and gave an awkward wave at the crowd.

The tension in the crowd broke. Some stood and clapped while others jeered. Many just gathered up their things, eager to move on with their day.

"This way." Incedis' familiar voice came from behind them.

Pax glanced over to see his advisor had moved to the edge of stage, waving them over. He could see the top of another set of stairs moving off the back of the stage, a great way to avoid conflicts with the crowd in front.

Amil and Rin hastened toward him, but Pax hesitated for a moment to look back over his shoulder and cement a memory. He stood in front of the entire academy body, recognized as the best among all the first-year students, rich and poor alike.

When they'd forced him to endure the Awakening, he'd known he'd lose control of the rest of his life or maybe even die. He could have never imagined this moment in his wildest dreams. And now?

He would claw and fight for every bit of power and coin he could and use them to teach the empire to respect and fear the power of a light mage and his new family. They had no idea what was coming.

As he walked after his friends, Pax couldn't help pulling up his menu to look one more time.

~

NAME: *Pax Vipersworn*
  Race: *Mixed Human (monster-touched)*
  Age: *16*
  Bound Location: *Shieldwall Mage Academy (provisional monthly)*
  Class: *Mage*
  Element: Light (Hidden)
  Specialization: none (Hidden)
  Paths of Understanding: *(Hidden)*
  Flame: Level 1 - 45/100 (+5)
  Air: Level 1 - 71/100 (+2)
  Water: Level 2 - 35/200 (+3)
  Earth: Level 1 - 29/100 (+11)

Level: 1
Mage Leveling Points: 1/5
Health: 43/43
Mana: 31/31
Attributes:
Strength: 7
Agility: 9
Endurance: 8
Intelligence: 8
Insight: 8
Charisma: 6 (+1)
Skills:
General Active:
Identify Level 1 (Common) - 89/100 (+15)
General Passive:
Skinning Level 1 (Common) - 93/100 (+55)
Butchering Level 1 (Common) - 96/100 (+42)
Clubs Level 1 (Common) - 53/100 (+14)
Mage:
Light Mana Manipulation Level 2 (Epic) - 15/300 (+12) (Hidden)
Light Mana Sight Level 1 (Rare) - 67/100 (+2) (Hidden)
Elemental Meditation Level 1 (Common) - 11/100
Light Healing Level 1 (Rare) - 42/100 (+13) (Hidden)
Runes Level 1 (Uncommon) - 11/100
Mana Merge Level 1 (Epic) - 66/100 (+11) (Hidden)
Universal Beast Tamer Level 1 (Rare) - 21/100 (+21) (Hidden)
Companions (1/1) (Hidden)
1. Talpa: Level 0 Earth-based Baby Talpasauria Shade
Spells:
Light (1/3):
Haste Level 1 (Common) - 47/100 (+8)
Water (1/1):
Water Blade Level 1 (Common) - 41/100 (+15) (Hidden)
Class Evolution Points Unused: 1
Inventory: 0/20 available.

Assignments:
Academy Workshop Trainee
6/30 hours (+2)
0/1 Supervisor approval
Exterminator Intern
223/300 Vermin killed (+133)
0/1 Supervisor approval
Misc.: *First-year Point Ranking (expand)*
Coin Count: *1 Gold, 5 Silver, 3 copper (+8 Silver, +5 Copper, -2 silver fine)*
Academy Points: *51.5 (+33)*

~

As Pax stepped off the back of the stage following Amil and Rin, he finally let his full smile spread across his face. A rush of happiness and excitement filled him at how far he'd come in his first week at the Academy.

Ravalar's punitive fine had barely scratched the mass of points they'd been able to earn with the help of Mistress Nymeli. His grin widened further as he realized the three of them had all beaten the *new record* set by Aymer.

Glancing over his other gains, Pax was pleased to see the new point in Charisma, knowing it was more important than he'd realized at the start. With how much he'd pushed himself in the final battle, he was a bit disappointed that none of his other attributes had leveled. Rin had mentioned that each level was harder to achieve, but they had to be close.

Both his Skinning and Butchering were close to leveling up. That would let him harvest more and better-quality beast parts in his workshop assignment and jobs for Mistress Nymeli.

Thinking of earning more coin drew his eye back to his total. His heart still almost stopped at the astounding figures in his menu. An entire gold coin. That was a thousand copper. An astronomical amount no street rat could ever dream of. And he'd earned it in a week!

Even more would come in soon. Mistress Nymeli hadn't finished negotiating the sale of all the beast parts she planned to split with them. The job of earning the five gold tuition for the term suddenly didn't seem so impossible.

Pax pushed aside the sour thought of paying all that wealth to the academy and instead thought of the spending spree he and his friends had planned for tomorrow. They would ignore tuition for now. They needed strength and power first, so they could grow fast enough to succeed later.

By the time class started again on Monday, he and his friends would have new equipment and spells to give them a significant boost ahead of their colleagues.

And he still had that evolution point. Pax just needed an hour or two of quiet so he could carefully go through his choices. Only then would he feel comfortable discussing the subject with his friends and getting advice from Incedis. He got excited just thinking about the possibilities.

Pax's mind whirled with everything he had to do. Just redeeming their prize scrolls would offer them so many powerful options. They desperately needed to make the right choices. Spending their coin wisely would require just as much research. Hopefully Mage Incedis and Crafter Jacoby would offer them decent advice on what spells and equipment to choose.

A real air magic spell was at the top of his list. Pax only had a day and a half to finish his air path and practice with the new spell before Basic Spell class on Monday. Thinking of spell training made him remember the mysterious light manual he absolutely had to find time to uncover the trick to opening.

Talpa squirmed in his backpack, making Pax add another thing to his list: level up his beast companion. Thinking of his new family prompted a thought of his first one, lost for so long. The small sliver of hope that came with Rin's yearbook idea was more than he'd had for years, and he couldn't wait to squeeze in a trip to the library.

As Pax stepped out of one of the stadium's back entrances, he felt both determination and excitement. After the amazing adventures of the last handful of days, he couldn't wait to see what happened next.

His backpack shifted again, pulling him from his thoughts. Talpa squirmed harder this time and sent a pulse of alarm and distress strong enough to make Pax's step falter. Rin noticed immediately and aimed a concerned look his way. Pax tapped his backpack in answer and winced as the emotions coming from Talpa intensified.

Hunger, need and even pain warred with a strong need for something to help push outward, to grow.

"Got some things to take care of back in my room." Rushing the quick excuse, Pax ignored Incedis when he opened his mouth to object and took off running.

"My office," Incedis called after him. "First thing in the morning!"

"Got it," Pax yelled back over his shoulder, too distracted by Talpa to think about all the things he should discuss with Incedis tomorrow.

They'd been feeding the little guy meat from earth beasts and doing their best to give him chances to join in the occasional easy battle during their forays in the catacombs. Talpa had even managed the occasional flicker of camouflage and could travel short distances underground at an amazing speed. Was he leveling up already? He'd heard beasts leveled up a lot faster than people.

A grin broke across Pax's face as he ran and did his best to send reassuring emotions back to the newest member of their family.

EPILOGUE

ANOTHER MONTH and the first eggs would hatch! Eyes closed, and his breathing focused in a long slow pattern, Fortysecond Spawn spun the soul energy out of him in a small, steady thread that moved from egg to egg with a regular cadence he could keep up indefinitely.

Sitting in the still darkness of the warm cave, Fortysecond Spawn suppressed any sense of impatience or hunger and focused on calm. The perfect conditions of the environment aided immensely. The small pool of water kept the air moist enough to relax his hide, and the soothing stillness of the quiet earth pressing in from all sides enfolded him in its comforting embrace.

Like an egg, he realized, proud of the epiphany. *Protective and nurturing, but ready to break open when the time is right.*

Fortysecond Spawn let a proud grimace pull at his mouth for a moment as he envisioned how he was single-handedly saving his colony, the hero to bring fresh blood to their beleaguered troops.

No. A painful twinge popped his visions of grandeur, and Fortysecond Spawn shifted his thoughts quickly back into line.

Master is the hero. He was the one brilliant enough to use Fortysecond Spawn as an effective instrument to discover the paradise of souls here. He had the plan to harvest and return with breeders that would save them all.

Master knew best. He'd investigated the ancient legend of a long war, one which mentioned the bounteous life on the other side of the great Chaos Wall. And then, despite the continuous battle with their enemy, Master had diverted valuable resources to probe the Wall.

Over and over. He never gave up, sending younger and younger martyrs to find a way through. Fortysecond Spawn had been Master's most expensive effort, gifted with a priceless amount of soul energy while incubating. Master had bestowed his valuable attention on Fortysecond Spawn during his first days of life, impressing the Master's plan upon him and the importance of it. Fortysecond Spawn had a brief twinge of loss that he'd missed out on bonding with his clutch mates during that time. Instead, he'd had to make do with the impersonal ancestral knowledge every hatchling was born with.

He'd been only a week old when Master had brought him to the barrier and encouraged him to fulfill his purpose. A mix of pride and anxiety shuddered through him at the memories of that day. The harrowing journey that followed was even worse.

The shiver of memories made his stream of soul energy falter. Fortysecond Spawn quashed the weakness, steadied the energy and focused back on his Master's brilliant plan.

So many cycles of continual battle with their enemy had transformed their entire world into an empty desert, producing barely enough to maintain the status quo. Master knew that an outside source of soul energy and food had to be found if they were to triumph against the archenemy.

Fortysecond Spawn felt the soft flickers of life in the surrounding eggs, and its mind settled back into the comforting patterns of obedience. They would stay hidden and grow, sending the occasional new hatchling back through the barrier to ensure one made it through to report.

Once they received word back, and Fortysecond Spawn had hatched and trained enough hatchlings to make the first cadre, he would send them through. Master had given him specific training programs to implement. Fortysecond Spawn just needed to follow the plan and be patient.

He settled back, enjoying the life-giving aura of the soul energy slowly spiraling out of him. Even better was the knowledge that there was much more in the world above him, ripe for the harvesting.

YOUR REVIEWS ARE IMPORTANT! If you could take a minute to leave a quick review on Amazon, you'll help my books reach more people. That means I can keep writing! Sending you a virtual high five right now! :D

KEEP READING for a sneak peek of *Emerging Rebel: Shieldwall Academy Book Two.*

FREE BONUS STORIES, ROYAL ROAD, PATREON AND DISCORD

Join my newsletters for updates and Free Bonus Stories:

How did Incedis become an Academy teacher?
What happened to Tomis?
How did Mage Lorkranna get that scar?

https://storyoriginapp.com/giveaways/317003e8-1f8b-11ee-bdb9-73003f7eb555

Read more of the series for free:
royalroad.com/fiction/58482/awakening-horde-shieldwall-academy-series

Support me and read the latest chapters:
patreon.com/mzaugg

Or say hi on Discord:
https://discord.gg/XZ5NnhuQrD

FREE PREVIEW - EMERGING REBEL

PROLOGUE: TITUS

Titus and his two squad mates ran through the alley as roars and screams echoed off the dank walls to either side of them.

"Faster," screamed a voice behind them, so shrill with fear it could have been a woman's.

Despite the danger, Titus couldn't help a snicker at the man who'd held so much power only hours ago reduced to a bedraggled fugitive peeing his pants in fear.

"Yes, sir," he yelled over his shoulder while rolling his eyes at his buddies.

A bestial shriek ahead of them jerked their attention back sharply and the three warriors hefted weapons in tired arms, eyes alert. They slowed at the exit of the alley. Girrec to the right, his sword and shield up. Echo took the left, his spear and shield held tight and ready. They had him covered as he stepped out into the open intersection, eyes on a swivel.

The dark night was lit by the flicker of orange glow from various fires. Acrid smoke stung the eyes and bit at the back of the throat. The statue at the center of the small fountain ahead epitomized the state of the rural town. The battles had cracked the once-proud milkmaid in half, her upper torso and bucket in pieces among the rubble. Her head seemed to stare accusingly at Titus from the ground, despite missing the left half of her face.

"There ain't no coming back from this breach, is there, Sergeant?" Echo's grim question didn't need an answer.

"Why'd you stop? My compound is just up the street. Get me there. Now!" Magister Arlin Blackwood was practically spitting with desperate rage as he crowded up behind them. He was a tall elf, pure-bred enough for it to show on his stats, and arrogant to match.

But getting caught out during Northville's worst breach had taken him down more than a few pegs. His fine clothes hung torn and soot-stained. Dirt and blood streaked his face, mixed with his fancy make-up. His hair stuck up in all directions, substances much worse than his normal hair gel mixed in. He was missing one fancy shoe, and Titus wondered if the man even noticed the blood seeping through rips in the expensive sock on his injured foot.

"Of course, sir. We'll get right to it." Titus said the words with the practiced calm subservience that had become second nature years ago when dealing with his superiors. "Square up on our asset," he called to the rest of his squad and waited a heartbeat for the three in the back to form up closer to Blackwood. Mage Crissim stepped in closer to the 'crat and placed a hand on the man's shoulder, ignoring Black-wood's flinch.

Crissim gave Titus a grim nod, and Titus knew he'd use his precious mana to spread his shield over the idiot in an emergency. Blackwood was their ticket to freedom, after all. He just didn't know it.

"Ready?" With a quick glance, Titus met everyone's eyes, including the archer and swordsman covering their backs, who Titus had pressed to join their squad during the chaos.

"Move out."

With fast strides, the seven of them snuck out into the open inter-section and, for once, Blackwood had enough sense to stay quiet. Titus kept his eyes moving. Broken shop windows gaped like open mouths to his right. Piles of broken fountain stone were big enough to hide plenty of beasts. Enough smoke drifted above to hide an aerial attack if the beast was small.

The sudden disappearance of a thin strip of stars from the night sky was his only warning.

"Turtle!" he snapped out the order, his own body already crouching down, as three shields snapped up at an angle to face the sky.

With instincts honed by years of fighting, he Identified the beast.

$\backsim$

Nocturnal Birseg - Level 5
 Element: Air
 Health: 185/205
 Attack: Deafening Howl, Buffet, Dive
 Defense: Wind Shield
 *Increase **Identify** Skill for more information*
 *Skill Boost: +6 to **Identify** Level 5 - 60/500*

$\backsim$

"Air. 185 Health. It's got Dive, sound and wing attacks. Wind Shield defense." Titus yelled out the details so others could save their mana.

The shadow blocking out the stars grew at an alarming speed. The birseg slammed into their shields with alarming force. Somehow, Echo and Girrec kept their feet, making Titus glad he'd had time to warn them about a diving attack. He'd given them just enough time to activate their versions of a stand fast ability. Otherwise, the beast would have simply smashed them all flat into the rubble.

Knowing the beast would be stunned, Titus sprang into action. His two swords flashed up into the dark bulk that smothered them like a heavy, dangerous blanket. Next to him, Echo's spear darted out. On his right, he glimpsed Girrec stabbing out from behind his shield. A twang from behind Titus let him know their archer was joining the counterattack.

The birseg was so close, Titus could smell the odor of rancid oil and blood coming from whatever nasty things had accumulated under the plates of hardened hide that overlapped each other in natural armor. He stabbed up with his off hand, aiming to hit under a flap of hide while he wrenched his other sword back for a follow-up strike. When Titus' short sword skittered along the plates without making it through, he knew they were in trouble.

A flame spear from Crissim lit up the underside of the monster, stabbing into its chest and heating a section of plate. With a screech of pain, it struck back with huge wings that buffeted their group.

"Brace together," Titus yelled over the roar of the wind and was glad when Echo and Girrec moved in close, backing up to the others and bending knees so they could support each other.

Before the wings stopped their attack, claws tore at the shields protecting them. Grunts of effort and pain filled the air as they fought to protect each other.

Titus was proud that his squad didn't let the powerful beast's attacks set them off balance. They struck back at the first chance, hitting fast and hard to inflict damage while the thing was close enough to hit.

Power Thrust! Titus shifted out from under Echo's shield and activated his mainstay ability. He stabbed his main sword straight up into the joint where the beast's wing met its body. The beast's hide seemed to bow inward for an alarming moment before Titus' sword punched through, penetrating with half of its length before the beast thrashed and pulled free.

"Target the base of the bleeding wing." He stabbed again, trying to land another blow before the vulnerable area was out of reach. But the birseg flailed back, making Titus's swords fall short.

Titus roared in frustration, not daring to leave the protection of his comrades' shields. Even Echo's longer spear skittered off the hide as the beast's convulsive motions made it impossible to hit the injury streaming hot red blood that steamed in the brisk night air.

Then an arrow landed true and must have had an ability behind it, because it buried itself all the way to the fletching. Before Titus could cheer, a bright spear of flame slammed into the same spot, making the arrow burst into flames before the flame buried itself deep into the muscles at the base of the wing.

An angry roar of pain slammed into the squad and then crescendoed into an all-encompassing shriek that drove into Titus' ears like two ice picks. Titus groaned in pain, ducked down and a moment later had two wads of wax from his inventory shoved into his ears.

Despite how fast the birseg had ambushed them, Titus should have found time to do it earlier, especially knowing about the beast's Howl attack. The others were going to give him grief if they survived this.

The birseg used their distraction to take back to the air. Powerful down gusts kicked up dust and debris. Everyone blinked and coughed while straining to keep the beast in sight as it ascended.

"It's gone. Run. Now." The previously catatonic Blackwood was suddenly active and full of energy again.

If there was a benefit to Titus' ringing ears, it was that it muffled Blackwood's whiny voice. Though Titus had to give him some credit for being back on his feet, despite the trickle of blood dripping from one ear.

"Birsegs don't give up," Mage Crissim had moved closer, a wary eye on the sky. "It's just getting higher for another Dive."

Both Echo and Girrec gave grim nods in agreement. Titus pushed himself straight and looked over their small group. Everyone ignored Blackwood's ranting, and the coward was too scared to make a break for his compound on his own.

It gratified Titus to see his squad facing outward, weapons ready and eyes scanning their surroundings with quick glances at the sky.

Titus did a fast and dirty evaluation of their choices. They needed somewhere sturdy to take cover. But none of the ramshackle buildings nearby looked like they'd last long on their own, much less with a wagon-sized birseg crashing down on top. Titus knew the added danger of falling beams and bricks smashing into them, along with the beast, would be worse than staying where they were.

Making a fast decision, he snapped out orders. "We have to survive the next Dive here in the open and kill it while it's stunned."

His squad shifted into a tight formation, overlapping shields. Crissim pushed the protesting Blackwood down to their center.

"Prep your best abilities. With three attacks back-to-back, it can't have much mana left. It's blowing through all its mana because, with our levels, we're a juicy target. We'll have one chance to kill it. After the Dive, while it's stunned. We'll recover at Blackwood's. So, use everything." Titus checked his mana and, with a hard swallow, prepared to use his most expensive ability, despite how little he'd have left afterward.

Blackwood was right about one thing. His compound was just down the street. Titus knew the rich flick had reinforced the place and stocked it well with potions and supplies. If they made it, they'd recover and try to salvage something from this whole mess of chaos.

"Incoming!" Echo had the best long-range sight in the group.

The slight rush of wind and the rapidly growing shadow were their only warnings.

Chaos, the thing was fast! This Dive looked much faster than the first one. Suddenly unsure, Titus shot a glance at Crissim. The mage was already staring at him, one cultured Elvin brow raised in question.

Titus glanced at those not in on the secret. Blackwood had curled into a ball, hands over his head and already moaning they were going to die. The new archer and swordsman had been fighting with them all evening, but Titus didn't know how much they'd notice in the middle of a battle.

Would they even care?

The better question: would they survive if Crissim didn't use his air spell? The mage's illicit spell, Diverting Gust, seemed specially made for this situation. He could push attacks off target with a single powerful blast of air. Right now, it could mean the difference between life and death. They had to risk it.

Titus gave Crissim a sharp nod before turning to face the sky. For some inexplicable reason, a fierce grin spread across his face, made even wider when he tasted blood from a split lip he hadn't noticed.

The loot from a birseg this level would top off the treasures they'd accumulated fighting the fall of the town tonight. Combined with their plan for Blackwood, he and his squad might just come out of this disaster on top. If they survived.

And then on to Thanhil, his brother and the other Vipers. The old dream, despite time and impossibility wearing it to a threadbare state, still kept him going.

And he just knew. He knew. Wherever Pax was, he'd be fighting just as hard as his older brother.

He had to be.

CHAPTER 1: AMBUSH

Pax barely noticed as the empty paths of the Academy raced by underfoot. He'd heard Rin and Amil yell out when he'd taken off so suddenly back at the arena and expected they'd be close on his tail. Almost everyone else was just leaving the arena after the first big assembly. Pax's breath whistled in the afternoon's quiet as landscaped bushes and manicured patches of grass passed by to either side.

From his backpack, Pax could feel an urgent emotion from his baby Talpasauria Shade demanding his attention right now. It felt like a mix of agitation and excitement, combined with a growing hunger for something the little creature needed. Pax's grin widened as the wind pushed his short, dusky hair back from his face and his boots pounded on the gravel.

Hold on. We'll be home soon. Pax sent the thoughts to Talpa along with reassuring emotions, hoping the little guy would get the idea and calm down. Acting on instinct, Pax's boot dug into the gravel as he made a hard turn onto a thin dirt trail. The narrow path cut through the small forested area near his academy dorm building. He'd explored the nature area near his dorm two days ago. It was perfect when he wanted a break. The quiet pond with a single bench deep in the grove had been just what he'd needed.

For a kid who'd grown up in underground tunnels and cobble-stone streets, the haven of quiet trees felt like another world entirely, a welcome refuge he already treasured. The quiet woods enveloped him with a welcome calm, and the springy bark lining the path absorbed his pounding footsteps.

Almost there, Pax reassured Talpa, but only got incoherent feelings back.

Whatever was happening, Pax knew he needed to get behind closed doors before it started. With the strait-laced academy environment, the last thing he could afford was to draw attention to more unapproved activities. With all his secrets, it was crucial he kept up the appearance of being a diligent rule follower.

Pax thought about pausing for a beat to grab more earth meat from his inventory and stuff it through the top of his backpack for Talpa to gnaw on. He definitely had privacy now, but what if the extra energy from the beast meat accelerated things and something happened before he could get to his dorm room?

Probably not a good idea. Pax just ducked his head and pushed a little faster, his thighs burning and air whistling through his lungs. His grin widened as he marveled at how fast he could run now compared to back home.

Not that there had been this much open space to run back on the streets of Thanhil or in the sewers, but still. The increases in his Strength, Agility and Endurance had definitely made noticeable improvements.

His feet skidded as he took a turn into the clearing, the late after-noon sun just high enough to glint off the still surface of the pond. Wood chips flew in the air as he angled for the path leading to his dorm building through the foliage ahead.

A sudden skitter of dread ran up the back of his neck. A warning from paranoid instincts that had kept him alive as a street rat. Only this time, they were a beat too slow. He'd been too complacent and wrapped up in his thoughts to react in time.

He'd just flinched and spin toward the tree on his right when a shadowy figure leaped out of the undergrowth and slammed into his side, sending Pax flying toward the bank of the pond.

Stunned, Pax still twisted, trying to keep from landing on his pack and hurting Talpa inside. He caught his weight with one arm, feeling a sharp pain stab from wrist to shoulder before the rest of his body smashed into the grassy bank.

Before he could push up, a solid blow slammed into the back of his head. The pain exploded in his head, making him cry out and forget all about his arm. The momentum behind the blow sent him rolling further across the grass.

A black curtain rushed in from the sides of his vision. The world spun around him. Pax fought to keep from passing out.

Someone tugged at his backpack, prompting a surge of adrenaline that gave him a moment of clarity. Pax lashed out, whipping a backfist up toward the shadowy figure crouched behind him.

A satisfying crack, followed by a yelp of pain, put a grim smile on Pax's face. He jerked his pack around to the front and wrapped his body protectively around it.

An angry cry rang out, followed by a torrent of blows in retaliation. Boots and fists landed one after the other, soon indistinguishable as they blended into a spreading layer of pain that poured in on him from all sides.

Pax pulled himself into an even tighter ball. He focused on protecting Talpa while his spark flared up in rage, insisting he fight back. But the attackers weren't using magic, and some instinct warned Pax that if he brought magic to the fight, the escalation could become deadly.

And he had Talpa to consider. The small beast had suddenly gone silent, likely an instinctive response to danger. Pax couldn't sense any of Talpa's previous emotions at all. Their connection was still there, just quiet.

His breath whistled in and out as he fought to endure. Pax had just enough sense to hold back. There were too many to fight, and they surrounded him, blocking any chance of escape. If Pax could just endure until either they finished, or help came, he could recover from this. It wouldn't be his first beat-down. He just needed to make sure it never happened again.

Unable to fight back, Pax instead pushed his senses to their max, struggling to hear and sense movement while the pain insisted he pay attention to it instead. There were at least three attackers, and sneaking a quick glance didn't give him anything he could use to identify them. They wore dark clothes and hoods, even staying quiet, only letting the occasional growl or grunt of effort slip out.

Identify! Pax was so accustomed to using the skill on beasts, he'd forgotten it worked on people too.

~

Identify attempt blocked.
  Skill Boost: +5 to Identify Level 1 - 94/100

~

Blocked? What did that mean? Pax couldn't afford to waste mana trying again. So, he focused on surviving. Gritting his teeth, knowing it would draw out the painful beating, Pax activated the only spell he could get away with.

Haste.

Time slowed a beat around Pax, giving him the bit of extra time he needed to avoid the worst blows. A foot scuffed to the left. Pax, still in a tight ball around his backpack, shifted in time to take the blow to his shoulder instead of his head. A harsh breath from the opposite side made him tense his back muscles as another kick landed, shooting pain through his kidneys.

Endurance. The word popped into his thoughts, and he stilled. What if he could use more than Haste? He had attributes and many mage skills. With a mental kick at himself, Pax focused inward and summoned his mana. He might not be able to fight back with magic without escalating the attack, but that didn't mean he couldn't protect himself with it.

Pulling on his healing and mana manipulation skills, Pax grabbed half of his mana and pushed it up to his head, focusing on the throbbing headache there that was making his thoughts swim and drift in and out through the pain.

Heal. He urged as he spread his mana over his mind, envisioning a soothing blanket, cool and healing.

It took a moment, but he groaned in relief when the technique took the edge off the pain in his head. He could focus much better and pulled on his mana sight to get a better handle on what was happening in his mind. But focusing any further was too hard with his attention trying to track the attackers and avoid the worst blows at the same time.

Desperate, he burst the mana in his mind into a cloud with a generic command to boost his natural healing there as he turned his attention to the rest of his body.

A quick scan was overwhelming. Injuries were swelling everywhere, his skin already bulging in places while deeper down his organs took damage and did their best to keep performing vital functions.

He couldn't heal it all, not with the blows still coming, though they seemed to have slowed some. Harsh laughter punctuated the beating as the attackers seemed to be taking their time now to cause maximum pain. Pax kept Haste running despite the drain on his mana. It was the only thing allowing him to protect his head from the worst blows.

Putting the idea of healing aside, Pax tried to come up with another use for his remaining mana. Too bad he couldn't make it solid. Then he'd just wrap it around himself in a protective egg and let the idiots break their toes and fists on it.

And then Pax had an epiphany. Mana *could* turn solid. That was what his Water Blade spell did, didn't it? He obviously couldn't form a visible shield around himself with it, which would draw too much attention, but why couldn't he use his mana to reinforce his body somehow?

He clenched his teeth as another kick landed on his bent legs, making the pain there flare up to compete with his back that had taken the brunt of the beating.

Pulling on his remaining mana, Pax forced his mind to focus. He had to make this work to protect both himself and Talpa.

Continue Pax's adventure in Emerging Rebel: Shieldwall Academy Book 2!

ABOUT THE AUTHOR

About M. Zaugg

I started Kenpo Karate at 13 because my mom found a coupon for a free lesson. I sold candy at school (and got in trouble for it) but earned enough to carry a jar of small bills and change to pay for my first month of lessons. I fell in love with martial arts and obsessed about leveling up to black belt in three years time.

Married at 26, I decided to switch classes to healer and four years later was awarded the rank of doctor.

And through it all I devoured stories and played games. I bought Starcraft for my husband when we first got married, but I secretly played it for a couple of weeks before giving it to him, because you know . . . competitive. :) My kids loved it when I helped moderate the Minecraft server they played on.

And now? I write stories with a mix of it all.

Tell me what you think. I'm always looking to connect with readers and improve my writing. I love a good adventure and hope my stories deliver that.

Say hi - I answer.

-- Misty :)

Misty's Website
https://www.MistyZaugg.com
https://www.amazon.com/stores/M.-Zaugg/author/B0CC432MY5

facebook.com/mistyzauggauthor
bookbub.com/profile/misty-zaugg

Made in the USA
Las Vegas, NV
28 August 2024